After all the month[...] : the
nightmares would h[...] 't. If
anything, they were [...]

Murderer, the inner voice whispered.

Arren closed his eyes and tried not to think. In spite of
his exhaustion, though, he couldn't sleep. He never slept well
any more. It was partly the dreams, but it was also the fear.
It troubled him every time he lay down to rest: the fear that
somehow, this time, he wouldn't wake up.

Murderer.

Once again the memory of Lord Rannagon's dead body
rose up in his mind. *The boy has lost his mind. Murderer.*

Arren curled up, wrapping his arms around his knees and
hugging them to his chest. *No,* he thought. *No. They wanted
me dead even before I was a murderer.*

"I couldn't help it," Arren whispered. "I couldn't help it."

*Every Northerner has a madness inside him. One day it
will come through in you.*

"No," Arren whispered again.

The boy has lost his mind.

He rolled over onto his other side, covering his ears with
his hands, trying to blot it out. But the accusations were in
his memory, not in the world around him, and they could not
be escaped.

Murderer.

Ace Books by K. J. Taylor

The Fallen Moon

THE DARK GRIFFIN
THE GRIFFIN'S FLIGHT
THE GRIFFIN'S WAR

The Griffin's Flight

THE FALLEN MOON
BOOK TWO

K. J. TAYLOR

WITHDRAWN

ACE BOOKS, NEW YORK

THE BERKLEY PUBLISHING GROUP
Published by the Penguin Group
Penguin Group (USA) Inc.
375 Hudson Street, New York, New York 10014, USA

Penguin Group (Canada), 90 Eglinton Avenue East, Suite 700, Toronto, Ontario M4P 2Y3, Canada
(a division of Pearson Penguin Canada Inc.)
Penguin Books Ltd., 80 Strand, London WC2R 0RL, England
Penguin Group Ireland, 25 St. Stephen's Green, Dublin 2, Ireland (a division of Penguin Books Ltd.)
Penguin Group (Australia), 250 Camberwell Road, Camberwell, Victoria 3124, Australia
(a division of Pearson Australia Group Pty. Ltd.)
Penguin Books India Pvt. Ltd., 11 Community Centre, Panchsheel Park, New Delhi—110 017, India
Penguin Group (NZ), 67 Apollo Drive, Rosedale, North Shore 0632, New Zealand
(a division of Pearson New Zealand Ltd.)
Penguin Books (South Africa) (Pty.) Ltd., 24 Sturdee Avenue, Rosebank, Johannesburg 2196,
South Africa

Penguin Books Ltd., Registered Offices: 80 Strand, London WC2R 0RL, England

THE GRIFFIN'S FLIGHT

An Ace Book / published by arrangement with the author

PRINTING HISTORY
HarperCollins Australia mass-market edition / February 2010
Ace mass-market edition / February 2011

Copyright © 2010 by K. J. Taylor.
Maps by Allison Jones.
Welsh translation on pages 150, 164, 370, 375 by Janice Jones.
Cover art by Steve Stone.
Cover design by Judith Lagerman.
Interior text design by Kristin del Rosario.

ISBN: 978-0-441-01997-7

ACE
Ace Books are published by The Berkley Publishing Group,
a division of Penguin Group (USA) Inc.,
375 Hudson Street, New York, New York 10014.
ACE and the "A" design are trademarks of Penguin Group (USA) Inc.

PRINTED IN THE UNITED STATES OF AMERICA

10   9   8   7   6   5   4   3   2   1

For my grandmother.
You listened to my heartbeat and gave me
your name, and I know you loved me,
even though we never met.

Acknowledgments

Thanks to everyone at Griffins_Eyrie for never losing faith and for being just generally awesome. Thanks to my parents for not using birth control, and my sister for telling me the truth even when I don't want to hear it. Thanks are also due to Stephanie for not sending me another rejection letter, and to Vanessa for making a neat list of all my screwups like every good editor should. And, once again, thanks to Janice Jones (camlas@hotmail.com) for knowing more Welsh than I do.

Author's Note

Once again, the language of the Northerners is Welsh, and "dd" is pronounced "th."

Hence "Arenadd" is "Arrenath," "Saeddryn" is "Saythrin," and "Arddryn" is "Arthrin."

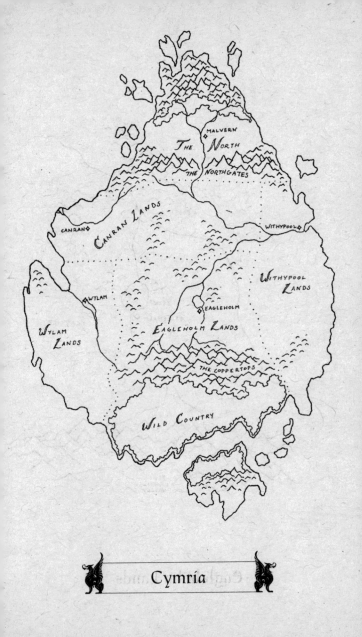

Cymria

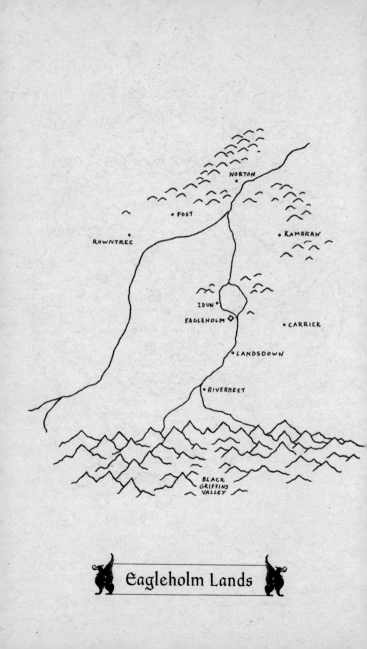

Eagleholm Lands

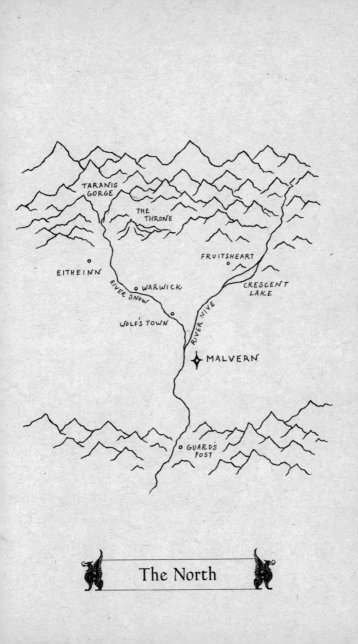

The North

1

Revenge

Dawn over the city of Eagleholm. The light of the sun was pink and yellow, but from the ground it looked red.

Smoke billowed into the sky.

Most people in the mountain-top city were used to rising at dawn. Every morning at sunrise the city would come alive with the calls of the griffins as they screeched their names, signalling their presence and strength to the rest of their kind and to the humans they helped rule over.

But today it was different.

The sky was full of griffins. They were circling over the ruins of the building that had once been the Eyrie, seat of the ruler of the city, and the sounds they made were not mere territorial calls. They were wailing; it was an endless high keening sound, full of despair. Some were calling the names of friends or family they had lost. Others mourned without words. On the ground below them, where humans mourned as well, Bran picked his way through the rubble, pausing every now and then to stoop and examine something. Most of the survivors had already been found, and now Bran, along with most of his fellow guardsmen and dozens of bystanders, had the unpleasant task of retrieving the bodies.

Most of those left, though, had been burned to the point where it was impossible to tell who they were or even what gender they had been.

Bran paused in the act of sifting through a heap of ashes and glanced over his shoulder. He could see a cluster of people standing at the edge of the devastation, distinguished from the rest of the crowd by their fine clothes. Nearly all of them had a griffin crouched beside them. In their midst, a young man was trying to comfort a girl a little younger than him, who was crying.

Bran sighed and gestured at a nearby guard. "You take over, Dan. I don't think we're gonna find much else here."

"Yes, sir."

Bran wandered toward the group of people. Most of the humans ignored him, but the griffins immediately began to hiss at him, their metallic eyes fierce. Bran bowed low to them, and most lost interest, but others continued to eye him and dig their talons into the ground. Bran kept as far away from them as he could. Even a griffin brought up among humans was perfectly capable of attacking a perceived threat to its human partner.

"Flell!"

The young man looked around sharply. "What d'you want?" he demanded.

Bran hesitated and bowed. "I'm sorry, sir, just wanted t'see if Flell was all right."

Flell turned at the sound of his voice, and then hurried toward him. There was a griffin chick following at her heels. It stood by and chirped anxiously as Bran and Flell embraced.

Bran let go quickly, somewhat embarrassed. "Flell, are yeh hurt?"

There were tears on Flell's face, but she shook her head. "No . . . no, I'm fine."

"Did yer father get out?" said Bran. "I—someone said he was hurt."

Flell started to sob. "He's dead."

Bran forgot his awkwardness and hugged her again. "Flell, I'm sorry." He looked over her shoulder at the group of shocked and bewildered griffiners. "How'd this happen?"

The young man had come to join them. A griffin had followed him, this one much larger than Flell's, with a brown coat and blue eyes. The young man, too, had blue eyes.

Bran inclined his head respectfully as he let go of Flell again. "Are you Lord Erian?"

The man nodded. "And who are you, guardsman? How does my sister know you?"

"Uh, Branton Redguard, lord. We're friends."

Erian looked him up and down, then looked away rather dismissively and surveyed the ruins. "I had hoped to live my life here," he said. "With my father."

"Did Lady Kaelyn get out?" Bran asked.

Erian glanced at him. "No," he said briefly, and turned away.

"We can rebuild it," said Bran.

"No, we can't," said Erian. "The Mistress is dead, and so is most of the council. There can be no rebuilding."

"What happened?" said Bran. "D'you know where the fire started, my lord?"

"Yes," said Erian. "Everyone knows. It began in my father's rooms."

"You mean—?"

"It was not his fault," Erian snapped.

"How do you know, my lord?"

"This was no accident," said Erian. "The fire was deliberately lit. And by then my father was already dead."

"What?" said Bran.

Flell looked up at him. Her eyes were bloodshot, and she was trembling. "It was him," she whispered. "Bran, he did it. He murdered my father. He burned the Eyrie."

"Who did?" said Bran.

"The blackrobe," Erian spat. "This was his doing."

"What, my lord?" said Bran.

"Bran, it was Arren," said Flell. "He's alive. He came back. He killed my father. I saw him do it."

Bran froze. "What? But—but—"

Erian had paused to watch him, and now he started forward suddenly. "Wait. Aren't you—Flell mentioned you. You were his friend, weren't you?"

"I knew him, my lord," said Bran.

"And you were the one who brought us the report that he was dead," said Erian. "Could you, perhaps, explain how he managed to break into the Eyrie last night and commit murder?"

The brown griffin had been listening. As Bran started to speak, she came closer to him, hissing and lashing her tail. Bran backed away slowly. "Please, my lord, I ain't done anythin'."

"Don't play stupid with me," said Erian. "You know something about this. I refuse to believe it was a coincidence that your best friend could escape from prison when *you* happened to be on guard duty there. What were you thinking? That he would just leave the city? You didn't think that, perhaps, releasing an insane blackrobe would have consequences?" He was getting closer, reaching for the sword that hung from his waist.

Flell put herself in the way. "Erian, no. It wasn't Bran's fault. He was the one who arrested him in the first place. And he wasn't on duty that night anyway."

"Is that true?" Erian demanded.

Bran nodded. "If yeh ask the commander over at the prison district he'll show yeh the roster, my lord. I was on duty that day, but off at night. He was still there when I left."

"Well, then how did he escape?" said Erian. "You"—he pointed at Bran—"*you* told us he fell more than five hundred feet from the edge of the city, and yet *somehow* he looked to be in perfectly good health when I saw him last night. Explain that, if you can."

"I *don't know*," said Bran. "I only told 'em what I saw. I saw him shot with arrows, and I saw him fall. I nearly fell, too, tryin' t'catch him."

"He would not have thanked you," said Erian. "And nor would anyone else. Could he have survived the drop? What was underneath? Did he fall into the lake?"

"No, my lord. There was nothin' but bare rocks down there. He must have . . . I dunno what happened. I went down there an' looked for his body after the sun came up, and there was nothin' there. But I found the spot where he must've landed. There was blood on the ground."

"And that's all you saw?" said Erian.

"Yes, my lord. That's all."

Erian looked blank. "But how is that possible?"

"I don't know, my lord."

The brown griffin had returned to her partner's side, and now she nudged him with her shoulder. *"Ae ee, kraen aee o,"* she rasped.

Flell looked at her. *"Kre ae oe aa?"*

The griffin shivered her wings. *"Ae a'ai, kroe an ee—Kraeai kran ae."*

"Kraeai kran ae, a ee ai o?" said Erian.

Bran looked on uncomprehending, wondering if he should leave.

"Magic," Erian said at last, reverting to the human tongue. "Evil Northern magic."

"But blackrobes don't *have* any magic," said Bran, unable to stop himself.

Erian gave him a withering look. "Don't you have something more useful you could be doing?"

"Erian, don't talk to him like that," said Flell. "He hasn't done anything wrong."

"No, no, he's right," said Bran. "I'm sorry. See yeh later, Flell. My lord." He bowed to Erian and the brown griffin, and left.

Erian watched him go. "Why do you waste your time with him, Flell?"

"He's a good man," said Flell.

"Like your pet blackrobe?" said Erian.

Flell slapped him in the face. "How *dare* you?"

Instantly the brown griffin sprang forward, hissing. In spite of her much smaller size, Flell's griffin moved to protect her, and for a few tense moments the two of them confronted each other, occasionally making threatening almost-charges before backing off.

Flell scooped the chick up in her arms. "Thrain, no. Erian, control your griffin."

Erian put his hand on the brown griffin's neck. "Senneck, calm down. It's not worth it."

Senneck subsided, casting sulky looks at her partner while still keeping an eye on Flell.

She did not look intimidated. "You're forgetting your place," she said coldly to Erian. "I am Rannagon's full-blooded offspring. You are a bastard. Being a griffiner won't change that, any more than it stopped *him* from being a Northerner—not even a griffin can change what is in your blood. Never let yourself forget that."

Erian gave her a look of barely concealed fury. "No," he said, through gritted teeth. "I will not. And neither should you."

Flell glared at him and stalked off.

Senneck watched her go. "Do not let her upset you, Erian," she said. "You did not choose to be illegitimate. It was your father who was disgraced, not you. But she—her time will come soon enough. When the world finds out what she did."

"I should send her away," said Erian. "Our father would have, I'm sure. I owe it to her to ensure that the world doesn't find out."

"Why bother?" said Senneck. "It was her folly, not yours. You owe her nothing."

"But she's my sister."

"Yes, a sister who mated with a blackrobe and will bear his child. You would be well advised to disown her."

Erian watched her as she walked among the rubble, trying to catch up with the retreating Bran. "No," he said. "She's suffered enough."

"And so has this city," said Senneck. She looked up at the griffins flying overhead, and sighed. "You came to me too late, Erian Rannagonson. You and I could have risen to rule this city and its lands. But Eagleholm cannot recover from this. Our allies will turn on us soon enough. We have no option but to leave."

"But what about the other griffins?" said Erian. "The ones without humans—what will happen to them?"

"They will find a way to secure their own futures," said Senneck. "We know what must be done. Look." She raised her head, pointing her beak eastward.

Erian followed her gaze, and thus it was that he was one of the first to see the huge shapes that arose from the roof of the hatchery.

"Bran!"

Bran turned. "Oh. Hello, Flell."

Flell caught up with him. She was pale but looked in control of herself. "I'm sorry for how Erian acted. He's not—well, he's arrogant."

Bran snorted. "Yeh don't say? Wasn't he brought up on some farm somewhere?"

"Yes, near Carrick. But our—he had special tutoring from a griffiner in the town. That's how he learnt griffish. He was brought up believing he'd be a griffiner himself one day."

"So he got his wish," said Bran. "Lucky old us."

"He means well," said Flell.

There was silence for a long time. Bran was avoiding Flell's gaze.

"You saw him, didn't you?" she asked softly.

Bran glanced briefly at her, and then looked away. It was all the answer she needed.

"I saw him, too," she said.

Bran stopped dead.

"What did you see?" said Flell.

"I saw him at his parents' house," Bran almost whispered. His eyes, turning toward her, were full of fear. "Went there before I went looking for him. To tell 'em what happened. To say sorry. An' I—we heard him callin', and he came in through the back door. He—he—"

"What, Bran?" said Flell, putting a hand on his arm. Beside her, Thrain stirred uneasily.

"He still had an arrow sticking out of him," said Bran. "He hadn't even noticed it was there. I saw him pull it out and throw it away like it was a thorn."

"But how?" said Flell. "How? He can't be alive!"

"I dunno, Flell. But it was him. He wasn't a ghost. His parents could see him. He recognised me. He shouted at me to get out an' never tell anyone I'd seen him, so I—I ran, and that was the last time I saw him."

"I saw him, too," Flell said again. "Just before it . . . happened. I went into my house, and suddenly Thrain was scared. I couldn't understand why. She panicked and tried to hide. And then he was there. He just appeared out of nowhere, and he looked . . ."

"Wrong," said Bran.

"Yes. I don't know how, but there was something I just didn't—it was terrifying. Like there was something evil hanging over him. Like he *was* evil."

"What'd he say?"

"He—he talked about what happened," said Flell. "He told me it wasn't his fault and he didn't mean for it to happen. He said he stole the chick, but everything else was a lie. And then he asked me . . ."

"What?"

"He asked me to forgive him," said Flell. "He kept saying it, over and over again. 'Please forgive me.' I didn't understand, but that was all he would say. Just 'Forgive me.' "

"He must've already been planning it," said Bran. "An' he must've known yeh'd find out it was him."

"He disappeared again after that," said Flell. "He climbed out the window, and when I ran after him he wasn't there. I went to the Eyrie later on. I was just so frightened—I went to find Erian, and I told him what had happened. He said we should tell Father, but when we got to his study the door was locked and we could hear—something was happening inside.

It sounded like screams and thumping. Father called out to us. He said, 'I'm being attacked.' Senneck broke the door open, and we saw . . ."

"What?" said Bran.

"It was the black griffin," said Flell. "It was there. It had killed Shoa. My father was there. He was hurt. And Arren was there. He killed my father in front of us."

Bran shuddered. "But *why?*"

"He's insane," Flell said harshly. "You know that, Bran. Everyone knows it. I saw him in the councillors' chamber when he was tried. He was mad. Yelling and screaming. He said terrible things. He tried to attack my father after he was sentenced. The guards had to hold him back. It was horrible."

"But Flell, he ain't *like* that," said Bran.

"He didn't used to be," said Flell. "But he is now. He's not our Arren any more, Bran. He's changed into something else."

"How'd he escape?" said Bran.

"It was the black griffin," said Flell. "He was controlling it. I *saw* that he was. It attacked us. Defended him from us. And then he set the room on fire and ran away, and it carried him off. That was the last time I saw him." She shuddered, on the verge of tears. "I keep seeing it in my head. Over and over again. I see his face in front of me. I can't stop—the last thing he said to me was 'Run.' And he's—he's—he was wearing a black robe. And his beard was pointed. He looked like a blackrobe out of a book. He looked evil."

Bran put his arm around her shoulders. "Flell."

"And he's destroyed our city," said Flell. "This was his *home.* And he's k— he's killed all those people, and griffins. How could he? How *could* he?"

"I dunno, Flell."

She pulled away from him. "I should go home," she said abruptly, and walked off.

Bran watched her, full of a terrible helplessness. He wanted to go after her, but he forced himself to leave her alone. What good could he do?

He sighed and turned away. With Arren gone, he and Flell had very little in common. She had been wealthy and privileged even before she became a griffiner, but he had never been anything more than a lowly guard. And now he would probably lose his job over what had happened. Though it wasn't his fault, he knew he would be blamed anyway. Why would anyone believe his story, when even he didn't? Humans did not have magic, Northern or otherwise, and a man could not come back from the dead.

Or at least that was what he wanted to believe.

There was an outburst of screeching from above. Bran glanced up. The calls from the griffins circling over the ruins had become louder and taken on a different note, and they were being answered. Bran looked eastward, and his heart leapt.

Over the rooftops of the city, from the hatchery that housed unpartnered griffins, huge shapes were rising into the sky. The adult griffins were coming.

They landed among the rubble of the burned Eyrie, scattering the humans in fright, and from there the group broke up and spread out. Bran watched them, bemused. He'd only ever seen all the hatchery griffins leave their home as a group once before: on the night Arren Cardockson abducted a griffin hatchling and ran away with it. The adults, discovering the empty pen, had flown out over the city to hunt for him. Bran still remembered seeing them fly over the market district, their voices loud and full of terrifying rage. When they had found and cornered the fleeing thief, Bran and his fellow guards had had to physically interfere to stop them from killing him on the spot.

But this was different. This time they did not look angry—but there was a uniformly intent look about them as they set out into the city.

More strangely still, he realised that many of them were carrying something.

Chicks. Dozens of them dangled from their elders' beaks. As the adult griffins landed they put them down and allowed them to run off, which they did at high speed, their little talons scrabbling on the blackened stone.

Several of the griffins were coming straight toward him. Bran backed away, being careful to keep his motions slow and deliberate. Sudden movements were liable to make a griffin anxious and then aggressive.

These ones, though, did not look as though they were going to attack him. Two of them walked past him, but three more slowed down and began to circle around him, heads down and tails up, as if they were stalking him.

Bran stood as still as he could, not daring to move, his heart pattering frantically.

One of the griffins pushed at him with her beak, nearly knocking him over. She bumped him in the shoulder and side, not violently but with a kind of assurance. He could hear her sniffing at his clothes and skin. She withdrew and watched him for a time, then turned and left. One of the others went with her. The third paused to scent him as well, and then followed.

Bran watched them, bewildered. It was as if they were searching for something. Was it Arren? Did they already know what he had done?

More griffins passed him. Some stopped to examine him before they moved on. He could see them doing the same to other people. The chicks were joining in, too. The people were either retreating or prudently keeping still; even non-griffiners knew how to behave around a griffin.

Bran started to walk toward the group of griffiners. Though he had no idea of what was going on, his instincts told him to keep close to them. They would know, and it was his duty to help them.

Before he was halfway there, a large griffin landed directly in front of him. He tried to walk around it, but it moved to block his way, its eyes fixed intently on him.

Bran bowed. "I mean no harm," he said. It was more or less the only griffish phrase he knew how to speak; Arren had taught it to him, saying it could be useful.

The griffin eyed him. It was female, and powerfully built. Her feathers and furred hindquarters were a rich shade of russet. Her eyes were yellow, and disconcertingly intelligent.

"I mean no harm," Bran repeated, hoping she would understand him.

The griffin moved closer, shoulders hunched. He stood still and let her scent him, and when she had done this she circled around him as the others had done, occasionally prodding at him with her beak. Then, returning to her original spot, she sat back on her haunches and simply stared.

Bran, sensing that she wanted something from him, said, "I—uh—what d'yeh want me to do?" He'd been told that most griffins understood the human tongue, though they were unable to speak it themselves.

The griffin appeared to listen. And then, without any warning, she opened her wings wide and reared up onto her hind legs. Her front talons snatched at the air, the sharp points gleaming in the sun, and she opened her beak wide and screeched.

Bran jerked in fright and started to back away as fast as he dared, his boots snagging on the rough ground underfoot. "I mean no harm!" he shouted.

The red griffin dropped back onto her paws and advanced on him, hissing and snarling, talons clicking on the ground, beak snapping. Bran continued to inch away until his back slammed into a wall and he was trapped, staring straight into the blazing eyes of the mad griffin.

She held him at bay for a few moments and then abruptly began to hit out at him with her beak, tearing his tunic. Bran flattened himself against the wall, still shouting that he meant no harm, looking desperately past her for help.

The red griffin backed away suddenly and then reared up again and lashed out with one forepaw. The outstretched talons caught him square in the chest, making a loud noise as they scraped across his leather breastplate, and she hurled him to the ground.

He landed hard, but then his guard training took over. He rolled when he hit the ground and managed to get up, and his hand went to his waist and wrenched his short sword out of its sheath. As the griffin ran at him, he pointed the weapon at her, causing her to back off. When she made another charge he made a warning swing at her beak and then ran for shelter. She chased him and cornered him yet again, and he held her at bay with his sword. "I mean no harm!" he said yet again.

The red griffin stopped. She drew back, regarding him, suddenly placid, and then she came forward slowly, her head bobbing up and down. Bran watched her warily.

She stood still, so close they were almost touching, and then very gently pushed his sword arm away with her beak. Then she sniffed at his face and rubbed the top of her head against his chin, like a cat.

Very carefully, Bran put his sword back into its sheath.

Apparently satisfied, the griffin backed away from him and moved aside. She made no move to stop him when he began to walk away.

Bran went toward the griffiners, almost sick with relief. Then he stopped and looked back.

The red griffin was following him.

He paused and then carried on, pretending to be unaware of her presence. But she continued to follow him all the way across the patch of rubble, and to the group of griffiners.

As Bran walked, he could see a strange thing happening. All around him, people were still being inspected by griffins. But others—others were being followed, just like him. Some looked confused; most looked afraid. When Bran turned back, the red griffin was right behind him.

"What d'yeh want?" he asked her.

She said nothing, and merely regarded him.

Bran shook his head and walked on. He found a fellow guard, this one being harassed by a grey chick.

"Dan, what's goin' on? What are they doin'?"

"I don't know, sir!" the other guard exclaimed. "The damn thing just won't leave me alone! It came up and sniffed at me and now it's following me." He stopped, seeing the red griffin. "What in the gods' names—?"

The red griffin sat down by Bran's side. She looked, he thought, rather amused.

"It's like they're lookin' for something," he said.

"I just hope it's not food," said Dan, eyeing the red griffin. The grey chick sat down by his boot, purring to itself.

"Bran!"

Bran looked up and saw an elderly yellow-bearded man hurrying toward him. There was an ancient griffin with him.

"Roland, sir," said Bran. "What's goin' on, d'yeh know?"

Roland was looking at the red griffin. It said something to him, and he nodded and then looked at Bran.

"You, too, Bran." He was looking pale and shaken, but a little excited.

"What's gotten into them, sir?" said Bran. "Does Keth know?"

The old griffin was watching him sternly, but at the sound of her name she glanced at Roland and spoke to him. He replied, and then said to Bran, "Keth knows. She said I can translate for her if I want to."

Keth started to speak, her griffish dry and rasping.

"'The Eyrie is destroyed, and the council with it,'" Roland translated. "'Our leaders have gone, and more cannot arise in time. The city of Eagleholm is no more. The griffins have spoken among themselves, and they have decided that they will leave this place now. New homes must be found and new nests built. But those griffins without partners know they cannot survive long without a human to be their ambassador and companion. Therefore, the griffins of the hatchery have come to choose humans to take with them.'"

Bran went pale. "What?" He looked at the red griffin. She looked back calmly. "I can't be a griffiner!" he almost shouted. "I ain't a noble; I can't even read!"

The red griffin spoke.

"She says those things don't matter now," said Roland. "She has tested your courage, and you impressed her. You are a fighter, and strong, and she likes you."

In spite of himself, Bran felt a little flattered. "Well, can yeh tell her I said I don't think I'm right for it?"

Roland listened to her reply. "She said she understands you perfectly and that in time you will understand her, too. She said you are worthy because she has made you worthy. And also . . ."

The red griffin rasped something.

"She asked what your name is," said Roland.

"Oh." Bran looked at the griffin. "Do I just tell her?"

"It works with other humans, lad," said Roland.

"Oh." Bran turned to the griffin and put a hand on his chest. "Branton Redguard," he said, slowly and carefully.

She cocked her head. "Raanton Redgurd?"

"My friends call me Bran."

The red griffin nodded sharply. "Ran," she said.

"Er—"

"Griffins cannot pronounce the 'b' sound," Roland explained gently.

"Oh. What's your name?" said Bran, a little more boldly.

The red griffin paused, then raised one forepaw from the ground and touched it somewhat clumsily to her chest, imitating his own gesture. "Kraeya," she said.

"Kr-a-ya?" Bran tried.

She spoke to Roland again.

"She said you can give her a different name if you'd prefer," he said. "But her proper name is Kraeya."

"Kraeya," said Bran. "Kraeya."

Kraeya looked at him encouragingly. "Ran," she said.

Bran started to smile. "Kraeya."

She dipped her head and gently tapped him on the top of

the head with the tip of her beak. *"Kraeya ae ee, Ran ae o,"* she said.

"She said, 'Kraeya and Bran are friends now,'" said Roland.

Kraeya bowed her head so that it was level with Bran's chest.

"Touch her," said Roland. "Gently."

Very carefully, Bran put his hand on the griffin's neck. The feathers were warm and soft, and he marvelled at their rich colour. Kraeya lifted her head, tilting it upward, and he scratched her under the beak as he had seen griffiners do. She liked that and closed her eyes, crooning deep in her throat.

Bran looked at Roland. "Now what do I do?"

"You'll have to be trained, but, really, the only thing you need to know is griffish, and Kraeya will teach you that," said Roland. "And you can learn a few things about how to clean her talons and what food to give her and how to treat diseases. Flying takes some practice, too."

"Flying?"

"But of course. Griffins never leave their humans behind if they can possibly help it."

"Where'm I gonna learn all that?" said Bran. "Who'll teach me?"

Roland sighed. "The griffiners are leaving," he said. "There won't be a single one left in the city by the end of the week. Everyone who hasn't been chosen will have to stay behind. What are you going to do, Branton Redguard?"

The question caught him by surprise. "I don't—I dunno, sir, I ain't got anywhere else t'go."

"No doubt Kraeya will have suggestions. But you needn't go until you're ready. If you would like, I can teach you a few things before you go."

"Why, ain't you leavin', too, sir?"

"I doubt it," said Roland. "I'm too old to go gallivanting around the countryside, and Keth's wings are too stiff for much flying. Besides, the people here need us."

"But what about later on?" said Bran. "I mean, someone said we'll be invaded soon as the other cities find out what happened here."

"Of course," said Roland. "They certainly will not be slow to recognise land for the taking. But I doubt they will be very concerned if they find one old griffiner left behind. I'll be no threat to them. If I'm still alive when the city finds a new ruler,

I shall ally myself with him or her. No doubt I could be useful. But you, I think, have other things in store. You're young, and so is Kraeya. You could do great things, given the chance."

"Where will I go, though?" said Bran.

Roland shrugged. "There are other cities out there and other countries. Places that need griffiners. Choose someone to ally yourself with. You will be invaluable in the right place among the right people."

"But this is my home," said Bran. There was very little conviction in his voice, though.

"No, Bran. This is no-one's home any more," said Roland. "It's a graveyard."

Bran bowed his head. "Yes, sir. I know."

2

Nightmares

Murderer.

M He could see it again. It was rising out of the darkness, utterly silent, almost glowing.

Blood was everywhere. He could feel it matting his hair, running down his face and into his beard, soaking into his robe. It was coming from his neck and from his eyes. And from his hands. They were bleeding. They would not stop bleeding.

He held them out, as his boots were slipping and sliding out from beneath him. The floor was slippery with blood. *Help me. Please, help.*

The shape was there in front of him now, its eyes turned accusingly toward him. He could see the blood coming from its throat, from the terrible wound. Flames were coming from it, too. He could smell the smoke.

Arren, what have you done?

There was pain in his neck. It was weighing him down, pulling him down, tearing his flesh, bringing the blood out of him like rain and tears.

Somewhere in the gloom he saw a griffin, her feathers white as snow. *Arren, what have you done?* she whispered.

I'm falling. Help me, I'm falling, I'm falling, help me . . .

And then he was falling.

Murderer.

Arren Cardockson woke up on his side, breathing heavily. Sweat had plastered his hair to his head. He could feel more of it trickling down his back, and he sat up, trying to wipe his face clean on his sleeve. The fabric was full of ingrained dirt, so it only served to spread a layer of sticky mud over his forehead, and he lay down on his back, trying to breathe deeply.

He could hear the faint rumble of Skandar's breathing, somewhere to his left, and realised that he must have rolled away from the griffin's flank in his sleep. But he couldn't summon up the energy to move back. Instead he lay and stared up at the sky. It was still night, and a crescent moon was shining. That comforted him slightly.

He sighed. The terror of the dream was fading now, and he tried not to think about it. After all the months that had passed he had hoped that the nightmares would have left him by now, but they hadn't. If anything, they were getting worse.

Murderer, the inner voice whispered.

Arren turned over on his side again, fighting down the impulse. But it wouldn't leave him alone. Unable to stop himself, he put his hand to the side of his neck and waited.

Nothing.

He had been expecting that, but it still sent a dull shock through his chest. It always did.

He closed his eyes and tried not to think. In spite of his exhaustion, though, he couldn't sleep. He never slept well any more. It was partly the dreams, but it was also the fear. It troubled him every time he lay down to rest: the fear that somehow, this time, he wouldn't wake up.

It was strange. He was so afraid of dying, and yet he *wanted* to die. The idea followed him day and night. If he died, there would be no more fear. No more pain. No more nightmares. No more running, no more hiding, no more hunger. And yet, when he touched the side of his neck and felt nothing, he was terrified. And when he looked up at the sky and thought he saw wings coming for him, he would panic and run for cover. There were so many ways to die out here: poison, cold, starvation, wild animals. More than once, when food had been scarce, he had been convinced that Skandar was going to eat him. But the griffin never did. He'd gone without food for several days at a stretch but had never once attempted to eat the human that he had adopted.

Arren had thought of leaving him, but he couldn't make himself do it. Skandar was his only company, and the closest thing he had to a friend. Most likely he was the only living creature in the world who did not want Arren dead.

Murderer.

Once again the memory of Lord Rannagon's dead body rose up in his mind. *The boy has lost his mind. Murderer.*

Arren curled up, wrapping his arms around his knees and hugging them to his chest. *No,* he thought. *No. They wanted me dead even before I was a murderer.*

Blackrobe.

"I couldn't help it," Arren whispered. "I couldn't help it."

No man chooses his heritage. He can only try and make the best of it. But you . . .

Arren clasped his throat. The wounds had long since healed, but the scars were still there, large, deep, swollen and occasionally still painful. He knew he would have them forever.

Every Northerner has a madness inside him. One day it will come through in you.

"No," Arren whispered again.

The boy has lost his mind.

He rolled over onto his other side, covering his ears with his hands, trying to blot it out. But the accusations were in his memory, not in the world around him, and they could not be escaped.

Murderer.

Arren's black eyes became hard and cold in the darkness. *I don't care,* he shouted back mentally. *You hear me? I don't care that you're dead. I'd do it again if I got the chance.*

But still the voice would not leave him alone.

He woke up again at dawn, to the sound of Skandar's screeches. He got up, rubbing his back, and squinted muzzily at the sky. The black griffin was flying overhead, calling his name.

"Darkheart! Darkheart!"

Darkheart. That was the name they had given him when he was a captive in the Arena at Eagleholm. As punishment for his crimes, he was used as entertainment there. Skandar was a man-eater. He had been born wild and had turned to preying on livestock and then on human beings as well. Arren, as a junior griffiner, had been sent by Lord Rannagon to capture him and sell him to the Arena. He had succeeded, in spite of the fact that he had been sent on his own and had no prior experience—but his griffin, Eluna, had met her end at Skandar's talons. Arren had returned home grieving for her, only to find that his mission had not been authorised as he had thought it was. Rannagon then claimed that Arren had gone without permission and in defiance of the rules binding griffiners to stay at their posts unless given leave by the Mistress of the Eyrie. No-one believed Arren's story, and he had been disgraced and cast out of the order of griffiners.

Alone, bereft, without a griffin to protect him, he had lost first the respect of those around him and then all his respect for himself, and from then on his life had begun to spiral out of control.

It was strange, he thought, that it had ended like this, with his having become a partner to the griffin that had killed Eluna and destroyed his life. But then again, it hadn't, he remembered with a little chill. It had ended months before, when he had fallen from the edge of the great mountain-top city and into space, his bid for freedom over and his last hope gone. That was when his life had ended. This, whatever it was, was something else.

Skandar screeched again, and Arren sighed. He still had not been able to persuade the griffin to stop making his territorial calls at dawn and dusk; one reason why he had thought of leaving him. But even if he did leave, he doubted he would get far. To his knowledge no-one else had ever refused a griffin's companionship. Though Arren had tried to, Skandar could not be dissuaded. And in spite of everything the black griffin had done to hurt him, Arren couldn't help but feel a certain bond with him. Every time he tried to make himself hate the black griffin—for his savagery, his bloodlust, for the killings he had committed—he would be forced to confront the cold truth: that he himself was no different, and that whether he liked it or not he had thrown his lot in with Skandar and was now his partner and companion until one of them died.

His calling done, Skandar beat his wings hard and flew away. He was going to hunt. With any luck he would bring back something for Arren to share, but there was no certainty of that.

Arren got up and walked slowly around their temporary camp, stretching his legs. The fire had burned down, and he wondered if he should bother relighting it. No. Not much point. They would be leaving it again soon enough. Instead he rummaged in the pocket of his robe, hoping to find food. There were some dried berries and a couple of squashed mushrooms, and he ate them while he set out to forage for something more substantial.

The campsite was in the middle of thick bushland and quite a long way from the nearest human settlement. Tall spice-trees covered the landscape in every direction, with thick brush growing between them. The spice-trees hereabouts had smooth trunks and no low-growing branches, making them more or less unclimbable, but there were some scrubby wattle trees as well, and Arren wandered around among a nearby stand of them. Clinging to their trunks were thick lumps of sap that could be eaten; he picked off a bit and chewed it unenthusiastically. It didn't have much flavour.

As he was poking around its roots, a chirping from above made him look up.

There was a bird's nest built between two small branches high up in the tree. A bird was sitting in it; he could just make out its tail.

Arren grinned. He unlaced his boots and put them aside, and then pulled himself into the branches. His toes were long and flexible, and he nimbly scaled the tree until he was as high as he could reach, just high enough to be within grabbing distance of the nest.

The mother bird flew off when she saw his hand coming, and he groped his way over the side of the nest and into the bottom, straining to stretch his arm as far as it would go. Sure enough, his fingers brushed against the warm shells of three eggs. He picked them out one by one and ate them raw, perched there in the branches like a possum. They tasted delicious.

Some of his hunger satisfied, he began to climb back down. When he was at the halfway point, he heard the sound of rustling grass and froze instantly. The rustling came again. It was coming from the base of the tree. Something was moving down there. Arren looked down, searching for movement, and eventually spotted something in the undergrowth beneath the tree. It was far too small to be a human, and he relaxed and continued to climb down, watching closely. Maybe it was something he could catch.

There was more rustling, and then he saw it properly. It was a huge lizard, nearly as long as he was tall, its throat pulsating gently. It was examining his boots, its great thick tongue flicking in and out.

Arren descended to another branch, moving as slowly and quietly as he could. The lizard still hadn't spotted him. He shuffled out onto the branch until he was just above it, tensed and dropped.

He landed inches away from the lizard, which turned and dashed off at high speed. Arren went in pursuit, his robe snagging on the bushes. The lizard's legs were short; he caught up with it in a few strides and then pounced. He landed squarely on top of it, knocking it flat on its stomach. The lizard struggled, its entire body thrashing with astonishing strength. Its tail whipped at him, and as Arren tried to pin it down it turned itself onto its back and tore at him with its claws. One caught him on the back of the hand, cutting him, but the others snagged in the thick fabric of his robe, unable to penetrate it. Arren could feel the lizard wriggling its way out from beneath him, and knew that if it reached the nearest spice-tree he would never be able to get it down again. He snatched up a rock from the ground and bashed it over the head. The blow didn't kill it but did manage to stun it. Quick as thought, he grabbed it by the head and twisted its neck hard. There was a dull snap and the lizard began to twitch and convulse violently, its mouth opening wide to hiss. Arren flicked it over onto its stomach and bashed its head in with the rock, and it finally became still.

Flushed with triumph, he carried the dead lizard to the fireplace and began to gather more wood. He'd eaten lizards like this one before, and they had rich, fatty flesh. He could live off one this big for days.

It took a while to build up the fire again; fortunately there were still some coals that had a bit of heat left in them, and he added some dry grass and blew gently on it until it caught. Once it was ablaze he added twigs and leaves and then a couple of larger branches, working patiently until the fire was going again. This done, he took his knife from his belt and turned his attention to the dead lizard. His stomach was already rumbling in anticipation as he skinned and gutted it. The flesh was thick and oily; evidently this lizard had been eating well recently. It would taste delicious.

As he was sharpening a stick to serve as a crude spit, he heard the sound of wings from overhead and looked up sharply.

But it was only Skandar. The black griffin had spotted him and was coming down to land. Arren shuffled back a little way to give him room, and he landed in the middle of the clearing, his four huge paws hitting the ground with scarcely a sound. He paused to preen his wings and then came toward the fire, his tail swinging gently behind him.

"Good morning," said Arren. "How was the hunt?"

Skandar paused and looked at him. "No food," he said briefly. His speech was slow and clumsy, though Arren had been helping him to improve.

"That's not good," said Arren. "You could try hunting on the ground. There's a few ground-bears around and some rabbits, I think."

Skandar came closer, ignoring him.

"Well, maybe the next place we go to will be better," Arren went on. "There could be some sheep there for you."

Skandar wasn't looking at him. Arren realised with a horrible start that the griffin was intent on the dead lizard.

He got up sharply. "No, don't even think about it, that's m— *oof!*"

Skandar knocked him aside almost casually and snapped up the lizard. He swallowed it whole with scarcely a pause.

Arren got up. "*Skandar!* That was *mine*, damn it!"

Skandar looked at him and then started to groom.

Arren rubbed his forehead, trying to restrain his temper, "Listen, you greedy idiot, you can't take other people's food like that. I'll starve if you keep doing it."

Skandar glanced up. "Not understand," he said, clicking his beak.

"Yes you do;" Arren snapped. "You understand perfectly well. Don't try and get around me with that excuse. I caught that lizard. If you wanted one, you should have caught your own."

Skandar yawned. "We go now?" he said.

Arren could see he wasn't going to get anywhere. "Fine. We might as well."

Skandar watched while he kicked dirt over the fire to put it out and then scattered the ashes as far as he could. He had left his sword leaning against a tree, and now he picked it up and strapped it to his back, making sure it was secure. Once he'd checked the campsite for anything that might have been left behind, he approached the griffin as slowly and respectfully as he could.

"Can I get on?" he asked.

Skandar regarded him for a moment, then crouched low to the ground and waited.

Arren climbed onto his back, being careful not to pull out any of his feathers, and settled down in the space between his neck and wings. It had taken a lot of persuasion to get the griffin to agree to this; to begin with Arren had had to put up with being carried in Skandar's claws like prey. In the end, though, he'd explained to Skandar that carrying him on his back would both let him fly faster and leave his talons free.

Riding a griffin was harder without tack; Arren leant back as Skandar straightened up, and then put his arms around the griffin's neck and held on as tightly as he dared. Skandar made a short, rough dash across the clearing and then leapt, his wings opening wide. They beat hard at the air, lifting the pair of them in a brief and unstable prelude to true flight before he found his balance and settled into a glide.

Arren relaxed his grip and sat back a little. Riding a griffin wasn't as easy as it looked; human beings were heavy, and griffins weren't built to carry large burdens over long distances. Making a sudden move or leaning too far in any direction could unbalance a griffin in flight, and that could have all kinds of unpleasant consequences, from making the griffin lose control and fall or collide with something, to simply causing it to become angry and refuse to carry such an inept rider any further. Fortunately, Arren had been trained and was fairly competent in the air. And over the last few months he had had a great deal of practice.

The sun was well up by now, and as Skandar flew high over the treetops, its light reflected off the silver feathers that covered his front half. He was not all black; no griffin was entirely one colour. But his furred hindquarters were: Arren had noticed that even the pads on his back paws were black. The rudder of feathers on the end of his tail was white, and his wings were mottled with black, silver and white. His scaly front legs and his beak were black, and so were the two pointed tufts of feather that grew over his ears, but the feathers on his neck and chest were silver. Arren had never seen or heard of a griffin with this sort of colouration; silver was uncommon though not unheard of, but as far as he knew there had never been a black griffin anywhere.

When they had first met, Skandar's feathers had been thick and strong and his fur glossy with health. But the time he had spent caged behind the Arena had changed that. Now there were two rings of pale, weak scales on his forelegs—scars left by the manacles he had worn—and there was a patch on his neck where the feathers had not yet finished regrowing after the collar had rubbed them away. And there were scars and bald patches on his hindquarters and chips in his beak, relics of his many fights against both humans and griffins.

One of them had been against Arren himself.

Skandar's condition made Arren feel slightly ashamed, but he knew that he, too, was far from a picture of health and perfection.

At twenty years old—he had celebrated his last birthday in prison—he was tall and lean, almost gaunt. He'd always been thin, but months of poor and sporadic food supply had made him even thinner. His face was pale and angular, with a raised, twisted scar on one cheek that looked almost like a tear track. He had curly black hair that had grown long and wild and permanently tangled—much to his dismay—and he had a pointed beard, which had also become unkempt and needed trimming. His eyes, too, were black—cold and glittering and wary—and the ragged robe that was his only garment had once been black as well, though now it was stained and grubby. It had no collar, and thus there was nothing to hide the deep, ugly scars on his neck. There were dozens of them, making a ring clear around it, like a necklace. It looked as if he had been stabbed repeatedly with a dozen small daggers.

Arren rubbed the scars without thinking, and sighed. He hadn't seen another human in a very long time; neither of them dared go too close to inhabited areas. The trouble was that he was too recognisable, even on his own. Northerners were fairly common in Cymria, but not Northerners like him. No-one would look twice at a Northerner under normal circumstances; after all, slaves were hardly worth looking at. But a *free* Northerner— one without a collar or a brand—would attract attention straight away. Even if he managed to go on his way without being harassed, people would remember him. And then they would tell other people, and sooner or later a griffiner would hear about the wild-looking Northerner with the scar on his face.

By now they all must know that he was a wanted man. The different griffiner-owned city states were not unified by a single ruler, but they were allies. Capturing and handing over a fugitive would be an excellent way to foster good relations with a neighbour, and no Master or Mistress of an Eyrie anywhere in the country would want to be discovered harbouring someone who had committed his crimes. Stealing a griffin chick was enough to warrant an immediate death sentence, but murdering a griffiner was a hundred times worse.

Arren knew perfectly well that if he was ever caught he would be hideously punished, most likely tortured to death. Unspeakable things had happened to the few people found guilty of killing a griffiner. They had been burned at the stake, buried alive, starved to death, cut up and fed a piece at a time to vengeful griffins—punishments that would never be meted out to any criminal but the very worst and most hated of all.

Why am I afraid? he thought, and not for the first time. *Why should any of that scare me? I'm already dead.*

But he knew why. He could still be hurt. He could still feel pain. And if those things happened to him . . .

Arren shuddered and held on to Skandar to reassure himself. The black griffin wouldn't let anything happen to him, not while he could still fight. He had already saved Arren's life several times. Whatever his faults were as a travelling companion, he would always protect his human partner.

The only problem, Arren knew, was that they had nowhere to go. They were trying to reach Norton—a town that was part of Eagleholm's territory—but Arren didn't have a map or much idea of how to navigate. He knew it was north of Eagleholm, and indeed they had been heading north, or at least roughly north, but Arren had an unpleasant feeling that they were too far west. At this rate they would reach the Northgate Mountains before they got anywhere near Norton, and the idea of turning back from there wasn't at all attractive. Skandar wasn't much help, either; until their flight from Eagleholm he'd never flown anywhere outside of the Coppertop Mountains, where he was born, and he had no knowledge or experience of long-distance travel. He seemed content to fly wherever Arren suggested, apparently believing that his partner knew things and had skills he lacked.

Arren could understand why; to Skandar, all humans had mysterious powers. And he, Arren, had had the power to capture him and put him in a cage and then take him to Eagleholm, where he had sold him to the Arena. In Skandar's mind, Arren had the power to make cages, and therefore the power to unmake them. And he was the only human at Eagleholm the griffin had known back in his old home. Therefore, the black griffin had decided that Arren was the key to escaping and going home. He must have formulated a plan of some kind, though when and how Arren didn't know.

The punishment for stealing a griffin chick was death. But while waiting for his sentence to be carried out, Arren had been offered an alternative: volunteer to fight in the Arena and win his freedom. He agreed, but insisted that he fight the black griffin, alone. After all, it had killed Eluna, and perhaps this would be his chance for revenge.

They had fought, and Arren had lost. But instead of killing him, Skandar had pinned him down and promised to spare his life if he in turn promised to free Skandar from his cage. After Arren had escaped from prison he had returned to keep that promise, and it had both saved and cost him his life. Though Skandar was wild, though he was fierce, in his own way he was as intelligent as a human. And he understood gratitude.

Humans did not have magic. Griffins did.

3

Skade

Noon, and it was fiercely hot. Insects chirped and whirred in the damp air. There were clouds drifting over the sky, thick and grey and growing in number. Thunder rumbled very quietly, but it was getting closer.

As the first few drops began to fleck the ground, Skade stood on the edge of a rocky shelf and stared fixedly at the pool far below her, while the rising wind tugged at her long silver hair. The water was dark with rotting leaves, almost black, and its surface captured the sky and the trees above like a mirror, rippling gently as the raindrops struck it. When she leant forward over it, she could see her own face looking back up at her, faint and wavering, but there.

She was shuddering. Even now, she couldn't bear to look.

Her whole body hurt. Her feet were cut and bleeding, and dirt had worked its way in to make them sting. There were cuts and grazes on her face, arms and legs, and her clothes were torn. Her head ached with exhaustion, and her stomach felt like a gaping void inside her.

She was weak now. The knowledge of it filled her like a disease. She lifted her head and tried to call, but her voice was feeble and the sound would not come properly. All she could manage was a pathetic rasping sound, like a sick chick.

She turned away from the water, unable to make herself look any longer. *Weak,* her mind shouted at her. *Weak!*

The image of her own face still swam before her eyes. She could not make it leave her alone.

Tears wet her cheeks. She hated them. They were weak. They weren't natural.

But she could still see. Her eyes were blurred by tears and

exhaustion, but they showed her what she needed to see. She took a few unsteady, clumsy steps back and picked up a large chunk of stone. It was heavy, and it grazed her fingers, but she could lift it. She carried it to the edge of the cliff, and there put it down and rested. Her back heaved, and she could feel her pathetically tiny heart pattering away inside her chest, protected by nothing but thin little ribs.

She thumped her fist into her chest, hissing to herself. "Weak! *Weak!*"

Once some of her strength—such as it was—had returned, she picked up the rock again, hugging it to herself. It bruised her, but she didn't care.

"I will not live like this," she rasped, and jumped.

She hit the water and immediately sank, weighed down by the stone. She held on grimly and let it drag her downward until it landed on the bottom and she was dangling upward, anchored in place. Even then, she did not let go. Her breath escaped in great silver bubbles; she forced her eyes open and saw it rush past amid the suspended debris, shimmering and almost beautiful. Her lungs started to hurt, and her head pounded, but she did not let go of the rock.

She opened her mouth wide and breathed in water. It flooded into her body in a torrent, and she began to jerk and convulse, her legs kicking as if she were being strangled. Her vision went red, and then black, and then she lost consciousness. A few moments later she went limp. Her grip on the stone slackened, and she drifted slowly back to the surface and floated there, face-down. The sun, strong despite the grey cloud, warmed her exposed back, but she did not feel it.

The wind was picking up. Arren awoke from a shallow doze to find that the sky had darkened. Clouds were gathering, and with them came wind. It blew through Skandar's feathers, lifting them, and pulled at his wings, making him buck slightly in the sky. The griffin put his head down, trying to streamline himself, and without it to shelter behind, Arren was nearly wrenched off his seat. He threw himself forward, lying flat against Skandar's neck, and held on grimly.

As the wind increased steadily, he heard thunder rumble

overhead. Lightning flashed a few moments later. They were right on top of it.

Arren thumped Skandar on the side of the head. "Go down!" he shouted over the noise.

Skandar jerked his head irritably but gave no other response.

"I said fly down!" Arren yelled. "We'll be blown away if you don't!"

For a few horrible moments it seemed that Skandar either hadn't heard or was ignoring him. But when the rain started to fall a short time later the black griffin finally began his descent. It wasn't easy; the wind gathered under his wings and wrenched them backward, making the feathers bend ominously, and his tail was whipped this way and that, unable to steer properly. As he flew lower, trying desperately to home in on a landing site, the wind continually pulled him away from it, forcing him to make several attempts and once nearly flipping him over backward. Arren did his best to help or at least not be a burden; he moved forward as far as he could, using his weight to counteract the effect of the wind. It helped; Skandar finally dipped below the level of the trees, and there the wind dropped dramatically. Still, he landed clumsily, ploughing through a thick stand of soap-bush and stumbling to a halt at the base of a tree. The landing threw Arren off, but fortunately he landed on a heap of dry grass.

He got up, rubbing his back, and hurried toward Skandar, who was disentangling himself from the broken branches, and hissing.

"Skandar, are you all right?"

Skandar managed to get up and struggle out of the undergrowth into a clear spot, where he sat on his haunches and began to groom his feathers. He limped very slightly and looked irritable, but he appeared to be fine.

Arren waited until he calmed down and then patted him on the leg. "Are you hurt?"

Skandar's head turned sharply toward him, so he backed off immediately, but the griffin only got up and inspected him. "You hurt?" he rasped.

Arren shook his head. "I'm fine, are you?"

Skandar sniffed at him and then sat back and resumed his grooming. "Not hurt."

"That's good." Arren looked up. The clouds were clearing

already, but there were still a few drops of rain falling. He
scowled. "It wasn't even a proper storm. Just a quick sun shower.
Bloody thing. We may as well rest here for a while. I'll see if I
can find anything to eat."

Skandar looked up as he started to walk off. "You go?"

"Not far," Arren promised. "I'll stay close enough for you to
hear me, all right?"

Nevertheless, Skandar got up and followed him at a distance
as he set out to explore the area.

They were in a stand of tall spice-trees that looked virtually identical to the last one they had been in that morning.
The only real difference he could see was that the ground was
rockier and less flat: they were in more mountainous country
now. Arren headed downhill, hoping to find water.

The ground flattened out a little, and as the trees began to peter
out he saw why: the soil was thin, and here and there patches of
stone were showing through. Up ahead, stone took over from soil
almost entirely; there was a bare stretch of it, without any vegetation except for lichen and the occasional patch of grass clinging
on. But he could also hear the gentle sound of running water.
There must be a stream somewhere up ahead.

The rocky stretch ended in a sharp drop, more a shelf of rock
than a true cliff. Arren went as close to the edge as he dared
and looked down. Sure enough, there was a large pond below.
It was fed by a thin trickle of water that spilt over a heap of
tumbled rocks. Though it was so thin it was a rivulet rather than
a stream, it would do. He didn't like the look of the pond itself;
it was murky and full of dead leaves. In fact—

He froze.

"Oh my gods."

Skandar came up behind him. "Danger?" he inquired.

Arren fumbled with the fastenings of his robe. "There's
someone in the water," he said.

It seemed to take forever to undo the straps holding the sword
to his back and then struggle out of his robe; he wrenched it off
his shoulders and tossed it aside, sword and all, and then dived
from the edge without waiting to take off his boots.

He hit the surface of the water with a loud splash and a cold
shock, and for a moment he was struggling to recover himself.
But he broke through the surface and began to swim toward the

floating body as fast as he could. It was a woman, face-down, her long hair waving in the water like weed.

Arren grabbed her by the arm and managed to turn her over; for a moment she started to sink, but then she bobbed to the surface again. She wasn't moving. Panicking, he swam for the shore, dragging her behind him. She was heavy, and the struggle to keep her on the surface kept forcing him downward. He reached the rocky lip of the pool, half-drowned, and climbed out backward, pulling her with him. She came slowly, the remains of her dress catching and dragging on the dry stone, and he let go once she was half out of the water, legs still partly submerged. He began to pound her on the chest, between her breasts. It was a crude method; he'd learnt it years ago and never tried it before, but now the knowledge flooded back into his mind without being called. He stopped to check her pulse and breathing; there was a weak heartbeat, but he couldn't detect any breath coming from her mouth. Desperate, he put his mouth over hers and blew air down her throat as hard as he could, trying to reinflate her lungs, then put both hands on her chest and pressed down on the bony plate that supported her rib cage. He blew into her mouth again, then turned her over and thumped her on the back, hoping this would help.

Without warning, she gave a jerk and began to vomit up water. Arren laid her on her back and she coughed and vomited. The water bubbled out of her mouth and onto her chest, mucky pond water with fragments of rotting leaf in it. Arren fought down his disgust and pushed on her chest a few more times, encouraging her to breathe. Once she had brought up the last of the water, she opened her mouth wide and started to cough and wheeze. After a while, it settled into true breathing, and Arren sat back, giddy with relief.

There was a thump, and Skandar landed behind him. The griffin came over to inspect the woman, and Arren moved instinctively to protect her.

Skandar sniffed at her, and then looked up. "Food?" he asked hopefully.

"No," said Arren. "Absolutely not. No more eating humans. I've told you before."

Skandar sat back on his haunches. "Strange human."

Arren couldn't help but agree with that. Now that he had

time to look more closely at the woman, he found her appearance very puzzling indeed. Her hair was silver. Not grey or light blonde, but silver. Yet she didn't look old. In fact, she looked about the same age as he was. Her skin had an odd silvery sheen to it, and her features were sharp and hard; she had a pointed nose and small chin. She was barefoot and wore a very torn and dirty grey dress, which, sticking to her skin because it was wet, revealed how thin she was.

Arren stood up and lifted her onto his shoulder, then staggered away from the pool, with Skandar in tow. She hung limply, apparently still unconscious. He found a patch of sunlit grass and laid her down as gently as possible, placing her arms by her sides and pulling her dress over her as well as he could.

This done, he turned to Skandar. "Skandar, could you just—" He broke off. Asking the griffin to keep an eye on her for a few moments did not seem like the most intelligent idea. "I mean," he went on, "could you just get my robe and my sword? I left them on top of the cliff."

Skandar appeared to listen, but he didn't move.

"If you go and get them, I'll catch you another lizard," said Arren.

Skandar stood up. "Big lizard?"

"The biggest I can find. Now go and get the robe."

Skandar paused to consider the offer and then flew off. He returned a few moments later and dropped the robe and sword next to Arren, then looked at him expectantly. "Lizard?"

"Later," said Arren. He picked up the robe and used it to cover the woman. She looked as though she was starting to recover; she stirred when he touched her, and he put his hand on her forehead. "It's all right," he told her. "You're safe."

Bored, Skandar started to take an interest in her again. "Food?"

Arren pushed his beak away. "*No*, Skandar."

"Hungry," the griffin complained.

"Well," said Arren, deciding to use a different tack, "there's no point in eating her. Look how thin she is. She's even thinner than I am. Why don't you go and catch something bigger? A goat, maybe."

Skandar made a grab for the woman, but Arren smacked him in the face. "Don't you *dare*."

The black griffin hissed at him and snapped his beak, trying to intimidate him, but Arren glared at him until he looked away.

"I go find food," the griffin muttered sullenly and flew off.

"Thank gods for that," Arren said aloud. He patted the woman's face. "Hello? Can you hear me?"

The woman's eyes opened, and Arren jerked backward in shock.

Her eyes were not human. They were burning gold from edge to edge, without any whites or irises, and the pupils were jet black. As Arren sat there staring in bewilderment, they turned and focused on him.

The woman suddenly came alive, starting up and scrabbling at the ground beneath her, hissing. But she was still weak; she couldn't sit up and fell back onto the grass, breathing heavily.

Arren tried to restrain her. "You're safe," he said. "I'm not going to hurt you."

The woman recoiled at his touch. "Do not touch me, slave," she rasped.

The words were spoken in griffish. "I'm not a slave," he snapped, unable to bite back on the anger that word automatically provoked. "I saved you."

She snarled back at him. Her eyes, fixed on his face, were full of hate. "Come near me and I will kill you with my teeth," she promised.

Arren drew away, both shocked and concerned. "Please, don't try and get up. Just lie back. I promise I won't come near you if you don't want me to, but you need to rest. You nearly died."

She subsided, panting. "I—am—not weak, human."

"I didn't say you were. No, you're strong. I can tell."

That seemed to mollify her a little. "How did you find me?"

"You were in that pond," said Arren, gesturing toward it. "I saw you in there and pulled you out. How did you get in there? What's your name?"

The woman was silent for a time. "Named Skade," she said at last.

"Skade," said Arren. "That's a nice name. I'm—well, no-one much."

"You are blackrobe," said Skade.

Even now, the word struck a painful blow. "Yes," he said. "I suppose I am. How do you feel?"

She made another attempt to get up, and then lay back again. "Do not touch me."

"I won't," Arren promised. "Rest there. I'll look after you."

She didn't reply. She stared up at the sky for a while, unmoving, and then closed her eyes. Arren got up and wandered around, hoping to find some food. There were a few berries growing on a bush not far away; he cautiously tasted one and found it was sweet and juicy. He picked the rest of them and stuffed them in his pocket, then found a sharp stick and dug around for grubs and roots. He eventually found some; they were thin and dirty, but he pocketed them anyway. This done, he started to hunt through the grass and turn over rocks, looking for lizards. The odds of finding another as big as the one he had caught that morning were very poor, but he tried anyway. Patient searching eventually turned up a skink about as large as his hand. He knew Skandar wouldn't be happy, but it would just have to do.

When he returned to the clearing he found Skade still asleep. She had rolled onto her side and was curled up, one hand resting under her chin. Arren pulled the robe over her and set to work building a fire. He'd done it a hundred times before, and by now it was almost a reflex action. He cleared a patch of earth and laid out a circle of rocks, then heaped dry grass and twigs inside it. Larger sticks went on top, and he found a chunk of a fallen log and laid that in the centre. Then, sitting cross-legged beside it, he took a piece of flint from his pocket and struck it against the blade of his knife, directing the sparks onto the dry grass. It caught, and he dropped the flint and blew on the grass as gently as he could, until it began to smoke. The smoke increased, and then true flames appeared and the grass began to burn. Arren sheathed his knife and added more grass and twigs until the whole thing was well ablaze, constantly glancing over his shoulder to check on Skade. She hadn't moved, but he could see her breathing. She would be fine.

His stomach was churning with hunger, so he spitted some grubs on a stick and cooked them over the fire. They didn't actually taste bad, but the texture still made him pull a face. He put a few aside for Skade, along with some roots and half of the berries he'd gathered, and ate the rest. It would probably be more sensible to save some of it for later, but he was too hungry to care.

Once he'd eaten, he added more fuel to the fire and went to check on Skade. His curiosity was so powerful that he couldn't help it. He wanted to know about her. Who she was, where she had come from, why she was out here. And how she knew griff-ish. Could she be a griffiner? But surely if she was, then her griffin would be with her. She looked thin and exhausted and ragged, like himself. Was she a fugitive?

And if so, what was she running from?

He sat close, watching her and debating whether to wake her up and ask, but before he could make a decision he glanced up and saw Skandar flying overhead.

The black griffin landed not far from the fire and dropped a bloody bundle in front of Arren. "Food," he said, almost sternly.

It was a dead sheep, whole and virtually undamaged. Arren examined it, utterly astonished. "Skandar, where in the gods' names did you get this from?"

Skandar sat back and made a rather unpleasant choking sound, almost a burp. "Many food," he said. "Field, fence. I eat many. This one yours."

Arren went cold. "Did anyone see you? Were there any humans there?"

"No. I look first."

"Are you sure?"

Skandar rolled onto his side. His stomach was bulging. "I look first," he said again. "Then eat. You eat now."

Arren didn't need telling twice. He dragged the sheep a short way into the brush and began to butcher it, clumsy in his eager-ness. The sheep was fat and healthy, and its wool was thick. It must have come from a rich pasture. In spite of his hunger, Arren skinned it before he began stripping the meat from the carcass. The hide could be extremely useful. Once he'd scraped it clean and laid it out flat to dry, he cut several large pieces of meat from the sheep's hind legs and spitted them over the fire before he began on the rest, not noticing the mess or the blood coating both his arms.

Skandar watched him with a lazy, indulgent air, having eaten so much he could barely move. "Good food," he muttered.

"Oh yes," said Arren. He could already smell the meat beginning to cook. "This is wonderful, Skandar. Perfect. I'm so hungry I was starting to wonder if I could eat ants."

Skandar looked at him with an almost fond expression in his silver eyes. "My human," he said.

Arren paused in his work and sighed. Skandar wasn't Eluna, but he cared in his own way. He was self-centred and unpredictable, but he was every bit as loyal as any griffin was toward his partner.

Arren remembered the night of Rannagon's murder, when Skandar had come to help him fight. The black griffin had stood between him and Rannagon's griffin, Shoa, head low, hissing and menacing her. "Mine!" he had shouted, again and again. "Mine! My human."

Skandar was looking at Skade. "Human dead?"

"No," said Arren. "She's just sleeping."

The black griffin did not look happy. "You help her. Why?"

"Because she needs it," said Arren. "That's why."

Skandar was silent for a time. He looked deep in thought. He often looked that way when he was about to say something. His griffish was slow and clumsy, but it was improving steadily. Much of the time he was monosyllabic only because using longer sentences took more effort than he was willing to give.

"You say—other human dangerous," he said eventually. "You say, hide. Not be seen. If human find us, they kill you. Kill me."

"Yes, I did," said Arren.

Skandar looked pointedly at Skade. "She human. She see you."

"That's different," said Arren.

"Different?"

"She's on her own," said Arren. "She's not looking for us. And anyway, she doesn't know who we are."

"She remember," Skandar said darkly. "She talk. Tell them. They find you. Take you. Kill you."

"I know, but—look, if we help her, maybe she'll help us. She'll be grateful. You know? I helped you and you didn't kill me. So it's the same."

"Not same," said Skandar. "Human enemy. Kill her."

"No."

"Kill her," Skandar said again. "You say, kill anyone if they see us. Kill her."

"I can't do that," said Arren.

Skandar started to hiss softly. "You kill Rannagon. Kill her like him."

Murderer.

"No, Skandar," said Arren. "I won't do that again. Skade

hasn't done anything to hurt me, or you. She could be our friend. And I want to know who she is."

"What Skade?"

Arren nodded toward the sleeping woman. "That's her name. She told me."

Skandar stood up. "If you not kill, I kill."

"Skandar, *no*. I won't let you."

Skandar's head turned sharply toward him. "Why?"

Arren moved to Skade's side, laying a protective hand on her shoulder. "She could help us," he said urgently. "Don't you understand? We're lost, Skandar. We've been lost for months. Maybe she can tell us where we are, help us get to Norton at last. We have to get there as soon as we can. If my parents get there before we do, what if they get caught? If the news has spread, they'll be arrested. Maybe tortured. The griffiners won't rest until they find me. Find us."

Skandar listened. He sat back on his haunches, apparently digesting all this. "Skade help?"

"Yes. She speaks griffish, Skandar. Like me. She must be educated."

"Edu-ded?" Skandar tried.

"Educated. It means knowing things. She could know things we need to know. Understand?"

"And if Skade not know? Not help?" said Skandar.

"Then we'll leave her. Make her promise not to tell anyone. In return for saving her life."

Skandar retreated and lay down on his belly. "I do not like this," he said. It was one of the first phrases Arren had taught him.

Arren realised he'd left a smear of sheep's blood on Skade's forehead. He wiped it off with a corner of the robe and went back to the carcass. "I know it's risky," he said. "But sometimes we have to take risks. We can't just wander around forever. We'd starve."

It took him some time to finish cutting all the meat he could off the dead sheep, and he also took the heart, liver, kidneys and brain. He wove grass into a crude frame and put it over the fire, held up by sticks just high enough to avoid it catching alight, and then laid as many pieces of meat on it as he could manage. He left them there to cure and ate the pieces he'd already cooked. They were burnt on the outside and raw on the inside, but absolutely delicious. He had to force himself not to bolt it all down in a few bites.

Curing the rest of the meat was a crude and unreliable process. He'd had to figure out how to do it through trial and error, and his technique still wasn't perfect, but if this worked there was enough to keep him going for at least a week. The organs, though, would have to be eaten today. Not immediately, however. He wrapped them up in leaves and put them aside for later. Skade would probably want some.

Now for the hide. Here he was at more of an advantage; his father, a tanner and leather worker, had taught him how to cure a fresh skin when he was just a boy. It was a smelly and unpleasant business, but he'd had practice.

He didn't have a vat or a bowl, so he gingerly lifted the hide in his arms and carried it to the pool. The water was brown not just because of the decaying leaves in it. There was a kind of bush growing around the edges that he recognised; it was known as leatherbush because its leaves could be used for tanning. It had turned the water brown, and it could do the same to leather.

He made a small hole in the edge of the hide and threaded a thin strip of torn cloth through it, tied one end to the trunk of a leatherbush that stood on the very edge of the bank, and then dropped the hide into the water. It sank, and he left it there to soak. He'd come back later to check on it. The sheep's brain would be useful, too, so he made a mental note not to eat it.

When he got back to the camp, he found that one of the sticks holding up the frame over the fire was starting to char. He hastily moved it and then turned the pieces of meat over. They were starting to dry out already.

Skandar was still sitting where he'd been before. He was watching Skade balefully, and when Arren looked at her he realised she was returning the look. She hadn't moved, which was why he hadn't noticed that she was awake, but her eyes were open and fixed on Skandar.

"Are you feeling better?" said Arren.

She looked at him, and then at Skandar. "You are a griffiner?"

"Uh—well, this is Skandar," said Arren. "D'you want something to eat?" he added, indicating the meat. "There's plenty."

Skade looked away. "No."

"Come on," said Arren. "You've got to eat. You need to get your strength back. You look half-starved."

Skade stared blankly at the sky and said nothing.

"Honestly," said Arren. "I don't mind. I just want to help you, Skade."

She looked at him. "Why?"

The question caught him by surprise. "What d'you mean, why? Why do I need a reason? You're human, that's why."

Skade laughed softly. "Fool."

4

Fugitives

Skade remained uncommunicative for the rest of that day and continued to refuse the food Arren offered her. She also refused to let him dry her dress over the fire. In fact, she showed no interest in anything around her, though she watched both him and Skandar closely as they moved around the camp, her golden eyes taking in everything. Arren left her alone and busied himself with smoking the rest of the mutton and then tanning the sheepskin. It was hard work, but the pleasant prospect of having a blanket of sorts did a lot to motivate him. Once he had thoroughly cleaned the hide and had cured it with a combination of leatherbush-infused water and brains, he rinsed it off and then hung it up to dry. Tomorrow he'd soak and clean it again and give it a good going-over to make it more supple. It would be stiff and smelly, but he didn't care.

The sun began to go down, and he began to cook the sheep's organs. He didn't like liver or kidneys very much, but they'd do. He offered some to Skandar, but the griffin groaned and looked away. "Not hungry."

"All right. Oh, I got you the lizard I promised."

Skandar regarded the pathetic corpse of the skink, and then snapped it up. "Good lizard," he mumbled, with what Arren was just able to recognise as sarcasm.

"It was pretty big," he said. "I haven't seen many skinks that big." He looked in Skade's direction and saw she had finally moved. She'd pushed the robe off and was sitting with her back to a tree, still watching him.

"Feeling better now?" said Arren.

Skade was looking at the offal staked over the fire. "I am hungry," she said at last.

"Well, you're welcome to it," said Arren, very relieved. "I'll give you some once it's ready."

He gave her the heart and a large chunk of liver, and she ate them ravenously. She also ate the berries he'd been saving and the roots and even the grubs.

Arren couldn't help it; he grinned. "So, you really were hungry," he said.

Skade licked her fingers clean. "Yes."

"Do you feel better now?"

"A little," said Skade. She still looked wary, but her demeanour was less hostile.

"So," said Arren, sitting down with his own food, "where are you from, Skade? How did you get out here?"

Skade was silent for a long time. "I am from Withypool," she said at last.

Arren gaped at her. "You're what? But that's on the other side of the country!"

"Yes," said Skade.

Withypool was one of the great griffiner capitals, and its lands bordered those of Eagleholm. Arren had never been there, but he'd heard it was near the coast. "What's it like?" he asked.

Skade thought about it. "Beautiful."

"Is it really next to the sea?"

"A small flight away," said Skade. "But the land is flat. You can see it from the top of the Eyrie."

"I've never seen the sea before," said Arren. "Does it really breathe?"

"It moves," said Skade. "The water rises up and throws itself onto the land. At night it rises, and in the morning it returns."

Arren tried to imagine it. "Magic," he said aloud. "I'd love to see it one day. I've seen griffins use magic, but magical places—I've never seen one of those." He cursed internally: he shouldn't have said anything about griffins. If she realised he was—he cursed internally again. She already knew he spoke griffish. She'd been using it since the moment they had met, and though he had been answering her in Cymrian, he obviously understood it. "What's the city like?" he asked hastily.

"It is very large," said Skade. "Stone and mud brick, mostly. The Eyrie is at the top of a mountain, above the other buildings. But there is a great wall around the city, to protect it. And there is a fortress near the sea. We flew out to it every day. There are always three of us there, watching the sea."

Once Withypool had constantly had to defend the coast against raiders from the East, Arren knew. But that had died down recently. "Who was the Master of the Eyrie?"

"Arakae."

That didn't sound like a human name. "Is he a good ruler?" said Arren.

"Yes. He is just and brave, and his human is cunning."

"Wait—Arakae is a griffin?"

"Of course," said Skade. "A griffiner is not master of his griffin. Without Arakae, the Lord Ruel would not be a ruler of humans."

Arren supposed that was true. In Eagleholm, people had deferred to the griffins at least as much as to their human partners, if not more so. After all, as soon as he had lost Eluna and the news had spread, he had lost everything. Without her, there was no respect from anyone. Even so, it was always the human who was the lord or lady, and the one people thought of first. Arren knew why: though the griffin was the more powerful and revered of the two, the human was the one other humans understood and could relate to. Humans saw the world in terms of other humans. And that would mean that griffins would see it in terms of—

He realised that Skade had asked him a question. "Sorry, what?"

"I said, where are you from?" said Skade.

"Oh. Uh, well, nowhere really. It's not important." Arren cursed inside yet again. He hadn't been ready for the question and didn't have a lie prepared.

"I can understand that you do not wish for other people to know," Skade said more gently.

"I prefer to keep things to myself," said Arren. "I can tell *you* do. You're on the run, aren't you?"

She tensed. "Why do you say that?"

"It's obvious. You're from Withypool, but you're not there. You're hundreds of damn miles away, in the middle of the countryside, all alone and with no shoes. Why in the gods' names would you be out here by choice?"

Skade looked at him, unreadable. Arren wondered if he had made her angry, but then she relaxed and sighed. "You are not a fool," she said.

So he'd guessed correctly. "Are you trying to get somewhere?" he asked.

"Why should I tell you?" said Skade. "I do not trust you, blackrobe."

Arren winced. "But you told me where you were from. You told me your name. That's enough for me to tell other people who you are and where you are."

Skade laughed at him. "You cannot threaten me. You are a fugitive as much as I am. You would not go near anyone to tell them."

Arren relaxed. "And neither would you."

"No," said Skade. "I would not. Tell me your name, and I will tell you where I am going."

"Why do you care?" said Arren.

"I do not care," said Skade. "But I will trust you if you trust me."

"Fine. I'm Taranis."

Skade looked away. "Why are you out here, Taranis? Are you a slave who has escaped?"

"Do I look like one?"

She examined him. "You are a blackrobe. You are hiding. There are collar scars on your neck."

Arren nodded. "That's a good guess," he said. "But there's one problem." He held up his right hand, showing her the grubby skin on the back of it. "No brand," he said.

"Yes," said Skade. "I noticed that. And"—she looked at Skandar—"a slave would not be travelling with a griffin. And he would not know griffish."

"And how do *you* know griffish?" said Arren. "Wouldn't it be easier to speak human?"

Skade's expression hardened. "I have the right, blackrobe. Who taught you to speak it? Was it this griffin?"

"It doesn't matter," said Arren.

"But I want to know," said Skade. "Tell me."

"No. You said you'd tell me where you were going if I told you my name. You know my name, so tell me where you're going."

There was a tense silence. They looked challengingly at each other while Skandar watched, ready to attack if Skade showed any sign of hostility.

She glanced quickly at him, and then looked at Arren again. "I was looking for a cave."

"A cave?" said Arren. "What sort of cave?"

"Have you ever heard of a spirit cave?" said Skade.

"I don't think so."

"There is more than one spirit cave," said Skade. "I was looking for one that is said to be near the Northgate Mountains. It is a magical place."

"Why are you looking for it?" said Arren.

"The spirits of the dead dwell inside it," said Skade. "The cave has magic. It can do things no griffin can do. Answer questions. Give guidance. Reveal the future. And . . . it can heal a soul."

"Heal a soul?" said Arren. "How? Is it a holy place or something?"

"No," Skade hissed. "It is a griffish place. Griffins have no gods. The magic of a spirit cave can undo other magics. It can remove even the most powerful curse."

Arren froze. "Curse? What sort of curse?"

"Any that is woven by a griffin," said Skade. "Even a death curse."

His hands closed around the now-cold meat, squashing it. "Where is this place?"

"It does not matter," said Skade. "I am not going there now. I have been travelling toward it for more than a year, but now I have seen sense. It does not exist."

"But it has to," said Arren. "I mean, how can people talk about—you shouldn't give in until you know."

Skade looked at the ground. "No. My heart tells me it is not there. There is no hope. A griffin's curse cannot be healed."

"Not even by another griffin?" said Arren.

Skade shook her head. "I do not know."

"Take me there," said Arren. "Let me come with you to this place. I'll help you, Skade."

She looked up, all fire and anger again. "No. I travel alone."

"But if we travel together, we can work together," said Arren. "Protect each other. Help each other find food, keep each other company. And you can travel faster if you're with me. I think Skandar could carry both of us."

"I do not need company," Skade hissed. "I am not going to this cave."

"Well then, where *are* you going?"

Skade said nothing.

"You really do want to find it, don't you?" said Arren. "Don't give up. I'll help you get there, I promise."

"Why do you want to go there?" said Skade.

"Because I want to see it. Why do *you* want to go there?"

Silence.

"You're cursed, aren't you?" Arren said softly. "That's why you're out here, isn't it? There's a curse on you."

She snarled softly and looked away.

"Is that why you look like that?" said Arren.

"Yes," Skade said at last.

"I'll help you, Skade," said Arren. "I'll do whatever it takes."

Skade hesitated. "I will . . . think about it."

"Thank you," said Arren.

He ate the cold offal, not noticing the unpleasant taste. His mind was abuzz. *She can take me to this place. We'll find it together, she and I. I'll go in there and talk to those spirits, I'll ask them . . . I'll ask them to save me.*

He glanced at her and smiled very slightly. *She's beautiful,* he thought. *In a strange way.*

Skade was watching him. The blackrobe was difficult to read, but she could sense his hopefulness, along with a kind of buried fear. She saw his glance toward her, and her eyes narrowed. *You want something,* she thought. *And I will find out what it is.*

Arren finished eating, and stretched. It was dark now, and he wrapped up the smoked mutton in a scrap of dirty cloth from his pocket and hung it from a tree to protect it from animals. Skandar was already asleep, his back rising and falling gently in time with his breathing.

"Well," said Arren, "I'm ready to sleep now. Keep my robe. I'll see you in the morning."

Skade watched as he curled up beside the griffin, sheltering under one wing. She was tempted to throw the robe aside—but the night air was cold, and though the garment was very dirty and was trimmed with ragged edges, it.was still thick and warm. She wrapped it around her shoulders and watched in the dying firelight as Arren fell asleep. He looked tired, but after a few moments she saw his face crease as if in pain. His lips moved as he muttered something to himself, and one hand twitched.

Skade lay down by the base of a tree, pulling the robe over her exposed shoulders. In spite of herself she was feeling better now. The food had filled her up, and she was warm. And perhaps, after all, the blackrobe could help her. Perhaps the spirit cave really did exist. Perhaps, when she got to the place she had been striving to reach for so long, the cave would be there after all. *I will get there,* she thought. *I should not have given up. I will find it. And afterward, it will be time for my revenge.*

She looked at Arren again, at his scarred face. She had never seen a Northerner who was not a slave. This one was bolder and far more well-spoken than the rest of his race. And he was intelligent, as well. But clearly desperate—for something.

You will help me, she decided. *You and the black griffin. I do not care any more. I will break the curse.*

Arren stirred in his sleep, and his lips formed a single word: *falling.*

Skade sighed. *You are right to sleep uneasily,* she thought. *Murderer.*

Skade was still there next morning when Arren woke up. He'd half-expected her to be gone, and when he was woken at dawn by Skandar's screech the first thing he did was look toward the spot where she'd been lying the previous night. She was there, and stirred when Skandar screeched again, though she didn't wake. Arren felt curiously relieved to see her.

Skandar finished his calling and came down to land at the edge of the camp. He stretched and fluttered his wings a few times and then strutted over toward Arren. "We go now?"

Arren scratched his head. "Not yet. I need to eat first. And"—he looked at Skade—"we have to talk to her."

Skandar shook his head irritably. "Why talk?"

"She hasn't agreed to help us yet," said Arren. "I have to talk to her some more and see if she's made up her mind yet. And if she says no, then I'll just ask her if she knows which way to go."

The black griffin started to preen his feathers, hissing to himself. "Not like. Human smell wrong. Look wrong."

"If she can help us, I don't care what she looks or smells like. Try and be pleasant to her, Skandar."

Skandar didn't reply. Arren left him to sulk and went to check on the sheepskin, which he'd hung from a tree. It was smelly and still a little damp, but it looked to have cured nicely, and he draped it around his shoulders, wool side down, to try to stave off the early-morning chill while he set to work getting breakfast ready. There was still some meat left on the sheep's carcass that he hadn't smoked, so he refuelled the fire and cooked it. Skandar, apparently still satisfied from the previous day's gorging, gnawed on a couple of bones.

While the meat was cooking, Arren walked back to the pool. It still looked filthy—and it hadn't been improved at all by his having used it as a tanning solution—so he climbed the rocks by the stream that fed it and followed it for a while until he found a spot where it was a little deeper. He drank from it; the water here was clear and fresh, and the taste of dirt in it didn't bother him. Once he'd satisfied his thirst, he looked speculatively at his reflection. His face looked thin and grubby, and his beard was a mess. So was his hair. *I look ridiculous,* he thought glumly.

Well, he had some time now. He wandered off and picked branches from a soap-bush and took them back to the water's edge, where he wet his hair, then crushed the leaves. They released an oily sap, and he washed his hair as well as he could with it. The sap helped soften and dislodge some of the dirt, and from his pocket he took a comb—he'd carved it himself, rather crudely, from a piece of wood—and started to try to put his hair into some kind of order. It wasn't easy. Skandar generally insisted on leaving shortly after dawn and landed when it suited him. Time not spent in the air generally went toward looking for food, and he couldn't remember the last time he'd had a moment for personal grooming. His hair had worked itself into a horrible mess.

But he combed away diligently at it until it was as neat as he could make it and then used some more soap-bush sap and his knife to try to do something about his beard. It didn't work very well: the knife was too blunt to be much good as a razor, and the sap was a pathetically inadequate substitute for real soap. He persisted anyway, removing the moustache that had started to sprout. He hated having hair around his mouth. It made him feel scruffy.

He cut himself a couple of times before he achieved what he

was aiming for: a pointed tuft perched on his chin. He'd only started wearing a beard very recently, but when he checked his reflection again he decided it rather suited him.

The faint image in the water smiled grimly up at him. Everyone in Cymria could recognise a beard like this one. It was in all the history books, the ones that described the savage Northerners trying to invade from the cold lands beyond the Northgate Mountains centuries ago. Unlike the brown-haired people of the South, the Northerners had never forged an alliance with the griffins. They had come south in great numbers and had waged war with the Southerners, a spectacularly idiotic thing to do. Today, the only surviving Northerners were either slaves or vassals.

Arren ran his fingers through his still-wet hair. It looked a lot better now. Maybe Skade would take him more seriously if he didn't look like a beggar.

Sudden realisation dawned. Arren scrambled to his feet and dashed off, swearing.

It seemed to take forever to get back to the camp. He stumbled through the trees, still cursing. *Idiot!* He must have spent half the damn morning mooning over his reflection, and the gods alone knew what could have happened while he was gone.

He finally reached the clearing and slumped against a tree, panting. Skade was there, awake now and sitting near the fire. Skandar was on the other side of it, and the two of them were glaring at each other.

Arren came closer. The meat he'd put over the fire was still there, burned to a crisp.

"What's going on?" he asked, using griffish.

Skade turned to look at him. "Where have you been?" she said abruptly.

"I was—getting a drink," said Arren. "Why did you let the meat burn?"

The silver-haired woman nodded toward Skandar. "Your friend would not let me touch it."

Arren crouched beside her and pulled the spit out of the ground. He examined the meat, but it was patently obvious that it was inedible. He dumped it in the fire. "Why did you do that?"

The black griffin clicked his beak. "Your food, not hers."

Arren hesitated briefly. He had to concede that made sense. Regardless, he said, "Well, it was for her, too. Now you've forced her to let it go to waste. Can't you stop being a pain in the neck for once?"

Skandar dug his talons into the ground, obviously aware that he had just been insulted. "You ask," he snapped. "She tell. Now."

Arren groaned inwardly. So much for diplomacy.

Skade, however, laughed. She had an odd, harsh laugh, but it was sincere enough. "Your friend knows what he wants, doesn't he?"

"I'm sorry," said Arren, reverting to Cymrian. "He doesn't speak griffish very well, and . . . he's not very good with people."

"I can see that," said Skade, using Cymrian for the first time since they'd met. She spoke it quite well, but with what Arren easily recognised as an Eastern accent, typical of someone from Withypool or its surrounds.

Skandar was watching them. Now the griffin suddenly advanced, tail swishing ominously from side to side. "You talk, talk to me," he hissed.

His voice was low with anger, and Arren quickly saw that he had made a mistake. He turned to Skade. "Look, Skandar and I have talked," he said, speaking griffish now, "and we've agreed that if you want us to help you, then you have to help us first."

Skade glanced quickly at Skandar. "I do need your help," she said. "I confess that now. And you have been a great help to me already. What exactly do you need me to do for you?"

"We go North," Skandar said instantly. "You tell us way."

"No," said Arren. "Not yet. Skade, I want to go to this spirit cave with you. If you'll let me, I'll come with you. Afterward, we can go our separate ways."

"No," Skandar rasped. "Norton. You say we go to Norton. Not cave. Norton."

"Well, the plan's changed," said Arren. "Norton can wait."

Skade was giving him a long, slow look. "And why do you want to go there, Taranis?"

"Because . . ." Arren faltered. "Because there are things I want to see there. If there really are spirits living there, then they could give me guidance. Besides," he added, with a sudden burst of inspiration, "there's no reason for you to come with us to Norton. If you want to be cured of this curse, whatever it is, then we should go to the cave first. What do you say?"

Skade was silent for a long time. "Agreed," she said at last. "But there is a problem."

"What's that?" said Arren.

She fiddled with a lock of her silver hair. "I do not know the way to the cave," she said. "I am as lost as you are."

Arren's heart sank. "But don't you know anything about where it's supposed to be? What it looks like? Anything at all?"

"It is said to be near a river," said Skade. "Between two mountains. The legend says it is not far from a place called Healer's Home, where herbs of every kind grow."

Arren scratched his beard. "I've never heard of any place like that. But I've never been that far north, so—"

"We could find it by following the river, maybe," said Skade. "The mountains must be part of the Northgates."

"Yes, but there must be dozens of caves in the mountains," Arren said wretchedly. "How are we supposed to know which one it is?"

Skade shook her head. "The spirit cave must not be too far from the river. If the Healer's Home is a village or a city, it would need to be built near water."

"Wait a moment," said Arren. "Healing—does that mean there's a temple there?"

"It could," Skade conceded.

"Well, if it's an important place for healers and healing, it makes sense for the priesthood to be running it or at least supporting it," said Arren. "So if we can find a temple near the river—"

"What temple?" Skandar interrupted.

Arren glanced up. "Oh. It's a building, Skandar. It would have a roof shaped like this"—he made a dome shape with his hands—"and a big gold disc on top."

Skade looked thoughtful. "That makes sense. I am willing to try."

"We'll do it, then," said Arren. "All we have to do is find the river."

"Norton," said Skandar.

"What, Skandar?"

"Norton," the black griffin repeated. "We go to Norton. Not cave. Not want go there."

"I don't care what you want," Arren said coldly. "I am going to this cave, and you can't stop me,"

It was the wrong thing to say. Skandar snarled and lunged forward, scattering the fire with his claws. His beak struck Arren directly in the chest, knocking him violently to the ground, and before he could get up, the griffin had pinned him down, his huge talons threatening to crush him. Skade darted out of the way, but neither of them paid her any attention.

Arren found himself looking up into a pair of blazing silver eyes. Skandar brought his beak down toward him, hissing. "My human," he rasped. "Mine!"

Arren struggled. "I am not yours, damn you!"

Skandar pressed down harder. "Mine!"

"Gods damn you!" Arren yelled. "Get off me! Get away from me! I hate you!"

"Mine!"

"No!"

Man and griffin stared each other in the face for a few moments, challenging each other. Arren knew that, if Skandar wanted to, he could crush his chest to a pulp. He had done it to men in the Arena, dozens of times. It had made him famous. But he glared back anyway, not caring what the griffin did.

"Now you listen to me," Arren rasped, the pressure on his rib cage making his voice sound strange and hoarse. "This is your fault, griffin. What happened to me was because of you, understand? I am going to the spirit cave and I am going to be healed there, and you can go to Norton or anywhere else you want, but you can go on your own. Because I've had enough. I've had enough of you, and I've had enough of this, and you can help me or you can go away. I don't care."

The silence stretched out for what felt like an eternity. Skandar did not move. Arren could feel the griffin's hot, rank-smelling breath on his face and see the myriad of tiny black veins that crossed the silver in his eyes. The only sounds were the wind in the trees and the faint crackling of the fire.

Skandar removed his claws and backed away, hissing.

Arren sat up, wincing. He said nothing but continued to stare coldly at the griffin, full of anger and a kind of hot, sick guilt.

"I go," Skandar said at last. Without another word, he turned and walked away. When he was a good distance from Arren, he opened his wings and broke into a stumbling run. Arren scrambled to his feet, suddenly afraid, but there was nothing he could do. Skandar took off in a clumsy flurry of wings and flew up and over the forest and then northward, growing smaller and smaller.

Arren stared at the sky, full of shock. "He's gone," he said blankly.

"So it would appear," said a voice.

Arren looked around, and froze.

It was Skade. She was walking toward him, her sharp face wearing an expression of steady, cold determination. She was holding his sword.

5

The Pact

Arren backed away. "Skade, what are you doing?" he said, reaching for his knife.

The silver-haired woman stopped, resting the tip of the sword on the ground. "You should put your robe back on," she said. "It is by your feet."

Arren glanced down and saw it lying discarded by the base of a tree. He snatched it up hastily and pulled it on. "That's my sword. Could I have it back, please?"

Skade gripped the hilt more tightly. "No. I will keep it for now, thank you."

Arren did up the fastenings on his robe and grasped the handle of his knife, though he didn't pull it out. He didn't want to risk provoking her. "What are you doing?"

"I am sorry," said Skade. "You have—you saved my life. But I cannot risk trusting you more than I have to." She glanced at the sky. "Your partner is gone. You are not much of a griffiner if you cannot stay in harmony with your griffin."

"He's not my griffin," said Arren. "He's just—well, he's not my griffin."

"But he let you ride on his back, and he protected you," said Skade. "To me that makes him your griffin. It would be an insult to him to say otherwise. Unless you have a reason to think he is not your griffin?"

"It's none of your business," Arren snapped.

"But I am making it my business, Arren."

"You shouldn't. What I do is my business. I—" Arren broke off and clenched his fists. "Gods, he's gone. I didn't think he would do that."

"You told him to," said Skade. "He knew he was not wanted.

You should not have spoken to him like that, Arren. You insulted him and rejected him. He will not forget that. Either way, it is no concern of mine." She held out a hand. "And now you will give that knife to me."

Arren drew it. "Why should I?"

"I do not trust a murderer," said Skade.

The word felt like a dagger blow in his chest. Arren backed away further. "What? I'm not a—how dare you say I'm a—"

Skade's expression hardened. "You are a liar, Arren Cardockson," she said, "And not a good one. I know who you are, and I know what you did."

Arren's stomach started to churn. "Who's Arren? Why are you calling me that?"

"I called you that twice already," said Skade. "And you did not notice. That was the only confirmation I needed."

Arren felt a strange calm come over him. He looked at her, quickly judging how much of a threat she could pose. She was shorter than him, and thin, and from the way she was holding the sword it was obvious that she did not have any training in weapons. He could probably disarm her if he wanted to. And there was no-one else out here for miles. He decided to play along.

"How did you know?" he asked.

Her look was withering. "You are a Northerner," she said. "You have a scar on your face. You are travelling with a black griffin. You are a fugitive. And you were carrying this sword." She tapped the weapon's hilt; it was bronze and decorated with a frieze of griffins. "A sword this fine could only belong to a griffiner. And you speak griffish. The signs are hardly difficult to see."

"So, people know about me," Arren mumbled, not quite able to take all this in.

Skade gave an incredulous laugh. "You cannot be serious."

"I've been out here for months," said Arren. "I haven't spoken to another human being in all that time. I have no idea what people know about me."

"They know everything, Arren Cardockson," said Skade. "It has been months since you destroyed Eagleholm. More than long enough for word to spread."

Arren stared at her. "I destroyed—?"

Skade blinked. "Is there anything you *do* know about yourself?"

"I never destroyed Eagleholm," said Arren. "How could I have?"

"You murdered the Mistress and her council, and you set the Eyrie on fire," Skade told him. "It burned to the ground. Dozens of other griffiners and griffins were killed. The city is no more. The griffins and the griffiners have abandoned it."

Arren was aghast. "I didn't kill the Mistress! *Or* her council! I—"

"But that is the story I heard," said Skade. "That is the story many people are telling. You destroyed the city in one night, with the help of a black griffin, and now every griffiner in Cymria will be looking for you."

Arren closed his eyes. "Oh gods."

"I cannot believe that you did not know this," said Skade. "Or that you trusted me! I could have killed you in your sleep if I had wanted to."

"And are you going to try and do it now?" said Arren.

She spat. "No. What do I care what you have done? I have no love of griffiners or partnered griffins. I only want to know why you did it."

"Well, what are people saying?" said Arren.

"That you did it because you are insane. I did not believe it then, and I do not believe it now. Madness is not a reason. So tell me why you did it," said Skade. "There is no reason to hide it from me," she added when he didn't reply immediately. "Who would I tell?"

"I *didn't* do it," said Arren. "And I'm not mad."

"Oh? Then if you did not set fire to the Eyrie, who did? The city did not destroy itself."

"I only killed one of them," Arren blurted. "Just one. And I did set the Eyrie on fire, but I didn't know the whole thing would burn down. I just did it so they'd be too busy trying to put it out to chase after me. I didn't know that . . . oh gods." He closed his eyes. The Mistress dead and dozens of others . . .

Skade looked curious. "Who was the one you murdered? And why?"

"Rannagon," said Arren. "It was Lord Rannagon, the reeve. And his griffin, Shoa. But I didn't kill her; Skandar did."

"Why did you kill them?"

"Because Lord Rannagon betrayed me. He was—" Arren fiddled with his hair, caught between guilt and fear. "I was a griffiner." He paused and laughed bitterly. "I was. I really was. A real griffiner. My griffin was white, and her name was Eluna. She chose me when I was just a small boy; they couldn't persuade her to leave me. The other griffiners didn't want to accept me because I was a Northerner, but one of them offered to train me. I learnt griffish from him, and other things. When I was old enough I expected to be given a place in the Eyrie, but I didn't get one. I had to live out in the city with the commoners. I didn't mind. I always thought that one day they'd accept me. I did well. They made me Master of Trade. And then one day . . ."

Before he knew it, the story was tumbling out of him, all of it. Rannagon's betrayal, Eluna's death, and the misery and despair that had taken over his life once he returned to Eagleholm in disgrace.

"I finally did get another job, though, working in the hatchery," he said at last. "I hoped another griffin would choose me, but none did. Why would they? I was the lowest of the low by then. And then one day some people broke into my house. I still don't know who they were—whether Rannagon sent them or whether they were doing it for some other reason. They destroyed most of what I owned and stole the rest, and when I got home they were waiting for me. They attacked me, beat me up. They put a slave collar on me and left me alone to suffer. I got better, but I couldn't get it off, and it hurt all the time . . ."

Skade was listening. She didn't try to interrupt but let him talk on.

". . . and a while after that I snapped and stole a griffin chick," said Arren. "I couldn't stand it any longer. Without a griffin to protect me, I had become worthless. I wanted my life back. But they caught me, and Lord Rannagon sentenced me to death. I told them all the truth at my trial, but nobody listened. It was my word against his. Lord Rannagon told them I was mad." He realised he was breathing hard and tried to make himself slow down. "That was why I killed him. After Skandar helped me escape from prison. I came back to the Eyrie and killed him, and Skandar helped me. Someone saw me kill Rannagon. I set a fire in the room and then ran, and Skandar carried me out of there."

Skade waited for some time after his story had finished, as if to make certain that he had said all he had to say. "That griffin saved your life," she said softly.

Arren paused and nodded. "I suppose so."

"No. There is no supposing about it. If he had not carried you away, they would have caught you. You would have suffered a hideous death at their hands if they had."

"He killed Eluna."

"In self-defence, perhaps," said Skade. "I would say that a man in your position cannot afford to choose his friends. Anyone who stays by you now should be a hundred times more precious than the friends you had in your old life."

"He'll come back," Arren said unconvincingly.

"You will have to hold on to that hope," said Skade. "But I would not blame him if he did not return." Her look became bitter, almost angry. "A griffin who thinks he can protect a human forever is a fool, and few humans deserve their protection at all."

Arren stood up, watching her intently. "And you'd know, wouldn't you, Skade?"

She said nothing, but the certainty had already hardened in Arren's mind.

"You're not human," he said. "You're a griffin."

Skade froze. "You cannot know that."

Arren watched her closely, taking in the golden eyes, the claw-like fingernails, the silver hair. "You're a griffin," he said again.

She took a step closer. "How can you know? I have worn this body for so long, no other human—"

"I can . . . smell it," said Arren. His own voice sounded puzzled, but the moment he said it he realised what had been nagging at him all this time. "You're a griffin in a human's body. That's why you feel wrong to me. You've felt wrong from the moment I met you."

Skade turned away. "Leave me alone."

Arren thought back to what she said when they first spoke. "A year," he half-whispered. "You've been like this for a year. And you're trying to find the spirit cave so you can change back."

Skade, her back still turned, began to make a strange hoarse sound. With a shock, Arren realised she was sobbing.

He ventured closer. "I'm sorry, I didn't mean—"

With a sudden motion, Skade flung the sword away and put her hands to her face, rubbing it fiercely in a wild effort to remove the tears that had begun to wet it. He could hear her snarling, trying to stop herself from crying, but she only sobbed the harder.

Arren reached out to touch her shoulder, but then thought better of it. He surreptitiously kicked the sword away from her. "Skade, I—"

She turned. "Leave me alone!"

"It's all right," said Arren. "You don't have to be embarrassed about it, I can understand if you're—"

Skade let out another half-strangled sob and continued to rub at her eyes. "I hate it!" she screamed. "They will not stop doing it! I tr— I have tried everything, but I c-cannot—make it stop—"

Arren couldn't bear it any longer. He put his arms around her and held her to him. She tried to pull away at first, but finally stilled. "Do not touch me," she mumbled.

"It's all right," Arren said again. "I'm not hurting you, I'm just trying to make you feel better."

"And how will this make me feel better?" said Skade, her voice slightly muffled.

Arren couldn't help it; he smiled. "You're crying," he said. "It's what humans do when they're unhappy. Holding on to someone makes them feel better. See?"

She shuddered in his arms. "Why?"

"I don't know, but it's always worked for me. It's a human thing."

Skade pressed herself against him; she was thin and bony, and he could feel her heart pattering. "I wanted to die," she said at last. "I wanted to drown in that pond. I hated you for pulling me out."

Arren felt an ache in his chest. "It's okay, Skade. We'll find the cave, and you can change back. You'll be healed."

Skade said nothing. She did not try to return the embrace, but she did not try to pull away from him, either.

"Do you want me to let go now?" Arren asked gently.

She pulled his arm away from herself, and he released her, but she did not move away. She looked him in the face. Hers was tear-stained, but her gold griffin eyes were as fierce as ever. "Thank you, Arren Cardockson," she said, rather stiffly. "I . . . thank you."

Arren wanted to touch her, to try to comfort her further, but he didn't want to risk making her angry again. "Who would do something like this?" he asked softly. "Who would—why would anyone turn a griffin into a human? It's monstrous!"

Skade turned away. "I will travel to the spirit cave with you. If I can. But I am—I do not know if I will be healed there, if we ever do find it. Spirits are treacherous. They do not help all those who come to them, only those they deem worthy."

Arren felt a sick twisting sensation in his gut. "Why would you not be worthy?" he asked, trying desperately to block it out.

"I am not an innocent victim, Arren," said Skade, without turning around. "I was not cursed out of malice. It was punishment."

"Punishment for what?" said Arren.

She turned to look at him. "I am—I was a rogue griffin. I lived in the city, but one day I turned on the humans around me. I killed many. I was judged to be unstable and therefore worthless, and when it was clear that I had declared myself an enemy to humankind, the great council of griffins decided they would punish me, not with death but by forcing me to live as a human." She closed her eyes. "Arakae cast the spell on me, and when it was over I was banished and told that my fate was to wander the world in human form, with no hope of ever changing back." Her eyes opened. "That is why I have decided to trust you, human. Because you and I are alike. We are outcasts and murderers, and both of us are cursed."

"Cursed?" Arren repeated dully.

She nodded. "That is why you are so desperate to go to the cave, so much so that you decided to take my side rather than Skandar's, even though you barely knew me." She sighed and sat down with her back to a tree, evidently exhausted. "It only makes sense. When so many griffins want you dead, there is every chance that those with the power have death-cursed you by now."

Arren looked away. "Yes."

There was silence after that. Arren gazed up at the sky, scanning the endless blue. There were a few birds up there, but no sign of anything that could be a griffin. His feeling of sickness increased.

"I'll just fix the fire now," he mumbled. "Are you hungry?"

"Yes," said Skade. She got up. "I will help."

Arren opened his mouth to tell her she should rest, and then shut it again. He wandered off into the trees and gathered wood. When he returned, Skade was using the sword to cut some more meat from the sheep—not a very efficient process. The blade was blunt, as sword blades always were—after all, they were made to slash bodies open, not perform surgery.

Arren went over and offered her his knife. "Here, this might work better."

She took it. "I cannot eat raw meat any more," she muttered as she worked. "It makes me ill."

Arren piled more fuel onto the fire and blew on it to coax it back to life. "The food isn't very good out here, is it?" He sighed. "If only we were back in my house at Eagleholm. I could cook a proper meal for you." The dry bark he'd put onto the coals caught and began to burn brightly. "Potatoes—now, I haven't had those for as long as I can remember. I'd give anything for a plate of boiled potatoes."

Skade came over carrying a bloody hunk of meat. "Eggs," she said. "I would love some eggs."

"Ooh, yes," said Arren. "A couple of poached eggs with some sage sprinkled on top, and maybe a cup of strayberry milk to go with 'em."

She gave him an odd look. "Strayberry milk? You can get milk from strayberries?"

Arren laughed. "No, no, of course not. No, it's something I invented." He took the meat from her and impaled it on a stick. "What you do is take a cup of ordinary cow's or goat's milk, and then you crush a few strayberries—as many as you like— and mix the juice in with the milk. You can add some honey to sweeten it, and warm it on the stove for a while if you want, and then you drink it. It tastes delicious."

Skade shook her head. "You humans cannot eat anything as it is, can you? You must always insist on burning it or mixing it with something else."

"Well, if it tastes better that way, I'm not going to complain," said Arren.

Skade snickered. "You are a strange man, Arren."

He looked at her. "How do you mean?"

"I knew many Northerners in Withypool," said Skade. "To me, nearly all of them looked the same. They were not like you, not at all."

Arren touched his neck. "They wouldn't be like me, would they? They were slaves, and I'm not."

Skade watched him with a gleam in her eye. "I have known only two free Northerners in my life," she said, "and I think you are a better people when you are free. There is a spirit about you that other humans do not have."

Arren smiled. "Thank you, Skade," He checked on the meat, moving it closer to the fire. "Who was the other one? The other free Northerner you met?"

Skade did not reply. When he looked at her, he saw she was watching the sky.

Arren looked skyward as well, thinking that maybe she had seen Skandar. There was nothing.

"Skade?"

She looked at him. "Yes, Arren?"

"Do you think he's going to come back?"

He waited for her reply, almost desperate to hear it, as if she somehow knew what Skandar would do.

"Do you want him to?" she said at length.

Arren glanced skyward again. "Yes," he said.

"Why?"

"Because—I don't know. I keep wanting to hate him, but—" Arren gave her an agonised look. "What if he doesn't come back? What if something happens to him? He doesn't know where he's going. What if he gets lost? If I'm not there to help him, he might start eating people again, and then they'll catch him and kill him."

Skade smiled to herself. "I am sure he can look after himself. I suggest you wait here for him to return."

"But what if he doesn't?"

"I think he will come looking for you sooner or later," said Skade. "You saved his life, and he will remember it. Besides, where else does he have to go?"

Arren calmed down a little. "Yes, I suppose that's all we can do for now. I don't want to leave here without him. When I see him again I'll apologise to him and hope he forgives me."

"If he thinks of you as his human, he will come back," said Skade.

Arren looked at the sky. "I hope you're right, Skade. I hope you're right."

* * *

The sun was high overhead, and the screech of a griffin echoed over the rooftops of Norton to signify that it was noon. The town was right on the border between the lands belonging to Eagleholm and the neighbouring territory of Malvern—the city that ruled over what had once been black-robe land—and though the fortified walls that surrounded it had fallen into disrepair after a hundred years of relative peace, there was a large stone tower in the centre which was still in use. The top was flat, and large platforms jutted from its sides, built specifically for griffins to land and perch on.

Senneck circled above it a few times rather than landing immediately. There were no other griffins in the sky here or any perched on the tower platforms, but there was a small gathering of people on the ground at the base of the tower, and she made her decision and descended toward them. They moved away to let her land, and once she had folded her wings, Erian slid off her back. He paused to pat her on the shoulder and then turned to look at the little group that had come to welcome him.

"Why are there no griffiners here?" he said, without pausing to greet them. "I expected Lord Galrick to be here to meet me. Where is he?"

One of the group came forward, bowing low. "I am sorry, my lord. Lord Galrick left here only two days ago."

"Left to go where?" Erian demanded.

"Uh, we, uh—we understand that he has gone to Malvern, my lord, to offer his services to Lady Elkin."

Erian swore. "Already? Curse him! How many others were here with him?"

"Seven, my lord. The lords Sumner, Manolis, Mervis and Dirke, and the ladies Stellana, Katriona and Liyah."

"And where have *they* gone, may I ask?"

"I am not certain, my lord. Sumner and Mervis went with Lord Galrick and his wife, Lady Stellana, but the others—they left without notice, shortly after we received word of what had happened at Eagleholm."

Erian breathed deeply, trying to contain his anger. "So am I to take it that there are no griffiners left here at all?"

"No, my lord," said the man. "The Lady Kitaen is still here, at the temple."

"Go and tell her to come here at once," Erian snapped.

"I believe she is already on her way, my lord," said the man. "She was delayed by the noon rites, but they will be over by now. If you would like to retire indoors, I am sure that—"

"I have no time to waste," said Erian. "I shall wait for her here. Bring water for Senneck."

"Yes, my lord."

The man nodded to one of his companions, who dashed off and returned a surprisingly short time later with a very large dish and a jug of water. He placed the dish on the ground at a respectable distance from the two of them and filled it with water, keeping his head bowed and not daring to look directly at Senneck as he retreated. The brown griffin watched him disdainfully, and once he was out of the way, she stepped over to the dish and sniffed at its contents. Apparently satisfied, she dipped her beak in the water, tossing her head back to tip it down her throat.

Erian stood by and watched her, careful not to do anything that might annoy her. She had flown a long way in a brief period, and she was probably far more tired than she would be willing to admit. She had only had a human partner for a few months now, and carrying him in the air must still be hard work for her.

He stifled a yawn and adjusted the hang of his sword. It was a fine weapon; it had a long, straight blade made from the finest steel, and the hilt was gold set with large red stones. The swordsmith who had made it for him according to his exact specifications had said that such decorations were unnecessary and impractical, but Erian had been unmoved. He had spent nearly all his life on a farm and had always dreamt of the wealth and grandeur that would be his once he became a griffiner like his father; even if he didn't have any land or riches yet, nothing could make him put up with a plain sword. Nonetheless, this sword—fine though it was—was nothing but a temporary stand-in. Erian knew which sword he should be carrying. He had seen it only a few times, but he remembered it very clearly. Old, its bronze hilt decorated with images of flying griffins. His father's sword, now in the hands of his murderer.

Erian's jaw tightened as the crowd parted to let someone through. He saw the griffin before the griffiner: it was female, with yellow-brown feathers and tawny hindquarters. She looked a little too small to be ridden—not that her partner would be

able to ride a griffin anyway. Erian had nothing but contempt
for the priesthood. Every major temple in Cymria was headed
by a griffiner, but very few griffins would allow their partner
to join the priesthood voluntarily. A priest was not allowed to
own property or to command anyone outside of the spiritual
world, and the priesthood was traditionally a dumping ground
for unwanted griffiners: younger siblings, cowards, cripples—
in essence, anyone judged unable or unfit to fight or command
as every griffiner was expected to do.

This one wore the traditional pale-blue gown of a priestess
and had rather grubby blonde hair. She was very fat and walked
with a slow, heavy-footed gait. Erian sneered inside. No wonder
she'd been shunted sideways into the priesthood. There was no
griffin on earth that could carry someone her size.

Senneck went forward to meet the griffin, dipping her head
respectfully. The other griffin held her own head high, raising her wings slightly to make herself look larger as she sized
the newcomer up. Neither of them spoke, but Senneck clicked
her beak rapidly as the yellow griffin sniffed at her head and
neck, and made no move when she bit her lightly on the nape
of the neck to assert her dominance. Erian looked on, slightly
annoyed to see his partner deferring to the other griffin, but he
knew better than to interfere.

Finally, Senneck backed away and sat on her haunches, her
tail curled around her. "I am Senneck," she said. "My human is
named Erian Rannagonson."

The yellow griffin flicked her tail. "I am Kreeak, and my
human is Kitaen Sunborn, Priestess of the Norton Temple."

The formalities over with, the two griffins moved to stand
behind their humans, giving them tacit permission to talk to
each other.

Erian inclined his head briefly to the priestess. "It's an honour to meet you, my lady."

She returned the gesture. "May the light of Gryphus embrace
you, my lord."

Erian paused. "Please, my lady," he said, "there are urgent
matters to discuss, and I think we should do so in private. Shall
we retire indoors?"

"Of course." Kitaen glanced at the various officials who had
been loitering in the area. They had already taken the hint and

were retreating toward the tower, whose doors had been opened to let the two griffiners enter.

Lady Kitaen and her griffin led Erian and Senneck into the tower and thence to a large room where a good fire was burning in a finely carved fireplace. There were two comfortable chairs set up in front of it, and wine had been placed on a small table, along with a bowl of strayberries. A fresh haunch of meat had been put on a plate for Senneck, who bit into it without hesitation.

Erian sat down in the chair nearest to her, pleased. They must have been keeping a lookout for him to have everything so well organised.

Kitaen sat down in the other chair and poured wine for the two of them. "I truly am sorry for the circumstances, my lord," she said. "I assure you that I did all I could to persuade Lord Galrick to stay here at least long enough to greet you himself, but there was very little I could do."

Erian took the cup offered to him. "I don't blame you," he said. "But I am . . . disappointed. Not in you, but in Galrick. Does the man have no loyalty in him at all? Riona has barely been laid to rest but her so-called loyal city governor has already flown off to swear himself to a different Eyrie?"

Kitaen smiled slightly. "I'm afraid you mustn't have had too much experience in dealing with your fellow griffiners, my lord. Lord Galrick did what was best for himself and his family. This garrison here is weak, too weak to repel an invasion from the North. If he offers himself to Lady Elkin now, she will be far more likely to accept him than if he waited for her to send her armies to his doorstep. The same goes for the others."

"Have they all gone north, then?" said Erian.

"Most of them, I believe. They did not tell me, but Lord Manolis was a friend of mine and he confided to me that he planned to go west, toward Canran. If he did, then Liyah, his wife, would have gone with him."

"I suppose I shouldn't really blame them. These lands aren't ready to fend off invasion, and an attempt to resist would be suicide, and pointless suicide at that. I've no intention of staying here any longer than I have to, either. I understand why Galrick did what he did. Either way, it's not really any of my business." Erian sighed. "I'm only irritated with him because I had hoped he would show me the courtesy of staying to meet me. I suppose he didn't consider me worthy of that honour," he added sourly.

"Well, *I* am more than happy to meet you, my lord," said Kitaen. She paused to drink some wine. "I had been wondering whether you were coming here to take Galrick's place."

"Perhaps, one day," said Erian. "But becoming governor of this city is not my biggest concern at the moment. No, I have come here for a different purpose."

"And what would that be, my lord?" said Kitaen.

She bloody knows already, Erian thought. He leant forward. "I am looking for a certain person, my lady, someone I have a very large obligation to find. Someone *every* griffiner should be honour-bound to hunt down."

Kitaen sighed. "You are looking for Arren Cardockson."

Erian's grip tightened on his cup. "Arren Cardockson, Arenadd Taranisäii, the mad blackrobe, the destroyer of Eagleholm—I don't care what you call him. I want to find him before he escapes from Eagleholm's lands. If he falls into the hands of Canran, or *any* other Master or Mistress, I will—there will be consequences."

"Consequences for whom?" said Kitaen, choosing her words carefully.

"I am going to be the one to find him, my lady," said Erian. "And I intend to be personally responsible for what happens to him after that. Lord Rannagon was my father, and I saw him die in front of me. I have the right to avenge him, and I will go to any lengths to bring that about. Do you understand?"

Kreeak was hissing softly. Kitaen took a strayberry from the bowl and turned it over in her fingers. "I understand perfectly, my lord, and I have no intention of trying to get in your way."

"Then you'll help me?"

"As far as I can, yes," said Kitaen. "What is it you want from me?"

Erian relaxed slightly. "You have his parents."

She nodded.

"Where are they?"

"They were kept in the prison out in the city at first," said Kitaen. "But once Lord Galrick found out who they were, he had them moved. They are in the dungeons beneath this tower as we speak."

"I read that in the last message he sent to Eagleholm," said Erian. "How were they caught? When?"

"Only a week or so ago, by my guess," said Kitaen. "According to what I was told, they were found camping in the forest just outside the city and were arrested on suspicion of being bandits or escaped slaves." She smiled thinly. "Or possibly both. When Galrick found out that the blackrobe's parents were wanted, he thought this couple could well be them, so he interrogated them himself and managed to find out their names. Since then they have been living in the dungeons."

"Have they been tortured?"

"No. Threats and starvation were enough to make them give their names. Beyond that, they have given nothing away, but Lord Galrick thought it would be best to refer to Eagleholm before he took any further action."

Erian smiled grimly. "Then he did at least one thing right." He finished off his wine in a few mouthfuls and put the cup down. "I want to talk to them."

"Certainly, my lord. When?"

"Immediately."

6

Calling

Arren sat and prodded the fire despondently. It needed more fuel, but he couldn't summon up the energy to go and get any. He sighed. He was hungry, but he was forcing himself to wait until nightfall to eat. The sheep's carcass had been picked clean by now, and he and Skade had been steadily eating their way through the meat that he had already smoked. It would all be gone in a day or so and, even combined, their foraging hadn't turned up much.

He rubbed his eyes. It had been four days since Skandar had left them. Four days, and neither he nor Skade had seen a sign of the black griffin anywhere. For the first day, Arren had remained hopeful; Skandar had occasionally gone on extended hunting trips in the past, sometimes for nearly an entire day. He could still come back. But by noon on the second day, he began to lose hope, and there was little he could do but try to accept the fact that Skandar was not coming back. It was all over. Finished. Without Skandar to help him, he would never get to the spirit cave, or to Norton, or anywhere else for that matter. He had made the half-hearted suggestion that they begin walking, in the hopes of finding a better place to stay, but deep down he knew it would be pointless. There was nothing but forest for miles in every direction, and they could never find enough food for them both. If they left the camp, they would get lost in no time, and after that they would both die of starvation. Even so, he might have given it a try and hoped for the best, but only if he had been on his own—and he wasn't willing to leave Skade behind.

He glanced at the spot where she preferred to sit, close to the crude shelter he had built for the pair of them. It was unoccupied. Skade had been much weaker than he had realised at first, and for most of the time they had spent together since Skandar had flown away she had remained in the camp resting and eating. She had a voracious appetite once she stopped suppressing it, and Arren hadn't had the heart to tell her they should try to preserve the food they had. He had done his best to look after her, giving her as much food as she wanted and making sure she had plenty to drink. He let her use the sheepskin as a blanket, and after he'd built the shelter he had offered to let her have it to herself. She had refused the last offer, insisting that they share it so that they could keep each other warm. Arren had been embarrassed by that, but he hadn't protested much. He liked Skade, liked her very much.

The silver-haired woman had recovered her strength with surprising speed, and for a while she had apparently been content to stay close to the camp and help him look for food. But he had woken up that morning alone, and he had only seen her once since then, briefly, when he had gone looking for her. He had found her crouched by the base of a tree, glaring at the sky, and when he ventured too close she hissed at him and stalked off.

Arren glanced at the sky. Nothing.

They've both run off on me, he thought miserably.

The silence among the trees was oppressive. He couldn't even hear any insects chirping. Here the sky seemed huge, a massive presence hovering above him, the trees reaching up toward it like pillars. He hated this place. It made him feel as if he were in a cage, being steadily crushed by its great thick bars. He missed his home then, missed it as he had never done since Skandar had left. He thought of his little house on the edge of the city, with the small iron stove and his hammock hanging from the rafters. On cold mornings, when thick mist obscured the view, he would venture out onto the balcony and enjoy the feeling of the wind on his face, hearing nothing but the soft clinking of the bone wind chimes he had bought in the market district. Eluna would be there with him, too, saying nothing, maybe running the tip of her beak through the feathery rudder on the end of her tail to straighten the plumes.

Arren closed his eyes. He hadn't thought of Eluna for a

long time, but she was in his head now. He remembered her
so clearly, too clearly, but somehow when he thought of her,
he couldn't make the image of her in his mind stay still. It was
always moving, wavering, as if it were about to fade, and every
time he concentrated on it an image of Skandar would flash
across his consciousness, as if to remind him of the white griffin's fate.

He forced his eyes open again, and shivered. He missed
Eluna, and yet he missed Skandar, too. Just as he missed everyone he had known in his old life. Bran, his best friend, and
Gern, who had died, and Flell, Flell whom he had loved, Flell
who had abandoned him, Flell . . .

He thought of her, feeling a sickness inside him. *Flell, I'm
sorry. I'm sorry.* He had tried so hard to forget her face as he
had last seen it, full of terrible shock. It was futile.

Misery was starting to overcome his senses. He struggled to
get a grip on himself. *Don't think about it. Don't think about
her. Make yourself forget it.*

He thought of Skade instead. She was beautiful. The idea
crossed his mind before he could squash it, and he instantly felt
disgusted with himself. Flell *is pretty,* he told himself sternly.
*She's human. With her fine brown hair and blue eyes, and the
way she—no, don't think about her. Think of Skade.*

Skade was beautiful. He sighed and let himself admit it. She
looked odd, but there was something about her that he found
attractive regardless. Perhaps it was her ferocity. She was cou-
rageous. Yes, that was a safer thought. She had recognised him
as the murderer he was, but where another person might have
fled or pretended to be oblivious, she had dared to confront him,
when she was weak and starved, holding a sword she could
barely lift, let alone use. True, she had waited until Skandar
was gone, but for all she knew, Arren was a dangerous lunatic
who might try to kill her, too. And yet she had faced him anyway. She had *challenged* him. She had not shied away; she had
not betrayed fear. And her golden eyes, the way they seemed to
burn from within, the way the light caught her hair . . .

Arren tangled his fingers in his own hair and wrenched at it
until it hurt, gritting his teeth savagely. "Stop it, stop it, *stop it!*"

Well, it doesn't matter, he thought, trying to calm himself
down. Skade was his friend now, and he would help her and

protect her as far as he could. If need be, he would starve himself rather than let her die. She deserved more than he did to live, and for her sake he would just have to do his best to act normally. If she knew what he was feeling—

No. I'm not feeling anything. It's just a few ridiculous thoughts. She's a bloody griffin, you sick bastard! What's wrong with you?

Actually, she's not a griffin, a treacherous inner voice whispered. *Not any more.*

Arren shut it out and shambled off to find some more wood. Luckily there were plenty of fallen branches in the area, and it hadn't rained again since he had pulled Skade out of the pond, so they were dry enough. He gathered an armload and carried it back to the camp, where he carefully restocked the guttering fire. Once it was burning strongly again, he went to gather some more wood to pile beside it. It would be sunset fairly soon, and they couldn't afford to run out of fuel while it was dark.

Once he had done that, he relented and took a chunk of smoked meat from the bark-wrapped bundle that hung from a nearby tree. He'd eat this much for now and hope it would be enough.

As he was impaling it on his knife, the sound of rustling bark behind him made him look up sharply.

It was Skade. The instant he saw her, his stomach started churning. He said nothing but watched her re-enter the camp, moving quickly and picking her way through the rocks and sharp sticks that littered the ground. She reached the fire and sat down opposite him.

"Hello," Arren ventured. "D'you want something to eat?"

Skade said nothing. She looked into the fire, blinking slowly, like a lizard. He could see her chest heaving, as if she had been running, and a hot shiver went right down his spine.

"Uh," he said. "Uh, ahem, sorry. I was just—" He pulled himself together. "I'm just going to warm this up a little. Do you want some, too?"

Finally, Skade turned her face to his. She remained silent but looked him up and down, her eyes moving slowly and deliberately, as if she was looking for something.

It did very little to make Arren feel less awkward. "Uh, Skade? Is something the matter?"

Finally, Skade appeared to relax. "Sorry," she said, looking away. She shook herself with a quick, sharp motion, as if trying to ruffle the feathers she no longer had, and the distant look vanished from her eyes. "I will take some," she said.

Arren went to get another piece of meat, massively relieved, as if he had just passed some kind of very important test. "I'm sorry I blundered into you like that before," he said. "I was just worried about you. I didn't know that—well, I can understand it if you wanted some time alone."

She nodded. "I am sorry. I should not have hissed at you like that, but you took me by surprise."

"Sorry. I didn't realise you hadn't seen me."

Arren put the piece of meat on a flat rock beside the fire and held the other piece over the flames on the end of his knife. "Skade? I'm sorry if this is too personal, but I can't help but wonder—"

She looked at him sharply. "Yes?"

"What was your power?" said Arren. "Before you were—I mean, I know every griffin has a power, and I was just wondering—" He broke off awkwardly.

Skade smiled and glanced at the sky. "Up there," she said softly. "That was my power."

Arren followed her gaze. "The sky?"

"The storm," she said. "I had the power to summon the storm."

Arren thought of the sudden squall that had forced him and Skandar to land. "You mean, you made it rain that day? When we met?"

Her smile faded. "No. I cannot use my magic any more. That storm was a natural one."

"Are you sure?"

"Yes," Skade snapped.

"Sorry, sorry, I just—" Arren paused. He couldn't help himself. "What does it feel like? To use magic?"

She looked amused. "Why do you want to know?"

"I've just always wondered," said Arren. "You see"—he turned the meat over—"I never did ask Eluna. She never discovered her own magic before she died, but she always promised me that when she did, she would tell me what it felt like. And now I'll never know."

"Did you ask Skandar?"

"No. I don't think he knows his own magic, either. As far as I know, he's never used it. Besides, I don't think he could speak well enough to describe it. So I thought maybe you could tell me."

Skade paused and then got up and moved to sit closer to him. Arren shrank away from her slightly, but she only reached past him and took the piece of meat he had put next to the fire. She bit a piece off it and chewed slowly, almost blissfully. "Even I could not describe it to you," she said at last, just as he had begun to wonder if he had offended her in some way. "Not properly."

"I think I understand," said Arren. "It's too far outside what humans understand. It would be like trying to tell a rock what it feels like to be in love. Is that right?"

She appeared to think it over, and then nodded briefly. "Yes. Exactly right."

"But could you try anyway?"

"Heat," Skade said simply. "It feels like heat. A heat so intense that you feel it should destroy you, but somehow you can contain it. You feel it rushing through you, from every part of your body, into your throat. You cannot move or think. The magic controls you and forces your beak open wide, as if you were going to scream, but what comes out is not sound but light." She paused. "That is what it feels like."

Arren sat back, holding the knife in one hand without really noticing it. "That's—that sounds amazing."

"It is," said Skade. "And I would give anything to feel it again." She ate the rest of her meat in silence.

Arren, bringing himself back to reality with a little effort, pulled his own portion free of the knife and chewed unenthusiastically at it. After four days of very little else, even mutton was losing its appeal.

"I wonder what power Skandar has?" said Skade, breaking into his thoughts.

Arren stared at the fire. "I don't know. Something very intense, I think. Something wonderful—or terrible."

"Yes," Skade said slowly. "I had a feeling when I was near him."

"What kind of feeling?"

"I do not know. This body does not understand it. But something. That griffin is strong. Who knows what his magic could do?" She glanced at the sky. It was a gesture both of them had been repeating very often over the last few days. "Are you going to call for him again?"

Arren sighed. "I don't know. What's the point? He must be miles away by now."

"Maybe, maybe not. Have you given up on him already?"

By way of an answer, Arren got up and walked away from the fire. The sun was close to going down now. The light would start to fade soon.

He lifted his face toward the sky, braced himself and screamed. *"Arren! Arren!"*

He repeated it again and again, sending his name into the sky as a griffin would. It was a griffiner trick, one he had been taught very early in his training as a way to signal to his griffin that he needed her. After Eluna's death, he had used it once more before the burning of the Eyrie, and that time it had not brought her but Skandar. Maybe now it would bring him back, but Arren didn't believe it. He called anyway, on and on, as he had called every evening since his friend had abandoned him, until his throat hurt too much to continue and he fell silent and wandered back to the fire.

Skade was watching him with an odd expression; he couldn't read it, but it unsettled him.

He slouched down as close to her as he dared and buried his face in his hands. "There, that's that done," he croaked. He glanced up. "Why are you looking at me like that?"

Skade looked away, "Sorry. I was . . . thinking."

"About what?"

"I am not certain yet." She shifted slightly. "Is there anything more to eat?"

"What? Oh. Yes, of course. Just give me a moment." Arren went to fetch her some more meat.

As he was unwrapping the bark, the quiet was shattered by a loud noise from behind him. It was somewhere away from the camp, in the trees, and was muffled a little by distance, but it was the unmistakeable sound of breaking wood. And, behind that, a thud.

Arren turned sharply, reaching for his sword. "What in the gods' thundering toenails was *that*?"

Skade had scrambled to her feet and was standing by the fire, hunched slightly, like a cat poised to run. She paused briefly and then pointed. "That way." Without waiting for an answer, she ran.

Arren snatched up the sword and followed, blundering through the trees, his boots catching on rocks and branches and clumps of grass. He had a fair turn of speed over better terrain, but Skade was shockingly fast when she wanted to be. He managed to keep up with her by dint of considerable effort, until she disappeared through a soap-bush thicket. When Arren tried to follow, the branches snagged on his robe and tripped him up, and he lost his patience and hacked his way through with his sword.

The first thing he saw when he emerged on the other side was Skade. She had stopped and was standing and looking at something big and dark lying on the ground. Something that was trying to get up, one wing flailing awkwardly.

"Skandar!"

Arren dashed forward, dropping the sword, and Skade had to leap out of the way to avoid being knocked over.

Skandar managed to roll onto his stomach, and stared blankly at him. "Arren," he rasped.

Arren halted before he got too close, knowing the griffin might see it as an attack if he kept coming. "Skandar," he said again. "Skandar, for gods' sakes, I . . ."

Skandar didn't seem to hear him, and Arren suddenly felt his insides twist as he saw the strange, rigid posture, the dull, desperate look in the eyes, the saliva glistening around the beak. "Oh no," he whispered.

Skandar tried to drag himself closer. "Sick," he said, the word gurgling in his throat.

Arren went to him. "No, no, don't move, Skandar. Lie still. Don't move too much, I need—"

The black griffin slumped. "I die," he said. "Die now, Arren Cardockson."

"No," Arren snapped. "Skandar, listen. I need you to tell me what's wrong. Where do you feel sick? Where does it hurt?"

"Hurt," Skandar repeated, as if he didn't understand what the word meant.

"Where, Skandar? Where? Is it your stomach? Your chest? Please, just tell me where it hurts and I can help you. Please, Skandar. *Skandar!*"

Skandar's eyes had closed. Arren dared to touch his head, trying desperately to coax him back into wakefulness. At first the griffin did not respond, and for a horrible instant Arren thought he was dying. Then, without warning, his head jerked forward. Arren darted out of the way as Skandar started to heave and retch, his neck extending as far as it could go, back arching, hind paws scrabbling at the ground. More saliva drooled from the end of his beak, and he made an awful hacking, gagging noise. Then, just as abruptly, he groaned and slumped back down again.

Arren watched, horror-struck, trying desperately to think what to do. Memories sleeted through his mind, memories of days long gone, days spent in a dusty room with his old mentor, memories of books he had read, books that had seemed boring at the time, but books whose knowledge could help Skandar now. And as Skandar convulsed again, it clicked into place. Arren started to unfasten his robe as fast as he could.

"What are you doing?" said Skade from behind him.

Arren threw the garment aside. "It's his throat," he said. "There's something stuck in his throat!"

Skandar slumped again as Arren came closer. He made no further attempt to speak, and it was plain that he was reaching the end of his strength.

Arren knelt by him and touched his beak. "Skandar, listen to me," he said. "Listen. Please. Look at me."

Skandar opened one eye and turned it toward him.

"I need you to open your beak," said Arren. "There's something stuck in your throat, and I have to pull it out. Understand?"

Skandar retched again, and then again, more violently, and Arren scrambled aside as the convulsions returned. The griffin rolled onto his side, legs jerking, beak opening as wide as it could. A wing lashed at the air, so hard it nearly bowled Arren over, and his forelegs kicked out wildly. One blow from the right angle could kill Arren instantly.

Skade darted over and grabbed Arren by the arm. "Arren, get away from him!"

Arren pulled himself free. "No!"

Skandar continued to jerk and twitch, his talons clutching at nothing. Arren dodged around them, threw himself down by the griffin's head, and thrust his arm deep inside the wide-open

beak and down his throat. Skandar's gagging worsened, and
he wrenched his head sideways, nearly breaking Arren's arm.
But it was too late to stop now. Arren grabbed hold of his beak
with his free hand and pushed the other further in, searching
desperately for the obstruction. Skandar made another jerking
motion, but then, far worse, he began to still. His legs stopped
kicking out, and his breathing became rapid and desperate. He
was suffocating.

Finally, Arren's questing fingers struck something hard and
unyielding. With a little jolt of triumph, he began to feel his
way around it, trying to find the best way to get a grip on it and
pull it out. It was long and thin, like a branch, and was jammed
sideways inside the fleshy tube that led to Skandar's stomach.
Arren, his shoulder now stuck against the corner of the griffin's beak, searched as fast as he could for any sharp edges.
There didn't seem to be any, so he grasped the thing by one
end and pulled. It came unstuck, and he increased his grip and
continued to pull it toward himself until, at last, it was out of
Skandar's throat and in his beak, and in a moment Arren was
slumping back on the ground by his head, holding something
soggy and glistening in his hands.

Skandar sighed and became still. Arren watched him anxiously, but the griffin's breathing had deepened and slowed.
The unnatural rigidity was gone. He was exhausted, but he
would live.

Skade appeared silently behind him. "You saved him."

Arren panted. "I hope so." He got up, still holding the thing
in his hands. "I need to wash my arm. It's—" He grinned suddenly, full of the strange euphoria that panic leaves behind. "I
had no idea griffin spit was so . . . sticky," he said, trying to
wipe it off on a nearby tree.

Skade hid a smile behind her hand. "There is water just over
there," she said, pointing to the creek.

"Thanks."

The creek was a little deeper here, and he drank and then
washed himself, scrubbing his skin with a handful of sand. He
was still carrying the object, and gave that a quick rinse as well.
He frowned at it, puzzled. It wasn't a branch but something
else; obscured by something that looked like—

His happiness started to drain away as quickly as it had

come. Cloth. The thing was wrapped in cloth. He pulled it away; it was perished, and disintegrated almost instantly, leaving the hard object inside it to fall onto the ground.

Arren picked it up, and the sick, anxious feeling he had had before came flooding back. He got up and ran to the clearing where Skandar lay.

"Skandar!"

Skade was there, holding his robe. "He is asleep," she said. "You should let him rest. What did you find in his throat?"

Arren showed it to her.

Skade's face fell. "But that—"

"Yes."

She came closer, staring at it. "I do not understand. How did that come to be in his throat?"

It was a long dagger, still in a leather sheath. Arren drew it cautiously; the blade was straight and looked quite sharp. Not an extremely expensive weapon, but good quality.

"Oh gods," Arren groaned. "What's he done?"

"Tried to eat a dagger, I think," Skade said dryly.

"No," said Arren. "Isn't it obvious? He's eaten someone. He's killed another human."

Skade's reaction caught him completely off guard. She looked at him for a moment, and then she laughed.

"It's no laughing matter," Arren snapped. "Don't you understand? If he's killed someone, that means all kinds of terrible things. For one thing, someone's dead, and for another, someone else could have seen him do it. It'll draw attention to us— for all we know there could be a hunting party out there right now looking for us!"

Skade lost her smile. "And what will you do if that is true, Arren? What if they are out there now and come across our camp without warning? What will you do?"

Arren gripped the dagger. "I'll fight. Not to win, but to escape."

"And if there is no escape?"

"Then I'll fight until I'm dead. I am not going to let myself be captured, not for anything."

She nodded. "Yes, that is what a warrior would do," she said in an oddly satisfied tone of voice.

"Here." Arren gave her the dagger. "You can keep this if you want. It'll probably be useful. I'm going to wake Skandar up. I have to know if there are people near here." He strode over to the griffin and nudged him with his boot. "Skandar? Skandar, wake up."

Skandar stirred and coughed softly. "I . . . wake, Arren."

Arren paused. "Skandar, do you feel better now?"

Skandar raised his head. "You help me," he said simply.

"Of course I did," said Arren. "You're my—" He suddenly felt a little awkward. "Well, you're my friend," he mumbled at last. "I'm sorry, Skandar. I shouldn't have said those things. I don't hate you, and I don't want you to go away. I missed you when you were gone."

Skandar blinked slowly. "I not—did not want—not want you to—" He gave up. "I heard you. You calling for me. I should not fly away. I cannot fly without you." He sighed and lowered his head onto his talons. "My human," he mumbled. "Mine."

Arren smiled. "I'll be your human for as long as you want me to be, Skandar. Truly. But—" Somehow, asking now felt almost cruel. But he had to do it. "Skandar, listen. Have you killed someone? A human?"

Skandar said nothing.

"Where did you go?" Arren persisted. "Where did you fly to?"

"Mist," Skandar said softly.

Arren's forehead wrinkled. "What? What's that, Skandar? Mist?"

"Mist," the griffin repeated, not raising his head. "Place . . . mist. Whispering."

"Whispering mist?" said Arren. "What are you talking about? Where was this?"

Skade had come closer to listen. "What did he say?"

"He said something about whispering mist," said Arren.

She stiffened. "Skandar, where was this? Where did you see the mist?"

"Place," said Skandar. "Place in ground. Hole. Space." He was growing frustrated searching for the words.

"Was it a cave?" said Skade.

Skandar sighed. "Yes. Cave, yes. Rocks, hole. Two mountains. Singing hill."

"Skade?" said Arren. "What's he talking about?"

Skade had become very still. "The cave," she said softly. "He's found the cave!"

Arren stared at her. "What?"

"The cave!" Skade said again. "The spirit cave! Don't you understand? Two mountains, a whispering mist—those were the spirits!" She went closer to Skandar, stopping only when he started to hiss warningly. "Where is it?" she said. "This cave with the mist in it, where is it?"

"Mountains," said Skandar. "Singing hill, then mountains. Big mountains. Cold. There was mist."

"Did it speak to you?"

The black griffin shuddered softly. "Yes. Whispering."

"What did it say?" said Arren.

Skade laid a hand on his arm. "No. Don't ask him. What the spirits tell must not be shared with another living soul."

Arren touched Skandar's beak. "Skandar, where is this place? Can you—*will* you take us there?"

"Yes," Skandar rasped. "I take you there."

Arren sighed. "Thank you, Skandar. A hundred times."

Skandar raised his head. "We go tomorrow," he said, with a touch of his old brusque authority. "Fly at dawn."

"Yes, of course. But Skandar, were there people there? Did you see people there?"

"Yes," said Skandar.

Arren groaned. "How many? What happened?"

"Humans near cave," said Skandar, sounding almost bored. "They see me, I kill them."

"You killed them?"

"And eat them," Skandar added blandly. "Good food."

"You probably shouldn't have tried to eat their weapons as well. Did any of them get away?"

"No. One run, I chase him. Eat him. Then sick."

"That was when you got the dagger stuck in your throat," Arren summarised. "And then you flew back."

"Yes." Skandar yawned. "I sleep now," he said abruptly, lowered his head back onto his claws and closed his eyes.

Skade took Arren by the arm. "We should leave him alone," she said softly.

Arren went reluctantly. It was nearly dark. "How are we going to find our way back to camp now?"

"Here." Skade gave him his robe. "We can follow the fire-light. Don't forget your sword."

Arren struggled back into the robe and found his sword

lying on the ground where he'd dropped it. Skandar was fast asleep. He'd be able to find them in the morning.

The two humans trudged back toward the camp. Arren was quick to spot the light of the fire showing through the trees and led the way to it. It was fortunate that he had added more fuel not very long ago; otherwise it could well have gone out by now.

He put the sword down by the lean-to and put some more wood on the fire.

Skade took meat out of the parcel. "We are lucky some animal did not steal this while we were gone," she commented.

Arren watched her take a generous amount of mutton out. "We really should try and save it," he said weakly.

"Perhaps," said Skade, who was already laying it out to warm up by the fire. "But I am sure we can find better food at the next place we stay. And besides, we should finish it now. Humans eat more when they have something to celebrate, and we have a great deal to celebrate."

Arren brightened up. "Yes, we do, don't we?" He paused and then laughed. "My gods! Can you believe this? Skandar found it for us!"

Skade nodded. "He is as remarkable as his partner."

Arren smiled bashfully. "Thanks. It's odd, though," he added. "How do you think he did it? He can't have had much idea of where he was going, and yet—it's bizarre."

"Not so bizarre," said Skade.

"What d'you mean by that?"

"The spirit cave is a place for griffins," said Skade. She moved closer to the fire, light and shadows playing over her face. "It calls," she half-whispered. "Its magic reaches out, drawing griffins toward it when they come close enough. He was meant to find it. And so are we."

Arren scratched his beard. This sort of thing sounded a little too mystical for him. Griffin talk. "You mean, it's destiny?" he ventured.

"I suppose it could be called that," said Skade. She shrugged. "Never mind."

They were silent for a time, busy with their own thoughts. Skade checked on the meat every now and then, and eventually passed a piece of it over to him.

Arren ate it, chewing slowly. "You know, we really should try and spice this stuff up a little," he said. "You can use soap-bush leaves as seasoning, I think. We could try it, if you want."

Skade wasn't listening. Arren glanced at her and saw she had that distant look about her again. He shrugged and decided to leave her alone.

Skade closed her eyes for a moment. "The spirit cave is so close," she breathed. "After so long, when I had begun to think I would never find it, it is within my grasp. Soon my curse will be lifted."

Soon, Arren thought. *Soon I'll be there, and the spirits will make me whole again. I can feel it. It's so close.*

Skade looked up at him. "Soon I shall be a griffin again," she said. "And you shall see me as I should be. You shall see my beauty."

"You look beautiful already," said Arren without even thinking. He cringed the instant the words were out of his mouth. It was such an idiotic thing to say, and it was bound to make her angry with him.

Skade smiled, though. "I hated being a human," she said. "Every moment of it was torment. I despised what I saw reflected in the water when I went to drink. It made me hate my own self. But you have helped me, Arren Cardockson."

"Helped you do what?" said Arren.

She glanced quickly at him and smiled again, almost shyly. "These last few days have been the only time I have not hated myself. And now, here with you, I almost feel as if I could be happy again."

"Well," said Arren. "Well, uh, it's the same for me," he said in a rush. "I like you, Skade. I've been so lonely out here for so long with nobody but Skandar. I felt like the whole world hated me. Sometimes even *I* hated me. But you were—well, you're a friend to me, Skade. A good friend."

She was watching him with that searching look. "You did a very brave thing tonight, Arren," she said softly. "What you did to save Skandar's life took great courage, and compassion as well. I did not think you would be able to do it, but you proved me wrong."

"I had to do it," said Arren. "Skandar's my friend. You were right, Skade. Any friend I have now is worth a hundred times what the friends I had in my old life were." He paused, and sighed. "I miss them all the same, though."

Skade nodded and picked up a piece of mutton. She teased at it with her fingers, shredding it, and ate the pieces one by one. "I have great admiration for you, Arren Cardockson," she said abruptly. "I spent this day thinking of you, and other things as well. I am sorry that I left you, but I needed to be alone."

"I understand," said Arren. "We all need to be alone sometimes."

"I was thinking," Skade said again. "I have made a decision."

"What kind of decision?" said Arren.

She looked him in the eye. "You saved my life," she said matter-of-factly. "I owe you a debt. And you—I have been watching you these past few days. You are strong and intelligent and kind. I have been thinking it over and over today. I was still uncertain when I returned to you before sunset, but after I saw what you did for Skandar, I was certain."

Arren swallowed. "Certain of what?"

"You have proven your worth to me," said Skade. She was moving closer, watching him intently.

Arren tried to keep calm and stopped himself from pulling away. "Thank you."

Skade stopped. "I felt a change in myself today," she said. "It made me angry and afraid. That is why I hissed at you. I did not think it could happen now that I am human, but it has."

"What has?" said Arren. He was feeling more and more bewildered, almost afraid.

Skade sat back. "I am ready to mate," she said calmly. "All day I have felt the urge to find a high place and call for a male to come to me, but this body cannot do that, and nor can it pair with another griffin."

Arren backed away. "What?"

She watched him, unwavering, showing no sign of embarrassment. "I want a mate," she said. "I need a mate. I have made my decision. I want you, Arren Cardockson."

"But I . . ."

Skade ran her fingers through her hair. "Do you not find me attractive?" she asked, with a hint of mischief. "You said you thought I was beautiful."

Arren stared at the ground. "Well, I—"

"Answer me!" Skade said sharply.

Arren looked up. "Look, I can't—it's not—you're *a griffin*!"

"No. Not now, Arren Cardockson. Now I am human. A human needs another human, and you are all I want in a mate." She came closer, so close he could feel her warmth; her eyes were aglow. "Tell me I am beautiful," she breathed. "Hold me like you did before. I want you to."

Arren didn't know what to do. Part of him wanted to move away; part of him wanted to move closer. "It's wrong," he said. "It's wrong."

She laughed. "And what do we care for what is right and wrong, Arren? We are murderers. There is nothing we can do that would make others condemn us more."

"Yes, but, but—" He could not find words to complete the sentence.

Skade's eyes narrowed. "If you will not hold me, then I shall hold you," she said, and pounced.

She collided bodily with him, knocking him flat on his back. He yelped and almost shoved her off, but she was surprisingly strong. She brought her face close to his, her hair brushing against his cheeks. "I am not a fool," she whispered, her eyes fixed on his. "I know how to be human, I know—" Then she kissed him. She did it clumsily at first, but she followed it up with another kiss, and this time there was more certainty, and when her lips touched his, Arren's buried feelings boiled over, sweeping away all his doubts and fears. He kissed her back, reaching up to put his arms around her. They rolled over, holding each other close, and after that there was nothing, no thought, nothing to propel them but instinct and an inner heat that changed itself to passion.

Arren could feel Skade's warm body pressed against his own, separated by nothing but a few layers of cloth. She was thin, but so strong, and delicate as well. She was beautiful; she was wonderful; she was wild; she was untamed. She was Skade.

As their embrace tightened, Skade's heart began to beat faster, pattering inside her chest. But Arren's heart was completely silent.

7

In This Together

Erian sat at a table in a dank stone room, hands folded in front of him. Senneck wasn't with him; much to her irritation, the brown griffin had been told that the dungeon passages were too small for her to fit. She was outside, waiting for him impatiently.

Meanwhile, Erian waited, jaw clenched, as a barred door in the opposite wall opened and a trio of guards entered, leading two manacled prisoners. The foremost guard shoved them toward the pair of chairs that had been placed on the other side of the table, facing Erian, and once they were seated, the guards stationed themselves just behind them, ready in case they made any sudden moves.

Erian regarded the prisoners. They were both middle-aged and had the black hair and pale skin of Northerners. The man had curly hair and wore a ragged beard that had probably sprouted during his imprisonment, and the woman had a haggard look about her. Both of them were watching him silently, their black eyes unreadable. Anger rose in Erian's chest almost instantly. He did not need any proof that they were the murderer's parents. The resemblance was obvious.

"So," he said, as coldly as he could, "I am told that you are Cardock the bootmaker, formerly of the village of Idun."

Cardock stared at the tabletop, unspeaking.

"And you," Erian went on, "are his wife, Annir, yes?"

"Yes," Annir whispered.

Erian nodded. "You both lived in Idun, very close to Eagleholm itself," he said. "I have seen the house you had there, and I cannot help but wonder, why are you not there now?"

They kept silent.

"It seems odd," Erian continued, "for you to suddenly abandon your home and your livelihood as you did. Your neighbours said you left in a great hurry. In fact, you didn't even stop to say goodbye. Could you, perhaps, provide some kind of explanation?"

More silence. For a moment Annir looked as if she was about to speak, but her husband touched her arm and shook his head.

"Cardock," said Erian. "You have an interesting name. And yet, somehow, I find it familiar. As if I have heard it before somewhere." He scratched his chin. "Cardock . . . Cardock . . . oh, yes. That was it. Cardockson." His voice hardened. "Do you, perhaps, know of a man with the last name of Cardockson?"

They stared at him, unyielding.

"I believe it's the tradition in these parts for a man to take his father's name," said Erian, his voice becoming louder. "So it's not unreasonable, perhaps, to assume that a man called Cardockson would, in fact, be *your* son, Cardock. Is that so?"

Annir and Cardock had drawn a little closer together, their hands clasped. Somehow, it only increased Erian's hatred of them.

"I haven't given *my* other name, have I?" he said. "Actually, I haven't given *either* of them. How rude. Please, forgive me." He touched his chest. "I am Lord Erian Rannagonson, and now you know my name, and the name of my father as well."

Cardock closed his eyes for a moment. The knowledge must have warned him that he could not expect any mercy.

Erian decided to stop playing games. "I'm the son of Lord Rannagon Raegonson," he said. "And three months ago I saw him murdered in front of me by a man who bore a striking resemblance to you, Cardock. A man I believe visited you before he committed his crime."

"We don't know anything," Cardock said at last.

Erian leant forward. "Don't think you can hide information from me, blackrobe," he hissed. "Your position is dangerous enough already. I could have you both killed instantly if I wanted. Who would care about the fate of Northern filth like yourselves? You're in my power now, and what happens to you depends on whether you give me what I want."

Annir clutched her husband's hand more tightly. "We can't lead you to him," she said in a strange, flat voice. "We don't know where he is. We don't know anything."

"You were expecting to meet him in Norton, weren't you?" said Erian. "That's why you were still here. You were waiting for him to come to you. But he didn't come. Or did he?"

"No," said Cardock. "He didn't come here. We don't know where he is. We haven't seen him."

Erian rolled his shoulders as he mulled this over. "But you knew he planned to come here, didn't you?" he said at last.

Silence.

Erian nodded. "I see. He knew you would be wanted by the authorities once he had become a murderer, so he told you to run here. But he didn't come. He lied to you. He and the black griffin have flown away and left you to your fate. But what more could you expect from a monster?"

"My son is not a monster!" Cardock burst out. He lurched forward, only to be hauled back by his guard. "You listen to me, boy," he snarled at Erian. "Your father deserved to die, understand? He deserved to die for what he did to us. He was in the North; he helped them massacre our people there. He was just as much of a murderer as you call our son. What Arren did was not murder. It was justice."

Erian lashed out, striking him hard in the face. Unable to contain himself, he followed it up with a second blow, which broke Cardock's nose. Cardock cried out, struggling to get free of the manacles, while Annir tried desperately to help him. It was a futile effort. Erian sat back as the two of them were restrained.

"You listen to me," he spat. "Arren Cardockson is a wanted man. Wanted by me. I intend to find him and see to it that justice is carried out. Now you're going to tell me what I want to know, or suffer until you do. Tell me where he's going. Where is he *really* going? Where is he hiding? *Where—is—Arren—Cardockson?*"

Cardock spat a mouthful of blood onto the table. "I don't know, and I wouldn't tell you if I did."

Erian sighed. "Very well." He looked at the guard holding Annir. "You, guardsman."

"Sir?"

"How are your quarters?" said Erian. "Are they comfortable?"

"They're not bad, sir," said the guard.

Erian looked at Annir. "But could they perhaps be a little more pleasant than that? A little less . . . lonely, maybe?"

The guard grinned. "We're always up for some company, sir."

"Excellent," said Erian. "Take her away and let her keep you company for a while. I'm sure she can find ways to entertain you."

"Certainly, sir."

"No!" Cardock lunged toward his wife, grabbing her hands as the guard began to haul her away. "For gods' sakes, no!"

Erian raised a hand to stop the guard. "You have something to say, Cardock?"

Cardock leapt at him with a scream of pure fury; Erian drew back a little in surprise, but the guards already had the matter in hand. The one near the door came over to help, and he and his colleague dragged Cardock away from the table, throwing him to the floor. He tried to get up, still fighting with all his might to get at Erian, but the guards threw him down again and began to hit him, kicking him in the stomach and groin. He curled up, trying to protect himself, but they continued to kick him; his yells were punctuated by horrible thuds and thumps.

Annir, still in the clutches of her own guard, started to sob. "Stop it! Stop it!"

"That's enough," said Erian.

The guards stopped at once, and Cardock rolled over on the floor, gasping in pain.

"Let him go," Annir sobbed. "He hasn't done anything, he's—"

Erian stood up. "Just tell me what I want to know," he said. "And it will all be over. Why protect a murderer? Do you know how many people died in that fire? It wasn't just my father he killed. There were others. Dozens of others. Innocents. *Children.*"

Annir sobbed harder. "No. Don't. Don't—"

"Just tell me where he went," said Erian. "Tell me where he was going to go after he met you. Tell me and you'll be out of these dungeons for good."

"North," Cardock rasped.

"I'm sorry?" said Erian.

"North," said Cardock, struggling to get up. "My son is going north. To his own country. He'll f— he'll fight you there. All of you, you murdering tyrants. You can't—can't win against him. He'll punish you, he will, for what you did to us. He'll—"

Erian sighed. "North," he said in an undertone. "Now it all makes sense. Of course he's going north. He thinks he can hide there. Well then," he said aloud. "If Arren Cardockson has gone north, then north is where I'll go. You, help him up."

The guards hauled Cardock to his feet, and Erian stepped around the table to face him.

"That wasn't so hard, was it?" he said. "And if your beloved son wants to fight us, so be it."

Cardock looked him in the eye. He was bleeding badly and swaying, but he stood tall—taller than Erian—facing him proudly. "He'll kill you, brat," he said. "When you find him, he'll kill you."

"He can try, if he wants to," said Erian.

Annir broke free of her guard and went to her husband's side; they made no effort to stop her but let her reach him and clasp him to her. She let go and turned to look at Erian. "Set us free," she said. "We gave you what you wanted."

"I'll do to you what should be done with every blackrobe," said Erian. He nodded to the guards. "Brand them, collar them and sell them."

S omething nudged Arren in the shoulder, waking him up. He groaned and rolled over. "What's—?"

He opened his eyes and saw something huge looming over him. He gave a yell of fright and scrabbled away from it as fast as he could go. Skandar backed off, wings opening, hissing. Arren sank back down again. "Skandar, what the—?"

The griffin sat back on his haunches, clicking his beak. "You sleep," he said reproachfully.

Arren sat up and made an effort to pick the bits of leaf out of his hair. "Well, yes, that's what I generally do at night." He looked at the spot where he had been lying. Skade was still there, curled up. She was starting to wake.

The recollection of the previous night came back to Arren. He rubbed his face. "Ye gods."

Skade turned over. "What, Welyn?" she mumbled.

Arren shook her gently by the shoulder. "Skade, it's me. Wake up."

She sat up, yawning. "Is it morning?"

"Yes." Arren looked around at the camp. The fire had gone

out. Skandar was sitting next to it, tail twitching impatiently. He'd eaten the last of the meat and had sharpened his talons on a nearby tree. He looked perfectly alert and healthy.

Skade followed his gaze. "Are you better?" she asked Skandar.

The black griffin regarded her for a moment. "Not sick any more," he conceded.

Arren got up. His robe and the front of his trousers were hanging open, and he refastened them hastily. "There's no pain?"

Skade yawned. "Hungry."

"I'll take that as a no." Arren looked at the sky. The sun was well up. "I suppose we should get going, then."

"We should conceal all of this first," said Skade. "We do not want to be tracked."

Arren shook himself. "Yes, you're right. I'll demolish the lean-to; you bury the fire."

"As you wish."

Arren quickly dismantled the crude shelter, saving the sheepskin blanket. He found his sword and strapped it on, and retrieved his knife from the fireside. Skade quickly finished covering the heap of ash and coals with leaf litter, and then scattered the sheep's bones.

Arren watched her surreptitiously. She looked completely unflustered, as if nothing had happened at all. It made him feel strangely embarrassed. He tried to think clearly, but it was hard. His head was full of memories, little snippets, little pieces of speech. *I want you for my mate, I want you, I want . . .*

His hands fumbled with the crude straps holding his sword to his back. He tried his best, letting himself remember it all, trying to identify the emotion beneath it.

Skandar had grown tired of waiting. He got up and came forward. "We go," he said.

Arren returned to the present. "Yes, of course. Skade?"

She came to his side, looking speculatively at Skandar. "Can he carry both of us?"

Arren shrugged. "I think so, but not all day. He carried two sheep at once just a few days ago."

Skade glanced at him. "I only saw one."

Arren smiled slightly. "The other one was in his stomach. Skandar, what do you think?"

The black griffin clicked his beak; if he had been human, he would have been scowling. "Can carry you," he said.

Arren knew he was annoyed by the suggestion that he couldn't. "Of course you can," he said soothingly. "I'll get up first."

Skandar lowered his head and let Arren climb onto the gap between his neck and his wings. Arren settled down there and then looked at Skade. "Now you get up behind me."

She approached carefully, not wanting to provoke Skandar in any way. He didn't react, but merely ruffled his wings irritably. Skade paused uncertainly, apparently trying to decide how best to get on without hurting him.

Arren reached down to her. "Here, take my hand."

She did, and he pulled her up over Skandar's shoulder. She managed to get her leg over and settled down behind Arren, putting her arms around his waist. Skandar didn't like this much; he shifted around, hissing softly. For a moment, the horrible thought crossed Arren's mind that he might try to throw them off. He didn't, but now would be a very bad time to provoke him.

"I've never done this before," said Arren. "Griffins aren't supposed to carry two people at once, but Skandar's very large for a griffin, and he's strong. Aren't you, Skandar?"

"Am strong," said Skandar, mollified. "We fly now."

"Just hold on to me, Skade," said Arren, tensing as the griffin spread his wings. "Try and move as I move, and for gods' sakes, don't let go."

"I am ready," Skade said calmly.

Skandar, too, was ready. He paused a moment, then set off in a rough, shambling run across the campsite. His wings opened wide as he ran, and he began to beat them, harder and harder. They lifted him a little each time, but his paws remained stubbornly on the ground; he ran on, faster, beating his wings with all his might as the trees at the edge of camp loomed up in front of him. Arren started to panic. He'd been through dozens of take-offs, and none of them had been like this. Skandar couldn't get off the ground, he'd—

The trees were there, directly in front of him, and then they were gone, rushing past as Skandar broke into a sprint, folding his wings to fit through the forest. The motion jolted Arren violently up and down, and he lay as flat as he could, doing his uttermost to keep still and not throw the griffin off balance. He could feel Skade's arms wrapped around his waist, holding on tightly. She was light, but not enough; they were going to fall off.

The landscape cleared again as the trees opened up at the banks of the pond. In a moment they were going to plough straight into the water.

Skandar's wings opened again, and he jumped. They were stuck in midair, gravity dragging at them, and then Skandar's wings beat, hard, and Arren's stomach felt as if it had dropped straight into his boots as they finally made it into the air.

Skandar flew higher, lurching a little, but struggling on determinedly. For a few moments it looked as if they weren't going to clear the trees, but they made it, passing so close to them that the griffin's tail snagged briefly on a branch.

Skandar levelled out with some effort and began to fly away over the trees, heading directly north, and Arren felt his heart soar. They had made it.

He sat up, letting himself relax, moving with Skandar. "It's all right!" he called to Skade when she tensed behind him. "We're in the air!"

"Thank the stars in the sky!" she called back over the wind. "I thought we were going to fall into the pond!"

"I don't know how long he can keep it up, though!" said Arren. "And landing will be a bit tricky as well!"

Skade leant forward so that she could talk directly into his ear. "I am sure we will be fine," she said. "I have faith in him, and in you."

That made Arren feel better. He smiled to himself, some of his inner turmoil cooling.

"You know," he said, "I feel—"

"What?"

"I said I feel—" Arren shouted.

"What do you feel?" said Skade.

"I feel that—" Arren gave up. "Never mind. We'll talk later!"

And that was how the day's flight began. Arren had been right; Skandar could not carry two people for an entire day. He was much clumsier in the air now and could not fly as high; he could only soar for much shorter distances and constantly had to resume beating his wings in order to regain the height he kept losing. But he toiled on regardless, and Arren knew what he was probably thinking. Taking off was more strenuous than remaining in the air, so stopping to rest would actually wear him out faster. It was easier to just keep going. Arren only hoped that he wouldn't push himself too hard.

Noon drew closer and they stayed in the air. Arren dozed briefly and woke up again with a start. Falling asleep now would be a bad idea. To distract himself, he watched the landscape below them. It was still thick with trees, but he could see the creek peeking through here and there. They were following it. He nodded to himself. Sensible.

Then Skade shifted behind him, reminding him of her presence. He started slightly, his mind instantly refilling with uncomfortable thoughts. *What have I done?*

His stomach was churning. It had felt right. It had felt more than right, but—

Well, how do you feel about her? he asked himself, almost sternly.

The answer came slowly, nearly obliquely, as if it was embarrassed to do so. He examined it, forcing himself not to push it away, trying to accept it, and that was when it all became clear in his mind. Arren knew he was falling in love.

Again! he raged. *So soon after Flell—you bastard! How could you be so—?*

Then, without warning, he laughed. The sound was snatched away by the wind the instant it was out of his mouth, but he laughed on regardless. He couldn't help it. Here he was, Arren Cardockson, the heartless one, the destroyer of Eagleholm, worrying about right and wrong. The sheer ridiculousness of it was almost too much to bear.

It was as if the laughter cured him of his fears and his guilt. The moment he stopped, he felt a new and powerful certainty that swept them all away. What did it matter whether it was right or wrong? If he didn't care, and Skade didn't, then that was all that mattered. Who else would even know about it? *Nobody,* he thought. *Skade was right. What do we care?*

He sat up straighter on Skandar's back, suddenly relishing the feeling of Skade's warm body pressed against his. Fierce Skade. His mate.

* * *

Arren's euphoria lasted until partway through the afternoon, when Skandar slowed his progress and started to circle, looking for a place to land. By now the creek had joined itself to a river, and the griffin found an open space by its banks and began to fly lower. Arren leant forward, holding on tightly.

"Brace yourself!" he shouted.

The landing was not a pleasant one. At first it seemed they were going to be all right; Skandar managed to retain his balance as he descended, wings half-folded, tail turning sideways to steady himself. But Arren was quick to see their danger. He leant forward as far as he could, yelling at Skade to do likewise as the wind whipped his hair away from his face. He could see the ground below getting closer and closer very fast, too fast. Panic shot through him. Skandar couldn't slow himself enough; the extra weight was dragging him down. And then the ground was no longer below them; it was *there*, directly in front of them. Arren closed his eyes and braced himself.

Skandar's talons hit the ground with a massive thud, ploughing up sand and dirt. His momentum pitched him head forward, and Arren was thrown from his back. He smacked into the ground so hard it knocked all the breath out of him and made his vision go black, rolled down a steep embankment and fell straight into the river. The cold shock of it engulfed him, and the next thing he knew he was floundering in the water. It was deep and the current was powerful. All his instincts screamed at him to get out, and he started to flail desperately, trying to swim. Too late, he remembered the sword still strapped to his back. He managed to break the surface once, and gasped in a lungful of air before it dragged him down again. He rolled over and over as he sank, wrestling with the straps, but they had expanded in the water, and the shock of landing had nearly knocked him senseless. Panic-stricken, he grabbed hold of the sword by the hilt and tried to pull it out, but he couldn't get purchase. His lungs were bursting; he was going to drown.

Something snagged on the back of his robe. He let go of the sword and made a grab for it, and then he was being dragged inexorably backward. He forced his eyes open and saw nothing but dark water and a whirl of silvery bubbles escaping from his mouth and nose. Then something wrapped itself around his waist and hauled him upward, back to the light.

He re-emerged into the open air, coughing and gasping, pain shooting through him as he breathed in at last. Skandar, moving on three legs with Arren's sodden form clasped to his chest, scrambled up the bank and dumped him on the sand. Arren lay there on his back, head spinning.

Skandar nudged him with his beak. "You hurt?"

Arren coughed. "Sk-Skandar."

The griffin flopped down on his belly and laid his head beside his partner. He was breathing hard and his feathers were soaked. "Drink later," he muttered.

Arren managed a laugh. "I think I've—had enough—for now."

"Arren?" It was Skade. He turned his head and saw her coming toward him, moving slowly and carefully. She kept glancing at Skandar, but the black griffin only groaned and closed his eyes. The silver-haired woman came to Arren's side. "Are you well?"

Arren stayed where he was, looking up at her. "I'm all right."

Skade touched his forehead, pulling away the damp locks of hair. "I thought you had drowned."

Arren lifted his head briefly and then let it drop. "I've had landings that went better."

She smiled. "I am sorry I did not try and rescue you myself, but Skandar looked very . . . upset. I did not want to provoke him."

Arren watched her, and the wonderful certainty became stronger. "You really care about me, don't you?"

Skade looked uncertain. "What do you mean by that?"

Arren didn't answer. He pulled himself into a sitting position and kissed her. She started a little, but she returned the kiss willingly enough.

"You like that," she said once they parted, smiling slightly.

Arren looked into her eyes. "You're right, Skade," he said softly. "You're right. It doesn't matter. We shouldn't care what people think, or worry about right and wrong. We're different; we're not bound by their laws; we're . . . free. Free to do and think what we choose. I shouldn't have tried to push you away like that or been ashamed of the way I felt. I'm sorry."

Skade looked a little taken aback by his outburst. "You were thinking all of that while we were flying?"

"Yes, I was. I didn't know how I felt at first, but now I do."

"You were not certain," said Skade. "But you paired with me willingly enough last night."

Arren looked at the ground. "Yes. I—I was attracted to you. While you were thinking of me yesterday, I was thinking of you. I'm such a terrible person, Skade. I killed Lord Rannagon in front of his children. I set a man-eating griffin free. My parents—they're in danger right now because of me. That's why I was going to Norton. I warned them to leave their old home before they were arrested, and I promised to meet them in Norton and help them escape. I don't know if they ever made it there, but Skandar still wanted to go. But I chose not to. I chose to go to this cave . . . with you."

Skade stared at him. "You mean you only chose to go there because of me?"

Arren couldn't look her in the eye. "Yes," he mumbled, hating himself for lying to her.

She smiled and touched his arm. "You are not a terrible person, Arren Cardockson. You are . . . sweet."

Arren smiled back. "You're wonderful, Skade. You're the most amazing woman I've ever met. Human, griffin—I don't care which one you are. You're you, and that's all that matters to me."

Skade looked wistful. "You would make a magnificent griffin."

Arren struggled to his feet. "It's said all griffiners are part griffin already anyway. I sometimes wonder what it would be like to be a griffin. To have wings."

Skandar was asleep. He looked to have fallen asleep almost immediately after rescuing Arren from the river.

"We should not disturb him," said Skade. "He exhausted himself today." She gestured at Arren. "Come. We should make camp."

Arren surveyed the area. They were on a patch of open sand close to the river, and further ahead of them there was a thicket of wattle trees. Plenty of firewood and water, and the sand would be comfortable to sleep on. "We'll have to move in under the trees," he said reluctantly. "We can't risk sleeping in the open; if anyone flies over they'll see us."

"Yes, you are right," said Skade. "We shall have to ask Skandar to move. But later. Once he has slept a little."

"I'm not going to argue with you there," said Arren. "Let sleeping griffins lie. Especially if they're the kind that rip people's limbs off."

Skade laughed as they entered the trees and began to search for a new campsite. The wattles were thick; Arren had to draw his sword and hack a way through. Once they were through those, they picked their way through a patch of marsh and gained the higher ground. It was studded with large rocks and dozens of fallen branches, but it would have to do; they were too tired to go further. Arren gladly took his sword off his back and leant it against a tree before the two of them set about clearing the area, removing rocks and sticks. Arren made a fireplace with a ring of stones, and he and Skade began to gather wood for it.

Arren paused in the act of breaking a large branch in half. "Skade?"

She looked at him. "Yes?"

He snapped the branch over his thigh and turned to look at her, holding the two broken pieces. "I never did ask as much about you as I should have."

"I probably would not have told you," said Skade.

"Ah, but you have to tell me now," Arren said, and grinned. "Tit for tat; I answered your questions, and now you have to answer mine."

"What did you want to know?" said Skade.

Arren tossed the wood toward the fireplace and bent to pick up another branch. "The answer to the same question you asked me. Why did you do it?"

"Do what?" said Skade.

"You know what I'm talking about, Skade. Why did you kill those people?"

"I killed them for revenge," Skade said softly. "You and I are more alike than you think."

"Revenge for what?" said Arren.

She looked away. "They had killed someone I cared for, someone who did not deserve to die."

"Who? Another griffin? One of your family?"

"No. My human."

Arren started. "You had a human?"

"Yes. I chose him, and they killed him."

Arren moved closer to her. "Who was he?"

Skade turned and looked him in the face. "His name was Welyn, and he was a Northerner."

8

The Man Without a
Heart

Skade told her story that night, when she and Arren had lit
the fire and eaten a frugal meal of reed-roots and berries.
Skandar had recovered somewhat and was dozing nearby, his
great flanks rising and falling gently in time with his breathing.

"I lived in a nest near the Eyrie," the silver-haired woman
said, the firelight flickering in her eyes. "There were two other
griffins there, my siblings."

"Only three of you?" said Arren, surprised.

"Yes. Unpartnered griffins lived where they chose. The state
granted them food and shelter, and every nest had an atten-
dant to clean it every day and bring food and water and fresh
bedding. My siblings and I had grown up together after our
mother died of disease. They were always looking for humans
to choose; they would go out into the city most days in the
hopes of finding one. I had gone with them a few times, but I
was the smallest of the clutch and did not want to risk invading
another griffin's territory. And I was not interested in choosing
a human. I looked upon humans as weak, stupid, inferior beings
whose only purpose was to serve us."

"What about the griffiners?" said Arren.

"They were servants to griffins even more so than the rest,"
said Skade. "The only difference was that other humans admired
them for it."

Arren thought of Shoa. "Yes, I suppose that's true in a way.
Plenty of griffins—never mind."

"So I stayed in the nest most of the time," Skade resumed.
"Sometimes I would go flying, away from the city. I enjoyed
that. I even thought of leaving, flying out into the wild to live

on my own. But what would have been the point? I did not know how to hunt or build a nest for myself, and I knew what humans did to wild griffins. A silver griffin's hide to decorate some human's nest," she snarled. "So I stayed. The only human I came to know well was the blackrobe slave who brought my food. His master owned the nest and sent him to maintain it; he was too lazy to do it himself."

Arren sighed. No wonder Skade thought of his race as inferior: one had been cleaning up her dung for years. Slaves got all the worst jobs. Although, when he thought of it, he'd been the one who had cleaned up after Eluna. That was the menial side of a griffiner's life; if the griffiner was too poor to own a slave or to pay someone else to do it.

"One day," said Skade, "one day the slave stopped coming. I found out later on that he had fallen ill. Instead, his son was sent to do his work. He was just a boy, no more than ten years old."

"Welyn," Arren guessed.

She nodded. "His name was Llewellyn, but I shortened it to Welyn." She smiled sadly, her gaze becoming distant for a moment. "My little Welyn. He was too young to have a collar yet, but he wore a black robe, like all slaves. He had never been close to a griffin in his life, and when he came to the nest for the first time, he was terrified. I could *smell* his fear. But he came in anyway and gave us our food. My siblings thought it was amusing to snap at him and watch him run away; I thought they were acting like chicks and ignored them."

"I'm surprised he kept coming," Arren remarked.

"Surprised?" Skade blinked. "Of course he kept on coming. He would have been flogged if he had disobeyed."

"Ah."

"It went on like that for a long time," said Skade. "And then, one of my siblings chose a human. It happened suddenly; one day he was there and the next day he had left the nest for good and moved in with his new partner. My sister must have been jealous, and perhaps that made her more anxious to go. She chose a human a month or so later, and after that I was alone. I became depressed; I had been so used to their company that I did not know what to do now that they were gone.

"Welyn was my only company, and I began to look forward to his visits. He had become more confident around me; he knew I would not attack him. He used to speak to me; he would talk about everything under the sun while he took out the old straw, and I would listen. Sometimes I thought he was annoying, but after a while I came to enjoy listening to him." She prodded the fire. "He saw how unhappy I was. I was eating less, and it worried him. In the end, he went and told his master that I was ill. They brought a healer, who examined me and found nothing wrong. I bit him for his trouble.

"The next day, when Welyn came he was walking strangely. Limping. I knew he was hurt, and when he came closer I smelt blood on him. It unsettled me, made me angry and upset. When he tried to lift the bucket to refill my trough, it was too heavy for him. He kept trying, but he could not do it, and then he collapsed. Fainted in front of me. I went to him, and I saw the blood on the back of his robe."

"He'd been flogged," Arren said grimly.

"Yes. His master was angry with him for wasting his money and the healer's time. But it was too much. He was not strong enough for it." Her lips drew back, exposing her teeth as she snarled her rage. "He was a *boy*. And when I saw what they had done, I suddenly felt something I had never felt before. It was so powerful, like magic. I felt as if he were a chick and I were his mother who must care for him. I did not want him to be hurt or to feel pain. But I did not know what to do. I pushed him into my nest and curled up with him lying against my belly, where it was warm and soft." She smiled a little. "I even tried to groom him, as if he were another griffin. Foolish. He woke up after a time, and I expected him to be afraid, but he was not. He looked up at me and smiled, and I let him touch my beak. He stayed with me all that night and slept lying against me. They came looking for him the next morning; they were all angry, threatening. When Welyn saw them he was afraid; he stayed close to me, and suddenly I felt furious. He tried to go to them when they called, but I blocked his way, and when they came toward us to drag him from me, I threatened them. His master tried, but I knocked him down. Later on, a griffiner came, sent by Arakae himself, and commanded me to give him up. But I would not. Welyn was still there by my flank, still frightened and hurt, needing my protection, and I came forward and faced them, and I said"—she breathed in deeply—"*mine*."

Arren shivered. *Mine. My human, mine, mine.*

"I did not understand what I was saying," said Skade. "I said it as if I were being controlled by something else. But I said it anyway, again and again. *He is my human. My human. Mine!*"

"My gods," Arren mumbled. "What did they do?"

Skade shook her head. "There was nothing they could do. They were angry, but they left us in peace, Welyn and me. I have never felt so relieved in my life. By that afternoon the news was all over the city that a griffin had chosen a slave as her partner. People came to the nest to see us, Welyn sitting next to me with his hand on my wing, unafraid. I felt so proud of him. He had accepted what had happened, and from now on he and I would be friends and would live our lives together." She paused. "And two days later he was dead."

Arren groaned. "Gods. My gods. They couldn't stand it, could they? A blackrobe griffiner? It violated everything they held dear, didn't it? They couldn't just respect your choice, could they?" His voice was getting louder, anger behind every word. "So they murdered him. Just as they murdered Eluna. They had to get rid of us. Welyn and me, we were dangerous." His fists clenched. "I'm glad I killed Rannagon. I'm glad I killed all those griffiners in the Eyrie. I'd do it again. I'd do it a hundred times." He looked at Skade, almost glaring. "So you did what I did, didn't you? You went for revenge against them."

"No." Skade was hunching her shoulders, threatened by his rage. "No, Arren, I did not. That was not what happened."

Arren stopped abruptly. "What? What do you mean?"

"Griffiners did not kill Welyn," said Skade. "Other blackrobes did."

Arren stared blankly at her. "What?"

"I tell you, they did it," said Skade. "I saw it happen."

Arren couldn't help it. He let forth a string of Northern obscenities, startling Skade, who pulled away from him. "What *for*?" he shouted at last.

"He had *betrayed* them," Skade said sharply. "Do not take such a rosy view of your race, Arren. They are not all free and educated men like you. Most of them have been slaves from birth. That is their station in life, and they accept it. Those who do not, die. There were no free Northerners in Withypool, none at all. Everyone knew about the actions of the Lady Riona in

Eagleholm, and they saw it as dangerous insanity. No. What Welyn had done violated the way of the world, and it had to be stopped. He was killed by his father."

"His own—?"

"*Yes,*" she rasped. "You hear me: his father killed him. He came to the nest with some of his friends; he was in a violent rage and shouted at Welyn, told him he had endangered all their lives and if he did not abandon me, Welyn would see the Northerners all killed in the end. The gods did not will our partnership, he said. But Welyn was bold now he had me; he told his father it was his choice and mine and that he would become a griffiner and use his power to make the city great."

Skade hissed. "The man was a fool. He killed Welyn in front of me, hit him so hard that he fell against the wall and broke his neck. I rushed to try and stop it, but I was too late. My talons hit Welyn's father, tore him open. He died there on the floor, and the others fled. I should have let them go, but I had gone mad. I killed them. All of them. Hunted them through the city, every last one, and I killed anyone who tried to stop me. When the city guard came to capture me, I attacked them and killed some before they snared me. After that I was brought before the council of griffins, who were quick to condemn me as mad and beyond saving. Arakae wielded his power to trap me in human form, and after that there was nothing but anger and misery. I had nowhere to run to, and I did not care, because Welyn was dead."

Arren laughed, a flat, bitter laugh that had no humour in it whatsoever. "And after all that you decided to throw your lot in with another Northerner. Haven't you learnt your lesson by now?"

Skade hissed at him. "Do not mock me!"

Guilt hit him instantly. "Sorry. I'm sorry, it's just—I just didn't know what to say." He reached out and took Skade by the hand.

She made no effort to pull away. "That is why I decided to trust you, and why I came to look on you as worthy of being more than a friend. We are of a kind, you and I. The gods willed us to meet; that our stories are so alike is a sign."

"The gods!" Arren snorted. "Hah. The way I see it is that the gods piss on your head and then condemn you for being wet.

They never let me in the temple back at Eagleholm, but I never really wanted to go in there anyway. Gryphus and Scathach can lick my boots for all I care."

"But you are a Northerner," said Skade, surprised. "Your god is the moon."

"The moon," Arren spat. "The moon never did anything to help me. I prayed to it to save me when I was in prison, and it was the last thing I saw before I—"

"Before you what?" said Skade.

Before I died. "Nothing," said Arren. "It's nothing. Sorry." He glanced at the sky. The moon was up now, its white light outshining the stars. "But you're right," he added more quietly. "You and I are of a kind, Skade. You and I together. We can do anything."

She was watching him carefully. "Yes," she said slowly. "Anything."

Their journey resumed the following day, and it was one of the happiest times of Arren's life. Part of the reason was Skandar's return, and another was the knowledge that they would soon reach the spirit cave and the healing it offered. But the biggest part of it was Skade. The silver-haired woman had recovered her strength and every evening helped him make camp and forage for food. She was taciturn a lot of the time, even unemotional, but her looks toward him were warm and her affections aggressive, almost violent. It was not in her nature to be gentle, not in anything, but Arren didn't mind. He loved her. He loved her as he had never loved anyone before, more than he had loved Flell. He didn't care that her eyes were gold or that her fingernails were sharp claws. He did not care that she had been born as a griffin. Nor could he make himself think about what might happen when they reached the spirit cave. For now, all that mattered was . . . now.

As for Skandar, he didn't seem to be aware of what was going on. Every day Arren appreciated the griffin's help more and more. He carried both of them as far as he could, starting at dawn and flying for much of the day, though each flight was growing shorter as they went on, and they were covering less ground. It was plain that he wouldn't be able to keep it up for too long; he was wearing himself out. He slept a great deal and ate voraciously, and yet he never complained or even mentioned that he felt burdened. Arren and Skade were careful to wait until he was asleep before they touched, but one day he caught them locked in a passionate embrace by the fire. His only reaction was to blink and wander off as if he had seen nothing out of the ordinary, and Arren was left to thank his lucky stars that the griffin had spent very little time around human beings.

Four days passed as they travelled steadily north, and the mountains began to come into sight. They would be there in another day or so. On the fifth day they passed a fairly large town, and Arren briefly saw in the distance a little flash of gold from a sun-shaped disc on the dome of a temple. He had already guessed that it must be Skandar's "singing hill." They were nearly there.

The landscape had changed. They were very close to the mountains; the plains had ended and they were in hilly country. Large areas had been cleared to make way for farmland, and Skandar had to fly quite a long way to be well clear of it before he finally landed at midafternoon. Their landings were becoming smoother; by now Arren and Skade had both learnt to throw themselves backwards when the griffin's forelegs hit the ground, to avoid being thrown over his head. Nevertheless, they both fell off shortly afterward.

Arren got up and rubbed his bruises. "Well," he panted, "I think we're nearly there. Are we, Skandar?"

Skandar had already flopped onto his stomach, but he clicked his beak in response. "Not far. We fly there now, maybe."

"No," said Arren. "It's not necessary. We can wait until tomorrow. You should rest now, Skandar. I'll try and find something for you to eat."

Skade was already building a fireplace. "Did you see the town?"

"Yes," said Arren. "D'you think . . . ?"

"Healer's Home?" said Skade. "Maybe. Who can say? It does not matter either way. If Skandar knows where the cave is, then we do not need to worry about directions any longer."

"It makes me uneasy being this close to human lands. We'll have to take extra care to hide our camp."

Skade laughed. "Human lands, is it? You sound like a griffin!"

Arren shrugged. "I'd probably be better off if I was. Skandar wouldn't have to carry me, and I'd be stronger."

"There is no point in thinking that kind of thought, Arren," said Skade. She broke off the conversation and walked toward the remains of a fallen tree that lay near the camp. Arren followed her, and the two of them gathered as much dead wood as they needed and brought it back, ready to build the fire. They didn't light it; a fire wouldn't be necessary until nightfall and, besides, Arren was nervous that someone might see the smoke, even if they were over a day's walk away from the nearest farm.

Once the fire had been built ready to be lit, they set off to forage for food. The pickings had been poor the last couple of days, and both of them were hungry, but by a stroke of luck, some way from the camp Skade found a wild apple tree. The fruit was unripe, but they picked it anyway and bundled it up in Arren's robe. On the way back they found the burrow of a ground-bear.

Ground-bears had no relation to actual bears, which were widely found only in the North, but were so called because of their round ears and heavyset bearlike shape. Since they were nocturnal, the burrow had to be occupied. Arren had caught ground-bears many times during his weeks on the run, and had worked out a method that generally worked. It was crude but effective: he gave his sword to Skade, along with the robe full of apples, put his knife between his teeth and crawled into the burrow. Luckily he was thin and the burrow quite large; he fitted easily enough and scrabbled his way underground a couple of body lengths until it opened up into the ground-bear's home. It was pitch-black, but he took the knife out from his teeth, located the animal's head as it woke up and swung around to bite him, and stabbed it in the neck. Warm blood wet his hand, and the bear went into a maddened frenzy, rushing at him in a flurry of claws and flying dirt. Arren had no room to fight; he stabbed it again as hard as he could, trying to protect his face and eyes with his free arm. A short and nasty scuffle ensued, but he managed to get in a decisive blow with the knife, and the bear finally started to weaken. Arren clenched the knife in his teeth again and shuffled out backwards, dragging the animal by the shoulders.

He emerged into the open air, filthy and exhausted, both arms covered in painful scratches and his chin smarting horribly from where the bear's chisel-shaped teeth had caught him.

He hauled the carcass out after him and slumped down beside it, panting but triumphant.

Skade was already bending to look at it. "The creature is massive!"

Arren had to agree; standing up, the bear would have been about as high as his knee. It was covered in coarse brown fur, and its body was basically shaped like a barrel; its heavy, blunt head looked almost as large.

He grinned. "Skandar will love it."

"Oh." Skade looked disappointed. "I assumed it was for us."

Arren got up and stuffed his knife back into his belt. "Don't be ridiculous; we've got all those apples. Anyway, Skandar needs it more than we do. He's too tired to hunt for himself. Could you carry my sword for me? Thanks." He heaved the bear over his shoulder and set off, staggering slightly under the weight.

Skandar was still asleep when they returned to the camp, but the sun hadn't yet begun to go down. They had a while yet. Arren dumped the dead bear next to the fireplace and then straightened up, stretching his back.

"Argh. Ooh. Ow." He rubbed it. "It's never been the same since . . ."

Skade put the sword and the apples down close to the bear. "Since what?"

"What?" said Arren. "Oh. I took a bit of a nasty fall a while ago." He glanced at the bear. "I'd skin it, only there's not much point. I just wish I had some tools—a needle and some thread at the very least. Then I'd be able to collect a few skins and make them into a blanket or something. I tried carving a needle out of bone, but I couldn't get it to work. I'm going to go to the river and wash myself. I'll be back in a moment."

In fact the river was too far to walk to; they'd had to make camp well away from it to avoid farmland. But he did find a small stream that had branched off from it, and there he washed the blood and dirt off himself. He ached all over and found himself thinking wistfully of his hammock. Just at that moment, he would have given anything to sleep in it again.

No hammocks for murderers, he thought irrelevantly, and walked back to camp.

Skandar was still asleep. Arren moved the bear closer to

him and nudged the griffin gently to wake him up. "Skandar. Skandar!"

Skandar's eyes opened slowly, and he groaned.

"Look," said Arren, pointing at the bear. "Food."

There was a soft whistling noise as the griffin breathed in. He appeared to wake up more completely when he caught the bear's scent, and he tore into it immediately.

Arren moved away and left him to it while he sat down with Skade and munched on the unripe apples. They were sour but juicy, and he relished them. After days of very little food, just about anything tasted good.

Skade swallowed a mouthful, and sighed. "These are good."

"Aren't they?" said Arren. "Ripe ones would be better, but even so—" He reduced an apple to the core, paused a moment and then ate the core as well. No sense in wasting it. He picked up a second. "We can cook some of these later. That might make them a bit less sour. Could I have my robe, please?"

Skade passed it to him. "What is that on your arm?"

"What, this?" said Arren, touching the tattoo on his shoulder.

"Yes. I saw it before, but did not think to ask you."

He turned slightly to let her see it more clearly. The tattoo was of the dark blue head of a wolf holding a great yellow globe in its jaws. The eye was shut and the ears laid flat, as if the wolf was howling.

Skade leant closer to look. "A picture on your skin," she remarked. "How is that possible?"

"What, you've never seen a tattoo before?" said Arren, surprised.

"Ta-too?"

"It's ink," he explained. "Ink under your skin. Someone takes a needle and dips it in ink, and then they stick it in you. They do it over and over again, leaving a little bit of ink every time, and they use it to draw a picture."

Skade looked at him as if he was mad. "Why would you let them do that to you? Did they do it while you were in prison? Was it torture?"

"What? No! I paid to have it done, and it was very expensive, too."

"You . . . paid . . . someone to hurt you?" said Skade, very slowly.

"Yes. No. Look," said Arren. "You don't pay to have it done

because it hurts; you pay to have it done so you can have the tattoo afterward. The pain is the nasty part, but it doesn't kill you. Tattoos are important. They're stories. Signs. They tell other people things about you."

Skade was giving him a long, slow look. "And what story does *that* tell?"

"The wolf's head is a symbol," said Arren. "It means—did I ever tell you my proper name?"

"What? What proper name?"

"Arren is—well, it's a nickname. You see, I grew up among Southerners and I wanted to fit in. 'Cardockson' just means 'son of Cardock'—Southerners give themselves second names after their mothers or fathers. If I called myself Arren Cardockson, it meant people wouldn't know I was a Northerner just from hearing my name." He sighed. "My father didn't like that. He always refused to call me Arren. Said I should go by my proper name, out of pride. But I don't take any pride in being what I am, and I never have."

"I did not think your name sounded Northern," said Skade. "So what is it?"

"It's Arenadd," said Arren. "Arenadd Taranisäii."

Skade frowned. "How do you say it?"

"A-ren-ath Tah-ran-is-eye," said Arren, sounding it out for her. "I always thought it was a stupid-sounding name myself."

"Arenadd Taranisäii. It sounds Northern enough," said Skade. "It suits you," she added.

"Huh," Arren scowled. "Maybe I should start calling myself that. Arren Cardockson's probably too dull a name for a murderer to have."

"Perhaps, but what does it have to do with the drawing on your arm?" said Skade.

"Oh. 'Taranisäii' means 'of the blood of Taranis.' My family descends from the Northern tribe known as the Wolf Tribe. The wolf's head holding the moon is the symbol of the clan. It's a sign of my ancestors."

Skade nodded slowly. "I think I understand. It is like a form of plumage."

"Yes, I suppose so."

"And yet," said Skade, "you said you take no pride in being a Northerner."

"Yes," said Arren, "I had some silly ideas back then. My

father was always trying to fill my head with nonsense about how the Northerners are an ancient and noble race and so on and so forth, and I agreed with him for a while."

"You don't believe they are?" said Skade.

"Look," said Arren, more sharply than he needed to, "as far as I'm concerned, any race stupid enough to try and invade the South and try and fight *griffiners*, for gods' sakes, can't be as wise and cunning as they like to think. My father can be romantic about it if he wants to, but most Northerners are slaves, and the rest of them are uneducated peasants who can't even govern themselves, and I'm damned if that's anything to be proud of. I spent most of my life trying to cut myself off from them and show people I could be more than that. I even changed my *name*. I never spoke the Northern tongue, never worshipped the moon, never. I never *acted* like them. I acted like a Southerner. I *was* a Southerner. I could read and write, I could administrate—I was *Master of Trade*, for gods' sakes. I didn't even spend much time with my parents. All my friends were Southerners, and yet"—his voice was getting louder and louder, suddenly impassioned—"it wasn't enough! Nothing was ever enough! Nothing I ever did could convince them that I should be treated like one of them. And why? Because of *this*!" He pulled at his hair and beard and waved a hand over his face, indicating his black eyes and sharp features. "All this! It wasn't anything I did; it was all about how I looked! As if that was my fault! Even when I was a griffiner, people called me 'blackrobe' behind my back. And the moment Eluna was gone and people knew about it, they stopped pretending to respect me and took away everything I had. My job, my home, my dignity—d'you know how I got this?" He was pointing at the scar on his throat now. "D'you know how I got this, Skade?"

Skade was staring at him, shocked. "Yes, you told me. Calm down—"

"Some people put a slave collar on me," Arren snarled. He couldn't calm down now; red-hot rage was filling him, taking away his self-control. "They put it on me! Not because I'd done anything, but just because they wanted to humiliate me. What did I do to deserve it? Nothing. I—" His voice cracked. "I don't want to be like this, Skade, I don't want it. I can't stand it. I don't want to be a blackrobe. If I could tear all this away, I would. I'd hurt myself to do it. I didn't want to kill Rannagon, but after what happened, I couldn't—it's the madness. We're all mad inside, we blackrobes. Something just breaks inside us and all we can think of is fighting and killing. I wanted revenge. I thought that if I went back there and killed him it would all be over. I could rest; I could . . ." His words ran out at last, choked with sobs.

Skandar was staring at him in confusion, not knowing what was wrong with him. Skade, too, was staring, but after a moment's hesitation she moved closer to him—not reaching out, but edging nearer. Arren turned and put his arms around her, holding her to him, and she finally embraced him in return, holding him awkwardly as he cried.

"It is not your fault," she said. "Arren, please. Don't do this."

Arren tried to control himself, tried to speak. "Skade, I'm—I'm not—I don't—"

"Be still," said Skade. "Breathe deeply."

Arren did, and his sobs started to die down. But he could not stop himself from saying what he said next. "Skade, I'm dead."

She let go of him. "What?"

Arren shuddered. He'd said it. It was too late to take it back. He took Skade's hand and lifted it. "Touch my neck," he said softly. "Touch the side."

She did, her expression bewildered. "Arren, what—?"

Arren carefully let go of her hand. "What do you feel?" he said.

Skade was silent for a time, and then she shook her head. "Nothing."

He looked her in the eye. "You feel nothing."

Skade took her hand away. "Arren, what is this?" she said impatiently. "What are you trying to tell me?"

"Don't you understand?" Arren hissed. "You touched my neck and you didn't feel anything."

"Yes, but—"

"You felt nothing!" he repeated. "Nothing! No heartbeat!"

Skade froze. "What?"

"I have no heartbeat," said Arren. "I'm dead, Skade. I've been dead for months."

She was staring at him, utterly lost. "What? But how can that be?"

He looked away. "I don't know. But my heart hasn't made a sound since what happened. I don't know why I'm still here. All I know is that I died . . . and then I came back."

"But how?"

"I fell," said Arren. "From the edge of the city. Eagleholm is built on the top of a mountain. There are platforms—they expanded the mountain top to make room for new houses. I lived on the edge, but I was always afraid of heights. After I escaped from prison, after I came back and set Skandar free, guards saw me and I ran from them. I was trying to escape. They chased me to the edge of the city, and I surrendered. There was nowhere left to run." He looked up at her. "And they shot me," he said simply. "Hit me with arrows. Here." He touched the scar over his heart. "And I fell from the edge, fell hundreds of feet. No-one could have survived it, and I didn't."

"But you must have."

"I didn't," Arren said sharply. "I died. I landed on hard rocks. I felt every bone in my body break." He glanced at Skandar. "He found me. Skandar. Came looking for me. The last thing I saw was him. Him, and the moon behind him. And then I died."

"You fainted," said Skade. "That is all. From the pain."

Arren shook his head vaguely. "I don't know what happened after that. I was in darkness. And then I felt something, as if I were on fire. Like something had taken hold of me and wouldn't let go. Something hit me. Hit me all over. And then I woke up and it was morning, and Skandar was there watching me. There was nothing, no pain. I could stand and walk without any trouble, even though there were still two arrows stuck in me. And everything felt . . . different. For a while I couldn't remember my own name. I thought it was a miracle. I'd survived. I'd come back. But when I tried to check my pulse—nothing."

"Let me try," said Skade, coming closer.

Arren did not resist as she touched his neck. He closed his eyes, hoping against hope that she would find something, anything. Maybe he had been missing it all along, maybe he'd made a mistake—

Skade withdrew her hand abruptly. Arren opened his eyes and saw her looking at him, an expression of utter horror on her face. "No," she whispered. "No. This cannot—this is impossible!"

Arren bowed his head. "I thought it was a dream, a nightmare. Or that I really was dead and this was the afterlife." He turned to stare at Skandar. Skandar stared back. "It was him," Arren half-whispered. "It was Skandar. He made it happen. He used magic on me, to bring me back. He can't tell me how he did it, but—"

Skade stood up and approached the black griffin. "Did you?" she said. "Skandar?"

Skandar stirred nervously. "I see him die," he said at last. "And then I scream."

"Was there light?" said Skade. "Did you see something come out of your beak, some kind of light?"

"Something come," said Skandar. "Like fire. The scream, I see it."

"Magic," Skade breathed. "It was your fault."

Arren stood, too. "Skade, I'm sorry. I should have—but how *could* I have told you? How could I tell anyone that I'm a walking dead man?"

She turned to face him. "That is why you want to go to the cave. You believe the spirits can heal you."

"I have to try," said Arren. "I can't bear it. I feel dead inside. It makes me terrified to know my heart doesn't beat. It makes me an abomination."

She came closer. "It is not your fault. You did not make it happen; the fault lies with your partner."

"It's not Skandar's fault," said Arren. "He'd never used magic before and hasn't since. He doesn't understand it any better than I do. I don't know, maybe I should thank him. But"—he came toward her, holding out his hands in supplication—"that's why I killed Rannagon. Do you understand now? Every story I'd ever heard where the dead came back to life, it was always because they had something, some great purpose, something left unfinished. I thought that if I avenged my own death and Eluna's, then it would all be over. I could go to my rest and be buried as I should. But it didn't work. All that happened was that I became a murderer and destroyed all those lives. Nothing changed except for the worse, and *I don't know what to do.*"

Skade touched him on the arm. "Hush. Do not despair. There is still hope. For you and for me."

Arren gave her a wretched look. "Do you really think the spirits can help me, Skade?"

"I believe they can," she replied, almost gently. "And I believe they will."

9

The Spirit Cave

Arren slept very little that night. Skade showed no interest in coupling after they had eaten, but she nestled beside him when he lay down to sleep against Skandar's flank, sheltering under his wing. The feeling of her warm body against his helped to comfort him, but he lay awake for ages anyway, too miserable and upset to sleep. He felt ashamed of his tirade and of his tears as well. What right did he have to cry?

And yet . . .

And yet Skade had not turned away from him. She had been shocked and frightened and upset, but she had not become angry or disgusted, and she had not abandoned him. And, as Arren lay awake brooding, he dared to hope that maybe she would accept him even with his curse. Maybe it would be all right, and she'd help him.

Even so, he did not fall asleep until well after midnight.

Skade shook him awake. "Come," she said softly. "We must eat before we leave."

Arren sat up, yawning.

It was dawn, and Skandar was stirring, too. Skade had gone over to the remains of the fire and was picking up the last of the apples.

Arren got to his feet and stretched. He was stiff and sore and chilled to the bone, and he had that light-headed bewildered feeling that indicated that he wasn't ready to be up yet. He ignored it and wandered over to Skade, who silently passed him an apple.

Skandar had stood up and was busily preening and stretching

his wings. Birds were calling everywhere, but the griffin hadn't added his voice to theirs. In fact, now that Arren thought about it, he hadn't done it in quite some time. He wondered about it briefly, but his brain wasn't in the mood for any hard work just then, and he forgot about it fairly quickly and started on his breakfast. He was tempted to sit down but made himself pace around the campsite instead. If he stopped moving, he'd probably start wanting to go back to sleep.

No-one was talking. Skade was busy chewing on an apple and wasn't looking at him. Skandar looked irritable and kept twitching his tail. Arren felt uncomfortable in their presence. The camp was full of quiet tension, and he couldn't help but believe it was his fault. The previous night's talk kept running around in his mind, and it almost made him afraid, or angry with himself. He looked at Skade, wanting to talk to her, but no words felt adequate.

Skade, however, paid almost no attention to him. She finished eating and walked off to the stream to drink, and Arren watched her go, feeling anxious and depressed.

Meanwhile, Skandar had finished his grooming and loped over to him. "We go now," he said shortly.

Arren flung away the remains of the apple. "Yes, you're right. Wait a moment." He found his sword and strapped it on, and stuffed the last few apples into his pockets.

Skandar fluttered his wings. "Now go. Call your mate."

Arren blinked. "What?"

"Mate," Skandar repeated. "Your mate. The female. Call her."

"How do you know?"

Skandar clicked his beak. "I am not stupid. I know mating. Even human mating."

Arren grinned despite himself. "How did you realise it?"

"You groom each other," said Skandar. "Hunt together. Sleep together. Mates do that." He drew himself up. "I had a mate."

"You did?" said Arren. "When?"

"Long ago," said Skandar. "Before you came. In the mountains. I live there, alone. No mother, no brothers or sisters. And then one day my mate comes. Yellow, like the sun. She did not tell me her name. She was looking for me. For a male. We mated, many times, on a mountain top, and then she show . . . showed me humans."

Arren was staring at him with something close to astonishment; this was the most Skandar had ever said about himself before. "Showed you humans? Where?"

"Human nests," Skandar explained. "I did not know humans; she showed them to me. She said—" He paused. "Said things. I did not understand them all, but she said 'Find a human.'"

"Find which human? What for?"

Skandar shook himself irritably. "She said I must have a human. Find a human, not let go of it ever. I did not understand. She flew away, and then I watched humans. Wanted one. Picked them up, took them home. Talked to them." He hissed to himself. "Stupid human. I talk, they say nothing. Looked for one who would speak. Did not find one. Eat the ones who did not speak. Good food."

"And the griffiners found out about it," said Arren. "And they sent me to stop you."

"You come," Skandar agreed. "I see you. Want you. You different. Look different. But you"—he made a little hacking sound in his throat—"you fight me."

"I'm sorry, Skandar," said Arren. "But you were trying to—"

"Brave!" Skandar said sharply. "You brave! Brave human. You talked. Stronger than me. Hated you. But wanted you." He looked at him proudly. "My human."

Arren couldn't help but feel flattered. "I haven't been as nice to you as I should have, have I?" he said.

"Nice!" Skandar repeated in contemptuous tones. "What nice?"

Arren patted him on the beak. "Nice means kind. Friendly."

Skandar sighed and looked away. "You did not want the white griffin to die."

"No," Arren said quietly. "I didn't."

"Did not want to fight her," said Skandar. "Wanted you, not her. She came at me. Hit my talons. Too fast."

"I know you didn't mean to kill her, Skandar," said Arren. "I mean, I've . . . forgiven you for it."

"White griffin," Skandar said abruptly, "she tell me help you."

The sudden change of topic threw him off balance. "What, Skandar?"

"The cave," said Skandar. "Sleep near it, after they speak. White griffin came."

"You met another griffin?" said Arren.

"No." Skandar shook his head. "Not real. Sleep-picture."

"Oh, a *dream*," said Arren. "You dreamt about a white griffin?"

"Yes. White griffin come. She say go back to you. Go back to human. She say find both human. Dark human, silver human. Not leave them. She say you bring great change, make good home for Skandar. Make all world better."

Arren shivered. "Skandar, what—?"

"Arren?"

It was Skade, returning from the stream.

Arren pulled himself together. "Hello."

The silver-haired woman had her hands tucked under her arms for warmth, and still looked a little unsettled. "Shall we go now?" she asked.

"Yes," Skandar interrupted. He came toward her, tail swishing. "We go," he said. "Now go. The cave waits."

"Hang on," said Arren. "Shouldn't we cover over the fire before—?"

"No," said Skade. She was breathing heavily. "We are going now. I will not wait any longer."

Arren didn't have the energy to resist. He got onto Skandar's back and held on while Skade got up behind him. Once the two of them were in place the griffin took off in a series of quick, rough wing beats and they gained the air. The sun was still rising and the sky was mushroom grey, tinted with pink on the horizon. The wind tingled with ice.

Skandar turned northward and set out on the last push to the cave.

Skandar flew through the morning, moving steadily straight toward the mountains, big and craggy and bare, capped with snow. They were much bigger than the Coppertops, where the black griffin had grown up, and far colder. Beyond them lay the North. Arren felt nervous inside when he realised that, though he wasn't sure why. Perhaps it was because he was seeing the Northgates for the first time. They looked so huge and so inhospitable, and the prospect of trying to pass through them frankly scared him.

Skandar didn't seem bothered. He flew unhurriedly, wings and tail angling to keep him stable in the air, like a griffin who knew exactly where he was going. Arren, leaning over slightly to look past his head, couldn't see anything that might be the place they were trying to reach; he hoped Skandar knew what he was doing. There were plenty of mountains within striking distance now, but none of them looked like the twin mountains Skade had described. At least, not as he had imagined them.

The sun was well up by the time they cleared the last of the hills and were among the mountains themselves. The trees were much sparser here and the ground rocky. Arren had scarcely registered this before Skandar suddenly leant to one side, nearly tipping him off. He flung himself forward, wrapping his arms more tightly around the griffin's neck, while behind him Skade clutched at his robe to anchor herself as Skandar made a wide circle in the air. He beat his wings a few times and then began to fly lower, still circling. He was coming in to land.

Skandar made a short, stumbling run as he landed, slowing himself by digging his talons into the ground. It helped to make the landing gentler on his passengers, who slid off his back.

Arren rubbed his own back and looked around. They were on a nondescript patch of ground, where the only decorations were a few tufts of grass and the remains of a long-dead tree. They were at the base of one of the mountains at the very edge of the Northgates, and the ground was covered in the shattered remains of rocks that had fallen down its sides. It was no place to camp, and no place to find food, either.

He looked at Skandar. The griffin had sat down on his haunches and was preening himself, apparently unconcerned. Skade, meanwhile, had wandered off and was rather disconsolately poking around.

Arren groaned. "Well, this is wonderful. We're lost." He couldn't resist glancing quickly at Skade as he said it, in the hope that she would say something to contradict him.

She limped toward him, wincing as the stony ground hurt her feet. "I think we should ask Skandar about that," she said. "Skandar?"

Skandar glanced up at her. "Skade?"

Skade hesitated and then bowed slightly to him. "Is this the place where you found the cave?"

The griffin yawned briefly. "Yes."

Arren stared at him, and then at the mountain. "Where?" he said. "I can't see anything."

Skandar pointed his beak toward the mountain. "There. See, there, Two. One, two."

"It looks like just one to—"

Skade nudged him heavily in the side. "No, look up," she said. "Skandar is right."

Arren did. There was another mountain almost directly behind the first, but slightly taller, giving the impression of a double peak. "So?" he said impatiently. "There's dozens of damn mountains here. It could be any of 'em. Anyway, I don't see any caves here, do you?"

Skade turned to Skandar. "If this is the mountain, then where is the cave, Skandar?"

"There," the griffin answered, looking at the base of the nearest one.

Arren moved closer to it. The only thing that Skandar could be indicating was a heap of boulders at the base of the mountain, by a dead tree. It was slightly higher than Arren was tall, and looked dangerously unstable. He kicked it as hard as he dared. "You mean it's behind these?"

"Don't know," said Skandar. "Cave here, before. Now, not here."

Arren kicked the heap again, and swore. "Godsdamnit! A godsdamned rock fall! *Now* what are we going to do?"

Skade examined it. "Perhaps we could move them?"

"Oh, but of course," Arren sneered. "I used to lift boulders twice my weight all the time back home, didn't I tell you?"

She gave him an irritated look. "Sarcasm will not help, Arenadd."

He calmed down slightly. "All right. Then what will?"

Skade was running her hands over the stones. "I don't know, perhaps we could make a lever of some kind? A push from the right direction could make them all fall."

"Maybe." Arren sighed. "I don't know, Skade. We're both tired and neither of us has been eating enough. I don't know if I've got the energy for it."

"Oh? You cannot summon up the energy to do something toward making your heart beat again?"

The sharpness in her voice stung him. "No, I didn't mean that—look," he said hastily, "we're tired. I suggest we rest a little while first. Have something to eat, think it over."

She paused a moment and then nodded. "Agreed."

Arren took the last of the apples out of his pockets, and the two of them sat by the dead tree.

Skandar had finished his grooming and loped over to them. "Food?" he said hopefully.

"Sorry, Skandar," said Arren.

Skandar shook himself. "I go hunt," he said. "You stay here. Come back later."

"A good idea," said Skade.

Apparently satisfied, Skandar flew away. Arren and Skade watched him go in silence.

"Well," Arren said eventually, swallowing a mouthful of apple, "I suppose we could break a branch off this tree, maybe see if that would work."

Skade nodded. "I will be willing to try it. I am not going to give in when we are this close."

"Yes."

Skade picked up the last apple. "Do you want this?"

Arren shook his head. "You have it."

"Thank you."

There was silence while Skade bit into it.

Finally, Arren looked up. "Skade?"

"Yes?"

"Skade, I—" He paused, trying to hold on to his courage. "About last night."

She tensed. "Yes?"

Arren gave her an agonised look. "You don't . . . mind, do you?"

Skade lowered the apple. "What do you mean by that?"

"It's just that"—he twisted his fingers together—"I don't know if I should have said it. I felt bad hiding it from you. I thought maybe you were better off not knowing, but there are some things that shouldn't go unsaid when—well, I just couldn't stop myself from telling you. It felt like the right thing to do."

She didn't reply immediately, and he watched her, almost feeling pain in his anxiety.

"I do not know," she said at last. "If you thought it best to tell me, then so be it. But my advice to you—you have been a good mate," she said. "And a good friend. I have enjoyed your company. I cannot repay you, but I can offer my advice."

"What advice?"

"This curse," said Skade. "If the spirits are not kind and you are not healed, or if we do not uncover the cave, and the curse remains, then you must never tell another living soul about it as you told me. If the world were to find out—"

"Yes. I know. But it won't."

"But what if I were to tell someone?"

Arren stared at her. "You wouldn't!"

"I might. You should have made certain of it before you told me. But no, I will not betray you. In return for all you have done for me, Arenadd."

"Please don't call me that."

Skade gave him the same impenetrable stare he had come to know so well over the last few days. "You go under a Southern name when you have made yourself an enemy to every Southerner in Cymria. Do not keep trying to pretend you are one of them, Arenadd Taranisäii. You will only suffer for it, even more than you have already done."

"Yes, but—"

"You should never be ashamed of what you are," Skade said softly. "I thought you would know that already. You have taught that lesson to me yourself."

Arren shivered. A cloud had covered the sun, and suddenly it seemed much colder. "I suppose you're right, but what have I got to be proud of?"

She shrugged. "What does anyone have to be proud of?"

Arren huddled down beside her, hugging his knees. He glanced upward. "I think it's going to"—a drop of water landed on his nose—"rain."

Skade sighed. "So now we must be wet as well as hungry."

It was a light, cold drizzle, not enough to soak into their clothes right away but more than enough to be unpleasant. Arren and Skade drew back under the feeble shelter offered by the dead tree and waited resignedly for it to clear. The rain fell thicker and faster, making the mountain appear hazy. Arren watched it gloomily. It almost looked as if there was mist or smoke rising from the ground.

"Well," he said, "isn't this fun?"

There was no reply from Skade. He glanced at her and saw she was sitting very still.

"Skade?"

She put a hand on his arm. "Can you hear that?"

Arren listened carefully. "What does it sound like?"

"I hear a voice."

"What? Where?"

Her grip tightened on his arm. "Look," she whispered.

Arren followed her gaze. The fog around the heap of boulders looked very thick. In fact—

He froze.

"Do you hear it now?" said Skade.

Arren nodded silently. There was a sound coming from the boulders. It was faint, but insistent. It sounded like voices. A soft muttering of voices. He stood up slowly and stepped toward it, heedless of the rain. Whiteness was swirling around the stones, growing thicker even as he watched. The muttering was coming from somewhere inside it. It sounded like many voices, but the words were impossible to discern.

"The spirits," he breathed. "My gods. Skandar was right."

The mist thickened. Arren watched it, almost hypnotised, but something stopped him moving closer. The voices grew louder and took on a harsh edge.

Arren backed away. "Skade, I don't think we should go near it. Skade?"

Skade stepped slowly forward, staring straight at the mist. Her lips were moving, forming words, but Arren couldn't hear them.

Inexplicable fear rose up inside him. "Skade, what are you doing?"

She reached a hand out toward the mist. "Welyn."

"What? Skade, don't—"

She turned her head sharply to look at him. "Can you hear it?" she demanded. "Can you hear him?"

"I can hear the voices," said Arren. "I don't know what they're saying."

She paused a moment. Listening. "It is Welyn. I can hear him. He is calling me."

The mist rose up higher and higher, obscuring the stones. Arren could see a faint glow inside it. And still the voices swirled and whispered in his ears, hissing and threatening.

Skade stood tall. "I come," she said.

Arren grabbed her arm. "Skade, no!"

She turned on him suddenly, all hissing anger. "Let go of me! I must go!"

Arren tugged at her arm, trying to pull her away. "Welyn's

not in there, Skade. There's no-one in there! Please, don't go in. It's dangerous. They'll hurt you."

She wrenched herself free. "No. I must go. Welyn is among the dead, and that is where I must go."

"Please," said Arren. "Please, I don't want you to go. Stay with me."

"Why?" She snarled the question, all her affection toward him gone. She was quivering slightly where she stood, full of pent-up rage and aggression.

"You don't understand!" Arren burst out. "Skade, I love you."

She stared at him. "What?"

"I love you," Arren repeated. "I want you to stay with me. Please."

Skade looked at him, then at the mist, and then back at him. "I do not understand you."

Arren took her hand. "I mean that I—it's like choosing. When a griffin chooses a partner. You said you wanted me for your mate. And now I know that I want you, Skade."

She shook her head. "Stop it. You are raving, Arenadd."

"No! Skade, please don't say that. I'm not mad. Please, try and understand—"

Skade pulled her hand free. "Listen to yourself!" she snapped. "Think of what you are saying! This is insanity!"

"It's not. I swear it's not. I wouldn't lie to you, Skade."

She moved a little closer to him. "You were a good mate," she said more softly. "And I am glad that you were pleased to be mine. But that is all we were. Our pairing is over now. We have had our time. I am a griffin, and you are a human. You knew that when we found the cave I would enter it and be changed back into my true form. My kind do not linger together. We pair, and then we part. Always." She turned away from him, toward the whispering mist. "And now I must go. Goodbye, Arenadd Taranisäii."

Arren knew he couldn't stop her. He stood there, filled with pain and confusion, all his strength and all his certainty gone. "Skade—"

But Skade did not look back. She stepped forward, her damp hair hanging over her shoulders, and did not look back. The mist opened up, and now Arren saw that the boulders were no longer there. There was nothing in front of him but the mist, and beyond that there was a great space, full of whispering whiteness and pale light. Skade stepped into it, and the mist rolled silently back to fill the place where she had been, leaving no sign of her.

"Skade!"

Nothing now, nothing. Only the voices and the drumming of the rain. And then, as Arren watched, he saw the mist begin to fade. It was dying down, thinning out and vanishing into the air. The light at its heart dimmed, and he began to see glimpses of the heap of boulders that had been there before. There was no trace of Skade.

Panic-stricken, Arren began to walk toward the boulders. Instantly the voices rose up around him, no longer muttering but loud and full of anger.

Go, they rasped. *Go now. Turn back. Go!*

Arren felt sick with fear. But the thought of Skade gave him courage, and he drew his sword. "No," he snarled, and ran forward.

The mist swallowed him.

Inside the spirit cave there was nothing but whiteness. And cold. It wrapped itself around Arren, numbing him, making him slow and clumsy. He stumbled on blindly, clutching his sword for comfort, calling Skade's name all the while. The voices had gone now, at least, and he felt stronger. He broke into a run.

It was impossible to tell how fast he was going, or where he was going. The mist was utterly featureless, a blank void in which he could see nothing but himself.

"Skade? Skade! *Skade!*"

Arren stumbled on something and fell forward. He landed heavily, and the sword flew out of his hand. He got up, swearing, and groped around for it, but he couldn't find it.

"Godsdamnit! Skade, are you there? Skade, for gods' sakes—"

Arren.

Arren froze. "Who said that? Is someone there?"

Arren.

He suddenly realised that the whiteness was gone. He hadn't seen it disappear; it was simply there one moment and absent the next.

Arren blinked, puzzled. There was no mist. No voices. No

light. He was standing in a perfectly ordinary stone cave dimly lit by a hole in the ceiling. The floor was sandy, the walls and roof jagged. There was no sign of Skade anywhere.

"Hello?" he called, a little uncertainly. "Is there anyone—?"

Arren.

He turned, and there she was. Real and solid, large as life, sitting on her haunches, watching him, her tail wrapped around her talons.

Arren gaped at her. "Eluna?"

The white griffin put her head on one side. *You should not be here,* she whispered.

Arren backed away. "No. No, this isn't right. This isn't real. You're not real. You're dead."

Eluna stood up. *Why have you come here? You were not meant to come here.*

"I've come to—I want—Eluna, where is this? Why are you here? You're dead!"

We did not call you here, said Eluna, and Arren knew it wasn't her voice. It was soft and whispering, like the sound of distant wind. It sounded like many voices speaking at once.

"Eluna, are you a spirit?"

We are the dead, said Eluna. *Why have you come here to us?*

"I have come to be healed," said Arren.

Then tell us what may be healed, said the white griffin.

"There's a curse on me," said Arren. "My heart—"

Yes. But it is a curse that needs no healing.

"Please!" said Arren, starting toward her. "Please, make my heart beat again. I beg you."

There was a curse upon the man called Arren Cardockson, said Eluna. *We know this. He was cursed by the griffin called Shoa. She wove her spell around the skull of a griffin chick, and her partner, Rannagon, gave it to him. The instant he touched it the curse was upon him. He was doomed to die within less than a year. It was fulfilled on the night after his twentieth birthday. He fell from the edge of the city and died among the stones, in the moonlight. Now the curse is complete.*

"No!" said Arren. "No, not that curse, I mean the other one."

There is no other—

"My heart!" Arren half-shouted, thumping his chest. "Please, you have to make my heart beat again."

There is no other, Eluna's whispering voice repeated.

"It's a curse," said Arren. "I have no heartbeat."

Eluna's shape began to waver, becoming misty and unreal. *You have no heart, Kraeai kran ae.*

"I want it back," said Arren. "Please. Give it back to me."

You cannot be healed, said Eluna. *A curse cannot be lifted that does not exist.*

"But you have the power! You have to—"

Mist began to swirl around Eluna. She was disappearing, fading into it. *You dare command us, Kraeai kran ae?*

"If you can help me, then do it," said Arren. "I don't deserve this. I don't want to be this way. I didn't do anything wrong."

Whiteness was rising from the floor, surrounding him. Eluna disappeared, leaving nothing but a glow of light from her eyes. *You,* the voices hissed. *You dare to come here, monster, you monster, you murderer without a heart, you dare come here and tell us we must help you? You dare that?*

"Yes," said Arren. "I do. Give me my heart back."

It was closing in around him now, cold and smothering. *And who are you who dare do this?*

"I am Arren Cardockson, and I—"

No. Arren Cardockson is dead. You are not him. You are Kraeai kran ae. You are the man without a heart.

"Then I am Arenadd Taranisäii," Arren shouted back. "I am the man without a heart. Give it back to me, and I'll do whatever you ask."

The cave had vanished, covered up by the mist. It wrapped itself around him, taking him into itself, lifting him from the floor and holding him, suspended helplessly. He struggled, but the mist would not let go.

Kraeai kran ae, Kraeai kran ae! the spirits hissed, again and again.

"Let me go!"

No faith, they whispered. *No mercy. No rest. No heart. No life. The dead who walks among the living cannot be one of them, any more than north can be south.*

Arren tried to speak, but his voice died in his throat. *My heart,* he thought. *Give me back my heart.*

A heart is not a thing that can be given or taken, said the spirits. *And we do not wish it. You are not cursed, Kraeai kran ae. You* are *a curse.*

No. No. I'm not, I'm—

The force holding him grew stronger, pressing in on him, spreading a crushing pain through his whole body. It was a feeling he knew, one he had felt in his dreams. It was the pain he had felt as he lay at the foot of the mountain, staring sightlessly up at the moon and the looming presence of Skandar, blood trickling down over his fingers.

Hear us now, the spirits said, their voices needling, cold, full of contempt. *There is no place for you. You are not wanted; you should not be here. We shall tell you now that when your end comes, you shall be alone. Your body shall rot and your bones shall be left for animals, and no living soul shall ever mourn for you.*

Arren couldn't reply. All he could feel was the pain. It was everywhere, inside and out. His bones were breaking; he could feel them twist and crack inside him. He couldn't move or breathe or even think. His heart was pattering frantically.

While you walk, hundreds will want you gone, the spirits promised. *They will hunt you their whole lives, seeking your destruction with their every breath. But where you go, death shall always follow. They will hate you,* Kraeai kran ae. *Hate you with their very souls.*

He could feel his heart beating now. But slower and slower, weakening as the blood flowed out of him. He was dying. His heart was dying.

Seek out the Night Eye for your hope now, said the spirits. *Take up your own pagan ways. But we do not want you. Farewell.*

Arren felt his heart stop.

Go back to the North, blackrobe, the spirits said, their voices full of sneering mockery.

And then there was nothing but silence, and blackness.

10

Herbstitt

It was very cold. Arren shivered and curled up more tightly. His robe was wet.

Something grabbed him by the collar, and he was being hauled to his feet. He flung out an arm as his eyes snapped open, but too late. A rough hand grabbed him by the wrist, and there was a loud metallic snap as something closed tightly around it. Someone had grabbed his other arm, too, and before he knew what was happening he was being dragged backward. It was dark, and rain was still falling, but the moon had come out, and there were lights nearby. Lights and people.

The hands that had dragged him upright flung him down against a tree, and as he fell he realised his hands were manacled together. Terrified, he tried to get up and run, but someone kicked him in the stomach, and he keeled over, wheezing.

"All right, you son of a bitch," a voice snarled. "We've got you, so don't try anything on."

Arren managed to sit up as someone brought a torch over. The guttering flame showed him a group of men clad in rough leather armour. They were armed and had the easy confidence of people used to travelling and fighting.

Arren's hand went to his belt, dragging the other with it as he groped for his knife, but it was gone. He tried to get up, but one of the men grabbed hold of the manacles and dragged him forward, nearly tipping him onto his face.

Arren struggled wildly, wrenching at the chain. "Let go of me!"

They hit him again, this time in the head, but he barely felt it in his terror. He twisted sideways, breaking free of the man's grip, and hurled himself at the nearest of them. It took the man by surprise; Arren knocked him sideways and ran for it.

Footsteps came up fast behind him, and something hit him in the back of the knees. His legs folded, and he stumbled to the ground. They were on him instantly, hitting him from all sides. He made a few attempts to defend himself, but the blows continued to fall, hard and merciless. Finally, half-conscious and bleeding badly from a cut lip, he slumped onto his side and lay there, gasping. The next time they dragged him to his feet, he didn't resist.

One of them hit him hard in the face. "Thought you could get away, did you, blackrobe?"

Arren sagged, groaning. "Please stop hitting me."

The man hit him again. "Shut your face!"

"Come on, Russ," another voice cut in. "I'm getting soaked here. Let's just get him back to camp."

"Wait a moment," said the one called Russ. "You"—this was to Arren—"is there anyone else here with you?"

"No," Arren said without hesitation.

Russ drew back his hand to hit him again. "You sure about that, blackrobe?"

"There's no-one else!" said Arren. "I swear!"

Russ lowered his hand. "Fine, whatever. I don't see why we should be wasting our time with this kind of crap anyway. Here," he said, turning to one of his companions, "toss me that rope, will you?" He caught it and wrapped it around Arren's manacled wrists, binding them tightly together. He tugged at it a few times to make sure it was secure and then took hold of the loose end. "Right, let's get going. Daen, could you bring my horse over here?"

He tied the end of the rope to the back of the animal's saddle while his companions mounted, and then got up himself. "Let's go. You go ahead, Jono."

The group set out, four in all, riding in single file. Russ was at the back, and Arren had to walk behind him, the rope threatening to drag him down if he was too slow. He knew it would be pointless to try to pull back; the rope was thick, and besides, they'd only start hitting him again. He limped along after the column, looking back desperately over his shoulder at the mountain. He could just see the dead tree and the heap of boulders. There was no sign of anything unusual there, and no sign of Skade or Skandar, either. He was on his own.

They rode out of the clearing and away over the rocky

landscape, heading southward. As Arren walked, he tried to untie the rope pinning his wrists together, but it had been tied expertly and refused to budge. His fingers were longer than those of a Southerner, but even so he couldn't get hold of the knot. It had been tied on the side furthest away from his mouth, too, making it nearly impossible to get his teeth into it. He did manage to after a few tries, but it was too tight to be undone that way, and it was slick with rain. Even so, he continued to wrench at it, trying again and again to get a grip on it. He fell too far behind and was instantly pulled to the ground when the rope went taut. The horse dragged him along behind it while he tried to get up, but Russ quickly noticed and called a halt. He dismounted, strode over to Arren and pulled him upright.

Then he hit him again. "Bloody well keep up or I'll cut your ears off, understand?"

After that Arren gave up and walked obediently along behind the column, rain slicking his hair to his head and trickling down his face. His robe was already soaked, and its weight slowed him down. He ached all over from the beating; his legs and back were starting to stiffen. Little spots of light flickered in his vision, and his head was spinning. He groaned softly. The encounter with the spirits still loomed large in his memory, but it was already starting to feel hazy and unreal. Like a dream. Or a nightmare. But deep down he knew it had been real.

Hatred started to roil in his chest, and the despair that went with it only made it worse. They hadn't helped him. They had mocked him, condemned him, turned him away, tortured him with the memory of his own death. And then they had thrown him out of the cave, delivered him straight into the hands of his enemies.

He closed his eyes. They would have him soon. Griffiners. These men would give him straight to them. After that there would be no hope, none at all.

The rope grew taut again. Arren jogged forward a short way, and once he had enough slack he lifted his hands to his neck and felt it carefully, checking yet again.

His heart was absolutely silent.

They rode on through the night, still heading away from the mountains. After a while the ground became more level and the trees thicker. The rain slowed to a few light spots, though by now every member of the party was already wet through. They rode on regardless, keeping up a steady pace, while Arren trudged along on the end of his rope, head bowed.

Finally, a shout from the front made him look up. The others had sped up. Russ nudged his horse's sides, and the animal lurched forward without warning, nearly dragging Arren over again. He had to break into a clumsy run to keep pace, his boots catching on rocks and sticks and threatening to trip him. Tired panic started to grip him. If they went on like this for too long he'd never be able to keep up. To his relief, they slowed down again a short time later, when they reached the edge of a stand of trees. And as they went in among them, he heard voices from up ahead. There was light there, too, the flickering light of a campfire.

The horses finally came to a halt, and the riders dismounted. Two people were waiting for them by the large fire. Russ turned and took hold of Arren's rope before he slid out of the saddle. The instant he hit the ground he pulled hard on the rope, dragging Arren toward him, and then shoved him into a kneeling position. "Sit there and don't move."

The two who had been waiting came over. "You got him, then," said one.

Russ kicked Arren casually in the stomach. "Yes, thank gods," he said as Arren doubled over, wheezing. "Little shit gave us some trouble, though."

"Where'd you find him?"

"Up north, near the mountains," said Russ. "Found him asleep under a tree."

"That's that sorted out, then," said the other. "No sign of Raen's group, then?"

"Not a damn thing. We found their last camp, or something that might've been it, but other than that—it's the bloody rain. Covers everything up. Nothing more we can do about it; either they've gone back or they're still lost somewhere. We've done half the job, and they'll just have to be happy with it, because I'm not staying out here any longer."

The other man took Arren by the shoulder. "I hear yah. I'll get this son of a bitch secured; you go get yourself warmed up. There's some warm wine over by the fire; help yourself."

Russ sighed. "Thanks, mate. That's just what I need."

He walked off purposefully toward the fire, and his friend pulled Arren upright and gave him a shove. "Go on, move it."

Arren, too exhausted to resist, allowed himself to be taken to the foot of a large tree. There his bonds were removed, and his hands were shackled behind his back and tethered to an overhanging branch, pulling them upward. Once he'd tugged on the rope to make sure it was secure, the man walked off and left Arren alone.

Arren pulled at the rope, but without much hope. When it refused to budge he sat down with his back to the tree trunk and watched his captors relax around the fire. They were talking among themselves, but he couldn't catch most of it, and the bits and pieces he did pick up weren't very useful. All he could gather was that they had agreed to start heading back the next day; just where they were heading back to wasn't certain, but they all seemed keen to go there. They ate and passed around a jar of wine that had been warmed up by the fire, and Arren had to sit and watch them, burning inside with both fear and hunger.

He had hoped that he could find a way to break free while they were busy, but it was futile. The rope wouldn't budge and neither would the manacles, and in any case they were still keeping an eye on him; those of them who were facing toward him kept glancing at him. And once they had eaten, one of them came over and sat down just out of his reach, watching him in silence.

Arren looked back uneasily, but the man didn't seem about to do anything other than watch. He thought of saying something but decided against it.

The man looked him up and down, and then sighed. "Trying to go north, were you?"

There was no point in hiding it. Arren nodded.

The man shook his head in disgust. "North!" he said. "Why do you sods always go north? I mean, what's the point? D'you think you're going to find some sort of paradise there? Ye gods. Bloody blackrobes. You've all got snow between your ears."

Another man wandered over. "You all set for the night, Jono?"

The man identified as Jono shrugged. "Some more wine'd be nice, but I'd better not risk it. See you later."

"Yeah, all right," said his friend. "You come and wake me up when you're ready to turn in, okay?"

"Yeah, right. Good night."

"Huh, I'll bet." The man walked off. The others had finished off the wine and were busy setting up bedrolls around the fire. The horses had been tethered on the other side of the camp.

Arren's guard yawned and pulled his waterproof cloak around his shoulders. "Get some sleep, blackrobe," he advised. "You're gonna need it for tomorrow, and I don't want to have to sling you over the back of my saddle, understand?"

"Where are we going?" Arren dared ask.

"Back to Herbstitt," Jono said briefly. He squinted at Arren. "I don't get it. Why run? I mean, where did you think you were going? Did you really think you were going to get away?"

Arren said nothing.

Jono shrugged. "You just don't make any sense to me, that's all."

He didn't say anything more after that. The rain had stopped, and Arren sat and watched his guard, hoping he'd fall asleep. But the man was obviously too well-trained for that sort of thing. He stayed at his post, his attention never wandering. Occasionally he would hum a tune under his breath or mutter something to himself, but he showed no sign of falling asleep or letting his attention waver. Eventually he did start showing signs of tiredness, but at that point he got up and went and woke his companion, who came to take his place, muttering and irritable but alert. After that, Arren gave up. It wasn't as if he could have done anything, even if there hadn't been someone watching him; he'd already searched the ground for a sharp rock that he could use to cut the rope and found nothing. And if he could get loose, he wouldn't get very far with his hands chained together behind his back.

The rope was too short for him to lie down. He had to try and make himself comfortable sitting up against the tree, the manacles digging into his back. He fell asleep with the resolution that he would keep looking for an opportunity to escape. It had to happen sooner or later.

It was a four-day journey to Herbstitt, and by the end of the second day Arren had long since realised that there was no hope of escape. He was forced to walk behind Russ' horse all day, with only a few short breaks, and at night he was tied to a tree in the same manner as before. His hands were kept chained together at all times, and he was never left unguarded.

His captors were obviously experienced and must have been expecting him to try and escape. They kept their distance from him most of the time in case he tried to attack, and searched the ground around him for sharp objects. Every morning and evening they patted him down and turned out his pockets to make sure he had nothing hidden on him he could use to escape.

Other than that, they generally ignored him, speaking to him only to give him orders and showing little interest in his wellbeing, although they did give him plenty to eat. The food mostly consisted of dried travel rations, but it was far superior to what he'd survived on for the last few months, and he ate it very gratefully. He needed all he could get. It had been a long time since he'd walked any great distance, and by the end of the first day he could barely stand upright. The second day was nightmarish. He forgot any notion of escaping and focused all his efforts on simply keeping up as the day stretched out into an endless slow pounding of hooves and his own boots dragging on the ground. He was so exhausted that he collapsed the instant the rope was untied and had to be dragged over to the tree where he would spend the night.

His captors, aware that he couldn't keep on going like this, left a little later the next day and took more breaks. He was able to cope with that. By the middle of the third day they were back in inhabited country, riding through large stretches of farmland toward the river. That night they took shelter in the home of a farmer, who let them sleep in his barn for a handful of silver oblong. Arren was locked up in a small storeroom under the floor, but at least he could lie down now, and they provided him with a heap of straw.

The day after that was easier. There was a decent road following the river, and it was far easier to travel along it than through damp forest. There were other people using it, too: farm carts and mounted travellers and even a few boats on the river, which was wide and looked to be very deep. One or two of their fellow travellers paused briefly to greet Arren's captors, and it was from one of those encounters that he finally learnt something useful.

"Heading straight for Canran," said the traveller, a roughly clad man on a horse. "Seems they're preparing themselves for a fight. As for me, I'm keeping well out of it. Got better things to do than worry about what the griffiners are up to."

"Well, Lord Holm's not a fool," one of Arren's guards replied. "I doubt the Eagleholm lot are gonna put up much of a fight. Most of 'em would've flown off by now anyway."

Arren's heart leapt. Lord Holm! That was a name he knew: Lord Holm was Eyrie Master at Canran, and that meant Arren was out of Eagleholm's lands and in those of Canran. He and Skandar had flown further than he had realised.

The conversation ended after that, as the rider went on his way, and Arren trudged on. The truth was that he had no idea what Lord Holm would do with him. Once he would have assumed that he'd be handed over to Lady Riona at Eagleholm, for a price. But now that she was gone, what then? If the Canran griffiners were going to invade Eagleholm's lands—something he'd gleaned from listening to the talk around him—then they were hardly likely to be interested in doing them any favours. Even so, he couldn't expect mercy from Lord Holm. He was still a Northerner, and he had still killed griffiners, which made him an enemy to every griffiner in Cymria. There was no doubt whatsoever that they would kill him. The only question was when, how and who would do it.

Arren brooded obsessively on it as the day wore on, trying to imagine what was going to happen to him. The traitor's death, perhaps. That was the punishment meted out to anyone whose crimes went beyond mere ordinary murder; it was done only rarely, but always in public, when the griffiners wanted to make an example. Arren had witnessed a few executions in his life, but the traitor's death was something else. Mere hanging or beheading was one thing; they were unpleasant, but quick and clean enough. The traitor's death, though . . .

He'd read accounts of it in books. The condemned would be hanged until he was nearly dead, and then cut down and manacled to a rack. Then he would be torn open and disembowelled, forced to watch as his own intestines came out of his body. After that, he would be finished off by being hacked into four crude pieces, and his heart would be taken out and shown to the crowd. The vilest death the griffiners had ever devised.

Arren felt sick when he thought of it. It didn't matter that he was already dead; he could still feel pain. And he would not survive that punishment.

He thought of Skandar. The griffin must be looking for him; maybe he would come and try to rescue him. But Skandar could have no way of knowing where he was by now. Again and again he had wanted to call for him, but it would be suicide. If these men knew anything about griffiners then they would know what he was doing if he started calling. They had bows. If he called and Skandar did come, they would be forewarned. They could shoot him down the instant he flew within range. Arren watched the sky surreptitiously, always on the lookout for a pair of dark wings, but he never saw anything. He hoped Skandar was safe. And Skade—he thought of her, too. He wondered where she was now and whether the spirits had granted *her* request. Was she back in her old shape now, or was she still out there somewhere, trapped in human form? Arren didn't like to think of her, but he couldn't help it. As the journey continued, he relived their last exchange over and over in his mind, and nursed his hurt. He felt like an idiot. But though he was angry with her as well as himself, he still wanted to know if she was safe.

Herbstitt came into sight shortly before sunset, and Arren's suspicions were confirmed the instant he saw the dome of the temple rising over the rooftops: it was the same town he had spotted from Skandar's back.

There was a large wall around the city, or at least part of one. The stones were crumbling and the gates missing, but there were signs that they were being rebuilt; scaffolds had been set up around them, and there were heaps of newly cut blocks stacked just beyond the nonexistent gates. The workers must have retired for the night; the sun was sinking, and he could see people in the streets heading for home.

Herbstitt was bigger than he had thought. There was a mill built on the riverbank and a small dock where a number of boats were moored. The houses looked old but well kept, and there was a good-sized marketplace. The temple was near the centre of town, and not far away from it was a great stone tower. Arren recognised the design immediately: the wide balconies without railings and the flat top. A griffiner tower. This would be the place where the town's administration took place. And the place where prisoners were kept.

He was led through the streets, directly to the tower, and he felt his insides crumble. This was it. Soon he would be in the tower's dungeons, ready to be interrogated.

He looked away. The streets here were cobbled, but there

was a layer of dirt over the stones. He examined them closely, trying to think of anything except the tower and the dungeons. There were plants, he noticed. Plants growing in the cracks between the cobbles, and in the gutters and along the walls of the buildings they passed. Some of them had flowers. He started trying to identify each one he saw, concentrating almost fiercely. There was soap-bush, mint, spleenwort, bloodroot and catweed. Arren trod on a clump of spiny griffin-tail, and the sharp smell of it filled his nose. Herbs. They were growing everywhere. Quite suddenly, he found himself biting back a snigger. Herbstitt, the Healer's Home. The place where herbs grew.

A tug on the rope brought him back to reality. They had come to a halt in the yard in front of the tower, and Russ and his men were dismounting. Russ untied the rope from the back of his horse and yanked on it, and Arren stumbled toward him. Guards were already emerging from the tower to come and meet them, and Arren's captors held him by the shoulders as Russ untied the rope, leaving only the manacles.

"G'day," Russ said, nodding to one of the guards. "How's things?"

"Not bad," said the guard. He and his companion took up station on either side of Arren, grabbing him by the elbows. "We'll take charge of him now."

"Right," said Russ. He nodded to his friends. "Go on. I'll stay with him and meet you later with the money, all right?"

Jono nodded briefly in return. "Come on," he said to his fellows, and the group of them left, leading their horses and leaving Russ behind.

Russ tethered his horse to a ring set into the wall and entered the tower. The guards followed, with Arren walking between them. No-one seemed particularly interested.

"So, where'd you catch him?" one guard asked.

"Near the Northgates," Russ answered briefly.

"Bastard got his collar off," said the other guard.

Russ shrugged. "Some of 'em figure out how to do it. There's a trick to it."

Somewhere in the midst of the terror constricting his throat, Arren felt a hint of confusion.

"I take it the others haven't shown up?" said Russ.

"Not a sign," said the guard.

"Well, it's not my problem," said Russ. He reached the end of the corridor and knocked on a large door. It was opened by another guard, and Arren was taken through and into a big stone room with a table in it. There was a fireplace with a good fire burning in it, and a large dog curled up on the rug in front of it looked up as the door opened.

There was a man sitting at the table, but Arren knew instantly that he wasn't a griffiner. He was too plainly clad, for one thing, and there was no sign of a griffin. The interior of the tower had been built specifically to allow a griffin inside, and if this man had one it would certainly be with him.

Russ strode over to the table. "Evening, sir."

The man stood up. "I was expecting you back days ago."

Russ shrugged. "We stay out as long as the job takes." He gestured at the guards to bring Arren forward. "Anyway, we got him, sir."

The man looked Arren up and down, and then blinked in a puzzled kind of way. "Where did you find him?"

"Near the Northgates. No sign of the other group, though. My guess is they're lost somewhere. Anyway, it's no concern of ours. We're just here to hand the blackrobe over and get our pay."

The man looked at Arren again. "It's not him."

Russ paused. "What, sir?"

"You heard me," said the man. "That's not him. You've got the wrong man."

"Are you sure, sir?" said Russ. He sounded surprised.

"Yes. I know what he looks like, and this isn't him. He's too young. The runner doesn't have a scar on his face, either."

Russ looked at Arren. "Oh."

The man leant over the table. "Show me your hand, blackrobe."

Before he could obey, one of the guards grabbed Arren's forearm and yanked it forward. The man examined the back of Arren's hand. "No brand. Where is his brand?" He looked up at Arren. "Where's your brand, blackrobe?"

Arren gaped at him, too bewildered to speak.

The man made a sound of irritation and let go. "This is wonderful. Instead of bringing back that cursed runner, you've brought me this idiot."

"Well, I'm sorry, *sir*," Russ snapped. "How was I supposed

to know? A blackrobe on his own with collar scars on his neck—what else could I have done?"

"You *could* have checked his hand," the man said acidly.

"Look, sir," said Russ, calming down, "we were out near the mountains, it was freezing cold and pissing with rain, and we were running out of supplies. I figure one blackrobe's pretty much like another. Now are you going to pay me, or should I take him somewhere else?"

The man paused to think it over. "You," he said to Arren, "can you talk, blackrobe?"

Arren swallowed. "Uh, yes. Sir."

"Thank gods for that. Where did you run away from?"

Arren's mind raced. "I—uh—W-Withypool, sir."

"You're not local, that's obvious," said the man, in an oddly satisfied tone. "Don't they brand slaves over there?"

"Uh—no, sir," said Arren.

"Why wouldn't they?" said Russ.

The man, though, waved him into silence. "It's this new system: some people just mark the collars. Makes no difference to me. What's your name, blackrobe?"

"Er—Taranis, sir," said Arren.

"And what are your skills?"

Arren looked at him blankly.

"What can you do, blackrobe?" the man said impatiently. "What sort of work did you do in Withypool?"

"Oh. I—uh—" Arren pulled himself together. "I know some carpentry, sir. And I can—" He was about to say that he could read and write, but decided against it. "I know how to cook," he said lamely.

The man snorted. "Educated, are you? Do you know anything about building, then?"

"A little. Sir."

"Excuse me, sir," said Russ.

The man looked at him, irritated. "Yes, what?"

"If this isn't the one that ran away from here, then what are we supposed to do with him? You know you'll be in trouble if—"

"If what?" the man interrupted. "If the Withypoolians find out we picked up one of their runaways? Don't make me laugh." He looked at Arren. "Blackrobe, this is your lucky day. If your master had been the one to catch you, you'd probably have your tendons cut." To Russ he said, "He's not ours, but he'll do. I'll buy him from you."

"Are you sure that's a good idea, sir?" said Russ, in a tone that suggested he didn't think so. "He's a rebel, fought back something fierce when we caught him. He'll try and run off again, sure as fate."

"Yes, I'm aware of that," the man snapped. "But the new lot are late, and Lord Holm will have my head if we don't get the wall ready in time. We need the extra manpower. Now, how much do you want for him?"

"I'll take the standard fee for catching him, plus the regular sum for a decent slave," Russ said promptly. "I make it nine hundred oblong, sir."

"Absolutely not. You can have four hundred, and that's flat."

Russ nodded. "Fine." He took hold of Arren's shoulder. "I'll just be taking him away with me now—"

"Six hundred, then," the man snapped. "That's my final offer."

"Seven hundred and we'll call it quits."

There was dead silence while the two of them glared at each other. Finally, the man shrugged. "Seven hundred it is. Take him down to the dungeon with the guards and I'll have the money ready when you get back."

Russ nodded. "Deal."

"Have him branded with the Herbstitt iron," said the man, now speaking to Arren's guards. "And when you've done that, give him a flogging and fit him with some leg-irons. I don't want to have to deal with another runner. And find a collar for him, double time. I don't want anyone asking questions."

Arren's blood ran cold. "You can't—"

The man looked sharply at him. "Do you have something to say, blackrobe?"

Arren opened his mouth to protest, and then shut it again and looked away.

"I didn't think so," said the man. "When you're done, take him over to the slave-house and let Caedmon deal with him. As for you, blackrobe—look at me, damn you."

Arren did.

"You are not to tell anyone about this, understand? Not a word."

"Yes, sir."

"I mean it," said the man. "If I hear you've let anything slip, anything at all, I will give you more than just a flogging. Understand?"

"Yes, sir," said Arren.

"Good. Take him away."

11

The Slave-House

Arren had expected the dungeons to be dark, given that they were underground, but the passage leading down to them was well lit, and so was the guardroom at the end of it. The two guards who had brought him down handed him over to their colleagues assigned to the dungeon, and passed on the instructions their master had given. It all happened with efficient speed. Two of the dungeon guards replaced the others and led Arren to a small stone chamber. There he was pushed into a chair and one guard stayed to watch over him; the other left. While he waited, Arren looked around the room, and immediately regretted it. He was in the interrogation chamber: a set of manacles hung from the ceiling, and there was another pair attached to the floor. A whip hung from a hook on the wall, and there was a brazier intended for heating the torture implements. There was nothing in it but glowing coals, but Arren couldn't look away from it.

A few moments later the guard returned carrying a long metal rod with a wooden handle. He thrust the tip of it into the brazier and stood by to wait.

Arren stared at the branding iron as it slowly heated up. A single metal rune was attached to the end, pitted and blackened from countless heatings and coolings. The coals were already beginning to do their work. He felt cold sweat prickling on his forehead.

When the guard finally took the brand out, the end of it was glowing red. He put it back in and nodded to his colleague who removed Arren's manacles. He grabbed Arren's left arm and twisted it behind his back. Arren cried out and pulled his free arm away from the table in front of him, trying to keep it out of their reach, but they were ready for that. The guard behind him gave him a shove, and as he flung out his arm to steady himself the other one grabbed him by the wrist and wrenched it forward, stretching it out over the table. The guard's other hand reached for the handle of the branding iron.

Arren tried to pull free. "No, wait, st— *aaaaargh!*"

The glowing metal was pressed into the back of his hand and kept there. Arren struggled wildly, yelling, but they held him still, both of them, and the guard pushed down hard with the brand, keeping it in place for a hideous moment. The flesh made a vile sizzling noise, and Arren's nose was full of the stench of burning skin and hair—*his* skin and hair—and he retched as the guard finally took the brand away and let go of his wrist. The other one let go of his left arm, and Arren slumped in his chair, gasping. He cradled his wounded hand against his chest and stared blankly at the two of them, as if he couldn't quite comprehend what they had just done.

The guards didn't seem to notice. The one behind him took him by the shoulder and pulled him to his feet.

Arren didn't resist as he was taken to the middle of the room. A strange numbness was spreading through his body, almost a euphoria. His head was spinning, and he had such a powerful sense of unreality all of a sudden that he could almost believe it was a dream.

The guard tore his robe off and forced him to kneel. He did so, not really able to think about what was going on. His hand felt as if it were on fire. He could still smell it.

There were bloodstains on the floor around him, he noticed dully as the guard shackled him to a large iron ring set into the stone. The guard then left the room. Behind him, the other guard took down the whip.

It was very cold without his robe. He shivered. If only Skandar was there. He thought of the griffin's warm fur and feathers. Then the whip came down for the first time.

Arren gasped and shuddered. The pain was so intense that he could scarcely believe it. The guard couldn't possibly do it more than once; it was ridiculous. He'd kill him or break his back, surely.

But it was not over, and it wasn't over for what felt like half the night. The whip cut into his back, again and again, and each time it did, it felt like the guard was striking him harder. At

first Arren did nothing but jerk under each blow, too shocked
to do anything else. But as the flogging continued and the pain
intensified, something inside him snapped and he tried to get
up, wrenching at the chains with all his might. It didn't do any
good at all. Blood trickled downward and soaked into his trousers, and that was when he started to scream. Scrabbling at the
floor, trying to break free and attack his tormentor, he screamed
and yelled at the top of his voice, cursing and pleading. That
could not help him, either. The whip rose and fell until his voice
ran out, and all he could do was cry out every time it struck
him, too weak now to struggle any further.

Finally, the guard stood back and returned the whip to its
hook, and Arren was left cringing on the floor, his back a mass
of torn and bleeding flesh. He made an attempt to get up, but
his legs gave way and he fell onto his face. He lay there, half
propped up by his hands, still tugging feebly at the chains. The
manacles had cut into his wrists, and sweat was soaking into
the burn on the back of his hand, making it sting. He could feel
the blood running over the bare skin on his sides to drip onto the
floor, darkening the stains there even further.

He tried to get up once more, but all the strength seemed to
have gone out of him. His vision was fading. From somewhere
far away he heard a door open and the sound of footsteps. The
other guard had come back, maybe, he thought.

". . . don't have any we can find; he'll have to go without,"
a voice said, but Arren couldn't think about what it meant. He
blacked out.

A rren didn't stay unconscious for very long. He woke up as
the guards were undoing the shackles but stayed limp, eyes
shut, hoping they wouldn't notice.

"Poor sod couldn't take it," one muttered. "Probably won't
need the irons at all."

"Get them anyway," said the other. "Go on. I'll wake him up."

Footsteps retreated as a pair of hands rolled Arren onto his
side. He kept still.

A few moments later there was a cold shock as a bucket of
water was thrown over his head. Arren jerked in surprise and
started to cough.

"On your feet," said the guard, brusquely but not unkindly. "Come on, blackrobe, we haven't got all night."

Arren managed to lift himself into a sitting position and rubbed his hands over his face. His back was a mass of pain, and his burned hand was throbbing horrendously. His wrists hurt. His legs hurt. Everything hurt.

The guard grabbed him by the upper arm and pulled him to his feet. "Come on, stand up. That's right. Here."

A cup was thrust into his hand. Arren managed to grasp it, and drank the contents. Water. He coughed again and nearly dropped it. His fingers were stiff and clumsy; it hurt to move them.

"Here." The guard draped Arren's robe over him.

Arren screamed the instant the rough cloth touched his wounded back, and the cup fell out of his hand as he tried to pull it off.

The guard, though, took him by the arm and thrust it roughly through the sleeve. "Go on, put it on, it's not going to kill you."

Arren continued to resist as the robe was forcibly put back on him, but the guard ignored his protests. As he was pulling the garment over his chest, his friend returned.

"He's awake, then."

"He'll be fine," the first guard said confidently. "Just a bit of shock. Did you get them?"

The second guard rattled the pair of leg-irons he was carrying. "Of course I bloody did; what do these look like, chopped onions?"

"Har har, very funny. Keep them with you for the moment; we'll put them on him once we've got him to the slave-house. He'll have enough trouble walking as it is."

"Good point. Let's go, then."

Arren leant gratefully on his guards as they took him out of the room and back into the main passageway of the dungeon. Now they had finished dealing with him as they had been ordered to, all they wanted to do was be rid of him, and they had nothing to gain from forcing him to walk unaided. They helped him out of the dungeon and back above ground, into the tower, and out through a side door. It was dark outside and the stars had come out. As they emerged into the night air, Arren looked up at them and felt strangely comforted. They were still there, at least. Going into the dungeons had felt like being buried alive, but now he could see the sky again. And it was cold out here, too. The hint of frost in the air helped to soothe his burned hand.

The guards led him away from the tower, toward the edge of the city. They walked through the near-deserted streets for a while, until they had passed through the market district and were in the residential area. From there they walked on until the last of the houses had gone and crossed a small patch of open ground between them and the crumbling wall. There was another building there, quite large, with a low, flat roof. Faint lights were showing through the windows, and Arren could hear voices coming from inside.

There were guards there, too. Arren was taken to a small room attached to the side of the building. Inside, several guards were sitting around a brazier warming their hands. One came out to meet them almost as soon as they were within striking distance.

"Hello, what's this?" he said, eyeing Arren.

"We've brought the new one," said one of Arren's guards. "You should've had word from the tower."

"Yes, of course. Bring him in, then."

Arren was brought into the guardhouse and allowed to sit down on a bench. The guards there looked at him with a certain amount of curiosity.

"So, this is the runner," said one. "Doesn't look like much to me. Where's his collar?"

"Couldn't find one," said one of the tower guards. "Don't suppose you've got any over here?"

"I doubt it, but we'll have a look. Are you going to put those irons on him, or what?"

"You do it," the tower guard snapped. "We were supposed to be off duty ages ago."

"Fine, hand them over and get lost," the other replied, taking them. "We'll take charge of him now."

The tower guards nodded briefly to their fellows and left.

"Right," said the one holding the irons. "That's that sorted out. Now then." He turned to Arren. "What's your name, blackrobe?"

"Taranis," Arren mumbled.

"And where are you from, Taranis?"

"Withypool."

"Right, I expect that's what they told you to say. If that

accent's from Withy then I'm a griffin. Well, it doesn't make any difference to me where you're from, and I don't imagine anyone else will care, either. You're in our hands now, and as long as you stick to the rules you'll do well enough. Now hold out your legs."

Arren did, and watched resignedly as the irons were snapped into place around his ankles.

The guard tugged at the chain to make sure it was secure. "Good. Get up. We're going to hand you over to Caedmon now, and he'll get you a bed and tell you anything you need to know. Up you get."

Arren stood up, and the guard who'd spoken to him shoved him toward the back of the room where there was a heavy iron gate. He unlocked it with a key from his belt, and they went through. Beyond the gate there was a long wooden corridor lined with doorways. Torches set into metal cages were attached to the walls, and light spilt out from the doors as well. Arren, his gait slow and shuffling thanks to the chain attached to his ankles, could hear low voices mixed with the occasional laugh.

The guard closed the gate behind them. "Caedmon!" he shouted. "Get your wrinkly arse out here right now!"

The voices died down, and a few cautious faces peered out of the nearest doorways.

"Caedmon!" the guard yelled again.

There was a brief silence, and then a small boy appeared from the nearest doorway. "I think he's asleep, sir," he said.

The guard turned to look at him. "Well, I'm in no mood to wait around for him." He gave Arren a shove. "Take this son of a bitch into your quarters and give him something to eat, and then go and tell Caedmon he's got a new man to sort, understand?"

The boy looked at Arren, wide-eyed. "Is he dangerous?"

"Not as dangerous as I'm going to be in a moment. Get on with it."

"Yes, sir," said the boy. He darted closer to Arren. "You're to come with me."

Arren glanced quickly at the guard, but he was already leaving. The boy retreated through the doorway he'd come out of, and Arren followed.

There was a simple wooden room on the other side. A fire

was burning in a metal drum in the middle of the floor, and a large pot was hanging over it. The only furniture was a privy-hole in one corner and a row of hammocks hanging from the roof. But there were people there, too, at least a dozen men of various ages, leaning on the walls or sitting cross-legged on the floor. One or two were asleep in their hammocks.

Arren, standing in the doorway, stared at them with a kind of bewilderment. He knew he shouldn't really be surprised, but he was weak from pain and couldn't quite grasp what he was seeing.

The boy tugged at his sleeve. "Come on. You can lie in my hammock for a while, and I'll give you some food."

Arren pulled himself together and followed the boy. His back was too painful to allow him to lie down, but he sat on the proffered hammock, cringing and holding his hand against his chest.

The boy regarded him solemnly. He looked about twelve years old and was clad in a roughly sewn black robe. His grubby hair was pitch-black, and so were his eyes. He had pale skin, long fingers and angular features, and a thick metal collar was clamped around his neck, the skin above and below it an angry and swollen red.

Arren looked back, his head spinning. Meanwhile, others were coming over to look at him. He stared at them, too. Pale skin, black hair, black eyes, robed and collared. Slaves. Northern slaves.

They were watching him warily, apparently not quite sure what to make of this newcomer. The boy, though, was more forthcoming. "I'm Torc," he said. "I'm gonna get you some food, and then I'll go find Caedmon an' tell him to come." That said, he smiled nervously and walked off toward the fire.

"So," one of the others said eventually, "where'd you come from, then? I ain't seen you before."

Arren opened his mouth to answer, but stopped when he saw Torc returning. He was carrying a small bowl and a spoon, and held them out toward him. "Here. I got you some stew."

Arren finally found his voice. "Thank you."

The bowl contained some kind of thick concoction that appeared to be mostly potatoes. Arren ate it and started to get some of his strength back.

Torc was watching him. "What's your name?"

Arren put down the spoon. "I'm Taranis."

"What clan?" said Torc. "I'm Deer."

"Wh— oh." Arren hesitated. Nobody had ever asked him that before. "Wolf," he said at last. There was no point in pretending it was something else; the moment anyone saw his tattoo it would give him away.

"Wolf, eh?" said one of the others. "Same with me. Nice to meet ye then, Taranis. I'm Nolan."

"I'm gonna go get Caedmon now," Torc interrupted.

"That lad's too helpful by half, if yeh ask me," said another slave, though not without affection, as the boy hurried out. "Dunno why they brought him here, really."

The one who'd identified himself as Nolan came closer to look at Arren. "Where'n the moon's name did you come from, then? Not seen many who just shows up in the middle of the night like that. Where's your collar?"

"It came off," said Arren.

Nolan picked at the one around his neck. "Wish mine would. How'd you get it off, anyway?"

Arren remembered the night that he had fallen from the edge of the city. When he had woken the morning after, the collar had simply come off. The landing had bent and twisted the metal beyond redemption. "I fell over," he said. "It hit a rock and broke."

Nolan whistled. "That's damn lucky. Could've driven the spikes right into y'neck instead. Heard about this man had that happen. Poor bastard ended up crippled an' had his master put him out of his misery. Well, no point in livin' like that, is there?"

"You shut up about that friend of yours, Nolan," another slave snapped. "I'm sick of hearin' about it, got that?" He looked at Arren. "Where'd you come from, then? You ain't said yet."

"Well, he's a runner, ain't he?" Nolan said resentfully. "They only puts irons on runners. Where'd you run from, then, Taranis?"

"Withypool."

"Ah. I came from Canran, meself. Horrible cold place. Got sent here, though, to help with this cursed wall. But if you ran off from there, why didn't they send you back?"

Arren squinted. His back was agony, and thinking was difficult. "Manpower," he mumbled. "They said they needed . . ." He realised he was swaying.

"Hold on a bit, are you okay?" said Nolan, suddenly concerned.

Arren tried to sit upright. "My back," he said.

Someone took him by the arm, and someone else prodded the wet patch on his back.

"Ah, gods damn the bastards, they've flogged him. Here, Nolan, help me with him."

"I'm all right—" Arren began, but they ignored him. Someone took the bowl of stew from him, and the rest of them helped him out of the hammock and took his robe off, exposing the marks of the whip.

Nolan groaned. "Ye gods, they made a nasty mess out of you, didn't they? Annan, go get some water."

The water was fetched, and Arren sat on the floor, gasping in pain as the wounds were cleaned with a wet rag. "I r— *ah*—I really d— *ow*—I really don't th—"

"You got to keep 'em clean," Nolan told him. "These gets infected so easy, and then you're a dead man. Tomorrow I'll see if I can get some griffin-tail. Does just right for wounds."

There was a thump at the doorway. "What are ye lot doing?" a voice demanded.

They turned. An elderly Northerner was walking into the room, Torc trailing behind him. His hair and beard were greying and his face was lined, but he looked quite strong as he pointed a heavy stick at Arren. "All right, let's be having ye, runner."

Arren got up with some help from Nolan and watched uncertainly as the old man came toward him. "I'm Taranis," he said, hoping this would help.

The old man looked him up and down. "Taranis, did ye say? What clan?"

The question still caught him off guard. He hesitated. "Wolf Clan, *hynafgwr*." It was a Northern term of respect that his father had taught him, which meant, roughly, "wise one." He hoped he had pronounced it correctly.

The reaction was not at all what he had expected. There were sharp intakes of breath from the men around him, and Torc looked horrified.

The old man stood a little taller. "*What* did ye say?"

Arren ducked his head slightly. "I'm sorry, I didn't mean to offend you, but it's been a long time since I've spoken N—"

The old man hit him with his stick. "Shut up! Are ye mad, boy? D'ye want to get yerself killed?"

Arren clutched at the bruise forming on his arm. "What?"

The old man looked disgusted. "I always said runners were stupid, but now you've proved yer worse. I'm not going t'waste time askin' questions, so I'll just make it plain. I don't care what yer mam told ye; speaking that tongue's a fast track to getting yer arms broken, and I ain't going to try an' protect ye, understand?"

Arren looked blankly at him, and then glanced around at the others. They were looking at him as if he was mad. Realisation finally dawned. "Oh! Of course, you're not allowed to—sorry. Sorry. I forgot . . . *sir*?"

"Caedmon will do fine," said the old man, mollified. "Anyway, so, where was I? Oh, right. Taranis, I'm told yer a runner, but they're makin' ye part of our group instead of sending ye back to yer master. It's not up to me to say what they should and shouldn't do with ye, so I'll just do my duty so's I can get back to my hammock. I'm in charge of the men here, so if there's ever a squabble or somethin' else what needs sortin' out, I'm the one ye come to. I gets my orders from the tower, and then I pass 'em on to ye, so I'll be the one ye'll be gettin' yer directions from. Now, here's the rules, an' I'm expectin' ye to listen."

"I'm listening," Arren said politely.

"Good. The slave-house here is where we live when we ain't workin', but we've got a big job to do here before we're off, so you'll be spendin' most of the day out of doors. Do as yer told, no laggin' or complainin', no backchat—the usual. What job did ye do before ye ran off?"

"Wh— uh, carpentry," Arren said hastily. It was the most menial of the jobs he'd done over the years; during his time as a junior griffiner he had been briefly assigned to help the government division that dealt with the extension and repairing of the huge wooden platforms that made up most of Eagleholm. It hadn't gone very well, but he had picked up a few skills.

"Well, it's a start," said Caedmon. "Ye don't look to be in very good shape, so I expect ye'll be given lighter stuff to do at first. Haulin' blocks, mostly. Not too tricky. But here's the part I'm most interested in makin' sure ye're aware of." He jabbed at Arren with his stick. "Ye're a runner. And we don't look too kind on yer sort. Ye can blather on about how yer master beat you an' didn't give ye enough food and how runnin' away was the only option an' anyway all men were meant to be free, but that ain't gonna win ye no respect from me or anyone else here, understand? I don't care what happens to ye if ye run away; it's yer risk. But if ye manage to get them irons off and do a runner, it's not ye I'm worried about. Let me promise, if any of us catches ye tryin' to run off, we'll stop ye."

"Why?" said Arren.

"Why? I'll tell ye why. Because if ye run, we're the ones who gets punished. There was one of us run off from here a few months back, and afterward none of us ate for three days. Two of the bastard's bunk mates were flogged for helpin' him get away. That's what'll happen if ye run. Ye hear me, Taranis?"

Arren nodded miserably.

"Good," said Caedmon, straightening up. "Just as long as we've got an understandin'. An' now I'm off to bed." He paused, and then smiled at last. "Welcome, Taranis. We'll be glad to have ye here, I'm sure. The lads always like havin' someone new to talk to. Maybe tomorrow we can chat properly, an' ye can tell me more about yerself."

Arren held out a hand. "I'm very pleased to meet you, sir."

Caedmon gave him an odd look, but shook it anyway. "Talk fancy, don't ye? Well, g'night, Taranis." He inclined his head slightly and left the room.

Arren sat down again and reached for the bowl of stew. It was cold, but he ate it anyway.

Torc had come over and was looking at his back. "That looks horrible! Does it hurt bad?"

Arren swallowed. "Yes."

"How'd you get that scar on your face?" Torc added.

Very briefly, Arren thought back to the night of his arrest, when his house had burned down and the kidnapped griffin chick, terrified by the flames, had twisted in his grasp and torn his face with its beak. "I was in an accident," he said.

"What sort of accident?" said Torc, apparently fascinated.

"Leave him alone, Torc," said the man who had snapped at Nolan. "He's had a hard time."

"Sorry," said Torc. "D'you want to use my hammock?" he added, to Arren. "You can have it if you want."

"No, Torc," said Nolan. "There's a spare one at the end of the row. He can have that."

"Thank you," said Arren. "I mean, I—" He cringed at the pain in his back.

"Say no more, Taranis," said Nolan. "Just eat that up and have something to drink afore you turn in; you need plenty of good rest if you're gonna heal up. Try not to move too much; send Torc if you need anythin'. Stick close to me tomorrow, an' I'll try an' help you keep goin'. Time like this, you needs all the help you can get."

"I . . ." Arren trailed off, looking at Nolan. Nolan stared back guilelessly. Around him the other slaves were still watching, their expressions not hostile but curious and sympathetic. Even welcoming. And there was something about them, he realised, something about the way they looked at him and the way they spoke, something he couldn't quite put his finger on. He felt frustrated that he couldn't decide what it was, but his mind was in a haze and he couldn't concentrate properly.

"Thank you," he said at last.

12

Northerners

In spite of his pain, Arren was so weak and exhausted that he drifted off to sleep fairly quickly, but what sleep he got was uncomfortable and disturbed. He lay on his side in the hammock, covered only by his robe and a grubby woollen blanket, stuck in a horrible half-waking state in which time seemed to stand still. He kept dreaming that it was morning and he was getting up and talking to his new companions; it was the kind of vivid dreaming that felt frustratingly real. He lived the next day over and over again in his head, only to wake up in his hammock to find it was night-time, not quite certain if the events had actually happened or not.

After that, when deeper sleep came, he dreamt the falling dream again. But now, instead of Rannagon, it was Skade who confronted him. Feathers were sprouting from her hands and arms, spiking through the skin like daggers. Blood poured down them, turning the plumage red, and she screamed and grabbed at him, trying to hold on to him with fingers that kept twisting themselves into long talons. He tried to tell her she was hurting him, wanted to pull away from her but wasn't able to, and then he was kissing her, but her lips were hard and sharp and tasted of blood. Then he was being dragged away from her, and he tried to hold on to her, desperate not to lose her again.

She stared at him, her great golden eyes filling the world. *Arren, what have you done?* her voice whispered from far away, and then he was falling, falling . . .

He woke up slowly and found himself lying in the gently swinging hammock and staring at the wooden wall directly in front of him. The night had ended, and the room was full of dull grey light filtering in through the cracks in the roof. Arren lay still, trying to think. At first, still befuddled by sleep, he thought he was back in his old home. The wood-plank wall and the hammock dragged his mind back there, and just for a moment he was filled with wild, impossible joy. But then the memory of the last few days returned to him, and all his fears and misery came rushing back. He was not home. He was not safe. He was in captivity, trapped in a slave-house with a pair of heavy irons clamped to his legs and whip marks all over his back. And they had branded him. Marked him as a slave.

And then, without warning, he heard a sound that he had been longing to hear ever since he had been captured: the screech of a griffin. It was faint, coming from somewhere outside, but the instant he heard it his heart leapt. He jerked upright in the hammock, which tipped sideways and dumped him onto the floor. He hit it hard, and almost instantly he cried out as pain spread all over his back. The lash marks, which had scabbed over during the night, tore open, and he felt fresh blood wet his skin.

He struggled to get up, moaning softly. Around him the others were climbing out of their own hammocks, woken up by the screech and by the thump of him hitting the floor.

Arren managed to lift himself into a sitting position. The skin on the back of his hand felt taut, as if it had shrunk, and when he moved his fingers it hurt unbelievably. He squinted muzzily at it. A single rune—the first one in the word "Herb-stitt"—had been burned into his flesh. Most of it was black, but the skin around it was swollen and had turned an angry red. He would have a deep scar there once it healed. His back wouldn't be much better.

There was the sound of footsteps, and Nolan appeared. "Morning. Did yer sleep well?"

Arren managed to stand up, hampered by the irons. "Not really. Nolan, did you hear that?"

"Hear what?" said Nolan. "I heard you hittin' the floor, no problem." He grinned, showing a couple of missing teeth.

"No!" said Arren. "I meant that screech! Just now—did you hear it?"

Nolan peered at him. "You feelin' all right there, Taranis?"

"It sounded like a griffin," said Arren.

"Oh!" said Nolan. "I see. Yeah, course I heard it. Wakes us up every mornin'."

Arren's heart sank. "I didn't know there were any griffins here."

"There used t'be a few livin' in the tower. Now there's just the one over at the temple, see. Wakes us up in the morning." Nolan gestured at him. "C'mon, no time to waste. Gotta get somethin' t'eat before we goes out on the job."

Arren followed him over to the fire, which was still burning. Someone must have added more fuel during the night. "Where did the griffiners go?"

"Bin called back to Canran, from what I heard," said Nolan. "Eyrie Master probably wants to talk to 'em about what's goin' on right now with Eagleholm."

There were bowls stacked near the fire. Arren took one and filled it with stew from the pot. "And what *is* going on?"

"Dunno much about it," said Nolan. "Just what you picks up from listenin' in on people. Eagleholm's finished, though, that's certain. Griffiners all leavin'. My guess is they're gonna go in, try and take as much of the land as they can get." He shrugged and dipped his spoon into his stew. "Griffiners' business," he said, as if that were the final word on the matter.

Arren started on his food. He hadn't really thought about what would happen now that Eagleholm's Eyrie and its Mistress had been destroyed, but it didn't surprise him at all to learn that the neighbouring states were already preparing to start taking over its lands. Troops were probably moving in already, and as soon as the forces of two different states met, there would be fighting. Everyone would be grasping for a piece of Eagleholm's land. His former state had been one of the largest and had included a lake and an enormous stretch of river, not to mention a great deal of fertile ground and several mines. Winning some of that would be more than worth the fighting for it.

Around him the others were getting ready to start the day, some partway through breakfast and others still lacing up their boots. They were talking among themselves in calm voices; they almost sounded like—well, like ordinary men preparing for a day's work. He was surprised.

Eagleholm had no slaves, at least not during his lifetime. He had never actually seen a slave until the previous night, and until then his parents had been the only other Northerners he had ever known. Consequently he'd never seen the inside of a slave-house before and had no idea what to expect from one. But the picture his imagination had painted for him had been nothing like this. In his mind he'd seen rows of dank cells in which the slaves sat chained to benches, constantly watched over by guards, unable to move free or enjoy the comfort of proper bedding. But here he was seeing—well, the quarters were rough and the food was poor, but it was comfortable enough. He had seen poor people back in Eagleholm whose living conditions were far worse. The slaves weren't even being guarded, at least not here.

And yet when he saw the collars, it was all the reminder he needed. These people still weren't free men; they were property, and that was how they were treated. What they had here was enough to keep them strong and in reasonable health, and that was all.

Arren finished the stew and took a second helping; his stomach was aching with hunger. No-one said anything, but he noticed many of the others were making do with just one bowl, and he felt a twinge of guilt, as if he had just stolen something.

He was finishing the second bowlful when the call came for them to leave; there were shouts and a series of thumps from the corridor, and Arren saw Caedmon pause briefly in the doorway and smack the frame with his stick, shouting, "Up! Up! Get up, move out! Move! Move!"

Arren sighed and put the bowl back down with the others. Torc had appeared from somewhere with a tub of water and was already cleaning up, and the others formed themselves into a rough column and began to file out of the door in the manner of people who had done this a hundred times before.

Nolan nudged Arren in the side. "C'mon, Taranis. We'll go at the back; you won't be able to move too fast with them things on."

Arren fell in behind him. "Why are you helping me?"

Nolan gave him an odd look. "What sort of question's that, then?"

"I didn't mean to offend you or anything," Arren said hastily. "But we've only just met, and—I'm sorry, never mind."

Nolan whistled. "Ye gods, where'd you learn to speak like that? Where'd you say y'came from again?"

"Oh. Er. Uh." Arren cursed himself; he'd been too distracted to try and disguise his voice. Not that he would have been any good at it. "Withypool," he said. It would do. Skade had told him enough about it that he could describe it fairly well. He should be able to bluff unless he met someone else who had come from there.

"Withypool, eh?" said Nolan. "Damn long way away. Never met anyone from there before; you got to tell me all about it."

"Of course," said Arren. They were out in the passageway now, in front of a long row of others who had emerged from the other dormitories. Up ahead, their own column was slowly filing out of the iron gateway, where a guard was giving each slave a quick going-over before letting him through. Arren looked over his shoulder and was surprised by how many men were behind him; the slave-house had looked large from the outside, but he hadn't realised it had this many people in it. He estimated that there were at least a hundred slaves all told.

"Well," said Nolan, as the guard turned out his pockets, "we're both Wolf, ain't we? You're my clan. My dad always said, 'We helps other Wolf as and when they needs it, because that's our way.'" He glanced at Arren and grinned. "I'm sorta lyin', of course. I'd be helpin' you even if y'weren't Wolf. Way I see it is that a man in our position only gets what the people around him will give him, and we needs all the help we can get."

Arren flinched as the guard patted him down. "Thank you, Nolan. If there's ever anything I can do . . ."

"Don't worry, I'll tell you if I needs anythin' in return," said Nolan, flashing another gap-toothed grin. "Now"—they had emerged into the open air—"we got work to do, eh?"

There were more guards waiting outside for them. Caedmon was there, too, and he gave the commands. The slaves split themselves into groups according to which room they slept in, and each group was then led off to its place of work. Arren saw two groups head off toward the quarry that lay just outside the town walls. Another one was sent to help carry back the stone blocks they would cut there, and the rest were taken to the wall itself. Arren's group were directed to the spot where they must have been working the day before; there was a large gap in the wall where the mortar had crumbled away and the stones had come tumbling down. Some had been broken in the fall, and others looked to be missing, probably carried off to build houses.

Tools were being brought over by another group of slaves: buckets, sticks, ladders and large sacks of sand. Arren's group obviously knew what it was doing; ladders were quickly set up at the edges of the gap, where fresh stones had been laid, and the buckets were set up in a long row beside the bags of sand. The group that had brought the tools returned again with more buckets, these full of water, and put those beside the rest.

"Right." Caedmon strolled over. "Ye, runner," he said, pointing at Arren, "yer in no state for carrying blocks, and ye can't climb the ladders with them irons on, so ye can mix the mortar with Nolan and the rest. Think ye can manage that?"

It sounded fairly straightforward. "Yes, sir."

Nolan looked pleased. "Looks like y've already done me a favour," he said as they took up position by the buckets. "I'd've been set to haulin' blocks most like if I weren't with you. This is the easy job."

"Thank gods for that," said Arren. "How does it work, then?"

"Easy as fallin' off a log," said Nolan. "Only tricky part is gettin' the balance right. Here, I'll show you."

Arren watched as the other man gave a quick demonstration, measuring out sand, water and lime, and stirring them with a heavy stick. It was simple enough, and before long Arren was working on his own bucket. Once the mortar was ready, another team hauled it off to the wall, and the mixers began again with fresh buckets. It was simple work, though fairly tedious, and Arren was glad. The stone blocks being used on the wall were enormous, and carrying even one of them would have been backbreaking. He was even half-glad that he was wearing the irons; the mere thought of having to climb one of the ladders made him feel dizzy.

While he worked, he watched the other slaves at work. His father had always told him the Northern people were proud warriors, but these didn't look much like warriors to him. As for pride—well, there wasn't much to be proud of in the life of a slave. The gang of robed men—there were no women that he'd seen so far—worked steadily, not lagging or digging their heels in, but not rushing, either. They worked with the efficiency of men who had a task to carry out and didn't particularly care about when it would be over or whether their overseers would say they were doing a good job.

And really, why would they? he thought as he scooped sand into the bucket. *It's not as if they can expect a pay rise.*

A line of men trudged past carrying more blocks to the

wall. To his surprise, Arren noticed two of them were, like him, wearing leg-irons. One was about his age, the other a little older, and they hunched slightly as they walked.

He nudged Nolan. "Did those two try and run off?"

Nolan followed his gaze, and spat. "Hah. Yeah, that they did. Them and a couple of others. You want to stay away from them, Taranis."

The dislike was obvious in his voice, and Arren was surprised. "You're not staying away from me," he pointed out.

"Yeah, well, that's different," said Nolan. "That lot are bad news. They're Northerners."

Arren gave him a long, slow look. "And that's . . . unusual, is it?"

Nolan laughed. "You're funny. I mean they're *from* the North. Born there. Not like the rest of us. From the way they act, you'd think that made 'em royalty or somethin.' They're only workin' under sufferance. It was one of them did a runner a while back. Those two tried to go with him but got caught."

Arren watched them curiously. "I thought you were all from Canran."

"Most of us, but not all," said Nolan. "See, this is a temporary assignment thing here. They sent a gang of us here to fix up the wall, an' a bunch of others got brought in from other places. They want the job done fast, see, and that means more men."

"I haven't seen any women here," Arren remarked.

"Of course you ain't. Buildin's not a job for womenfolk. They're all at home. Most of us have got wives waitin' for us. Not me, but there's my three sisters back at Canran." He paused to scratch at a flea bite. "We've been here a while now, an' most of us just want to go home."

"What about Torc?" said Arren. "What's he doing here?"

"Orphan," Nolan said. "They couldn't find anythin' else to do with him, so they sent him out here with us. He does odd jobs. Runs errands, takes messages, makes the food. He'll be bringin' out some lunch later on. We're all fond of the lad."

Arren nodded. "Remind me not to complain about that stew when he's listening, then."

One of the shackled slaves shuffled back past them, on his way to get another stone. Arren watched him. "So, tell me about those Northerners," he said. "How did they try and escape?"

Nolan dragged another bag of sand over and opened it. "Way

I heard it was that one of 'em found a loose board at the back of his dorm. They worked together to pull it out and then slipped out through the hole and ran off."

"What, it was that easy?" said Arren. "Those guards must be bloody stupid."

"Ah, well, no-one was expecting them to try, see," said Nolan. "Herbstitt's the only settlement for a long way, an' any-one out on their own in the countryside is bound to starve to death in a few weeks. They didn't think anyone would be stupid enough. Course, you can't expect that lot to have any sense. Bloody tendernecks."

"Tendernecks?" said Arren.

"What, you don't know what it means?"

"We must call it something different in Withypool," Arren said hastily.

"Newly collared," said Nolan. "You can see how their necks is all swollen when you gets close enough. They weren't born slaves like the rest of us; they were born free in the North an' got collared as punishment for some crime or other."

"I was trying to go north when they caught me," said Arren.

"Why?" said Nolan.

"To live free, of course," said Arren. "Where else could I have gone?"

"Is that why you done a runner, then?" said Nolan.

Arren thrust his stick into the bucket and began to stir. "Yes. I'm a human being, and I have no intention of living out my life as someone else's property, and I'd rather die than wear a collar again."

Nolan was giving him a slightly nervous look. "That's danger-ous talk, Taranis. You ain't gonna try an' run off again, are you?"

"No," Arren lied. "What's the point? I can't run anywhere in these irons, and they'll only catch me again."

Nolan relaxed. "That's good. We'd all get it in the neck if you did. Anyway, I like you."

"You do?" said Arren. That surprised him.

"Yeah, I do," said Nolan, unembarrassed. "You're good to talk to. An' I liked how you were with Caedmon. You did the right thing, bein' respectful to him an' all. Runners don't usu-ally; they think he's a traitor for workin' with the Southerners."

Arren had never heard anyone refer to Southerners like that, as if they were a different race. It was odd, seeing it from the other side like this. "I don't see why I should look down on him for that," he said. "It's not like he has any choice."

"You're right there," said Nolan. "Caedmon doesn't like 'em much, but he gets better rations and extra bedding an' a bit more freedom than the rest of us, an' really—"

"You get what you're given," Arren finished.

"Yeah."

They worked on through the morning, mixing cement. Arren found it monotonous, but he didn't care much. It gave him plenty of time to think. His back wasn't too painful now; it was his hand that hurt. In spite of his efforts to keep it clean, it quickly became encrusted with sand, which actually soothed it a little once the initial stinging had stopped. The sand and water formed a kind of mud poultice, he realised, but he made a mental note to try to pick some griffin-tail if he saw any. Nolan had been right when he'd said that his wounds needed to be kept clean. An infection could kill him.

Noon finally arrived, and they were allowed to stop work and have some lunch. Torc had appeared carrying an enormous basket full of bread and had left it by the wall then scurried off and returned with a huge earthenware jug and a stack of wooden cups. Caedmon gave the command, and the slaves put down their tools and eagerly crowded around the basket, where Torc doled out a small loaf of bread and a cup of water to every man. They were still being watched closely by guards—Arren had the uncomfortable feeling that they were paying special attention to him—but they were allowed to sit down on the grass at the base of the wall to eat. Arren had been anticipating this; he lost Nolan among the crowd and went looking for the two Northerners he'd seen before. He found them sitting a little way off, using some of the blocks they had been carrying as seats. They were talking in low voices and looked up sharply when Arren came near them.

"What d'ye want?" one said immediately, standing up to confront him.

Arren straightened up, trying not to flinch when his back hurt in response. "I was wondering if I could sit with you. My name's Taranis."

The man looked at him askance. He was the older of the two; he looked about forty, and there was a hint of grey in his hair.

The skin above and below his collar was swollen, and there were traces of dried blood underneath it. "Ye're the runner from Withypool," he said.

Arren shrugged. "I suppose so."

"Well, what d'ye want with us?" the other man asked. Like his companion, he had a harsh accent to his voice and looked at Arren with deep suspicion.

"To talk," said Arren. They obviously weren't going to offer him a seat, so he chose a chunk of rock nearby and sat on it. "I'm told you two are from the North," he added, hoping this would mollify them.

The older man sat down again. "What's it to ye, Southerner?"

Arren had been diffident, but this was too much. "So, now I'm a Southerner, am I? That's news to me."

"Ye're Southern born," said the man, unmoved. "Like the rest of them water-bloods. Ye speak Southern, boy, and that makes ye Southern to me."

Arren took a deep breath and decided he wasn't going to let himself be provoked. "I was wondering if you could tell me how your friend escaped from here."

The younger man tore off a chunk of bread. "Why, are ye hopin' to follow him, maybe?"

"Are you?" said Arren.

The man glared at him. Arren stared back, unblinking. Finally, the other appeared to relax slightly. "Name's Prydwen."

"What clan?" said Arren.

"Crow. And ye?"

"Wolf." Arren looked at the older man. "And you?"

The man shrugged. "Olwydd. Bear Clan. So, ye think ye can run from here the same way Gwydyon did, do ye?"

"I'm willing to give it a shot," said Arren. "I'm damned if I'm going to stay here and build walls for griffiners. Let the bastards do their own building."

They liked that. Olwydd grinned. "Show me a griffiner can put one stone atop another and I'll show ye a deer with wings. So"— he looked down—"how exactly do ye plan to get those off?"

Arren tugged at the iron ring locked in place around his right ankle. "I don't know; if there was some way to pick the lock I'd do that, but if they search us every day . . ."

"They do. Ye'd be seen, anyway."

"So I was planning to bide my time," said Arren. "Do as I'm told, not make any fuss. Sooner or later they'll decide I'm not going to run and take them off."

"Talk fancy, don't ye?" said Prydwen. "How'd ye get here, anyway?"

"They caught me because they were after your friend," said Arren. "They thought I was him, and when what's-his-name— that man at the tower—found out, he said he'd take me anyway because he needed the extra pair of hands. He told me to keep quiet about it."

Olwydd snorted. "Man's a damn fool. There's no secrets among slaves. Where's yer collar?"

"It came off," said Arren. "They were supposed to put a new one on me, but I don't think they could find one. Thank gods," he added.

"Aye, they comes off if ye know how to break 'em," said Olwydd. "Or so I'm told." He paused. "So, that's yer plan, is it? Wait around, be a good boy and hope they give up watchin' ye and give yer back yer legs?"

"It's got to be better than trying to run off in these things," said Arren. "Why, what were *you* planning?"

"And why should we tell ye?" said Prydwen, sullen again.

So, they didn't have a plan. "Fine, if you'd rather keep it to yourself. Where do you intend to go once you've escaped?"

"Home," Prydwen said instantly. "Where else? Back to Tara."

"Tara?"

All their grudging respect disappeared in a moment. Olwydd spat. "Ye're pathetic, Southern boy. Like the rest of them, ye're no true Northerner. Ye don't know the name of yer own homeland, do ye?" he sneered and bit into his bread.

Arren had had enough. He lunged forward, grabbing the front of Olwydd's robe, and dragged him forward until they were face to face. *"Dwi chan 'r Gogledd. Gwna mo amhercha 'm,"* he rasped.

For a few moments the two of them were frozen, until Arren let go and sat back. He started on his lunch, calmly, as if nothing had happened.

There was silence. Then Olwydd coughed. "Ye're brave or mad, but ye're no fool, I'll give ye that. Very well, then. Tara's the true name of the North, though there's not many call it that now. I take it ye meant to go there."

"Yes," said Arren.

Prydwen was watching him with renewed interest. "An' why would that be, Taranis?"

"Because where else could I go?" said Arren. "It's the only place where our people live free."

"Free!" Olwydd growled. "There's scarce more than a hundred Northerners could call themselves free, even in Tara. We're slaves or vassals. Even in our own land we can't marry or move house or buy land without leave from the griffiners at Malvern. And if ye stand up an' be yer own man, gods help ye then."

"Is that why you're here?" said Arren.

Prydwen nodded. "They caught us tryin' to leave our village to join the others up north, near Taranis Gorge, where the standing stones are."

"Others?"

"Free Northerners," said Olwydd. "Rebels. The ones who left the cages and went to the wild, where the land is too cold for Southerners." He snarled to himself. "We went to seek freedom with them, and so Lady Elkin took what freedom we had already."

"Is it even possible to get through the Northgates?" said Arren. "On foot, I mean."

"There's passes and suchlike," said Prydwen. "There's a few who've made it."

That wouldn't be a problem, Arren thought. If he ever did get back to the Northgates he wouldn't be passing through them on foot. He would go there with Skandar or not at all. And before then he would have to go to Norton to find his parents.

There were commanding shouts from nearby and a general stirring among the slaves.

"Looks like we're back on duty," said Olwydd. He gulped down the last of his water and stood up.

Arren stood, too, holding the remains of his bread. "Well, it was good to meet you."

Prydwen nodded as he rose. "Makes me happy to know there's at least one darkman here who's still got his balls."

Arren glanced quickly over his shoulder and moved closer. "So, we're agreed?"

"I never agreed to anything," said Olwydd.

Arren shrugged. "If you say so. But since I know you're interested in escaping, and you know I am, too—well, I'm sure it wouldn't hurt for us to share any plans or ideas we might come up with."

The others were already returning to their work. "So, we're to take ye with us if we escape, and ye're to do the same for us?" Olwydd said quickly.

"Something like that," said Arren. He nodded to them. "I'm in the first room nearest the gate. You know where to find me." That said, he walked back toward the mortar buckets, hastily wolfing down the last of his bread. It was hard and made from poor-quality flour, but just then it tasted delicious.

13

Tales of Tara

Arren's feeling of pride lasted a good way into that afternoon's work. He wasn't completely sure why, but he had to admit that things were looking up. Nobody had any suspicion of his true identity or was asking any really probing questions yet, and now he had a couple of allies. Prydwen and Olwydd looked like tough and resourceful men; there was no doubt whatsoever that they were looking for ways to escape, and Arren had every intention of helping them. If he could find a way of getting the leg-irons off, that would be the most important first step. But it had to be done quickly, he decided. He couldn't expect to remain anonymous forever. People were already taking something of an interest in his background. The man who seemed to be in charge was obviously too harassed to waste time talking to runaway slaves, but if anyone here had a description of what Arren looked like . . .

Arren started to feel slightly sick again. He dumped more water into the bucket and stirred rapidly with the stick, distracting himself with the work. If only there was some way of hiding the scar on his face and the tattoo; he made a mental note to keep his robe on at all times.

Nolan had stopped making conversation. He was working away steadily next to Arren, now apparently bent on finishing the day so he could get back to the slave-house and rest. Arren felt curiously guilty for having dodged him at lunch.

The afternoon seemed longer than the morning had. Arren mixed what felt like a dozen buckets of mortar while the others carried blocks from the quarry and a third group worked on the wall itself. The gap, which had been big enough to drive a wagon through at the beginning of the day, was slowly beginning to shrink. It would probably be fixed within a week or so, but doubtless there were others. There were only about thirty slaves working at this spot; those who hadn't gone to the quarry had spread out to other parts of the wall. Arren wondered if they worked in rotation. It would give him a better picture of how close they were to finishing the job. He would be in a lot of trouble once the wall was fixed and the slaves began to be sent back to their homes. They couldn't very well send him to Canran, and if they still didn't know who he was by then—which didn't seem likely—he could be sold anywhere. The gods alone knew where he might end up. Wylam, Withypool, even over the sea at a place like Amoran. He would never find Skandar again if that happened. And Skade.

Arren wondered where she was. Alive, dead, lost. He thought of the last thing she had said to him. *Our pairing is over . . . We do not linger together. We pair, and then we part.* He tried to remember if she had pushed him or hit him. It didn't matter. What she said was painful enough. He had confessed and been spurned. She had chosen the imagined whisperings of a long-dead boy over him. And now she was gone, and he knew he would never see her again.

The thought made a lump form in his throat. He gripped the stirring stick fiercely, until his knuckles whitened. *Why do you care?* he asked himself. *She used you. Bedded you, toyed with you and then abandoned you. If you'd never met her . . .*

But he couldn't disguise his misery as anger for very long. If he had never met Skade he would still be lost in the countryside, surviving on grubs and beetles. If he had never met her . . . *then you wouldn't be here in Herbstitt, wearing a pair of leg-irons, with a brand burned into you and whip marks on your back,* his mind whispered.

Arren sighed as the completed bucket of mortar was carried off and an emptied one dumped next to him, ready to be refilled. He started to measure out the sand and lime for what felt like the hundredth time that day. He wished Skandar was there.

"What's the matter, Taranis?" Nolan's rough voice broke into his thoughts. "You look all miserable."

"What?" Arren shook himself. "Oh. Just thinking."

"Thinking about somethin' sad, by the looks of it," Nolan observed. "Ooh, watch out, here comes the governor."

Arren followed his gaze and froze. It was the man from the tower. He was nearby, talking to the guards, and as Arren watched he turned to look straight at him. Arren looked back, full of a wild impulse to run away. They were all looking at him. He could see the man—the governor, Nolan had called him—saying something to the guards, asking them some question. They were too far away to be heard, but Arren thought he could hear them in his head. *I've just had word from Canran. There's a blackrobe they're looking for; his name is Arren Cardockson, and he has a scar on his face. He's wanted for killing a griffiner. I want to question that new slave that was brought in yesterday.*

But then the governor looked away, and Arren thought he was going to faint with relief. They weren't coming any closer. He went back to work, still watching them surreptitiously. The man wasn't a griffiner; all he had with him was that big hunting dog, and if he hadn't suspected anything the night before, why should he start suspecting now?

Arren tried to convince himself that was true, but he kept an eye on him anyway.

"Ah, don't worry about him," said Nolan. "He don't take that much interest in us. He's just come to check on how the work's goin,' like usual."

"How long has he been governor here?" said Arren.

Nolan scratched his beard and yawned. "He ain't the proper governor; he's just fillin' in while Lady What's-Her-Name is off at Canran."

"And how long will it be before she comes back?"

"Don't ask me. Could be weeks, could be months, could be a few days. Makes no difference to me."

Arren watched as the governor finished his conversation with the guards and then walked away to talk with those nearer to the wall, his dog following at his heels. His path took him quite close to the mortar buckets, and as he passed, Arren ducked his head in the hopes that he wouldn't be noticed. The governor barely favoured him with a glance, and Arren breathed easier. But his breath caught in his throat as the man glanced over his shoulder and then stopped abruptly, turning around. Arren shrank back, but then he realised what it was that had made him stop.

It was the dog. The animal was backing away from its master.

Arren stopped to watch, vaguely interested. The governor called to his pet, but the dog didn't move. Finally, he strode over to it and grabbed it by the collar. The dog went with him for a few steps, but then began to dig in its heels. Arren could hear it whimpering. A lifetime spent around griffins had taught him a lot about how animals behave, and dogs weren't that dissimilar to griffins. This one was crouching low, ears laid flat. It was terrified.

The governor seemed to know that; he crouched and petted the dog's head. "Now, what's gotten into you?" he murmured. "There's nothing to be scared of. Come on."

He stood up, still trying to coax the dog into following him, but it wouldn't. Arren could see the creature's yellow eyes staring straight at him as it whined and cowered, wanting to flee but loath to leave its master.

Finally, the governor lost patience. "Fine," he muttered, and strode off. The dog lingered a few moments and then ran away with its tail between its legs.

"What was *that* all about?" said Nolan.

"I think it was frightened of me," said Arren.

Nolan glanced at him, apparently trying to decide if he was joking, and then laughed. "Yeah, I can see that. You look scary enough."

Arren smiled, but his heart wasn't in it. Maybe the dog could smell griffin on him. Most animals were afraid of griffins. But he had seen other animals cower and run when he came near them. Not all of them did, but the more intelligent creatures, like rats, always did. It frightened him more than he would admit.

The governor didn't stay much longer. He talked briefly to the guards by the wall and to Caedmon as well, who had spent the day walking among the slaves and supervising them, and then headed back toward the town, having shown little interest in Arren.

Nevertheless, Arren felt much calmer once he had gone.

Little by little the sun dipped toward the horizon, and the day's work started to draw to a close. The slaves were working more slowly now, and Arren could feel himself flagging. His hand burned, his back throbbed and his head ached, and the leg-irons were starting to chafe. All he wanted to do was go back to his hammock and sleep.

Finally, just as the sun was beginning to set, Caedmon gave the command, and the slaves began to pack up. The last of the mortar was either used up or thrown away, the ladders were taken down, and hammers, chisels and the flat mortar spreaders— Arren couldn't remember what they were called—were packed into their boxes while a pair of guards watched closely and counted them to make sure nobody had stolen one. Closely watched all the time, Arren and a group of men carried them to the small stone hut where they were stored, and after that he and his fellows were formed back into a column and marched to the slave-house.

Arren shuffled into his dormitory, forced to take small steps because of the irons. The others were already flopping into their hammocks or sitting down cross-legged near the fire to rest. Torc was there, busily throwing chopped potatoes into the pot along with a few other vegetables. Arren wasn't surprised to see that there was no meat. It was far too expensive to feed to slaves. He wasn't in the mood for conversation and made for his hammock. His back was bleeding again, but he was too far gone to care. He lay on his stomach, arms dangling over the sides, and let himself relax.

He must have dozed briefly; he was woken up by voices and the sound of metal on metal. Torc was serving out the stew, and the others were crowding around to fill their bowls.

Arren got laboriously out of his hammock. The prospect of another bowl of overcooked vegetable slop didn't appeal to him very much, but lunch had been a long time ago and he knew he had to keep his strength up. As it was, he was already thinner than he should be.

Torc grinned hopefully at him as he ladled out a generous helping of stew. "You gonna tell us about where you come from, Taranis?"

"Hm?" Arren blinked at him. "What? Oh. There's not much to tell, really."

Most of the others had their food now and had seated themselves around the fire to eat. Annan leant over to prod Arren with his spoon. "Go on, don't be shy. Why'd you run away? We all like a good story."

Arren sat down. "It's really not very interesting," he said, playing for time.

"Tell us anyway, an' we'll be the judges of that," said Nolan.

Arren shrugged. "I was a carpenter, at Withypool. Building houses, that sort of thing. And then one day—" He hesitated. "My collar got infected," he said. "It hurt all the time, day and night, and nobody would do anything about it. I was desperate; I tried everything. And then one day I hit it accidentally, and it broke. It came off, and I didn't know what to do; I knew I'd be in big trouble when my master found out. And then I thought—" He paused again, feeling rather pleased with himself. "Withypool is near the sea, and I liked to watch the water and think about faraway lands. Amoran and Erebus and Liawinee and Eire. I thought—I knew—I'd never see those places. I'd never see anything but Withypool and building and work and my master treating me like his property, which was what I was, and after my collar came off, I thought, why shouldn't I have a choice? Why should I let myself be a *thing* that belongs to someone, instead of a man? Don't I have two hands and a mind of my own and a soul? Why should where I go and what I do be someone else's choice? And so that night I broke out of my cell and I ran away, vowing I'd never let myself be a slave again. I went to the North because it was the only place I could think of, the only place where I thought I could be free. And here I am."

Silence followed. Arren looked at the others nervously, not quite sure what it meant and whether he had gone too far.

"Aren't they going to send you back to your master, then?" one man asked eventually.

"I hope not," said Arren. "I shouldn't think he'd want me, anyway."

"You're *brave*," Torc piped up. "You're like a wolf."

Arren glanced at him. "Wolves aren't brave."

"Well, you are," said Torc. "Running away is brave. If they catch you, you die. I could never do it, not ever."

"Couldn't you?" said Arren. "Are you sure?"

"There ain't no point in it," another slave interrupted. "Really, there ain't. Why go north? You've never been to the North. I've met Northerners. Most of 'em hate us. Call us Southerners and water-bloods and suchlike. Anyway, from what I'm told, the North's a terrible harsh place. Ice an' snow and bears, an' savage people living out in the wilderness, catching travellers to eat."

Arren looked around at them all. "Why go north? Yes,

indeed, why go north? That's a good question. I've been asked it many times. I've asked it myself. Why—go—north?"

"There's nothin' there," said Annan, though he sounded a little uneasy.

Go back to the North, blackrobe, Arren thought. "Because the North is our home," he said. "It has to be. What do we have out here in the South? What is there out here for us except collars and whips and chains and hard labour all our lives? We're slaves here, and we're lost. This isn't our land; we're not *made* for it. This land belongs to Southerners, and while we're in their land, so do we. But the North—if the North is where we came from, then the North is the only place we could ever call home. I've never been there, either, any more than you have, but I say that if our ancestors would fight even against griffiners to defend it, and die to do so, then the North is where I belong. And so do you."

Nolan chuckled. "You sound like my old grandad goin' on about that. Northern pride! And what'll you do when y'get there, then, Taranis? Try an' hide out in some peasant village? Run off into the forest to join the savages? There's griffiners there, too, you know. Lots of 'em." He became serious. "Now, look here, Taranis. It's good to have somethin' to dream about, if it keeps you goin' an' so on, but you need a good dose of the real world. The North ain't ours; it's theirs. None of our lot have lived there free since before my great-grandad was born. Griffiners own it, just like they own the rest of the country, an' nothin' an' nobody can stand against them or ever will."

Arren was silent for a long time. "Tell me about the North," he said at last. "I've told my story, now it's someone else's turn. Tell me a story about Tara."

Nolan sat back. "I'm no storyteller. Get Torc to do it."

Torc nodded. "I'll tell a story, sure. Which one do you want to hear?"

"Tell us about Taranis," said a voice.

It was Olwydd. The shackled Northerner walked slowly into the room, closely followed by Prydwen.

Nolan started up. "Here, you're not supposed to come in our dorm."

Olwydd shrugged. "Caedmon's asleep; who's gonna stop us?" He went over to the fire, stepping between the men seated around it, and managed to wedge himself in next to Arren, whom he pretended not to see. "Go on, boy," he said to Torc. "Tell us the story of Taranis the Wolf."

Torc looked uncertain. "Taranis already told us his story," he said, trying to grin.

Prydwen gave him a withering look. "He means the *other* Taranis, boy. Don't play stupid."

Torc cast an appealing glance at Arren. Arren hadn't missed the tension that had come into the room with the two Northerners, and he shrugged with exaggerated care. "I'd like to hear it if you're willing to tell it, Torc."

The boy nodded unhappily. "All right. I'll tell it, then."

Prydwen had sat down by his friend. He picked at his collar and settled down to listen, deliberately looking away from Arren.

Torc began. "Long ago," he said, "hundreds of years ago, before your grandfather's grandfather was born, the North was called Tara. Our people owned it; it was their land and their blood was in the soil. The clans lived there free—Deer and Wolf and Crow and Bear—and roamed wherever they chose. They made their houses from sticks and snow, and hunted wolf and deer and boar, and they herded black sheep and used their wool to make robes that would protect them from the cold. They called themselves the darkmen or the moon people, and they had healers and shamans who spoke with the voices of the gods and were given magic by the light of the moon. But one night, when the half-moon was out—the time when great things happen and the world turns—a boy was born. His name was Taranis, man of Tara, and he was born to the Wolf Clan. He grew up swift and strong, and cunning like a wolf, and some say he learnt to change his shape and become a wolf, with a wolf's pelt and sharp teeth. His elders said that one day he would become leader of his clan, and he did, when he fought the old leader and killed him, which was the way of the darkmen.

"But Taranis was not content to lead just one clan, just one people. He had a brother, Taliesin, who was fierce and wise, but wild, and he and Taranis decided they would make themselves greater than any clan chieftain. Taranis called the other chiefs together at a gorge where there was a stone circle built by giants long ago. Now that gorge is called Taranis Gorge. When the chiefs came together, Taranis told them he would become master of their clans as well as his own, and they told him he must defeat them and their people in battle if he would. But Taliesin was too cunning. He wove his magic around the chiefs as they sat there within the circle, and all of them were turned to stone. Now they still sit there, a circle inside a circle.

"When the clans learnt of what Taliesin and Taranis had done they were very afraid. But they did not attack the Wolf Clan, because their chiefs were dead and they had no-one to lead them. And since Taranis and Taliesin had killed them, they must replace them. That was the law. So Taranis became master of all the tribes, and he told them, 'You shall not be four clans, but one: the greatest clan, the Moon Clan. And I shall give you riches and glory such as you have never seen.' And he led them south, toward the mountains of Y Castell, where the land was warm and rich. They passed through the mountains, a hundred thousand strong warriors, united. And Taranis led them against the people of the South, and he humbled them, and took their land and their wealth for his own. Even when the terrible griffin-lords united against him they could not win; the men of Tara stood strong and fought strongly and with courage, and even mighty griffins fell before them. It was said even the gods could not stand against them, certainly not the soft Southern god. And Taranis was strong and proud and said that he would live forever, and that one day all the land would be his."

Arren had heard a version of this story before, but he listened anyway. It was close to its ending now.

Torc's small face grew solemn. "But Taranis fell. Before he could have his glory, he fell. Taliesin grew jealous, and the two of them argued, and then Taliesin left and vowed he would not return. Taranis was too proud to turn back; he marched on with his people and fought the griffiners one last time. But in the midst of the battle an arrow struck him, and Taliesin was not there to heal him. And so Taranis died there alone, calling Taliesin's name with his last breath. And as soon as he died, his men had no leader and could fight no more. The griffiners smashed them that day, and when the battle was done the Moon Clan was no more. They were Bear and Wolf and Crow and Deer once again, and they would no longer fight as one. Some fled, some stood and fought. But after that there was no more hope. The griffiners killed all those who fought, and chased the rest back through Y Castell and into Tara, and there they took it for themselves and broke the clans and made them all into slaves. And from then on there was never another leader to fight them and no more hope, and the moon itself wept as the snow turned red with Northern blood."

The story ended there, and Torc fell silent.

"What happened to Taliesin?" said someone.

Torc shrugged. "Some say he killed himself when he found out that Taranis was dead; others say he turned himself to stone. And others say he never died."

Arren sighed. "You're a good storyteller, Torc. It's not quite the same tale as the one I heard, though. In the one my father told, it was Taliesin who killed Taranis. And they weren't brothers; they were father and son."

"In the one I heard they were only friends," Prydwen put in. "But still, a well-told story, boy. Well done."

Torc looked nervous but pleased. "Thank you. It's not my favourite story. It always makes me sad."

"Well, why shouldn't it?" said Olwydd. "It's a story of our fall and our shame."

"*Your* shame, maybe," Annan muttered.

Olwydd glared at him. "*Our* shame," he repeated. "We are all Northerners, and the story is ours." He cast a quick glance at Arren as he said this. "All of ours," he said again.

"Oh, quite," said Arren, not liking how this was going. "But remember that stories are stories."

"And what do ye mean by *that*?" said Prydwen. He sounded irritated.

"I mean that there's no point in getting worked up about it," said Arren. He put aside his empty bowl. "As for me, I've always liked stories, but I prefer the ones about real people."

"Taranis *is* real," said Olwydd.

"How do you know?" said Arren.

The older man laced his fingers together and looked down his nose at him. "It doesn't matter if there was truly a man called Taranis," he said. "At the heart, all stories are true."

Arren nodded. "Yes, I suppose you're right there. But tell me"—he took in a deep breath; this was going to be a big risk— "I don't suppose there are any stories about real people that you'd care to tell?"

Olwydd gave him a look. "Which real people?"

Arren leant forward. It was now or never. "What do you know about the man called Arren Cardockson?" he asked softly.

Silence followed. The slaves around the fire shifted uneasily. Even Prydwen looked unsettled.

"Why d'you want to hear about *him*?" said Nolan.

Arren shrugged with forced casualness. "I've been hearing things. Not many things, but I've heard that name mentioned. I ran away months ago; I don't have any idea of what's going on in the world right now. All I know is that people have been mentioning someone called Arren Cardockson. Why?"

"Why d'you want to know?" said Annan.

"Idle curiosity," said Arren. "What can you tell me about him?" He glanced around at them. "Anyone?"

There was more silence.

"Eagleholm's destroyed," Nolan said at last. "Did you know that?"

"Yes, of course," said Arren.

"Well, Arren Cardockson's the man what destroyed it."

Arren blinked. "What? How?"

"No-one really knows—" Nolan began.

"I'll tell ye what *I* heard," said Olwydd. "Shall I?"

"Go on," said Arren.

"Arren Cardockson lived at Eagleholm," said Olwydd. "He was—is—a Northerner, like us."

"Stuff and nonsense!" Nolan interrupted. "Man's a griffiner; everyone knows that. One of their own, turned mad."

"A *Northerner*," Olwydd repeated. "I tell ye, he's a Northerner. He was a slave to the Eyrie Mistress, Riona—"

"Shut up!" said Nolan. "You dunno what yer talkin' about, you ignorant snow-blood. There *are* no slaves in Eagleholm. Don't you know bloody anything? The Lady Riona sent them all away. While she was in the North she fell in love with a Northerner, but he broke her heart, and when she came home and became Mistress she couldn't bear to look at a Northerner any more, so she rid her lands of them all for good."

"Well, she must have kept one behind, then," said Olwydd, unmoved. "Just this one, Arren Cardockson, who she kept as her lover. But one day he went mad and decided he could be a griffiner like her, so he stole a griffin chick, and then he murdered Riona and set fire to the Eyrie and ran off, him and the griffin."

"That's the stupidest thing I ever heard!" Nolan stormed. "Listen, the man was a griffiner."

"Oh?" said Olwydd, "Then *ye* can tell us what really happenèd, if ye're that certain. Go on."

"Fine, I will. Arren Cardockson was a griffiner, but his griffin was killed in an accident—"

"Because he killed it," Torc put in. "He went mad and killed it."

"Shut up, Torc. His griffin died, and he went insane and tried to steal another one, but he was caught and sentenced to death. But on the day of the execution he broke free and used magic to turn himself into a terrible black griffin, and he killed the Eyrie Mistress and her council and broke the Eyrie to pieces before he flew away. He's still out there in the wild somewhere, mad and lusting for blood. They say he'll be back to destroy the other Eyries some day."

Arren groaned quietly. "So, that's the story, is it?" he said, raising his voice. "Arren Cardockson is a Northerner who was a slave in lands where there *aren't* any slaves any more, but he was also a griffiner, and he went insane and stole a griffin chick and then turned *into* a griffin and killed the Eyrie Mistress. Do I have that right?"

Olwydd and Nolan glared at each other.

"It's not his fault, Taranis," said Nolan, looking away. "He's come straight from some peasant village over the mountains; how would he know anything about what's goin' on in the rest of the world?"

Olwydd half-rose at that, raising his fist. "Why ye little—"

Arren pushed him back. "Stop it! Do you want to get us all in trouble? Nolan, don't talk to him like that." He turned to Olwydd. "I'm afraid Nolan's right about there being no slaves in Eagleholm. There haven't been any there in about twenty years. But"—he couldn't stop himself from giving Nolan a sour look—"it's *not* because of some unrequited love story, I'm sorry to say. It's because Eagleholm was nearly bankrupt, and they couldn't afford to go on supporting a thousand-odd slaves, so Riona sold them all to refill the treasury. And I know that because I heard a griffiner say so. As for Arren Cardockson . . ." He shrugged. "Looks like nobody has any idea."

"*I* do," came a voice from the doorway.

It was Caedmon. The old man limped into the room. "So, *there* you are," he said, looking pointedly at Olwydd and Prydwen. "I had a notion ye'd be in here, filling this poor lad's head

with yer nonsense. I warn ye right now, if yer lookin' to talk
him into another escape yer going to have me to answer to."

Olwydd bowed his head toward him. "Not at all. We're here
for a little storytelling, that's all."

"He's speaking the truth," said Arren. "Right, Nolan?"

Nolan nodded a little sullenly. "I told 'em they shouldn't be
here, but they wouldn't listen. But we're just talkin'."

"About Arren Cardockson," said Caedmon.

"Well, I was *hoping* someone would be able to tell me who
he is," said Arren, affecting an air of slightly contemptuous
frustration. "But I'm not having much luck."

"And so it should be," said Caedmon. "That's not a thing
we're permitted to talk about."

"And who is going to stop us, old man?" said Prydwen.
"Yerself, maybe?"

"Don't talk to him like that," Arren snapped. He stood up.
"Caedmon, I'm sorry. I don't mean to be rude. Would you like
to sit down? Something to drink?"

Caedmon inclined his head graciously. "I'd appreciate it.
Thank you, Taranis."

Several men moved aside to give the old man room to sit down,
and Arren passed him a cup of water. "So," he said once Caedmon
was comfortable, "what's this all about? Can you at least tell me
who this person is and what he's supposed to have done?"

Caedmon looked reflectively at the fire. "I s'pose there's no
harm tellin' some of it. I heard the story up at the tower myself,
so I know the tale the griffiners are telling."

Arren tensed. "And what would that be?"

"This man," said Caedmon, "Arren Cardockson—Olwydd
was right. He is a Northerner. His true name is Arenadd Taranisäii, and he is one of the freed slaves of Eagleholm who stayed
behind. But there's more: Arren Cardockson was a griffiner."

Several people made incredulous noises.

"Oh, *come on*," said Annan. "One of us? A griffiner? Next
thing you'll be sayin' he lives in a castle in the clouds."

Caedmon shrugged. "That's what I heard. A Northern
griffiner. Not like to have been popular at the Eyrie, I'd say.
He was a griffiner, and his griffin died. Some say he killed her;
others say it was illness or an accident. But after that he lost his
mind. He broke into the Eyrie late at night and murdered Lady

Riona in her bed, along with most of her councillors, an' then he set a fire and fled. No-one knows where he went, but most say it was northward, to kill Lady Elkin at Malvern." He shook his head. "That's all I know, but whatever else this Arenadd is, he's a murderer."

"No," said Prydwen.

Everyone stared at him.

"No," Prydwen repeated. "I tell ye, no. Arenadd Taranisäii is no murderer, and no madman. He's a hero."

Arren had taken the condemnation in Caedmon's words like a physical blow, but even so he baulked at this. "Since when is a murderer a hero?" he snapped.

Prydwen gave him a look with more venom than a bag of snakes. "Shut that mouth of yers before I shut it for ye, yer soft-headed Southern slave. Ye know nothin'. What Arenadd did was for us, all of us." He glanced appealingly at the others. "Don't ye see? It was justice. Lady Riona was in the North, did ye know that? Her and her brother." His face darkened. "I know of him. Rannagon. Lord Rannagon, the bloody bastard. My grandfather told me he destroyed three villages, all on his own. Sent his soldiers in, killed everyone and burned the buildings to the ground. But did *he* get called a murderer? No, an' I'll tell ye why. Because he was a griffiner, that's why, an' when the griffiners are the ones dolin' out justice, what chance is there that they'd condemn one of their own? So it was left to Arenadd to do justice on him, an' on the rest, too. Justice for the dead."

Arren didn't know which was worse: that he was being called a villain or that he was being called a hero.

The others were looking uncertain. "Well," said Nolan, "I don't see how it's any of our business either way."

"Of *course* it's our business," said Prydwen. "We're his people, all of us. Even ye. What he did was for us."

"I'll bet," Arren muttered.

Prydwen stood up. "Arenadd Taranisäii is a hero, an' I name ye traitor if ye deny it." He gave the assembled slaves a disgusted look, and spat. "I tell ye, ye make me ashamed to be a Northern man. Once I thought ye were my brothers, but ye're too craven to even love yer own homeland. I'm glad ye're in chains. Ye're what ye make of yerselves, and I say ye deserve to be slaves. All of ye."

14

Breaking Chain

Every day, Arren and his fellows were woken up at dawn by the screech of the griffin at the temple—heard but never seen—and marched out to the wall to resume their work. Arren spent the first few days mixing mortar, until the supervisors decided he was ready to move on to something more strenuous. He was re-assigned to the quarry, where he had to help cut and haul blocks of stone.

Soon he was longing to return to the buckets. Mixing mortar had been tedious and tiring, but quarry work was backbreaking. Every evening he returned to the slave-house bruised and sore, his fingernails broken and his robe covered in stone dust. His wounded back couldn't take the strain; the lash marks opened and re-opened, becoming encrusted with thick, dirt-filled scabs. Inevitably several of them became infected, and Nolan and Caedmon had to clean them out with a stinging paste of crushed griffin-tail, which eventually did its work. The infection cleared up and the wounds healed, little by little, until he could lie on his back again. But he knew, even without the benefit of mirrors, that the wounds had left deep scars behind.

His hand was little better. The branding iron had killed off a large patch of skin and destroyed the flesh underneath. It itched and burned appallingly and wept thin, watery blood. He didn't dare scratch it, because that caused the kind of pain that made him think he was going to faint, but after a time the itching died down, and he lost all sensation in the back of his hand. That was when the worst part came. The dead skin had already sloughed off, and now the flesh underneath did the same. It stank of decay, and once it was all gone it left a deep, bloody wound behind. Arren did his best to keep it clean, packing the hole with griffin-tail and then covering it with a scrap of wet cloth, and fortunately it didn't become infected. But it took a long time to begin healing.

By the end of a week or so—Arren had soon lost count of the days—the gap in the wall that he and his fellows had been working on was completely closed and the top levelled out. But there were other gaps elsewhere and other places where the wall needed reinforcing, so Arren's squad was moved to a different spot, and the work continued.

A month dragged by. Arren worked without complaint and did as he was told; he never answered back, never looked a superior in the eye, never lagged or hesitated. He did his best to behave in the slave-house, too; when squabbles erupted he kept out of the way and never flared up or showed aggression toward anyone. It helped keep attention off him and stopped others from thinking of him as a troublemaker or untrustworthy. He hoped that the guards would notice and that, sooner or later, they would relent and take the irons off him. As for Olwydd and Prydwen, he stayed away from them as much as possible, knowing that being seen in their company would only raise suspicion. They obviously shared that view and made no attempt to talk with him again, but he knew they were watching him; they were waiting, like him, for a signal.

Arren behaved himself, but he wasn't passive by any means. Every waking moment he was aware of the danger he was in and of the need to escape. He never let himself relax; he kept his distance from the guards as much as possible. He was tempted to rub dirt on his scar, but he didn't dare; someone would see him do it and would ask questions.

That was the main reason he soon began to despair of having any chance to escape: he was never alone. Waking or sleeping, day or night, there was always someone there. He was watched by guards every moment when he was outside at work. The rest of the time it was the other slaves watching him, and though he liked their company, he knew they wouldn't hesitate to betray him if they saw him trying to run away. And, he eventually conceded, he didn't want to hurt them, either. They didn't deserve to suffer on his account, and he knew that if he ran, then they would be punished.

He thought about it constantly, brooding over the problem while he cut and hauled blocks of stone to build a wall for his enemies, a defence made necessary by a conflict he had started. There had to be a way to get out of Herbstitt unseen without casting suspicion on the others. But whatever that way was, it refused to come to him, and time was running out.

One day, nearly two months after his capture outside the spirit cave, Arren was helping Nolan wrestle a large stone block into position among its fellows at the base of the wall when a shout came from somewhere behind him. He glanced up automatically, and the block lurched in their combined grip.

"Come on!" Nolan gasped. "Don't drop it, damn yer!"

"Sorry." Arren took a few extra steps sideways, then he and Nolan lowered the block on top of a stack of its fellows. Once it was down, he straightened up and rubbed his back, groaning. "Argh, godsdamnit—what?"

Nolan gazed past him. "Hey, will yer look at that, then?"

Arren looked. They weren't far away from the town's gates, which hung open. A large wagon had just been driven through them and had come to a stop not far away. Arren squinted at it, confused. There was a kind of cage built over the wagon, and inside there were—

"Oi!" Caedmon had seen them and came over, scowling. "What d'ye think yer doin'? This ain't a puppet show. Get back to work!"

Arren shook himself. "Sorry, sir."

Nolan had already taken the hint and was walking back toward the quarry. Arren lagged behind him, chains rattling.

"Looks like the new lot have got here," said Nolan, glancing over at the wagon. The governor was there with a couple of guards, talking to the driver. "Not before time, either," he added sourly.

"New—?" Realisation dawned. "Oh. Those new slaves who were supposed to be here by now."

"That's right. Looks like there's a lot of 'em. Hope we got the room."

Arren sighed unhappily as they walked toward the side gate that would take them to the quarry. More slaves would mean the work would go faster, and escape would become even more urgent. Still, he was curious to know about them and where they had come from. Perhaps, he thought hopefully, there would be someone among them who could help, someone else who wanted to escape.

By the time he returned from the quarry, carrying another huge block, the wagon had been driven over to the slave-house and the occupants had been unloaded and taken inside.

"They'll be restin' the day out," Nolan observed. "None of them'd better take my hammock, or I swear they'll be sorry."

Arren grinned. "Don't worry, Torc will make sure they don't." The boy was in the slave-house that day, cleaning and repairing things with the help of a couple of other slaves who were injured and unable to work.

Noon came, and the boy reappeared as if by magic to bring them lunch, which as well as the usual bread included a basket of green apples. "They was brought into the tower, but the governor didn't want them," he explained. "We get 'em 'cause he's in a good mood now the new lot are here."

Arren took one gratefully. "So, have you talked to any of 'em yet?"

"Yes, sir. They was sent here from Wylam, sir, but they came through Eagleholm lands on the way. One of them said they was delayed there because a griffiner wanted to look at them all. He said he looked at all of 'em and asked their names an' such."

Arren's blood ran cold. "I wonder why?"

"Looking for someone maybe, sir," said Torc. "But that's why they're late."

"You really don't have to call me that, Torc," said Arren.

"Yes, sir." Torc grinned at him. "You'll like the new lot, sir. They've got all sorts of stories about Wylam an' such, and there was one said he come from Eagleholm once, too."

"How many of 'em are there?" said Nolan.

"Dunno," said Torc. "Fair few. We'll get this wall done in no time with them here."

Arren grinned and ruffled his hair. "What d'you mean, *we*?"

Torc grinned back. "Well, you know, *you* will, then. But you can't work if you ain't got any food, sir."

"He's got yer bang to rights there, Taranis," said Nolan.

Arren laughed as the two of them went off to eat, but his good humour was feigned. Underneath he was worried. He knew perfectly well why the new slaves had been inspected. This griffiner, whoever he was, had been hoping that one of them was something other than what he claimed to be. Arren could imagine him examining each face, looking for a scar.

And a further horrible thought occurred to him shortly afterward: that one of the new slaves would know what the fugitive looked like and begin to suspect Arren. And then they would ask questions he couldn't answer.

They were back at the quarry now, and Arren suddenly paused and scooped up a handful of damp soil. He straightened up and rubbed it onto the side of his face, grinding it into the scarred skin as fast as he could.

Nolan noticed, however, and gave him an odd look. "What in blazes are yer doin', Taranis?"

"Got an itch," Arren muttered.

"Well, fine. C'mon, help me with this."

The rest of that afternoon seemed to last forever. Arren never quite knew how he managed to keep going with all the anxiety burning inside him, but he got through it one way or another, and when the sun began to set he walked back toward the slavehouse with Nolan and the others, full of dull exhaustion. He could feel an odd fluttering sensation in his chest, and without thinking he put a hand to his neck. Nothing. Still nothing.

"You're always doin' that," Nolan said suddenly.

Arren started. "What?"

"I said, you're always doin' that," said Nolan. "Touchin' your neck."

"Oh. It's just a habit."

"I know what it is," Nolan said slyly. "You're checking, ain't you? Still can't quite believe it's not there any more."

Arren stared at him, horrified. "What?"

"Stop gawping at me like that," said Nolan. "I meant yer collar. You still ain't used to not having it, eh?"

"Oh." Arren felt giddy. "Yes, you're right." There had been several attempts to fit him with a collar, but it seemed Herbstitt only had two, and neither of them were the right size. Arren had noticed that the collars on these slaves had been fitted much more tightly than the one that had been put on him back at Eagleholm. *That* collar had been loose—he had been able to fit a finger underneath it—and had constantly shifted around, causing the short spikes on its inside to tear into him every time it moved. These collars, however, never moved. Each one was properly fitted to its owner's neck, and Arren had noted with horror that the skin grew to suit it. Caedmon's neck had actually begun to absorb his collar, the skin growing over it to claim it for its own. Also, nobody seemed to be suffering from infections. He had managed to get Nolan to explain why: every collar was boiled in alcohol before it was fitted, and the metal itself was a special alloy that discouraged infection. The idea had come from elsewhere and been adopted by Cymrian slavers. Arren had already learnt that from his studies as a griffiner: slave collars had been invented in Amoran, and the griffiners in Cymria had copied them for their own slaves to wear. Arren wondered if these ones caused constant pain, as his own had done.

"You're a strange one, aren't yer?" said Nolan as they filed into the slave-house. But it was said warmly, and Arren finally realised that since he had first come into the slave-house and taken his place among the slaves, no-one—*no-one*—had drawn attention to the fact that he was a Northerner. There were no stares, no comments, no condescension or jokes, light-hearted or otherwise.

Arren felt inexplicably ashamed as he realised this was what he had noticed that first night, the cause of the nagging sense that something was different here. He looked at Nolan and knew that his new friend was doing something nobody had ever done in the past: he was accepting him, Arren, for who he was.

Arren pulled himself together. "Strange?" he said. "Yes, probably. So people say, anyway."

Now in the corridor, they waited patiently until the way was clear for them to enter their dormitory. "Sorry," said Nolan, "I didn't mean to insult yer or nothing—oh my *gods*."

Arren looked past him into the dormitory, and groaned. The room was packed. Everyone who normally slept there was having to get past the knot of new men who were now sharing their quarters. There were at least a dozen of them loitering around the fire, all travel stained and weary looking. Caedmon was there, busy haranguing them, but he didn't seem to be having much success.

Arren gritted his teeth. "Godsdamnit, what do they think they're playing at? This lot can't fit in here!" But he could barely hear himself over the babble of voices. He waded through the crowd, elbowing people left and right, trying to get to Caedmon. "Caedmon, what in the gods' names is going on?" he yelled.

A hand grabbed his arm. Arren shook it off. "Caedmon, are this lot going to be—*will you leave me alone?*" He turned

to confront the person harassing him. "Look, bloody w—"
He froze.

The other was a middle-aged man whose curly hair was
greying and whose ragged beard was speckled with white. He
had a worn and exhausted look about him, and his nose had
been broken, but the instant Arren saw him he felt as if he were
falling.

"Dad?"

The man gaped at him. "What—what—?"

Arren grabbed him by the arm and dragged him away,
unnoticed in the general confusion. There was a clear spot in
the corner, and he hustled him into it, glancing around constantly to make sure they were unobserved. Once he was sure
nobody was watching, he turned to him. "Dad, what are you
doing here?"

Cardock's face was pale. "Arenadd! Thank the moon you're
alive."

"Shut up!" Arren hissed. "I don't know who you're talking
about, old man. My name's Taranis, understand? I've never
seen you before in my life, so stop giving me that look."

Cardock understood. He looked past Arren and then moved
closer to him. "What are you doing here?"

"They caught me," Arren said in an undertone. "But look,
it's all right, they don't know who I am; they think I'm a runaway slave. I told them I was from Withypool. Dad, what are
you doing here? And"—he grabbed his father's arm—"you're
wearing a collar! Who did that? Who put that on you? For gods'
sakes, where's Mum?"

Cardock's eyes were bright with unshed tears. "Arren, listen, listen, you've got to understand, they know where you were
going. They caught us at Norton. There's a young griffiner,
Erian. You know that name?"

Arren stared. "Rannagon's son."

"Yes. He's out there, and he's looking for you." Cardock
bowed his head. "I'm sorry. I had to tell them. I said you were
going to the North; now he's going there, too. If you go there—"

"I don't care," said Arren. "Where's Mum?"

"I don't know. They sold us both, and I don't know where
they sent her."

"Oh gods." Arren moaned. Female slaves often had it far
worse than the men did. There was every chance that his mother

had been sold to a brothel somewhere. "This is all my fault," he whispered. "All my fault."

Cardock grabbed his arm. "Listen! Listen, damn it, there's no time. He's after you. Erian. He won't rest until he's found you, and when he does—"

"When he does I'll kill him," Arren spat. "I'll kill him with my own hands, I swear. I'll rip his smug little bastard's head off." He saw the shocked look his father was giving him. "I don't know why you're looking like that. What's another murder to me?"

"Be quiet," said Cardock. "Someone could hear you. Just tell me what you're going to do."

Arren stared at him, genuinely taken aback. "I'm going to get us out of here," he said, full of a sudden certainty. "I'll find a way—"

"Here, ye!" Caedmon had seen them. "Yes, ye, yer blasted tenderneck, get over here."

Cardock darted closer to Arren. "Listen, there's no time, you've got to run for it; he's coming here, he's coming—"

Caedmon hit him with his stick. "I gave you an order, damn ye! Stop harassing the lad and get moving!"

Cardock gave Arren a desperate look as he was hauled off, and that was the last Arren saw of him. Caedmon, who had finally managed to bring some sort of order, took all those who couldn't find hammocks out of the dormitory with him. He eventually returned, bringing back a few who hadn't been able to find hammocks in the other dormitories, either, and would have to sleep on the floor. Cardock wasn't among them. Arren longed to go looking for him but didn't dare; it would only raise questions. And besides, the more time he spent near his father, the more likely it was that someone would spot the resemblance between them.

He had no appetite and went to bed that night full of fear and terrible guilt. It had been bad enough that he was in this situation, but now his father was as well, and his mother. How could he tell them why he had not come to meet them in Norton? And how was he going to free them now?

Another sleepless night was ended by the screech of the griffin at the temple. It seemed louder and longer than usual this time. Arren climbed out of his hammock, feeling dreadful. A bit of sleep had done absolutely nothing to soothe his nerves. His stomach ached as if he had been punched, and his hand itched and burned. And there was a strange sensation in his chest, too—not pain, but a strange feeling of emptiness, as if there were a gaping hole there. He touched his neck again, unconsciously. Nothing.

Nolan, who was pulling on his boots, paused to look up at him. "Are yer all right? Y'looks a bit pale there."

Arren took his hand away from his neck. "I'm not feeling well."

"I know how y'feel," said Nolan. "I didn't get a wink of sleep last night with that lot all over the damn floor, snoring." He glared at the new slaves, who were also stirring. Arren doubted they'd had much sleep, either.

Torc was already up and was adding fuel to the fire. There probably wouldn't be enough food in the pot to feed everyone, but Arren didn't think he could stomach it anyway. He sat down with his back to the wall and waited while the others ate, his mind full of a picture of his father as he had seen him the previous night: his lined face gone pale and gaunt, eyes hollow, the nose crooked from the blow that had broken it. And his mother was still out there somewhere, suffering once again the life of slavery she had been freed from when she was a child—and all because of him.

Arren clasped his hands together and wrenched, gripping and pulling until it hurt. He wanted it to hurt. *You should have died,* he thought. *You should have stayed dead, you should—*

Nolan appeared from out of the crowd of tired slaves, holding a bowl. "Hey, I got you some food. C'mon, get up, there ain't much time before we got to get out there."

Arren looked up, red-eyed. "I'm not hungry."

"C'mon, you gotta eat," said Nolan. "You'll be good f'nothin' if you don't get somethin' down yer."

Arren took it and ate a few spoonfuls. It was the same thing he'd eaten every day for months, and he'd grown used to it, but this morning it was like trying to eat vomit. He managed to swallow it, but it caught in his throat and he put the bowl down, retching.

Nolan looked concerned. "You don't look good at all. What's wrong?"

Arren groaned and put a hand to his chest. "It's my—there's

a funny feeling here. I don't know what's wrong. I need something to drink."

"Here, I'll get it for yer," said Nolan.

Arren watched him go, feeling more grateful than ever for his company. Nolan had more or less attached himself to him since their first meeting, and Arren had come to like him a lot; he was a simple man, but honest, and kind as well.

Nolan returned with water. "Here, drink up. You'll be fine."

Arren drank it in one long swallow. It made him feel a little better. "Thanks, Nolan."

"No trouble," said Nolan, treating him to a gap-toothed smile. He glanced over his shoulder, and sighed. "Ah, here we go, then."

The others had begun to file out. Arren went with them, knowing he had no choice and full of an overwhelming sense of dread. The feeling didn't leave him as the column marched out of the slave-house or when they went out into the open air. In fact, it grew worse. He flinched as he stepped into the open, feeling as if something were about to fall out of the sky and land on him. As the groups were split up and sent off to their different places of work, he looked about frantically for his father but failed to spot him among the dozens of faces.

Arren's group was marched toward its place near the gates. As he walked at the back of the line, head bowed, Arren caught a snatch of conversation from the guards flanking them. ". . . found them just lying there. I dunno, that's just what I heard. There aren't supposed to be any in Canran, but that's what they think it is . . ."

They reached their destination, and the group spread out to resume its different tasks. Arren joined up with the team that would go to the quarry, and they walked together to the gate. It had already been opened for them to pass through, and after that there would be a short walk through the scrubland outside, to the spot where the stone-cutters stacked the newly made blocks.

As he was passing through the gate, Nolan suddenly grabbed him by the arm. "Hey! Look at that!"

Arren turned. "What? I can't see—"

"On top of the tower!" said Nolan. "Right there, see!"

Arren looked straight toward the tower and saw it, saw the

dark silhouette against the sky. His blood turned to ice. He faltered in his step. "No."

"One of 'em must have come back," said Nolan. "I wonder what for."

The griffin shifted on its perch, great beaked head turning toward them as if it was looking straight at him. Arren, heedless of the other slaves jostling him on their way past, saw the shape of a man appear by the griffin's side and climb onto its back.

A guard thumped him in the side. "Move it!"

Arren couldn't. His boots seemed to be stuck to the ground, and his whole body had gone cold. Nolan grabbed him by the arm and more or less dragged him away, but Arren went backward, his gaze locked on the tower. He saw the griffin crouch and then leap, wings opening wide as it took off, flying straight toward the wall. And, as it came closer, he saw that its wings were brown, mottled brown like bark, its hindquarters the colour of straw. It was coming straight at him.

Arren's nerve broke. He turned and ran. Nolan's grip on his arm fell away, and he headed straight for the trees, not hearing the shouts of the guards.

The irons dragged, catching on sticks and plants, weighing him down and making him slow and clumsy. Arren could not have run far anyway. The empty feeling in his chest had risen and expanded, spreading a coldness through his limbs. There was a roaring in his ears, blotting out all other sounds. He felt as if he were drowning.

A hand caught him by the shoulder, pulling him up short. He staggered, trying to break free even as they started to drag him back. Someone hit him, but he didn't feel it. Blackness was closing over his eyes; everything had turned hazy. From somewhere far, far away he heard the screech of a griffin.

There was a babbling of voices around him, all faded and confused. Then the veil was ripped away from his eyes, and he saw the starry sky above the city, and the white half-moon shining on the armour of the knot of men in front of him, pointing arrows straight at him. The one in front of them, the one nearest, had no bow, but his short sword was in his hand. His red-brown hair and beard matched his tunic, and he was reaching toward Arren, saying something, telling him to do something.

Arren could hear his own voice, high and thin with terror.

"They're coming! They're coming for me, please don't let me fall, no!"

He grabbed at the man in front of him, trying desperately to save himself, but it was too late. One arrow hit him in the leg, and he staggered back, screaming. The second hit him in the chest. The bearded man lunged at him, one hand reaching out, and then he was falling, falling . . .

Arren didn't feel himself hit the ground. He landed with a crunch amid the wet bracken and lay there, unable to move. The vision ended and he knew where he was, but there was something wrong. His entire body had gone numb. He could feel the water soaking into his robe and the irons weighing him down. Sticks and broken fern stems were jabbing into him, and his head hurt from where it had hit the ground, but he couldn't move. His eyes refused to open, and his arms lay at his sides, as heavy and useless as bits of wood, and his legs were the same.

Someone was hitting him, slapping his face. Above the roaring in his ears he could hear voices, rough and impatient. "Get up! Damn it, get up now or . . ."

Arren tried with all his might to obey, knowing that if he didn't he would be in trouble—but he couldn't. He tried to speak, wanting to tell them there was something wrong, but nothing happened. He lay there, unmoving, eyes closed. They continued to hit him for a while, cursing at him, but although he could feel the blows they didn't hurt.

Finally, someone grabbed him by the front of his robe and pulled him up. He hung limply in their grasp, head lolling.

A hand touched his chest. "I don't think he's breathing," said a voice.

"Check his pulse."

The hand moved to the side of his neck and lingered there for a while, and then he was suddenly released, flopping back to the ground like a broken doll.

"Godsdamnit! He's dead!"

There was a brief silence, and then, "You bloody idiot! What did you go an' hit him like that for! You've killed the son of a bitch! What're they gonna do when they find out?"

"I didn't hit him that hard!"

"Well, I didn't hit him at all, an' I'm damned if I'm taking the blame for this."

"Look, the bloody griffiner's gonna be here any moment. Just get the body out of here, an' we'll dump it in the scrub. We'll send someone out to bury it, an' tell the governor about it later."

"Tell him what?"

"The truth. He just dropped dead in front of us, an' we don't know why. It's nobody's fault, so you'd better back me up. I'm not gonna pay to replace him, understand? I've got a family to feed."

"Fine. You get rid of the body, an' I'll get back to the slaves an' get 'em moving again before anyone notices something's up."

There was a brief silence and then the crunching steps of the second speaker leaving. The guard grabbed the back of Arren's robe with his rough hands and dragged him upward before lifting him onto his shoulder and carrying him away through the scrub. Arren's head and arms hung over the man's back, the irons still weighing him down on the other side. Eventually, the guard cursed and stopped, dumping him on the ground. He unlocked the irons and took them off, and then picked Arren up again and went on.

Arren didn't know how far they went. The paralysis had spread into his mind now, and thinking was hard, as if he were trapped in a moment of half-sleep, unable to wake.

Finally he was dumped on the ground, and he heard the guard walk off. Once he had gone, Arren made another effort to move. Still, nothing happened.

A dull panic took hold of him. The irons were gone, but he couldn't move. He was helpless, trapped inside a body that had ceased to obey him. *I'm dead,* he thought. *I'm dead again, I'm dead* . . .

He lay there for a long time, trapped in that waking sleep, and at that moment he knew what he wanted above all else. *Skandar. Skandar, please, come and find me. I need you. Please, Skandar. Skandar, I'm your human, please come! Please!*

But Skandar was not there and he would not come. He was lost, somewhere out there in the world on his own. Maybe he was looking for his human, or maybe he had forgotten him and had gone back to his wild life. And why should he come now; why should he want to come back for a half-broken slave, or for a dead man? *I sent you away, I told you to go. I told you, Skandar—*

A voice intruded on his thoughts, calling to him through the darkness.

"Taranis! *Taranis!*"

Hands were patting his face, trying to wake him up.

"*Taranis!* Taranis, please, wake up! Please, don't be dead, please!"

Nolan, Arren thought.

Nolan stopped crying out, and gave a soft sob. "No."

"Get on with it!" a harsh voice rapped out. "Go on, you can mourn later!"

"Yes, sir," Nolan mumbled.

Arren felt his hands move away, and shortly afterward he heard a strange thud and scrape from somewhere nearby. It went on for some time before he realised what it was. Metal on soil. Nolan was digging a hole.

No, he thought. *No, Nolan, don't! I'm not dead! Please, don't!*

He struggled with all his might, trying desperately to speak, to tell them not to bury him, to say he wasn't dead, but his mouth wouldn't move and neither would his throat. There was no breath in his lungs. He was blind and voiceless.

The scraping stopped, and there was a thud as Nolan threw the shovel aside. Arren felt himself being dragged over the ground a short distance, and then he was dropped into the grave. Nolan lifted Arren's arms and laid them neatly over his chest, smoothed down his robe and brushed the hair away from his face.

"There," his distant voice said. "You look much better now. I've—this is all I can do. I'm sorry." There was a silence, and the voice grew a little fainter. "Sir, can I say the words? Please, just quickly for him?"

"Fine, but be quick about it."

"Thank you, sir." Arren heard the sound of Nolan's boots on the ground as he shifted his position, and then his voice spoke again, low and murmuring. "Of earth born and in fire forged, by magic blessed and by cool water soothed, then by a breeze in the night blown away to a land of silver and bright flowers. May the gods receive the soul of Taranis of Withypool, may he look down from the stars and may his wisdom embrace us. This I ask in the names of the lost gods, by the sacred light of the moon." A pause. "I'm—I'm done, sir."

"Good. Now fill it in."

Arren heard Nolan pick up the shovel, heard him dig it into the ground, and a few moments later the first load of wet earth thumped onto his legs. *No! Nolan, don't bury me, please, I'm not dead!*

More dirt was piled on top of him, more and more, until it had covered his face. The sound of the shovel grew fainter, muffled by the soil, until there was nothing but the silence of the grave.

15

To Stone

Erian Rannagonson nocked the arrow onto the string and pulled it back, balancing the tip on his other hand. The wood creaked softly as it bent; he loved the familiar feel of it in his hands as he sighted down the arrow at the target. He paused for a moment to line it up, and then loosed the arrow. It hissed softly as it shot through the air and hit the target with a *thunk*, right in the centre, where it stuck, quivering. Erian lowered the bow and grinned. He'd hit it dead centre. Perfect. His teacher had told him he had a gift for archery. Still, wooden butts were dull to aim at. Maybe he should leave the city for a while and see if he could find some game instead. But he'd have to wait for Senneck to get back first.

He selected another arrow. This one stuck in the target right next to the first, so close the heads were touching. Growing bored of this, he decided to challenge himself by testing his speed, grabbing, nocking and loosing each arrow as fast as he could; the butt was soon a forest of wooden shafts. He didn't stop until he had run out of arrows, and then strolled over to begin pulling them out.

He had had a dull morning. The temporary governor had explained—albeit apologetically—that the wall had to be finished within a few weeks, and hence he couldn't afford to stop work even for a short time so that Erian could inspect the slaves. Erian had visited each worksite and tried to examine each nervous face in turn, searching constantly for the one that had burned itself into his mind. It had been a tedious process; the only face he recognised was that of Cardock, who had shot him a look of pure and utter hatred before the guards had ordered him to get back to work.

Erian didn't care. It was only natural that the old man should hate him, and it simply wasn't possible for him to place the blame for his predicament on his black-hearted son, where it belonged. Erian had no remorse for having sold him and his wife—in fact he was rather pleased by his cunning in having done so. Herbstitt was desperate for slaves, and he'd managed to get a fair price for Cardock. The Wylamese slavers had bought Annir as well, for a lower sum, but it had added up, and Erian was pleased.

Being a griffiner didn't automatically make you rich, and Erian was painfully aware of that. His father's property had naturally passed to Flell, as his only true-born offspring, leaving Erian with nothing but the allowance he'd been given before his father's death. His sword had been expensive, and he had had to pay for it with borrowed money. Selling the murderer's parents had gone some way toward paying it off. He'd been lucky, too, to find that Lord Galrick had left plenty of his clothes behind in Norton. They fitted him quite well, and nobody had stopped him from helping himself.

He paused to adjust the hang of his new tunic. It was blue velvet, and the shoulders were decorated with griffin feathers dyed to match. He'd even found a pair of blue leather boots to go with it. Now he looked like a proper griffiner.

Erian pulled the last arrow out of the butt and stuffed it into his quiver. As he walked back to his spot, the sound of wings made him look up.

It was Senneck. The brown griffin landed neatly over by the archery butts, sending up a small cloud of dust. She folded her wings and came toward him, tail swishing behind her.

Erian went to meet her. "Hello, there you are."

Senneck's blue eyes were cold. "What are you doing?"

Erian held up his bow. "Just a little archery practice. I thought I should keep my hand in, since we're here."

"I see." She sat back on her haunches, but she still towered over him, watching him.

Erian started to feel uncomfortable. "Why, is there something else I should be doing?"

Senneck stood up abruptly. "Why are we here?"

"I *told* you already," Erian snapped. "We're here to check the slaves. I want to be sure he's not among them. As soon as they finish work for the day I'm going to have them lined up and talk to them."

"You think he is here?" Senneck hissed. The tip of her tail was twitching.

"He could be," said Erian.

"That is not good enough," said Senneck. "Be exact. What are the chances that he is here?"

"Well, they're low," Erian admitted. "But—"

The griffin clicked her beak sharply. "They are low! So then, why have we come here, may I ask?"

"Because I wanted to see this place for myself," said Erian. "Just on our way, so I could ask a few questions, scout things out—"

"You are looking for him here," Senneck sneered. "You think he could be here, hiding among the slaves!"

"He could have come this way!"

"You have already spoken to the governor, and there has been no word of anything. He is not here, Erian. You and I should be in the North by now, and yet you have insisted that we waste our time here. Why?"

Erian failed to spot the danger signals. He shrugged. "Do we need a reason?"

Senneck lashed out with lightning speed, sending him flying. He hit the ground hard, and his bow shot out of his hand. He tried to get up, winded and gasping, but she was too quick for him. She stood over him, hissing and furious. "Do not presume to speak to me like that, bastard."

Erian scrabbled at the ground, trying to pull himself away. "Senneck, no! I don't—"

Senneck lowered her head so that they were eye to eye. Hers were blazing. "You are not my master. Understand that? You do not tell me what to do. I am not your pet; I am not your beast of burden. You are mine now, and if I decide that we should or should not do a thing, then you are the one who must obey me."

There was enough defiance in Erian to make him say, "And what will you do if I don't?"

She straightened up, head turning to look to her left. The governor's dog had wandered into the yard and was regarding her cautiously. "This is what I shall do," the griffin said. She lowered her head and braced herself, placing her forelegs well apart. For a moment she stood like that, unmoving, and then she suddenly went rigid. Something changed around her, something unseen. The ground shook gently, and the air thrummed silently. Without warning she lifted her head, beak opening wide as if she was going to scream. But what came forth was not sound.

A great beam of light, pure green with a core of brown, came from Senneck's throat. It enveloped the dog, hiding the animal from view. For a few moments there was nothing but silence, and then Erian heard a horrible cracking, groaning noise coming from within the great green glow. It lasted only briefly before Senneck abruptly closed her beak and sat back on her haunches, the light disappearing like a flash of lightning.

Senneck turned to look at him again as he struggled upright. "That is what I shall do," she said softly.

Erian was not aware of the dirt besmirching his new tunic. He stared, dumbstruck. The dog was still where it had been before, but it had stopped moving. Its entire body had become grey and rigid; it sat there, locked into place, frozen in an attitude of cringing terror. It had turned to stone.

Erian found his voice at last. "You—you—"

Senneck refolded her wings. "You asked me what my power was. Now you know. That dog shall be trapped like that forever, neither alive nor dead. And the same shall happen to anyone I choose." She turned her terrible gaze on him. "No matter who they are."

"You wouldn't!" Erian whispered. "You're my griffin!"

The brown griffin's blue eyes were full of terrible contempt. "*Your* griffin?" Her tail started to twitch. "You are beginning to displease me, Erian Rannagonson."

"Why?" said Erian.

"Hear me now," she said. "You wish to have revenge. That is your desire. To find the man who killed your father and kill him in return."

"Yes," said Erian. "You *know* that, Senneck."

"Understand that I am sympathetic to your desire," said Senneck. "I despise that creature as much as you do, and if I find him before you, I shall kill him." She sighed. "I spent many long years living in the hatchery, unpartnered. I had food and shelter, but that was all I had. A griffin without a human has no status, any more than a human without a griffin does. I wanted a human to call my own, but I rejected all those who came to me. I wanted a human worthy of me, a noble—wealthy, respected. A human I could help become great. But none were worthy.

I rejected some; others were claimed before I could reach them. And then . . . you came."

Erian felt a little glow of pride. "Yes. I'll never forget the day we met."

"I knew you were a commoner the moment I saw you," Senneck said icily. "From your clothing, from the way you carried yourself. You had no status; you looked like a peasant. That blackrobe had sent you in alone to amuse himself, in the hopes that you would make a fool of yourself. I did not like him, but I agreed with him. I rejected you the instant I saw you." She paused. "And then you spoke, and spoke *griffish*. You proved you knew something. And you told us you were Lord Rannagon's son. I already knew that Lord Rannagon had a bastard son, and so did my fellows. They rejected you because you were a bastard; they would not dishonour themselves. They all knew what had become of Eluna when she partnered herself to a blackrobe. Even her own parents rejected her for it."

"But you chose me," said Erian. "You chose me."

"I took a risk," said Senneck. "I had grown tired of waiting. And if Rannagon had favoured you enough to acknowledge you as his son, then that meant there was a chance you could overcome your bastardy. It was my hope that, if you became a griffiner, you could persuade Lady Riona to legitimise you. Together, we could have become something more."

"And we will," said Erian. "I swear."

"Then *become*," Senneck rasped. "I command you. That blackrobe robbed me of my chance when he killed your father and Lady Riona, and I wish to see him dead. But if you continue to allow yourself to be this—this landless, penniless vagabond without even a lordship—I shall abandon you."

Erian went pale. "No. You wouldn't do that. We belong together. We're partners. You chose me."

"I chose you," she said. "Understand this, Erian. I made you. If it were not for me, you would still be a lowly farm boy. And if I left you, you would become that once again. All you are, you owe to me." She drew herself up. "So tread carefully, bastard."

He hesitated. "I—I will, Senneck. I promise. I won't forget. I'll do whatever you want."

Satisfaction gleamed in her eyes. "Then do as I say."

"I will."

"We leave tomorrow," said Senneck. "No more delays; time

is short. We shall go to Malvern immediately and swear our service to Lady Elkin. She will want youth and strength on her side if she chooses to invade Eagleholm's lands. But first you must go to the Wylamese slave-trader and speak with him. Command him to send the traitor's mother to Malvern to await our arrival. Return his money to him and say you are buying her back."

"Why?" said Erian.

She gave him a contemptuous look. "You truly know nothing, bastard. The woman will be useful. Use her as your personal slave. And when her son resurfaces, you will have the perfect bait to lure him to you."

Very slowly, Erian began to smile. "And when he comes . . ."

"You shall have a fine statue to sell," said Senneck.

It was raining. Drops landed on the bracken fern in a soft pattering that made them glisten and bob gently. More struck the mound of freshly dug earth surrounded by trampled vegetation. There was no marker there, nothing but a heap of dirt to show the spot.

There was a rustling among the ferns, and a long grey-green shape waddled toward the heap. It was a lizard, nearly as long as a man, moving surprisingly fast on its squat legs. Its tongue flicked in and out, tasting the air. It hated rain. The cold slowed it, made it feel confused and weak. But just now its mind was on something else. There was a smell coming from up ahead, a smell that rid its mind of all else.

Food.

The lizard made for the mound of disturbed soil and inspected it, tongue still flicking. It was faint, but unmistakeable: dead flesh lying just under the surface. The lizard paused briefly and then began to dig. Sharp black claws scooped the earth aside with ease, and the creature thrust itself downward. Before long it had dug a sizeable hole, and the scent was becoming stronger. Finally, its questing snout encountered something soft.

The lizard shovelled more dirt aside and found something pale and reeking of flesh. It took it between its teeth and bit down, shaking vigorously from side to side until the skin broke and it tasted blood. Encouraged, the lizard tugged more strenuously. But its efforts were not rewarded. The lizard's teeth were small and short, lacking the sharp serrations of a predator. This meat was too fresh to be easily torn apart.

The lizard hissed to itself in frustration. A find like this would be perfect if it had been allowed to rot for a week or so. But that was far too long to wait; it needed to eat now.

The lizard dug further, uncovering more of the corpse. It was human, mostly covered in a second skin of the kind humans had. The lizard found the soft midsection, just below the ribs, and nuzzled into it, pulling and biting. The flesh was thin there and could be opened with tooth and claw to expose the innards. Those would be far easier to eat, and they were the lizard's preferred food.

The creature dug its claws into the outer skin and pulled hard until it tore, exposing the pale second skin beneath. It bit into that, and began to pull.

Engrossed in what it was doing, its senses dulled by the cold, the lizard failed to see its own danger. There was a sudden flurry in the rain, a faint crash, and something enormous hit the lizard square in the back. The lizard jerked and began to thrash wildly, hissing, but the struggle was over almost as soon as it had begun. Huge talons closed tightly around its middle, and a black beak larger than a man's head struck, shattering the lizard's skull and breaking its neck in one blow. The lizard abruptly went limp.

Skandar hissed to himself and ripped the lizard in half with a jerk of his neck. He swallowed the front section in one go, gulping a little as it went down.

The second half was larger, but he was too impatient to tear it into smaller pieces. He threw his head back to tip it down his throat and then, part of the lizard's tail hanging from his beak, looked down for anything he might have missed.

That was when he saw the hand.

Skandar got up, tossing his head again quickly so that the last of the lizard slid down his gullet. His tail twitched. There was a smell, damped by the rain. A smell he knew.

It took him only a few moments to drag Arren out of the makeshift grave. He wrapped his talons around him and pulled him free as if he weighed nothing. Arren hung from his grip, cold and limp. He was deathly pale, his hair and beard tangled and matted with dirt.

Skandar lay down on his belly with Arren's still form cradled between his forelegs, and nosed at him.

"Arren," he rasped. "Arren. Wake now. Wake."

Arren did not move. He was dead.

A feeling of desolation rose up in Skandar's chest. The dark griffin continued to shove at Arren and call his name, waiting in vain for him to respond. His scent was still strong, the same scent he had had during all their time together in the wild. A cold, metallic scent, unlike anything a living creature could have. But a scent Skandar had come to know and to connect with the human he had claimed for his own.

Finally the griffin gave up and slumped disconsolately over Arren's body, rain dripping from the tip of his beak.

All his life he had been alone. His siblings had died, and his mother. The humans he had abducted had died as well. He hadn't meant to kill most of them, but they had all been so fragile, and most of them had made him angry with the strange whining and moaning noises they made. They were stupid animals who did not know how to speak and could not fly or fight. All of them but one. Just one, this human who had set him free, the one with the special powers, the one who could talk. Skandar had seen him use his magic many times. When they had first met, he had used some power to take away Skandar's strength and make him sleep, and had trapped him and taken him to a different place, as easily as if he were a newly hatched chick. And he could control other humans, make them do things. When Skandar had known he would face him in the arena, he had known at once what he must do. The human had talked to him; now he must talk to the human, and so he had. He had commanded him to use his magic once again to set him free, and left him alive so he could do as he had promised.

That night he had waited. The other griffins in the cages had mocked him, calling him a coward, saying he would be killed for refusing to fight. But Skandar had waited and said nothing, watching in silence, willing the human to come. And he had come. He had fallen out of the sky, fallen into the place with the cages. He could fly. And he had opened the cage and taken away the chains as if they were nothing, bending them to his will, and Skandar had been free.

Night was coming. Skandar looked down at Arren's pale face.

He had seen him like this before, just once. He had looked for him and had found him lying among the stones beneath the mountain where the humans nested. He had seen him stir and look up, eyes gleaming like two spots of blood. He had whispered a name before he died, and Skandar had watched, not knowing what to do.

But he had woken up. Somehow, he had died and then woken. Skandar had felt something in his own throat, something he had felt before when the human was there, and that night it finally came out. The scream. The black scream that looked like lightning and felt like fire inside him. It had frightened him then, and it frightened him now.

The rain had soaked through his fur and was beginning to soak through his feathers as well. His flanks twitched, but he stayed where he was and tried to think. Had *he*, Skandar, done something? Had he helped somehow?

He nudged Arren again. "Magic," he rasped. "Magic now."

Only silence and the drumming of the rain replied.

Skandar thought of the trapped thing in his throat. He had never felt it again after that night. It was gone, like a thorn that had been winkled out of his paw. By now he could barely even remember it. He opened his beak and tried to make something come out, but nothing emerged except a faint strangled whimper. He hissed to himself and pushed Arren further in toward his chest to protect him from the rain, as if he were an egg to be incubated.

Not knowing what else to do, he settled down to wait.

He dozed briefly and woke again. It was completely dark, and so he did not see Arren open his mouth and begin to breathe again. But he did feel him stir and hear him groan.

Skandar got up sharply, beak opening to hiss. But there was no scent of anything else nearby and no sign of an intruder. Arren was moving, trying to lift himself.

Skandar went to him and nudged at him again. "Arren, get up," he said. "Get up now."

Arren heard him. The griffin's voice sounded strangely muffled, as if he was dreaming it, but it was really there, dry and commanding as always; the sound of it put a sudden strength into his paralysed limbs. He struggled mightily, all his confusion vanishing as his mind buzzed with one sudden thought. *Skandar. Skandar's here. Skandar.*

He sat up and levered himself to his feet, opening his eyes, and the world came rushing back, the wet, cold, wonderful world. And Skandar was there.

Arren staggered to him and half-collapsed against his chest. "Skandar," he whispered, and coughed. He coughed again, harder, bringing up dirt and blood. His chest felt as if it were on fire, but he didn't care. He clutched onto Skandar, burying his face in the griffin's silver feathers. "Skandar. Skandar, it's you. You found me. You f—" And then he coughed again.

Skandar chirped and nipped at the back of Arren's neck as if trying to groom him. "Arren," he answered. "Arren Cardockson."

Arren finally let go. "Skandar, where are we? What's going on?"

Skandar shook the rain off his feathers. "Find you dead," he said. "You wake again."

Recollection came back. "I dreamt . . ." Arren felt cold all over. "I dreamt I was dead. I dreamt I was buried. I couldn't move, and it was so cold."

"Die, come back," Skandar said proudly. "Magic. You magic human. Lucky human."

Arren wrapped his arms around himself. "Lucky." He shuddered. "Yes. Skandar, where have you been? I thought you were dead, or lost."

Skandar clicked his beak. "*You* lost," he said. "You lost. I say, I go hunt. Go, come back, you gone. You *gone*."

"I know," said Arren. "Skandar, I'm sorry. I didn't mean for it to happen; it wasn't my fault."

"Where go?" said Skandar.

"They caught me," said Arren. "I was—look." He held out his hand. "This is what they did to me."

Skandar stared at the terrible scar. His tail began to lash. "They . . . hurt?"

"Yes, Skandar. They tortured me. They made me into a slave."

The dark griffin started to hiss. "They hurt you. Hurt human."

"Yes. They were our enemies."

Skandar's talons tore at the wet ground. "I see them, I kill. Not let them hurt."

"I'd like to do the same," said Arren. "Skandar, I—" He sat down suddenly.

Skandar nudged him. "Hurt?"

"No. Skandar, I'm . . ." Arren took a deep breath. "Skandar, I'm sorry. I'm so sorry."

"What sorry?" said Skandar.

"You're a magnificent griffin," said Arren. "The best and strongest I've ever seen. You don't deserve this. You didn't deserve to be caught and put in the Arena like that, and you don't deserve to be here with me now. A griffin like you should never—I shouldn't have treated you the way I did or spoken to you like I did. I was cruel and I was ungrateful. You saved my life so many times; you helped me to fight Rannagon. You're the only real friend I've got. And I ignored you, I insulted you, I didn't take your advice. You were right, Skandar. We should never have gone to that cave, and we should never have helped Skade. We should have made her tell us which way to go and flown to Norton without her, like you wanted to."

Skandar listened. "We go now," he suggested.

"No. It's too late now." Arren coughed. "I owe you everything, Skandar. If—if I weren't a Northerner, and if you had chosen me back at Eagleholm, we could have lived there together, you and I. I'd have given you a proper home and brought you food and bedding and clean water every day. We would have had respect. Other griffins would have bowed to you; you're so big, they would have respected you. You and I could have been on the council together, and I would have been your ambassador, like I was Eluna's once. I'd have been your human. Your servant, your partner, your friend. We could have been rich and powerful, and you would have had silver bands to wear on your forelegs, and female griffins would . . ." He closed his eyes and sighed. "So many things I could have given you. If only I was a Southerner, and you weren't a wild griffin, and if neither of us were murderers. I could have married Flell and had children of my own, and you would have had mates and eggs and chicks. Our names would have been carved on the wall of the temple."

Skandar seemed to understand. "I mate once," he said. "You mate."

Our pairing is over. "Yes. But that's not what I meant. What I meant was that we could have had a home. But we can't, and it's my fault. I'm a Northerner. A blackrobe. A darkman."

"What Northerner?" said Skandar.

"I look different," said Arren. "I *am* different."

"Am different, too," Skandar said softly.

Arren was caught completely off guard by that. "W— Yes. Yes. We're both different, aren't we?"

"Different," Skandar repeated. "Other griffins say 'You, Darkheart. You freak. Stupid chick. You cannot talk. You know nothing, Darkheart. Know nothing. Speak, Darkheart, speak.' I speak, they laugh. Hate them. Want to fight, but—not."

Arren thought of the huge griffin fighting furiously against his chains in the cage behind the Arena, trying to break free and attack the other griffins that mocked him. "People are cruel," he said. "And griffins are cruel, too. But I don't laugh at you, Skandar, and I never will. And maybe I can't give you all the things I want to give you, but I'll do my best to give you what you want." He touched the griffin's shoulder. "What *is* it you want, Skandar? What do you want me to do?"

"You . . . give me?" said Skandar.

"Yes. I'm your human, Skandar, for as long as you want me. A griffiner serves his griffin before everything else. What do *you* want?"

Skandar was silent for a long time.

"Just tell me," said Arren. "No matter what it is."

"Home," Skandar said at last. "Want home, Arren Cardockson."

Arren's immediate thought was of the home Skandar had once had, in the Coppertop Mountains, miles away to the south. His heart sank. "What home, Skandar? Where?"

"Want home," Skandar said again. "Mountains. Big mountains. Food. No human, only griffin. Want cave and river and sky, big sky."

"There's mountains in the North," Arren said slowly.

"Big mountain?"

"From what I've been told, yes. Huge mountains, covered in snow. And there are white deer and a giant lake and a big empty sky. My father said that in the North you can travel for a week and never see another living person."

Skandar cocked his head. "You come?"

"Yes, if you want me to. We could make it our home, if that's what you want."

The black griffin thought it over. Then he stood up. "We go," he said firmly. "North, go north."

"It could be dangerous, though," said Arren. "There are griffiners there."

Skandar hissed. "Not afraid. I fight, you fight. We go."

"Yes, Skandar. You and I. But would you do something for me first? Please? Just one thing?"

"What thing?" said Skandar.

Arren held up his hand to show the brand. "Revenge," he said softly. "You and I, Skandar. We can do it together."

16
Theft

The day had been long and exhausting, but Cardock had no appetite. Or at least not enough of one to want to elbow his way through the crowd around the stew pot in his dormitory. The other slaves were a loud and unruly lot, and he disliked their company. They had already made it plain that they disliked his; the fresh blood beneath his collar betrayed the fact that he was a tenderneck, not born into slavery, and therefore a troublemaker or a criminal.

Cardock was happy to keep his distance. He sat huddled in a corner, hugging his knees, and tried to think, while the others jostled and argued among themselves.

He had spent that day in agonies. Even now his stomach was churning. His son was here, in captivity. And Erian the Bastard was here, too. They knew each other by sight. Cardock had already seen the bastard inspect every single one of the Wylam slaves that had come here with him, examining each face as if he expected one of them to become Arenadd's. And he had seen him again that day, watching the slaves at work. Searching.

Every moment of that day, Cardock had expected to hear something or see something, expected to see people rushing to the tower in agitation, or to hear the news he dreaded: that Arren Cardockson had been found. When nothing happened, it did nothing to ease his mind.

Cardock laced his fingers together and tugged at them. He could feel sweat trickling down his back. Erian was still here. If he hadn't found Arren yet, then he soon would. He would recognise him the instant he saw him.

His stomach was knotting. He had to do something, but what? He had tried to warn his son the previous night, but he didn't know if Arenadd had understood. If he went to talk to him again now, someone might see the resemblance and ask questions. Or would the other slaves protect them? It was impossible to say.

The evening dragged on. Cardock ate nothing and ignored everyone who tried to talk to him. *I have to do something,* he told himself again and again. *I can't just sit here and do nothing. I have to see him again, make sure he's all right. I have to know.*

He got up, moving stiffly, and walked slowly toward the doorway.

Nobody paid much attention to him as he left the dormitory. Reaching the corridor outside, he shuffled along it, rubbing absent-mindedly at the brand scar on the back of his hand. It had healed cleanly enough, but it still itched occasionally.

He reached the door at the very end of the corridor, nearest to the guardroom, and carefully looked inside. It was still very crowded in there; some of the new slaves were busy sewing additional hammocks, but there wouldn't be enough room to hang one for each of them. Many of them would still have to sleep on the floor. Still, it was a little better than what most slaves could expect.

"Here, you. What're you doin' in here?"

Cardock looked up at the hefty slave who had come over to him. "Nothing, I—"

"You're not supposed to be in here, old man," said the slave. "If yer lookin' t'take extra rations out of our pot, forget it. There's scarcely enough for us."

"I'm not," said Cardock. "I'm just looking for someone."

"Lookin' for who?" said the man. "Who are you, anyway? Don't recognise yeh."

"Cardock Skandarson," said Cardock. There was no point in lying about it; the other slaves he had arrived with already knew his real name. "I'm looking for . . ." He frantically searched his memory. "Taranis," he said at last. "I'm looking for a man called Taranis. Have you seen him?"

The man looked him up and down. "You may as well come in," he said gruffly.

"Thank you." Cardock entered, looking around him for any sign of Arenadd, but he failed to spot him anywhere. "This *is* Taranis' dormitory, isn't it?" he asked.

"It was," said the man.

"Where is he, then?"

The man nodded toward a small group of people sitting by the back wall. "Ask Nolan. He was his friend; he'll tell yer."

"Thank you." Cardock made for the little group.

None of them looked up as he approached. They were sitting in a rough square, four of them, all looking grim and subdued.

"Excuse me," said Cardock.

One of them glanced up. "What d'you want?" he said roughly.

"I'm sorry to bother you," said Cardock. "Can I join you?"

"Now's not the best time," said one of the others.

"Sorry," said Cardock, "but I'm looking for Nolan. Someone said he could help me."

"That's me," said the first man. "What is it?"

"I'm told you know Taranis," said Cardock.

Nolan looked away. "I knew him, yeah."

"I'm looking for him," said Cardock. "Do you know where he is?"

They all stared at him in silence.

Finally, Nolan shuffled aside. "Sit down."

Cardock did. "Thanks. Crowded in here, isn't it?"

"Since you lot came along," the man sitting next to Nolan said unpleasantly. "Why are you looking for Taranis? Y'just got here."

"Never mind why," said Cardock. "I just want to know where he is."

"Did yer know him?" said Nolan.

Cardock hesitated. "We've . . . talked. Look, I don't want to keep annoying you; can you please just tell me where he is?"

Nolan sighed. "It's not a problem. What's yer name?"

"Cardock. Where's Taranis?"

"He's not here," said Nolan.

"Why? Where did he go? Is he okay?"

But Nolan couldn't seem to reply. The man beside him gripped his friend's shoulder and looked accusingly at Cardock. "He's dead, all right? Can you just leave us alone?"

Cardock only stared at him. "What?"

"He's dead," Nolan repeated. "Taranis died. This morning."

Cardock felt as if his stomach had been torn out. "That's not true," he said flatly. "I don't believe you."

Nolan shook his head. "I was there. I saw it with me own eyes. He just dropped dead in front of us." He shuddered. "It was horrible. He was acting funny. White and sweating. Muttering to himself. Said he felt wrong. An' then he just . . . went mad. Ran away like there was wolves on his tail. Guards caught him, an' he just started yelling."

"Yelling what?" said his friend.

" 'They're coming,' " said Nolan. " 'They're coming, don't let them get me.' An' after that it was all just babble. 'Don't let me fall.' He kept sayin' it over an' over. 'Don't let me fall.' An' then he just . . . died. Guard thumped him; he fell over an' never got up. They made me bury him. I checked him, tried to wake him up, but he was gone. Just like that. Dead."

"No," Cardock whispered. "No, no. Oh gods. No."

Nolan had gone pale, his eyes red rimmed. "What's wrong with you?" he snapped.

Cardock lurched forward and grabbed him by the front of his robe, shaking him violently. "Stop it!" he shouted. "Shut up! You're lying! He's not dead!"

Hands grabbed him and pulled him away, and he didn't resist. He sagged limply in their grasp, sobbing hoarsely. "No," he moaned. "No, this isn't . . . can't . . ."

Every man in the room had turned and was staring at him.

Nolan stood up. "Look at me," he said softly. "Look me in the face."

Cardock didn't have the strength to resist as the two who had restrained him lifted him to his feet. He knew he had given himself away, but he didn't care. What did it matter? What did anything matter now?

Nolan stooped to look at him, and squinted. "What in the gods' names?" he breathed.

"What's your name?" someone else said sharply. "What did you say your name was?"

"Cardock," he mumbled. "Wolf Tribe. Son of Skandar."

"You an' Taranis," said Nolan. "You—Annan, look at him. Look at his face."

The one called Annan did. "By the Moon," he muttered eventually. "It's him. Taranis. The spitting image."

"You were related, weren't yeh?" said Nolan. "Y'were, weren't yeh? You an' Taranis."

Cardock looked up. "I was his father."

Absolute silence reigned in the chamber. Every slave there was looking uncertain.

"His father?" said Nolan. "Wait. Wait. Cardock? Did yer say yer name was Cardock?"

"Yes."

"Cardock . . . Cardockson," said Nolan. *"Cardockson."*

"No," said Annan. "That ain't possible. Stop it. Taranis was—"

"Taranis wasn't his name," Cardock burst forth, not caring any more. "His name was Arenadd. Arenadd Tanarisäii. My son."

"Arren Cardockson?" someone shouted.

Nolan grabbed Cardock's arm. "Are you sayin'—are you sayin' that Taranis was *Arren Cardockson*?"

"Yes," said Cardock.

"But that's ridiculous!" said Annan. "You're tellin' me that Arren Cardockson was sleepin' in the hammock next to mine?"

"But that explains it, doesn't it?" said Nolan. "That explains *everything*. Why he never had no brand. Why he knew all that about griffins. Why he was so scared of griffiners comin' back here."

As suddenly as it had gone quiet, the room erupted into shouting. Cardock found himself being accosted by a dozen different people, all shouting questions and accusations at him. He backed away, frightened and bewildered, but he wasn't left to face them alone. Nolan and Annan moved in front of him, shielding him from the mob. Cardock cowered behind them, panic-stricken.

"What in the gods' names is going on in here?"

The voice lashed out like a whip. Most of the slaves went quiet instantly, and the rest were quick to follow suit as Caedmon limped into the room, his face a picture of fury.

The crowd parted to let him through, and he stumped toward the centre of the room, holding his stick menacingly and glaring at everyone as if daring them to challenge him.

"What's goin' on in here?" he said again, jabbing the stick at them all. "Own up. Who started this?"

As if acting on an unspoken agreement, Nolan and Annan took Cardock by the shoulders and led him straight to the old man.

Caedmon regarded them suspiciously. "Nolan. You ain't the type t'stir up trouble. Can't say the same for *you*, though," he added, to Annan. "What's this about? An' who's this?"

"We're sorry, sir," said Nolan. "It's just that . . ."

"It's this bugger's fault," said Annan, nodding at Cardock.

Caedmon squinted at him. "Who're you? Tenderneck, obviously. You look . . . familiar."

Nolan darted closer. "He's Taranis' father," he hissed.

Caedmon blinked. "His father? Here?"

"Yes, he just came—"

"He was Arren Cardockson!" one of the other slaves shouted suddenly. "Tell him, you old bastard. That Taranis was lyin' about his name. He was Arren Cardockson, and *you're* Cardock, his father."

Caedmon had become very still. "Is this true?" he said sharply. "Or are ye playin' some prank? I warn ye, tenderneck, I am not to be trifled with, an' I do not take kindly t'being lied to or played with. What's this nonsense ye're spewin'? Out with it."

Cardock watched the older man as he spoke, his mind racing. But one look at Caedmon's unbending expression told him there was no point in trying to lie. "It's true," he said, so quietly the others barely heard him. "I am Cardock Skandarson of Eagleholm. I was a freed slave and I lived in Idun with my wife, Annir. Arenadd was our only son. Our only child." He shuddered, and tears started to trickle down his face.

Caedmon listened closely. "You're admitting that?"

"He's dead," Cardock mumbled. "Why lie?"

"Why are ye here, then?" said Caedmon. "How'd ye get to be here?"

"We were captured," said Cardock. "In Norton. Waiting for him to meet us. Erian the Bastard forced us to tell him what we knew, and then he sold us. I don't know where Annir is."

Caedmon said nothing. If he was shocked he hid it well; he stood very still, wearing a frown, apparently deep in thought.

"He's got t'be tellin' the truth," Nolan put in. "Look at him. Taranis—*Arren* looked just like him. They got to be father an' son. Anyway, why would he lie about somethin' like that? It doesn't make no sense."

Finally Caedmon nodded. "Right. I believe you. Now listen"—he turned to look around at the others—"an' I want *all* of you to listen." He paused to make sure he had their full attention. "We're tellin' nobody about this, understand? *Nobody*. Not even the men in the other dorms. Nobody."

"Why?" someone demanded.

"Because I say so," Caedmon snapped. "Cardock's one of ours now, an' he's had a hard time. How would ye feel if you'd lost yer only son an' yer wife as well? So we're gonna help him. It doesn't matter if Taranis was Arren Cardockson or if he was the High Priestess of Amoran. He's dead now. Cardock is one of us, an' we stick together, so I expect ye to treat him like one of ye. If anyone even *talks* about going and ratting him out, I swear by the Night God's eye that man will suffer for it. An' believe me when I say I have the power to make that happen. Cross me, an' ye'll pay." He glared at them. "That clear enough for yer?"

Nobody spoke.

"I said, is that clear?" said Caedmon.

"I reckon so, Caedmon," said Nolan.

There was a general mumbling and nodding from the others.

"Right, then," said Caedmon. He nodded to Cardock. "Ye've nothin' to fear. They won't lay a hand on ye. Not unless they want to lose it."

Cardock smiled shakily as the others wandered off. "Thank you, Caedmon."

"It's nothin'," said Caedmon. "Now you just sit down an' try an' rest. I'll get someone t'bring ye some food. Y'need plenty to eat."

In a kind of trance, Cardock allowed himself to be led to a comparatively private corner behind some hammocks and accepted the food he was given. He stirred it listlessly, feeling as if there were a huge void inside him, a hole where his son had been.

Nolan and Annan stayed with him, curious and concerned. Caedmon stayed, too. Others hovered close by, obviously wanting to come closer and ask questions but loath to do so while Caedmon was there.

"Eat," the old man urged. "I know ye ain't hungry, but ye've got t'eat. Wastin' away won't help nobody."

Cardock managed a few spoonfuls. He sought for something to say, but nothing came. His mind was a blank.

"I still don't believe this," Annan said at last. "I mean, *Arren Cardockson*? Him? Here?"

"I always thought he was odd, y'know," said Nolan. "I liked him, but I always thought there was something—"

"I know," said Annan. "There was somethin' not quite right about him. He always looked so . . . I dunno. Just not right somehow."

"I heard him talkin' in his sleep," said Nolan. "Did you?"

"Of course I did," said Annan. "Everyone did. Madog said he heard him speakin' some different language once. All sorts of clicks an' trills an' things. I told him he was talkin' out his nethereye, but—"

"Griffish?" said Nolan. "Y'think maybe it was griffish?"

"Maybe, who knows? It scared me, though," Annan added. "What you said about the stuff he shouted before—" He broke off awkwardly. "I heard him say things like that in his sleep. 'Help me, I'm falling,' over an' over again."

"I knew about that," said Nolan. "He was scared of heights. Whenever we was at the quarry an' went over that bit where there's that drop, he'd go all pale."

"He was afraid of heights," said Cardock. His voice sounded flat and distant, as if he had become detached from it somehow. "Ever since he was a boy. He loved to climb. All the time. But someone, someone, someone . . ." He could hear himself starting to wander now. "Someone pushed him off a roof. He was twelve. Broke his arm. I asked him over and over to tell me who did it, but he never said. After that he was always frightened. Even stairs made him nervous. He hated heights, and he lived right at the edge of the city. I kept telling him to move, but he wouldn't; he said Eluna wouldn't let him."

Caedmon leant forward and touched him on the shoulder. "Hush. Calm down. Ye're all right. Here, just have some water."

Nolan and Annan exchanged glances.

"I can't believe it that he was a murderer," said Nolan. "He didn't—well, he didn't *feel* like a murderer. He was too nice."

"Kind." Annan nodded. "Good sense of humour. I still haven't told Torc he's dead. The boy loved him like a brother."

"I liked him," said Caedmon. "No matter what they say he did, I thought he was a good man. Good mind, well spoken, respectful. A good friend. Always did his share an' never complained or made trouble."

"He was a good boy," Cardock's faraway voice mumbled.

"Yes." Caedmon tugged gently at his arm. "Come on. I should take ye back to yer dorm now before people start askin' questions. C'mon."

Cardock heaved a sigh and got up. "Yes, I need to be alone for a while."

As he started to leave the room with Caedmon, Nolan caught up with him and touched his arm. "Listen," he said, "I'm sorry if we was unkind to you before. Your son was a good friend to me. So, for his sake, I'll be a friend t'you to, if yer want."

Cardock looked at him, taking in his rough, honest face, and smiled sadly. "Thanks, Nolan. I'd like that."

Caedmon escorted him back to his dormitory and guided him to a hammock, roughly ordering its occupant to find a spot on the floor. Cardock thanked him and lay back in the hammock while the others around him got ready for bed, their voices low and unconcerned. Even content.

Eventually the lights were snuffed out, and darkness closed in. Cardock lay in silence, not really aware of his surroundings, staring fixedly at the ceiling.

Part of him wanted to cry, but his tears had dried up, leaving him feeling dead inside. Part of him wanted to curse or to scream, but he had no energy for either. Besides, what was the point? And part of him wanted to pray, but the words wouldn't come to him. What could he possibly say? What could he say that would help him now? Nothing, nothing.

Helpless anger filled him. There was no window here, but he could see the moon in his mind's eye: the great silver orb that he had prayed to and kept faith in all his life. *Curse you,* he thought. *Curse you. You gave me back my son and then took him away again. He was all I had left, and you took him.* Curse *you!*

He lay awake like that for a long time, mourning his son and cursing the gods and fate for taking him away along with Annir and everything else. He cursed the Night God, he cursed Gryphus, and most of all he cursed Erian. The sneering brat with the glittering sword and the velvet tunics looted from another man's wardrobe, whose partner liked to snap and hiss at the slaves and watch them cringe in fear. Erian the Blue, he liked to call himself. Erian Rannagonson. *Lord* Erian. Erian the Bastard. Erian the Brat. Erian, who wanted nothing more than to see Arenadd tortured to death.

You'll never get him now, Cardock thought. *He's out of your reach.*

It was cold comfort. Outside, the rain fell harder than ever.

A storm was building, and the slave-house creaked and rattled in the gale. Thunder rumbled somewhere, low and threatening.

Eventually, Cardock slid into an exhausted, uneasy sleep. He dreamt of Arenadd as he had been as a child: six years old, his black hair neatly combed in spite of his rough clothing. He was playing alone, as he always did, with the little leather griffin his mother had made for him, prattling away to it as if it were alive. The other children, though, were never happy to let him keep to himself, and they wandered over in the hopes of finding something to taunt him with. *Blackrobe,* one yelled at him. *You're a blackrobe. Da said so.*

Arenadd turned to face them. *I'm a griffiner,* he told them haughtily. *You've got to bow and say "sir" when you talk to me.*

That's not a real *griffin,* a little girl shouted.

My griffin's real, said Arenadd. *If you don't leave me alone she'll bite you.*

Cardock knew what had happened after that. The other children, provoked, had begun to throw rocks and handfuls of mud at him until he had run back home in tears. But now the stones were sharp and drew blood when they hit him, and when he cried out it was a man's voice and full of mortal pain.

Someone shook Cardock awake. He stirred and moaned. "What?"

"Quiet," a voice hissed. "Come on, get up an' keep quiet."

Tired and disorientated, Cardock climbed out of the hammock and found his feet.

It was quite dark in the room; the torches on the walls hadn't been re-lit, and the fire had burned low. The gale was rattling the shingles on the roof. Even though it had to still be nighttime, he could hear the others stirring around him: soft thumps and mutterings and the rustle of cloth. As his eyes adjusted he could see their shapes by the dim light of the coals under the stew pot; it looked as if everyone was up now and getting dressed.

Cardock was still wearing the rough robe they'd given him and had forgotten to take off his boots, so he shuffled over to the nearest silhouette. "What's going on?" he asked, trying to keep his voice low.

"I dunno. We've just got to get dressed an' go out into t'corridor like normal."

Cardock rubbed his eyes; they were sore. "In the middle of the night?"

Someone shoved him in the back. "Move it, you, I can't see where I'm goin'."

Others were making for the doorway, and Cardock resignedly followed them. There was very little point in trying to find out what was going on, and if he was slow he would be in trouble. But he wondered vaguely why they were being made to get up at this time of night. What sort of work could anyone do in the dark, and while it was windy and raining as well?

The corridor was already jam-packed with slaves, all talking in low voices. They were as orderly as always, but there was an undercurrent of fear and bewilderment there as well. Cardock could hear them questioning each other, apparently all as confused as he was.

There was light coming from one end of the corridor, the opposite end to where the gate to the guardroom was. And there seemed to be a draught coming from the same direction as the light, he realised. Odd.

Someone jostled him. Cardock shoved back irritably, but before he could say anything there was a sudden disturbance among the crowd.

"Cardock!" someone called quietly.

The cry was taken up by others. "Cardock? Where's Cardock? Someone bring him forward, hurry!"

Cardock started to push his way in the direction of the voices. "I'm here," he said. "I'm Cardock. Hello? What's going on?"

Someone grabbed him by the arm. "There y'are. Quick, come with me."

"Caedmon. What's going on? What do they want me for?"

Caedmon's face, only semi-visible in the gloom, looked pale. "He asked for ye. C'mon. Out of the way! Let us through, damn ye!"

The two of them made an awkward scramble between the mass of bodies, making for the light at the end of the corridor. As they drew closer to it, Cardock began to hear other things being said around him.

"Griffin!"

"He's got a griffin."

"It's him, I know it's him."

Caedmon got through first and came to a halt. "I've got him, sir."

Cardock shoved his way through a knot of people, and the first thing he saw was the hole. Something had torn away a great chunk of the wall at the end of the corridor, leaving a gaping hole edged with splinters, on the other side of which something huge lurked—and then someone rushed forward and was embracing him, someone tall and bony and soaking wet.

"Dad! It's me. I'm back. I'm all right!"

Cardock's heart seemed to slow in its beating. "Arren," he gasped. "Arren, is that—?"

Arren let go of him and regarded him carefully by the light of the torch he had handed to Caedmon. "Gods. You look terrible. Have they been starving you?"

Cardock choked. "*Arren*. Arren! You're not—but they said you were—"

Arren clasped his shoulder. "It's okay. Calm down. I'm fine."

He did not look fine. Cardock saw that straight away. His face was deathly pale, his eyes hollow. His beard was no longer neatly pointed but a tangled mess of dirt-encrusted bristles, and the hair he had taken so much pride in was crusted with mud. But he was alive.

Caedmon was watching them. "So ye really *are* his father," he breathed. "And ye . . ." He regarded Arren with deep wariness.

Arren looked back impassively. "Well done, Caedmon. Trusting you was obviously the right thing to do."

"What do ye want us to do next, sir?" said Caedmon, as sharply as he dared. "I've woken everybody up and ye have yer father back as ye asked. What else d'ye intend t'do, may I ask?"

Arren nodded. "It's time to act. Bring everyone wearing irons to the front, and we'll be ready."

"Ready for *what*?" said Caedmon. "What are ye doing, sir?"

Arren smiled very slightly. "I'm stealing you."

"What?" said Caedmon. "Sir?"

"You and your friends are slaves, aren't you?" said Arren. "Property. Property can be stolen, and that's what I'm doing. Now move. We don't want to be kept waiting."

Caedmon bowed stiffly. "Yes . . . sir."

Cardock went to his son's side and took him by the elbow. Arren gave him a concerned look. "Dad, are you all right?"

"They told me you were dead," Cardock said softly.

"I thought they would have. I'm sorry, Dad."

"It's not your fault," said Cardock. "I'm just—I'm so happy you're alive. I thought I'd lost you again."

Arren winced. "I'm not going anywhere, Dad. And I'm not leaving you again. That's a promise."

"But how can this be?" said Cardock. "How did you—?"

"It was an escape. I was only—" Arren stiffened. "Don't move. He's coming."

"What? Who's—?"

Arren started to back away from him, moving very slowly. *"Don't move."*

Cardock turned to see what was going on, and his stomach lurched. Something—a big, shadowy something, the same thing he had glimpsed before—was coming toward the hole in the wall. Arren moved out into the open again to meet it, and several of the slaves nearest to the hole cried out and threw themselves backward as the monstrous griffin appeared from out of the night. A dark griffin, his silver-feathered head capped with black, his hindquarters the colour of jet, big mottled wings opening slightly as he walked.

"Darkheart," Cardock groaned.

The griffin stopped and sat on his haunches close to Arren, his silver eyes glaring at the slaves inside the building. But he made no move, and Arren went closer and touched his shoulder, saying something to him in griffish. The griffin replied, and the two of them conversed briefly.

Arren turned back to look through the hole. "Where's Caedmon?" he asked. "Tell him to hurry up! Skandar won't wait forever, and if guards come . . ."

Cardock looked over his shoulder, but it was too dark to tell what was going on back in the corridor. He stepped through the hole and toward his son instead. Instantly the griffin tensed, his tail lashing.

Arren touched the beast again. *"Kri oo,"* he said urgently. *"Kri oo kra ae ee a."* He punctuated it with a few sharp clicks of the teeth, mimicking the sound a griffin made with its beak.

The griffin rasped something back. Cardock couldn't tell if it was hostile or not; all griffish sounded angry to him. "Arren, what are you doing?" he said. "That griffin—"

"This is Skandar," said Arren, turning to him. "He's my—well, we're friends."

"Skandar?" Cardock repeated.

"I called him that." Arren looked slightly nervous. "He didn't have a proper name before then. Don't worry. I told him you're my father." He looked past Cardock. "Oh, thank gods."

Caedmon was back. The old man came forward, leading a group of four men who were weighed down by leg-irons.

Arren nodded to them. "Right," he said. "You four, sit down on the edge of the hole. This shouldn't take too long."

The four men, however, were gaping at the griffin. "What in the gods' names?" one said.

Arren stepped forward. *"Do it!"* he snarled, his voice suddenly full of cold command. "I am a griffiner, and I am giving you an order!"

They obeyed hastily. Once they were seated, Arren took a hammer and chisel from his belt and quickly broke the chains. "Good," he said once this was done. "You'll be able to walk now. Caedmon, give the order. We're walking out of here. All of us. Tell them to stay in a column, and no straggling. The weaker ones should stay at the front. Tell everyone to stay as far away from Skandar as possible. If anyone touches him or comes too close to either of us without permission they will be attacked and probably killed. I mean it. I can't control him, and he's perfectly capable of killing people if he wants to. Understood?"

"Yes, sir," said Caedmon.

"Good. D— Cardock, you'll stay with me."

"Sir," said Caedmon. "What if the guards come after us, sir? It's a miracle they ain't been alerted already."

"They're not coming after us," Arren said flatly. "Trust me. And if anyone *does* come after us, Skandar and I know how to deal with our enemies. Now move."

"Yes, sir."

Caedmon turned and began to relay the orders to the slaves. They—used to doing as they were told—formed up and filed out of the slave-house. Arren began to walk away with the griffin beside him, and they followed at a safe distance. At first Cardock kept well back, too, but Arren silently gestured at him to join him, which he very nervously did, keeping Arren between himself and the griffin, which was watching him menacingly.

It seemed Arren had everything carefully planned out. He led the slaves directly to the little stone building where the tools were kept. The door had been broken down, and he commanded everyone to go in and take something—an axe, shovel, pick, chisel or hammer—anything sharp or heavy. There were some sacks of potatoes there, too, and he told them to take those as well before leading them away to the wall. They passed through a gap in it and walked into the wilderness beyond, the rain still pouring down.

Cardock managed to keep pace with his son. "Arren, where are we going?"

"North," Arren answered briefly. "To Tara."

"But *why*? And why take everyone?"

To Cardock's surprise, Arren sniggered. "Aren't you proud of me, Dad? I don't think I've ever done anything this brilliant before. I really don't."

"Brilliant?" Cardock snapped. "What's brilliant about this?" He paused to untangle his robe from a sodden bush. "This— *argh!* Damn it! This is madness, not brilliance!"

"Well, thank you," Arren snapped back. "I'm sure some gratitude for getting you out of there was too much to expect."

"Getting me out, maybe," said Cardock. "But taking *everybody*? How in the gods' names do you expect to get them all to Tara?"

"They've got legs. They can walk."

"And what about food?"

"There's farmland most of the way there," said Arren. "We'll take what we need. And we can forage. I've learnt a few things about that over the last few months, you know."

"Foraging?" said Cardock. "Forget foraging! We're not going to get more than two miles. The moment they realise we're gone, they'll send people after us. Men on horseback. We'll be captured or slaughtered."

Arren laughed. "Captured? Slaughtered? Listen to yourself, Dad. There were nearly a hundred slaves in that building, and that was before you came with the others. I counted them myself. All strong, fit men, used to obeying orders, and all carrying something sharp. It'd take at least a hundred more to capture this lot. And in case you haven't noticed, you have me with you. And I have Skandar. If anyone tries to lay a hand on me, he's dead. You *know* what Skandar can do. You saw him in the Arena yourself."

"Arren, what are you doing with that griffin?" said Cardock. "That *is* Darkheart, isn't it?"

"He used to be."

Cardock eyed the massive shape of the griffin, which had pulled ahead of them and was shouldering his way through a soap-bush thicket. "Why is he helping you?"

He listened to Arren's explanation. "I don't like this," he said once Arren was done. "That's a wild griffin there, not a city one. A man-eater. He killed Eluna, didn't he?"

"Accidentally," said Arren. "He saved my life, Dad. I trust him."

"But you can't control him," said Cardock. "What if he decides to attack?"

"Control?" said Arren. "Dad, nobody controls a griffin. I didn't have any control over Eluna. Griffins make their own decisions. They'll go along with yours if they agree with you or if they don't care, but the rest of the time—"

"So, what you're saying is that if he attacks, you can't do anything."

"I can put myself in the way if I have to. But look, griffins don't attack unless they're hungry or if they feel threatened. Or if there's a female in heat, which doesn't apply here. As long as Skandar stays well fed and no-one does anything to provoke him, we're fine."

"Well fed?" said Cardock. "On *what*, exactly? He's a man-eater!"

"Not any more." Arren tried not to think of the men Skandar had slaughtered and eaten by the spirit cave. "There's no *meat* on a human, Dad. He'd only do that if he was starving. There are cows and sheep here for him to eat. And we've been travelling together for months and he hasn't eaten me yet. It's fine, I swear."

"I hope so," Cardock muttered.

17

An Entourage

At dawn the slaves were still marching. They had spent much of the night struggling over a series of forested hills, in pouring rain all the while, rain that was still falling by the time morning came.

The light of the rising sun revealed a miserable and exhausted group moving in a column but now showing definite signs of flagging. Everyone was soaked, and they had collected plenty of cuts and bruises along the way. But nobody was complaining or showing any signs of rebellion. Arren, noticing this, was grimly pleased. Slaves didn't complain, and they didn't rebel. They did as they were told and nothing more.

Caedmon was still among the forerunners of the group and looked surprisingly strong and alert given his age.

"How are they?" Arren asked him. "How much longer can they keep going?"

"Quite a bit longer, sir," said Caedmon.

"Good," said Arren. "We need to get as far as we can as fast as we can. They'll find us impossible to track through all these hills, especially with the rain. Is Torc all right?"

"He looks well enough to me, sir," said Caedmon. "Nolan's looking after him."

Arren nodded. "You should probably get them to come closer to the front so I can keep an eye on him."

"Yes, sir."

Arren watched the old man leave, and shook his head. It was strange to have people obeying him so unquestioningly. Even back at Eagleholm during his time as an official he'd grown used to being questioned when he gave orders, but this was different. No questions, no arguments. He was completely in control.

Cardock had been watching. "You still haven't told me why you . . . stole them," he said.

Arren shook himself. "Oh, it's simple enough."

"What is?"

"Look at this, Dad." Arren held out his hand. "See this?"

Cardock saw the brand, and hissed to himself. "Gods damn them."

"They flogged me, too," Arren said calmly. "I was there in Herbstitt for over a month, wearing those damned leg-irons and working from dawn until dusk. After I got out of there, I had to rescue you. And I wanted revenge."

"Like the revenge you took on Lord Rannagon?" said Cardock in an undertone.

"No," Arren said sharply. Too sharply. "I have no interest in killing more people. One was too many. No, revenge doesn't have to be murder. They made me a slave because they were short on slaves, so I went back and stole the lot of them. They'll never finish that wall now."

"What about the guards?" said Cardock. "How did you stop them catching you?"

Arren scratched his ear. "There were only two in the guard-room, and both of them were asleep. I picked the lock, snuck in and tied them both up. They never saw me."

Cardock relaxed. "Thank gods. I thought you'd—"

"Killed them?" Arren was giving him a furious look. "You thought I'd killed them?"

"No. Calm down, I wasn't—"

Arren looked away. "Well, what else should I expect you to think? Now that I'm—after what I—I suppose I should get used to it."

Cardock opened his mouth to speak but found himself unable to. A painful lump had formed in his chest, although what emotion it was made from he didn't know.

Arren looked at him again, and his expression was so full of fear and guilt and longing that for an instant it was as if the years had fallen away and he was a small boy again, looking to his father for punishment or approval. "Do you hate me, Dad?" he asked quietly. "Please, just tell me. Do you hate me for what I did? And Mum, what does she think?"

Cardock couldn't bear to look at him any more. "I don't know what to think, Arren."

* * *

The march continued well into the day, through endless rainy forest. Arren led them in a roundabout direction, weaving here and there, climbing over some hills and going around others, and made them wade through several streams. The reason was obvious: he was making sure that when people inevitably came after them, they would be extremely difficult to track. The slaves trudged on until the sun was high overhead and the rain began to thin. By then the pace had slowed considerably, and Caedmon and one or two of the weaker ones were showing signs of exhaustion. Arren, seeing this, finally called a halt.

They settled down in a rocky gorge, taking shelter among a series of large overhangs. Arren managed to find some dry wood and lit a fire with the help of a tinderbox stolen from the guardroom. Skandar curled up close to it to dry his feathers, while his partner sat down by his flank. The griffin looked annoyed and kept making quick jerking motions with his head, and everybody made a wide berth around him.

Arren, apparently unconcerned, summoned Caedmon again. "I'm sorry to bother you now," he said, "but I need you to go and bring a few people here to see me."

Caedmon stood straight, supporting himself with his stick, all respectful attention. "Yes, sir. Who do ye want me to bring, sir?" He paused. "If ye prefer, I can call ye 'my lord.'"

Arren sighed. "'Sir' will be fine. Bring me Nolan, Annan, Prydwen, Olwydd and both of their friends who were wearing irons. And bring Torc as well."

"Yes, sir."

Once he had gone, Arren rubbed his hands over his face and sighed. "Gods, I'm starving. I'd give anything for some roasted goat right now."

Cardock was sitting on the opposite side of the fire, well away from Skandar. "I could put some of those potatoes in the fire, maybe."

"Not right now," said Arren. "We need to try and make the food last. Later on I'll take some men and go foraging. And Skandar will want to hunt once he's rested."

Cardock eyed the griffin. "You named him after my father."

"Yes. Your grandfather, really." Arren looked slightly

bashful. "Skandar here is a great warrior, just like you said your grandfather was. I thought the name was right for him."

"He's really your friend, is he?" said Cardock.

"I think so. Haven't you ever wondered why he didn't kill me in the Arena? It wasn't because of anything I did. He wanted my help, so I gave it." *I sacrificed my life to set him free. If I hadn't gone back, I would never have died. And he knows it.*

"He chose you?" said Cardock. "Like Eluna did?"

"He believes I have magical powers," said Arren. "He's— he's like a big child, really."

Cardock looked at the massive beast that was now nibbling at the skin between its toes. Each toe was as long as his arm, and considerably thicker, tipped with a curved talon the size of a dagger. "A child," he said flatly.

"Yes. He doesn't know anything about human beings; he doesn't understand magic, not even his own. I speak griffish better than he does. As far as he's concerned, I know everything and can do anything. Not that that stops him from bullying me and taking my food when he wants to."

"Aren't you afraid of him, though?" said Cardock. "I saw everything that happened in the Arena. He nearly killed you!"

"Not really. He only disarmed me and pinned me down. Eluna did that to me a few times, you know. Not when anyone was watching, though."

"*Eluna* did that? When?"

"Every now and then," Arren said carelessly. "When she was angry or had a point to make. Griffins are violent creatures, Dad. They like to dominate; it's their way. But yes, I am afraid of Skandar. Not as much as I used to be, but a little. That's how it is. No matter what happens, we're in this together."

This was said with a certain amount of pride, and Cardock shook his head ruefully. "You keep strange company, Arenadd."

Arren looked over at the slaves sitting huddled on the sandy floor of the overhang, some sleeping, others trying to wring the water out of their robes. "True. Ah, here they come."

Caedmon returned, leading the men he'd been sent to find. Torc was keeping close to Nolan, looking pale and exhausted.

Arren stood up to receive them. "There you are. Come on, come closer and sit down. Don't worry about Skandar; he's too sleepy to snap at you."

They came closer, all watching him.

"Sit down," Arren said again. "You, too, Caedmon. I want to talk to you as well. Go on."

"Yes, sir," said Caedmon. He looked to the others. "Ye heard him; sit down."

They did, huddling with Cardock, well away from Skandar. Arren stepped around the fire to confront them. Behind him, Skandar stirred and raised his head to watch them, the tip of his tail twitching ever so slightly.

Arren sighed and ran his fingers through his hair. "I'm very sorry about all this. I know you're all tired and cold and probably hungry, but I did what I thought was best."

"Yes, sir," said Nolan. "We understand, sir." He was very pale.

They're afraid of me, Arren realised. "Now listen," he said. "I brought you all here because I trust you. You, Nolan, and you, Annan, and you, Torc—I counted you as my friends before, and I hope I still can. And you, Olwydd and Prydwen— it's obvious to me that you're both tough and resourceful men, and willing to fight." He eyed the remaining two Northerners, both still wearing the remains of the leg-irons. "And you two. I've seen you, but I don't think we've been introduced. What are your names?"

They shifted nervously.

"Garnoc, sir," said one, a heavyset man with curly hair.

"Dafydd, sir," said his slimmer companion.

"Pleased to meet you," said Arren. "I'm Arenadd Taranisäii, and my friend is Skandar. And this is my father, Cardock."

"So ye really are him," Olwydd mumbled. "Ye're Arren Cardockson."

"Yes," said Arren. "Arenadd will be fine. Now tell me"— he started to pace back and forth—"I'm going home, because that's the only place I can go, and I intend to take you with me. I intend to take *all* of you. If you want to come."

There was silence from the slaves. *They're not used to think- ing for themselves,* Arren thought unhappily.

"I'll go," Prydwen said at last. "I want to, sir."

"And so do I," said Olwydd. "I'll follow ye, sir."

"So shall we," said Garnoc.

"Aye," said Dafydd. "Tara's home for us, sir. Returnin' there's all we want."

"Good," said Arren. "Then you'll come. What about you, Caedmon?"

Caedmon looked back at him, stone-faced. "We'll be comin' to Tara with you, sir. All of us."

"I'm not going to accept that," said Arren. Everyone must make their own decision."

"No, sir," said Caedmon. "They're going to follow ye, sir."

"You can't make the choice for them, Caedmon," said Arren.

"I haven't, sir. Ye did that, sir. Ye stole them; they're yer property now, sir. They'll do what ye tell them to do. Sir."

Arren sighed. "We'll see. So"—he turned to the four Northerners again—"I can rely on you, then, can I?"

"Yes, sir," said Olwydd. "Me, anyway."

The other three nodded.

"Good," said Arren. He put his hand behind him and pulled a short sword out of his belt. He held it out to Olwydd, hilt first. "Here. This is for you."

Olwydd took it very carefully. "This is . . . ?"

"Yours, yes. I took it from the guardroom. I suppose you know how to use it?"

"No, sir. I've never handled a sword before, sir. In Tara it's against the law for us to own them, sir."

"Well, you own one now," said Arren. "Take good care of it. If we get into trouble, use it." He took a second sword from his belt and offered it to Prydwen. "Yours."

Prydwen was quicker to take it than his friend. "Thank ye, sir!"

"You're welcome." Arren had a third sword, which he gave to Dafydd, and a fourth, which he kept for himself. "I'm afraid I don't have one for you," he told Garnoc. "But an axe will probably do the job as well. See if you can find one. It's going to be a long journey, and I intend to keep all of you close by me. I'll need your help to keep everyone together, and if we're attacked, it'll be up to you to protect us."

The four of them sat a little straighter, eyes shining with pride. "Yes, sir," said Olwydd.

Prydwen tested the edge of his new blade. "But what if we're attacked by griffiners, sir? What do we do then?"

"If we're found by griffiners, then you leave them to us," Arren said grimly. "Skandar and I will fight them."

"Are ye sure, sir?" said Olwydd.

Arren's black eyes were as cold as death. "I've killed one griffiner, Olwydd. I can kill another."

Olwydd backed away slightly. "Yes, sir."

"As for you—" Arren turned to look at the others. "Caedmon, I'll need you to help organise everyone. You know how to do that, I'm sure. And if you ever have any advice to offer me, offer it. I don't want to make a mistake and then find out you could have stopped me doing it, understand?"

"Yes, sir," said Caedmon. "I can do that, sir."

"Good. Nolan, you and Torc and Annan are in charge of food. You'll keep an eye on everything we're carrying and make sure everyone gets their fair share."

"Yes, sir."

Arren nodded. "That's everything. You can go now. Get some rest. If anyone wants their own fire, they're welcome to light it from mine." As they began to depart, he said, "You stay behind a moment, Nolan."

Once the others had gone, Arren went to his friend and touched him on the shoulder. "Nolan. Look at me. Please."

Nolan did. "What is it, sir?"

Arren could feel him trembling. "I'm not going to hurt you. Look, Nolan . . ." He hesitated, not knowing what he could possibly say. "I didn't mean to scare you."

"It's all right, sir," said Nolan. He was sweating.

"No, it's not," said Arren. "You're terrified. Is it because—look, I'm sorry I lied to you, but I had to. If any of them had known who I was . . ."

"I understand, sir."

"Please, call me Arenadd. I have a name, you know."

"Yes, s— Arenadd."

"That's better. Nolan, just tell me what you're thinking, would you? I'm not going to have you flogged if you talk to me like a human being."

Nolan stared at the ground. "Can I go now, please, sir?"

"No. Stop that. Look me in the face."

Nolan did. "I don't want—"

"Out with it," Arren commanded.

"You were dead," Nolan said at last. "You were dead."

"No." Arren gripped his shoulder. "Nolan, I wasn't dead."

"You . . . ?"

"I was faking." He'd spent most of the trek rehearsing these words and launched into them now. "Understand? It was all an act. To get me out of there. They took the irons off so I could run."

"I buried you," said Nolan.

"Not very deeply. I dug myself out again after you'd gone." Arren smiled weakly. "I heard you say the words for me. You didn't have to do that. Thank you."

"Everyone's got to have the words," Nolan mumbled. "So the gods come for them."

"Yes." *When you die, it will be alone. No-one will mourn.* "You were a good friend, Nolan. I didn't come back just for my father; I came back for you, too."

Nolan appeared to have calmed a little. "You did?"

"Yes." Arren let go of him. "I really am all right, Nolan, I swear. I think I'll be coughing up dirt for a week, but I'll be fine."

Nolan gave a shaky laugh. "I really believed you were dead, you know. I even slapped you to try an' wake you up, but you never moved."

"Nolan, when it comes to playing dead, I'm one of the best," said Arren. "Trust me on this. Now, I probably shouldn't keep you up any longer. Go and get some rest. We've got a long journey ahead of us."

Finally, Nolan grinned the gap-toothed grin Arren knew so well. "Yes, s— Arenadd. I will."

When he was a boy, Erian had dreamt of griffins. They had been in his fantasies, night and day. And, like all young people who dreamt of something, he had idolised them, imagining they could go anywhere and do anything. Flying all day with a rider on their back sounded like nothing.

But it wasn't. Erian had his father's solid build and was well-muscled, and the ornamented sword added significantly to his weight. So did his bow and arrows. Senneck had allowed him to bring them, though she had sneeringly suggested that he have the sword melted down and made into a set of bracelets. Erian had held firm on that issue. He loved his jewelled sword, and not even Senneck's threats and contempt could make him get rid of it. He hadn't admitted it to her because he knew exactly how she would react, but he had secretly named it Bloodpride. He knew it was childish, but he didn't care. Senneck wouldn't understand. Nobody would.

There was no way Senneck, who was light and slender by

griffish standards, could fly all day with him on her back along with Bloodpride. It meant that their progress northward had been slower than he had expected.

Still, they were getting there. Immediately after the argument by the archery butts, he'd sent a messenger to the departing slavers to instruct them to send the woman Annir to Malvern at once, and then she and Erian had left Herbstitt. Erian hated the idea of having Annir with him at Malvern. She had her son's eyes, and she hated him. He'd have to keep a close eye on her, and the prospect of doing so upset him. Nobody had ever wanted to kill him before, and nobody had ever truly hated him, either. Not in the way Annir and her husband did. It was a new experience for him, one that bothered him more than he would admit, certainly to Senneck. The prospect of seeing her angry with him again terrified him.

Their journey had progressed in stages since then. They would fly for half a day, sometimes a little longer, and take shelter in the homes of farmers and other common people. They were more than happy to help; the common people held griffiners in deep awe. It was thought of as extremely lucky to have a griffin in your home. On the farm where he had grown up, Erian had known a man living nearby who owned a feather he claimed came from a griffin. Everyone who visited him would ask to see it and perhaps touch it, and there were stories of miraculous cures and wonderful good fortune coming as a result. Perhaps it was true.

After a week or so of this, they had reached the Northgate Mountains, and then the real test of endurance began. There was a pass leading clear through to the other side, with a road weaving through it used by traders and other ordinary travellers, but it was by no means easy to navigate. Senneck flew above it, keeping low. Too high and it would be dangerously cold. The vegetation was sparse here and the landscape exposed. When they stopped at night, Erian had to lie down against Senneck's flank and shelter under her wing. Even so, the cold was nearly crippling at times. He had had no idea it could be like this. It was only early autumn, and yet here it felt at least as cold as midwinter had at home. Erian wondered grimly how much worse it would be when they reached Malvern.

It took them four days to pass through the mountains, and it grew colder all the while. Fortunately they didn't have to camp in the open every night: on the third day they arrived at Guard's Post, an old fortress built centuries ago, during the great war against the Northerners. Once, guarding the pass had been a matter of life and death. Now, though, Guard's Post was thinly manned and had fallen into disrepair. Only a handful of men now lived there, opening the gates to let travellers through. But their captain assured Erian and Senneck that Lady Elkin had sent word that she was going to appoint two of her griffiners to take up residence in the fort very soon.

"A very sensible move, too, my lord," he added. "If it comes to war, like."

Erian nodded. "Do you know if she's planning to send troops into Eagleholm?"

"I don't know, my lord." The captain gave an ingratiating smile. "But if she does, I'm sure she'll welcome your help, my lord. A strong-looking young fellow like yourself—"

"That's enough," Erian snapped. "You're forgetting your place, captain."

The man's smile froze. "Yes, my lord. I'm sorry, my lord. Come with me and I'll show you to your quarters, my lord."

Erian couldn't resist glancing quickly at Senneck as they were led away. She looked impassively back, but he knew she was pleased with him.

Guard's Post had quarters for several griffins and griffiners, a relic of a time when ten of them had lived there at all times. Erian and Senneck were taken to one; it was a little run-down but had obviously been cleaned out and refurnished recently. There was a bed and a writing desk for Erian, and for Senneck an enormous sleeping mat made from moth-eaten but well-padded velvet.

"Ridiculous," she muttered and tore it open with her beak. "Straw would be far more comfortable. Do they think I am a cat?"

Erian stretched out on the bed. "Still, it's better than sleeping in the open, isn't it?"

"Sufficiently. Bring me food."

"Of course, but couldn't I just—?"

"Now," said Senneck. She laid her head on her talons and closed her eyes. "Venison, if you can find it. And water."

Erian bit back a sigh and strode out of the room. He'd grown used to Senneck doing this: even when there were servants or other people ready and willing to bring her food, she preferred him to do it himself. When he had complained, she had fixed him with an icy stare and said, "I carry you. I protect you. I give you your status. And this is the thanks I receive?"

Since then he had never even thought of protesting again, but, he comforted himself, at least this was nothing unusual. He'd known about it before he'd become a griffiner. Griffins were notoriously selfish and demanding creatures. They expected the best of everything, and if it wasn't vital for them to do something for themselves, they wouldn't do it. Many of those partnered with high officials in cities spent most of their time eating and sleeping and enjoying all the luxuries their humans could provide, and Erian knew well enough that Senneck resented his inability to do the same for her.

And she was right, he thought as he made for the kitchens. Under the circumstances, bringing her some food was a very small price to pay.

This time, however, it proved too much. There was no fresh meat in the kitchens or in the stores. The best he could find was a side of salted beef and some cheese. He carried those up to Senneck, dreading her reaction, but, thankfully, she merely gave him a steely look and ripped into the slab of meat with a little more force than was necessary.

Erian sat down on the bed and chewed listlessly at an apple. "How far do you think it is to Malvern?"

She tore the rib cage apart before she replied.

"Another day should be enough to take us out of these accursed mountains. Beyond that is farmland. I do not know exactly how long it will take to reach Malvern from there, but the travelling should be easier."

"Thank Gryphus," Erian mumbled.

They spent the rest of that day resting and left the next day at dawn, without waiting to say farewell to their hosts. The captain had already been ordered to be on the lookout for the supply wagon that would be coming his way some time over the next few weeks. Erian's belongings would be on it, along with his new personal slave, and he had asked for a message to be sent to him at Malvern to inform him when it had arrived safely.

Meanwhile, Senneck flew on. Erian sat comfortably in the hollow between her neck and her wings and felt the wind whip through his hair. He was feeling oddly cheerful that day and sang to himself as they flew.

"For the traitor's reward is the blade of a sword, and Scathach the One-Eyed became . . ."

At noon they stopped to rest, and Senneck preened her feathers and then napped while Erian walked around on the barren grey road, stretching his legs and munching on some dried travel rations he had stuffed in his pocket.

A while later they were ready to go on. Paradoxically, though, Erian felt tired and listless now and passed the rest of the flight in a kind of trance, wanting to slip into a doze but forced to stay awake, leaning in harmony with Senneck as she flew.

But as evening drew closer he saw signs that they were near their destination. The mountains were growing smaller, and he could see hills and plains beyond them in the distance. Senneck's estimate had been correct; they would be there soon.

At long last, as the sun dipped close to the horizon, Senneck slowed and began her descent. She landed at the very edge of the mountains, by a strange landmark.

Erian carefully slid off her back and went to inspect it. It was a huge stone—taller than he was—standing on its end. Its pitted grey sides were covered in intricate spiral patterns, the carvings weathered by time. Picked out among them, fitted in elegantly among the swirling lines, was a ring of thirteen globes.

"The full moons of the year," said Senneck, coming up behind him. "This is a blackrobe stone."

"I didn't know they made things like this," said Erian. He ran his fingers over the carvings, marvelling at them.

"Their ancestors are said to have made many stones like this," said Senneck. "Great circles, built on hilltops. One stone for every phase of the moon. They used them as temples. On their holy nights they would sacrifice children and cover themselves in blood."

Erian shuddered. "Why?"

"They believed it gave them power," said Senneck. "The blood could change them into wolves or reveal the future. The 'Blood Moon,' they called it. Or so I have heard."

Suddenly the stone looked far less beautiful. Erian took his hand away from it. "Gods. If they'd overrun Cymria—why is this stone here, anyway?"

"The blackrobes put it here to mark the edge of their territory," said Senneck. "This is the boundary. As soon as we pass beyond it, we will be in the North."

18

Mutterings

The camp wasn't so much one camp as it was many. The slaves, one hundred and fifty men in all, had split themselves up into smaller groups, which were now scattered among the trees. Most of them had been able to light fires, each one carefully placed at the base of a tree so that the branches would dispel some of the smoke and make it less visible from a distance.

All of it had been planned and directed by Arren, or Lord Arenadd as the slaves were calling him. Cardock walked among them, watching and listening.

It had been close to a week since their escape from Herbstitt, and they were making steady progress toward the mountains. Arenadd had taken every precaution, frequently consulting Caedmon and the handful of men who had become something of an inner circle for him. Very few of the slaves at large had spoken to him directly yet, although Cardock had seen him make several attempts to put them at their ease. They remained deeply wary of him. They did as he commanded, through Caedmon, who remained a go-between as he had been back at Herbstitt, but they kept as far away from Arenadd as they could, and to a man they refused to look him in the eye.

Cardock walked among them now, listening in on their conversations. Most of them fell silent as soon as they saw him, but he picked up the gist easily enough.

"What are we gonna do when we get there? When's he gonna tell us?"

". . . wanted to say goodbye at least. Gods, I miss her."

"Look at his eyes. You can see it. Next time he's near you, look at them, proper like. He's mad."

". . . mad."

Cardock had heard talk like this dozens of times over the last few days, and it failed to surprise him now. He didn't know if Arenadd was aware of what his new followers were saying among themselves, and so far he hadn't had the will to tell him. Then again, telling him anything was next to impossible now.

Hunger made his stomach twinge, and he sighed and walked back to the largest fire, which was right at the centre of the camp. By now he knew the eight figures that sat around it: Caedmon, Nolan, Annan, Torc and the four Northerners. Olwydd and his friends had taken to carrying their new weapons everywhere with them and had formed themselves into a kind of bodyguard for their leader, who had taught them a few things about basic mêlée combat.

Cardock approached the fire on the opposite side from where they sat. Caedmon and Nolan quickly shuffled aside to make room for him.

"There you are," said Nolan. "There's some mutton left. Want a bit?"

Cardock sat down and helped himself to a chunk of the over-cooked, greasy meat, which had been cut from a sheep stolen from an unattended flock by one of the raiding parties they had formed. "Where's Arenadd?" he asked tersely.

"*Lord* Arenadd is up on the hilltop with his griffin," Olwydd told him.

"Has he had anything to eat?"

Olwydd hesitated at that. "I don't know."

Cardock looked at Torc. "Has he?"

The boy looked nervous. "No, Cardock, sir, I don't think so."

"Didn't you offer him anything?"

"Yes, sir. He didn't want it, sir."

"He didn't eat anything yesterday, either," said Cardock. "Did he?"

"No, Cardock, sir," said Torc, staring at the ground.

"Why not?" said Cardock. "Didn't you insist?"

"No, sir."

"You should have," Cardock snapped. "He ordered you to make sure every man here got his fair share of food, and that should include himself."

"Go easy on him wouldya, Cardock?" said Nolan, coming to the defence of the petrified Torc. "You think the boy could tell Lord Arenadd what to do?"

"He's your master now," said Cardock. "You can't let him starve himself. If he isn't eating, then at least tell me about it."

Nolan looked hesitant. "I see where ye're comin' from an' that, but I don't think he'd be happy if he found out we were spyin' on him, like. I knew about this one slave, told his master's secrets to someone else an' got his—"

"This isn't like that," said Cardock. "I'm his father, understand? I have the right to know."

Nolan sighed. "All right."

"Good." Cardock stood up, taking some cold mutton and a couple of apples. "I'm going to go and talk to him."

"Watch out for the griffin, sir," Torc piped up.

"I plan to," Cardock muttered, and set off up the slope of the hill where Arenadd was keeping a lookout with Skandar.

He made the short climb, slipping a little on the wet leaves. It was late evening, and the stars were beginning to come out. Soon it would be full night, but for now people and objects were visible, albeit as detailed shadows.

The top of the hill was obscured by a large rocky outcrop. Cardock paused at the edge of it to rest, panting. His neck throbbed under the collar, and he rubbed pointlessly at it. Even now the thing was a torment; a slave collar never allowed the punctured flesh beneath to heal completely, and the pain drove some slaves mad.

He pulled himself together and walked in among the stones. "Arren?" he called, not wanting to draw too much attention to himself but afraid of what might happen if he surprised him.

This was absurd, he thought. Beyond absurd. He was frightened of his own son. Or at least of the thing that followed him everywhere like a shadow.

There was no reply to his call. It was growing darker, and he sped up, watching and listening, every sense alert for a sign of the griffin that had to be lurking somewhere on the hilltop.

As he reached the crest proper, he could see the remains of a pale, watery sunset still lingering on the horizon. Just up ahead, the fading light showed him the silhouette of his son, alone, sitting in a bare patch of ground amid the outcrop.

Cardock stepped closer. Arenadd was sitting hunched, hugging his knees, something Cardock hadn't seen him do since he was a child trying to hide away from the world.

Cardock thought of calling out to him, but something held

him back. He stayed where he was, clutching the little bundle of food, just watching, his insides beginning to churn with a sense of inexplicable dread. Something was wrong.

Very slowly, he realised that Arenadd was crying. Not loudly or passionately, but with soft, half-stifled sobs that sounded as if they had been going on for a long time.

Cardock's throat felt constricted. "Arren?"

The instant he spoke, the strange stillness vanished. There was a thump and a scrabbling sound, and in a heartbeat something huge and horrible was rearing up in front of him, all feathers and talons and lashing tail, hissing and spitting like a piece of hot iron. A hard blow to the chest hurled him to the ground, the bundle of food flew out of his grasp and then the thing was on him.

Cardock couldn't even scream. He lay there, pinned to the ground by a massive set of talons, half-crushed, his chest exploding with pain. He struggled feebly, but it was hopeless. All he could do was gasp his panic, sharp stones grinding into his back as the griffin pressed down yet harder.

Skandar brought his huge beak down and sniffed at the trapped human, the air hissing through the griffin's nostrils. He recognised the scent, and relaxed. He knew this one; it wasn't dangerous and sometimes brought food. He removed his paw and went after the other scent he had caught, one he found much more inviting.

Cardock struggled upright, groaning, and was in time to see the monstrous griffin scoop the chunk of mutton out of the dirt and swallow it with a quick toss of his head. He searched the ground for more but only succeeded in finding the apples, which he flicked aside before lifting his head to glare reproachfully at Cardock.

Cardock didn't dare do more than bow his head. "Sorry," he gasped. "Sorry." He didn't know if the griffin understood.

Skandar stared at him a moment longer and then looked away, apparently no longer interested. Cardock looked past him but couldn't see any sign of Arenadd. He knew there was nothing he could do.

"I'll go," he mumbled to the griffin, and stumbled back down the hill.

Skandar watched him go with a dispassionate eye. Inwardly, though, he was pleased. He didn't want another human near, confusing him. Not while his own human was unwell.

The pair of fruits the old male had brought were still lying nearby. He couldn't fathom why humans liked to eat them, but perhaps Arren would want them. Perhaps they would make him better somehow.

Skandar nudged them together and managed to pick them up in his beak. They sat there precariously, threatening to fall out, but he kept his head carefully still and walked back to where Arren was. He had stood up when he heard the other human and was staring at Skandar now, black eyes glimmering in the faint light left from the Day Eye.

Skandar put the fruits down in front of his human. "Eat," he rasped. "Food."

Arren looked at them but didn't pick them up. "I don't want them," he said.

"Eat," Skandar repeated patiently. "Eat now. Sick, need food."

Arren made that strange shuddering sound that he had been making a lot lately. "It won't help, Skandar."

"Eat," Skandar said yet again.

But Arren turned away. "Nothing can help me," he said quietly.

Skandar's tail began to lash. "You eat," he said. "Eat now. Eat, get better."

"I'm not sick, Skandar."

"You sick," said Skandar. "A sick griffin, not eat. Sick human, not eat. You not eat, you die."

The shuddering again, but Arren turned back and picked up the apples. "Fine. I'll eat them if that's what you want."

Skandar watched approvingly as he bit into one. "I want you—do not want you die."

"I know."

"Want you live," said Skandar. "Want keep you, Arren Cardockson. Keep you forever. Mine. Mine always. Mine."

"I won't leave you, Skandar," Arren said softly. "I can't. I understand that now."

"Mine," Skandar repeated.

Cardock reached the edge of the rocky outcrop at a staggering walk, but then his terror finally bubbled to the surface, and he broke into a sprint. Once he hit the slope, the treacherous ground and poor light forced him to slow down, but he moved as fast as he could, tripping over rocks and branches, and stumbling through thickets of damp soap-bush and piufex grass.

When he reached the edge of the firelight that marked Caedmon's camp he came to a stop and leant against a tree for a few moments, panting and clutching at his aching chest.

Once he had calmed down, he straightened up and walked into the circle of light.

The others glanced up. "How was he?" Caedmon inquired.

Cardock stared blankly at him for a couple of heartbeats, his mind flitting back to the sobbing figure at the top of the hill. "I . . . don't think he was hungry," he said at last. "But the griffin was."

Nolan winced. "Took the meat, did he?"

"Uh, yes. He did. Could I—" Cardock realised he was shaking slightly. "Could I sit down, please?"

They shuffled aside hastily, and Caedmon got up. "Ye gods, ye're as white as a lily. Come, siddown, warm yerself up. Someone get him some water, hurry up."

Cardock sat down and tried to slow his breathing. The warmth of the fire touched him, soaking through his clothes, and he shuddered slightly, but it helped to soothe him. Torc put a water bottle into his hands, and he drank.

After a little while he began to feel better. "Gods," he mumbled, putting the bottle aside and rubbing his hands over his face. "I didn't know what'd happened—the thing just leapt out at me."

Nolan looked sympathetic. "Did the same thing t'me once, sir. Nearly vomited up me own heart, I did, sir. No surprise you're a bit shaken up."

Cardock took his hands away from his face. "You really don't have to call me sir."

"I do, sir," said Nolan. "You're Lord Arenadd's father, ain't you? An' you're a free man, too. Everyone knows about that. You was set free, an' Erian the Bastard sold you back. But you're a free man far as we're concerned; you didn't do nothin' wrong. We're just slaves, us. We call every free man sir. I was *born* knowin' that."

"Well, if that's the way, I'd like t'know why ye ain't callin' *us* sir," Garnoc put in suddenly. "We're free, same as"—a polite nod toward Cardock—"yer new master's father here, but I ain't heard no sirs from ye to me yet, Southerner."

Another man would certainly have flared up in response to this, but Nolan only ducked his head nervously. "Sorry, sir. I didn't mean no disrespect or nothin', only—"

"Only we're wearin' collars, too," Garnoc muttered savagely.

"Moon damn it!" Olwydd burst forth. He snatched at his collar, trying to hook his fingers beneath it, but in vain. "These damn things! I hate them! If I could get this off by tearin' my own arm off, I'd do it. I'd do anything. I'd get it off and melt it down an' piss on it t'cool it off." He looked wildly at Caedmon. "How can ye bear it? Tell me true, old man, how d'ye bear it? How can ye live a life with that thing around yer neck an' not go mad or kill yerself?"

Caedmon sighed. "They don't hurt forever, lad. Once it heals—"

"I'm not talkin' about that!" Olwydd shouted. "I'm talkin' about how can ye wear it an' just—I mean, don't ye know what it is? What it means? It's more than torture, Caedmon. It's *more* than that. They put this—when they put this on me, when it snapped on, an' the spikes went into me like they was gonna—it *changed* me. I was a man, but after they put the collar on me I wasn't any more. I was a *thing*. Something ye could buy or sell. A *thing*."

"Oh, yes."

Olwydd broke off and turned sharply to look behind him to see who had spoken.

It was Arenadd. He emerged from the shadows like a ghost, and Cardock felt sick to his stomach at the sight of him. He looked half-dead. Grey-faced and gaunt, his eyes hollow, as if he was deathly sick.

The others recovered themselves hastily. "My lord," said Caedmon, standing up. "Please, come, sit—move out of the way, all of ye, the Master needs—"

Arenadd waved him into silence with a rather listless gesture, as if his arm was very heavy. "Don't worry about it," he said. "Just—I just want to sit down. And some food. Skandar's behind me. Give me some meat for him, or he'll take it."

They obeyed with the speed of men accustomed to it: Nolan and Torc took the remains of the sheep carcass they had been cutting meat from and put it at the edge of the camp, and Skandar loomed out of the darkness and hooked it with his talons. While the griffin settled down to eat, Arenadd sat down by the fire. The others, including Cardock, moved to the other side, as far away from him as they could get, leaving him surrounded by a ring of empty space, as if he were at the centre of an invisible wall that only Skandar could pass through. Arenadd watched them dully and sighed, the only sign he gave.

Torc served him some mutton, potatoes and an ear of corn, and retreated, bowing and ducking. Arenadd gave no comment but started to eat.

When the silence became too uncomfortable, Cardock said, "So, which way are we going to take next?"

Arenadd said nothing, but Prydwen answered for him. "Around this hill and on through the valley, split up like Lord Arenadd said. One half on the east side, other half on the west, an' we meet up on the other side an' follow Lord Arenadd from there. Should be just a day or so before we're at the edge of Y Castell."

Dafydd smiled. "T'will be good t'see Tara again, lads."

"I'll drink t'that, Dafydd, or I would if I had any wine," Olwydd said, and grinned.

Cardock rubbed his forehead. "But what are we going to do when we get there? We still haven't talked about that."

"We join the rebels, of course," said Prydwen.

"We'll do what Lord Arenadd wants us to do," Caedmon snapped. "I should remind ye, my lad, that he's master of ye now, an' that it's him who'll be tellin' ye what to do from now on."

Cardock coughed loudly. "I'm sure he'll tell us what he's got in mind when he's ready." He glanced at Arenadd, expecting him to say something at this point, but he was still sitting by the fire, chewing slowly at his food and apparently oblivious to the discussion going on in front of him.

"So he will," said Caedmon. He gave Cardock an approving look. "Right an' sensible as always, Cardock Skandarson."

Cardock chuckled. "Always right! If I had an oblong for every time my wife told me that—" He broke off abruptly, his smile fading as his mind suddenly filled with pictures of Annir. Poor sweet Annir, so far away, so lost and afraid, not knowing where her husband and son were or whether either of them was alive. His dear Annir. He closed his eyes.

"I'm sure you'll get her back some day, sir," Torc said.

Cardock looked up. "I'll never give in. I'll do anything I have to in order to set her free."

"I'm sure ye will," Caedmon said kindly. "If a man's determined enough, he'll—"

"I had to do it."

For the second time that night, everyone stopped.

"What, Arenadd?" said Cardock.

Arenadd looked up. "I had to do it," he said again. His eyes were bloodshot. "You have to understand that, Dad. I had no choice."

Cardock dared to shuffle closer to him, stopping when Skandar looked up. "What are you saying, son?" This was the first time Arenadd had spoken to him directly in days.

Arenadd shuddered a little. "I had no choice," he said huskily. "I had to kill him. Please, you have to understand." He looked briefly at him, and then stared at the ground, fists clenching. "I had to do it. He killed Eluna. He sent us to our deaths. I was honour bound, had to avenge her, had to punish him for what he did. It was my duty. They made me swear. 'By friendship bound, by blood sworn.' The words—I said them at the ceremony. When they made me a griffiner. Protect each other, always. And if one is killed, the other must—it was honour. I swore an oath. His life for Eluna's, and mine—I had to do it." His fists clenched harder. "I had no choice," he intoned.

Deathly silence followed. No-one dared make a move.

Finally, Olwydd spoke up. "We don't blame ye, my lord. Ye're no murderer; we know it. What ye did was for everyone, all of us. The North knows it. Yer people know it. *We* know it. Ye stood up, avenged us, showed the griffiners our people aren't conquered, showed them we can still fight. Ye set us free, my lord. We won't ever forget that."

The other three Northerners nodded fervently.

"I'll never forget seein' ye," Dafydd put in, "when ye came to us at Herbstitt. Every night I was there, I swore I'd get free some day. Nothin' an' nobody could ever make me give up. I prayed every night, looking for guidance. A sign for what to do. For a while I thought maybe the moon had left me, stopped caring about me. But I was wrong." He laughed incredulously. "Wrong! I prayed, an' the moon sent ye." He looked at Arenadd with something like adoration. "It sent ye to us," he said, eyes shining. "It brought ye to that slave-house to set us free, take us home. I'm no slave, sir, an' never will be, but that doesn't matter. Ye'll always be a master to me."

Arenadd's face betrayed no reaction to this. He stared dully at Dafydd, who looked back for a few moments before he turned nervously away, his air of bravado suddenly gone.

Arenadd appeared to wake up in some way. "How are they?" he asked in a tone of forced calmness, looking toward the trees beyond which the light of the other fires was visible.

Caedmon looked relieved. "Doin' well, sir," he said. "Everyone looks t'be in good health to me. Few scrapes an' whatnot from the last couple days' walk, but that's to be expected. We picked up plenty of food at the last farm, an' I've seen to it the load's distributed properly."

"How long will it last?"

Caedmon clicked his tongue thoughtfully. "Few days. Four, five maybe. More'n enough to get us to the mountains, sir."

Arenadd nodded vaguely. "Good. That's good." He glanced at Olwydd. "The mountain pass—a week to get through it, didn't you say?"

"Yes, sir," said Olwydd. He hesitated. "But that's only a guess. I went through there before by cart. On foot it could be longer. And that still leaves Guard's Post. How're we gonna get past it, sir?"

"I'm . . . thinking about it," said Arenadd, staring at the ground again. There was a crunching sound from behind him, and Skandar appeared, gulping slightly as he swallowed the last of the carcass. The others around the fire drew back in fright, and the griffin sat down on his haunches behind his partner, the feathers on his chest brushing the top of Arenadd's head. He stayed there, watching them balefully.

Arenadd made no move. "I only hope there'll be enough game around there," he said. "He needs a lot of food."

No-one replied, not even Cardock. Arenadd watched them in silence for a while and then stood up abruptly. "I'm tired," he said. "I think I'll go and get some sleep. See you tomorrow." Without waiting for an answer, he turned and walked back toward the shadows he had emerged from. Skandar hissed softly and followed.

Cardock, watching them go, suddenly felt a little pang of fear. He scrambled upright and went after them. "Arren!"

Skandar turned sharply, beak opening, and Cardock backed away. "Arren!"

There was no reply, and for a moment it seemed that

Arenadd had abandoned him yet again. But there was a rustling from up ahead and he stepped forward, ghostly in the gloom. "What is it?"

Cardock almost reached out to grab his arm but stopped himself, knowing that would only provoke the hissing griffin. "I want to talk to you."

A brief silence followed. "Fine," Arenadd said at last. "Follow us back up the hill if you want."

Cardock waited a while to let Skandar get well ahead of him, and then followed at a distance. Night had fallen, but fortunately the moon had risen and was bright enough to see without a torch. He climbed the hill, following Skandar's massive shape, and the three of them navigated the stones and finally came to a halt in a sheltered spot where a small fire was smouldering.

Arenadd crouched down by it and added more wood, blowing on it until it had rekindled. Skandar paused to watch him for a moment and then made an easy leap to the top of a nearby chunk of rock and crouched there like an enormous gargoyle.

Cardock stood at a safe distance, watching until Arenadd beckoned him closer. "Come on," he said, his voice suddenly taking on a more familiar note of impatience. "Sit down."

Cardock obeyed, still watching Skandar. Even now, though, father and son sat well apart.

Arenadd sat cross-legged, watching the fire. "It's a good spot, this," he said, again sounding much more normal than he had with the others.

Somehow, that gave Cardock some of his courage back. "I wanted to talk to you, Arren," he said. "It's been—well, it's been almost a week since you took us out of there, and you and I have barely spoken."

Arenadd had looked up at him. "Was there something you wanted to ask me?"

"Well, yes," said Cardock. "Several things. Where were you? Your mother and I went to Norton; we left the same day you came back to us. We were there for weeks, waiting for you. We spent all our money. Your mother started to say we should go back, but I said we had to keep waiting. But you never came. Why?"

Arenadd groaned softly. "I'm sorry, Dad. I meant to come. I swear, I meant to."

"Then why didn't you?" Cardock said harshly. "Well?"

"Dad, I was *lost*. Skandar and I were out in the middle of nowhere, trying to find Norton. We didn't have a map, and we couldn't exactly ask anyone for directions. All the time, I knew you were waiting for me and that you were in danger, but there was nothing I could—I was trying, Dad. I tried for months. Half the time we were starving."

Cardock stared at him.

"Lost, Dad. That's all." Arenadd couldn't look him in the eye.

"Arren, I'm sorry," said Cardock. "I shouldn't have doubted you. I should have known it was out of your hands." He sighed.

"It's all right, Dad," said Arenadd. But inside he knew he was lying. He could see his father's face in the firelight, could see how thin it looked, even half-obscured by a matted beard as it was. He could only guess at what he must have suffered. *You miserable, self-centred bastard,* his inner voice whispered, full of furious hatred. *While you were romancing a griffin and running after idiot fantasies, your own parents were being tortured. Because of you.*

He shuddered. "Well, you're free now," he said loudly. "And I swear I'll die before I let anything else happen to you. And we're going to find Mum as well. One way or another, we'll set her free, and I'll take care of both of you. I'll find a way to fix things, I promise."

Cardock sighed. "In the North, maybe."

"Do you think I'm doing the right thing?" Arenadd asked. "Taking them all to the North, I mean."

"Olwydd and the rest couldn't be happier," said Cardock.

"I know. But what about the others? What do *they* want?" Arenadd buried his face in his hands. "I've tried to ask them so many times, but they won't tell me anything. All they'll do is what I tell them to do, and they never disagree with me about anything. Olwydd was right. They're not men any more. They're broken. *Objects.* They've got no will of their own."

"They've been slaves all their lives, Arren," Cardock said gently. "You can't expect them to be able to forget it overnight. These things take time."

"Was it like that when you were a slave?" said Arenadd.

"I don't know," said Cardock. "I barely remember any more. I was only very small. Too young to be used for labour, too young to sell, and my parents were both dead. Until the Bastard

sold me, I hadn't seen another Northerner besides you and your
mother in more than thirty years."

"I don't know what I'm going to do with them when we
get to the N— to Tara," said Arenadd. "I was planning to free
them, let them go their own way." He tugged at his beard. "I
thought I was setting them free!" he raged suddenly. "I thought
they'd be *happy*! I thought they'd thank me! I'd be their saviour,
some kind of hero. But all I've done is become another master
for them to serve, who's probably even worse than the last one
they had. Now instead of living in a leaky barn and doing what
they're told, they're wandering through some gods-forsaken
wilderness with no shelter and doing what they're told. And
they probably hate me far more than they hated—" His voice
broke. "I thought I was doing the right thing, Dad. I thought I
was being brave."

"You were," said Cardock. "Arren, you *were*. What you did
was one of the bravest things I've ever known. You knew that if
they caught you, you'd be killed; you knew you could be seen,
but you came back anyway, just to help me and your friends."

Arenadd didn't seem to hear him. "I thought I was redeem-
ing myself," he mumbled. "I thought that if I did that, it would
somehow make up for what I did. I don't know what I'm doing
any more, Dad. I don't know why I'm doing it. Everything I do
only makes things worse."

"It hasn't," said Cardock. "Are you listening to me? It *hasn't*."

His voice was a father's voice now, stern and no-nonsense.
It pulled Arenadd up short. "What do you mean?" he said, a
little timidly.

"I mean that what you did at Herbstitt was a good thing,"
said Cardock. "It made things better for me, didn't it? And it did
for Olwydd and his friends. And the others—they'll thank you
one day, Arenadd, I swear they will."

"But it doesn't change anything," said Arenadd. "It doesn't
change what I did . . . Rannagon." The name was half-whispered, almost fearfully, as if it were a curse. "I still killed him.
But I had to. Eluna died because of me, it was my fault as well
as Rannagon's. If I'd only done something. If I hadn't gone to
Rivermeet, if I hadn't run, if Eluna hadn't—and I knew it was
my fault. I had to kill him. Eluna put her trust in me. I had sworn
to—we were partners. I served her, she served me. I had to
avenge her, to make amends . . ."

He was mumbling, his words wandering here and there, and Cardock knew he was bringing up everything he had thought of since Rannagon's death, trying desperately to find some way to justify himself. "If Rannagon tried to kill you, then he was a traitor," Cardock said. "And if he could have been brought to fair trial for it, he would have been sentenced to death."

"Sentenced to death?" There was suddenly a sneer in Arenadd's voice. "For what? For trying to kill me? I'm only a *Northerner*, Dad. Who would have cared? Without Eluna, I was nothing. Less than nothing."

"For Eluna, then," said Cardock.

"Perhaps, but it never would have happened. I was the only witness. Nobody would have believed me, and I knew it. That's why I never said anything. And when I *did* tell the truth, at my trial, they didn't listen. Rannagon told them all I was mad, and they believed him. Killing him was the only way to make him pay."

"Then you made him pay," said Cardock. "For Eluna, and for the North."

Arenadd watched him miserably. He wanted to scream it out. *His children saw me do it! They saw their father die! I burned the Eyrie; I killed Lady Riona and all the others. I can't sleep. I can't sleep any more. I can't—*

Cardock watched him. "Don't torture yourself," he said. "You can't change the past."

Arenadd said nothing. He stared out at the stars, blank-faced but breathing shakily.

Cardock moved closer to him. "Arren?"

Arenadd didn't look at him, but he stirred at the sound of his voice. Then he began to speak. "I'm a bad person." His voice sounded jerky and emotionless. "I've always been a bad person. There's something wrong inside. I know it."

"You're not a bad person, Arren." Cardock touched him on the shoulder. "Stop it."

Arenadd didn't react to the touch. "I ran away from home when I was only ten. But after that, I never really did grow up. I did things I shouldn't have. Bad things."

Cardock felt cold all over. "What things?"

"I wanted to be a griffiner," Arenadd mumbled. "A real griffiner. That's all I wanted all my life. They did everything to stop me, but I kept on going no matter what I had to do. All those apprenticeships, and they never let me finish one. Every time I got close, they moved me on to a new master. One day, I realised they'd never let me finish. I'd never be a master of anything."

"But you did finish, and I'm proud," said Cardock. "I was always proud."

Arenadd ignored him. "My last master. I remember him. I hated him so much, and he hated me. He wanted me to leave, but I knew it was my last chance. I stayed no matter what he did. I wanted his position, and I knew there was no way he'd ever let me have it. I did what I had to do."

"Arren, you didn't—?"

"I poisoned him. And when he was dead I took his position for myself. They couldn't stop that."

"Arren—"

"But it still wasn't enough. The Master of Gold wouldn't pay me fairly. I got less than half of what my old master had. They wouldn't even let me live in the Eyrie or have a place on the council. I needed money; I had to feed Eluna. Roland helped me, but he couldn't keep on doing it. So I took what I needed from other people. I framed people for smuggling, so I could take their belongings. I made people pay me twice the correct amount for their licences. And when people complained, I threatened to kill them if they did anything." Arenadd laughed in a flat, discordant way. "Half the city hated me. And when Eluna was gone, they came back for revenge."

Cardock said nothing.

"I'm sorry, Dad," Arenadd said at last. "I'm sorry for the things I did and for the things I'm going to do. I'm sorry I abandoned you, and I'm sorry for all the things I said. I was just a child in a man's body. A stupid, selfish child. So I'm sorry for that. I'm sorry I took your only son away from you and turned him into this."

Silence followed; yawning, aching silence.

Cardock felt sick and frightened. "Arren, I—"

At last, his son turned to look at him. "Arenadd. Call me Arenadd. I'm done with Arren. That was my name when I was pretending to be a Southerner, and that time's done." He sighed a long, weary sigh. "I don't think I know what I am any more, but I do know one thing. I'm a Northerner. I've always been a Northerner, and I will not be ashamed of it any more. And from now on, I'm going to do what you always told me to do, and be proud."

Cardock finally lost the battle with himself. He let out a sob and hugged Arenadd tightly.

Arenadd hugged him back, and father and son held each other for a long time.

"I *will* keep them safe," Arenadd muttered. "No matter what. I'll fight for them, and lead them if that's what they want. I did anything I had to for myself once, now I'll do the same for them. I'll kill for them. Die for them. Anything."

19

Malvern

So this was the North. During his boyhood, when he had listened to stories about it, Erian had always pictured it as a vast snowfield broken up only by bare craggy mountains and pine forests. Now that he was seeing it in reality, he couldn't help but feel slightly cheated to discover that it looked little different from the Southern lands they had just left.

Senneck flew over hills and plains, much of it covered in farmland. There were indeed pine forests here, interspersed with a kind of spice-tree whose trunks were ghostly white. It was cold, but there was no snow anywhere.

"Obviously," said Senneck when he pointed this out. "It is not winter. If there were permanent snow here, farming would be impossible."

"*Is* there any part of the North where there's always snow?" Erian asked.

"Further north, perhaps. We shall find out."

One important difference he did see, however, was in the people. Northerners. They passed through several villages on their way toward Malvern, and at the first one they visited, Erian was openly shocked to see its inhabitants. Every single one of the villagers was a Northerner. There were only a few dozen of them, but the sight of them sent a chill down his spine. They weren't all tall and thin like their murderous cousin; like ordinary human beings, they came in all shapes and sizes. But he looked almost wildly at them, and everywhere he turned it was the same: pale skin, black hair, black eyes. Many of the men wore small, pointed beards, and the women had their hair braided and occasionally decorated with crow feathers.

They wore rough peasant clothing, not black robes, they had none of the spiral tattoos or painted faces he had expected their kind to have, and they all spoke proper Cymrian, though with harsh, coarse accents. And they welcomed him humbly, bowing and scraping and looking at Senneck with awe.

Erian relaxed then and let them provide him with food and shelter for the night. These people weren't savage warriors like the Northerners in stories. They were just stupid, frightened farmers, who looked at him as if they expected him to sprout wings or produce fireballs out of the air. Timidly they approached and asked him to heal wounds and sickness with his touch, and bless a couple of squalling black-haired brats.

Now that he thought about it, his secret fears over coming to the North seemed more than a little comical.

He confessed as much to Senneck. "I don't know what I was expecting, but I was frightened inside. I suppose, after what that man"—he generally avoided calling his father's murderer by name—"did, I couldn't help but imagine they were all like that."

Senneck chirped her amusement. "Lady Elkin would have my eternal respect if they were. Governing an entire realm of people who were like the Cursed One would be a task worthy of Gryphus himself."

"Why do you call him that, Senneck?" said Erian. "You've been doing it ever since we met."

She clicked her beak. "He is *Kraeai kran ae*. He is the Cursed One. We have known it for a long time."

"But what *is* a Cursed One?" Erian persisted. "And how do you know it?"

"It is not a thing for humans to know," said Senneck. "But there was a griffin I knew, at Eagleholm. Okaree was her name, and she was a silver griffin. She had the power of insight, and she recognised him for what he was when he came to the hatchery, hoping to be chosen again. She named him *Kraeai kran ae* for what she sensed in him."

"What does it mean?" said Erian. "Is there a curse on him? Is that what it means?"

"*Kraeai kran ae* is an old name," said Senneck. "Its meaning is complex. I do not understand it fully, but it means 'great evil.' One day, if you meet a griffin wiser than I am, he or she may tell you." She fixed him with a pale blue gaze. "But it may interest you to know a little more about that day. When he came before us, in all his arrogance, demanding to be made a griffiner again, many of us merely laughed at him. Others left in disgust. I was one of those who stayed."

"What happened?"

"I went closer," said Senneck. "To examine him. I was curious. I had heard the tale already. Eluna chose him when she was a mere chick. A fool she was. She could have become great and powerful, and yet she crippled herself by choosing him. A Northerner! But perhaps they were a fine match: she was as mad as he. And she died because of his stupidity. A fitting end to a sordid partnership. Yet he dared to return, looking for a second chance. I spoke to him briefly, questioned him."

"So, what happened?" said Erian.

She flicked her tail. "You probably did not notice it when you saw him."

"Notice what?"

"His ear. His ragged ear."

Erian shook his head. "I saw the wound on his face."

"If it comes to pass that you see him again, look at his ear," said Senneck. "There is a piece missing." She blinked smugly. "I removed it. I tore his ear to humble him, after the others had rejected him. That is why I do not fear him. I have tasted his blood once, and one day I shall do it again."

Erian couldn't help but grin. "You're wonderful, Senneck. A wonderful griffin. You really are."

She made a show of looking aloofly away from him. "Work hard to please me, Erian Rannagonson, for I begin to grow fond of you."

Erian grinned again. "I will, Senneck." Inwardly he was as happy as he sounded, for since they had left Herbstitt, Senneck's mood had improved greatly and she had lost the constant air of tension and irritability that had surrounded her during their stay there. Most likely she, too, was relieved that their journey was nearly over.

They spent the first night in that village and left early the next morning, following the River Snow, and from there the going was far easier. They were able to shelter in a different village every night, and once they even came across a small town. There were a few traders and craftsmen there, and Erian noticed that the wealthier of these were all Southerners like himself, come to live in the North. They were the first Southerners they had seen.

He explored the town and visited most of the shops and stalls, curious to know what kinds of things would be for sale here, and by the time he had finished he was puzzled.

"I don't understand," he said to Senneck. "The Northern craftsmen don't seem to be any worse than the Southern ones, but they own all the smaller shops and sell everything more cheaply. Why?"

Senneck clicked her beak. "I think, most likely, the Southerners are taxed more lightly than the rest."

Erian scratched his nose. "Why, though?"

"To force the Northerners to keep their place, of course," said Senneck. "It seems clear enough to me, and suitably cunning. Lady Elkin is said to be famed for her mind."

Erian was instantly reminded of his desire to meet the Mistress of Malvern's Eyrie and didn't argue when Senneck told him they shouldn't linger in the town. They left again the next day and flew on, still heading northward. The locals they had spoken to said that Malvern wasn't too far, and Senneck had studied a map and estimated that they would be there in under a week.

All the while, Erian could feel the cold growing. The landscape grew steadily rougher; the hills became larger and closer together, frequently dotted with rocky outcrops. The River Snow formed itself into lakes and pools, and the forests became thicker and darker. Wild country.

And then, one morning, they saw it. Up ahead, perched on a hilltop, was a dark, hunched mass, all jagged and tumbled like a heap of fallen bricks. Malvern.

"We shall reach it today," was Senneck's only comment.

Erian watched as they drew steadily closer, his heart quickening with anticipation when he began to make out the shapes of towers and rooftops. After a time he could also see dark shapes in the sky: griffins, circling lazily in the updrafts.

Senneck was spotted well before they passed over the stone walls that surrounded the city. Half a dozen griffins flew out to intercept her, and she slowed and let them surround her, careful to show no sign of hostility.

Erian swallowed hard. None of the other griffins had riders, and many of them were larger than Senneck. He knew that if either of them made a false move they were likely to be attacked. He bowed his head, staring fixedly at the back of Senneck's neck as a sign of humility toward them, while she recited the ancient codes of friendship, promising to enter their territory without designs on their food, mates or nests, and to be a friend to them in time of need.

The griffins listened, and the largest responded with one word. "Follow."

He turned and flew back the way he had come, and Senneck fell in behind him, riding his slipstream. The others flew either beside or behind her, still watching for signs of trickery.

Meanwhile, the city passed below them. Far larger than Erian had expected, it took the form of levels that had been carved out of the hillside. The tiers of the city were separated from one another by walls. He had never seen a city as heavily fortified as this. Nor had he seen one as *dark*: the stone used to build it was very dark grey, almost black from this distance. It gave the place a slightly grim look, and he began to think he understood why many griffiners saw Malvern as an unpleasant place to live.

The Eyrie stood at the very centre, as expected. It was larger than the one at Eagleholm, which was the only Eyrie he had ever seen. Like all griffiner buildings, it was a tower—or, rather, a series of towers—much like the griffiner tower at Herbstitt, flat-topped and festooned with ledges. Covered walkways linked the towers, but Erian could instantly tell that the Eyrie must be a nightmarish place to try to navigate. The centremost tower was the largest and tallest. Their guides forced Senneck to land at the very top.

Erian slid off her back. The wind up here was icy and very powerful. He could hear it whistling softly between the stones. The tower-top, which was large enough to hold several houses, had been partially converted into a garden. Trees and other plants grew in enormous stone pots and troughs, and there was even an ornamental pond.

But Erian had very little time to take any of this in. The griffins had landed around them in a ring and were moving closer, all staring straight at him and Senneck.

It was all he could do to stop himself from shrinking back against his partner's flank. Yet he knew what was expected of him, and he knelt hastily, saying nothing. It wasn't his place to speak now. He spoke to other humans, not to griffins, unless they spoke to him first.

Senneck took a few slow, careful steps toward the male griffin who had spoken to her earlier. The two of them sized each other up for a moment, and then Senneck bent her forelegs and lowered her beak until it touched the ground. "I greet you in the names of the sea and the sky," she intoned. "I am Senneck, hatched in Eagleholm but no longer of that land, and this is my human, Erian Rannagonson, born of Carrick."

The male griffin made a quick upward jerking motion with his beak. "Why have you come to Malvern, Senneck?"

"We have not sworn ourselves to an Eyrie," said Senneck. "Therefore, we have come to Malvern with the intent to swear loyalty to the Mighty Kraal, and to his human, the Lady Elkin. That is our only purpose."

The male griffin eyed her. "You believe you shall be welcomed, Senneck?"

"I do not," Senneck replied coolly. "I hope, and that is all. My human and I have come many miles to Malvern, and all we ask is for the chance to speak with your masters. If that is not permitted, we ask for food and shelter."

After a brief silence the other griffin yawned and gave a dismissive flick of his tail. "We shall allow you entry to the Eyrie. Kraal has commanded that all partnered griffins be brought to him at once so that he may speak with them and know their scent."

Senneck bowed again. "I thank you."

"Follow me now," the male griffin said. "I shall take you to Kraal and his human."

Senneck rose to follow him. "Come," she said curtly to Erian.

Erian didn't need any prompting. He walked by his partner's shoulder, and the two of them were led to a hole in the roof, which opened into a ramp leading downward.

Their guide walked ahead, talons clicking on the stone, and the three of them climbed down the ramp and found themselves in a large and pleasant corridor. The floor was covered by a long, thickly woven rug, and tapestries hung from the walls. It was as sumptuous as anything Erian had seen at Eagleholm, if not more so, and he wondered if the whole Eyrie matched it. He didn't, however, feel brave enough to ask their guide, who loped to the end of the corridor and turned a corner into another, this sloping downward just like the previous one. They did this twice more before the corridor levelled out, and after that they made a short trip through a couple of attractive antechambers to an archway leading into a very large audience chamber.

A guard was stationed on each side of the arch, both of them human and unaccompanied by griffins. Neither made a move.

Here, their guide stopped. "Kraal and his human will be waiting for you beyond," he said to Senneck. "Go in and meet them. I shall leave you here." He walked back the way they had come, pushing past Erian on the way.

Senneck stood a little taller and nudged Erian with her beak. "Come," she said. "It is time. Do not embarrass me, Erian."

"I won't," he promised.

Senneck flicked her tail and passed through the arch. Erian paused a moment, then squared his shoulders and followed.

The audience chamber was unlike anything he had ever seen. It was huge and high-ceilinged, lined with white marble. Elegant pale-blue drapes edged with gold hung here and there, and three large fireplaces were set into the walls. There was no furniture, but there was a raised dais at the centre, incongruously covered by a heap of dry rushes, and some large cushions lay on the floor at its base. The dais was unoccupied.

Erian and Senneck stopped by the cushions and waited. Erian was about to ask where the Lady Elkin was when he saw Senneck draw herself up expectantly and heard the sound of talons on the floor on the other side of the dais.

There was another, smaller archway beyond it, and through that stepped—

Erian gaped. His stomach lurched. For a moment his legs felt as if they were going to collapse.

Through the archway came what was quite simply the largest living thing he had ever seen in his life.

It was a griffin, male, his coat pure white and his eyes burnished gold. Erian had never seen a griffin so big. He was at least twice as large as Senneck and many times heavier. Each foreleg looked as thick as Erian's entire body, and the shoulders were wider than those of an ox. The head, towering above both of them, looked like a white-feathered boulder with a beak. Not even Darkheart, the one-time legend of the Arena, was as big as this.

Erian regained some of his senses and dropped to his knees. "My lord," he breathed. Instantly he knew he had made a blunder, and crumbled inside. Griffins did not have titles, and if he acted as if he didn't know what he was doing . . .

He glanced up, hoping that the colossal griffin hadn't heard him. To his intense relief, the gold eyes were fixed on Senneck rather than him. The brown griffin had already backed away and was bowing, even more humbly than she had up on the roof.

"The Mighty Kraal," she said, in awestruck tones.

The white griffin regarded her impassively for a few moments. "I do not know you," he said at last. His voice was rough and deep.

"I have only just come to your city," Senneck explained. "I am Senneck of Eagleholm, and this is my human, Erian Rannagonson. Most humbly do we come before you."

Kraal looked at Erian for the first time. "Rise."

Erian did so, saying nothing. He glanced around quickly for any sign of Lady Elkin, but failed to spot her. Returning his gaze to Kraal, he was careful to avoid making eye contact and stared instead at the griffin's talons. They were huge and pitted, and did nothing to ease his nerves.

He felt something enormous move just above him and closed his eyes tightly as Kraal brought his beak down and scented him, hot breath ruffling his hair. It lasted for a few heart-stopping moments, as visions of that great beak cracking his skull danced through Erian's head. Then the white griffin abruptly withdrew and he dared to breathe again.

"Southerners, are you?" said a voice.

Erian looked up, surprised, and was in time to see a small figure appear from somewhere beside Kraal, as if she had been hiding in his feathers, which, he thought later, she quite possibly had.

He looked at her, confused. She was a teenage girl, no older than fifteen or sixteen. Where her partner was huge, she was tiny: Erian could have encircled her waist with his hands. Her face was delicate and pointed, her shape elegant but almost alarmingly fragile. She wore a simple white gown, and her hair was so blonde it nearly matched it.

She smiled at him. "Hello, Erian, and welcome to my city. I am Lady Elkin."

Erian blinked stupidly. "You're . . . ?"

The smile widened slightly. "Lady Elkin, yes. Do you want to sit down?"

"We shall," Senneck interrupted sharply. "Erian, sit."

Erian hastily selected a cushion and sat down on it, cross-legged. Senneck crouched beside him. Kraal, apparently satisfied, stepped up onto the dais and lay down on the rushes. Elkin sat in front of him, nestling between his front paws.

"Welcome to the North," she said sweetly. "I'm happy to see you."

Senneck glanced at Erian, giving him his cue to speak.

"Th-thank you," he stammered. "My lady, Senneck and I are honoured to be here in your lands."

"How do you like them?" she asked.

Erian hesitated. "They're . . . not what I expected."

"Things rarely are," said Elkin, nodding solemnly. "But do you like them?"

"I do, my lady," said Erian. He pulled himself together. "My lady," he said in his most measured, respectful voice, "Senneck and I have come here from Eagleholm with the inten—"

She waved him into silence. "I'm glad you like my lands, Erian. I do. Many people don't like them; they say they're too cold and barren, and too full of Northerners."

She tittered. "I suppose some people would complain that the sea is full of fish. Do you know, some people thought we should destroy them? Kill them all, or make *all* of them slaves, which isn't practical, and why should we? It isn't the North without them, I think, and you get used to them. Anyway"—she fixed him with a suddenly intent look—"I expect you've come to work for me."

"Wh— yes," said Erian. "We never swore ourselves to any other Eyrie, but we have chosen to swear ourselves to you, my lady, if you will have us."

She sighed. "Many griffiners have already come here to say the same thing. Well, except for the first part, because they were all older than you. Do you know, I think you're the youngest griffiner we've had here apart from me? How old are you?"

"Uh, sixteen, my lady."

Elkin smiled. "Oh! So am I! Isn't that odd? So, Erian, won't you tell me about yourself? Where are you from? What was your family like?"

"Well, I was born in a village near Carrick," said Erian, feeling unexpectedly flattered to have been asked. "My father was Lord Rannagon Raegonson of Eagleholm."

"And your mother?" Elkin interrupted.

"Oh. She died giving birth to me," Erian mumbled. "I was raised by my grandparents. And my father—"

"Wait," said Elkin. "You are the son of Lord Rannagon, but you weren't born at Eagleholm?"

"Yes."

"Ah!" Her eyes lit up. "Of course! You're Lord Rannagon's bastard, aren't you?"

Erian winced. "Yes, I am, my lady."

"I knew Lord Rannagon," said Elkin. "Or at least my mother and father did. Many of the griffiners here did. And his sister, too. They were both here once, during Arddryn's Uprising. There was a rather terrible war. But your father fought very bravely. Lord Anech, who was Eyrie Master before me, wanted him to live here for good, but he said no. He wanted to go home. And then he fathered you."

She favoured him with another smile. "And you grew up to be a griffiner, just like him. I expect he was very proud."

"He was," said Erian. "I saw him only once after Senneck chose me. His wife didn't like me, so she kept away, but my father saw me. He hugged me and told me how happy he was and how he always knew I would become a griffiner, and Senneck said . . ." He trailed off, suddenly aware that he was rambling.

Elkin was watching him keenly. "Why didn't you swear yourself to Lady Riona, then? Didn't she want you?"

"I never spoke to her myself," said Erian. "She was very ill. But my father said he was arranging for Senneck and me to swear loyalty to her in her absence. That was the last time I ever spoke to him."

"Why?" said Elkin. "Did he change his mind?"

"No." Erian felt his throat squeeze in upon itself. "It was the last day of his life. He was murdered that same night."

"Oh." Elkin ran her fingers through her hair, and sighed. "Yes, I see. I did know about that. I never heard the story from anyone who was there, though. Is it true he was killed by another griffiner?"

"No." Erian couldn't stop himself from spitting the word. "A Northerner did it."

"But a Northern griffiner," said Elkin. "There was one at Eagleholm, wasn't there? My councillors were very unhappy when we heard about it. In fact, we sent a message to Eagleholm about it. We told Lady Riona that letting a Northerner be a griffin's partner was a very dangerous thing and she should know it better than most, and that if she wanted to protect her lands she should put a stop to it straight away."

Erian shook his head. "Everyone at Eagleholm knew it was wrong. Especially my father. But there were a few griffiners there—a few of them took his side, helped protect him. One of them owned the hatchery, and some of the others he worked with liked him. My father says that Lady Riona believed he could be useful and that trying to get rid of him would cause too much trouble. And he *was* useful, my father said. Did well at every job they gave him, until they made him Master of Trade. There was even talk of putting him on the council. But after his griffin died because he disobeyed orders, he went mad. He blamed my father for what happened, and he killed him."

Elkin nodded gravely. "Lady Riona was a good Mistress. I always thought so. But she brought what happened on herself. Northerners weren't meant to be griffiners, and that isn't just what I think. It's against the gods for it to happen." She frowned. "Don't get me wrong. I like the Northerners, you know. Some of them are very clever, and they're good craftsmen. I like their music, too. And those little spirits and things they believe in—it's interesting to study them. It teaches you so much about what our own people were like before they discovered true religion. But they can't be griffiners. They're just not right for it. They're too simple-minded, they don't have any understanding of things like law and governance, and they're too undisciplined. They can't help it; it's just in their nature to be that way. But I've seen it so many times. Let Northerners govern themselves and they end up killing one another. It's our duty as griffiners to protect them and look after them, but we can't ever let them try and join us. This isn't the first time it's happened, you see."

"It isn't?" said Erian.

"Oh no," said Elkin. She fixed him with a pale-green gaze.

"It's happened. Not very often, but it's happened. Do you know how Arddryn's Uprising started?"

"Yes, of course," said Erian. "A peasant woman called Arddryn incited a rebellion, and her followers took over a couple of cities before they were put down."

"That's the story they all tell," said Elkin. "But didn't you ever wonder why so many people wanted to follow her? And why the fighting went on so long?"

Erian blanched. "She wasn't a—?"

"Yes. It was kept quiet, you know," said Elkin. "Out of shame. Because we here at Malvern let it happen. She lived here once, you know. But one day—well, a griffin chick escaped from the hatchery, you see, and somehow she got her hands on it. She kept it hidden in her house, and it grew up knowing just her. By the time people found out about it, it was attached to her, and it was big enough to escape again when they took it back to the hatchery. Every time they tried, it flew back to her.

"A pair of griffiners decided to help Arddryn, out of charity, you know, and they gave her the training. Nobody thought anything would come of it. The griffin was obviously mad, and she was only some Northern woman who couldn't read or write. We thought they would live together as just friends and nothing else would happen. After all, there wasn't any chance they'd be given status or anything.

"But it turned out differently than that, didn't it? Arddryn found out that now she was a sort of griffiner, people wanted to do what she told them to. When she started using that to get things she wanted, Master Anech found out about it and sent the city guard to put a stop to it. But her griffin attacked them, and Arddryn and her griffin flew away before they could be arrested. After that they started moving around the countryside, gathering followers, and that was how the uprising started. And all because Master Anech let a griffin choose a Northerner." She shook her head sadly. "And now it's happened again."

Erian rubbed his head, unable to hide his shock. "By Gryphus' talons—so, Riona *knew* about that?"

"Of course. We sent to the other cities asking for help, you know, and she was one of those who came, along with her brother Rannagon. They were only young then. Lord Rannagon was the one who tracked Arddryn down and fought her and her griffin—Hyrenna, her name was. That's why everyone here remembers him so well." She smiled solemnly at Erian. "And now his son has come."

Erian smiled back. He felt warm and happy inside. "The more I learn about my father the prouder I am to be his son," he said.

"And so you should be," said Elkin.

Kraal had been idly grooming his feathers, apparently uninterested in the conversation. Now he raised his head and looked at Erian. "Lord Rannagon was the catalyst that ended the uprising," he rumbled. "We in the North owe him a great deal, and I was sorrowful to learn of his death."

Erian bowed his head. "Did you know him, Kraal?"

"I did," said the white griffin. Close to, Erian saw that his hindquarters were not white but pale gold. Those burnished eyes focused on him. "You look very much like him, Erian."

"Thank you," he replied. It wasn't the first time he'd been told that, but it made him happy even now.

Kraal watched him for a moment and then turned to Senneck. "Tell me, young griffin," he said, "there is something I wish to know."

Senneck raised her head, instantly alert. "Ask and I shall tell," she said promptly. "I am at your command, mighty Kraal."

If Kraal had noticed her overeager tone, he gave no sign of it. "The Northerner who murdered Lord Rannagon," he said. "Rumour has it that he has been caught and killed. Is this true?"

Senneck flicked her tail. "It is not true, though it pains me to admit it. He has not been seen since the night of the murders, but my human and I believe that he is going north."

"North?" Kraal repeated. "What is it that makes you believe this?"

"We apprehended his parents," said Senneck. "At Norton, close to the edge of Eagleholm's lands. They had gone there to meet with him, but he had not come. We interrogated them, and his father finally confessed that his son was going north. I was inclined to believe him. Your lands are the only place he could hope to find sanctuary."

Kraal inclined his head. "I believe your judgment was correct, Senneck. Further north there are uncharted lands. The murderer could hide there easily enough, assuming he could pass through our dominions without being apprehended." He looked at Erian and Senneck. "I thank you both for your warnings. Elkin and I shall warn our officials and the guard in the outlying cities to be watchful."

"What'll happen if he's caught?" Erian interrupted, unable to stop himself.

Kraal cast a slow blank look at him—not menacing but somehow far more frightening than anger could ever have been. Erian withered before it.

"He'll be brought here," said Elkin, coming to his rescue. "A criminal as dangerous as that has to be, you know. And then the council shall help us decide what to do with him. It would be a formality, though, of course."

"Execution, then?" said Erian, leaning closer without realising he was doing it.

"Of course," said Elkin, slightly surprised. "What else? The traitor's death, most likely."

"Could . . ." Erian realised he was sweating. "Could we—?"

Senneck silenced him with a glare. "We trust in the competence of your underlings, my lady," she said. "And in your justice. The Cursed One cannot survive long here, and he is a fool if he believes he can find safety in your dominions. After all, your leadership and your power are legend."

Elkin straightened up, her demeanour suddenly cool and reserved. But she smiled very slightly at Senneck's words. "Maybe I'm young," she said, "but I know how to lead, and Kraal knows more than you can imagine. And you can stay."

Erian started. "I'm sorry, my lady?"

"I said you can stay," said Elkin. "I like you, Erian, and you, too, Senneck. I think you both have potential, and it makes me happy to know that even though you could have gone anywhere, you chose to come to me. You'll have to work, of course."

"Oh!" said Erian. "Yes, of course, we understand that, and I'd be happy to—"

"One of my officials needs a new assistant," Elkin interrupted. "And I think you would be perfect, Lord Erian. You'll be a lord now, by the way; all my officials are. We'll have a ceremony for that later."

Everything seemed to have slowed down. Erian could feel his heart beating, and hear it, too, so loud it sounded like a massive drum. "My lady," he breathed. "I—I would be honoured."

She smiled that sweet smile again. "You haven't asked what your work will be."

"Oh. What will it be, my lady?"

"Lord Kerod, the Master of Farms, is the official who needs an assistant. He'll be your master," Elkin told him. "He's a good man, but he really doesn't know much about farming, you see. Since you grew up on a farm, I think you could be perfect."

Erian's heart sank. "Oh. What would I have to do?"

"It should be simple enough for you. The villages all have to meet a certain yield every year, and if they're well below it then you have to go out there and find out why. The Master of Farms has to monitor the villages and come up with new farming methods and send out people to train the peasants in how to use them. It makes it much more efficient. Malvern is the only city to have a Master of Farms, you know. The others prefer to leave the farmers to work it out for themselves, but I think that if you help them it can only help you. Don't you think so, Erian?"

"Oh yes!" said Erian, too quickly and much too eagerly. "After all, everyone has to eat, and if you help the farmers then there'll be more food," he added, hoping this would sound perceptive.

It seemed to work. Elkin smiled and nodded. "I'm glad you think so. Many other griffiners don't take me very seriously, because I'm young. I know you were surprised—you didn't hide it very well."

"I'm sorry—" Erian began.

"It doesn't matter," said Elkin. "Everybody is surprised. I tried to stop people from talking about my age. But, you see, it doesn't matter. I'm young, but I'm very clever. And Kraal is the strongest griffin in Cymria, you know. He has the strength, and I have the cleverness. We go very well together, I think." She sounded perfectly matter-of-fact.

"I am sure you do," Senneck said smoothly. "After all, a fool or a weakling could not have done what you both have done."

Kraal clicked his beak. "You had best be careful, Senneck. My human is vulnerable to flattery."

Elkin laughed. "We all are, you know. Even if we hide it. Well, then." She stood up. "I think we've talked long enough. I shall give orders for you two to be given quarters. You'll take up your duties in two days, once you've rested, and we'll have the lordship ceremony for you later. A feast would be good. I do like a feast, you know. And maybe a dance as well. Would you like that?"

"Very much," said Erian. He glanced at Senneck. "Very much, my lady."

"I thought you would," said Elkin.

20

One Beat

Prydwen's estimate had been an accurate one, and they reached the edge of the mountains within three days of his having made it. Cardock, still at the head of the column of black-robed figures, looked up at the peaks of Y Castell and felt nothing but a kind of dull relief. The last day or so had been thoroughly wearing for everyone, and he kept noticing how the column behind him was straggling. They would need some time to rest before they struck out into the mountains. Cardock had already said as much to Arenadd, and the others had backed him up.

Cardock had hoped that their talk on the hilltop, brief though it was, had been a sign that Arenadd was getting better and would begin to open up to him again, but he had been wrong. His son remained silent and shut in, unreadable, wrestling with some inner pain that he wouldn't allow to show through in front of anyone. Cardock suspected that he still cried from time to time when he was alone with Skandar. Perhaps he confided in the griffin, and that thought hurt Cardock more than he would admit. He felt as if he didn't know Arenadd any more, or at least not the grim, haggard man he had become. The old Arenadd, or Arren as Cardock now thought of him, had never been particularly sociable, but despite what Cardock now knew he had done, he had always been cheerful enough. Lord Arenadd Taranisäii, though, spent his time alone with his new partner, silent and brooding, all cold authority and distance. He had found a spare slave collar in the shed back at Herbstitt and spent a lot of his leisure time with it in his hands, endlessly toying with it, turning it over, examining the hinge and the spikes and the locking mechanism, and occasionally closing it partway but then pulling it apart again before it could lock shut.

Cardock sighed miserably. He had lost his wife, and now it felt as if he had lost his son, too.

He was very relieved when he heard the sound of wings overhead and looked up to see Skandar flying low and coming in to land on top of a smallish peak not far ahead. He was signalling to them to stop at its base and make camp.

They reached the new campsite well before sundown. It was on open land at the base of the mountain, fairly nondescript and not particularly sheltered. The trees thinned out here, and the ground was rocky.

Arenadd was waiting for them under a lone tree by a heap of tumbled rocks. Skandar was nowhere to be seen.

"Gone hunting," Arenadd said briefly.

Cardock looked around at the others, who were already setting up camp. "So, we're here," he said, for lack of anything else to say. "Y Castell at last."

Arenadd nodded and sighed. "I know this place," he said. "*This* is where I was captured. Right here by this tree." He kicked it. "Skandar insisted on coming back here for some reason, maybe because it's a place he knows, too. He doesn't have a territory, so this is the closest thing to familiar ground that he's got. Now—" He sighed again. "I'd better go and find a camp spot. See you later."

Cardock watched disconsolately as he walked off, and sat down at the base of the tree to rest his aching feet. The truth was that he simply couldn't fathom the way Arenadd had been behaving lately. Perhaps it was the fact that he was now among other people who all knew his real name and what he had done. Having a reputation like that couldn't be easy. If there was only some way to get him to talk about it, it might help.

Cardock stood up abruptly. There was work to do, and sitting around moping would help no-one. He willed his sore legs back into action and walked off to help with the setting up of the camp.

Caedmon and the others were busily gathering wood for their fire, and Cardock joined them. Unfortunately, the space they had chosen—right under the lone tree—had very little wood around it. Cardock told Caedmon to stay there and rest while he and the others went back the way they had come, where the trees were thicker. They reached the fringes of the forest and spread out.

The forest was already thick with other people setting up their own camps, and Cardock weaved his way among them, careful not to get in the way. Most of the obvious wood here had already been claimed, so he moved further in, where there were fewer people.

Eventually he had some luck: he came across a dead tree that had fallen some time ago and had plenty of dry branches on it. He began snapping some off, on the lookout for any larger pieces he could carry. He wouldn't have to go any further than this; the tree was very large and had more than enough. In fact, some others had already spotted it and were coming to help themselves.

Cardock moved to the far side of the tree, searching for a good solid piece of wood. A proper fire would need a log or two if it was going to keep burning all night. He found a good-sized bough that was nearly detached from the trunk, and began to pull at it.

"— killed them."

Cardock stopped to catch his breath and peered curiously through the branches. A couple of the men who had come to join him were talking as they gathered branches.

"Well, it only made sense," one of them said. "If he hadn't, we'd have bin caught, sure as fate."

"Right enough, yeah, but it's just, what I heard—well, I was right next door, see? And awake. Couldn't sleep on that damned floor. I was right near the wall, an' I heard what happened in there."

"You said so already. What'd you hear, then?"

The first man shuddered. "It was horrible. I swear, I hear it every night when I can't sleep. I heard these sort of—just thumping and a few yells. Hard to hear over the storm outside. Didn't think much of it, but I heard the last one. Everything sort of died down, and then I heard this voice."

"What'd it say, then?" said his friend.

"It was so *quiet*," said the first man. "That was what scares me most. It wasn't, like, screaming or anything. It just said, 'Please don't kill me. I have children. Please don't kill me.' And after that, nothing. Just another thump, an' something hit the wall behind me, and after that, just silence."

Cardock's blood ran cold. "Oh, gods," he whispered.

"No witnesses, then," said the second voice. "He gave their swords to those friends of his, you know. I wondered where they come from."

Cardock didn't hear anything else after that. He let go of the branch and began to walk back toward the mountain. He felt strangely numb. Even calm.

Of course. It all made sense. The silence, the hiding and the tears. He'd spoken to Nolan and the others, and according to them Arenadd had behaved normally enough at Herbstitt. So why this sudden change?

Cardock cursed himself. He felt betrayed, but he also felt like a fool. Only two guards for all those slaves! And both of them trained men, hardly likely to be asleep while on duty. And he, Cardock, had believed the lie, and he had utterly failed to see or understand what he was seeing in his son after that. Not the reserve of a wanted man but the guilt of one who had killed again, and recently. A man unable to face his own father.

The sun was beginning to go down as he reached the lone tree. Caedmon was attempting to light a small heap of kindling, while Olwydd piled larger sticks around it.

Cardock stopped, breathing heavily. "Where's Arenadd?" he said.

Caedmon looked up. "That was quick. Where's the firewood, sir?"

"The others will bring it. Where's Arenadd?" Cardock snapped. "I need to talk to him."

Olwydd gave him a jaundiced look. "*Lord* Arenadd went around the other side of the mountain."

Cardock nodded curtly and walked off. The mountain was a small one, but he had to walk for a while before he saw the little patch of firelight that marked Arenadd's camp.

Skandar was still absent when he reached the spot, and Arenadd was sitting alone by the fire, poking at it with his sword point.

Cardock didn't know what he had planned to do. He had thought of shouting at him, accusing him, even hitting him. But now, looking at Arren, it wasn't in him to do those things. He didn't know what to say.

Arenadd looked up. "Hello."

Cardock moved closer. "You killed those guards." It came out flatly, neither accusing nor questioning.

Arenadd's expression tightened. "I did what I had to do."

Cardock wanted to reach out, hit him or hug him, he didn't know which. "You said you hadn't," he said. "You told me—"

Arenadd was avoiding his gaze. "I didn't think there was any point in telling you. Knowing it wouldn't have helped you. I thought you deserved some peace of mind."

"Peace of—!" Cardock's voice finally sharpened. "Arenadd, how *could* you? I can't—what's happened to you? You're not the man I remember. How could you have done that? First your master, then Rannagon and all those people in the Eyrie— now this."

Arenadd stood up. "I thought you said Rannagon deserved to die."

"Well . . ." Cardock faltered. "You had just cause to do that. But you told me you couldn't live with it; you told me so. But you did it again."

"Not by choice," Arenadd snapped. He was gripping the sword now, not pointing it at his father but nearly so. "I had to do it. To get you out of there quietly. If even one of them had lived he would have raised the alarm. They all saw me; they'd have described me to someone. Can you imagine what would have happened then? It was for safety—mine and yours."

"Yes, but . . ." Cardock's voice weakened. "But killing people, just like that, I don't—it's not *like* you. I never believed that you could—"

Arenadd sighed a long, tired sigh. "I know. I never believed I could either. After I killed Rannagon, I was in a kind of shock for a long time. Sometimes I almost believed I hadn't done it, or that it was a dream I was going to wake up from. But after those guards—"

"You should have said something," Cardock said more gently. "I knew you were unhappy."

"No," said Arenadd. "It's not that, Dad. It's not that I—" He broke off, shaking his head. "It wasn't the same this time. I killed those guards myself; Skandar couldn't get in. I took them by surprise. Stabbed one in the back, slashed the next across the throat. The third one tried to run, but Skandar caught him. The last one surrendered, but I killed him anyway. Strangled him.

He died quietly. And afterward . . ." His face was pale. "And afterward, it was—I felt—I *still* feel . . ."

Cardock felt his stomach cramping. "I heard you crying," he said softly. "I know you must—"

Arenadd looked him in the eye. "I felt nothing," he said.

There was silence between them.

"I felt nothing," Arenadd repeated. "I felt nothing while it was happening, and I felt nothing afterward. And I still feel nothing."

"But you were—"

"I was frightened," said Arenadd. "I knew I should feel something, but . . ." He turned away abruptly, mumbling half to himself, "I am the man without a heart."

Cardock felt as if the ground had vanished out from beneath him.

"Go," Arenadd said quietly, without turning around. "Please, just leave me, Dad. I need to be alone."

His voice was flat and distant—not hostile, or dismissive, but terribly, painfully uncaring.

Cardock stepped closer to him. "Arenadd, please, don't do this. Don't be like this. You can't just hide yourself away like this. You have to talk to someone. I'm your father. Why don't you trust me any more?"

Arenadd was silent.

"Please," Cardock said again. "Just listen to me. You know what happened at Eagleholm. You hid yourself away then, remember? You needed help, but you didn't look for it. Not even from your own parents."

Arenadd turned sharply. "Why, do you think it would have helped?" he snapped. "Could you have given Eluna back to me? Can you stop me from being a murderer now? Is that it? A nice little chat and a cup of tea and everything's all right again?"

"I'm not your enemy," Cardock snapped back, "So stop pretending I am. I only want to help. You're my only son, Arenadd, and I care about you."

Arenadd's anger died down again. "No-one can help me, Dad," he said quietly. "Not you, not the gods, not anyone."

"Don't be childish," said Cardock. "You're a Northerner, Arenadd. Pull yourself together. There are a hundred and fifty or so men out there relying on you. If you won't let me help you, then try and help them."

Arenadd started as if he had just been slapped in the face. "That's not—I *am* helping them. Don't try and—"

At that moment the quiet around them was disturbed by a loud thumping and crashing from behind Cardock. He turned sharply; someone was coming, running toward them.

Arenadd raised his sword. "Who's that?" he called.

The crashing grew louder, and Cardock moved instinctively to stand behind Arenadd as a skinny shape emerged into the firelight.

It was Torc, pale and breathless. "Sir! Sir, come quickly!"

Arenadd relaxed slightly. "What is it, Torc?"

Torc paused to hold his chest. "They've—someone's found us, sir," he said. "We've been seen."

Arenadd tensed. "Godsdamnit. Who? How many? Are they armed?"

"It's just one person, sir," said Torc. "Olwydd and the others caught her; they said I should come and get you straight away."

"Right," said Arenadd. "Let's go."

The three of them dashed off, with Torc in the lead. The boy blundered through the undergrowth, making for the little patch of firelight on the other side of the mountain. Night had come, and none of them had a torch, but fortunately the terrain was fairly level here. Still, they had to negotiate a large stretch of damp bracken and soap-bush before the ground cleared.

There Torc broke into a full run, and Arenadd followed close on his heels. He drew level, passed him, and reached the spot before Torc and Cardock, which meant that he was the first to see the scene.

Caedmon, Nolan and Annan were there by the tree, keeping well back and staring at the knot of people standing on the far side of the fire. Dafydd and Garnoc were there, weapons drawn, keeping close to Prydwen and Olwydd, who were holding someone between them. They had twisted the prisoner's arms behind her back, in the manner of professional guards, and Olwydd was holding his sword to her throat. She stood still, breathing hard, her silver hair hanging over her face.

Arenadd stopped dead.

Garnoc saw him and stepped toward him, bowing low. "My lord," he said. "We caught her trying to steal food at the edge of camp. She was on her own." He sounded rather proud of himself.

Arenadd didn't seem to hear him. He moved closer, his eyes fixed on the woman. She wrenched her arm, hissing and snarling.

Prydwen hit her. "Look up, ye Southern scum," he snapped. "Show some respect."

The woman looked up sullenly at Arenadd, and their eyes met.

Arenadd stared at her, as if in a trance. "Skade?"

She stilled. "Arenadd?" ·

Arenadd waved at them. "Let go of her. Do it!"

They did, and Skade pulled away and walked toward Arenadd. The Northerners tensed, but backed away when Arenadd glared at them, and the two of them met by the fireside.

Arenadd looked her up and down. "Good gods," he said. "Skade. It really is you. What are you *doing* here?"

She straightened up. "What do you mean?" she said. "What do you *think* I am doing here, Arenadd Taranisäii?"

He put his sword back in his belt and folded his arms. "I don't know, you tell me."

She hissed at him. "I have been waiting for *you*, you faithless blackrobe. Where have you been? Where did these men come from?"

"They're friends of mine," said Arenadd. He paused. "Skade, what in the gods' names is going on? Why are you still here? And still—why are you still like that?"

She glanced at the onlookers. "Now is not the time for that. You still have not answered me. Where were you? I was waiting for you for days."

"Days? What d'you mean, days?"

"Don't you dare speak to me like that," Skade snarled. She was speaking Cymrian now, though in a slightly stilted manner. "I put my faith in you, Arenadd. I trusted you to be here. I came out of the cave, thinking you would be there, and you were gone. I waited for days; I nearly starved. You were the only—" She moved closer. "The spirits refused me," she said, reverting briefly to griffish. "As you can see. I have been condemned to live out the rest of my life in this body. I returned to the living world knowing that you were the only thing I had left. My only link to the new world I must live in. My only comfort. And you were gone." Her voice rose. "You were *gone*! You betrayed me. Abandoned me!"

"*Abandoned* you?" said Arenadd. "I'm sorry, I must have misunderstood the last thing you said to me." His voice took on a sour tinge. "I don't know, it's been a while, but I thought it was something about how our pairing was over and you had no more use for me. That was it, wasn't it?"

She hesitated. "Words spoken in haste can—I was confused, overexcited. I did not mean to hurt you."

"Well, that makes everything better, doesn't it?" Arenadd sneered. "You find me, make use of me, toy with me, and the moment I stop being useful you drop me like a hot coal. Or maybe I should say a hot iron, which is what they jammed into the back of my hand after they caught me and dragged me to Herbstitt."

Skade backed off a little. "They caught you?"

"Yes. Under this very tree, as it happens. Not that I wouldn't have left anyway if I'd had the choice."

"You *wanted* to come here," she said. "You believed they could—"

"Well, they didn't. Understand? They didn't care. They tortured me and then threw me out, and meanwhile my parents were being sold into slavery. Thanks for the advice, it was a big help. We come all this way, neither of us get what we're after, I get captured. Wonderful plan. Had you actually thought of another idea in case they didn't like us? Hmm? Or were you hoping you could get Skandar to carry you somewhere else next?"

"I did not know," Skade snapped. "And you agreed to it. You did not know what to do any more than I did. If they did not help you, then that is not my fault."

"All they told me was the exact same thing people used to shout at me in the streets back home. 'Go back to the North, blackrobe.' So that's what I'm going to do, and I'm taking these men with me."

"And me?" said Skade.

"You?" said Arenadd. "What about you? Go back to Withypool if you want; I don't care. Go your own way. I don't want any part of it, understand?"

There was silence. They had been shouting at each other, so loudly that the onlookers had backed away. Others had come to see what was going on, and several dozen pairs of eyes were staring straight at them.

Skade didn't seem to be aware of them, or of anything except Arenadd. She looked suddenly smaller, and lost. "I thought . . . I did not . . ."

"Did not what?" said Arenadd. His voice and face were full of dislike.

"I thought that you could help me," said Skade in a small voice.

"Really." It wasn't a question.

"Arenadd," said Skade, "I—I should not have said what I said. Ever since I returned and you were not here I thought of what I said, and thought that you had left because of it. And ever since then I have regretted it. I waited here because I did not know what to do, and every day I thought of you and wished you were here. And I realised that I missed you. I missed you every moment. I looked for you in every shadow, I thought of everything you had ever said to me, I—" She bowed her head. "I must learn how to live this way now, and you were the only teacher I ever had. Without you I am lost."

"And why should I care about that?"

Skade said nothing. She stared at him, her golden eyes pleading. The pupils were no longer slitted. They had become round, and the gold had been reduced to thin bands around them, barely noticeable to the casual glance. They were nearly human now.

Neither of them spoke, and the silence drew out between them.

Arenadd did not falter. He stood rock steady, arms folded, glaring at her with contempt and anger in every line on his face.

After a time Skade sighed, and her shoulders hunched in defeat.

Finally, Arenadd moved. His hand lashed out; grabbing her by the shoulder. He pulled her toward him, almost violently, his other hand reaching for her neck. But it clasped her other shoulder instead, and he pressed her against him and kissed her hard on the mouth. She started and tried to pull away for an instant, but Arenadd paid no attention. He wrapped his arms around her and held her close, his mouth pressed against hers, and after a moment she had relaxed into him and was kissing him back, her hands in his hair.

But it only lasted for a moment. Quite suddenly, Arenadd had broken free and staggered away from her, his face contorting. He slammed into the trunk of the tree and stood there, his hands pressed into his chest, gasping in agony.

Cardock ran to him. "Arenadd!"

The others started toward Skade. "What have ye done to him?" Olwydd demanded.

Skade ignored him and ran to Arenadd. "Arenadd!"

Arenadd was making a strange sound, half gasping, half sobbing. He raised his head and stared straight at Skade. "What did you do?" he whispered. "What did you do to me?"

"I did nothing," she said, "Arenadd, what—?"

His hand was still pressed into his chest. "My heart. My heart, I felt it . . ."

Skade took him by the arm. "What do you mean? Did it . . . ?"

Arenadd's eyes met hers. "Yes," he said softly. "Yes. I felt it. Not any more, but just then, when you kissed me."

"Arenadd." Cardock clasped his son by the shoulder. "Are you all right?"

Arenadd stood up straight. He was breathing heavily. "Yes. Yes, I'm fine. Olwydd—" The Northerner had reached out to grab hold of Skade. Arenadd met his eye and shook his head. "Don't touch her. Leave her alone."

Olwydd backed off. "Who is she, sir?"

Arenadd stepped away from the tree. "She's Skade. Skade of Withypool." He looked at her. "Lady Skade."

"Lady, sir?" Olwydd said doubtfully.

"Yes, Olwydd," he told him more sharply. "This is the Lady Skade, and no-one is to harm her. She is my—she's with me."

Skade had moved closer to him. "I am?"

Arenadd took her hand. "Yes, Skade." He looked at the others. "She comes with us," he said. "That is"—he looked at Skade—"if you want to."

"I do," she said firmly. "Where you go, I go."

He looked at the others again. "Is that understood?"

Dafydd was the first to speak. "Yes, sir. If she's with ye, then yes, sir."

An awkward silence had fallen. Most of the slaves were staring at Skade, some with fascination, others with deep distrust, but all with fear. She ignored them.

Cardock grabbed Arenadd by the arm. "Arenadd, what happened?" He could feel his son shuddering slightly under his hand.

Arenadd shook himself. "I'm fine. It's just my chest." He touched it. "That old wound where the guards shot me. It hurts sometimes. Skade accidentally put pressure on it."

Cardock gave him a suspicious look, but he finally shrugged and let the matter drop.

"Who are you?" he said, turning to Skade. "How do you know my son?"

"Oh," Arenadd interrupted. "Skade, this is my father, Cardock."

Skade looked at him, expressionless. "He looks like you." To Cardock she said, "I am pleased to meet you, Cardock of Idun." She paused. "I am Skade, and I am from Withypool. Arenadd and I met in the wilds, and he and Skandar brought me here. I owe him my life."

"And I owe her mine," said Arenadd.

"Well, if ye trust her, sir, so do I," Olwydd broke in. He bowed to Skade. "I'm sorry, my lady. If I'd known . . ." He looked at Prydwen. "Give her back her things, would ye?"

Prydwen started. "Oh. Right, yes." He hurried over and made an awkward bow to Skade as he held two objects out to her, a sword and a dagger. "Yer things, milady."

"That's my sword!" said Arenadd.

Skade smiled and gave it to him. "I kept it safe for you." She put the dagger into her belt.

He took the sword and turned it over in his hands. The blade was slightly rusty, but other than that it was as good as new. "I thought I'd lost it."

"You did," said Skade. "I found it."

"Here," he said, taking the short sword from his belt and offering it to her. "I don't need this now, but I think you might. I can teach you how to use it, if you want."

Skade examined the sword and then looked up at him. "Yes. I think I should learn."

Arenadd nodded. "Yes." He looked at the others. "I think we should all learn." He raised his voice. "We're going to stay here for a while. I have a few things to teach you. All of you. I don't claim to be a weapons master or a general, but I know how to handle a sword and a few other things about fighting, and very soon I think we'll be called upon to know those things." He paused and glanced up.

"For what?" said Cardock.

Arenadd wasn't listening. There was a swoosh of air and a sudden movement from overhead, and Skandar appeared from out of the night sky, landing neatly beside his partner. The others scattered, but Skade stayed where she was.

Skandar appeared tired and a little ragged as he took up his accustomed place behind Arenadd. He looked at Skade and dipped his head briefly to her.

She bowed back. "Hello, Skandar. I am glad to see you again." She looked at Arenadd. "I am curious. Why do you want these . . . men to know how to fight? I would have thought that your time would be better spent moving further north. Staying in one place for too long would only increase the risk of being found."

"Yes, I know," said Arenadd. "But it's a necessary risk. They need to rest, and I have to try and do something to organise them properly. They're not an army, but—"

"But why fighting?" said Skade.

Arenadd scratched Skandar under the beak and smiled a very small, enigmatic smile. "For Guard's Post," he said.

21

A Place in the World

Days passed, and Erian began to settle into his new life. He and Senneck had been given quarters in the Eyrie: a pair of rooms in one of the outer towers, which were spacious if not luxurious. Senneck took possession of the larger one, which opened onto a small balcony she could take flight from, and Erian took the other. There was straw in one chamber and a bed and desk in the other, and both were supplied with food from the kitchens two levels below.

The day after their arrival they were both introduced to Lord Kerod, the Master of Farms, and his partner, the rather oddly named Eekrae. Lord Kerod proved to be an elderly man, whose stooped appearance was even more pronounced when he stood beside the young and spritely Eekrae. Kerod's look toward Erian was friendly enough.

"A pleasure to meet you, young master," he said, holding out a hand.

Erian reached out in return, and the two of them linked fingers and gave a brief tug, the traditional griffiners' gesture of greeting.

"I'm honoured to meet you, my lord," Erian said when this was done. "Lady Elkin told me you were one of her finest," he added, lying.

Kerod gave a wrinkled smile. "I'm pleased to hear her ladyship hasn't forgotten me. So, you have been sent to help me, have you?"

"We have, my lord," said Erian. Senneck had already advised him not to reveal that this was his first official position, so he resisted that temptation and said, "I hope we can work well together."

"Oh, no doubt we can," said Kerod rather dismissively. "There's very little to it, you'll find. With two of us, there'll be even less, I'm thinking." He grinned again. "Leaves more time for the finer things in life."

"Such as?" said Erian.

Kerod jabbed the air. "Hunting! This territory has some of the best hunting anywhere in Cymria, my boy, just you let me show you some time. I know a few choice spots. You and Senneck," he said, bowing in her direction, "will probably find flying out there in search of deer and bear much more to your taste than staying here dealing with paperwork!" He nodded at Erian again. "Yes, Eekrae and I really must show you two. Soon. Remind me."

Erian smiled. "We will, my lord."

"Good!" said Kerod. "Now, we should go to my office, and I will show you the work we'll be doing."

"But you do not need to come, if you do not want," Eekrae put in, speaking to Senneck. He clicked his beak cheerfully. "Let our humans wrestle with papers, and you and I can fly together. I shall show you the finest places to soar in the evenings and the places to perch at sunrise. And perhaps we shall race each other between the towers—it is dangerous, but the best of us love it!"

Senneck hesitated very briefly before she gave a dismissive flick of her tail. "I am sorry, but I would prefer to accompany my human. I should see what it is he will be doing here, so that I may advise him." A gleam showed in her eye. "Not that I shall need to," she added, with unaccustomed pride. "My human is most cunning and learned."

Eekrae chirped. "Ah, but my human is old and wise."

Senneck dipped her head. "Then he shall teach my human," she said more humbly.

Erian blinked—it wasn't like Senneck to boast about him—but he said nothing and followed Kerod. The two griffins fell in behind him. Eekrae seemed to want to be close to Senneck, and the two of them made little darting mock attacks at each other with their beaks as they walked. Erian could hear them talking, but they were speaking far more rapidly than usual. Few humans could understand griffish unless it was spoken slowly.

Kerod reached a door and opened it, leading them into his large, ramshackle office. Papers covered every surface.

"And here we are," said the old man. "Apologies for the mess, but I don't let the servants in to clean it up. Don't want them seeing anything they shouldn't, even if none of 'em could read it anyway."

Erian shrugged. "I'm sure I can help tidy things up a little. If you'd like, my lord."

Kerod cackled. "Griffiners, tidying up! That's a fine joke. Come now, and I'll show you how it works."

Senneck and Eekrae stood on either side of the door, and Erian waited by the desk while Kerod unlocked a cabinet and brought out an enormous leather-bound book, which he dumped on the desk, disturbing a heap of paper.

"The Book of Farms," he said, opening it. "Very important."

Erian examined it. Every page was covered in endless rows of tiny runes. The one he was looking at now was headed with the word "Snowton" in larger runes. Underneath that were several columns saying things like "rufus, 500 head," and "dairy, 200 head."

"What does it mean?" he asked after a polite interval.

"Don't let all the numbers scare you; it's quite simple," said Kerod. He tapped the word "Snowton." "Every single town and village in the North is in here. This is Snowton's page, with a list of everything they have there. How many cattle, how many sheep, how many fields, orchards, beehives, mills—everything. The Book of Farms is updated every ten years—lucky for us the last one was two years ago so we won't have that hanging over our heads. Believe me, taking a census of a territory this big is more work than most people do in a lifetime."

Erian examined the book, trying to look keen and intelligent and hide his true dismay. "I see."

"This book is the most important thing you and I have to work with," said Kerod. "See, every village is taxed according to its resources, and it's our job to go through the book and work out the amounts, and then we submit that to the Master of Taxation. Meanwhile, we'll be getting reports from the countryside, which we have to record. Fires, cattle disease, that sort of thing. And Lady Elkin has given the farmers permission to send us their ideas and complaints, gods help us."

"So, we don't have to visit them ourselves?" said Erian.

"Oh, gods no," said Kerod. "Leave them to come to us if they want to; we have better things to do than fly around visiting every blasted darkman who thinks he knows more about how to fertilise corn."

Erian frowned. "A 'darkman'? What's that?"

Kerod gave him a bemused look. "What?"

"Sorry, my lord. I don't think I've heard that word before."

"Good gods," said Kerod. "*Northerners*, boy. Blackrobes, darkmen, moon-worshippers, whatever you want to call them. Don't tell me you didn't know that."

"Oh." Erian felt himself going red. "Yes, of course. I just haven't heard them called that before."

Kerod sniffed. "Well, in a manner of speaking, most of the ones living here aren't really blackrobes. Only the slaves wear robes, see. Free Northerners hate slaves. Look down on 'em and such. They get very upset if you call 'em blackrobes to their faces. Not like I care. But it's a bit less confusing if you call the free ones darkmen."

Erian grinned to hide his embarrassment. "So, are we the lightmen or something?"

"Don't be daft," said Kerod. He closed the book. "You and I, young Erian, are griffiners, and that's all anyone, darkmen or otherwise, should be calling us." He walked over to the cabinet and put the book back inside. "Anyway, now that's sorted out, I think I'm ready for a little lunch. Care to join us?"

"Of course."

Accordingly, the four of them retired to Kerod's own rather larger chambers and made themselves comfortable while a servant went to get some food. Erian was surprised to see that the servant, like most of those in the Eyrie, was a Northerner.

"I'm surprised you employ them," he said.

"Why shouldn't we?" said Kerod.

"Oh. Well, it's just that . . ." Erian paused, feeling inexplicably embarrassed. "I don't know; I just assumed that all the Northerners here were slaves."

Kerod threw back his head and laughed. "Hah! You young Southerners have some funny ideas, don't you?"

"I don't understand, my lord," Erian said rather stiffly. He hated being laughed at.

"Don't get me wrong, there *are* slaves here," said Kerod. "Not as many as you might think. See, we use slavery as punishment. If you aren't born a slave, you can be made one by breaking the law. After that, you're sold somewhere. Usually to somewhere further south, but we also sell plenty of slaves in Amoran as well. The Amorani have the biggest slave trade in the world, and they do like Northerners. Need plenty of labour to build those giant statues of theirs, I suppose. But most of the darkmen here are free, so why shouldn't we give them jobs? They outnumber us, for Gryphus' sake."

Erian blanched. "They do?"

Kerod nodded. "Hundreds to one," he said carelessly. "But there are about a hundred griffiners living here, and plenty of unpartnered griffins, too. They don't dare rebel. The last time—well, everybody knows about that, don't they?"

Erian nodded. "But aren't there still some rebels hiding further north? That's what I heard. And this Arddryn—"

"Oh, there's a few, I'll grant," said Kerod. "Fugitives, runaway slaves, outlaws. We've caught some over the years and got enough out of them to know they're there. There's only a handful of 'em hanging on. Land's too inhospitable to support large numbers, see; most likely they're barely able to feed themselves, let alone cause any mischief."

"Just one Northerner is enough," Erian said darkly. "In the right place."

Kerod looked keenly at him for a moment and then nodded. "Ah, right. Yes. You came here from Eagleholm, didn't you? Yes. Terrible story that was. Really a Northerner who did it, then?"

"Yes. I met him."

Kerod's eyes widened. "You did? Good gods, what was he like?"

Lunch arrived at that point, and while the four of them ate, Erian told the story of his meeting with Arren Cardockson.

"I didn't think much of him," he confessed. "I went to the hatchery looking for Lord Roland. I wanted to present myself to the griffins. But when I got there, the only person inside was a Northerner, wearing a slave collar and sweeping the floor."

"What did he look like?" said Kerod.

"Like a beggar," said Erian. "Dirty and scruffy, and wearing that collar. I thought he was a slave, of course, so I asked him where his master was. But when he talked, I was amazed. There he was—this blackrobe with a beard like an old carpet, and he talked like a noble."

"Educated?"

"Oh yes," said Erian. "Lord Roland taught him, gave him

the training after he became a griffiner. But of course after
his griffin died he lost everything. They say he lost his mind
after the wild griffin killed his partner. I didn't see anything of
his madness then; he was very rude, but he seemed perfectly
sane to me." Erian sighed and picked at his food. "It was that
same night he stole the chick. Right after I left, probably. I saw
him the next day, at his trial. He was . . . insane. His face was
torn open, his clothes were burned. He told all sorts of terrible
lies to the council, blamed everything he'd done on my father,
claimed he'd been victimised and beaten on his orders. And
then after he was given the death sentence he went mad and
started screaming that he was going to kill my father. He even
tried to attack him right there; they had to drag him out, fighting every step of the way."

"By gods," said Kerod. "That must have been a sight to see."
He scratched his chin. "The stories about him being a griffiner
are really true, then."

Erian nodded. "I never saw his partner, but I know her name
was Eluna. He came back to Eagleholm on the same day I
arrived."

"So, you're Lord Rannagon's son?" said Kerod.

"I am, my lord."

"That's a lineage to be proud of," Kerod remarked. He
yawned. "I don't doubt we'll work well together. Lady Elkin
seemed to think you were a promising young man."

Erian brightened up. "What can you tell me about her?
I'm—I'm curious about her, and Kraal, too." He cast a quick
glance at Senneck, but she was crouched on the far side of the
room with Eekrae, apparently deep in conversation with the
other griffin.

Kerod poured himself some wine. "I take it you were surprised when you saw her?"

"Well, yes," said Erian. "I had no idea. When I came here I
was expecting—"

"Some old lady in velvet?" said Kerod, grinning.

Erian thought briefly of his aunt, Lady Riona, and her aged
dignity. "Honestly, yes."

"That's what they all expect," said Kerod. He took a swallow of wine. "Hmm, good vintage, this. Try some. There's a
little bit of a story behind that, if you want to hear it."

"Oh, please tell me," said Erian, helping himself to some wine. "I'd love to know."

"All right, then. It all starts with Kraal, really. Most of the griffins living here were born in the North, but nobody really knows exactly where Kraal came from. I was just a boy when he came here, and he was huge even then. It's said he spent most of his earlier life flying from city to city, going wherever he chose. Supposedly he's the biggest griffin ever seen in Cymria. Powerful, too. Powerfully magical. Powers even other griffins are afraid of.

"Anyway, Kraal didn't have a partner, but everyone knew that if he ever did choose a human for himself that human would become a Master or Mistress straight away. But he wouldn't choose anyone. People said he was so powerful he thought he was above that sort of thing, and can you really blame him? He lived in the North for a while, visited Malvern a few times, but never stayed long. And then one day, one day—completely out of the blue—he chooses someone. And it's not a great lord or a mighty warrior; instead it's Lord Hemant's sickly daughter. Only twelve, and nearly mute. Most people thought she was touched in the head and wouldn't live to marry."

"Elkin," Erian breathed.

Kerod nodded. "But after Kraal chose her, everything changed. She started speaking, she got stronger and—well, you know the rest. She was made Mistress of the Eyrie the instant Lord Anech died, a year or so later."

Erian gaped at him. "She was—she became an Eyrie Mistress when she was *thirteen*?"

"Don't be fooled," Kerod said sharply. "I know what you're thinking. Many, many people here were against it. They said it was insanity letting her become Mistress. But Kraal had chosen her, and nobody dared stand in *his* way. It didn't take long for us to see what was going on—or *think* we saw, anyway. We thought he chose her because she was tiny and weak, so he could make every decision for her and she would do as he said. Of course no griffiner would do anything without consulting their griffin, but an Eyrie Mistress completely controlled by her partner? Unthinkable."

Erian thought of Senneck's threats at Herbstitt. "Yes."

Kerod shrugged. "But we were wrong. All of us were wrong,

and we were proven wrong less than a week after Elkin was named Mistress. That girl—that girl has the finest mind I have ever seen in my life. The whole taxation system we have now— all her idea. She reorganised all the trade routes, renewed the most important relations with our neighbours. We had plenty of officials who weren't doing their jobs properly. They were lazy or incompetent or corrupt, but they came from good families or had money, and Anech hadn't dared do anything because he couldn't afford to have them turn on him. Well, that's not a problem any more. They're all gone. Elkin booted every single one of 'em out of office or forced 'em to reform, and when some of 'em tried to rebel they didn't last half a day."

Erian listened. "She gave you your post, didn't she?"

"That she did. I'm only from a minor house, see, which means I couldn't get much in the way of status. Eekrae and I spent our time working for the Master of Farms, flying around the villages and talking to farmers and so on. But Elkin showed the old Master the door, and gave us his place."

Erian grinned. "*Now* I think I understand why you like her so much."

A shrug. "What did you think of her?"

That caught Erian off guard. "Oh. Well." He thought about it for a moment. "I was surprised at first, when I saw her. Kraal—*he* scared me. Scared both of us, actually. I didn't think Senneck was afraid, but afterward she confessed to me." He glanced at her, hoping she wasn't listening in. "She said he was the biggest griffin she'd ever seen, and she spent the whole meeting thinking about how he could tear her head off in one go if he wanted to."

Kerod grinned. "Yes, most people think that sort of thing around him. Griffins too, probably. And Elkin? What did you think of her?"

"My lord, I liked her," Erian said. The words seemed to fall out of him, taking him by surprise, but he knew they were the truth. "Is she betrothed?" he added, without thinking.

"Not so far as I know," said Kerod. "She tends to keep away from men. She *will* have to marry eventually, though. When it suits her."

Erian wished he hadn't asked, and drank some more wine to cover the moment. "We talked for a long time," he said. "She asked me questions about where I'd come from and about what happened at Eagleholm. It was like—well, it wasn't like having an audience with an Eyrie Mistress at all. It was like chatting to a friend. And then she told me I could stay, just casually, like it was nothing at all, and said she wanted me to become your assistant."

Kerod nodded. "Surprised you, didn't it?"

"Yes," said Erian. He smiled involuntarily, remembering it. He and Senneck had discussed it afterward, and though the griffin had misgivings, he knew what it must mean. Elkin hadn't spoken to him like an underling but like a friend. She liked him, and that was why—

"She's very clever," said Kerod, interrupting his thoughts. "See, she talks to everybody like that. It's her way. How did it make you feel?"

Erian gaped at him. "Uh—I—uh—relaxed? Welcome?"

"Exactly. She put you at your ease, acted like a friend. She isn't one to interrogate people or scare them into giving her information. She charms them instead, makes them want to tell her things."

Erian crumbled inside. "Oh."

"Fooled you, didn't she?" said Kerod. "You didn't even realise she was doing it, did you?"

"No," Erian mumbled.

"Not many people do," said Kerod, in what he probably thought was a reassuring voice. "I told you she was clever."

Erian realised that Senneck was giving him a warning glare. "Yes indeed, my lord. It will be an honour to serve her."

"No need to call me that," said Kerod. "Kerod will do fine. We're equals here, Erian."

That cheered him up very slightly. "Of course, my l— Kerod."

Kerod yawned. "Well, if you've finished eating then we should probably make our way back to the office an' see if we can't get some work done."

Erian was still hungry, but he nodded anyway. The prospect of spending an afternoon thumbing through the Book of Farms was a dismal one, but Senneck had already impressed on him the importance of making a good impression as quickly as possible.

Back in the office, Kerod sat him down at the desk and gave him a more thorough explanation of how he was to use the book. He had to go through it and check each entry against the stack of reports that had been brought in for that month, to see if each village still had its full complement of each resource. It was a tedious process, but straightforward enough, and once Erian had grasped it Kerod said, "And there you go. Now I've got some papers to sort through while you're doing that."

Senneck had been standing silently behind Erian's chair while all this was going on, listening to everything and ignoring Eekrae, who was watching her hopefully from a spot by the door. Erian, well aware of her watchful gaze, dipped the reed stylus in the ink and set to work.

Senneck stayed where she was for a long time, occasionally pointing out a mistake or helping him find something in the endless lists of figures. Eekrae, bored, dozed beside the door, and Kerod wandered here and there, rifling through cupboards in search of something or other. Eventually he looked up at the two of them and said, "That's a helpful griffin you have, Erian. I couldn't get Eekrae to do that if his life depended on it." He grinned when Senneck looked up at him. "Doesn't like to let you out of her sight, does she? What is she, your partner or your nursemaid?"

Erian flushed. Behind him, Senneck dug her talons into the wooden floor and hissed very quietly, so quietly that Kerod probably didn't even hear it.

"She wants to make sure that—well, we've only just become partners," said Erian, hastily stopping himself in mid-sentence. "You know how it is."

"Yes, I remember well enough," said Kerod. Another grin. "Takes a while for you to get bored with each other."

Senneck seemed to have decided that she was embarrassing her partner, and abruptly stepped away from him. "I think I have done enough here for now. Erian, do you wish for me to stay longer?"

"Oh. No, Senneck, I can do this on my own now. You can do what you want."

"Good," she said briskly. "Eekrae"—the other griffin had woken up and was looking at her now—"I feel in need of some fresh air. If your offer still stands, perhaps we can fly together after all."

Eekrae got up. He was a slim griffin with a slightly scrappy look, his grey and brown feathers tousled. "I would be glad to," he said. "More than glad."

If Senneck had been human, she would have smiled thinly. "Good. Let us go, then. Erian, I shall see you this evening in our nest."

Erian smiled at her. "Have a good time, Senneck. I'll have some food ready for you."

The two griffins left, tails swinging behind them. Once they were gone, Erian felt himself relax, though up until that moment he hadn't been aware that he was tense. He sat back.

"Well, then," he said to no-one in particular.

"She's very tough on you," Kerod observed.

"What? Oh. Yes, I suppose so."

"It's only to be expected," said the old man. "When a griffin first chooses a partner, she tends to be very fussy in the beginning. Like a mother with chicks. That's why it's mostly females who do the choosing, see. It's like a mothering instinct. They get attached to you. But at first they take it a bit too far. And she'll be wanting the best for you, of course. New griffiners have to prove themselves right away. Show their mettle, so to speak." He cackled. "Anyway, I wouldn't worry if I was you. She might be pushing you hard now, but if I'm any judge she'll have other things to worry about soon enough."

Erian scratched his ear. "Like what?"

"I mean that she's got a proper home now," said Kerod. "A nest. And everyone knows what griffins use nests for."

"I'm sorry?" said Erian, mystified.

"Good gods, boy, don't you know anything about griffins?" said Kerod. "Where did you grow up, anyway?"

"Uh, Carrick," said Erian, wishing he could have said something else.

"Carrick? Never heard of it. Well, look," Kerod said, and shrugged, "when a male griffin invites a female to go flying with him—"

Erian started, so violently he broke the stylus in half. "What?"

"Calm down, it's natural enough," said Kerod.

"Yes, but . . ." Erian tried to imagine Senneck submitting to a male, especially one as scruffy looking and eccentric as Eekrae, and failed. "You mean Eekrae . . . ?"

"A little slow on the uptake, aren't we?" said Kerod. "He likes her, obviously, and she finally said yes to his invitation, so—"

"So she'll lay eggs?"

"Maybe, maybe not. There's no promise it'll come to

anything. Plenty of times griffins mate but the female doesn't lay, or the eggs aren't viable. But if I were you, I'd take it as a good sign. If Senneck feels enough at home here to be thinking about breeding, it means good luck for both of you."

Erian rubbed his head. "So what happens if she lays eggs? I mean, where will the chicks go?"

"When they're old enough they'll have to leave," said Kerod. "They'll live in one of the roosts, unless they choose humans to move in with."

Erian tried to think, but his mind refused to accept what Kerod was telling him. "Good gods," he managed.

22

Choosing

Arenadd and Skade walked back toward his campsite, with Skandar leading the way. Skade kept her distance from Arenadd, still uncertain and a little afraid, but as they were negotiating a rough patch of undergrowth he reached back and took her hand. She held on to it for the rest of the way, until they reached the little clearing where a fire was still smouldering.

Arenadd let go of her hand and added more fuel until the fire was burning brightly again.

"Here, sit down," he said. "Come on. You look exhausted. I've got some food."

Skade took the undercooked meat and raw potatoes he gave her, and tore into them without a second thought. Part of her felt slightly ashamed and urged her to stop and ask all the questions burning on her tongue, but her hunger overrode that and she bolted the food down without even tasting it.

Arenadd ate nothing. He sat on the other side of the fire, with Skandar lying peacefully behind him and watched her, his pale face concerned. "You look so thin."

Skade swallowed the last bite. "I survived well enough. What you taught me helped me find food."

Arenadd moved closer to her. "Skade, what happened? Where were you, really? I don't understand any of this."

"I do not understand, either," said Skade. "How did you come back here from Herbstitt so quickly? And where did all those slaves come from? And why are they following you?"

Arenadd waved a hand. "Let's start at the beginning. You went into the cave. I followed you immediately afterward."

"What did you see in there?" said Skade. "May I ask?"

Arenadd thought briefly of the mist, the threatening voices

and the inexplicable sense of dread. "The spirits didn't want me to come in. They were trying to frighten me away. That was when I dropped my sword. But I got in anyway. I don't think the spirits are that powerful, you know. They couldn't physically stop me getting in; all they could do was get into my head, try and scare me. Anyway, after that I saw . . ."

"Saw what?" said Skade.

"I saw Eluna," Arenadd said simply. "My dead griffin. But she wasn't . . . her. She spoke, but it sounded like many voices, not one. She said she was the dead, and—"

"Do not tell me what they told you," said Skade. "It was between—"

"Between me and them, I know," said Arenadd. "But I don't give a flying turd about what they think and want. They told me to go away. I asked them to help me, but they cursed me, said terrible things, told me I was evil. They got inside my head. Made me remember things." He paused. "The night I died. They made me relive it. I felt the same pain I felt then, and after that—" He shrugged with exaggerated care. "The next thing I knew I was outside in the rain and people were grabbing me and shackling my wrists together. I can't have been in that cave for more than a few heartbeats, but it was night when I came out."

"And they caught you," Skade said softly.

"Yes." Arenadd's face twisted. "Those spirits—they didn't just refuse to help me. They gave me to my captors, let them get me."

"And they took you to Herbstitt," said Skade.

"Yes. They didn't realise who I was; they were out looking for a runaway slave, and I was there, so they dragged me back to Herbstitt. The man in charge there knew I wasn't one of his, but he decided to keep me anyway. He had me branded and put in with the other slaves. I was there for a month or so, but after I escaped and Skandar found me we decided to go back and free the slaves. So we brought them here with us."

Skade looked bewildered. "But how is that possible? For all that to have happened—how can you have been gone a month?"

"I don't know," said Arenadd. "How long were you in that cave?"

"Only a short time," said Skade. "I thought it must have been one night; it was dawn when I came out. And you were not there, and neither was Skandar. I waited for days, hoping you would return, and now you have."

Arenadd frowned. "Hmm. That's odd. Skandar?"

Skandar raised his head.

"Skandar," said Arenadd. "How long were you gone? When did you come back from hunting?"

The griffin appeared to think about it. "Not fly far," he said. "Tired. Fly east. Catch good food, big food. Eat, fly back, bring food for human."

"Was it night-time by then?"

"Yes. The Night Eye open."

"Was it raining?"

"No. No rain, not for days," said Skandar. "I wait. Waited one, two, three days. No food, so I fly away. Come back to look, but you were not there. Come back many times, but nothing. I did not go back any more. I think you have gone, so I look for you. Find human, watch human, eat cow. But humans not see," he added proudly. "I come at night, stay away. Like you said. Then I find you, near singing hill. Dig you up. You dead, but come alive. Magic! Magic human."

Arenadd scratched at the scars on his neck. "Gods. That means if Skandar had come back that night, but it wasn't raining and I wasn't there, I can't have been in the cave for only a short time. I must have been in there for a month or so without even knowing it. And you too, Skade."

Skade looked thoughtful. "I think that explanation makes sense. Spirits, after all—they have a different time from our own."

"So, they didn't cure you, either," Arenadd said bitterly. "Some help they were."

Skade shook her head. "We were wrong, Arenadd. Spirits cannot help us. I do not think they even had the power to do so. The old stories claimed they had all the magic of every griffin that has ever died, but magic is something that belongs to life. To nature. And they are not part of nature; they are what has passed beyond it."

"Well, then what use are they?" said Arenadd.

"They can do only what they did, which is to look into the future and into our minds, and advise us."

Arenadd spat into the fire. "Advice! That'll be the day."

She looked at him seriously. "Did they tell you to do anything, Arenadd? Anything at all?"

"Yes, actually," said Arenadd. "And a lot of good it'll do me."

"But what was it?" said Skade.

"Exactly the same thing people used to shout at me in the street. 'Go back to the North, blackrobe.'"

"Then that is what they want you to do," said Skade.

"Hah. And why, exactly, should I care about what they want?"

She shook her head. "I, too, was angered by the advice they gave to me, but now I think that it is the only thing I can do."

"Why?" said Arenadd. "What was it?"

Skade hesitated, and then shook her head again. "No, I will tell you another time, perhaps. Is that all the spirits said to you?"

You are not cursed. You are *a curse.* "They said . . . I don't know, I think that was all they said."

"You are sure?"

"Yes. No. Wait. I remember, they said something else, something about looking to my own pagan ways if I wanted help."

Skade looked upward. "Perhaps they meant that the moon could help you. It is your race's god, after all."

"No," said Arenadd. "Theirs maybe, but not mine. I already tried turning to the moon for help, Skade, and it doesn't care about me any more than Gryphus or those cursed spirits of yours."

"Why, have you prayed to it?"

"Yes," said Arenadd. "I prayed to it once, while I was in prison. I begged it to save me. That was the night before my last day on earth. The night after that I turned into . . . into *this*." He thumped himself in the chest, on the spot where his heart had once been.

Skade opened her mouth, then closed it again and sighed.

"Skade." Arenadd moved closer. "Will you—will you do something for me?"

"What is it?" said Skade.

He touched her hand tentatively. "Will you kiss me again? Please?"

Skade looked uncertain. "Arenadd, I do not understand. Our pairing—our mating—it is over now. We were not meant—"

"That doesn't matter now," said Arenadd. "Just kiss me. Please. Like you did before."

Skade hesitated a moment longer but then leant forward and kissed him lightly on the mouth. Arenadd tensed expectantly for a moment, but nothing happened. He kissed her in return, hesitantly, and she, once again seized by an energy and a passion she did not understand, pressed herself against him and kissed him as she had done before, lingeringly and lovingly.

They parted only reluctantly, and Arenadd touched his neck in a way she had become very familiar with. After a few moments' silence, he sighed. "Nothing."

"Why did you ask me to do that?" said Skade.

"Skade." Arenadd took her hand. "When you kissed me before, I felt my heart beat. Just once. You made it happen; I know you did, but I don't understand why."

"But how can that be?" said Skade. "Are you sure?"

"Yes. I'm sure, Skade. Surer than I've ever been in my life. You made my heart beat. It hurt so much, but . . . it felt so wonderful."

"But what does it mean?" said Skade.

"That gods and spirits can't help me, but you can," said Arenadd. "It's a sign. Don't you see?" He took her hand. "I'm sorry for the things I said, Skade. I was angry with you; I felt it was your fault that I was caught. My father and mother were sold into slavery while I was looking for the cave, and I blamed you for leading me there when I should have been going to Norton to meet them. I thought about that all the time. While I was in Herbstitt, I thought about the cave every day. And I thought about you." He let go of her hand. "And I know we can't be together, Skade. It was a dream. Nothing more. I'm a human and you're a griffin. It's wrong and obscene and . . . impossible. We never had a chance to be anything more than lovers for a short time. And how could anyone love me? After what I've done? What I've become? No. But I'll still protect you, Skade. I still care about you, and I still . . ."

"Still what?" said Skade.

"I still love you, Skade, I never thought I could have that feeling ever again, but I do."

"Love?" said Skade. "For me?"

"Yes. You're . . ." Arenadd shook his head. "I can't help it. I don't care that you're a griffin. You're the most amazing woman I've ever met. You're beautiful, you're clever, you're braver than anyone I know. And you accept me for who and what I am, like Skandar does. Even if the spirits didn't help me, you gave me back my—you made me feel like I was worth something again, and I can't ever repay you for that. And I thought that—" He looked away. "Well, it doesn't matter. None of it does. It's over with. It's done."

Silence.

"Arenadd," Skade said at last. "Do you know why it was that the spirits refused to change me back into my old shape?"

He looked at her. "No, how could I?"

"It was because of you," Skade said simply.

"Me? Why?"

"The spirits appeared to me as they did to you," said Skade. "In the shape of a dead soul I had known and cared for."

"Welyn."

"Yes. The spirits came in his form, and I asked them, as you did, to heal me. And then Welyn . . . changed. He became someone I did not recognise at first, but after a time I realised that it was you. But a younger you, without scars. And you—he—told me that I could never become a griffin again. He said that at first I had merely worn the shape of a human, but now it is too late for me to return. 'You ate with a human, travelled with a human, talked with a human as an equal. You shared yourself with him and so began to feel emotions as a human would.' He said that if I had not mated with you, I could still have returned. But when I did that, I made myself human in a way that meant there was no going back. He said, 'You sealed your own fate the moment you began to lust after him.' " She sighed.

"And so I returned to the living world and found I was still human, and I realised that there was no hope that I could ever change again. I am not a griffin now, Arenadd Taranisäii. I am a human, and shall be for the rest of my life. In a way, it is just as well that you were not there then, for I was angry with you, so much so that I would have attacked you if I had seen you. But you were not there, and in time my anger calmed, and I began to wish for you."

"But it was my fault," said Arenadd. "If I hadn't let you—"

"You do not understand," said Skade. "You, Arenadd, you were the saving of me. The times I spent with you were the only times I was happy as a human. And it is you who gave me a reason to believe that I could survive this way. It was you who gave me hope."

Arenadd looked wretched. "Yes, but I'm not *worth* it, Skade. I have no heart."

"You have enough of a heart for me," said Skade.

He was silent for a time. "Skade, since we were separated, I killed again. Four people. Guards. I slaughtered them. Even the one who surrendered. And I *enjoyed* it." He clasped his hands together. "I think I'm evil, Skade. It scares me—but what else can I be? I kill, I destroy. And what the spirits told me: not cursed but *a* curse. *Kraeai kran ae*. Heartless. Soulless. *Evil*."

Skade seized him by the shoulders. "Look at me, Arenadd," she commanded.

Arenadd did, black to gold. "Skade, I—"

"The evil do not love," Skade breathed.

"I don't—"

But Skade smothered his protests with a kiss.

Sunset over Malvern, and Erian walked back to his quarters, feeling tired but oddly satisfied. He had spent the entire afternoon and evening in his new office, searching, shuffling and scribbling. His shoulders ached, his eyes were sore and his favourite feathered tunic was spotted with ink. But in spite of all that, he had a sense of achievement as well. The endless turning of the pages had settled into a kind of rhythm and had lulled him into a relaxed half-dreaming state that prevented him from becoming bored. He had lost his sense of time and had almost been shocked when Kerod suddenly announced that the sun was going down and they may as well retire for the night.

They parted amicably, with Kerod's final words being "Goodnight, Erian. You did good work today; you've got good handwriting, and you work at a fine pace and don't make too many mistakes. I think we'll work well together." He gave his by-now-familiar wrinkled smile. "Once again, Elkin proves how good she is at seeing the potential of people."

That warmed Erian and gave him an extra bounce in his step as he walked back along the corridor. All the same, he couldn't help but wish Senneck had been there to hear it. She hadn't returned to the office and neither had Eekrae, and Erian assumed she must be waiting for him in her new nest. Remembering his promise, he stopped a servant on the way and sent him to get some meat.

His quarters had been cleaned out during his absence, and a bowl of fruit was waiting on the desk. Senneck hadn't returned yet, so he selected a pear and flopped down on the bed to eat it. Eventually the servant arrived, carrying a haunch of venison.

Erian ordered him to place it on the large earthenware dish in Senneck's chamber, and then took a bucketful of water to refill the trough. Still not entirely satisfied, he spent some time rearranging the straw to make it as comfortable for her as possible. He was pleased; he knew Senneck would be happy when she saw her favourite meat waiting for her, and his account of his successful first day of work would please her even more.

Filled with optimism and contentment, he wandered out onto the balcony to see if he could spot her in the sky.

The sun had nearly finished going down, but the sky was still full of griffins. Erian squinted at them, hoping to spot Senneck's mottled brown wings, but without result: in the half-light most of them resembled nothing more than black shapes, drifting lazily here and there. But it was truly a magnificent sight.

Once again, Erian reflected on how proud he was to have found a home here in this beautiful Eyrie, bigger and far more impressive than Eagleholm's had once been. And this land, too, had a beauty all its own beyond its harsh cold. Its inhabitants should be proud to belong to it.

Quite unexpectedly, he found himself wondering if the murderer had reached the North yet. Was he out there somewhere, hiding among his fellow darkmen? Or had he gone even further north, to the places where no civilised people went and savages lived and preyed on one another? Or had something happened to him before then; had he been captured or killed on the way and never even seen his people's home at all?

Erian clasped his hands together behind his back, his forehead wrinkling. "Where are you?" he said aloud. "Where are you hiding? Are you coming here? Are you hiding from me, or looking for me? Do you even remember me, or am I nothing to you at all?" He thought of the way the blackrobe had looked at him that night, the contempt and hatred in his torn face as he stood over his father's bloodied corpse. *If your father was such a great man, ask yourself why he fathered a bastard. Ask yourself why even death could not stop me—he fathered a bastard, he fathered—*

"It wasn't his fault," Erian mumbled. "He was a man of honour; my mother seduced him. He still cared about me. He—"

Erian shook himself abruptly. There was no point in torturing himself. His father would want him to be brave and keep his mind on what he should be doing.

Still no sign of Senneck. The sun had gone down, and the stars were coming out. Erian sighed and went back inside. A fire had been set in the grate, and he lit some candles from it and sent a servant to bring him some food. Lunch had been a long time ago, and his stomach ached with hunger.

When the food arrived he ate it alone at the table, his former good cheer now absent. He had expected Senneck to be there. He'd walked back to their home envisioning what would happen when he got there: they would eat together, and he would tell her everything that had happened and see if she would tell him about her flight with Eekrae.

Once he'd eaten, he poured himself a mug of warm cider and sat out on the balcony to drink it, feeling almost betrayed. He was Senneck's human, her partner, her friend, and yet she would rather spend her time with her new mate than with him.

Not for the first time, Erian felt resentful toward her. When he was younger and dreaming of being a griffiner, he had thought his partner would be his friend, his best friend, the one who understood him better than anyone else. They would talk together about anything and share their secrets and deepest feelings, and no matter what happened he could always confide in her and she would help him. And when they walked together down the street, people would bow to them in awe, and she would snap at anyone who bothered them, and they would watch them run off in fright, and laugh. It would be his pathway to a new life, a better life, and he would never be lonely or rejected again. But Senneck was—well, she was Senneck, and that was all.

Erian tossed back the last of the cider and hunched his shoulders against the cold. *She doesn't care about you,* he thought. *And she isn't your friend. All she cares about is using you for her own ends, to make herself powerful. She* told *you so. After all, she's the mighty griffin, and you're . . . nothing.*

Eventually tiredness caught up with him, and he got up and stumbled back inside. The cider had gone to his head, and he felt dizzy and a little disoriented. Part of him wanted to sleep, but he wanted to be awake when Senneck returned.

He sat down with his back to the wall and waited. She had to come back soon. After all, griffins didn't like to fly at night, and she would be hungry.

But Senneck did not come. The candles continued to burn in

the next room, providing the only light, and the effort of seeing made Erian's eyes hurt.

Eventually, he slipped into a doze and the dream caught up with him again.

He was standing in a room, surrounded by flames. Senneck was with him, and Flell, but both of them were shadowy: present, but unimportant in some way.

There was nothing unimportant about the shape in front of him, the one rising out of the fire to confront him. By now, he knew the face perfectly dominated by those soulless black eyes.

You, the face whispered. *You.*

Erian tried to speak, but his lips were stuck together. The hateful figure came closer, and he drew Bloodpride and swung it with all his might, but the blade crumbled away to nothing and he was trapped, while the monster danced in front of him, sneering and mocking.

As it was before, it shall be again, again Bastard, again, again. As it was before, was before. Where you go I go, here to there, then to now, we have the power, she and I have it, she and I, and it will be again, again, again—

A hard nudge in the ribs woke Erian up. He jerked awake. "What? What?"

"Calm yourself, Erian."

Senneck's voice. Erian groaned and rubbed his face. It was nearly pitch-black, but he could sense the griffin's presence in front of him.

"Senneck," he said. "You're back."

She moved away from him, allowing more light to filter in from the next room. "So I am. I see you were waiting for me."

Erian stood. "Yes. I didn't mean to fall asleep."

There was a rustling of straw from somewhere to his left. "There is no need to apologise," said Senneck. "The time is late." A dull *thunk*, and she said, "And I see you have left some venison for me."

"Yes. I knew you'd like it."

"I do," said Senneck. He heard a crunching sound. "Please, excuse me. I am hungry."

"Oh. Oh, it's all right. Shall I bring some light?"

"Yes, thank you."

Erian stumbled into the next room and brought a candle in a candleholder. There were some torches high up on the walls, well away from the straw, and he lit them. Once the chamber had been illuminated he could see Senneck, busily hunched over the meat. She looked a little tousled but otherwise fine.

Erian returned the candle to the next room before he came back to join her. He waited politely until she had finished eating and had drunk from the trough.

"I'm glad you're back," he said as she curled up on the straw.

Senneck yawned. "I am glad to be back. I did not mean to be gone so long, but—"

"It's all right," Erian lied. "You don't need my permission. How was . . ." He hesitated. "How was your . . . flight?"

"Ahhhh . . ." Senneck let out a great sigh and rolled onto her back, talons curled over her chest. "It went well for us both. And how was your work inside?"

"It wasn't too bad," said Erian. "I worked until sunset. And—and Kerod likes me. He said I did well and he was pleased to have me as his assistant and that Elkin had chosen well."

"Lady Elkin," Senneck corrected.

"Yes, of course. He said she had a great gift for seeing potential in people, and it must have worked well this time. So, he's very pleased," Erian added.

"I would expect him to be pleased," Senneck said tartly. "Now that he has an assistant upon whom he can lay all the more tedious aspects of his duty he should be very pleased indeed."

Yet again, Erian felt himself crumble inside.

"You do realise that what you did this afternoon was pointless, do you not?" Senneck added, almost casually.

Erian blinked. "What do you mean?"

"Come now. Do not tell me I chose a fool for my partner. I listened carefully to everything your master told you today, and I saw what he was truly saying. Do you honestly believe that after two years the taxes have not already been long since calculated for all those villages? If they pay every year, would it not be somewhat inefficient to conduct matters this way?"

"But . . ." Erian faltered. "But why? I don't understand. Why would he want me to do that?"

"To test you," said Senneck, "To see if you would do as you were told without question, and do it efficiently. I spoke to Eekrae today, and he told me a great deal about his partner. Kerod may be an eccentric, but he is not a fool. He loves the power that he has—slight though it is—and he does not want to lose it. When he was told that he was to be given an assistant, he was afraid that there was a warning in it, that he was to be replaced by a younger man. He and Eekrae agreed that they should get the measure of you first, to see how pliant or ambitious you were. So Kerod gave you a pointless task to carry out and watched to see how you would react."

All of Erian's pride vanished. "*What?* He—what in the gods' names . . . ?" But helpless anger quickly lost out to humiliation. "Oh gods. Senneck, I'm so sorry. I'm such an *idiot*! Why didn't I see it?"

"Be calm," Senneck urged. "No, Erian. Listen. What you did was precisely what you should have done."

"It—what?"

"You did the right thing," said Senneck. "You showed no sign of knowing what was happening, and now Kerod's fears have been soothed. If you do not appear to be ambitious, if you act as if your only desire is to do your duty and please him, if Kerod believes you are too unintelligent to pose a threat, then he will relax, and you will endear yourself to him."

"Oh. Oh, I see. Yes, of course. You're right, Senneck. As always. Yes." Erian relaxed and wiped his arm across his forehead. "Well, I was very friendly and polite to him. I liked him."

"Yes," said Senneck. "You conducted yourself well with him, and I was impressed. You were natural and polite and friendly, and you flattered him. Eekrae saw it, too. He told me I had chosen well."

"It sounds like he told you a lot," Erian observed.

"Oh yes," said Senneck. She chirped. "Perhaps you think that I was merely indulging myself today when I agreed to go with him. I assure you that I was not. I have done good work for us today."

"By mating with him?" The words were out before he could stop them.

"Eekrae wanted me," she said after a lengthy pause, "but not merely to fertilise my eggs. He wanted to know me better, to talk to me and try and get the measure of me, as Kerod did with you. But he is young and male, and he could not hide that he wanted more than that, even in spite of himself."

"But did you mate with him?" Erian asked quietly.

"You are jealous," said Senneck.

"Maybe I am—who cares? Did you mate with him?"

Another pause. "If you must know, yes. I paired with him. My first time," she said, almost shyly. "And afterward—afterward he was confused, caught up in the moment. He told me all I wished to know, and more."

Erian tensed. "What things did he tell you?"

"He told me that Kerod has no children and that he is the last of his house. He is not the wealthiest human in Malvern, but he owns some property. And he has no direct heir."

"So, what does that mean?" said Erian.

"Kerod is an old man," said Senneck. "When he dies, his Mastership shall go to you, and so will a portion of his wealth. And the more you charm him, the more he may choose to leave you."

"That could be a long way away, though," said Erian.

"Time we have. We are young, and secure here for now." Senneck paused and then got up and came closer to him. "I know that I have not been as kind to you as I could have," she said, almost gently. "And you know it, do you not?"

Erian hesitated. "I—I don't blame you. I understand—"

"No," said Senneck. "I have been harsh with you. Even cruel. What I said to you at Herbstitt was not—" She shook herself. "I did not like it there. There was a wrongness about that place. It made me feel sick and . . . afraid, as if there was some influence there. I grew angry with you for forcing me to stay there and so I threatened you, and when you resisted—well, it is in the past now."

"We shouldn't have been there, Senneck," said Erian. "You were right to want to leave, and I shouldn't have argued like that."

"To have a will of your own is no bad thing." Senneck sat on her haunches, her tail twitching among the straw. "You have done well, Erian Rannagonson. You have made me proud. For a time I had doubts; I worried that I had not—" She looked up. "Perhaps you do not understand. You are in a place you do not know, among people you do not know, either, you are afraid and uncertain, you are facing challenges you have never faced before. And so am I. You are afraid; you are uncertain—that is what I feel as well. You have only just become a griffiner, and I have only just become partnered. I want what is best for us both, and that has made me anxious. I have demanded a great deal from you. Perhaps too much. But you stood up under that burden, and so I know . . ."

"Know what?" said Erian.

"That you are worthy," said Senneck. "Worthy of me, worthy of the status we are in search of. Do not believe your own fears, Erian. You are worthy, and I am proud to have chosen you." She looked at him, her blue eyes serene. "I have chosen well."

23

Guard's Post

Captain Burd had gone to bed early. A good-sized mug of hot mead and a wedge of toasted cheese, then he had flopped onto his straw pallet, pulled the blankets over himself and quickly been lulled to sleep by the crackling of the fire in the grate.

It had been a stressful day. Burd had been the sole commander of Guard's Post for several years now, ever since his predecessor had retired, and he liked his life here. It was easy: organising the shifts, keeping everyone in order and, from time to time, vetting a traveller who looked suspicious. Comparatively few travellers passed through the mountains nowadays; most of them were traders making the journey to or from Canran or Eagleholm. It was the duty of the guards to search each cartload that passed through the two gates, in search of illegal goods, but they rarely bothered. Burd's men already knew most of the traders who used the road regularly, and if they were willing to put them in the way of some good cider or a little addition to their usual pay, then they weren't inclined to look too closely. Burd himself rarely went down to the gates any more.

Recently some of the sergeants had been half-seriously suggesting that they begin leaving the gates open, but Burd had put his foot down about that. If Malvern got wind of it he'd be put on duty in the fighting pits for the rest of his natural life.

He was deeply asleep, warm and comfortable under the blankets, when someone shook him awake. "Sir? Captain?"

Burd groaned and opened an eye. "What?"

"Sorry, sir, but something's happening and Sergeant Wiln sent me to wake you up."

The captain sat up in bed. "What kind of something? Is the sun up yet?"

"It's just before dawn, sir," said the guardsman. He looked a little tousled but alert. "I've been asked to say that you should probably go and wake the griffiners, sir. Some travellers have come, and they look a bit strange."

"Understood. Go and tell the sergeant I'm on my way."

"Yes, sir."

The guard left, and Burd splashed water on his face and pulled on his uniform with the speed of one accustomed to being woken up at short notice. The light coming in through the window was dull and grey, and he cursed as he stubbed a toe on the edge of the bed. Damn it all. Damn those griffiners. They'd arrived the previous day: two young idiots, minor lords from Malvern with shiny swords and big ideas about how the place should be run. What the blazes did they know? As if having a griffin could make you know better than someone with thirty years of experience.

Burd didn't like griffiners, and he didn't like griffins, either. They were damned dangerous creatures, no matter what the griffiners said. Supposedly only rogue griffins or wild ones ever attacked people with the intent to kill, but everyone knew that was nonsense. The cursed things were animals, and you couldn't rely on an animal to do anything other than look for food. And spending your time living next to these overgrown bird-things who had beaks strong enough to tear through solid wood and who could eat a whole ox in a day—madness. Bloody madness.

Burd paused outside the door to Lord Tuomas' chamber and straightened his uniform. He took a deep breath and knocked.

Nothing happened, so he knocked again, more loudly. There was a sudden *thump* from the other side, and the snarling rasp of a griffin. Burd backed away hurriedly.

The door opened, and Lord Tuomas appeared, still clad in his nightshirt. A large grey griffin was close by, trying to poke its head through the door to hiss at him.

"What?" The young man's voice was thick and irritable.

Burd coughed. "My lord. I'm sorry to wake you up, but I've just been informed that something's happening down between the gates—some travellers have shown up and it sounds like they need to be looked at."

"Why? Can't you deal with that?"

Burd forced himself not to react to the imperious tone. "Yes, my lord, but with all due respect, this is your command now, and part of your duties is to attend to this sort of thing when it comes up."

Lord Tuomas looked at him a moment longer and then said, "Delegation is the key to successful command, captain. See to it yourself." He shut the door before Burd could answer.

Burd sighed and walked away. Once he was out of earshot, he swore vigorously under his breath. *Bloody griffiners. They come here, take over everything. Their griffins eat all the damned meat. And they can't even be bothered to do their blasted duty.*

He wasn't going to bother wasting his time with Lord Rine, and instead he hurried to the staircase that would lead him down to the gap between the gates. As he reached the top, Sergeant Wiln came up the other way to meet him.

"Sir! There you are."

"Morning," Burd said curtly. "What's going on?"

"It's a griffiner, sir," said Wiln. "One's trying to get passage through the gates."

"What?" said Burd. "With a griffin?"

"Yes, sir. She's asking—"

"Why in Gryphus' name didn't she just *fly* over instead of bothering us?"

"Well, sir, it's because she's not alone," said Wiln. "She's brought a load of slaves with her, and they're all on foot."

"She—What the—? Which way are they going?"

"Northbound, sir. She says she's going to Malvern."

"From where?"

"Withypool, sir."

Burd scratched his head. "Why in the gods' names would a griffiner be taking slaves *to* Malvern?"

"She won't say, sir. Have you woken up the griffiners?"

"I tried Lord Tuomas, but he didn't want to hear about it," said Burd. "I didn't bother with the other one. But—" He thought for a moment. "This sounds strange. Go and wake up Lord Rine and tell him to come down. Don't take no for an answer. If this is griffiner business then it's our duty to let them know."

"Yes, sir." Wiln hurried away.

"Right," Burd muttered to no-one in particular. He descended the stairs, taking them two at a time.

The space between the two gates was very large, and today it needed to be. Both gates were closed, and a ring of guards had gathered around—

Burd stopped at the foot of the stairs, dumbfounded. The slaves were standing together in a large group, nervously watching the guards. There were more than a hundred by his count, all robed and collared, but they had a ragged, travel-stained look about them, as if they had walked a long way. He looked at the nearest one to him but couldn't read anything in his face other than a kind of steady, controlled fear, the kind of dumb animal look he had seen in all slaves. Pathetic, really.

Burd made his way to the head of the group at the northernmost gate. The griffin had been easy enough to spot: it was male, with silver feathers and black fur, and was the biggest griffin he'd seen since that day in Malvern when he had caught a brief glimpse of the Mighty Kraal himself.

The beast's partner stood beside him, and if she was a griffiner then she was the grubbiest one he'd ever seen. She looked just as ragged and desperate as her slaves: the grey dress she wore was torn and filthy, and her extraordinary long silvery hair was tangled. But her demeanour was full of cool pride and reserve, and she looked straight at him without hesitation.

"My . . . lady." Burd gave her a slightly hesitant bow. "I'm Captain Burd, and I'm in command here."

She watched him for a moment, shifting slightly so he could see the long sword slung on her back. "Greetings, captain," she said. Her tone was formal and a little flat, somehow lacking in emotion, as if she were reciting her words from a piece of paper. "I am Lady Skade, of Withypool," she told him distantly. "And I command you to open the gate and allow me and my slaves to pass through."

"Yes, my lady," said Burd, eyeing the griffin. He bowed again. "I would happily do that, but it's my duty to search you first."

She fixed him with a dreadful stare. "Search?"

"Yes, my lady," Burd said again. "In order . . . to . . . be certain . . ." He felt himself beginning to sweat. "We must search every traveller who comes this way," he said, pulling himself together. "If any of them are smuggling illegal items into Malvern's territory, then we're obliged to arrest them."

Skade's look did not waver. "Are slaves illegal, captain?"

"In some circumstances, yes, my lady," said Burd. "Slaves can only be sold by slave-traders licensed and authorised by an Eyrie."

"But I am not going to sell them," said Skade. "These slaves are my property, and I am taking them with me."

"May I ask where you're taking them, my lady?" said Burd.

"That is not your concern," said Skade. "I am taking them north, to my new home."

"And you say you're from Withypool, my lady?"

"I do. I purchased these slaves there, and I have documents to prove it. Is there anything else you want from me?"

"I'm sorry, my lady, but yes," said Burd. "If you'll just wait a moment, my commander is coming—a griffiner, who'll want to talk to you."

Skade sighed. "Very well, then we shall wait."

Fortunately, Wiln arrived only a short time later. Lord Rine was with him, his griffin walking slightly ahead of them both.

The instant the dark beast by Skade's side saw the other griffin, he began to hiss and lash his tail. Skade laid a hand on his shoulder to restrain him, and inclined her head toward Lord Rine. "Greetings," she said, speaking griffish now. "I am Skade, and this is Skandar."

Rine gave her a slightly shocked look but said nothing. He stood back and allowed his partner to come forward instead, toward Skandar, to greet him and size him up.

Skandar's reaction was immediate, and violent. He stood up and screeched, his wings opening, aggression vibrating in every hair and feather. The other griffin backed off, screeching in return and positioning himself to protect his partner.

For a moment it looked as if the two would come to blows, but Skade hurried forward and put herself in the way. "Enough!" she snapped, turning to face Skandar. "Skandar, no. *No.*"

Skandar hissed and moved to push her out of the way, but she made eye contact and shook her head very slightly. "No," she said again. "Do not move. It is not time."

They challenged each other with a glare for a few moments, before Skandar sulkily sat back on his haunches.

"My apologies," said Skade, apparently unaware that the griffin still looked more than inclined to attack. "Skandar has not seen another griffin in many months."

"So I see," said Lord Rine, appearing beside his partner.

"Then perhaps we can dispense with the formalities." He bowed very slightly. "I am Lord Rine of Malvern."

"I am pleased to meet you," Skade said stiffly. "I am the Lady Skade of Withypool, and my partner, as you have heard, is Skandar."

"Now," said Rine, seeing his own partner was still busy glaring at Skandar. "What brings you here, my lady?"

"I am travelling to the North," said Skade. "And these are my slaves, which I am bringing with me."

"Those are all yours?" said Rine.

"They are."

"And why are you going north?" said Rine.

Skade hesitated very briefly. "I plan to begin a new life. I have purchased land there, and I am taking my slaves with me to build a home for me. If you are wondering why I am travelling this way, it is because I spent the last of my money on the slaves. The trader asked for an outrageous sum—my family told me he had robbed me, but I did not care, for I wished to leave Withypool quickly."

"Why?" said Rine.

"My father intended to force me into a marriage I did not want," said Skade. "The only way to escape it was to leave as soon as I could, and so I made arrangements and left home at speed." She smiled for the first time. "Perhaps it was reckless, but I have always been reckless. I am chasing a dream, my lord, and we both of us know the power of dreams to disrupt our lives."

Rine still looked hesitant. "Forgive me, my lady, but we were given no forewarning that you were coming."

"I did not send word," said Skade. "I did not know that I should."

"I see," said Rine. "Well . . ." He glanced at Burd. "Well, then," he said, looking at Skade again and appearing to relax, "I see no harm in letting you through."

Skade's smile returned, more warmly than before. "Thank you, my lord."

Burd darted forward and whispered urgently in Rine's ear. The young griffiner nodded.

"However, we're still required to quickly examine your slaves, my lady."

Her smile vanished. "Why?"

"Because—I'm sorry, my lady, and please don't take this as an accusation—we have been warned that a very dangerous criminal is trying to enter the North. A darkman. He committed a series of murders; no doubt you've heard?"

Skade's eyes narrowed. "Are you suggesting that I am trying to smuggle criminals into Malvern's lands?"

"Not at all, my lady, but we have to observe the formalities. We'll want to see the documents proving that you bought these slaves legitimately, and after that the guards will check their brands."

Skade nodded. "Understood. I will search for the documents in my bag, and perhaps while I am doing that you can begin to inspect the brands."

"We should—" Rine began.

"Excellent," said Skade. She turned around. "You," she said, grabbing a slave at random and shoving him forward. "Show Lord Rine your brand, and be quick about it."

The slave, a thin young man with a scar on his face, stumbled toward Rine. "Yes, my lady." He bowed. "My lord."

Rine opened his mouth to complain, but stopped. "Where is your collar, blackrobe?"

The man shrugged. "Lost it. But I have a brand, see?" He held out his hand. "See? There."

Rine grabbed it by the wrist. "This isn't a Withypool brand," he said. "This looks like—I don't recognise it. Where is this brand from?"

"I'll let you see it a little closer," said the slave, and punched him hard in the face.

Rine toppled backward, stars exploding in his vision. As he hit the ground, he heard the shout.

"Attack!"

It happened in an instant. Rine's partner lashed out at the scarred slave, and as he dodged it the huge dark griffin rushed forward, slamming into Rine's griffin and bowling her over. In the same moment, every single one of the slaves pulled a weapon out of his robe and hurled himself at the guards.

Arenadd was almost completely unaware of the chaos breaking out around him. Even as he avoided the attack from the griffin, he ran straight at Rine. The griffiner was struggling to his feet, wide-eyed, mouth opening to shout something, but before he could speak Arenadd had reached him and attacked.

His boot lashed out, striking Rine under the chin and knocking him backward, and Arenadd leapt at him, pinning him down.

The two of them struggled together, each one wrestling for control for a few breathless moments. Rine snatched at the dagger in his belt, but Arenadd struck his hand away and began to hit him, punching him in the head with all his strength.

Rine landed a few blows on him in return, but Arenadd didn't feel them. He continued to strike, again and again, until the griffiner slumped, half-conscious. Arenadd pulled the dagger from his own belt and pressed it into Rine's neck, and for a moment there was stillness.

Rine said nothing, but Arenadd heard him groan. Blood was coming from his mouth and nose, and his fingers curled, grasping at nothing. From somewhere far away came the sound of two griffins screeching and tearing at each other. Fighting to kill.

Rine groaned again and stirred, and for an instant their eyes met. Rine's eyes were green, and dim with pain. There was fear there, too. He knew he was about to die.

I am the man without a heart, Arenadd thought. "Join me," he whispered, and pulled the dagger hard over the man's throat, tearing it wide open. Blood gushed out, staining his hands and soaking into his robe.

Rine died almost instantly, and Arenadd straightened up, looking down at him. It was so strange how different people looked when they were dead.

A hand grabbed his shoulder. Instantly his senses snapped back and he whirled around, raising the dagger.

"Stop! Arenadd, it is me!"

"Skade."

"Yes. Are you hurt?"

"No."

Arenadd looked around. The slaves had overwhelmed the guards, leaving them dead or wounded, and were already pouring up the staircases and into the building. Skandar was over by the other gate, tearing at the griffin, which had fallen and was still lashing out at him. But the fight was already won; even as Arenadd ran to help, Skandar struck the other griffin a blow that broke her neck.

"Skandar!"

Skandar turned away from the griffin's twitching body. His

sides were heaving, his face and chest were bloodied, and one front talon was broken. "Win," he snarled. "Kill."

Arenadd wiped his hands over his face, staining it with blood. "Yes. Are you hurt, Skandar?"

The griffin either did not understand the question or didn't consider it worth an answer. He came to Arenadd and nudged him roughly. "You kill?"

"Yes. He's dead."

"Good," Skade broke in. "Here." She held out his sword. "Take this, and go."

Arenadd took it. "Look after yourself, Skade," he said, and ran.

The slaves had entered the fort, and by the time Arenadd arrived a savage fight had already broken out. Most of the guards had still been in bed, but they were quick to appear when the slaves flooded into the rooms and corridors they called home. Captain Burd had escaped and run to wake up his men, and he and his officers were leading a counterattack.

Even though they were outnumbered, the guards were doing far better than Arenadd had expected. The slaves, unused to fighting, were often unwilling to kill, and some surrendered or tried to run away.

They died.

All the same, he could see that the training he had given them had worked. They were sticking together rather than letting themselves be split up and picked off and were using furniture as temporary barricades. Many of the guards were unarmoured, most were tired, and all were bewildered and ill-prepared.

Arenadd ran through several chambers and corridors, passing scenes of carnage and violence all the while. From time to time he caught a glimpse of someone he knew. There were Olwydd and Prydwen, fighting side by side. Garnoc was defending a group of slaves who had thrown down their weapons, one brawny arm raising his axe to bring it down on a guard's shoulder. He saw other things, too. Saw Nolan take a sword cut to the stomach. Saw Annan die, stabbed through the throat.

But he ran on, intent on finding the other griffiner and especially the griffin. The guards who saw him tried to stop him, and he swung Lord Rannagon's sword, thrusting and slashing, blocking other weapons and striking out at unprotected flesh wherever he saw it. Skandar ran ahead, uncontrollable, a raging demon, ripping into any man—friend or foe—who stood in his way. And still Arenadd ran, killing left and right, his body thrumming with the same dark thrill he had felt that night at Herbstitt.

Others fell in behind him as he ran. Olwydd, Prydwen and Dafydd, all shouting his name.

Arenadd uttered no sound at all.

When they reached the highest floor they found it a strange haven of quiet. The fight hadn't reached here yet. Arenadd paused and wiped the bloody sweat off his forehead.

"They should be up here somewhere," he said. "Come on."

Skandar had already gone on ahead. Arenadd caught up with him at a sprint, realising that all the noise the griffin was making would alert anyone up here who might have been caught off guard. But there was little point in trying to restrain him; Skandar charged along the corridor, snarling and berserk, all his natural ferocity let loose for the first time in months. He had been forced to travel with dozens of humans, constantly surrounded by creatures he saw as weak and irritating and edible. Only his respect for his partner had held him back. But now that was over. Now that was done. Now was the time to do what he had desired to do but been denied the chance to for far too long.

Arenadd knew him too well to be unaware of this. He slipped past Skandar and ran ahead of him, every sense on the alert. This floor looked disused; there was no sign of any guards about. The doors lining the corridor, all closed, were large and well made. Griffiner quarters, he knew. They had to be. The second griffiner he had seen flying over the fort had to be here somewhere.

The others had fallen behind. Arenadd and Skandar charged up a ramp, turned another corner, and there was a door bursting open. Something huge and horrible came rushing out: a griffin, beak open, screeching.

Arenadd caught a brief glimpse of the sword-wielding man behind the beast before Skandar shoved him aside and attacked.

Arenadd heard thudding bootsteps behind him as the others arrived. The two griffins were grappling with each other, but he quickly saw that Skandar was in trouble. His enemy, smaller than him but obviously strong, seemed to have wounded the black griffin's foreleg, judging by the way he was holding it when the two parted for a moment.

He made a quick decision. "Kill the griffin!" he yelled to the others, and ran at it, sword raised.

The blade came down on the creature's shoulder, and blood and feathers fell away. The griffin screeched and lashed out, hurling Arenadd aside. His head hit the wall with an audible crack, and he fell limply to the ground, his vision exploding into red before it abruptly faded to black.

From somewhere off to his left he heard Olwydd. *"My lord!"*

After that there was a confusion of thumping, screeching and the shouts of his friends. Pain brought Arenadd back to consciousness a few moments later. He groaned and opened his eyes, and his blurred vision showed him a strange grey-brown mass moving just above him. He lay there peacefully for a few moments, wondering what it was, then a high, thin scream cut into his ears. It was a sound he knew by now, filled with agony and despair. The sound of a dying man.

Arenadd groped at his belt. Miraculously, his fingers found the hilt of his dagger and closed around it. He drew it and pulled himself into a half-sitting position, squinting at the thing above him. His vision grew less blurry, and he suddenly knew where he was: lying underneath the enemy griffin. Its furred belly was directly above him.

The scream had stopped. Arenadd braced himself and thrust the dagger deep into the griffin's belly.

The creature reeled away, screeching yet again, and Arenadd wriggled out from under him and crawled away as fast as he could. The griffin lurched toward him, and it could well have been the end of him, but Skandar, who had fallen back after his partner was injured, took his opportunity and attacked.

This time he had the advantage. The other griffin, staggering from his wound, took a savage blow to the head and fell onto his forelegs. Skandar was on him in an instant, his beak shattering the back of the other griffin's skull. The griffin slumped, twitching, but these last throes were cut short when Skandar broke his neck with another blow.

Lord Tuomas was a witness to his partner's demise. He let out an inarticulate scream and charged, sword raised.

He never stood a chance. The three surviving Northerners ran to attack him, but Skandar cut him down before they reached him, leaving the griffiner to die in a pool of his own blood.

And after that, quite suddenly, it was all over.

When the others helped him up, the first thing Arenadd saw was Olwydd, dead. The Northerner's head had been nearly severed by a blow from the griffin's beak, but his sword was still held loosely in his hand.

"He died trying to save ye, sir," said Prydwen.

Arenadd found his sword and slung it on his back. "Come on," he said quietly. "Let's go. We'll carry him."

He checked Skandar; the griffin was panting and exhausted, bloodied in several places, but not seriously hurt. Before they left, Arenadd picked up Tuomas' sword. Skade would like it.

They returned to the lower levels to find the fighting over with. Most of the guards were dead; a few, including Captain Burd, had been taken prisoner. They had all been taken into the mess hall and their hands tied together.

Arenadd scarcely paid them any attention. "Have the dead brought in here, too," he ordered.

It took a long time for them all to be gathered, and Arenadd, unwilling to stay in the mess hall and do nothing, went to look for Skade.

He wandered through scenes of horror. Bodies lay everywhere, both dead and wounded, some screaming out for help or to be given a quick death. Arenadd ordered Prydwen and the others to kill anyone who was mortally wounded. His expression distant, as if his mind was on something else, he picked his way through the devastation while they obeyed.

"Skade, my father—where are they?" he said to everyone he met.

Most shook their heads. Eventually, though, he saw a face he recognised: Madog, who had shared his dormitory at Herbstitt.

"They're both a few rooms along, sir," he said. "I'll show you the way."

Something in his voice made Arenadd's scalp prickle. "Are they all right?" he asked.

"I don't know, sir," said Madog.

Skade was in what had once been a guard's bedroom. Cut and bleeding but alive, she crouched beside Cardock, who had been laid down on the bed. When she saw Arenadd, she jumped up and ran to meet him.

"Arenadd! Are you hurt?"

Arenadd embraced her tightly. "I'm fine. You?"

"Well enough," said Skade, letting go. "But your father . . ."

Arenadd walked over to the bed. Cardock was lying motionless on his side. His mouth was slightly open, and from its corner blood had trickled and dried.

Arenadd knew without even asking that he was dead.

Skade laid a hand on his arm. "I am sorry, Arenadd. Truly. I did my best to protect him, as you asked me to, but it was very confused. People were running everywhere; we were being attacked from all sides . . . Your father took a blow to the head."

Everything seemed to have become vague and distant, as if there were a wall around him. He was dimly aware of a buzzing in his ears and a dull throbbing from his head. He felt nothing.

"I am sorry," Skade said again. "If it comforts you, I killed the man who did this."

"It's all right," Arenadd mumbled. "I don't—I'm all right— I . . ." But his voice didn't want to come any more. It faltered and fell silent, and he closed his eyes and tried to breathe.

"Arenadd?" Skade's voice drifted toward him, quiet with concern. "Arenadd?"

Arenadd opened his eyes. "Here," he said, holding out Tuomas' sword. "It's—it's for you. Your own sword. It belonged to the other griffiner. He's dead. Him and the other griffin. Skandar killed them."

Skade did not take it. "Arenadd, you should not be—"

Arenadd couldn't make himself look at what was on the bed. He dropped the sword and turned away. He was in time to see Skandar ducking his head to get through the door. The griffin moved slowly and with pain, panting a little with his beak open.

The sight of him seemed to bring some of Arenadd's mind back, and he started toward him. "Skandar! Skandar, come here!"

Skandar looked up and limped toward him. "Hurt, human," he rasped.

Arenadd ignored him. He turned and pointed at Cardock's still form. "Heal him," he said.

Skandar merely blinked, uncomprehending.

"Heal him!" Arenadd shouted. "Do something!"

Skandar crouched down, holding his wounded leg off the ground. "Not understand."

Arenadd could feel his shoulders heaving. "You did it with

me," he said. "Do it again, damn you! Bring him back! Use your magic!"

Skandar shivered his wings. "Not have magic," he said.

"Yes, you do!"

"Not have," Skandar repeated.

"Gods damn you!" Arenadd screamed, suddenly losing control. "You insufferable cretin! What in Scathach's name is wrong with you? You're a bloody griffin! You've got magic; you've got magic I've never *seen* before! For gods' sakes, you *brought me back from the dead*. That was *you!*"

Skandar began to look slightly distressed. "Not understand."

"You—have—magic!" Arenadd bellowed. "Use it! Save him!"

He had gone too far. Skandar stood up, tail lashing. "Not understand," he said. "Not want. You should not shout. Do not want."

"Just do it!" said Arenadd, waving an arm at Cardock. "Just bloody do it, or I'll leave you and never come back, understand? Understand?"

Skandar started forward. "You mine!" he screeched. "Mine! You do what I say! *Mine! My human! Mine!*"

"Skandar, my father is *dead*," said Arenadd. "Understand? They killed him. You have to bring him back. Like you did with me. You've got to do it!"

Skade grabbed his arm. "Arenadd!"

"Let go!" Arenadd snapped. "This is none of your business." She kept hold of him. "Arenadd! Stop it, or I will bite you."

Arenadd calmed down very slightly. "Skade, he has to—"

"You are accomplishing nothing," Skade told him. "You are only making Skandar angry with you. For the sky's sake, look at him. He is hurt, exhausted. Even if he knew how to control his magic, wielding it now would damage him more than you could imagine."

Arenadd hesitated, but Skade's voice did not allow any argument. He looked at Skandar and saw that the griffin had faltered, panting again. There was blood on his foreleg, and more soaked into his feathers. He looked as if he were at the end of his strength.

Arenadd felt a strange calmness come over him. "Yes. You're right. Skandar, I'm sorry. I shouldn't have said that. My father wouldn't have wanted to live the way I do. He deserves to rest in peace, the way a man should."

"Not have magic," Skandar mumbled.

Arenadd bowed his head to the griffin and smiled. "If you say so, Skandar. Now, excuse me a moment—"

But as he turned back to look at Cardock's body, all his serenity vanished as abruptly as it had come. His strength left him, too, without any warning, and he dropped to his knees.

"Dad—"

And then he was crying, crying harder than he had done in weeks, his whole body shaking with sobs—not the half-swallowed sobs that he had allowed himself those few nights when guilt had overcome him, but great, gulping, shuddering sounds that gave him physical pain. He managed to raise himself a little, but collapsed again beside his father's resting place, grasping one of the cold hands and holding it close.

Skade did not try to interfere. She kept back and silently watched him cry, knowing there was nothing she could or should do.

Arenadd did not stop crying for a long time. Eventually, though, he found he could speak.

"Dad," he sobbed. "Dad, I'm sorry, I'm so sorry. I know there were so many things . . . wanted me to be, but I was . . . let you down, said all those things I shouldn't have . . . on my birthday. When you brought me the robe, and I wouldn't put it on, and I said those things—but I'm not ashamed, Dad, I'm not, I'm not. I'll never feel that way again; I swear. I'll lead them to the North; I'll keep them safe, I swear. I'll keep them all safe." That seemed to calm him. The sobs died down and he rested his head on the edge of the bed, still clasping his father's hand. "I'll keep them safe, Dad," he said again. "I swear it. I'll find Mum and set her free, I'll tell her what happened and I'll make the North my home. Always. I swear."

24

Dancing in the Dark

The ceremony that would mark Erian's appointment to lordship took place about two weeks after his and Senneck's
arrival at Malvern. Erian had spent most of that time working under Lord Kerod, who had become even more open and
friendly toward him since their first meeting. Erian had followed Senneck's advice and said nothing about the wasted
afternoon in the office, and that appeared to have done the
trick; Kerod made no reference to it the next day and gave Erian
the legitimate job of sorting through a stack of farmers' letters
full of complaints and suggestions. That was a little more interesting, at least.

Erian had hoped for another meeting with Elkin during that
time, and once or twice he thought of applying for another audience with her, but he didn't have to talk to Senneck to know
it wouldn't work. Even though he found himself thinking of
her almost constantly, Elkin had duties and so did he, and she
would be irritated if he wasted her time simply because he
wanted to see her again.

When the message arrived to let him know that he would
be officially anointed as a lord in three days' time, he felt his
heart soar.

"I thought she'd forgotten," he told Senneck. "I really did."

"Evidently, she did not," said Senneck. She hooted. "Erian,
my little human, our fortunes are improving all the time. Soon
you shall be a lord, and when you are married—"

"What?" said Erian. *"Married?"*

"But of course," Senneck said coolly. "That is what humans
do, is it not? And I am sure that there is another griffiner here
who will be willing to marry you, bastard born or not."

"But that's a long time away, isn't it?" said Erian. "I mean, we don't know when I'll meet the girl who's right for me."

"Erian, we are here to look for more than what your race calls 'true love,'" said Senneck, a hint of impatience showing in her voice. "We are here to find a place for ourselves, to secure our future together."

"Well, we're secure now, aren't we?" said Erian. "We've got a home and a job—isn't that enough?" He caught the whine in his voice, and winced to himself.

"I have already made it clear that I will not allow my partner to remain in as lowly a position as you are now," Senneck said tartly. "You have made a good beginning, but more is needed. The correct marriage can win you wealth and property and greater standing here."

Erian's heart sank. "I just hadn't really . . . thought of it yet."

"Do not trouble yourself overmuch," Senneck said more kindly. "All I ask is that you be alert. At the celebrations talk to as many females as you can and learn as much about their backgrounds as they will allow."

Erian nodded vaguely. *I can see Elkin again there,* he thought. *Maybe she'll dance with me. I should do some practice first.*

The next few days dragged. Erian fidgeted at his desk and often caught himself daydreaming, which Kerod noticed and teased him for. But the old man had congratulated him sincerely enough when Erian had passed on the news. At least he didn't seem to resent the fact that an acknowledged bastard was about to be given the title of lord.

As for Senneck, she maintained her usual reserve most of the time, but Erian knew her well enough by now to see how proud she was. After that first day, she had "flown" with Eekrae twice more, after which the two griffins abruptly ceased to show any further interest in each other. If Senneck was going to lay eggs she hadn't said anything about it, and Erian hadn't asked. Either way, the entire affair had served to make her even more self-assured than before. But she was happy here, and Erian knew it.

And then, at last, the day came. Erian rose at dawn, as usual, and brought Senneck some food. He had used some of the modest amount of money he had been granted by the Eyrie to have a new outfit made, and it had arrived the day before. He looked at it while he ate breakfast, and longed to try it on again. The ceremony wouldn't be until sunset, but his heart was already thumping.

That day felt like one of the longest of his life. He spent most of the morning at work in Kerod's office, but after lunch the old man said, "That's it for today. I'm thinking you and Senneck probably want to spend some time alone before the ceremony. Big step for you, eh?"

Erian nodded gladly. "More than I can say, my lord."

"Kerod, please. Well, there's no need to trouble yourself with trying. See you tonight!"

Senneck had been dozing by the door but roused herself when Erian got up from the desk. The two of them returned to their quarters, where Erian put on the simple harness that would help him stay secure on Senneck's back. He did up the straps around her head and neck. She submitted patiently, though her wings kept quivering in anticipation, and a few moments later the two of them were in the air.

Talking during flight had never been practical, but Erian knew that this wasn't a time for it anyway. Senneck soared upward into the sky, and he hung on, heart fluttering, but at the same time filled with a wonderful sense of lightness and power.

And after that, they flew.

Senneck circled over the Eyrie, weaving her way between the towers wherever the mood suited her, while other griffins soared and dived around her, flying not with a purpose but simply for the pleasure of it, as all griffins loved to do.

"The air was meant for griffins," Senneck had once told him. "It is we who are masters of the sky, and like all griffiners, you are privileged to share it with us."

Erian held on to the harness, the wind whipping through his hair, and watched the towers rush past. The sky was bright blue and looked endless, streaked with a few clouds the colour of Elkin's hair. *It goes to the end of the world,* he thought deliriously.

Senneck flew among the towers for a time, looping and diving occasionally, just for the sake of it, and then abruptly wheeled and flew out over the city instead. Fewer griffins flew there, and she had the sky more or less to herself. She flew lower, and Erian could see the streets below, alive with the shapes of people, all tiny and seemingly oblivious to their presence. And though they were so far away, Erian had the strange feeling that he could reach out and pick them up with his bare hands. He felt like a god.

Senneck's wings beat steadily behind him, and he looked back and watched the way they moved: held out rigidly from her sides, twisting slightly to steady her in the air. Further back her tail made a straight line, the feathery rudder at its tip tilting to one side as she began a gentle turn.

Not for the first time, Erian marvelled at her strength. But she was graceful, too, he thought. She could tear down a tree with a few blows, and yet she could ride the wind like a leaf. *The most perfect creature there ever was,* he thought. *And she chose to share all that strength with me.*

The thought made him feel peaceful, but awed as well.

Senneck flew on, and Erian began to lose track of time, lost in thoughts of her, and of other things: his father, his mother, his old home and his new one, and Elkin, too.

He roused himself when he felt Senneck begin a sharp turn, and saw that she was flying back toward the Eyrie. He looked at the sun and suddenly realised that more time had passed than he had thought. The sun had sunk close to the horizon, which had begun to take on the faintest of yellow tinges. It would be time very soon.

Senneck had obviously realised that, too. She flew directly back to their quarters and landed on the balcony. "Quickly," she said as soon as her talons had touched down. "Remove the harness and go and prepare. I shall groom myself here."

Erian, his heart pounding once again, took off the harness as quickly as he could. "Do you think you can remember the way to the councillors' chamber?" he asked.

"Of course. Now go!"

Erian nodded and hung the harness on a nail before running into his own chamber. The new outfit was still laid out on the bed where he'd left it. He stripped off his clothes and gave himself a quick wash with a sponge and some cold water. That done, he dried himself off, dabbed some scented oil on his chest and under his arms, and brushed his hair until it was as neat as he could make it.

Then he put on the new outfit. It was an elaborate affair, richer and grander than the velvets he had filched from Norton. This was a true ceremonial outfit, of the kind worn only by griffiners, and then only on very important occasions. The tunic was made of velvet dyed a rich gold-brown to match Senneck's feathers, and the leggings were wool of the same colour. The front of the tunic had been covered by a large patch of fox fur dyed blue, which hung down beyond the garment and reached to the level of his knees. Higher up, hundreds of tawny griffin feathers donated by Senneck had been stitched onto the fabric, and the shoulders and sleeves were weighed down by longer feathers taken from her wings, which hung down his back like a cloak.

Erian put the tunic on very carefully and smoothed it down. He felt magnificent.

Only one thing remained. He took a small jar from the desk and used some of the red paste it contained to draw a series of lines on his forehead just above his eyes, ancient signs of nobility that had survived since the oldest times of his tribal ancestors.

Senneck, her fur and feathers smooth and well ordered, entered just as he finished.

Erian turned to look at her. "How do I look?"

She looked him up and down. "Like a true griffiner."

He smiled. "And you look as magnificent as you always do."

Senneck purred. "Well, then," she said, "I suppose it is time we left."

"Yes, you're right," said Erian. "Time for us to take our place."

"Yes," said Senneck. "Our honoured place."

The corridors seemed very quiet when they set out. Erian wondered if every griffiner in the tower had gone to the council chamber. Would they all be there waiting for him?

They had both had the sense to make sure they knew the way to the chamber beforehand, and now they followed the route Kerod had first shown them at Senneck's suggestion. Up a flight of stairs, around a corner, over the bridge linking their tower to the central and largest of Malvern's towers, which they now knew as the Council's Tower, and downward until they were on the middle floor, where the tower was much broader. A single corridor girdled the circular tower, with large double doors spaced along the inner wall. Normally these were kept closed. Today, they were open.

Erian and Senneck stopped at the first one they reached, and Erian leant forward slightly to peer through. The space inside looked massive. He could already hear the faint murmur of voices beyond, hundreds of voices.

"Senneck, what do I do?" he hissed.

He expected her to be impatient with him for asking such a foolish-sounding question, but she sat down on her haunches beside him and lowered her head, pressing it against his head and shoulder. Her feathers were warm and soft on his skin, and her voice was the same. "Do not be afraid, my human," she breathed. "You have the blood of great warriors, and their courage is in you. I am by your side, and I shall not leave you. Now come. Let us face our destiny, side by side, as it was meant to be."

Erian wanted to bury his face in her feathers, but he forced himself to stand up straight and square his shoulders. "Yes. I'm ready. Let's go, Senneck. Together."

And he stepped through the door and into the council chamber.

The chamber was round, like the tower that housed it, and cavernous. It had a great domed roof, hundreds of feet high, covered in wood panelling that had been painted with clouds, stars and suns. Great griffins wove in among them, elegant and elongated, their wings painted in every colour of the rainbow, beaks open to breathe columns of bright magic.

The walls of the chamber were lined with benches placed in sloping rows, as if the chamber was an arena where an audience could come to watch the slaughter below them. But this audience looked down at a wide area of flat ground, where the councillors sat on a ring of benches. At the centre of that was a large wooden platform, cut into the shape of a great sun and painted gold, on which the Mistress and her partner stood.

Somehow, Erian had expected there to be a lot of noise when he and Senneck entered, but that was the very opposite of what happened. The chamber had been full of sound—people talking, griffins stirring and rasping at each other—but the instant the two of them appeared, absolute silence fell.

A thousand eyes turned toward them.

Erian faltered when he saw them, but only briefly. Senneck half-raised her wings and let out a great screech. "Senneck! Senneck! Senneck!"

Beside her, Erian raised his own face to the ceiling. "Erian!" he bellowed. "Erian! Erian!" The chamber erupted. Every single griffin and griffiner there responded, crying out their own

names, every voice melding with its fellows' until even that
great space vibrated with it.

The noise was so intense that it hurt Erian's ears; he nearly
covered them with his hands, and only a strong effort of will
held him back. But the cacophony did not last forever, because
at that moment, the massive white griffin standing on the sun-
shaped platform opened his own beak wide and screamed.

"Kraal!" As if by magic, every voice was silenced. Kraal
cried his name again, and beside him Elkin did the same, her
own voice thin and pathetic compared to his, but Erian heard
it all the same.

Then they fell silent, and Kraal turned his great golden
eyes on Senneck and Erian. "Come," he rumbled. "Senneck of
Eagleholm, come to me."

"Come," Elkin echoed. "Erian Rannagonson, come to me."

At the sound of her voice, all of Erian's fear left him. He
forgot the hundreds of griffiners staring at him, forgot the stern
eyes of the council, and walked toward Elkin, feeling light-
headed but exhilarated. Kraal stood by her, of course, as huge
as always, but Erian didn't notice him much, either. At that
moment, only Elkin existed for him.

Elkin wore a gown decorated in the same manner as his
own outfit, but pure white adorned with blue sapphires. Her
hair had been neatly brushed and set with pearls, but she wore
it loose in the manner of a virgin, and her smile toward him
was sweet. "Welcome, Erian," she said, for the whole chamber
to hear. "Welcome."

Erian's breath caught in his throat. He wanted to reach out
to her, but he remembered what was required of him and knelt
before her, while beside him Senneck folded her forelegs and
touched her beak to the ground.

Kraal spoke first. "Senneck of Eagleholm," he intoned,
"whose power is of stone and earth. I, Kraal, Master of the
Eyrie of Malvern, ask you your purpose and your desire."

"Mighty Kraal," Senneck replied, not raising her head.
"Kraal whose power is of purity and majesty, I come to your
nest with the purpose and desire to serve and to honour. I come
without design upon your mates, your food or your territory,
and do swear loyalty all my days to you, who shall be my Master always."

Now Elkin spoke. "Erian Rannagonson of Eagleholm," she

said, "whose birth is noble and whose nature is likewise. I, Elkin, Mistress of the Eyrie of Malvern, ask you your purpose and your desire."

Erian took a deep breath. "My lady Elkin," he said. "Elkin who is Mistress of Malvern, I come to your home with the purpose and desire to serve and to honour. I come without design on your wealth or your power, or with the desire to harm you or your realm, and do swear loyalty all my days to you, who shall be my Mistress always."

Elkin gave a small smile and laid a hand on Kraal's shoulder. Human and griffin stood tall and spoke in unison.

"Do you both swear this, in the name of Gryphus of the Day Eye, who is the god of all life?"

"This we swear in his holy name," Erian and Senneck said as one.

"Then you have sworn yourselves to us and to Malvern, and shall be friend and follower to us both, and to the council we lead," Elkin and Kraal replied.

The two of them separated and stepped down from the platform. Elkin came to Erian and laid her hand on his head. Her touch was soft and delicate, and sent a hot thrill through his body. "Rise now as the sun with the dawn, my lord Erian of Malvern," she said.

Kraal touched his beak to Senneck's head. "Rise as the Day Eye opens, Senneck of Malvern, and be blessed."

Erian and Senneck rose as one.

"Senneck," said Kraal. "You have chosen a Master as you chose a human, and in both things you have chosen well. Come forward now, and my human shall honour you."

Senneck stepped forward and bowed low to Elkin. She returned the bow and took a pair of enormous gold rings out of a pouch hanging from her shoulder. "Hold out your forelegs, and I shall bestow the signs of honour upon you," she said.

Senneck did, and Elkin knelt and snapped the rings into place around her forelegs, just below the knee. Once on they stayed firmly in place, locked shut like a pair of slave collars. But they had no spikes on the inside, and they shone as only gold could.

"Rise now, Senneck," said Kraal. "And return to your human."

Senneck did, her eyes glittering with pride.

"Now you are lord and partnered to a lord," said Kraal. He turned his head to look at the rest of the chamber: at the council and at the other griffiners and griffins all watching. "Now let us welcome them!" he screeched. "Griffin and human both, we are now joined by Senneck Earthwings and her human, Lord Erian Rannagonson! Now let us honour them!"

The crowd roared its approval.

Erian, down below them all, could hear them shouting his name and Senneck's, and felt a fierce pride burning inside him. *I am not Erian the Bastard any more,* he thought. *I am not a peasant. I am Lord Erian. I am a griffiner. I am Lord Erian.*

He felt a gentle touch on his arm and looked up to see Elkin smiling at him. "Welcome," she said, under the noise of the crowd. "You're one of us now, Lord Erian. Are you proud?"

"More than I've ever been in my life," he said.

"I'm glad," she said, moving a little closer so he could hear her. "Kerod tells me you're doing very well. I knew I was right to choose you for that job."

Erian felt a strange tightness in his throat. "Elkin—"

But Elkin had already moved away from him. She stepped back onto her platform with Kraal, and the griffin screeched once again.

"Now!"

Silence returned.

"Now!" Kraal bellowed. "Now the ceremony is done, and we are done. Now let us leave here and return to the open air, so that we may celebrate together. We shall feast in the starlight and fly together and rejoice. Now go!"

And with that the ceremony was over. The witnesses up on the stands began to leave and the councillors stood, bowed to their two masters, and filed out, too, leaving Erian and Senneck alone with Elkin and Kraal.

"Thank you, Kraal," said Erian.

The white griffin inclined his head without saying anything, but at that moment Erian became deliciously aware that he and Elkin were alone in the same room for the first time since his arrival. She smiled down at him from her platform, and he found himself looking at her, really looking, in a way he had not done before. At the fine, delicate lines of her face and her green eyes, so bright against her pale skin and hair, and the white gown she wore. She was so slight, almost fragile, but her body had a woman's curves beneath the cloth. And he could smell her, too; a faint flowery scent came from her, left by some perfume she must have anointed herself with back in her chambers, when she was naked . . .

Erian felt his mouth go dry. "Elkin—"

The moment ended the instant he spoke. "*Lady* Elkin," she corrected. But she inclined her head toward him much as her partner had done, the smile still lingering around her mouth. "My lord Erian Rannagonson, welcome home." She placed a hand on Kraal's neck. "We will see you in the garden," she said, and climbed onto his back. She looked almost lost, nestled among the griffin's feathers, but there was a surety about the way she sat, and a grace.

Kraal took off with a quick, powerful blow of his wings, and Erian and Senneck ducked instinctively as he flew upward, circled around the inside of the dome for a few moments, and then swooped down and flew through one of the entrances the assembly had used, folding his wings to fit through but not slowing down for an instant.

"Well," Erian said, his voice sounding small and lost in the huge chamber. "It's done."

Senneck nudged him playfully. "Done indeed, my lord Erian. And now we must go to the gardens above and celebrate with your fellow lords and ladies."

"Yes. And Elkin."

"You should not have spoken to her that way," Senneck added, more sharply. "She is your Mistress now."

Erian nodded vaguely. "She's just so young—I keep thinking—never mind."

Senneck looked down at the rings on her forelegs, tapping them with her beak and admiring their lustre. "Beautiful," she cooed. "Do you not think so, Erian? They are beautiful."

"Oh, yes," said Erian, not really thinking about it. "Senneck?"

She raised her head. "Yes?"

"Why do griffins choose humans?" said Erian. "I've been thinking about it for a long time, and I don't think I understand."

"Why should we not choose humans?" said Senneck.

"Well, you're griffins," said Erian. "You're strong, you're intelligent, you have magic. You're so much more powerful than we are. Why would you care about us? Why carry us around and live with us? What does a human even have to offer a griffin?"

Senneck clicked her beak. "Erian. My poor silly little human. Do you not know?"

"No, I don't. I just don't understand why you put up with us. You're always telling me how stupid and weak I am, and sometimes I wonder why you even need me." It came out in a rush. "I feel useless, Senneck. Weak. I don't know anything, but you know everything. So why? Why me?"

"Come," said Senneck. "Let us walk. We should follow the others to the rooftop."

"Are you going to tell me why?" Erian persisted as they walked away from the platform.

Senneck walked in silence for a time, her head bobbing slightly with each step. "Erian Rannagonson," she said at last, "you have known griffins for a long time. What have you seen in us?"

"That you're magnificent creatures," said Erian. "Better than humans."

She chirped. "Flatter me, if you wish. No. We are *vain*, Erian. Think carefully. You and I live side by side. I give you my help, my favour, and in return you feed me, clean my nest, bring me water, compliment me, do everything you can simply to please me. We are not like your kind, Erian. We are not interested in riches or possessions or friendship. Our wants are simple, and by living with humans we are given all we could wish for. We have warm homes that we do not have to build ourselves, food we do not have to hunt, treatment for our wounds and illnesses. And by choosing a human, we may have power and respect as well. These rings"—she tapped them again—"are the symbols of all I want, and without you I could never have them."

"Yes, but why humans?" said Erian. "Couldn't you just take everything you want and ignore us, or kill us?"

Senneck stopped in the doorway leading out of the chamber. "I have never understood human beings," she said abruptly. "And why you despise yourselves so much. Turn and look back."

Erian did. "What should I be looking at?"

"At everything," said Senneck. "Do you see it?"

"Yes, but—"

"Be silent and look."

Erian obeyed. The silence drew out, and he took in the painted dome, the shields and spears that hung from the walls below the seats. It must have taken years to build.

"It was not griffins that made this chamber," Senneck said softly.

The top of the tower, where Senneck had first landed, had been transformed for the celebratory feast. Long tables had been set up and covered in dishes of fine foods, interspersed with elaborate flower decorations. Braziers were burning brightly at the top of long poles placed into recesses cut into the stone, illuminating hundreds of men, women and griffins mingling freely. The humans helped themselves to food from the tables, while a line of freshly slaughtered sheep had been laid out for the griffins.

Erian pointed them out to Senneck. "It looks like the others are going to eat them all before too long. You should hurry if you want some."

"I would like to, but I shall stay with you," said Senneck. "No doubt more will be brought out later, and for now I should be with you. If I appeared to be more interested in food than in staying by you, it would look . . . unimpressive."

Erian hid a smile. "Of course."

They went in among the crowd, and Erian started to look for Elkin. He found her easily enough, with Kraal beside her, talking to some of her councillors. He wanted to go over to her, but the chances of that were next to nonexistent and became even more so when Kerod appeared.

"There you are!" he said cheerily. "Eekrae and I were wondering where you'd got to."

Erian tried to look past him toward Elkin. "Hello. Yes, Senneck and I were just—"

Kerod moved to the left, unwittingly blocking his assistant's view. "Well," he said, holding out a hand, "congratulations, Erian. Or Lord Erian, I should say. You did well at the ceremony. You've done well at everything since you got here, I'd say."

Erian tugged briefly at Kerod's fingers. "Thank you," he said, forcing himself to smile and look directly at the old man. "Senneck and I are very proud. This is everything we've always wanted."

"Except for the part where you had to read eighty-nine letters sent in from Nowhere Village, eh?" Kerod cackled. "Well, I've been thinking about that, actually."

"You have?" said Erian. He was already desperate to get away but knew he should stay where he was lest he insult his master.

"We both have," said Kerod. "Eekrae and I, that is. You may remember the first time we met, and I said you and I should go hunting some day. Eekrae and I—he's over there, with the sheep, by the way—think it's time we made good on that. What do you say, Erian? Shall we go tomorrow? It would be a good way to celebrate your lordship, and we know a good place. What do you think?"

"Oh." Erian's mind raced as he tried to recall what had just been said to him. "Oh, well, I suppose so. Yes, of course. I mean, I'd love to."

"We both would," Senneck added smoothly.

Kerod grinned. "That's wonderful. I'll expect you to be up here at dawn tomorrow, so try not to drink too much, eh?"

"Of course not," said Erian.

"Good, good. I for one wouldn't mind having a look at the eats over there, so if you'll excuse me."

Kerod wandered off.

"Good gods he's annoying," Erian muttered once he'd gone. "I really wish he'd stop trying to be my friend like that."

"I question Lady Elkin's ability to choose the finest officials," said Senneck, "if that is the best she could find to be Master of Farms. He cares more for hunting than for his duties."

"I'm sure she had her reasons," said Erian. "Maybe he was more interested before, and she thought he'd be like that forever." He realised he was being unduly defensive and shrugged to cover it. "I'm sure we can make certain the work gets done properly, anyway."

"No doubt," said Senneck. "Now, we should—"

But another lord had already wandered over to them. "Welcome to Malvern, my lord Erian. I hope you do well here."

Erian didn't recognise him. "Oh. Thank you, I don't believe we've—"

"Lord Dahl, Master of Taxation," said the griffiner. "My partner, Raekri, isn't far away; she was hungry. Now, Lord Kerod tells me you've been made his assistant?"

"Uh, yes, uh—"

"Excellent. You really should meet a few people. Here, come with me."

After that, Erian found himself swept up in an endless parade of greetings and platitudes poured on him by a series of benign but uninterested faces, each one attached to a name he forgot almost instantly. Lords and ladies and griffins, some with official positions and some without. He did his best, smiling and nodding and answering their questions about himself and his background, and trying to take in everything they told him.

In the end, though, he slid into a kind of trance from which he did not awaken until Dahl said, "And this is Lady Arden, the Master of Trade."

Erian froze. "What?"

The red-haired lady in front of him smiled. "Pleased to meet you, Lord Erian. Tell me, is it true that you are Lord Rannagon's son?"

Erian pulled himself together. "I have that honour, my lady. So, tell me," he added, once they had tugged fingers. "Did I just hear you say you were the Master of Trade?"

She laughed. "That was Lord Dahl, actually. I suppose *Mistress* of Trade wouldn't sound proper. Now, Erian, I'm interested to hear about your parentage. I wasn't aware that Lord Rannagon had any sons. Where were you born?"

Erian's heart sank, but the instant he opened his mouth to reply a deafening screech cut across the conversations going on around him.

The guests fell silent at once, and he saw them backing away from the point where the screech had come from. For an instant he thought a fight had broken out, but then he saw Kraal standing at the centre of a rapidly expanding ring of empty ground.

"My lords and ladies!" said Elkin, once again appearing beside him as if by magic. "It is time!" She raised a hand, and the little group of musicians that had been playing by the tables moved to the edge of the ring and settled down.

Elkin scanned the crowd. "Lord Erian," she called. "Come forward!"

Erian needed no prompting from Senneck this time. He all but shoved his way past the people standing between him and Elkin, until he had reached the edge of the ring, and then he stepped into it. "Here I am, my lady."

Elkin favoured him with her smile. "My lord," she said,

holding her hand out toward him, palm uppermost. "Would you honour me with a dance?"

Erian took her hand. "The honour would be mine, my lady," he said, aware of all the onlookers.

"Then let us begin," said Elkin, and before he knew it the musicians launched into "The Lordly Peasant," and she linked her arm with his and began the dance.

Erian felt giddy, but he knew the dance, and after a moment's stumbling he slipped into the proper rhythm of the steps, and he and Elkin danced alone at the centre of the circle.

But only for a brief time. The onlookers, having allowed the Mistress to begin, moved into the circle and joined the dance. Soon nearly every human there had found a partner, while a few stayed by the tables and watched, and the griffins moved back and settled down to eat or groom.

The ceremonial outfit made dancing awkward. Erian could feel the long feathers hanging from his back and shoulders weighing him down, and a constant fear nagged at him that they would catch on something and break, but he ignored the thought and put all his efforts into dancing as well as he could. "The Lordly Peasant" was a fast tune, and keeping up with it was no easy task; he mentally thanked the gods that he had practised the steps in private.

But Elkin made a good partner. Even though she was a head shorter than him, she was stronger than she looked and quick on her feet. And even though Erian had never liked dancing, his heart was singing. All the secret fantasies he had had about this night were coming true.

The first dance ended, and they launched into "Dance of the Griffins." Most of the other dancers chose new partners, but Elkin made no move to let go of Erian's arm. Nor did she part with him during the third dance. By the fourth, however, she moved on to a different partner, leaving Erian with a feeling of mingled elation and disappointment.

He danced with several different women after that, some better than others, but all the while he found himself looking for Elkin. She had disappeared among the mass of twirling figures, and he couldn't catch a glimpse of her pale hair anywhere.

Night drew in and the stars came out. Eventually the moon rose. By then Erian had danced several dances, and he was sweating and exhausted when he finally excused himself and went over to the tables to eat something.

He helped himself to some bread and cheese and a roasted chicken leg, and picked some strayberries out of a bowl. Jugs of drink had been laid out as well, so he poured himself a cupful and unwisely downed it in a few mouthfuls without tasting it first.

It turned out to be strong iced wine, and he put the cup down and started coughing. Moments later his stomach lurched, and he grabbed hold of the table to support himself. His head was spinning.

Idiot! he berated himself. But he had a second cup anyway, to steady his nerves. That made him feel a little better, and he had some more to eat before tackling a third cupful.

He wondered where Senneck was, and then dismissed the thought with a shrug. Doubtless she was enjoying herself with the other griffins. She didn't need him for now.

He finished the third cup and stifled a yawn. The wine had made him feel pleasantly warm and contented, and he eyed the nearest jug and wondered if he should risk having some more.

"My lord?"

Erian turned. "Hm? What? Oh!"

Elkin had appeared behind him, smiling. "There you are," she said. "I was looking for you."

"Oh," Erian said again. "I—uh—hello, my lady."

She held out her arm. "Will you honour me with the next dance, my lord?"

Erian smiled and accepted the arm. "Of course."

Elkin led him onto the dance floor as the musicians struck up a slow tune that he recognised as "The Flowers of the Field." This was a dance he didn't know.

Elkin took his hands in hers. "Come," she said.

Erian was nervous for an instant, but the wine boosted his confidence. He let her lead him into the dance, and watched the others around him to try and pick up the steps. He stumbled a few times, but Elkin helped him keep up.

"This is my favourite dance," she confided as she moved in close to him.

"I like it, too," Erian said and grinned back.

And even though he hated dancing, it was the truth.

The dance seemed to go on for a long time, and when it was over Erian said, "Do you want to go and have something to eat?"

Elkin paused. "Of course. Why not?"

They returned to the tables and picked at a few choice dishes, neither of them saying much. Erian tried desperately to think of something to talk about, but his mind had gone blank.

"The wine's good," he blurted at last. "Would you like me to pour you some?"

"Yes, thank you," said Elkin. She took the cup he offered her, and sipped from it. "This wine came all the way from Amoran, you know. I was waiting for a good time to bring it out of the cellars. Do you like it?"

"Yes, it's very good," said Erian.

"They make it in Syama," said Elkin. "Have some yourself, why don't you?"

Erian did. "It's very sweet. I've always liked sweet wines. Do they put honey in it?"

"I think so, yes." Elkin finished the cup and grinned wickedly at him. "I'm not supposed to drink too much wine, you know, but I do anyway, on special occasions."

"Why not?" said Erian.

"Oh, because I'm so delicate, you know," said Elkin, pouring herself another cupful regardless. "And I *am* Mistress here, too. Who knows what stupid decisions I might make?"

Erian laughed. "I don't think anyone would say anything. They all admire you, my lady. Every griffiner I've spoken to since I got here has told me you are the best Eyrie Mistress they know of."

"Have they really?" she asked seriously.

"Yes. And I think so, too," Erian added.

She gave him an amused look. "Is that so?"

He cursed himself yet again, and put the cup aside. He'd drunk too much. If he said or did something truly appalling in front of her . . .

"Well?" Elkin prompted.

"Uh, yes," said Erian. "I do."

She watched him for a while, sipping at her wine. "So," she said, once the silence had begun to be uncomfortable. "Tell me about yourself, Erian. And"—she picked up a strayberry and turned it over in her fingers—"I don't mean in the way you did when we first met. Tell me something *real*."

Erian felt hot all over. "Oh, well . . ."

"Go on," said Elkin. "I'm interested. I want to know you better."

"Well, I . . ."

And then, quite suddenly, he was telling her everything. He talked about his conception, when Lord Rannagon, on his way back to Eagleholm after the war in the North, had stayed for the night at a small village called Carrick, where a peasant girl named Belara had caught his eye and shared his bed for the night. Rannagon had left the next day.

She had tried to lure him back after she discovered that she was pregnant, but never had any response from him, and eventually died birthing the boy, leaving him to be brought up by her parents.

"So I grew up without a father," said Erian. "But they told me who he was, and told me stories about him, and I grew up believing—well, I always thought it made me special. He was my hero. I used to imagine meeting him; I'd try and think of all the things I would say to him and what he would say back. For a long time I believed that he'd come and see me one day; he'd come on his griffin, Shoa, and we'd fly back to Eagleholm together, and I'd grow up there, and . . ." He trailed off.

"But he never came?" Elkin said sympathetically.

Erian smiled sadly. "He did. He did come. He came and saw me several times. And he didn't take me away, but—but he was kind. He called me 'son,' brought me presents. Shoa even let me touch her once. Later on I found out he was doing it secretly, flying out to Carrick on a pretext so people wouldn't know. And then he stopped coming. But he gave orders to an old griffiner in the village to be my teacher. He taught me griffish and how to read and write and handle a sword and a bow. He never told me why, but I knew my father had got him to do it—paid him or bribed him somehow."

"You were lucky," said Elkin. "Not many griffiners would do that."

"I know." Erian smiled. "That's how I knew that he cared about me. I always knew it. And when I was sixteen I knew it was time. My grandparents expected me to get married, take over the farm and settle down there, but I wouldn't. They told me I was mad—stupid—but I knew I wasn't meant to be a farmer. I knew griffish, I knew things peasants didn't know, and the gods must have a different plan for me. And my *father* must have one, too. I kept expecting him to come and see me again, but he didn't, and so I decided that I had to go to him. So I went to Eagleholm, and I found him there. He pretended he wasn't happy that I'd come, but later on he said he knew I would. I asked him if he thought I should become a griffiner, and he said that wasn't for him to decide. But he told me only nobles become griffiners, and that just because I was his son I shouldn't get ideas above myself. He said he could get me a job in the city—maybe as a guardsman—but that was all he was willing to do. He told me he was sorry, but that having me there was an embarrassment and he was already in trouble with his sister for acknowledging me, even if it was only in secret." Erian rubbed his head. "Once he'd finished saying that, he gave me a piece of paper and told me to go and not come back."

Elkin sighed. "That was cold of him."

"Not as much as it sounds, my lady," said Erian. "I realised later on that people must have been listening in—Shoa was listening, and I know she didn't like me. But the paper—once I was outside I looked at it, and it was a map to the hatchery. There was writing on it. It just said 'Let the gods and the griffins decide.' And I went to the hatchery, and—"

"And all your dreams came true," Elkin finished.

"They did, my lady," said Erian. "They all did. And it was thanks to my father, and I am never going to forget that."

"Or forgive the one who took him from you," said Elkin softly, as if she had read his mind.

Erian felt his heart clench. He picked up the cup of wine and drank it, more quickly than he should. He didn't want to talk about that now. "Senneck wants me to marry," he said hastily, and thoughtlessly.

Elkin looked inexplicably unhappy. "Yes, I thought she would. If she wants you to succeed, then a good marriage would be an important part of it."

"I don't want to," said Erian. "At least, not like that. I want to marry the one who's right for me. I want to marry because I'm in love, not because Senneck wants me to be rich. Anyway," he added bitterly, "what woman here would want me? I might be a griffiner now, but I'm still a bastard."

Elkin reached out as if to touch his arm, but withdrew. "I understand," she said. "Kraal wants me to marry, too. So do

most of my griffiners—mostly the men, for some reason. Erian,
it might not look that way, but I know just how you feel. You
don't think anyone would want you, but my trouble is almost
the same. *Every* unmarried man here wants me, and even some
of the married ones would probably be glad to separate themselves from their wives for my sake. There are quite a few I
could choose, but—I don't like it. Why should I marry just for
the sake of convenience? Don't my feelings count? I give everything I have for my Eyrie and its lands, but I still own my body
and heart, and I don't want to give them to the first well-bred
idiot who puts himself in my way."

Erian blinked. "Er . . ."

Elkin winced. "Oh gods. I'm sorry, I shouldn't have—I
should go."

Without even thinking, Erian reached out and grabbed her
shoulder. "Elkin."

She looked at him. "Don't do that."

He let go. "Elkin, I just wanted to say that I . . ."

"Yes?"

"I really enjoyed dancing with you tonight," said Erian.

She smiled sadly. "That's nice. I'm glad you did."

It was growing late. Around them the crowd had dispersed;
many griffiners were leaving, and only a few were still dancing. The griffins, unused to being awake at night, had begun to
order their partners back inside.

Erian looked at Elkin, and struggled desperately to find the
thing he should say to reach through to her and express how he
felt. "Elkin, I . . ."

Something in her was pulling away, but she kept her gaze
on him. "Yes?"

"Elkin, Lady Elkin. I was thinking, have you ever . . . ? I
mean, it's so beautiful tonight, isn't it?"

Elkin glanced quickly over her shoulder. "Yes. It is. The
moon will be full soon."

"It's the same colour as your hair," said Erian. "Isn't it?"

"The same colour as Kraal's feathers," said Elkin "Yes. I've
always liked that. We're alike in that way I think. It's the same
with you and Senneck, isn't it?"

"Yes." Erian laughed weakly. "We're both the colour of dirt."

"Straw," Elkin corrected. "But I was thinking of your eyes.
Sky blue. It's a nice colour, isn't it?"

Erian felt close to trembling. "Yes, yes, it is." *Your eyes are like the colour of nothing I've ever seen before.* He wanted to say it aloud but couldn't put it into words and it sounded stupid and clumsy in his head. He stayed quiet, his whole body screaming out for him to do something, anything, while the moment slipped inexorably away from him.

"Well," Elkin said at last, and he thought he could hear something like disappointment in her voice. "It's late. I should go to bed. I have a busy day ahead. As always."

Erian wanted to cry. "Yes. We both—yes, I should go, too."

"Yes, we should," Elkin said more sharply.

And then, just like that, she was gone.

25

Arenadd the Conqueror

Cardock was not the only one to have lost his life in the capture of Guard's Post. When Arenadd, Skade and Skandar emerged from the room where his body lay and returned to the mess hall, they found a grim sight waiting for them. The bodies of the dead had been brought in and laid down in a row against one wall, and more were coming even now.

The final tally was chilling: more than forty of their companions had been killed, including Annan, Nolan, Olwydd and several other men who had shared Arenadd's dormitory back at Herbstitt.

Arenadd, red-eyed but outwardly calm, silently took all this in and afterward merely said: "What have you done with the wounded?"

"Morgan found an infirmary, sir. They've been taken there."

Arenadd nodded. "Is someone looking after them?"

"Yes, sir."

"Good. I'm going to look after Skandar and then go and help them. In the meantime, Prydwen, you and Dafydd go and open the southernmost gate. Find the others and bring them back. Garnoc, I want you to talk to everyone here. Find out if any of them know how to cook. They're to find the storerooms and take stock of what we've got, and after that I want them to find the kitchens and make enough food for everyone. Tell them to be as generous as they can afford to be. After all, we'll be celebrating."

Garnoc grinned. "Yes, sir."

"Right," said Arenadd to no-one in particular after the three of them had left.

Skandar had slumped down in a corner of the mess hall

while this was going on, his head hanging low. Everyone was keeping well away from him as usual.

Arenadd approached him carefully. "Skandar, how are you?"

The griffin looked up. "Strong. Am strong," he mumbled, his wings rising briefly before they fell back.

"Of course," said Arenadd. "But I think you've got a few injuries. Shall I have a look at them? I can make them stop hurting and heal faster."

Skandar's pride didn't hold out for long; he hissed briefly in protest when Arenadd came closer, but lay still and let him examine his wounds. His face and neck had several deep talon cuts on them, and a beak had laid his shoulder open. A sword had caught him on one knee, which explained the limp, but his wings and other legs looked undamaged.

Even so, Arenadd didn't want to leave anything to chance. "You," he called to a nearby slave.

The man looked nervous. "Yes, sir?"

"Go to the infirmary," said Arenadd. "Get some griffin-tail paste and some bandages, fast as you can."

"Yes, sir." The man dashed out.

"Will he recover?" Skade asked.

Arenadd groaned softly as he subsided onto a chair. "Unless one of those injuries gets infected, yes. If he'll let me put some paste on them, he should be fine."

The man returned a few moments later with the medicine, and after some cajoling Skandar allowed Arenadd to treat him.

"How do you know how to treat wounds like that?" said Skade, watching him apply the paste and then bandage the cuts as well as he could.

"Simple enough," said Arenadd, without looking around. "Nobody back home wanted me to have an official position, so I spent about ten years being pushed around the place. I worked for nearly every part of the government there was; they used to call me 'the one-year apprentice.' I worked for the Master of Arms, the Master of Taxation, the Master of Healing—well, the Mistress, really. I even worked for Rannagon himself for a while. See, nobody wanted me to be apprenticed to anyone for too long, because if someone died or was disgraced while I was their apprentice, I'd automatically be given their office. They even thought of making me the commander of the city guard for a while, but the one who was in the position at the time put his foot down about that. But it meant I learnt a lot about a lot of different things. Even carpentry, although that posting didn't last for too long."

"Why not?" said Skade.

"Oh, I had to help the people who kept the platform in proper repair," said Arenadd. "You know, the one the city was built on. The planks would rot, and people would steal pieces of them for firewood, so we had to keep fixing it. I was only there for a few weeks. Ow! Skandar, keep still, will you?"

"I hardly think that was the proper job for a griffiner," said Skade. "No wonder they moved you."

"Hah, as if they would have cared," said Arenadd. "No, they would have been happy to keep me there, but . . ." He paused, slightly embarrassed. "There was an accident."

"What sort of accident?" said Skade.

"I'm afraid of heights. Always have been. They sent me to the edge of the platform for something or other, and I panicked and stayed there for ages, too terrified to move. In the end, Eluna had to drag me away. It was—uh—very humiliating."

"Ah," said Skade. "I see."

"Unfortunate." Arenadd finished tying the last bandage. "There. All done. Stop shivering, you big coward, you're fine."

Skandar got up and pecked at a bandage. "Not want."

"I'm sorry, but you have to wear them for a while. They won't hurt you. They'll help make you heal."

The griffin flicked his tail. "I go find food," he muttered resentfully, and limped off.

"I hope he does not go to the kitchens," said Skade.

"I doubt it. He'll want live food; he'll probably look for the stables. Or he might—" Thinking of the other possibility, he shivered. "I'm sure he'll be fine," he said loudly. "Now, I'd better go. You should get some rest; I could be some time."

"I shall explore the fortress a little, I think," said Skade. "Perhaps I shall find another gown; this one is nearly in rags."

"Good idea," said Arenadd. "But I don't know if that's very likely. See if anyone here knows anything about tailoring; they could sew it up for you." He gave her a brief smile and left the room.

Once he had gone, Skade wandered away and began her exploration. She found the kitchens—which, fortunately, Skandar hadn't—where a group of slaves were already beginning to prepare the food they'd taken from the storerooms. She paused to help herself to some meat and wandered out again, chewing at it.

The fortress' interior proved to be bigger than she had thought. She explored various different rooms and found guard quarters, an armoury, a training gallery, a small forge and a treasury containing chests of gold oblong. She opened the various crates and boxes that shared the space with them, and found other items: boots, miscellaneous pieces of armour, several cloth-wrapped parcels of whiteleaf, bottles of liquid whose labels she couldn't read and bundles of clothing. All of it must have been confiscated from travellers caught between the gates and searched.

Skade rummaged through the clothing until she found some gowns that looked to be about her size. She tried those on and finally chose a simple one made from white wool; its long sleeves and thick weave could help protect her from the cold of the North.

Feeling much neater, she returned to the lower levels of the fort. Finding nothing particularly interesting there, she decided to go in the opposite direction this time and move further downward. There were a few chambers built below ground, including a wine cellar, cool storerooms for perishable foods and a small set of prison cells.

Skade examined this last area but found the cells unoccupied. A thought occurred to her, and she returned to the mess hall.

During her absence, Prydwen and Dafydd had gone to a spot back down the road and had brought back all those who had been unable to fight. Torc and Caedmon had been among them, and now the old man was standing beside the row of bodies, leaning on his stick and looking expressionlessly at them. Nearby, the captured guards were standing penned in a corner, hands tied together, closely guarded by Prydwen, Dafydd and the hulking Garnoc.

Skade looked briefly at the new arrivals before approaching the three of them. "Look at me," she commanded.

They did, and Prydwen betrayed a hint of nervousness before he bowed his head toward her. "Yes, my lady?"

"There are cells beneath us," Skade told him. "You should take them down there and lock them up securely."

Dafydd coughed, "Lord Arenadd—"

"Do it," said Skade. "Lord Arenadd wishes for you to think for yourselves."

"Of course, my lady," Prydwen cut in. "C'mon, let's go." He prodded the nearest prisoner with the point of his stolen sword. "Move, ye lousy bastard, and don't even think of doin' anythin' else."

Skade watched as the prisoners were herded away, and sighed. "They should be killed."

A hand tugged at her sleeve. "My lady?"

She looked around and saw Torc. Even now the boy's face reminded her of Welyn, and she had to stop herself from crying out. "Yes?"

Torc backed away. "I'm sorry, my lady. I just wondered if you could tell me where Lord Arenadd is."

Caedmon stepped in and grabbed him by the shoulder. "Torc! Don't ye dare question the lady!"

Torc yelped. "I'm sorry! I just wanted to know if he was hurt or anything. I'm sorry."

"He is in the infirmary, tending to the wounded," said Skade.

"He's not hurt then, my lady?" said Caedmon.

Skade gave him a look. "I see *you* have no troubles with questioning the lady."

"I'm the elder among the slaves, my lady," Caedmon answered calmly. "It's my duty to ask the questions and pass the answers on to the others."

"I see. No, Lord Arenadd is not hurt. But he is grieving for his father," said Skade.

Caedmon's face fell. "Not Cardock?"

"Yes. He died defending me, and Arenadd is distraught."

Torc groaned. "Oh, no."

"This was madness," Caedmon muttered. "How many are there dead?"

"At least forty of our men," said Skade.

"Madness! Using slaves as an attack force—and what exactly is Lord Arenadd planning to do with us next? First we were runaways; now we're killers. If we're caught, we'll all hang." Caedmon gripped his stick and muttered Northern curses under his breath.

"You forget yourself," Skade said coldly. "You are not in a position to question your master's decisions."

Caedmon bowed. "Forgive me, my lady," he said stiffly and walked away.

Torc watched him go. "I've never heard him say anything like that before."

"No, and he should not have said it, either," said Skade. "Now you should go to the kitchens, Torc. We are going to eat here tonight, all together."

Torc stared at her. "What, all in the same room? At the same table? My lady."

Skade smiled very slightly. *So much like Welyn.* "Of course. We have won a great victory here today and must celebrate. Now go. There is work to do."

By evening, the fortress had been fully occupied by the slaves. They had cleaned out the rooms, taking anything that looked useful. Every scrap of food from the storerooms had been brought out, and the armoury, too, had been emptied. The surviving guards had been locked away and provided with bread and water, and the dead had been removed from the mess hall. Prydwen had posted sentries on top of the walls, to watch out for any travellers coming up the road.

Meanwhile, the slaves assigned to the kitchens had been working their hardest preparing a range of dishes to be served that evening in the mess hall, where the long tables had been righted and stocked with enough chairs for everyone.

Amid all this work, however, one person remained conspicuously absent: Arenadd. Skade eventually lost patience and went to the infirmary to look for him, but was told he had left some time ago. When she went in search of him she failed to find him or Skandar, either, but questioning eventually revealed where they both were.

"Lord Arenadd went down to the vault, my lady. The griffin followed; they've been down there for a long while."

"They are with the bodies?" said Skade, startled.

"Yes, my lady. The door's locked, but I went past and heard some strange sounds."

"What sounds?" said Skade.

The man shook his head. "Like metal."

Skade felt an unpleasant churning in her stomach as she made for the door to the vault, which did indeed prove to be locked. She thumped on it. "Arenadd? Arenadd, are you there?"

There was silence, and then a scrape of wood from the other side. The door swung open and Arenadd appeared, looking pale and tired. He blinked at her. "Oh. Hello."

Skade looked past him but only saw the huge bulk of Skandar approaching. "How is he?"

"Better. Excuse me, I have to go upstairs." Arenadd pushed past her and walked up the corridor toward the stairs. Skade flattened herself against the wall to let Skandar through; the griffin glanced briefly at her and then limped off after his friend.

Skade hesitated, thinking of looking inside the vault for some clue, but instead followed Skandar, hoping to catch up with Arenadd. But the griffin, only just able to fit through the corridor, blocked her way, and she had to follow him at a distance as he struggled up the stairs.

The three of them made the short journey back up to the second level of the fort, where Arenadd opened a large studded door. Skandar followed him through it, and Skade ran to catch up.

"Arenadd!"

Arenadd paused in the act of closing the door. "Yes?"

She stopped. "What are you doing?"

Arenadd rubbed his eyes. "I found a razor and a comb in one of the rooms. I need to have a bath and neaten myself up a bit."

"In the *forge*?"

"I see you found a new gown," said Arenadd, ignoring her. "It looks good on you. I shouldn't be long; I'll see you downstairs later, all right?" That said, he closed the door.

Skade glared at it and walked away.

The slaves held their impromptu victory feast after moonrise, every man packed into the mess hall who wasn't on sentry duty or in the infirmary. The slaves assigned to the kitchens had done their best, and had provided roasted and salted meat, boiled potatoes, bread and butter, dried fruit and two barrels of mead. The slaves sat around the table in no particular order and eagerly bit in, and the air was soon full of their talk.

Skade, standing awkwardly by the doorway, watched them. There was an apprehensive feel in the room, but she could hear relief and even pride in the men's voices as well. They had fought a battle and won it, and now they had food and shelter and a true sense of safety for the first time in weeks. For now they could afford to enjoy themselves a little.

Skade scratched her neck. Arenadd hadn't reappeared since

he had locked himself up in the forge, and she had finally commanded the slaves to begin eating without him.

She chewed at the food she had taken from the nearest table,
and sighed. Caedmon and Prydwen had both invited her to sit
with them, but she disliked the idea of being surrounded by so
many humans, and hunger had forced her to stay in the mess
hall, feeling jittery and anxious. She hated being out of sight of
the sky and wished Arenadd was there to calm her down.

She wondered, abruptly, if he was all right. He hadn't looked
well when she had seen him, and there had been something
about the way he acted. She still didn't understand a lot of
human behaviour. They communicated things with their faces,
but she only knew a few expressions. Had there been something
in Arenadd's face that she should have noticed, something he
wanted to tell her but without words? His father was dead: was
there something she should have said or done, something he
needed from her?

She sighed miserably. *I am a cripple. Once I was strong, but
now my wings are gone and I know nothing. Once I was the
protector, but now—*

You failed to protect Welyn, her inner voice told her harshly.
*You watched him die. Why do you think you can protect Are-
nadd, who loves you? Your talons are gone; your magic is
gone; you know nothing and can do nothing. Fool. Weak fool.*

Skade hissed to herself and tore a piece of bread in half.

A few moments later, the back of her neck prickled. She
looked up sharply, alerted by something that took her a few
moments to identify.

The hall had gone quiet. Every man there was looking toward
the opposite door, and Skade quickly saw why. She dropped the
bread and almost ran toward it.

"Arenadd!"

He stepped into the hall and treated her to a genuine smile.
"Hello, Skade. Have you had something to eat?"

"I have, and so have your friends," said Skade. She looked
him up and down. "I see you have groomed yourself."

He had washed himself and paid particular attention to his
hair, which had been trimmed, cleaned and combed. It hung
in a curly mane over his shoulders. He had also shaved and
styled the tangled mess of his facial hair and now wore a small,
pointed thin beard that suited him quite well. He had even, by

the looks of it, washed and darned his robe, though there was a bandage wrapped around his throat that she didn't remember seeing before.

"Yes, and I'm very pleased about that," he said, patting his hair. "I looked like something out of a drainage ditch."

Skandar shoved his way past and into the hall at this point, and instantly limped over to the nearest table and dragged a platter of meat onto the floor. The slaves yelled and darted out of the way, but the griffin completely ignored them and began to eat.

Arenadd groaned. "Sorry! Sorry, he's not very—oh, never mind. Is there a spare seat anywhere?"

Caedmon came hurrying over. "Of course, my lord. Follow me. And you, too, my lady."

Skade fell in behind Arenadd, feeling oddly relieved, and let herself be ushered to a seat beside him at the head of one of the tables. Caedmon and Torc brought over the choicest dishes for them to share, and poured two cups of mead.

Arenadd started to eat at once. "Thank gods. I'm ravenous."

Skade watched him. "Are you . . . well?"

"Well enough," he said briefly. "And you? That cut on your forehead looks painful."

"I am fine," said Skade. "But I was—I did not know if—I thought that perhaps you were not well," she finished lamely.

Arenadd picked up his cup. "I'm fine. My head still aches a bit, but it should be okay."

"But your father is dead."

He paused at that, and she saw some expression move over his face that could have been pain. "Yes. We'll burn him with the others tomorrow, before we leave. I'm going to take his ashes north with me. It's what he would have wanted."

"Why?" said Skade, mystified.

"Because—well, it's symbolic. Even if he's dead, part of him can still come with us. Does that make sense?"

"Very little," said Skade. "But who am I to judge?"

Arenadd smiled slightly. "I'm sorry if I was a bit standoffish before. I had things to think about."

"What things?" said Skade.

"Things," he said enigmatically.

"Yes, and what things would they be?" said Skade.

"Just things. Go on, have something to eat. We should enjoy

it while it lasts; I don't know how long it'll take us to get to where we're going."

"Where *are* we going?" said Skade. "We were always going north, but do you know where in the North?"

"We obviously can't go into any of the villages," said Arenadd, "so we'll have to find somewhere else. An uninhabited place. Somewhere further north, where no-one lives."

"You think we can survive there?" said Skade.

"I hope so." Arenadd began spreading butter on a slice of bread and left it at that.

Skade considered pressing him further but decided there would be time for that later. In the meantime, she ate.

The feast went on, and the men ate their fill. Skandar finished his stolen meat and then settled down against the wall closest to Arenadd but as far away from the humans as he could get; he alternately tore at his bandages and glared at the slaves.

Eventually the food was gone, along with most of the mead, and the slaves had settled down, sleepy and contented.

That was when Arenadd stood up. "Excuse me."

The people at his table looked up, but most of the room's other occupants didn't hear him and continued to chat among themselves.

Arenadd drew himself up. *"Listen to me!"*

Silence fell at once, and every man looked toward him.

Arenadd gave a satisfied smile. "Thank you," he said. "Now, I have some things to say." He paused a moment and then walked around the table to stand at the centre of the room. "My friends," he said. "And friends are what I hope you are, and it's how I think of you. I don't like to think of you as my property or as my underlings. I've led people before, even into dangerous situations. When I lived at Eagleholm I had to work with the city guard to capture smugglers, and even though I was in command we worked together as a team and every man there had his say. That's how a group should always work." He began to pace back and forth.

"Tonight, while we celebrate our victory—and that was what it was—I want to talk to you about someone. That someone is my father. His name was Cardock Skandarson. When he was only ten, Lady Riona sold the slaves she had at Eagleholm. Only a handful of them stayed behind; they were children who were too young to be sold. My father was freed and given an apprenticeship to a boot maker. Many years later he fell in love with another freed slave, Annir. I was their only child, and they named me Arenadd after Arenadd the Sage." Arenadd stopped pacing and frowned, his shoulders hunching slightly.

"I grew up as the only Northern child in the village. The other freed slaves had returned to Tara as soon as they were old enough, but my parents didn't want to travel with an infant, and so I grew up in Idun. They were the only people of my race I knew. My father always wanted to return to the North when I was a little older, but I destroyed his dreams without even realising it: I became a griffiner. Lady Riona had me swear loyalty to her, and I became her man from then on. And my father—I know he was proud, in a way, but he didn't show it. After what griffiners had done to his people, he saw it as a kind of betrayal. We argued—fought. My father had always told me that I should be proud of my heritage, and at first I listened. But after we began fighting, all that came to an end. I refused to answer to 'Arenadd' and began to call myself 'Arren Cardockson,' like a Southerner. I moved into the city and almost never visited my parents at all; I refused to speak the Northern tongue. I even cursed my own people. I didn't want to be a Northerner. I wanted to be a Southerner, and I believed I was, with all my heart. I believed that it didn't matter how I looked if I was a Southerner at heart, if I made myself be *more* than that.

"I listened to what my tutors said; I believed everything they told me about my race. But I knew I was more than just a savage; I was intelligent, educated. I could rise above my birth, become something special." He looked at them intensely. "I want you to understand that. All of you. I was *ashamed*. Truly ashamed. I was at war with my own blood, my own race, my own self. My father never forgave me for it. And yet he never stopped loving me, and he never stopped hoping that one day I would understand the things he was always trying to make me see. And today, I did see." Arenadd spread his hands, holding them out palm up. "And it was you that I saw," he said. "All of you. Here, today, the men in this hall showed me the truth. You showed me why I should never be ashamed; you taught me that I should be proud. All my life people have spat at me and cursed me behind my back because I was a Northerner. But you never did. You made me be proud; you made me feel that I was blessed, by these eyes, this hair, this robe, this pale skin. Even though you were born into slavery, you had the courage and the strength to do what I asked of you. You showed me what true men of Tara can do. And even though my father died today, fighting beside you, I know he would have been happy to know that I know. And for that"—he bowed low—"I thank you."

There was silence once Arenadd stopped speaking. And then, without any warning, three figures rose from the table.

Prydwen, Dafydd and Garnoc. The three Northerners looked at Arenadd, then at each other, and then Prydwen lifted his face to the ceiling and howled. It was a wolf howl—long, low and mournful—and after a few moments his two friends joined in.

Arenadd looked startled for a moment, but then he grinned. He cupped his hands around his mouth and howled back, and soon every man in the room was doing likewise. The howls filled the hall, mingled with whoops and cheers, and Skade looked on, puzzled.

Skandar looked up, his tail lashing in sudden alarm. The howling made him bristle, and he began to hiss. Finally, provoked, he opened his beak and screeched. The noise cut across the howling, and everyone started nervously, staring at him. Skandar glared back, and then, as suddenly as the howling had begun, everyone there started to laugh.

Skandar looked affronted and opened his beak a few times, apparently considering another screech, before he decided to ignore them.

The laughter died away, and Arenadd wiped his eyes. "Don't mind him; I'm sure he just wanted to join in. Now," he said, once the fresh laughter this provoked had ended, "I've been thinking alone this evening." He looked seriously at them. "After a victory in battle, generals usually give their soldiers extra pay. But what use would money be to you? You're slaves. You've spent your whole lives doing as you're told and have been given nothing in return. But still, even slaves sometimes get rewards from their masters when they do well, don't they? And I have a reward for you." Arenadd pointed abruptly. "Garnoc. Come here, please."

The burly slave rose from his seat. "Me, sir?"

"Yes, you. Come here."

Garnoc did. "What d'ye want from me, sir?"

Arenadd looked him up and down in a calculating kind of way. "Do you trust me, Garnoc?"

"Yes, sir."

"Good. And do you want the reward I have for you?"

"I . . . think so, sir."

"Then I need you to do exactly as I say," said Arenadd.

"I will, sir."

Arenadd nodded. "Stand very still and raise your chin. Yes, like that. And stand absolutely still. Don't move for any reason. Not even slightly. Understand?"

"Yes, sir," said Garnoc.

"Good." Arenadd reached into his robe and brought out an iron blacksmith's hammer, holding it tightly in one hand. "Then you'll have your reward now."

Garnoc's eyes widened. "Sir? What are you doing?"

A strange smile came over Arenadd's face. "Join me, Garnoc," he said, and swung the hammer as hard as he could.

26

Rogues

Erian woke up the morning after the dance with a hangover and a feeling of utter misery. He dressed in semi-darkness, choosing his warmest clothes by the light of a single candle. The ceremonial costume was draped over the desk where he'd left it, but he tried not to look at it as he strapped Bloodpride onto his back and picked up his quiver, the un-strung bow packed inside with the arrows. With those, and a water bottle and some dried food in his pockets, he went into the next room.

Senneck was already awake and looked alert in the dawn light coming in from the balcony. "Good morning," she said, sounding unusually cheerful. "I expected to have to wake you."

Erian took her harness down from the wall. "I thought I'd sleep late after last night."

"Ah, but the excitement woke you up, yes?" said Senneck.

"I suppose so," Erian mumbled.

"Then put on my harness, and we shall go," said Senneck. "Kerod will be impressed if we arrive before he does."

"Of course." Erian put it on, fumbling with the buckles, and the two of them walked onto the balcony, he climbed onto her back and she took off, flying into the early-morning chill. The sky was light grey, tinged with pink on the horizon, and very few other griffins were in the air. A few lights burned here and there in the windows of the Eyrie, and a strange hush lay over everything, as if the city itself were asleep.

Senneck landed at the top of Council's Tower. Few traces of last night's celebrations were left; the tables had been removed, along with the torches, and the only things left were a few scraps of food that had been dropped on the floor and, at the edge of the tower, a partially eaten sheep carcass.

Erian got off Senneck's back and wandered around among the plants, trying to ignore his aching head. The hangover was only a mild one, but the memories of the previous night were more than enough to make up for that. His conversation with Elkin—both said and unsaid—replayed itself over and over again. The way she had looked at him, those green eyes so pale and sad, watching him. And after that, the sense he had got from her that he had somehow betrayed her, that she had asked him for something and he had failed to give it. He tried to tell himself it was nothing, that he had only imagined it, but the feeling refused to leave him alone.

He sighed and kicked the ground. And now he was going to have to spend the entire day with Kerod, the eternal grandfather trying to act like he was twenty. The prospect made him want to yell and throw something.

The sun began to rise, and Erian and Senneck were still alone. *Maybe he won't come,* Erian thought hopefully. *Maybe he forgot or something.*

But this small ray of light was dashed a few moments later when Kerod and Eekrae arrived, landing close to Senneck.

Kerod came hurrying to meet him. "Good morning, my lord! I can't believe you got here first!"

"Morning," Erian mumbled.

"Old men like me need their rest, of course," Kerod added. "Anyway, we'll be able to get an early start, which is good. The place we're headed for is a fair flight from here. Oh, you're not bringing that, are you?"

Erian realised he was looking at the sword. "Yes."

"I'd leave it here if I were you," said Kerod. "It's dead weight. No use for hunting. Not much use for anything, really, with that many jewels on it. Where'd you get it from?"

"It's mine," said Erian, a touch defensively. "I want to bring it."

Kerod shrugged. "Well, if Senneck doesn't mind. So," he added, as they walked back toward the griffins, "how did you like the dance? I saw you were lucky enough to dance with Lady Elkin more than once. That must have been a thrill for you."

That gave him a far more painful pang than he had expected. "Yes."

"She always dances with the new lords after they're inducted," Kerod went on blithely, adjusting the quiver on his back. "It's a ceremonial thing. Oh, Eekrae?"

The griffin had been watching him and now drew himself up. "Kerod and I were planning to go further northward," Eekrae said, addressing Senneck. "There are uncharted lands that way, vast areas of forest and mountains. We can find game there: deer, wolves—even bears if we have good luck. The flight will be a long one, and if the weather turns foul we may have to spend a night camping. Does that suit you?"

Senneck inclined her head. "I think we shall enjoy ourselves very much. Erian and I have camped and hunted together before, and we would be more than glad to see this hunting ground."

"Excellent," said Eekrae. "Then we shall go now. Kerod, climb onto my back."

The two griffiners mounted up, and they set out as the sun rose, flying over the city and beyond it on an early-morning gale.

The flight did indeed prove to be a long one. The two griffins stayed in the air for much of the morning, Senneck flying slightly behind Eekrae and riding on his slipstream. Erian, relatively protected from the cold by Senneck's feathers and the warm furs he was wearing, quickly became lost in his own thoughts. Or rather, thought.

Elkin. As the time dragged by, she filled his mind. All he could think of was her: her laugh, her smile, her bright green eyes. Little moments flashed behind his eyes, instants frozen in time. Her hands gripping his as they twirled apart on the dance floor. The way her hair moved over her face when she leant forward to pick a strayberry out of the bowl. The scent of her skin and the way the light caught the gems on her gown. They tripped through his mind, as sharp and real as if they had happened only moments ago.

The thought of her made him feel strange. His stomach churned and his heart beat faster, but he didn't know why. Was it fear or shame? Or happiness? He couldn't tell.

He kept on thinking of their last conversation. All the time they had been speaking, he had wanted to reach out and touch her, or to tell her how beautiful she was and how being with her made him feel so frightened but so thrilled.

He knew that if he had done either of these things Senneck would have been furious. Kraal would almost certainly have been the same way. And Elkin—he didn't know what she would have thought or said. But he knew she would have rejected him. She would *have* to reject him. She was a great lady, the Mistress of Malvern, the greatest Eyrie Mistress in Cymria, rich, well born, loved and respected. Whereas he was none of those things.

Erian clenched his fists and stared at them, filled with a terrible sense of helplessness and fury. He felt weak, clumsy, stupid, ugly. What could Elkin ever see in him? What could *any* woman see? He didn't deserve her, or anyone.

I don't have anything to offer, he thought bitterly. *No money, no lands, no connections. I don't even have looks or charm. I'm nothing and nobody.* The picture of Elkin smiled at him in his mind, and he shuddered and suddenly wanted to cry. Sweet, wonderful Elkin. He tried desperately to put her out of his mind, to think of something else, but he couldn't. Everything seemed to revolve around her now.

He occupied himself with these miserable thoughts for most of the flight, while below them the inhabited lands of Malvern receded from view. They flew over hills and plains dotted with villages and the occasional town, while the sun rose higher overhead.

They stopped at midday to rest in a small copse, and Erian dismounted and limped around in a circle, cringing at the cramp in his legs.

Kerod sat down on a log and massaged his knees. "Argh. Damn these old joints. How are you doing, Erian?"

"Fine. How much further is it?"

"Not far at all from here," said Kerod. "We'll be there by mid-afternoon, I'd say. But first we should rest and have something to eat, so we're ready."

Erian slumped down at the base of a tree. "Are we heading for something in particular? Some kind of landmark?"

"Yes," said Kerod. "There's a stone circle just beyond the last village—Eitheinn, I believe it's called. It's one of the few left standing, and a good base to use for hunting. There's forest all around it."

Erian's interest perked up at that. "A stone circle? How big is it?"

"Bigger than you'd expect," said Kerod. "Wait until you see it; it's damned impressive. Say what you like about the darkmen, but they definitely know how to move stones."

The two of them shared a chuckle over that, and the mood lightened a little. Erian chewed at some dried meat while

Senneck and Eekrae rested, and after a while they were ready to set out again.

The last part of the journey passed quickly enough. Erian watched the landscape now, knowing they were entering much wilder country. There were no more villages in sight, and the road they had been following had become narrow and winding, often passing through patches of thick forest. Even the River Snow, which ran almost parallel to it, looked wider and faster here.

They entered mountainous country, and the road petered out as it reached its destination: a tiny village nestled at the base of a large peak where the mountain range began. Eekrae flew on without pausing, passing between two mountains and entering a valley. He and Senneck flew the length of that and then flew on until the stone circle finally came into sight.

Eekrae banked upward without warning and landed on the slope of a nearby mountain, and Senneck followed, forcing Erian to cling on tightly.

It was freezing cold on the mountainside, and windy. Erian stood close to Senneck, shivering. "What's going on?" he called. "Why are we up here?"

Kerod grinned. "Look at the view!"

Erian did. A wide plateau lay just below them, white with snow, just as the ground for the last few miles had been. Most of it was covered by pine trees, but toward the centre a large patch of ground had been cleared to make way for the circle. They were close enough for Erian to see the stones quite clearly. They had been arranged in a perfect ring.

"Impressive, isn't it?" said Kerod. "No-one knows how they moved them all up here."

Erian thought briefly of the slaves who had built Eagleholm, hauling hundreds of split trees up the mountain to build the Eyrie and the platform. "It's amazing," he admitted.

"They call it Taranis' Throne," said Kerod. "Some people think a few darkmen still come up here to worship when the moon's out. It's forbidden, of course, but who's going to stop them all the way out here?"

Erian snorted. "Why should we even care about what they do? If they want to worship rocks, let them."

"It's never bothered me," said Kerod. "Let the gods deal

with their own affairs, I say. Anyway," he said, stretching and yawning, "we're here, and it appears we made good time, too."

Erian surveyed the landscape. "It doesn't look like there'd be much game up here," he said doubtfully.

"Oh, don't let appearances fool you," said Kerod. "Look, up there." He pointed. "See that?"

Erian squinted for a while before he saw a tiny white cross slowly drifting over the mountains.

"Ice eagle," said Kerod. "Very rare. The feathers are worth a fortune."

"Chasing down an eagle would be a fine challenge," Senneck put in. "I would be pleased to try it."

"I have done it," said Eekrae. "It is not easy, but if you are agile enough in the air it can be done."

"Or—" Kerod cocked his head and grinned. "Ah! Can you hear that?"

Erian listened. "I'm not sure . . ."

"Listen carefully," said Kerod. "You can just pick it up on the wind."

After a few moments more Erian thought he caught something. "It's . . . some kind of wailing?" he said.

"Howling!" said Kerod. "Fancy a wolf-skin rug for your room, Erian?"

Erian had never seen a wolf before. "How close are they?"

"Just down on the plateau, by the sound of it," said Kerod. "D'you want to go and see if we can catch them?"

"All right," said Erian. Hunting something on the ground sounded better than trying to hold on while Senneck chased an eagle. "Senneck, do you want to hunt wolves?"

Senneck was still looking speculatively at the eagle. "Well." She paused, and then relented. "If that is what you want, then we shall. Eekrae, do you agree?"

"I do," said Eekrae. "Wolves make fine prey." He cocked his head toward Kerod. "Come, get on my back. We will land in the stone circle."

The two griffiners mounted, and Senneck and Eekrae made the brief flight down to the circle, landing on the snow, in the centre. Erian slid off Senneck's back and admired the stones; now that he could see them more closely he was even more impressed by their size and how they had been laid out. Every stone was carefully spaced apart from its two immediate neighbours, and had been cut and shaped into a tapering oblong. The inner face of every stone had been carved with a triple-spiral symbol, and just above that was a circle.

"Thirteen stones," said Kerod. "Thirteen full moons. A 'wolf moon,' some people call it. The full moon, I mean. Now then." He unshipped the quiver from his back and took out his bow, stringing it with a fresh string taken from a pouch in his pocket.

Erian hastily strung his own bow and selected an arrow. "So, how do we do this?"

"We'll be doing the actual hunting from the air," said Kerod. "But we have to have our bows ready beforehand. And leave anything you don't need here in the circle—we'll pick it up later. You should probably leave that shiny sword of yours."

Erian reluctantly took it off his back, sheath and all. "I suppose it'd only get in the way." He leant it against the nearest stone and then walked back to Senneck, holding his bow in one hand. "That's everything except my arrows and my water bottle. So, do we just fly low until we spot them?"

"That's the idea," said Kerod. He paused to listen. "I want to wait here a moment. If we're lucky we might hear another howl; that would help us find them."

Erian nodded vaguely. "Yes, of course."

He strolled around the circle, easing the ache in his legs and listening half-heartedly. Then, without warning, a low, hollow call came drifting toward them from the trees. Erian stopped dead, blinking. "Was that—?"

Kerod had started bolt upright. "Yes! That's it! Listen."

Another howl sounded a few moments later.

"Ooh, it's close," said Kerod. "We're sure to catch them."

The next howl came from somewhere behind Erian. He turned sharply to look, but saw nothing. He fidgeted "Uh, Kerod, are you sure—?"

Kerod wasn't listening. "Quick, let's go!" he said. "They can move fast."

But Erian was still staring at the trees. "Kerod, I think they're here. That one sounded like it was coming from just over there."

"Are you sure?" said Kerod. "Maybe they—" He stopped as

yet another howl came, this time from somewhere to his left, just outside the circle. "Ye gods," he muttered once it had ended. "You're right. They must be just in the trees here."

They listened for a while after that but heard nothing more. Perhaps the wolves had moved on.

Erian scratched his head. "You know, my grandmother always told me wolves only howled at the moon."

"Nonsense," said Kerod. "Wolves howl whenever they feel like it. It's darkmen that howl at the moon."

"What?" said Erian. "You mean that's real? They actually do that?"

"Oh, not any more," said Kerod. "But they used to. It was their way of calling to each other. And they used it as a battle cry, too. A little like how griffiners screech when they go into battle. Now, I'll tell you, Erian, you haven't lived until you've seen that. Griffins and griffiners riding into battle together, it's—Erian?"

Erian was standing very still. Behind him, Senneck began to hiss, her tail lashing.

"Erian?" Kerod repeated.

Eekrae moved to stand close to his partner, wings raised, and the four of them stood together in a kind of nervous tableau as a dozen tall, ragged figures appeared out of the trees and walked into the circle. Every single one was a Northerner, black haired and pale, clad in furs. Their faces were tattooed with blue spirals, and they wore bone ornaments in their hair. Some of them had spears, but nearly all of them carried a bow, each with an arrow nocked and ready to be loosed.

Kerod pulled himself together. "Stay back!" he snapped. "We are griffiners!"

The Northerners did stop, just inside the circle, but did not lower their bows. Every single one of them was glaring, poised and ready, at the griffiners and the griffins.

Erian loaded an arrow into his own bow. "How dare you?" he yelled. "Lower your bows now or I'll arrest you!"

The Northerners glanced briefly at each other, and several of them sniggered.

"Arrest us?" said one, his voice rough and harshly accented. "Ye've defiled the Throne, Southerner. This is our place, not for ye or yer Southern demons."

"Don't you *dare* threaten us," said Kerod, starting forward and pointing his bow directly at the man's face. "You have no right to bear weapons, darkman."

The man spat. "An' ye have no right to be in the circle, Southerner."

"This is our land, and you'll obey our laws here," said Kerod. "Now get out of here, and maybe I'll forget this happened."

One of the Northerners shouted in some language Erian didn't recognise, apparently speaking to the leader. The others responded with jeers and mocking shouts in that same language, and Eekrae instantly reared up and began to snarl and hiss at them.

Kerod moved forward, putting himself in the way. "That language is forbidden!" he shouted. "How dare you?"

Erian had begun to feel more and more nervous while this exchange was taking place. He looked quickly toward his sword, but one of the Northerners was between him and it. The man followed his gaze and snatched the sword.

"Hey!" Erian yelled. "That's mine! Give that to me!"

The man pulled Bloodpride out of its scabbard and waved it at the others. "Lookit this! Nice shiny bit of metal, ain't it? Fancy I'll keep it. Could be useful as a spit, eh?"

The others laughed. Erian's fingers itched, wanting to let go of the bowstring, but he restrained himself. "Senneck," he said, switching to griffish. "Senneck, what do we do?"

"They would not dare attack us," said Senneck, but she sounded uncertain. "We must make them leave without attacking, or—"

The leader stepped forward, holding out a hand. "Give us yer money an' those bows an' anythin' else ye've got," he said. "After that, ye can leave."

Erian gaped. "They can't rob us!" he said to Senneck, still using griffish. "Senneck, do something! Scare them off!"

Senneck shoved him out of the way and began to advance on them. "Begone," she hissed, her tail lashing. "Begone now, or I shall attack."

They did back away at that, and for a moment Erian thought they were going to leave, but then the leader gestured at his friends to stay where they were. "We are going nowhere, griffin," he said, and to Erian's bewilderment and horror, he said it in fractured griffish.

Kerod had gone pale. "How do you know that language? Who taught you? Answer me!"

What happened after that, happened fast. Senneck, infuriated by the sight of her human being threatened, lunged straight for the leader. There was a screech and a shout, a dull *thunk*, and Erian turned to see Kerod fall, an arrow embedded in his chest.

"Senneck!" he yelled, and a heartbeat later something hit him in the shoulder, so hard it spun him sideways and sent him staggering to the ground. He landed on his back in the snow, stunned. When he reached for his shoulder he found something stuck there, something long and thin, like a piece of wood or an arrow, but it couldn't be stuck in him; that was absurd, ridiculous—

Then the pain hit him. He cried out. "Senneck! Senneck! I'm hurt! Help me! Senneck! Where are you? Help!"

But Senneck did not come, and he lay on his back, shuddering helplessly, his back wet and freezing cold from the snow, his shoulder turning hot and sticky with blood. He wrapped his good hand around the arrow and kept it there, not knowing what to do. He was bleeding, his shirt was turning red, there was an arrow in him, he was going to die . . .

Screechings and shouts came from somewhere away to his left, and panic flooded through him. Senneck was hurt, they were attacking her, and he couldn't help her; they were going to die together.

And after that there was nothing but a grey haze, and pain, and blood.

27

The Gift

The hammer connected with a sickening thump and a crack, and Garnoc screamed and toppled over like a falling tree.

Instantly the hall erupted. Cries of horror rent the air, mingled with shouts as the slaves moved, some to make for the doors, some to draw their weapons and others to run toward Garnoc, who lay bleeding on the floor.

"He's killed him!"

"He's mad!"

Prydwen and Dafydd ran straight at Arenadd. "Ye son of a bitch!" Prydwen yelled.

Arenadd laughed dementedly. "I did it! It worked! Look!"

Dafydd crouched by Garnoc. "Garnoc? Garnoc, talk to me!"

Garnoc sat up, groaning. "Me neck! Me bloody neck! What did ye do?"

Arenadd came forward, pushing Dafydd out of the way. "Gave you your reward. Look." He grasped hold of the collar and pulled. For an instant the two of them struggled, Garnoc screaming in protest, and then the collar came away, bloodstained but intact.

Arenadd backed away and held it in the air. "Look!" he bellowed. "Look!"

The commotion stopped for an instant, and then broke out afresh.

Garnoc, though, was silent. He stood up, clutching at his neck. Blood ran over his fingers, but he didn't seem to notice. He stared at Arenadd.

Arenadd looked him in the eye, and nodded. "A strike to the right spot. It was true." He threw the collar down at Garnoc's feet. "You're free, Garnoc. My reward to you." He turned, holding the hammer up over his head. "My reward to all of you!" he yelled. "If you come to me, I will break the collars and make you into men again! You won't be my property, or anyone's property! Afterwards, you can go. Leave. You won't have to take my orders; you can go wherever you want and do whatever you choose. That is your reward!"

The room had gone quiet, and Arenadd wrapped his fingers around the head of the hammer and smiled an odd, wicked little smile. "So," he said. "Who wants to be next?"

The silence drew out a few moments longer, and then Prydwen drew himself up. "I do!"

"And me," said Dafydd. "But look, is it dangerous, sir? Garnoc, did that hurt ye bad?"

Garnoc dabbed at his throat. "No. Tore me up a little, but it'll heal."

"But I don't like it," said Dafydd. "Are ye sure?"

"It's fine," said Arenadd. "I swear. I worked out how to do it a while ago, and this evening I tried it with the bodies down in the vault. They've all had their collars removed, including my father. And after that, I tried it on myself."

Skade gaped at him. "*What* did you do?"

"Tried it on myself," Arenadd repeated. "I found some spare collars in the smithy and put one on myself. Then I broke it off with the hammer."

"But why?" said Skade.

"To see if I'd survive, of course," said Arenadd. "I wasn't going to risk anyone else's life unless I was completely sure I could do it. It put a few holes in my neck, but nothing serious. The spikes are too short to do more than just penetrate the skin."

Dafydd and Garnoc looked horrified. Prydwen, however, stared at him with something like awe. "I'll do it, then," he said. "I trust ye, sir. Take this collar off me."

"Oh, no ye don't," a stern voice rapped out. It was Caedmon, limping toward them. He jabbed his stick at Prydwen. "Out of my way, snow-blood."

"What d'ye want, blackrobe?" Prydwen sneered. "I don't take orders from ye now, so get ye gone."

"Don't you dare call him that," said Arenadd, starting furiously toward him. "Don't you *ever* call him that, or anyone else, understand?"

Prydwen looked startled. "I'm sorry, sir, but—"

"But nothing. Look down at yourself, Prydwen. You're not wearing a spotted gown with feathers on the shoulders. You're a slave just as much as he is, and Caedmon is an old man. He deserves your respect, along with everyone else's. Now stand aside and let him speak."

Arenadd's stern voice and gaze put all the defiance out of Prydwen, and the Northerner silently moved aside, inclining his head politely toward Caedmon as he did so.

Arenadd looked at Caedmon. "I'm sorry about that. Speak, *hynafgwr*."

Caedmon smiled slightly and then, to Arenadd's astonishment, began to speak the Northern tongue. He spoke slowly and a little haltingly, as if he hadn't done so in a long time. "Lord Arenadd. I think I should say something that I should have said a very long time ago." There was an air of slight nervousness about him, a sense that he wanted to glance over his shoulder to check for a vengeful guard who might hear him speak the forbidden language. But he held steady and looked Arenadd in the eye. "I want to thank ye, lord," he said. "For bringing us here, and for protecting us, and for what ye're doing for us now. I am an old man, and I have not—I have been a slave most of my life. But I would like to ask ye now, Lord Arenadd"—he bowed his head—"take my collar off. Free me. I, Caedmon Taranisäii—"

Arenadd couldn't stop himself from interrupting. "*Taranisäii?*"

Caedmon nodded very slowly. "I haven't—" He sighed and reverted to Cymrian. "I haven't gone by that name in a long time. The Taranisäiis—we're an old family. It's said we're descended from Taranis himself. Nowadays that don't mean much of anythin', not with things the way they are. An' me, now—"

Arenadd moved closer to him. "How did you become a slave?" he asked quietly. "What happened to you?"

"A long time ago it was," said Caedmon. "I lived in Malvern then, with my parents. And my sister, my older sister, Arddryn—ye know her, don't ye?"

"Of course—the one who started the rebellion. She was a Taranisäii?"

"Yes. After she got to be a griffiner, the lords up in the Eyrie started harassing her, doing things to try an' stop her getting above herself. Our parents lost their business, an' then I lost my house. There was a fire. No-one ever said as much, but I knew they'd had it done. Arddryn took me in, an' we held up one way or another for a few years, her an' me an' the griffin, Hyrenna. But the last straw came when our uncle, Skandar, got arrested on some trumped-up charge for protestin' over what happened to our parents. He was sold into slavery, him an' his wife, an' both were sent southward, an' we never saw either of them again."

"Skandar," said Arenadd. "Not my grandfather?"

"Aye, yer grandfather. Yer own father must've been born after that; I never knew about it myself. Anyway, Arddryn finally decided she'd had enough, so she went to the Eyrie to complain to Master Anech. Later on she said he tried to have her arrested, but all I knew then was that she an' Hyrenna left in a hurry. Flew away out of Malvern an' went into the far North to hide. A few years later they came back, and the rebellion started. Long story short: when people from Malvern started defecting to her, I went with them to find her an' fought with the rebels for a while. But after those sons of whores called in others to help, the whole thing ended fast. That bastard Rannagon killed Arddryn himself, an' me and lots of others were sold as slaves. I was sent south in chains, an' never saw Malvern again."

"My gods," Arenadd mumbled. "Arddryn Taranisäii—I'm her *cousin*, for gods' sakes."

"Close to it, anyway," said Caedmon. He sighed and nodded again. "When I heard about what happened to Rannagon, I liked to imagine it was Arddryn did it somehow, that she came back from the dead for revenge on the one who killed her."

Arenadd looked away. "People don't come back from the dead, Caedmon," he said, and the lie made him feel sick inside.

"Aye, I know, I know. But now I know yer name ain't Arren Cardockson at all, like they said." Caedmon looked at him, bright-eyed. "Ye're a Taranisäii, just like her an' me an' all those brave men who gave their lives for Tara. I lost my freedom fightin' for Arddryn, but now the moon's sent ye, Arenadd, to give it back to me."

Arenadd gripped the hammer. "Are you sure?"

"Of course I'm sure," Caedmon snapped, sounding much more normal now. "Swing that hammer an' stop muckin' about, boy. I'm ready."

Arenadd nodded. "Stand still, then, and lift your chin."

Caedmon glanced to his left. "Ye an' ye," he said, pointing

at Garnoc and Prydwen. "I need ye t'hold my elbows for me, stop me fallin' over."

The two of them moved into position without a murmur, and Caedmon dropped his stick and lifted his chin. "Do it," he said quietly.

Arenadd only hesitated a moment. He took the hammer firmly in both hands and struck, hitting the collar directly on the thin line next to the symbol etched into it, where it had been sealed shut long ago. The hammer connected with a loud thump, and Caedmon jerked and let out a half-stifled yell.

But he recovered in moments, shouting, "Let go! Let go of me, damn ye!" The instant his arms were free his hands went to his neck, grabbing at the collar. He wedged his fingers in under the overgrown skin and began to pull, gritting his teeth and working the collar back and forth until it came open. Caedmon threw it down and wrapped his hands around his throat, his eyes wide with wonder.

The spikes left a line of pits in his neck, each one horribly red and swollen and dark with ancient dirt and sweat. The collar had been in place for so long that it had left an indentation of pale, warped skin, all wet and peeling and vile. A little blood was leaking from the spike marks, but not much.

"Are you all right?" Arenadd asked.

Caedmon finally looked at him, and then, spontaneously, he began to laugh. "It's gone!" he said, his voice light and almost young. "It's gone! It's bloody gone! Twenty-one godsdamned years of my life! Twenty-one cursed years! It's over!"

Prydwen grinned and offered him back his stick. "It's over, all right. It'll be over for all of us, won't it?"

Caedmon pulled himself together. "Aye," he said, taking the stick. "It'll be over." He turned to look at the other slaves in the hall, shaking slightly with emotion, and pointed his stick at them. "We're free, friends," he told them. "All of us. Come now, all of ye. Come forward an' let Lord Arenadd take yer collars. We'll have no need for them where we're goin'."

Arenadd came to stand at his side. "Caedmon's right," he said. "Come on, all of you. Come to me, and I'll give you your reward. All of you."

And they did. The slaves began to come toward their erst-while master, some fearful, some hesitant, but all of them wanting to come and take their reward. Arenadd was as good as his word. He freed the slaves, one by one, breaking the collars and then handing each man a bandage to help stem the bleeding. A couple of them took more than one blow to destroy the locking mechanism, but all came off in the end. Soon there was a heap of discarded collars by Arenadd's feet, and his hands were aching, but still more slaves were coming forward, eager now, some reaching out to touch his robe or shouting his name.

Skandar watched, bemused, for a time, before retreating into a corner to sleep, tail twitching. Skade kept back, standing behind Arenadd as she had once stood behind Welyn, and watched silently. She felt like an intruder, witnessing something that had nothing to do with her and wasn't her business to see. But she didn't want to leave, either. She kept her eyes on Arenadd, just watching him until the last collar clanged on the floor and he threw the hammer down next to the heap and wiped his forehead.

"It's done," he said. Then, pulling himself up, he said, "It's done!" more loudly. "It's finished. You're free. Now go. Search the fort and take whatever you want—clothes, weapons, food. In the treasury there are some chests of money. Share it out. It should be more than enough. There are horses in the stables; help yourselves. I'm sure most of you have relatives in Tara, places you can go and find new homes and be out of sight of the authorities. I trust you not to say anything about me or Skade or Skandar."

Prydwen was laughing wildly and had already torn off his robe. Bare-chested, he held the bundled cloth in one hand and waved it in the air. "I'll burn it," he said. "I'll burn the cursed thing, find myself a tunic to wear. What d'ye say, lads? We'll have a bonfire an' feed it with black robes."

Dozens of men, hearing him, cheered their approval.

"An' ye, sir," Prydwen added. "Ye can look in the griffiners' rooms, find some fine clothes like ye should be wearin' instead of that filthy thing ye've had to wear."

Arenadd smiled and fingered his ragged robe. "I'm going to keep this. I'll wash it and sew up the holes in it."

"Why?" said Prydwen, pausing abruptly in his triumphant jig. "It's a bloody robe, sir, beg yer pardon. It's a slave's clothes. Ye're a hundred times better than t'be wearin' somethin' like that."

Arenadd shrugged. "I like it. My parents made it for me."

Prydwen looked uncertain. "Well, all right then, sir. If ye say so."

The other freed slaves were already scrambling out of the hall, thumping into the tables in their rush, and not long after, the room was nearly deserted.

"C'mon, let's go," Dafydd said, gesturing at his two friends. They glanced quickly at Arenadd and went, almost running after the others.

Arenadd watched them go, and chuckled. "Ah, there's nothing like a little looting to set a man's blood afire, is there? This is just like back in the old days, cleaning out smugglers' houses. We were meant to hand in everything we found, but nobody cared if we took our pick first. I even took some whiteleaf once. That was the best part of the job."

Caedmon had remained behind. "So, we're all leaving tomorrow," he said.

Arenadd nodded. "Where d'you think they'll go, Caedmon? D'you think they'll be all right?"

"I think so," said Caedmon. "Tara is a big land. Plenty of places to hide. They'll do well enough, I think."

"Where are you going to go?" said Arenadd. "If you don't mind my asking."

"Don't know yet," said Caedmon. "Not Malvern, obviously. Somewhere remote, I think. There's still people out there who'd welcome a Taranisäii."

"I still can't believe that," said Arenadd. "You, Arddryn's brother."

"It was a long time ago," said Caedmon. "Afterward I wanted nothin' more to do with rebels or griffiners or any of the rest of it."

Arenadd smiled. "And you didn't want anything to do with me, either."

Caedmon shrugged. "Far as I was concerned, ye was just some griffiner gone bad. Some stupid young fool out to get revenge without stopping to think about the pain an' trouble he was givin' everyone else. I didn't even believe ye were really a Taranisäii. I thought that name'd been stuck to ye by people who saw ye as a hero. After all, plenty of darkmen still know that name an' believe it has a kind of magic connected with it."

"Yes, I can see that." Arenadd sighed and rubbed his eyes. "You should probably go and see if you can get some new clothes. Skade says there's some in the treasury; maybe you could try there."

Caedmon nodded. "I should get goin' before they take everythin' for themselves, the greedy beggars. But Arenadd"— he rested his hands solemnly on the younger man's shoulders— "it was an honour to be here with ye today, an' a greater one t'be set free by ye. Truly."

"The honour was mine," said Arenadd, bowing to him. *"Hynafgwr."*

Caedmon smiled at him and shuffled out, leaving Arenadd alone in the room with Skade and Skandar.

Arenadd yawned and rubbed his back. "Well," he said, half to himself, "that's it, then."

"Human go," rasped a voice. It was Skandar. The griffin rose from his corner and limped toward the two humans. He'd already torn the bandage off his foreleg, and the shredded remains were tangled around his talons. He paused to rip them away, and then nosed at the heap of collars, which toppled over in a shower of metal clangs. The griffin snorted and lifted his head away. "Collars."

"That's right," said Arenadd.

Skandar didn't seem to hear him. He scratched at the bald patch on his neck. "Collars. Collar."

"Yes. Just like the one you wore, Skandar," said Arenadd.

Skandar fixed him with a steely silver gaze. "You break collar for me. Now break for them."

"Yes. You were a slave once, too, Skandar. Just like them. Now they're free, just like you. Do you understand?"

Skandar was silent for a time. "You help them," he said at last. "Why?"

"Why did I help you?" said Arenadd.

"Because I say I kill you unless you help," Skandar said immediately.

Skade and Arenadd both laughed.

"Well, yes," said Arenadd. "But I didn't have to come back and help you. I could have run away and left you there. Yet I didn't, because I owed you my life. And because I felt sorry for you."

"Do you think they will help you in return?" said Skade.

"They already helped me," said Arenadd. "Skade, without them we'd never have made it past Guard's Post. We could have flown over it, but we would have been seen, and we'd never have found enough food to make it through the mountains, anyway. Thanks to them we've got all the supplies we need and safe passage into the North. I hope I did the right thing for them. It was the only thing I could think of that felt right."

Skandar made a harsh cackling sound in his throat. "You strange," he said. "Always worry. Always say, 'right thing, wrong thing, not know.'" He flicked him lightly with his wing. "My human," he added fondly. "Silly human."

Arenadd grinned and ducked. "Hey, don't take my head off, you big brute." He noticed Skandar wince as he put weight on his injured leg. "How do you feel?"

"Am strong," Skandar said instantly. "Not hurt."

"Of course. Skade, d'you want to go exploring together? I haven't seen half of this place yet."

She smiled and nodded. "I found some interesting things—would you like to see them?"

Arenadd took her hand. "I would."

Skade started a little, and then smiled. "Then we will. Skandar, do you want to come?"

"I come," said Skandar. "Come now."

At Skade's suggestion, they made for the nearer of the two towers that flanked the gates, whose tops were manned by sentries. "Look," she said, letting go of Arenadd's hand to point at a large pair of wooden doors set into the end of the passage they had taken. "That should lead into the tower. The doors look very grand."

"They do, don't they?" said Arenadd. "Doesn't seem like anyone's been in there yet—shall we have a look?"

"Why not?" said Skade. She went ahead, pushed the doors open and stepped through. After a few moments her voice drifted back. "A chapel! Come and see!"

"What's that?" said Arenadd.

Skade re-emerged. "I said it is a chapel. Too small to have a priest, but the guards must have come here to worship."

"Oh. I've never been in a temple, actually," he said. "I wasn't allowed in the one back at Eagleholm. I've always wondered what they were like inside."

"Come and see, then!" said Skade. "The decorations are impressive."

He smiled and followed her to the doors. "I wouldn't mind . . ." His voice trailed off.

Skade looked back, and saw that he had stopped in the doorway. "Arenadd?"

Arenadd's expression had changed. "Skade—"

She came toward him. "Arenadd? What is wrong?"

His face had gone pale. "I can't go in there."

"Why not?" said Skade.

"Don't know. Something feels wrong."

"There is nothing to be afraid of," said Skade, reaching toward him. "Here, come and see the paintings."

He shook himself, banishing the irrational fear that had come over him. "It's all right. I'm fine." He stepped into the chapel, and screamed.

"Arenadd, what—?"

He stood rigid for a moment, his face ghastly with sweat. "It hurts," he moaned. "It hurts."

"What does?" said Skade. "Arenadd, come here!"

He took a few lurching steps toward her, his hands pressed into his chest. "My heart . . ." The pain increased with every step, until he went staggering to his knees and was violently ill.

Skade ran to him. "Arenadd!"

In the blink of an eye, he scrambled to his feet and ran out of the chapel as fast as he could go. He collapsed in the corridor outside and lay there gasping for breath. "Oh gods. Oh gods."

Skade took him by the arm. "Arenadd, what happened?"

He looked up at her, wild-eyed. "I can't go in there," he said. "There's something wrong. It made my heart hurt. I felt like I was going to die."

"But why?" said Skade. "It is only a room."

"No. There's something different about it. Skade, close the doors. Please."

Skade got up and pulled them shut, and Arenadd began to look better almost immediately. She helped him up. "Do you feel better now?"

He breathed deeply. "I think so."

Skandar nosed at him. "Sick? Human sick?"

Arenadd patted him on the beak. "I don't know, Skandar. But I'm not going in there again." He looked at Skade. "Come on. Let's get out of here. I need some water."

He walked quickly, taking long strides that left the chapel far behind, and the further he went from it the more he recovered. By the time they reached the kitchens and he had drunk several cups of water he looked as if nothing had happened at all.

Skade still looked worried. "I do not understand. What could have made that happen? Will it happen again?"

Arenadd gave her a watery smile. "I suppose the gods just don't like me."

"Do not be foolish," said Skade. "A chapel is only a place; it has no power in it."

"Like the spirit cave?" said Arenadd. He shook his head. "Well, I don't like the gods, so I couldn't blame them for not liking me."

"Bah. Gods are human inventions, made out of vanity," she said.

"Maybe," he said. "What would I know? But—" He shook his head again, dismissing the idea that had occurred to him. "It's probably just a coincidence. It's been a long day, and I'm tired."

"We are all tired," said Skade. She took his shoulder. "Come. We should find a place to sleep. There will be many more things to do tomorrow, and we should take advantage of having proper shelter for the night."

"Good idea," he said, and wiped the sweat off his forehead. "Come on, Skandar."

28

Rebels

Erian never remembered what happened after the arrow struck him and he fainted. He woke up briefly as something shoved at him, and screamed as pain erupted in his shoulder. His vision went red, and he tried to crawl away from whatever was attacking him. But something sharp dug into him and he was dragged to one side, able to put up only the most feeble resistance before a roaring filled his ears and he blacked out again. All he remembered after that was a confused vision of trees and sky and wind dragging at him for what felt like days or weeks or months.

He woke again later and found himself lying on a hard surface. Voices were coming from nearby, and he felt hands patting his face as someone called to him. He stirred and moaned, his good arm rising to try to fend them off, before he was dragged sideways onto some other surface and he was lifted and carried away.

He did remember being taken down a slope, and a confusion of voices around him as he was laid down on something soft. Someone pried his mouth open and poured liquid down his throat, and he gagged on it before managing to swallow. It made him feel warm and sleepy, and he lay peacefully on his back, not feeling anything more than the vaguest sensation of pain from his shoulder. After a little while even that faded, and he slept.

He dreamt that he was in the barn back at his grandparents' farm, and in spite of the high windows it was dark inside. The air was full of the scents of hay and horses, and it made him feel safe.

But as he turned to look for the doors, he felt the back of his neck prickle. The air had suddenly become colder. *He's here.*

He turned sharply. "Where are you? Come out!"

Then, without warning, flames sprang up around him. They burned higher and higher, trapping him in a ring of heat, but somehow they gave off no light, and the barn remained full of shadows.

"Come out!" Erian shouted again.

I come, a voice whispered back, and he saw something move just beyond the flames. The shadows that filled the barn swirled in toward the thing, melting together to form a tall human shape.

The murderer stepped forward, robed in shadows, pale face leering at him. *I come.*

Erian snarled and reached for Bloodpride's hilt, but it wasn't there, and panic stampeded through him. He was unarmed, helpless, and when he looked up he saw the murderer coming toward him, stepping through the fire as if it were nothing. Erian tried to back away, but he couldn't move; he could feel the heat of the fire behind him, and icy cold came from the murderer's robe as he lifted a bloodied hand and drew a sword: Bloodpride, its blade blackened and horrible.

"Help," Erian called. "Help me! Senneck!"

The murderer laughed at him. He raised the sword and stabbed it into Erian's shoulder. *Erian,* his voice called. *Erian. Erian.*

"Stop it," said Erian. "Stop it!"

Erian. Erian, can you hear me?

"Erian? Erian!"

Erian moaned. "Stop it. That hurts. Don't . . . Senneck . . ."

Pain continued to stab at his shoulder, and he felt his fingers curl on the blankets.

"He's waking up!" a voice exclaimed from somewhere above him. "Come, quickly!"

Something hard and sharp, like a dagger blade, touched his arm and then his shoulder, and he heard a voice he knew. "Erian. Erian. Speak. Open your eyes! Erian!"

Erian stirred again. "Senneck?"

A hand touched his forehead. It felt light and soft. "Lord Erian? Can you hear me?"

Erian forced his eyes open. Something blurry was hovering

over him, and he blinked until it came into focus. It was Elkin's face, looking down at him with concern.

The instant he saw her, his heart leapt. He began to struggle, trying to sit up, but he felt weak and his entire body ached. He slumped back, groaning.

Senneck's beak touched him again. "Erian," she rasped. "You are back."

Erian's throat was dry and painful. "Senneck. I w—"

"Bring water," Senneck's voice commanded, and a few moments later some was poured into his mouth. He gulped it down, and some of his strength came back.

"Erian," said Senneck. "Speak. How do you feel?"

Erian coughed. "I . . . hurt. Senneck, where—? What happened?"

"Be still," said Senneck. "You are safe. We are at Malvern, and you are wounded."

"My shoulder," said Erian.

"Yes. It has been treated. Do you need more water?"

"Please."

"Bring it," said Senneck.

More water was brought, and Erian drank it eagerly. He could feel his confusion and dizziness beginning to die down now, and he was able to take in his surroundings. He was lying on a bed in a room he didn't recognise but which had to be a hospital. Senneck was sitting close by, her forepaws resting on the bed beside him. But Erian only had eyes for the other person in the room.

Elkin was sitting by his side, wearing a simple yellow gown, her eyes fixed on his face. She smiled weakly at him. "Erian. Thank Gryphus you're awake."

Erian smiled back. "Elkin. You're . . . Elkin."

Elkin laughed. "Well, you recognise me. That should mean you'll recover. But—" She became solemn. "But you were lucky, you know. I thought you were going to die. After losing all that blood."

"Elkin, if the first thing I saw after I died was your face, I wouldn't care," said Erian.

She looked startled. "Erian . . . !"

Once Erian would have apologised, but not now. He watched her steadily, but she was unreadable.

"How long?" he asked eventually. "What happened?"

"You were hit by an arrow," Senneck interrupted. "The blackrobes attacked us in the circle. Kerod is dead, and I do not know what happened to Eekrae. After his human was killed he attacked them. He was struck by at least two arrows; they ran and he chased them, and I do not know what became of him after that. I killed the one who wounded you, but the rest escaped. I would have chased them, but I did not want to leave you alone. You were losing blood—too much of it. I carried you back to Malvern as quickly as I could."

"My shoulder?"

"Badly damaged. That arrow went through it to the other side. It will be a while before you will be able to use your arm again."

Erian groaned. "Bloodpride. They took it."

Senneck cocked her head. "Bloodpride? What is that?"

Erian cringed. "My sword."

"I see," Senneck said levelly. "I did not know you had named it."

"Did you get it back?" said Erian.

"No. I am sorry, but Bloodpride was stolen by Kerod's killers."

"But couldn't you have just—?"

"No, Erian," Senneck snapped. "I could not 'have just.' Kerod was dead and you were dying, and I did not have time to waste over your pretty toy. Doubtless you will be able to purchase another one."

"I didn't mean that," said Erian. "I'm sorry, Senneck, I just—you're right, it was only a sword. I can get another one. Thank you," he added. "You saved my life."

"Of course I did," said Senneck. "It was only expected of me. A griffin who cannot protect her human is useless." She shook herself. "Now you should thank Lady Elkin. She has visited you many times since we returned."

Erian turned his head to look at her. "Elkin," said Erian. "*Lady* Elkin. Thank you for coming to see me. I'm honoured."

She smiled nervously. "It's only expected of me," she said. "I visit all my officials when they're unwell."

"What, even one as lowly as me?" said Erian.

Elkin shrugged. "Maybe you're not as high as the Master of Taxation or the Mistress of Law, but Master of Farms is still quite an important position."

Erian started. "Master of—*me*?"

"Well, of course," said Elkin. She sighed. "They haven't retrieved Kerod's body yet, but Senneck's testimony was enough proof. Now that Kerod is dead, his office goes to you as a matter of course. It's done like that in every Eyrie, you know."

Erian lay there, head spinning. Him, Master of Farms. Lady Elkin, visiting him in his sick bed. And in spite of what she had said, he knew it was only a half-truth. She hadn't come to see the Master of Farms; she had come to see him. He was sure of it.

A strange certainty came over him. "Lady Elkin," he said. "Can I talk to you?"

"Of course," she said. "I'm listening."

"Alone," said Erian.

Senneck stood up. "I do not think—"

Elkin didn't look at her. She kept her eyes on Erian. He looked back steadily.

The Mistress of the Eyrie drew herself up. "Senneck, could you please leave us?" she said. "Lord Erian and I need to talk."

Senneck looked at Erian, pure outrage burning in her eyes. But her voice was level when she said, "Eyrie Mistress, I would prefer to stay."

Elkin glanced at the door. "Please. We won't take long, I promise."

Senneck couldn't argue. She left the room, her tail swishing dangerously.

When she had gone, Elkin turned to Erian.

"Help me sit up," said Erian. "Please."

Elkin took him by his uninjured shoulder and helped him struggle into a sitting position, propping him up with a few pillows. The action made his wound scream with pain, but he gritted his teeth and waited for it to subside.

"I really thought you were going to die," Elkin told him. "You were unconscious for nearly two days. Senneck never left you. Not even to eat."

Erian hadn't taken his eyes off her face. "Lady Elkin. I wanted to—"

"Please, just call me Elkin."

"Elkin, then." Erian breathed in deeply. "I wanted to say sorry for how I acted at the dance. I got carried away—I said things I shouldn't have."

"Oh." Elkin sat down beside him. "It's all right, Erian. It really is. We were both—well, I understand."

Erian wanted to reach out and touch her hand, but his wounded arm refused to move. "But there's something I have to tell you. I have to say it, and I'm going to, even though I know it's wrong. I know I shouldn't say it, and I know nothing will ever happen, but I have to say it, because it's the truth. You don't have to say anything or do anything; you don't even have to talk to me ever again. But I want to say it to you because if I don't I'll regret it forever."

Elkin had become very still. "Erian, I don't think you should—"

Erian's heart was racing; it made him feel sick and light-headed, but he knew he had to do it now. "I love you, Elkin," he said. "I've loved you ever since we first met. I didn't realise it until the day after we danced together. I don't know if it is right to tell you, but I have to. I love you, Elkin, and I always will."

The instant the words were out of his mouth, a wonderful calm came over him. He lay back on his pillows, his chest heaving, and watched Elkin. He kept his eyes on her face, the face he knew he loved with more certainty than he had ever known anything before in his life.

Elkin looked back silently at him, and the moment stretched out into eternity. Erian didn't try to break the silence. He had said everything he needed to say, and now he waited.

Then Elkin turned away. She walked to the window and stood there, looking out, with her back to him.

"I've spoken to Senneck," she said at last. "We have a description of the men who killed Kerod."

"Elkin—"

"I haven't sent anyone out there yet," Elkin continued, her voice flat and distant. "But I'm certain the people living in Eitheinn know something. Even if the killers aren't living there, the Eitheinnians have to know they're in the area. I've spoken to the Master of Law, and we agreed to wait a while. They must know that we know about them by now, and they'll have gone into hiding. I'm going to send some griffiners to the stone circle to search, and they'll ask some questions at Eitheinn. After that they'll leave. Once the darkmen have decided they're safe again, they'll go back and search the whole village. We should learn something that way, and if we're lucky we'll make some arrests as well. I'll catch them, my lord, and they'll be brought

back here to be questioned. After that they'll be hanged, and
Kerod will be avenged."

Erian felt as if every word were a dagger in his heart. "I see."

Elkin turned back to face him. "You should get some rest
now," she said. "I'll make sure the healers keep me informed."

Erian sighed. "Yes. Thank you—my lady."

Elkin hesitated, and then came closer to his bed. She leant
down, so close he could smell the faint flowery scent that
hung about her, and touched his arm. "My brave warrior," she
breathed, and left the room.

Erian lay very still for a long time after she had gone, feeling the deep ache in his shoulder. The wound would leave him
scarred, he knew. Deformed.

He turned his face to the wall and began to sob. The tears
hurt, and went on for a long time.

Elkin returned to her own chambers. She locked the door
behind her before entering her bedchamber. It was a big
room; the Master or Mistress' quarters had always been large,
and when she had moved into them they had been expanded
even further for Kraal's sake. The giant griffin couldn't go into
many parts of the Eyrie, which didn't seem to worry him much,
but Elkin didn't like being separated from him for too long and
preferred to stay in the upper levels, where he could be with her.

She sat down on the bed and buried her face in her hands.
So many things to do, so much to plan and organise, officials
to meet and documents to write—she felt exhausted at the very
thought. She had already missed far too much by spending all
that time in the infirmary with Erian, talking to Senneck. Elkin
had made the griffin tell her story several times, knowing she
would bring up more detail every time, and that had meant
being forced to be in the infirmary with her for long periods of
time, since the griffin refused to leave it.

Elkin looked up at her sword hanging on the wall. It was
an elegant thing, its hilt decorated with embossed vines. She
had inherited it from her father but had never used it, mostly
because it was too heavy for her to lift. The Eyrie's swordsmith
had offered to make her a smaller one, but she had refused.
Fighting wasn't for her.

A *thump* came from the next room, and she got up and walked through the doorway. It led to Kraal's enormous stable. The griffin was there now, crouched among the straw and grooming his wings, and he looked up when she entered. Even though she made very little noise when she walked, he always seemed to know when she was there. He clicked his beak briefly in greeting and went back to his grooming.

Elkin moved closer to him. "Hello. Do you want some food?"

He flicked his tail briefly to indicate no, and dipped his beak into the trough.

"Lord Erian woke up," said Elkin. "The healer says he should recover."

Kraal lifted his head, water dripping from his beak. "You spoke to him."

"Yes. He confirmed what Senneck told me."

Kraal shook his head, spraying water over the straw. "I see."

"Kraal." Elkin moved closer and touched his feathers. "Kraal, why are you so interested in him?"

The griffin cocked his head in order to fix a huge golden eye on her. "Do you not like him?" he asked mildly.

Elkin faltered. "He's—well, he's a good man—brave, maybe not very clever, but—yes, I like him. But why are *you* interested in him, Kraal? You keep on talking about him—why?"

Kraal sighed and lay down on his belly, curling his tail around himself. "You must protect him, Elkin, and keep him close."

"He certainly needs protecting," said Elkin. "The first time he left the Eyrie he lost a good griffiner and nearly died along with him. But why does it *matter* so much?"

"Do not be complacent," said Kraal. "There is more to that boy than there seems. The time will come when we shall all be grateful that he is here among us."

Elkin started. "What? Why?"

The griffin closed his eyes, and for a moment his massive frame looked smaller. "Because *Kraeai kran ae* is coming," he breathed.

The morning after the capture of Guard's Post, the surviving slaves gathered on the road outside the gates and burned the dead. They had gathered all the firewood they could find inside the fort and laid each body on its own crude pyre soaked with oil and packed with coal.

Arenadd and Caedmon lit the fires, and the slaves stood in a solemn crowd and watched the bodies burn, while Caedmon recited the ritual words.

"Of earth born and in fire forged, by magic blessed and by cool water soothed, then by a breeze in the night blown away to a land of silver and bright flowers. May the gods receive the souls of Cardock Skandarson, Annan Caenborn, Nolan Nolanson . . ."

He spoke the names of every single one of the dead men, while the fires burned higher and the others bowed their heads and murmured their own farewells. Skandar circled high above, uneasy around fire and impatient to be off.

When Caedmon had finished he looked at Arenadd. "Do ye want to say something, sir?"

Arenadd looked at the dozens of expectant faces. "They were good men," he said eventually. "They were my friends. They were all our friends."

Some of the others took their turns, speaking of lost friends and family, while the fires burned lower and eventually burned themselves out. A cold wind gusted up the road and carried the ashes away and up over the mountainside.

Arenadd took a clay pot from his robe and hurried over to Cardock's pyre, where he scooped up some of the ashes that were left and then sealed the pot and stowed it away in his robe.

"You're coming with me, Dad," he muttered. "Just like I promised."

When he straightened up he found the others all watching him. They had all shed their slave robes and were wearing an odd assortment of clothing stolen from the guards. Most of it didn't fit, and more than a few of the former slaves looked faintly ridiculous, but there was a new pride about the way they carried themselves. Nearly all of them carried a sword or some other weapon. They had taken horses and a handful of small carts from the fort and were carrying food and spare clothing; all of them looked ready to leave.

Arenadd coughed. "It's time for us to go," he said, his voice sounding rather thin in the open air.

Skandar, seeing the fires had died out, came down to land close to his human. "Go," he rasped. "Go now."

"Yes, yes." Arenadd waved at Skade to join him, and then turned to Caedmon. "I suppose this is goodbye," he said. "To you and everyone. We'll get through the mountains before you do, so—"

"Where are ye plannin' to go?" asked Caedmon.

Arenadd shrugged. "We'll find a place."

Caedmon came closer. "I know where ye should be goin'," he said. "Here, come to me. I don't want that griffin too close."

Arenadd obeyed. "What is it?"

Caedmon frowned and glanced over his shoulder before he spoke. "Eitheinn," he said in an undertone. "Go to Eitheinn. It's the furthest north of all the villages—tiny place. We hid there once durin' the war, an' if any one of our lot got away they'll be there now."

"Eitheinn," Arenadd repeated. "How do I find it?"

"Follow the River Snow," said Caedmon. "It'll get ye there. Even if Eitheinn's no good, go into the mountains beyond it. You'll find a stone circle. Only one left standing, far as I know. Taranis' Throne."

"It really exists?"

"Yes, and it'll protect ye. It's a sacred place."

Arenadd nodded. "I understand. If you think Eitheinn is where I should go, then I'll find it."

"Go then, an' good luck," said Caedmon.

"Thank you. Caedmon, where are you going to go?"

Caedmon shrugged. "I'll find something. I'm takin' Torc with me. We'll find a place to settle down. Somewhere quiet. I'm sure no-one'll ask too many questions of an old man an' his grandson who've lost their home."

"But what about the scars on your neck? Won't people ask questions?"

"Listen, lad," said Caedmon, with a touch of his old impatience, "we're all darkmen in the North, and darkmen protect each other. If a man makes it clear he's got no interest in lookin' for trouble, then he'll be left alone nine times out of ten."

Arenadd grinned. "Understood." He backed away toward Skandar and, raising his voice so that every one of the former slaves could hear him, said, "Never talk about what happened here, but never forget. I hope you can find a way to survive, and that you find better lives for yourselves. And I hope that one day we'll meet again." He bowed and turned toward Skandar, preparing to get onto his back.

"Wait!" A man came running toward him. Instantly Skandar reared up, hissing.

"Stay back!" Arenadd yelled.

The man backed away hastily, until Skandar relaxed. "Let me come with you," he said.

"And us!" Prydwen added, pushing forward.

The three Northerners stood together in a little group, arms folded, watching him resolutely.

"Let us come with ye, sir," said Prydwen.

"I'm sorry," said Arenadd, "but you can't."

"Please, sir!" said Dafydd. "We want to follow ye!"

"After all ye did for me, I'd go with ye no matter what," Garnoc added. "It'd be an honour, sir."

"I told you, no," said Arenadd. "I'd be happy to have you with me, but we can't do it. Six people travelling together would draw far too much attention; just travelling with Skandar is bad enough."

"But we can protect ye, sir," said Prydwen.

Arenadd laughed. "Be careful, Prydwen, I think you just insulted Skandar."

"Sorry," said Prydwen, casting a quick glance at the griffin. "But sir, ye're goin' into Lady Elkin's lands. There's hundreds of griffiners living there, and if they knew ye was there they'd never stop chasing ye. An' if they catch ye . . ." He shuddered.

"Ye set us free, sir," said Dafydd. "I . . ." He hesitated. "I saw someone die the traitor's death once. If that happened to ye, sir . . ."

Arenadd shook his head. "I understand. But don't worry about me. I've got Skandar to protect me, and Skade as well. With just the two of us, we can fly most of the way. No-one will ever see us. And if I'm caught—well, I foiled the griffiners once, didn't I? I can do it again." It was empty bravado, but the three Northerners looked convinced.

"I trust ye, sir," Prydwen said reluctantly. "If ye could do everythin' people say ye did back at Eagleholm, then those sons of bitches at Malvern would be the ones in trouble if they ever caught ye."

Skade cackled. "Do not worry, Prydwen. My Arenadd can

look after himself. And if not, then Skandar and I shall do it for him."

Skandar had looked increasingly bored and irritable during the conversation, and now he abruptly limped forward and thumped Arenadd on the head with his beak, nearly knocking him over. Arenadd yelped and staggered sideways as the three Northerners hurriedly backed off.

Arenadd turned to Skandar, rubbing his head. "Ow! You didn't have to do that."

But Skandar had had enough. He made a sudden rush forward, and his outstretched talons snapped shut around Arenadd's body, pinning his arms to his sides before the griffin leapt into the sky, carrying his human with him.

Torc screamed. "Oh my gods, he's going to eat him!"

Prydwen snatched up a rock and hurled it, but Skandar was already well out of range, flying up and away northward with Arenadd dangling from his talons.

Skade ran after him, shouting. "Come back! *Skandar!*"

For a moment it looked as if Skandar was going to keep on flying, but then he leant on one wing and wheeled back before he tipped head-downward and made a spectacular dive. Skade stood as still as she could, and the dark griffin swooped straight toward her and snatched her from the ground before his trajectory carried him upward. He flew low over the Northerners' heads and back into the sky.

Almost completely immobilised by the talons wrapped around her body, Skade tried to catch her breath. Skandar's silver feathers fluttered over her head as he turned northward once again and resumed his journey.

Dangling beside her, Arenadd spat out the hair that had been blown into his mouth and grinned madly at her. "Now, this is the only way to travel!" he yelled.

"Are you hurt?" Skade yelled back.

"No! Are you?"

Skade shook her head.

"I don't think he'll hurt you!" Arenadd shouted. "He seems to like you! Thank gods he decided to bring you as well! I thought I was going to lose you again!"

The wind made further conversation close to impossible, and the two of them hung limply side by side and let Skandar carry them away. Arenadd kept his eyes screwed shut, but Skade watched him.

You won't lose me, she thought. *Not again. You're mine. And I'm yours.*

29

Homecoming

Deep down, Arenadd had never been as confident about his bid to find shelter in the North as he had acted. From the beginning he had thought of it as little more than a last-ditch effort, something he was doing simply because there were no other realistic options. Going north would be difficult and dangerous, and the odds were that before he was even close to finding a place to lie low he would be spotted and then inexorably hunted down. But hiding anywhere else would be even more dangerous and impossible, and so he had settled on the North as the least hopeless out of a range of even worse decisions.

But within days of crossing over the border into the land called Tara, he knew that he had made the best choice he could have.

Skandar, for all his naïvety and ignorance of human ways, was already well versed in travelling inconspicuously. He followed the river as much as he could, taking large detours to avoid even the slightest hint of human habitation, sometimes choosing to fly at night to make more progress. They camped in the thickest patches of forest they could find, sometimes forced to lie low in small patches of cover to snatch some sleep before they moved on to find a safer location.

Skandar still persisted in taking livestock to feed himself, and there was very little Arenadd could do to make him stop, but he occasionally brought some meat back for his human cargo and insisted that "human not see" whenever Arenadd questioned him.

Arenadd and Skade rarely saw any humans, and when they did it was almost always from a great distance. Once they saw a griffin fly overhead, early one evening, but they tucked themselves away in a patch of willow trees and waited there until long after it had vanished.

That was their closest brush with danger, and the more they travelled the more Arenadd began to feel that they were in a land that could provide everything they needed.

The North was very different country than the Southern lands they had left behind; here the spice-trees were smaller and paler, interspersed with pine and fir. They began to see deer—animals that Arenadd had never seen before. And sometimes, at night, they heard the distant howling of wolves.

The last leg of their journey passed far more easily and uneventfully than they had expected, and the further north they went the easier it became. They had passed over and around towns and villages, but then there were only villages. The villages became smaller and the distances between them longer, until Skandar was following nothing but a small and winding road that ran alongside the River Snow. Ahead, mountains rose out of the landscape, and Arenadd knew they had made it.

They found a village tucked away at the very edge of the mountains just as Caedmon had said it would be, and went to ground well outside its edge to rest and consider their next move.

Arenadd sat down with his back to a tree and rubbed his numb legs. "I suppose this is it. We've done it."

"What do now?" said Skandar. "Where go? Mountain?"

Arenadd shook his head. "Not yet. We need to find out if this is Eitheinn and if there are any of Caedmon's friends still living here."

"How?" said Skade.

"I've been thinking about this for the last few days—I think I should go in there in the morning and talk to someone, see what I can find out."

"Is that wise?" said Skade.

"Relax," Arenadd advised. "We're miles away from the nearest town; there's no griffiners here and no guards, either. I wouldn't be surprised if these people don't even know about Eagleholm, and if they do, why in the world would they guess who I am? I'll just look like another Northerner, won't I?" He sat back and grinned. "The North was the right place to come, Skade. The best place. I could have gone into any of those towns

we passed and no-one would have looked twice at me. Come to
think of it, *you're* the one who'll stick out here."

"I would stand out anywhere," Skade said acidly. "How
many Southerners have my hair or eyes?"

"They're not so obvious now," said Arenadd, which was true
enough. During the last month or so Skade's appearance had
been changing subtly. Her eyes had faded from gold to a kind
of brownish amber, and her hair had lost its metallic tinge and
become pale ash blonde. Her claws, though, had stayed, and so
had her nature and stilted conversation.

"Even so," she said, "I doubt these people see many visitors,
and you are still wearing that robe. They will ask questions."

"Obviously. But look, there can't be much harm in just going
in and having a look around. I've still got some oblong, so I
can buy food, and I can probably buy a lot of 'no questions' as
well if I need to. And if things turn ugly, we can always leave."
He shivered. "It's cold country here, Skade. Living in the open
would be far more dangerous than it was back in the South. If
there's even the smallest chance of finding shelter here, I want
to, because quite honestly, I want to sleep with a roof over my
head again."

"I understand," said Skade.

Skandar hissed. "Not want."

"What don't you want, Skandar?" said Arenadd.

The griffin paused, a sure sign that he was forming a sentence in his head. "I do not want—do not want to live—want
mountains," He said at last. "Want to fly to mountains." He
lifted his beak, pointing it skyward, and clicked it several
times. "Want mountains. You, me, go there, build nest. You
say. You promise."

"Yes, but—"

"You say!" Skandar bellowed. "You say, go mountain. You
say, we make home. I carry human, I fight. Not eat human, not
fly away. You ask, I do. I help human, you show me mountain,
give home. Want home."

Arenadd stood up. "Skandar, calm down. I'm not saying we
can't go there."

Skandar wasn't listening. His wings were fluttering in agitation, and he was beginning to hiss and tear at the ground.
"Want mountain! No human! Griffin nest, no human nest! You
give! Promise!"

"All right. All right. Skandar, calm down. Please, someone will hear you. We'll go to the mountains, understand? We'll go in the morning. You're tired now; you need to rest."

Skandar subsided a little, though his tail continued to swish. "Go mountain?"

"Yes, Skandar. Just as you want."

"No human?"

"No human. I promise."

Arenadd kept his voice level and his head slightly bowed, careful not to look the griffin in the eye, and Skandar eventually relaxed and lay down on his belly.

"We go," he said in a satisfied tone. "Morning, go. Rest now. You rest now, human."

Arenadd nodded quickly at Skade. "Of course. You're right, Skandar. We should rest. It's been a long journey."

Skandar looked placated after that, and the three of them rested and shared some meat Arenadd had smoked the night before. After a while Skandar fell asleep, exhausted from half a day in the air. The stars began to come out.

Once Skandar's eyes had been closed for a decent amount of time, Arenadd stood up. "Right. I'd better go then."

Skade pulled her cloak over her shoulders. "You are going into the village?"

"Of course. We still need food, and I still want to ask some questions. I'll be back soon. Keep an eye on Skandar. If he wakes up try and distract him and call for me as soon as you can—for gods' sakes, don't let him follow me." He took his sword from his back and leant it against a tree. "Better leave this here. See you later."

"Good luck," said Skade. "And be careful."

"I will." Arenadd dusted the snow off his robe and slipped away through the trees, eerily silent as always.

The village was quiet when Arenadd entered it. It looked even smaller than it had from the air, barely more than a handful of wood-and-stone huts clustered together as if to protect each other from the wind. The place was so tiny that it didn't even have a mill. An inn would be out of the question.

People were coming back from their work in the field when Arenadd arrived, and he quickly found himself attracting the stares he had been expecting. Most of them started when they saw him, and nearly all of them shied away, quickly turning their faces from him as if they expected him to attack.

Arenadd approached the nearest of them. "Excuse me."

The man glanced quickly around and then, apparently deciding there was no hope of escape, turned to face him. "What d'ye want?" he mumbled. He was clad in the typical rough peasant's clothing but with a layer of furs over the top, and his accent was even thicker than Prydwen's.

"I'm not looking for trouble," Arenadd said as kindly as he could, aware of the people scurrying toward their homes as fast as they could go. "My name's Llewellyn. Is this Eitheinn?"

"Yes," said the man, still extremely nervous.

"Good. I'm just on my way through to somewhere else, and I was hoping to buy some food."

The man straightened up. "We don't have much," he said, a little more confidently. "Just what we need to get by on. Money's not of much use to us."

"I don't need a lot," said Arenadd. "Just a few loaves of bread or some vegetables—whatever you can spare."

The man looked past him. "Hmm, could be I've got a few things I could sell. Where be ye goin', can I ask?"

"That's my business," said Arenadd. "I'm in a hurry, so could you please just—"

His question ended in a yell as, without any warning, something hit him hard in the back of the knees. His legs folded and he fell hard, as the farmer darted away from him, and before he knew what was happening a boot had been slammed down onto his chest and a sharp metal point was jammed under his chin.

Arenadd reached frantically for his dagger, but it was kicked away, and someone stamped on his hand. He looked up into three hostile faces.

"What in the gods' names do you want?" he demanded, hiding his fear.

The face holding the blade to his neck spat. "Who are ye? Tell me yer name, or the next thing ye say will be yer epitaph, blackrobe."

"Llewellyn," said Arenadd. "My name's Llewellyn. Please, let me up, I'm not going to—*argh!*"

The blade dug in a little further. "Llewellyn, is it? And what are ye doin' here?" The voice was sharp and aggressive and, he realised with a hint of surprise, female.

"I'm trying to buy food," he said. "That's all."

Hands hauled him to his feet.

"Food, is it?" said the woman.

"Yes," said Arenadd, and yelped as the two men holding him twisted his arms behind his back.

She looked him up and down. "Where did ye come from, an' why are ye here?"

Arenadd hesitated, and then decided to throw caution to the winds. "I'm trying to hide."

The woman regarded him keenly. "A runaway slave, are ye?"

"Yes. I'm from Withypool."

She kept her sword to his throat a few moments longer, and then withdrew it. "I wouldn't think Elkin'd be fool enough to send someone so clumsy to spy f'her. But don't think that means I believe all of that. How did ye get here? Are ye alone?"

Arenadd rubbed his neck. "Yes. And I'm sorry if I frightened people, but I didn't know what else to do."

The woman snickered. "Talk fancy, don't ye?"

"Uh, yes, I suppose so." Arenadd pulled himself together. "I was told to come here if I wanted to hide."

She tensed immediately. "By who?"

"By another slave," said Arenadd.

"Who? What was his name?"

"Caedmon Taranisäii."

Almost immediately, the hands holding his arms let go.

The woman looked as if he had just slapped her in the face. *"Caedmon?"*

"Yes. He said this place was a shelter for him once and that I should come here if I wanted to find people who could help me hide."

"He's alive?" said the woman.

"Last time I saw him, yes. Look, do you have a name? You don't have to tell me, but—"

The woman sheathed her dagger and glanced sternly at her two comrades. "So Caedmon sent ye. That changes things. We thought—" She coughed and held out a hand. "Saeddryn. My name."

Without even thinking, Arenadd linked his fingers with hers

and gave the quick tug of a griffiner. "Pleased to meet you, Saeddryn."

Saeddryn pulled her hand back very quickly, staring at her fingers as if she'd never seen them before. "What was that?"

"What was what?" said Arenadd.

"What ye just did," said Saeddryn. "That—who taught ye that?"

"I can't remember. Someone. Look, I don't plan to stay here long. I just need to know—"

Saeddryn waved him into silence. "Ye want something from us, don't ye?"

"Just food." Arenadd began to feel nervous. "And I really should go soon."

She was watching him intently. "Go? Go where? It's nightfall; ye'll freeze to death if ye sleep in the open."

"Maybe, but that's my business," said Arenadd. "I'm not going to stay here."

"Then where are ye going?" said Saeddryn.

"It's not important. Somewhere else."

She moved closer. "To the mountains, maybe?"

"And why would I want to go there?" Arenadd said carefully.

"I don't know," said Saeddryn. "Perhaps because ye're hopin' to find something there. Perhaps because Caedmon said ye should go there. Ye tell me, Llewellyn."

"Well, I would like to see Taranis' Throne."

She grinned. "Then ye'll see it, Southerner. I'll take ye there myself."

"D'ye think that's a good idea?" one of Arenadd's captors interrupted. "Takin' him up there?"

"Shut up," said Saeddryn. "He knows about us, an' he knows about the Throne. An' he's only one man besides, an' skinny. But we need him even so. After Ouen, we'll need every man we can find," she added sourly. "Now come." She held a hand out toward Arenadd. "Ye need food an' rest, an' ye'll have both. Ye can stay in my home, an' when the time's right, I'll take ye to the Throne. The rest will be up to the moon."

"Thank you, Saeddryn, I'd love to. But—"

"But?"

"I left my bag outside the village," said Arenadd. "I should go and get it first."

Saeddryn nodded. "I'll come with ye, then. Rhodri, Talfryn, ye come, too."

Arenadd crumbled inside. "You don't need to bother; I can do it myself. It's just a short walk—"

Saeddryn touched the hilt of her sword. "Then we'll have no trouble in going. Come, let's go quickly, before the sun is all gone."

Arenadd knew he was making them suspicious. "All right. Let's go."

He walked back out of the village, with the three Northerners following, not daring to try to run away. They, apparently sensing that he was up to something, stayed very close to him, close enough to grab him the instant he did anything suspicious.

Arenadd entered the patch of trees where the others were hiding, hoping to lose himself in the shadows, but his escort kept close, and after only a few steps Saeddryn said, "So, where is it? Is it here?"

Arenadd made a show of examining the undergrowth. "Uh, I thought it was here somewhere. It all looks the same. I'll just have a look around."

"I'll help," she said immediately. "What does it look like?"

It's got silver feathers and black fur, and it's big enough to rip a horse's head off. "It's quite small; I hid it in some bushes under a tree—maybe it's this one." He rooted through the clump in question, while Saeddryn and her friends stood over him and watched. He straightened up. "Damn. Maybe it was further in."

He "searched" several bushes after that, his mind racing, as Saeddryn became more and more impatient and suspicious. There was no chance of shaking them off: they obviously knew what they were doing and would probably kill him if they thought he was trying to trick them. They were getting closer to Skade and Skandar's hiding place all the while.

Finally, as the atmosphere became increasingly tense, he decided that there was only one option. He paused by a tree, pretending to look at something a short distance away.

"What is it?" said Saeddryn.

"I think I can see something odd over there," said Arenadd, pointing. "See it?"

One of her companions squinted in that direction. "Too dark t'see anythin'. What're ye goin' on about? Where's this bag, anyway? Moon's gonna come up before ye find the damned thing, ye Southern fool."

It was now or never. Arenadd cupped his hands around his mouth and shouted in griffish. "Skade! Skade, it's me! Quickly, run away! Take Skandar and go, before—"

That was as far as he got. One of Saeddryn's friends grabbed him by the throat and slammed him into the tree, and the other delivered two fast and powerful blows to his stomach, which silenced him and drove all the air from his lungs in a single burst.

Saeddryn grabbed him by the hair and wrenched his head sideways. "Who were ye callin' for?" she snarled. "Who's out here with us?"

Arenadd coughed and gasped. "I w-w-w—"

As if by magic, the sword reappeared in her hand and pressed into his throat, hard enough to draw blood. "Answer me! *Now*."

Arenadd opened his mouth to reply, and in that instant a screech split the air. The three Northerners' heads snapped around, and Arenadd took his chance. He grabbed Saeddryn's arm and wrenched it away, kicked one of his captors in the groin, wriggled out of the grip of the other one, shoved his way past them and ran.

There was a scream and a bellow of rage, and they were after him in moments, but he didn't run far. Even as Saeddryn bore down on him, something huge came crashing through the undergrowth, screeching all the while.

Arenadd ran straight at Skandar, colliding with him. The griffin reeled back, beak opening, ready to attack, before he recognised his human and enveloped him with one wing and began to hiss and snarl at Saeddryn and her friends. "My human! *Mine!*"

Saeddryn pulled up short. "By the—*get back!*"

Her two friends stopped and ran back the way they had come, taking shelter behind a pair of trees. They clearly wanted to run further than that, but neither was prepared to abandon their leader. Saeddryn stood her ground.

Skandar hissed even more loudly and advanced on her with murder in his eyes.

Arenadd managed to extricate himself from the griffin's wing. "Saeddryn, get out of here! He'll kill you if you don't—"

Saeddryn did not move. She put her sword away and bowed low. "Great griffin," she intoned, and Arenadd's stomach lurched as he realised the words were spoken in griffish.

Skandar hesitated at that, and Saeddryn went on.

"Please, do not attack us," she said. "I bow to you, for you are powerful and I am weak. I am Saeddryn, and I will do no harm to you."

Skandar stopped and held his head up, looking down at her. "You . . . speak," he said slowly. "Human speak."

"I do," said Saeddryn.

Skandar had begun to look uncertain. He turned to Arenadd. "You hurt?"

"No. I'm fine. Don't attack, Skandar, there's no need. They can't hurt us."

There were sounds from behind them, and Skade came running. "Arenadd!"

Arenadd grabbed her arm. "It's all right. I'm not hurt. But these three—"

Saeddryn was watching him and Skandar, poised to run. "Who are ye?" she said, reverting to Cymrian. "Why are ye here?"

"Do not tell her," Skade hissed, in griffish. "Arenadd, they have seen us—we should kill them."

Arenadd put a hand on her shoulder. "No. They know Caedmon. I think they could help us. They're not going to tell the griffiners about us."

"We'll tell the griffiners nothing," Saeddryn spat. "We are their enemies and always shall be. Now tell us who ye are. Tell us the truth."

Arenadd nodded. "Yes. I think it's time. I am . . ." He hesitated. "I'm—well, this is Skandar, and this is Skade. And I'm . . ."

"And ye?" Saeddryn said intently. "Who are ye?"

"I'm Arenadd. Arenadd Taranisäii of Eagleholm."

Saeddryn drew back for a moment, and then she nodded with a kind of joyful certainty. "I knew it." She bowed to him. "And I am Saeddryn Taranisäii. Welcome home, Arenadd."

30

Parting

Saeddryn's home turned out to be the largest in the village, with a tall peaked roof and a barn attached. Saeddryn led all three of them to it, reassuring them that the villagers could be trusted not to say anything if guards or griffiners ever came to Eitheinn again.

"They're not likely to," she added confidently. "We're too far away, too small, an' we keep watchers on the road. Moment anyone comes this way, ground or sky, we go up to the mountains f'r shelter, an' there's neither man nor griffin could find us there."

"Don't tax gatherers come here, at least?" said Arenadd.

"From time to time, but they don't usually take the trouble," said Saeddryn. "Too tiny, too poor, too out of the way."

She bade Arenadd, Skade and Skandar wait outside the barn while Saeddryn's two friends went in.

"Horses," she explained. "We keep some in here. Got to move them b'fore you go in."

Arenadd nodded. Griffins' hatred of horses was legendary, and Skandar was hungry besides.

Saeddryn peered into the barn, and then nodded. "We can go in now."

The barn was large and full of the smell of horses, though the animals themselves had been removed, presumably via the door in the opposite wall. A lantern was hanging from a beam at the centre, and Saeddryn dragged a bucket and a crate over to it and gestured at Arenadd to sit. He chose the crate, and she sat on the bucket, opposite him.

Skade looked askance at them and sat on the floor, cross-legged. Skandar wandered around the barn, sniffing in the corners, before making a sudden leap onto the ledge that lined the wall high above. The wood creaked alarmingly under his weight, but he dug his talons in and clung there, balancing on his narrow perch.

Saeddryn looked up at him. "He's magnificent."

"He's my best friend," said Arenadd. He looked keenly at her. "You know griffins? You obviously know griffish."

She nodded. "Some of us speak it a little."

"How? Who taught you?"

Saeddryn was looking at Skade. "I trust ye, Arenadd. Ye're a Taranisäii, one of us. But who are ye, Southerner?"

"Skade of Withypool," said Skade. She clicked her teeth nervously. "I come in peace, without designs on your territory, your mates or your food."

Saeddryn snickered. "What does *that* mean?"

Skade glared at her. "I come in peace," she repeated. "I am no threat."

"She can be trusted," Arenadd put in hastily. "Skade is an outcast. We met while I was on my way here, and she helped me."

"Outcast?" said Saeddryn. "Why? What was it ye did, Skade?"

"I killed a man," said Skade. "More than one."

Saeddryn hissed to herself. "A murderer, then, is it?"

"They had killed someone close to me," Skade snapped. "He was a Northerner, like yourself. A slave. I was his friend, and I tried to set him free, but he was murdered. In revenge, I killed the ones who killed him. Now I have no home, but Arenadd brought me to hide with him here."

"It's the truth," said Arenadd.

Saeddryn still looked suspicious, but apparently deciding that she was satisfied for the time being, she turned to Arenadd. "Tell me about yerself. Why have ye come here? Why did ye leave? Why are ye with a griffin?"

Arenadd chewed his lip. "How much do you know? About Eagleholm? About what happened there?"

"Rumours. It's said something happened, some kind of disaster," said Saeddryn. "Some said it was an attack from Canran." She shook her head. "We go unnoticed, but that means we don't know much of what's happenin' in the South. What d'ye know about it?"

Skade gave him a warning glance. "Arenadd, we should be cautious."

"No, Skade. She's a friend." Arenadd looked at Saeddryn. "At least, I hope you are."

"A Taranisäii is always a friend to another Taranisäii," said Saeddryn. "Tell me yer story, Arenadd."

She sat still, watching him intently, and Arenadd told her everything from the beginning. He told her about his life in Eagleholm, Rannagon's plot, the death of Eluna, his persecution at Rannagon's hands and the pact with Skandar, and finally gave an account of how he had come back for revenge. He left out the fall from the edge of the city and its consequences.

Saeddryn stayed silent the whole time, but an expression of shock quickly appeared on her face, and deepened every moment.

". . . and I set fire to the room to help me escape," continued Arenadd, "and Skandar and I flew away. Later on I found out the entire Eyrie burned down, and dozens of griffiners died, including the Mistress."

Saeddryn rubbed her hands over her face. "Ye destroyed the Eyrie?"

"Yes. I didn't mean to, but I did."

"An' ye killed Lord Rannagon."

"Yes."

Saeddryn looked up. "How do I know ye're tellin' the truth?"

"Here." Arenadd took his sword from his back. "Here, look."

Saeddryn took it and laid it across her lap, examining the blade and the bronze hilt with its pattern of flying griffins.

"Lord Rannagon's sword," said Arenadd. "I took it from his body."

Saeddryn fingered the sword, apparently deep in thought. "So," she said at length. "So, now ye've come here, then. Ye destroyed an Eyrie, ye and this griffin, an' ye murdered Lord Rannagon."

Arenadd shivered. "Yes. Afterward I knew I had to find somewhere to hide, and fast, and this was the only place I could think of to come."

"An' Caedmon?" said Saeddryn. "How did ye meet him?"

"It was at Herbstitt . . ." Arenadd, feeling decidedly uneasy now, briefly told the tale of his capture and the escape of the slaves, and how he had led them to Guard's Post and overrun it with their help. "And afterward I knew they deserved a reward, and I couldn't very well bring them with me, so I set them free and told them to go wherever they wanted."

"Ye freed them?"

"Yes, including Caedmon. I found a way to break the collars off. Afterward Caedmon told me he was a Taranisäii, and he said that I should come here to be safe. That was the last time I saw him."

Saeddryn stood up abruptly. "Ye an' Caedmon . . ."

Arenadd stood, too. "I did what I thought was—*oof!*"

Without any warning, Saeddryn had dropped the sword and taken him in a fierce embrace. He tried to break free, but she held on, squeezing all the breath out of him, and then she kissed him on both cheeks, again and again.

There was an offended screech from Skandar and a shout from Skade. "What are you doing?"

Saeddryn let go and backed off hastily. "Forgive me," she said, bright-eyed. "Forgive me for not trusting ye, Arenadd, an' forgive me for not givin' ye the welcome ye deserved."

Arenadd dabbed at his face. "It's all right. I wouldn't have expected anything else."

"But ye're *welcome*," said Saeddryn, still completely ignoring Skade and Skandar. "Ye're more'n welcome. After what ye've done . . ." She shook her head. "Come. Come with me. Ye've come so far—my home is yer own. Come with me. I'll give ye new clothes an' we can burn that foul rag yer wearin', an' ye'll have food an' a bed an' anythin' else ye need. An' tomorrow I'll take ye to the circle myself, so ye can see it."

"What about my friends?" said Arenadd.

Saeddryn favoured both Skade and Skandar with a brief smile. "Friends of yers are friends of mine. Skandar," she said, speaking griffish now and bowing, "Skandar, this place is yours, an' I will be honoured to have you here. You'll be brought meat an' clean straw an' anythin' else you need."

Skandar clicked his beak. "Human speak."

"Yes, Skandar, she's a friend," said Arenadd. "She'll bring you food."

"Not stay," the griffin hissed. "Not live here. We go. Mountain."

"Yes, tomorrow, as we agreed," said Arenadd. "Just for tonight we can sleep here, all right? And Saeddryn will bring food, lots of food, just for you."

"A whole deer," Saeddryn put in. "Killed just today. All for you, Skandar."

Skandar leapt down from his perch, making the floorboards shudder violently. "Food?"

"Food and straw," said Arenadd. "And then tomorrow we'll go to the mountains."

Saeddryn nodded. "Good. Now, Arenadd, ye come with me into the house, an' ye, Skade—"

Skandar screeched. "Not go!"

Arenadd moved closer to him. "Look, I'm sorry, but I really should stay here with him. He's not used to being indoors, and he tends to get worked up if I'm not there. He's come a long way, carrying two people—he's at the end of his strength."

Saeddryn nodded stiffly. "As ye wish. Stay here, then, and I'll bring food and clothes."

"Thank you."

"It's a small thing to ask," said Saeddryn. She bowed to them all and left.

Once she'd gone, Arenadd heaved a deep sigh. "Well, that was . . . unexpected."

Skade gave the door a narrow-eyed look. "I do not trust her."

"What's she going to do?" said Arenadd. "Call the guards? Don't be ridiculous. There can't be more than fifty people living in this village, and they wouldn't dare attack us with Skandar here. Anyway, if she wanted to kill me she could have done it twice by now."

"Not like," said Skandar.

"Skandar, you don't like *anybody*," said Arenadd. "And I think you'll like Saeddryn a lot more after she brings you food." He noticed the look Skade was giving him. "Oh, don't do that, Skade. This is a *good* thing! We found Eitheinn without being caught or seen, and what's more we've found exactly the right person. We've got an ally now—probably more than one—and we've got shelter and food. There's no griffiners about. This is the perfect place for us to hide."

"But this stone circle," said Skade. "Why is she so intent on taking you there?"

"It's an important place," said Arenadd. "To us. I want to see it. And I have a feeling that those rebels Caedmon mentioned might be hiding up there; Saeddryn obviously thinks we've come to join them."

"Which we have not," said Skade.

"They could help us," said Arenadd. "Think about it, Skade; if griffiners ever come here looking for us, we'll need help if we're going to hide from them. Have you thought of that? And besides, I can't stay here. Can I, Skandar?"

"Not stay," the griffin agreed. "You, me, go mountains."

"And *me*?" said Skade. "What about me? Where shall I go?"

Arenadd stared at her, caught off guard. "Uh, well, where do you want to go?"

Skade hissed. "Do not mock me."

"I wasn't mocking you; I wanted to know," said Arenadd.

"Not come," said Skandar.

They both looked at him.

"What, Skandar?" said Arenadd.

The griffin moved forward, thrusting his beak at Skade. "Female not come. Not want her. She stay, not come. I go to mountains, take human with me. Take Arren. Not take her."

"What?" said Arenadd. "Skandar, why?"

"Not like silver human," said Skandar. "Arren friend, magic human. Show me where go. You say if I fly here, bring female, I have mountain. Have mountain now."

Skade had gone pale. "You told him to bring me?" she said to Arenadd.

"Arren tell," Skandar confirmed. "Arren say, 'You bring female, I show you the way, we go mountain. You, me, live together.' You say fly, I fly. You say fight, I fight. Now you give me what I want, you do what I say, human."

Arenadd's heart sank.

"Have mountains now," Skandar said arrogantly. "Now they mine. My territory. You come. Tomorrow."

"And the female stays behind," Skade finished. She gave Skandar a deathly look. "So now the mystery is solved. I wondered, for a long time."

"So did I," said Arenadd.

"Yes. That a griffin of his size and power—a *wild* griffin— would do what a mere human told him, and refrain from eating other humans—" Skade spat. "So, that was your great power. The mutterings of some spirits, and a promise you intended to break. And tomorrow our time together comes to an end."

Arenadd reached out to her. "Skade—"

Skade turned her back on him and went to sit on a heap of

straw in the corner, well away from him. Arenadd watched her unhappily but couldn't think of anything to say.

Skandar didn't appear to care either way. "Come now," he said, and shepherded his human to a spot in one of the horses' stalls, where he dragged some straw together into a crude nest and then lay down in it. Arenadd sat down beside him, hugging his knees.

Skandar took a drink from the horse trough and then settled down with a contented sigh. Arenadd, watching him, wondered yet again why he didn't hate the griffin. He was so selfish, so brutishly strong—and yet so innocent, even vulnerable.

He really is like a big child, Arenadd thought.

He tried to imagine what it would be like spending the rest of his life up in the mountains with Skandar. Would he ever speak to another human being again? Would Skandar force him to stay in the wild, away from civilisation forever? No, almost certainly not. They would return from time to time, he knew, to steal cattle for food. And possibly more than that. If Skandar no longer believed that he had to please his human, then nothing could stop him from eating other humans.

And he would never see Skade again.

His thoughts were interrupted a short time later by Saeddryn, who came in dragging the whole carcass of a deer. "I'm sorry for the wait," she said. "Just a moment an' I'll bring food for ye, Arenadd, and yer friend."

Skandar roused himself and tore into the deer before Saeddryn had even let go of it. She grinned nervously and darted out the door, emerging a moment later with two bowls of food. After that she left again.

Arenadd's bowl was full of stew and topped with two slices of bread and cheese. He tucked in gratefully; this was his first proper meal in several days. While the three of them ate, Saeddryn returned several times, bringing a tub of water, soap, blankets and clothes for Skade and Arenadd.

Once Arenadd had eaten, he washed himself and put on the clothes. They fitted quite well, but he felt strange to be wearing an ordinary tunic for the first time in months. He washed his hair as well and sat back in the straw to comb it into shape.

"You are *always* grooming your hair," said Skade, breaking her silence.

Arenadd glanced at her. "Hair like mine tangles easily, you

know, especially when it's this long. I might be a fugitive, but that doesn't mean I have to look like a beggar. You could try it yourself."

Skade dragged her fingers through her hair and muttered something under her breath.

Saeddryn returned with more blankets. "Here, ye can bed down in the straw with these. I know it'll be rough next to what ye must've had back at Eagleholm."

Arenadd got up to help her. "Oh no, not at all. Straw will be fine." He smiled at her as he helped her to pile some straw in the stall next to Skandar's. "Back home, I slept in a hammock."

"A hammock?" Saeddryn repeated. She scratched her head. "Ye gods, I always thought griffiners slept in feather beds an' suchlike."

"A feather bed?" said Arenadd. "Don't be ridiculous. Those things cost a thousand oblong each. I couldn't afford something like that. Anyway, I lived on the edge of the city. There were rules about how much furniture you could have."

"Really? Ye must tell me about it," said Saeddryn. "I'd love to know more. I've never been in a city or inside an Eyrie." She reached out to smooth the corner of the blanket, accidentally touching Arenadd's hand in the process. "Sorry."

Arenadd backed away slightly. "Thank you so much, Saeddryn. You've been a great help to us."

"It's nothing," said Saeddryn. "Ye're a friend to us, like I said. There's not a man or woman in this village wouldn't do everythin' in their power to help ye, once they know ye killed Lord Rannagon."

"He was here?"

Saeddryn nodded. "Not in Eitheinn, but in the villages further south. He led a group of griffiners, chased Lady Arddryn's friends northward, an' massacred 'em, along with anyone who'd helped 'em. The people what live here now, most of 'em are survivors or descended from 'em. There's not many left in the North doesn't remember his name an' hate it, an' they'll love the man what killed him." The bed was finished, and she straightened up. "Now, is there anythin' more ye need?"

"Just one thing," said Arenadd. "Could I have a needle and some thread? And if you've got any cloth, I need that, too."

"I'll go an' see," said Saeddryn, and left.

She returned with a spool of thread with a needle stuck in it, and a large fur slung over her shoulder. "No cloth I could find, but ye can cut up a blanket if ye want. I brought ye this wolf skin, though, in case ye could use it."

Arenadd fingered it. "Yes, this should work. Thank you."

"Anythin' else ye need?" said Saeddryn. "More food?"

Arenadd looked at Skade, but she was still sitting on her straw stool and looked disinclined to move. Skandar was busy pecking at the remains of his deer.

"No, I think that's all we need."

Saeddryn bowed and smiled. "If ye think of anythin', I'll be in the house. Goodnight, Arenadd, and the moon's light bless ye."

Arenadd returned the bow. "And the moon's light bless you, too, Saeddryn," he said, speaking the Northern tongue.

Saeddryn looked shocked for a moment, but she recovered herself and left.

Skade stood up, "I am going to sleep," she said.

Arenadd was busy threading the needle. "I'm going to stay up for a while. I've got some work to do."

Skade ignored him and climbed a ladder up to the ledge where Skandar had perched; she curled up with her back to Arenadd.

"You can have the bed—" Arenadd called, and then thought better of it and decided to leave her alone. Skade showed no sign of having heard him, anyway.

Skandar finished gnawing on a bone and wandered back to his nest. "Sleep now, human."

"I'll be here, Skandar," said Arenadd. "Sleep well."

He finished threading the needle and put it down next to his seat before he went and fetched his robe from the nail it was hanging on. He took one of the blankets off the bed and brought it back as well, and used his dagger to cut a piece out of it. Once he'd shaped it, he turned the robe inside out and began to stitch the patch into place.

The night wore on, but Arenadd didn't feel tired. He rarely did any more. He sat on the overturned bucket, patching or darning every hole in the robe, pausing occasionally to re-thread the needle.

The oil in the lamp began to burn down, and he roused himself from his work and rubbed his neck. Skandar was fast asleep in his nest. Up on the ledge, Skade had rolled onto her other side, one arm hanging partway over the edge. Arenadd could see her face, its sharp features softened by sleep.

He sighed and took a blanket up the ladder for her. She stirred when he laid it over her, but didn't wake up, and he climbed back down the ladder and returned to his work. The lamp had nearly burned itself out by the time he was finished, and he snuffed it out and trudged over to his straw bed, yawning and carrying the robe in one hand.

The bed was prickly but comfortable enough, and he curled up under his robe and went to sleep.

For the first time in weeks, no nightmares visited him.

Arenadd woke up at dawn and crawled out of bed; Skade and Skandar were still asleep. He put on his robe and crept out of the barn, taking his sword with him just in case.

Outside, it was far colder than he had expected. An icy wind was blowing down off the mountains, carrying a few snowflakes with it, and the sky was grey.

The villagers were already out and about, of course. Several figures were visible in the fields just beyond the village, and a pair of boys were herding a flock of black sheep out to graze. A woman was busy grinding flour with a small hand-mill, and two men were tanning a fresh hide.

They were quick to see Arenadd. As he wandered out into the village's single street, heads turned to stare at him. Conversations were hushed into silence, and when Arenadd got too close to anyone they edged away, trying not to look him in the face. He thought of trying to speak with them, but the sight of all those pale, watchful faces made him feel depressed; he walked back toward Saeddryn's home.

As he neared it, Saeddryn emerged from behind the house, warmly dressed and leading a small, shaggy pony. She started when she saw him. "Arenadd!"

Arenadd nodded to her. "Good morning."

"Why are ye wearin' that?" said Saeddryn.

Arenadd touched the sleeve of his robe. "I fixed it last night. Thanks for the thread."

He'd stitched up or patched all the tears and had used the wolf skin to line as much of the inside as possible, for warmth.

Saeddryn, however, looked less than happy. "Why would ye want to wear it? I gave ye new clothes; didn't they fit?"

"They did, but I prefer to wear this," said Arenadd.

"Arenadd, ye're wearin' a slave's robe," said Saeddryn. "Ain't ye ashamed? D'ye want to be called a blackrobe wherever ye go?"

"My father made this robe for me," said Arenadd. "Our people used to wear them into battle. Why should I be ashamed?"

Saeddryn stared at him for a moment and then burst out laughing. "Into battle? Ye don't believe that story, do ye?"

"That's what my father told me," said Arenadd, with a lot less certainty.

"Well, I don't want to insult his memory, but yer father was wrong," said Saeddryn. "The idea of it—wearin' *robes* in a fight!" She laughed again. "Have ye tried it? The thing would snag on every bush ye passed an' ye'd be dead in a heartbeat!"

Heartbeat. Arenadd shivered despite himself. "So, only slaves ever wore robes like this?"

"No." Saeddryn became serious. "No, those were what our kings wore."

Arenadd went rigid. *"What?"*

"Aye, kings." Saeddryn nodded. "Did ye not know that? Has the whole world forgotten? We had kings once. That was who Taranis was. He was king of the North, an' he wore a robe woven from black wolf fur. The circle up there, Taranis' Throne, that's where he was crowned. The Night God had chosen him, see, marked him out to lead us, but after he was killed an' the North was taken by griffiners, they changed that. They made slaves wear robes like his, so it'd be shameful always an' forever to wear one."

Arenadd rubbed his neck. "So I'm wearing a king's robe. I don't see why I should be ashamed of that. Anyway, this is all I've got to remember my dad. He told me not to be ashamed, and so I won't. Never again."

Saeddryn was looking at him with something like admiration. "Well," she said, trying to restrain the pony, which had begun to shy away from Arenadd, "I won't tell ye what ye should an' shouldn't wear. Where's Skandar?"

"Still in the barn," said Arenadd. "I think we should let him sleep a while. He needs it."

She nodded. "I want to be at the circle with ye, but ye'll

reach it ahead of me, so I'll leave first. I know a quick way. I was just comin' to wake ye now."

"So, how do we get to this circle?" said Arenadd. "Do you know how to find it from the air?"

"It's easy," said Saeddryn. "The circle is just beyond the mountains, on a flat piece of ground. Ye'll see it at once, but I warn ye, land outside it. Don't go among the stones, not for any reason."

Arenadd nodded. "I'll remember."

"Now, I should go," said Saeddryn. She mounted the pony, tugging hastily on the reins when it gave another nervous jerk, "Damn ye, yer daft animal, what's wrong with ye?"

Arenadd backed off. "Sorry; I probably smell like griffin."

She managed to calm the animal down. "That's better. I'll take the shortest route; that should get me there by noon, an' I'll meet ye at the circle."

"What about Skade?" said Arenadd. "Will she be all right here on her own?"

"She'll be cared for, don't worry," said Saeddryn. "Tell her she's welcome in my house while we're gone; there'll be food enough there for her."

"I want her to feel safe," said Arenadd. "She doesn't like being too close to people or being asked a lot of questions; she's happiest if she's left alone."

"Don't worry," said Saeddryn. "The people here know to stay away from friends of mine. The less ye know, the less ye can say if ye're questioned. They'll keep their distance. Now I have to go. See ye at noon, Arenadd."

Arenadd stood and watched her as she rode away, half-wishing he was riding alongside her. He still had a dozen questions he wanted to ask her, but he sensed that she wanted to wait until they were away from the village.

At noon, he would know.

He walked back to the barn, thoughtfully fingering his beard, and pushed the door open. When he entered he found Skandar still asleep. Skade, however, was awake, perched on her ledge and glaring down at him.

Arenadd climbed the ladder. "Good morning. Did you sleep well?"

"Where were you?" Skade asked abruptly.

"I went outside to stretch my legs. I saw Saeddryn. She's

gone up to the circle; Skandar and I are going to meet her there at noon. She says that while we're gone, you can stay in her house. There's food there for you, and you won't be bothered."

"I will tell them," said Skade.

"What?" said Arenadd. "Tell them what?"

She turned her head to look savagely at him. "If you abandon me, I will tell them your secret. I swear it."

"Wh— Skade, what are you talking about? You can't possibly—"

"I will tell them," she insisted. She prodded him with her forefinger, her claw digging into him. "Do not pretend that you do not understand, Arenadd. You are not going to come back. You will go into those mountains and never return to me."

"Skade, you know I want to come back."

"And you will," said Skade. "If you do not, I will tell every human in this village the truth about you. That you are dead. That you have no heart."

"Skade." Arenadd grabbed her hand. "Skade, don't do that. Stop it. What's wrong with you?"

"Do not touch me!" she snarled, pulling herself free. "I hate you! I should never have come here with you, *human*, you heartless murderer, you blackrobe, you filth of the void!"

Arenadd jerked backward, as if she had slapped him. "Skade!"

But Skade's anger vanished almost as abruptly as it had appeared. She shied away from him further and began to sob. "Leave me," she moaned when he tried to touch her. "Leave me. Go away, Arenadd. Fly to your mountains and never return. I do not want to see your face again."

Arenadd managed to put his arm around her shoulder, and pulled her toward him. She made another quick effort to break away, but finally gave in and pressed herself against him, crying into his chest.

Arenadd held her and did his best to comfort her, murmuring and stroking her hair until she finally calmed down. But she made no further attempts to push him away. He could feel her heart beating against his chest, and the sensation made his throat ache as if he was going to cry as well.

"What is it, Skade?" he said. "What's wrong? Why are you acting like this? Can you tell me?"

"I do not understand," she said, her voice muffled. "Arenadd, I do not feel well. I think there is something wrong with me."

"What do you mean? Are you sick?"

"I do not know. I have never felt like this before. Last night, when I knew that you were leaving, I was angry with you. But after that, when I thought of how it would be if you were gone, I did not know how I felt. I hated you for going, I hated Skandar for taking you from me, but I wanted you to go so that I would not feel this way—this confusion, this fear, this . . . sickness."

Arenadd sighed. "Oh, Skade."

She didn't seem to hear him. She spoke on for a long time, trying to explain thoughts and emotions that were completely unfamiliar to her, things that were alien to a griffin's mind but which Arenadd recognised and understood almost immediately.

"Skade," he said when she finally fell silent again. "Skade, you're not sick. You're just—you don't want me to go, you want me to stay with you, and it's upset you, that's all."

Skade lifted her face away from his chest; it was reddened and tear stained. "But why? You are not my mate now, or my chick, or my sibling. I should have no attachment to you, so why do I feel that losing you would kill me?"

"Because . . ." Arenadd took her hand in his and held it. "Because . . ."

"Why?" said Skade. "You must tell me."

"Because you love me," said Arenadd.

She stared at him.

"Listen," said Arenadd. "You remember the cave, don't you? You remember what I said to you then? You said you had to go, and I begged you not to. I said I wanted you to stay with me forever."

Skade's eyes widened. "You were afraid that you would not see me again."

"Yes." Arenadd put his other hand over hers. "What you're feeling now is what I was feeling then. Do you understand, Skade?"

"I . . . think so. But what does it mean?"

"You're human now," said Arenadd. "Completely human. You're feeling human emotions, and you understand what love feels like. Human love."

"Arenadd, what shall I do?" said Skade. "What shall *we* do? If you are leaving . . ."

Arenadd chuckled. "You're feeling human emotions, but

you don't understand all of them yet, do you? Listen to me." He gripped her hand. "I still love you, Skade. That's why I let you come with me and looked after you when you needed me to. And that means that I would never abandon you—not for anything. I don't care what Skandar wants; I am never going to stop loving you or wanting to be with you. And you don't have to threaten me to make me feel that way."

"So you will come back?" said Skade.

"Yes, Skade, I will. I'll find a way to be with you, I swear. And I know we'll be together."

"How?" said Skade.

Arenadd touched his chest. "This told me. My heart. When you kissed me and it beat—I'm certain it was trying to tell me something. If you can make my heart come back, then you and I were meant to be. Maybe that's not true, but I believe it, and that's all that matters."

Skade smiled and placed her hand on his chest, over his heart. "It will come back. One day it will beat again. We will find a way."

Arenadd kissed her lightly on the lips. "We will. D'you know why?"

She touched his cheek. "No, why?"

"Because together you and I can do anything," said Arenadd.

They kissed again after that. This time, it lasted much longer.

31

Taranis' Throne

Arenadd left Skade in Saeddryn's house, with plenty of food and promises. The two of them shared a long embrace before he got onto Skandar's back, and the black griffin flew away.

Arenadd watched Skade become smaller and smaller the further Skandar flew, until she was nothing but a tiny spot among a cluster of larger spots that was the village. Then Skandar cleared the mountain, and she was gone altogether.

But I'll see her again, Arenadd promised himself.

Skandar reached soaring altitude and beat his wings hard so that he shot forward and went swooping out over the mountains in a great rush of wind. The mountains sped past below them: huge craggy peaks capped with snow, dark rock showing beneath. They were taller than the Northgates, taller than the Coppertops where the griffin had hatched, and far more hostile. They were huge and wild and stretched out into the distance, mighty peaks below and endless skies above, just as Arenadd had described.

Skandar opened his beak and began to screech as he had not done in months. *"Skandar! Skandar! Skandar! Darkheart! Skandar! Darkheart!"*

Caught up in the moment, he flew so fast that he reached the plateau and the circle in barely any time. But instead of coming in to land he began to fly around the mountains that surrounded it, going from peak to peak and continuing to call.

Arenadd, clinging on and sensing the exhilaration his friend must be feeling, knew that Skandar was doing what every wild griffin did. He was staking out a territory, choosing its borders and announcing himself to any other griffin who might be in the area. This place was his now, and gods have mercy on anyone who dared to invade it.

When he was done he finally began his descent, down toward the stone circle, choosing to land outside it among some trees.

Arenadd got off his back, landing ankle-deep in snow. "Damn!" He looked around at the trees. "This is your new home. What do you think, Skandar?"

Skandar clicked his beak. "Home, human, good home," he said warmly.

"Is it what you were hoping for?" said Arenadd.

Skandar took a moment to digest this. "Yes. Big mountain, big sky. You say right."

"Of course I did," said Arenadd. "Would I lie to you? I told you I'd show you the way to mountains, and I did. They're all yours. You can make a nest and fly wherever you want, and no-one will ever bother you."

"Yes, nest," said Skandar. "Look for nest now, good nest."

"We should find Saeddryn first, though," said Arenadd.

Skandar started up at that. "Human here?"

"Yes, she's here to meet us," said Arenadd. "Don't worry; she won't stay. She just wants to tell us about this place."

"Not want," said Skandar, instantly resentful.

"Well," said Arenadd, "do you want to go and look at the stones now?"

Skandar dipped his head. "Yes. Go look."

"It's this way," said Arenadd, and he began to walk in that direction, inwardly congratulating himself on his strategy.

Skandar walked beside him. "I see stones before," he said. "Strange."

"They are strange, aren't they?" said Arenadd. "Humans put them there. They're holy places for my people."

"You worship Night Eye," said Skandar.

"That's right. They—we go to the stones to worship. But I've never seen a circle like this one before."

They crested the hill, and the stones came into sight beyond the edge of the trees. Arenadd felt his excitement grow as he saw them, and sped up, heedless of the snow sloshing around his boots. He passed out of the trees and reached the edge of the circle, and there he stopped. Skandar caught up with him but showed no inclination to go inside the circle, instead approaching the nearest stone and tapping it with his beak.

Arenadd joined him. The stone was taller than him, much bigger than he had expected, and flatter than it had looked from above, too. The side facing him was covered in intricate spiral patterns, and he traced them with his fingers, fascinated.

"It must have been here for hundreds of years," he said. "See how weathered the carvings are? And just think, people must have cut and dragged them all the way up here without using wagons or oxen—you'd never get them up here, it's just too rugged. Isn't that amazing?"

Skandar yawned. "Rocks."

"Well, yes, but—" Arenadd gave up and turned to examine the circle as a whole, marvelling at its size. In the centre there was a raised mound, partly buried in snow, but it looked like a large stone block, probably an altar of some kind. He thought of going to have a closer look, but decided against it. If someone saw him in there, he would be in trouble.

Beside him, Skandar tensed abruptly and his tail began to swish from side to side.

"What is it?"

"Human," the griffin hissed. "Human, see, there."

Arenadd followed his gaze, and saw someone emerging from the trees. The figure was wrapped in furs, but he recognised the walk.

"Don't worry, it's just Saeddryn," he said. "Calm down, Skandar, she won't stay for long."

His words did very little to placate Skandar; he walked stiffly with his wings half-raised, and made a sudden rush at Saeddryn as soon as she was close enough. Most people would have run, but she stood her ground and drew her sword, and Skandar turned away at the last moment.

"Be calm!" Saeddryn snapped, in griffish. "I am a friend."

Skandar placed himself between her and Arenadd. "Mine! You, go! Mine!"

"I'm sorry," said Arenadd, stepping to the side in order to look past him. "Skandar has decided this is his territory now."

"It doesn't matter," Saeddryn said stiffly. "I've done all I needed to. They know ye're here; I've sent word. They're comin' now."

Arenadd tensed at once. "Who are?"

"The ones who own this place," said Saeddryn. "Don't try an' run, either of ye; ye'll get nowhere. While ye're here, ye'll do as they tell ye an' nothin' else, understand? If ye attack or run, or do anythin' ye ain't supposed to, ye'll be killed."

Arenadd drew his sword. "*Who* is coming?" he said. "Answer me now."

Saeddryn pointed at the sky, and in that instant a screech came echoing down from off the mountains. Skandar and Arenadd both turned, and Skandar began to screech and hiss, his wings opening wide and his feathers fluffing themselves up so that he appeared to double in size. *"Mine!"* he screamed yet again.

Beside him, Arenadd's insides twisted with terror as he saw the very thing he had dreaded for months, ever since he had fled from Eagleholm: the dark shape of a griffin, flying straight toward them.

"Oh holy *gods*. Skandar!"

Too late. Skandar made a stumbling rush forward and leapt into the air, flying straight at the other griffin and screeching at the top of his lungs. The other griffin turned sharply to avoid him, but he wheeled after it with astonishing speed and attacked.

Arenadd didn't see the two griffins actually meet, but within moments of the attack Skandar jerked in midair and dropped, falling head downward with his wings flailing ineffectually before they managed to open partway and slow him down a little. He hit the ground just outside the circle, sending up a shower of snow, and as Arenadd ran toward him the other griffin came down to land in the way.

As Skandar struggled to rise, the other griffin ran at him. He managed to regain his paws and reared up to attack, but then he reeled backward, grabbing at the air, and collapsed on his side, as if he had been hit by something. The other griffin did not attack but stood over him as he continued to struggle against some unseen force. It was plainly a losing battle. Finally, after being knocked down yet again by whatever was hurting him, Skandar lay down in the snow and made no further attempts to rise.

Arenadd acted quickly. He raised his sword and made a silent run toward the strange griffin, intent on its unguarded back. If he could disable it, then Skandar would be freed from whatever magic it was using on him and could finish it off in moments.

He reached the griffin and brought the sword down as hard as he could on its back legs. The moment the blade struck home, pain lanced through his hands. He screamed, and the sword went flying, spinning away into the snow. Before he could make another move, something hit him in the chest and he was flicked backward, tumbling like a leaf caught in a gale.

He landed on his back in the snow and lay there, stunned. The snow soaking into his robe helped to clear his head, and he began trying to get up, but his limbs had gone numb and clumsy and refused to move.

He heard a crunching sound from somewhere to his left, and a sword point was pressed into his neck. "Don't ye move, blackrobe," a voice rasped.

Arenadd coughed. "K-kill me now. Don't take me back to Malvern; just kill me."

The sword point was withdrawn, and a hand grabbed hold of his. "Shut up an' get up, ye damned fool."

Arenadd managed to stand. "Godsdamnit. Where's Skandar? Please, let him go. If you're going to take me to Malvern—"

"Malvern?" the voice repeated; it was dry, elderly and female. "Malvern my arse. Are ye Arenadd Taranisäii?"

Arenadd's vision cleared, and he looked at his captor properly: an old woman, her hair faded to dark grey shot through with white. It had blown over her face, but as she flicked it back behind her ear he recoiled. One eye was sharp and black. The other was lost in the middle of an enormous scar that cut through her face from her forehead to her jaw. It was old and gnarled, almost certainly inflicted by a sword blow, which had crushed the bridge of her nose and given one side of her mouth a permanent sneer.

"Who are *you*?" he said, without even thinking.

The sneer twisted even further. "Ask me questions ye ain't answered an' I'll see ye buried alive, blackrobe. What's yer name an' where are ye from?"

Arenadd bowed. "I'm sorry. My name's Arenadd Taranisäii."

"Son of who?" the old woman asked instantly.

"Uh, Cardock."

"An' grandson of who?"

"Skandar Taranisäii."

The part of her face that was still capable of it softened. "Skandar, ye say? Born where?"

"Malvern. He died in Eagleholm."

The woman moved closer. "When? How?"

"Only a year or so after he got there."

"An' his son?"

"Only a boy then. He grew up with the other slaves and was set free when he was ten, when they were all sold or freed. He married a woman called Annir."

"An' where is he now?" said the woman.

Moving slowly and carefully, Arenadd reached into his robe and brought out the urn.

"How did he die?" the woman asked.

"He was killed at Guard's Post," said Arenadd, putting the urn back in his robe. "When a group of slaves captured it."

She cocked her head. "Slaves? At Guard's Post? How?"

"They escaped from Herbstitt," said Arenadd. "Someone set them free and took them to the North. They captured Guard's Post along the way, and then their leader took their collars off and let them go."

"Leader? What leader?"

"It was me," said Arenadd. "There was a man with the slaves; his name was Caedmon Taranisäii. I set him free and he told me to go to Eitheinn and say he sent me."

The woman nodded. "So ye are Arenadd Taranisäii."

"Yes."

"Ye are the one who murdered Lord Rannagon Raegonson, at Eagleholm," said the woman.

"I am," said Arenadd.

"Can ye prove it?" said the woman.

"Yes. My sword. It's his sword. I think it landed over there somewhere."

The woman glowered at him and limped away to look for it. A short distance away, Skandar was crouched at the talons of the woman's partner, hissing but intimidated into staying still.

The woman found the sword and pulled it out of the snow, lifting it with evident difficulty. She was very thin, but there was a wiry strength about her in spite of her great age.

Arenadd went to her and helped her lift the sword. "See? That's his name, engraved there just below the hilt."

She waved him away and examined the sword herself, running her fingers over the hilt and then the blade, testing its edge with her thumb. "His sword," she muttered. "Then he is dead."

Arenadd knew by now that she wasn't an enemy. "I killed

him with a broken sword," he said, astonished by the steadiness in his own voice. "Skandar fought Shoa and killed her, and I killed Rannagon. I stabbed him in the throat with the sword, and he died at my feet."

The sword fell out of the woman's hands, and without a word she spun around and punched him in the jaw.

The blow was surprisingly strong, and so unexpected that Arenadd staggered and nearly fell. "What—?"

The woman pointed at him. "That was for stealin' from me."

"What? I haven't—"

She touched the scar on her face. "Sixteen years I waited. Sixteen years, swearin' that one day I'd kill him for what he done. Sixteen years of seein' his face every night an' swearin' with my whole soul he'd die for what he did to mine."

Arenadd bent and picked up his sword. "This sword did that to you?"

"Did that, an' took the lives of dozens of the best warriors who ever drew breath, aye. An' now I find ye stole my revenge from me, Arenadd Taranisäii." She snarled to herself. "Still, it had to be done, an' I'm happy knowin' it were a Taranisäii what done it. An' I'm grateful ye came to tell me yerself, Arenadd."

Arenadd rubbed his jaw. "I'm sorry, but who *are* you?"

She snorted and began to walk toward her griffin. "Who d'ye think I am, ye brick-headed Southerner? I'm Arddryn Taranisäii. Saeddryn's mother."

Arenadd followed her. "You're supposed to be dead!"

"Bah. I'm as good as. Rannagon cut my face so bad it near killed me, an' I'm too old an' sick t'fight now."

The griffin standing over Skandar turned to look at her partner. She was younger than Arddryn, middle-aged by griffish standards. She was thickset and compact, with mottled brown feathers and white patches on her face and wings. Her hindquarters were ash grey and her tail feathers white.

Arenadd bowed to her before he looked at Skandar. "Is he all right?"

The brown griffin yawned and sat back on her haunches. "I have not hurt him."

"Skandar." Arenadd went to him and touched his head. "Skandar, are you hurt?"

Skandar finally managed to stand, though he staggered a little. "Not hurt, human."

"Good. Now be respectful. This griffin is much older than you, and more powerful."

Skandar glared at the brown griffin. "My territory," he hissed. "You go, or die."

She hissed back. "This land is mine, dark griffin. I own it, and I will kill anyone who tries to take it from me. If you attack, I will use my magic on you again. If I want to, I can crush your bones."

"Easy, Skandar," said Arenadd. "We don't have to fight. They're friends."

"Not have, not want," said Skandar, but he had the sense to keep still and lower his beak toward the other griffin.

She looked satisfied. "So you are Arenadd Taranisäii," she said. "The grandson of Skandar."

"Yes," said Arenadd. "And you?"

"I am Hyrenna, and you are welcome in my territory. Tell me"—she looked at Skandar—"I am curious. How did you come to have the same name as your partner's grandsire, Skandar?"

Skandar only stared at her.

"He didn't have a name when I met him," said Arenadd. "So I named him."

Hyrenna cocked her head, much like Arddryn before her. "No name? Why?"

Arenadd explained.

"Ah," said Hyrenna. "So, Skandar, have you discovered your magic?"

"Not have," Skandar muttered.

"He hasn't," said Arenadd, lying.

"Then I shall teach you," said Hyrenna.

"Teach?" said Skandar.

"Yes." Hyrenna moved closer to him and nibbled at the top of his head. "I have been waiting for you, Skandar, for a long time. There is something I want from you. If you do as I ask, then I will let you stay in my territory and I will teach you everything your mother would have taught you if she had lived. You will learn how to discover your magic, and to use it."

Skandar began to sniff at her. "What want?"

Hyrenna brought her head close to his and began to speak in rapid griffish, too fast for Arenadd to follow properly, though he caught snatches of it.

". . . need . . ."

". . . not understand . . ."

". . . everything you want . . ."

". . . yellow, sun, want . . ."

". . . go, go, fly now . . ."

Then the two griffins began to make odd chirping and trilling noises, and went into a frenzy of sniffing and nuzzling, pawing and pushing at each other, as if they were wrestling. They lifted their beaks high and pressed their bodies together, chest to chest, and rose onto their hind legs to shove back and forth, paws scuffing in the snow. The two humans moved away and watched them until Skandar broke away and looked at them. "Human?"

Hyrenna bit at the nape of his neck. "My human shall look after him. Come, now. We shall find them again later."

That seemed to satisfy Skandar. The big griffin took to the air in a flurry of wings; Hyrenna inclined her head briefly toward Arenadd and Arddryn, and flew up to join him.

"Where are they going?" said Arenadd.

"Don't worry, they'll be back 'fore night," said Arddryn. "Leaves ye an' me t'talk."

"Yes, but where are they going?"

"Don't ask me. Somewhere in the mountains. Hyrenna'll have the place picked out by now, f'sure."

Arenadd watched the two dark shapes circle above, drifting away toward the mountains further north. "How did she do that? I've never seen Skandar obey someone like that before. I can get him to do things sometimes, but I always have to spend half a day arguing with him first."

Arddryn cackled. "Hyrenna knows some good methods of persuasion, I reckon. When it comes to males, ev'ry female does."

Arenadd blinked. "What, they're not—?"

"Aye, matin'," Arddryn said carelessly. "Been a long time, it has."

Everything fell into place in an instant, and Arenadd wanted to slap himself. "Ah. Of course. I didn't know even griffins could be that fast, though."

"When ye're in Hyrenna's situation, there's no such thing as too fast," said Arddryn. "It's been twenty-odd years since she's seen another griffin, an' she's gettin' old an' hasn't had chicks. She wants 'em. We both do."

Arenadd nodded. "I think I understand. More griffins here means there could be more griffiners one day—on your side. Am I right?"

"Aye. Ye know what's goin' on, right enough. I don't want t'be the last griffiner among the darkmen." She shivered. "Now, come. Come. The camp ain't far from here, an' I ain't wantin' t'stay out here too long. Come, I'll show ye the way."

Arenadd walked beside her. "You're not thinking of restarting that rebellion, are you?"

Arddryn gave him a sharp look. "Why d'ye ask, Arenadd?"

"Well, why else would you want more griffiners on your side? It's obvious."

"Then why d'ye even need t'ask, if it's obvious?" said Arddryn.

Arenadd, choosing his words with care, said, "The last rebellion failed, didn't it? Hundreds of people died. How many eggs does a griffin lay in one clutch? Three? Four? Even if every one of the chicks survived and then chose humans, you'd have three or four griffiners. How many are there at Malvern? Fifty? A hundred?"

"Griffiners ain't immortal," said Arddryn. "Ye should know that better than most, Arenadd."

"What difference does that make? You're outnumbered. They've got all the advantages. You've seen how they fight. You know the weapons they can use. Fire-jars, burning water, shooting stars. And magic. Who knows what powers some of those griffins might have?"

"Ye're blunt," said Arddryn. "I like that. But tell me"—she stumbled on a stray root but recovered herself and ignored his proffered arm—"how many griffiners were in the Eyrie at Eagleholm?"

"I think about fifty," said Arenadd. "Not including the ones who lived in the city."

"An' how many are there of ye?" said Arddryn. "One. Two. Ye and Skandar. No followers, no magic, no weapons but a broken sword an' a set of talons, an' what did ye do between ye, in one night? Saeddryn told me the story. The whole Eyrie destroyed, by ye and Skandar alone."

I didn't mean to do it, Arenadd thought, but he knew he couldn't say it out loud. "Yes, but—"

She waved him into silence. "D'ye know what that tells me?"

"Not really."

Saeddryn appeared. "That even one darkman is worth a hundred Southerners, griffiners an' otherwise," she said. "Hello, Mother."

Arddryn leant on her daughter's arm. "Well said, Saeddryn. Now, Arenadd, d'ye understand?"

"I suppose so."

She caught the sceptical tone and prodded him painfully in the ribs. "We're warriors, boy, an' we weren't meant t'be vassals, not in our own land or anywhere else. We were the chosen of the Night God, an' we're the ones what understands her power an' her mystery. She gave us this land t'be our home, an' we're its guardians until the end of time. The Southerners came here, they defiled the holy places an' knocked down the stones, an' they raised their temples to their false gods an' forced us to forget our ways an' our tongue. We must fight back. For us, an' for the Night God."

Arenadd felt humbled. "What do you want from me?"

Arddryn gave him a look. "What d'ye mean, what do I want? Ye've given me what I want; ye've given all of us what we want."

"Look, killing Lord Rannagon wasn't about—"

"We've been waitin' for ye," Arddryn interrupted.

"That we have," said Saeddryn. "We all have."

Arddryn nodded. "We take in fugitives here," she said. "Thieves, murderers, runaway slaves—any darkman who wants shelter an' protection, we take. But they're no army. We can't fight against Malvern unless somethin' unites every village and town in Tara. Somethin'—or someone."

"What, *me*?" said Arenadd. He tried to laugh. "Look, you've got the wrong idea. If you think I've come here to unite the tribes and fight Malvern and be a big hero, think again. I'm not a rebel; for gods' sakes, I wasn't even born here."

Arddryn looked steadily at him. "Ye're a leader, an' ye're a rebel, whether ye call yerself one or not. Didn't ye set the slaves free? Didn't ye destroy Eagleholm an' kill Lord Rannagon with yer own hands? Didn't ye lead a bunch of slaves against trained soldiers an' win? Didn't ye come here t'find us?"

Arenadd stopped. "Now listen," he said. "I didn't do those things for you, understand? I did those things for myself. I'm not a hero. I'm a selfish bastard. I killed Lord Rannagon in front of his son and daughter, and I did it to avenge myself, not you. I set the Eyrie on fire to help my own escape. I stole the slaves from Herbstitt out of spite, and I captured Guard's Post so I could steal the supplies I needed. I set the slaves free because I didn't want to take responsibility for them. And I came here because I wanted to hide. I was looking out for myself. I didn't even know you were here. Understand? I'm not here to help you. I'm here because I'm a criminal. That's all."

Saeddryn looked shocked. Arddryn only gave him a steady look. "But ye want to stay here?"

"If I can, yes. If you want me to leave, I will. But I'm not interested in fighting."

"An' ye want to be one of us?" said Arddryn.

"I already am," said Arenadd.

"Ye ain't," said Arddryn. "Ye're Northern by blood, but that's all. Ye never passed into manhood our way, did ye— never offered yerself to the Night God?"

"No."

"An' do ye want to?"

Arenadd hesitated. "I don't know. What would I have to do?"

Arddryn began to walk again. "In three months, it'll be the time of the Blood Moon. A sacred time. Some of us will go to the circle for the ceremony. The Blood Moon is a time t'honour the dead, and for initiation. If ye come an' take part ye'll be made one of us, through an' through. The moon'll touch ye, give ye protection an' insight an' blessing."

Arenadd reached into his robe to touch the urn. "So my father—"

"Aye, ye could bring yer father's ashes t'be honoured. An' ye would pass into manhood as well. It'd make yer father proud."

"In three months, you say?"

Arddryn nodded. "Three months an' three days."

"I'll do it," said Arenadd.

"Good. Thank ye, Arenadd. We'd be honoured t'have ye there."

They had climbed down the side of the plateau while they talked, following a path so narrow it looked like nothing more than an animal trail. Arddryn walked it without faltering, only intermittently relying on Saeddryn to help her. Arenadd, following them both, was impressed. The old warrior had to be at least seventy—probably older—but she carried herself like someone much younger. He realised that he was glad to have met her, and humbled as well. Even if she wanted things from him that he wasn't prepared to give, he would be happy to stay here in her land and learn what she had to teach.

The trail led through a narrow valley for a while, then descended and passed through a maze of tumbled stones, into a canyon that was nearly round. Trees and ferns had sprouted from the cliff sides, and the floor was covered with what looked like large boulders or heaps of dead branches. From the air they would be barely visible and far from noteworthy, but when Arenadd entered the canyon and looked closer he realised what they were: dozens of hide-covered lean-tos erected among the rocks and then disguised with branches and snow.

People began to appear almost as soon as Arddryn arrived: men and women emerging as if by magic from the undergrowth, all tough and weather-beaten, clad in skins, their faces tattooed with spirals and their hair decorated with bones and copper beads. Most of them had weapons, and all of them looked lean and wild and wary.

They crowded toward their leader, calling out to her in the Northern language, some calling her "my lady," others addressing her with a title he'd never heard before, something that sounded like "holy woman."

Arddryn nodded briefly to them and gestured for Arenadd to come forward. "Let them see ye," she said, speaking the Northern tongue.

Arenadd came to stand by her left side, leaving Saeddryn on the right. His palms were sweaty, and he wiped them on his robe before bowing to the tribe. "Hello," he said, speaking their language as well as he could, but wincing inwardly at how slow and clumsy it sounded. "I'm honoured to be here," he added.

They cast scornful looks at him.

"Who are ye?" said one, making an aggressive move toward him. "Slave, are ye?"

Arenadd straightened up. "I am Arenadd Taranisäii of the Wolf Tribe."

They faltered at that, and a muttering arose from them as they looked at Arddryn.

She nodded. "Aye, this is Arenadd Taranisäii. My nephew, an' a brave warrior. He's to become one of us, so make him welcome."

"Taranisäii?" said one. "How? Where'd he come from?"

"My mother's womb," Arenadd shot back. "Why, where did *you* come from?"

Several of them laughed, and some of the tension went out of the atmosphere.

"Good," said Arddryn. "Now get back to where ye were before. Arenadd must come with me, an' ye can talk to him later." They dispersed, albeit reluctantly, and Arddryn paid no further attention to them. "Ye should be goin' too, Saeddryn, if ye want t'be home before dark."

Saeddryn looked unhappy. "Yes, Mother. Is there anythin' ye'd like me to tell the village?"

Arddryn shook her head. "The less they know the better. Ye ain't told anybody about who's come here t'join us, have ye?"

"No. Some of them saw the griffin, though; there was nothin' I could do about that."

Arddryn looked annoyed. "Damn ye, boy, did ye have t'fly straight into the village for all t'see? I thought ye had more sense."

"I didn't," said Arenadd. "Saeddryn brought me into the village and Skandar followed. How was I supposed to stop him? Smuggling a griffin through a village isn't something I've ever had to do before."

"Can't be helped," said Arddryn. "Swear 'em t'secrecy, Saeddryn; find out who knows, an' keep 'em quiet. Give 'em whatever they ask. There's not much chance they'll ever be questioned, but it pays t'be cautious." ·

"Yes, Mother." Saeddryn hugged her quickly and took Arenadd by surprise by pausing to hug him, too.

She kissed him on the cheek, on the scar. "I'm glad ye came, Arenadd," she whispered in his ear, then she let go and walked away.

Arddryn looked after her and smiled a twisted kind of smile. "She's a good girl, my Saeddryn."

Arenadd touched the spot on his cheek where she'd kissed him. "She's not weak, I'll give her that. She certainly watches over that village carefully; I got about seven paces into it before she kicked me over and shoved a sword into my neck."

"She knows how t'deal with intruders," said Arddryn. "We all do. Now come with me."

She led him through the settlement to the far end of the

canyon and pulled some bushes aside to reveal a tiny passage-way leading out of it.

"We don't use this much," she said. "It leads t'my camp, an' normally Hyrenna an' I fly in."

If anything this path was even more narrow and disused than the last one. Arenadd waded through shoulder-high bracken encrusted with snow, which quickly soaked through his robe and left cuts and scratches on his hands.

"Is it much further?" he asked eventually, reverting to Cymrian.

"Ye'll speak yer own language while ye're in my camp, or I'll pretend ye never spoke at all," said Arddryn, without looking back at him.

Arenadd swore as he stumbled on a hidden stone. "I don't speak it very well."

"So I noticed. I'll teach ye. Come, hurry up, it's not far."

Arenadd quickly decided she had been underestimating: the trip through the wet branches seemed to go on forever before the path finally widened and they entered Arddryn's camp. It would be difficult to call it a camp, however. It was simply a slightly wider spot in the pass the canyon had led into. A heap of charcoal inside a ring of stones served as a fireplace, but there was no sign of a shelter anywhere.

"This way," said Arddryn, indicating a heap of rocks at the base of the cliff, behind the fireplace. At first glance it looked like nothing more than that, but when they had rounded it Arenadd saw a gap between it and the cliff, with darkness beyond.

"My home," said Arddryn. "Come, see for yerself."

She squeezed through the hole, and Arenadd followed. It led to a cave, its ceiling high enough for them to stand upright. Light filtered in through a hole in the roof, and the interior was surprisingly comfortable: the walls had been scrubbed clean and carved with odd symbols and spiral patterns, and the floor was covered in dry grass. A heap of skins lay against one wall to serve as a bed, and there were some pots and baskets of food stacked in a corner.

Arddryn sat down cross-legged on the bed. "It ain't much, but it serves. Sit down, why don't ye. D'ye want somethin' t'eat?"

"Yes, thank you."

"There's dried meat in that basket," said Arddryn. "Get some for me while ye're at it."

They sat together and chewed at the smoked venison.

"So," said Arenadd. "You've lived here ever since the war?"

"Aye, more or less. This was a hidin' place for me after I left Malvern. The griffiners defeated us at Tor Plain. There was a village there. Ain't there now, not any more. Rannagon did this t'me face, an' Hyrenna carried me away back here. I stayed in this cave a long time, half-dead, thinkin' everyone else was gone. But they started comin' back. Just a few who'd survived. Came to Eitheinn, then to the Throne, hopin' t'find me. Found the cave in the end, too, an' me inside it, an' that's when I found out my baby daughter was alive. I raised her here till she was old enough to go an' live in the village. She wanted t'stay here, of course, but I wouldn't hear of it. Why should she spend her life in some tiny cave? No-one knew her name or what she looked like, so she could live in a house an' have proper food. It's what she deserved.

"You're a good mother," Arenadd said politely.

Arddryn gave another ghastly smile. "Thank ye." They finished eating, and she stood up and dusted herself down. "Shall we go outside? I fancy seein' the sky."

They went outside and both examined the sky. There was no sign of a griffin up there.

"When d'you think they'll get back?" said Arenadd, uncomfortably aware that it would start to get dark soon.

"Oh, before night," said Arddryn. "It's nothin' t'be worried about."

"It's just that I don't want to be here too late," said Arenadd. "We've still got to fly back to the village."

"There's no need," said Arddryn. "Ye're welcome t'share my cave, or ye can have a shelter back in the gorge with the rest."

"Thank you, but I'd really rather go back to Eitheinn."

Arddryn shook her head. "You ain't goin' nowhere."

Arenadd tensed at once. "What? Why?"

"Don't be an idiot," Arddryn snapped. "What, d'ye think ye can go flyin' back into the village just as ye please? Ye think people won't notice? Ye should be thankin' the moon ye weren't spotted on t'way here as it is. Anyway, there's no need for ye t'be there. This is yer home now. Ye've got t'stay by me these next three months, too. The Blood Moon ceremony ain't somethin' what just happens. There's things ye must know first, things I have t'teach ye, understand? Everythin' ye should've learnt when ye was a boy. Ye've got hard work ahead of ye."

"Three—? Look, Arddryn, please—it's not that I don't want to stay," Arenadd lied. "But I left someone behind in the village. I promised I'd be back. I can't just vanish."

"Someone?" said Arddryn. "What someone?"

"Her name's Skade. She's my friend; I brought her with me."

"Don't worry about her," said Arddryn. "Saeddryn can look after her."

"I promised her I'd be back with her soon," said Arenadd. "If I don't, she'll be—I can't do that to her."

"Why, are ye married to her?"

"Well, no—"

"Then it doesn't matter," said Arddryn. "Ye've pledged yerself to me, an' now ye'll do as I say. She can wait for ye."

"Can I at least send a message to her?" said Arenadd.

"Maybe, if someone visits from t'village," said Arddryn. "Worry about it another time. Now come with me. I got somethin' t'show ye."

She limped toward a large clump of bushes over by the opposite side of the pass, and as they approached, Arenadd saw them quiver. A strange sound came from within.

"What's in there?" he said.

"This," said Arddryn, and pulled the bushes aside to reveal a griffin. It was a scrawny-looking brown male, lying on his stomach with his legs folded beneath him. As the bush was pulled away and sunlight hit his eyes, he lifted his head and made a horrible groaning noise through a beak that had been tightly bound shut.

Arenadd stood back, seeing the ropes around the griffin's wings. "What in the gods' names—?"

"This one flew into the circle a few weeks back," said Arddryn. "Some of our men caught him up there with his human an' another griffin with a partner."

"Oh no. What happened?"

Arddryn looked disgusted and shoved the bushes back into place. "Ouen, curse his hide. Griffiners come up here sometimes, t'hunt. We hide away from the bastards. But Ouen an' some of his friends were up there an' saw 'em inside the circle, an' decided t'go up there an' tell 'em t'clear off. Then Ouen decided to rob 'em as well, an' things got out of hand. They killed that griffin's human. Wounded the other, but he got away. The griffin went mad an' attacked. Killed most of Ouen's friends, but the idiots led him straight t'the hides. They tied him up an' then asked me what t'do—I ask ye, what am I supposed t'do with a griffin?"

"For gods' sakes, why don't you just kill him?" said Arenadd. "And if that other griffiner got away—"

"Calm down," said Arddryn. "They already came here. A few days after it happened. Group of griffiners flew into the circle an' searched around here. They never found us down here an' flew away before nightfall. Asked some questions in the village an' left it at that. I tell ye, that Elkin's losin' her touch."

"Well, you should still kill him," said Arenadd. "What use is he?"

Arddryn shrugged. "I say, never throw anythin' away. Dead he's useless. Alive, we could find a use f'him. Either way, leave him be f'now. I just wanted ye t'know he was here so ye wouldn't stumble on him by accident."

Arenadd tried not to think of the terrible dead look in the griffin's eyes. And he tried not to look at Arddryn either, at her deformed face, which made him feel sick.

Oh gods, he thought. *What have I got myself into now?*

32

The Hunt

Skandar didn't return that day, or the next. When he finally did, Arenadd immediately asked him to fly them out of the mountains and back to Eitheinn.

Skandar only gave him a blank stare.

"Skade," Arenadd tried to explain. "I have to get back to Skade, understand?"

"Not want leave," Skandar said at last. "Home now."

"But Skade—"

Hyrenna had been listening, and she came closer now. "You will not leave, Arenadd."

"I only want to go back to Eitheinn," he protested. "I can't just leave Skade there on her own; I have to see her, explain—"

"You will not leave," Hyrenna repeated. "Not until the Blood Moon has come and we give you permission."

"Human not leave," said Skandar. "Not need mate. Find new mate." Plainly, he was done with listening to Arenadd.

"Finish your learning," Hyrenna commanded. "Try to leave and I will hunt you down."

Arenadd shot her a venomous stare. "I've been imprisoned long enough, griffin, and nobody is making me stay." With that he got up and walked away.

Skandar bounded ahead of him and stood in his path. "Not go."

"Out of my way!"

"Not go. Stay."

Arenadd made several attempts to get past him, but Skandar was faster and eventually knocked him over with an angry snort.

"Stay!" the dark griffin ordered.

Arenadd gave up without saying anything and returned to his new home.

He'd been given a shelter to himself in the settlement in the canyon, which according to its inhabitants was called Taranis Gorge. It was tiny, just big enough for him to lie down in. He had to pile his possessions, such as they were, beside his feet. But it was cosy enough, in its own way, and warmer than he had expected.

He spent the first day settling in, but his lessons began almost immediately. Arddryn had ordered several of her followers to teach him different things. A man called Nerth began teaching him how to track and hunt animals, and a woman called Wynne showed him how to make a bow and arrows, while her sister Hafwen taught him about the properties of different herbs found in the mountains. And from Arddryn he began to learn all the Northern lore and legends she insisted were so important. He learnt the language from everyone, since he was forced to speak it all the time. If he ever used Cymrian he was ignored.

He stayed on the lookout for Saeddryn, but she never returned from the village, and he quickly saw that the settlement in Taranis Gorge was almost completely cut off from the outside world. Arddryn explained that they seldom left it and that their friends stationed in the village only came to visit very rarely, to bring supplies when times were rough or to carry important messages. As it was, Arenadd had no way of contacting Skade or even asking after her.

A day or so after his first attempt to leave he tried again. This time, he was more careful. He waited until nightfall and slipped out of the gorge, sneaking off through the snow as quietly as he could.

He didn't see Hyrenna or anyone else trying to follow him, but his attempt was foiled by the mountains themselves. The snow around the gorge was far deeper than he had expected. Before long he was soaking wet, chilled right through, and hopelessly lost. It took him half the night just to find the gorge again, and by the time he returned to his shelter the others were already getting up.

If anyone noticed his absence, none of them said anything. He suspected that Arddryn had guessed. Resentment simmered inside him, but he said nothing and did his best to at least take in what they were trying to teach him.

Life in the gorge was hard: food had to be gathered every day, and Nerth and a band of hunters devoted much of their time to hunting and trapping animals for skins. Arenadd went with them and by watching learnt most of the skills they used. He already knew how to tan the hides they gathered, which won him plenty of thanks and a little admiration. When he wasn't doing that he was helping his other teachers with their daily tasks and listening to everything they had to tell him.

On the evening of the fifth day, Arddryn's followers—twenty-two of them in all—gathered around a single fire to share their food and talk, and Arenadd was called upon to speak. He told the tale of Eluna's death and its consequences, and finished with a brief description of how he had escaped from prison and killed Lord Rannagon.

The Northerners listened, their faces unreadable. They were a silent, unemotional lot; Arenadd found himself worrying that he was saying the wrong thing. He wondered if he was anything like them. Old memories came back to him of the voices of his friends back at Eagleholm. Flell caressing his face and saying, "You should smile more, Arren. You're so solemn all the time!"

He shut that memory out.

". . . and Rannagon disarmed me and was going to kill me," he continued, "but I sent out a call, and Skandar came. He must have been looking for me. He stood between me and them, and he said 'Mine! Mine! My human! Mine!'—just that, over and over again. Then he attacked Shoa. After all that time he spent in the Arena, he'd learnt how to fight. He killed her, and I killed Rannagon a few moments later. He was distracted when he saw Shoa die, and I ran at him and stabbed him through the throat. That was how he died."

Arenadd wrapped his arms around his knees and looked at his audience. None of them had moved. "And that's about it, really," he added. "I took the sword, and Skandar and I flew away."

All of a sudden, Nerth began to laugh. "So that's how the mighty Lord Rannagon died, is it? Stabbed with a broken sword, by someone who'd never fought before?" He laughed even harder. "Lord Rannagon the mighty, killed by a broken sword! Hah!"

Some joined in the laughter, but others let out whoops and jeering. Half a dozen of them edged over to Arenadd and patted him on the shoulders, muttering to him.

"Thank ye, Arenadd, thank ye."

"We're honoured to have ye here, Arenadd."

"I'm glad to have met ye."

"Ye're the one we've waited for," said Wynne.

Being touched made Arenadd uncomfortable. "Thank you."

Once the camp had quietened down a little, he sat cross-legged and rested his chin on his hand, trying not to see all the admiring stares being directed at him.

Gods. Everywhere I go, people want something from me. Everyone wants me to be something.

"Some people think I'm a hero," he said aloud, not really meaning to.

"A hero is what ye are, Lord Arenadd," said Nerth. "An' don't ye think it's otherwise."

Arenadd sat back. "Some say I'm a hero, and some say I'm a villain. But—"

"Villain?" Wynne scoffed. "Ye killed a murderin' tyrant, brought him t'justice. Where's the villainy in that?"

Arenadd felt a sudden helpless anger go rushing through him. He stood up. "No," he said, so sharply that everyone stared at him. "I'm not a villain or a hero. I'm a human being. And that's all I want to be."

He stalked off to his own shelter.

He'd been provided with a simple bed of furs and a pillow stuffed with dry grass, and he got into bed and covered himself up. He stayed there, feeling both angry and embarrassed, hoping no-one would bother him.

They didn't, and he eventually drifted off to sleep.

That night he dreamt of Rannagon again, but this time he was in Skandar's body, looking out through his eyes. His shoulders were massive and powerful, and his fingers were long talons. He could feel his wings stirring on his back and his tail swishing behind him.

Rannagon pointed a sword at him. *Stay away from me!* he yelled, in Shoa's voice. *Kraeai kran ae!*

Arenadd felt no fear. He reared up and lashed out with his beak, and Rannagon fell, blood gushing from his throat. It was exactly the way it had been that night in the Eyrie, but this time there was no fire and no-one bursting through the door. Arenadd looked down at Rannagon's body and made a contented rasping sound deep in his chest. He could smell the blood and the flesh that contained it. The scents made his mouth water, and he tore into the food, ripping off great chunks and swallowing them. The taste of blood was like metal on his tongue, and he loved it.

Skandar returned at noon on the tenth day, appearing without warning as Arenadd was sitting outside Arddryn's cave, trying to fix a hole in his boot. He heard the sound of wings and looked up, and his face split into a smile when he saw Skandar coming in to land.

The griffin touched ground and strutted toward him. "Human!" he crowed.

Arenadd ran to him. "Skandar! There you are!"

Skandar rubbed his head against Arenadd's cheek. "Not leave! Always come back!"

"You sound cheerful," said Arenadd. "Where have you been?"

"Mating," Skandar told him, without embarrassment, "Hyrenna and I fly together, hunt together. Mate. Now I have had two females."

Arenadd laughed. "I'm sure you'll have more one day. Where's Hyrenna?"

"Coming," said Skandar. "She has been teaching me."

Arenadd stared at him. "You're speaking differently. How did that happen?"

"Hyrenna," said Skandar. "She make—makes—made me speak with her. Often. That make—makes me—made me speak better."

"What did you talk about?"

"Magic," said Skandar.

Arenadd tensed immediately. "She taught you how to use your magic?"

"I have magic," Skandar said proudly. "Powerful magic. You"—he shoved at Arenadd with his beak—"have no magic. You are human. Humans not have."

"I *told* you that," said Arenadd. "I told you *you* had magic. Do you know what it is now, Skandar? What's your power?"

Skandar backed off. "Not know," he said, reverting to his old curt tones. "Not tell."

"But do you know if you can help me?" said Arenadd. "Can

you—" He moved closer. "My heart. Can you make it beat again?"

"Not know," Skandar repeated.

A horrible thought occurred to Arenadd. "You didn't tell her, did you? You didn't tell Hyrenna about me, did you?"

Skandar looked away, and the awful apprehension rose up inside him.

"You didn't tell her, did you?" he said, more sharply. "Skandar—"

"Not tell," Skandar said at last.

"Good. You mustn't tell anyone, Skandar. No matter what happens. They can't know. Do you understand?"

Skandar looked upward. "Hyrenna."

Arenadd followed his gaze and saw the other griffin flying low over the camp. She landed neatly on top of the heap of rocks that hid Arddryn's cave, and leapt down to the ground from there. Skandar went to her and nuzzled her neck. She bit at his shoulders and half-playfully shoved at him until he moved, making those same high chirping sounds she had made before.

Arenadd waited politely until Hyrenna broke away and came toward him. He remembered his manners and bowed, hiding his anger toward her.

Hyrenna gave a quick yawn. "Greetings. Where is Arddryn?"

"In the cave, sleeping," said Arenadd. "Can I ask how your, uh, time away was?"

She dipped her head. "It was good for both of us. And how are you settling into your new home, Arenadd?"

"I think I'm learning a lot," he said shortly.

"Excellent. Now I am going to rest. Skandar, you should go and find a place to nest before it is too dark."

Skandar rasped his agreement and loped off to explore the area. By now the captive griffin had been moved into a make-shift cage hidden in the gorge, and Skandar began tearing up the bushes where he had been, looking for a hollow to lie in.

Hyrenna, meanwhile, chose a spot at the base of the rock heap, where there was some sunlight, and lay down.

Arenadd went to her. "Hyrenna?"

The griffin watched him serenely, looking for all the world like a giant house-cat curled up in front of a stove. "Yes, human?"

Arenadd glanced quickly at Skandar. "I hope you don't mind my asking, but did you and Skandar . . . ?"

"Yes." She flicked her tail and added quite calmly, "I am going to lay eggs."

Even though he had been half-expecting it, the revelation still took him aback. Eluna had died before ever choosing a mate, and as a result he'd never had any first-hand experience when it came to griffish mating habits. Since griffins could talk, it was easy to think of them as giant furred-and-feathered humans, but moments like this were a sharp reminder of how very un-humanlike they were. *Just like that,* he thought. *She saw him, decided she liked him, and half a moment later they're busy making eggs. Just like Skade did with me. Is that how they always do it?*

"My gods," he mumbled.

Hyrenna clicked her beak. "You should not be so embarrassed. Sit, rest."

Arenadd sat down not far from her head. "I'm sorry, I didn't mean—"

"You are human," she said kindly. "You do not mate the way we do."

"We do sometimes," said Arenadd, half to himself, "Trust me."

"And it is not a thing you should be ashamed of. Now tell me, how is Arddryn?"

"She's well," said Arenadd. "She's been teaching me how to read the spirals."

"As I expected her to," said Hyrenna. "For a very long time, she told me that if another Taranisäii ever came here she would teach him or her everything she knew."

"I don't think I understand why it's so important," said Arenadd. "Being a Taranisäii, I mean."

"It matters more than you think," said Hyrenna. "You know what the word means."

"Of the blood of Taranis. Of course I know. But we aren't actually descended from Taranis. Even if he existed it must have been more than five hundred years ago—there's no way of proving it, and anyway, hundreds of people could be related to him. I wouldn't be surprised if someone made the name up to impress people."

"But that does not matter," said Hyrenna. "The name of Taranis still means much to your people, Arenadd. To be a Taranisäii means that others will respect you and believe that you have a power others do not."

"I suppose so." *What does it matter?* Arenadd paused. "Hyrenna, I know griffins don't like to be asked, but—"

"You wish to ask me about magic?" said Hyrenna.

"Yes. I was wondering if Skandar had discovered his power yet. I asked him but he wouldn't tell me."

"That is not for you to know," said Hyrenna. "I instructed him not to tell you anything."

"I understand," said Arenadd. "But does he know what it is yet?"

"No. He is on the way, though. I will continue to teach him. When the time comes, he may tell you what his power is and you may see him use it—but that is for him to decide."

"Thank you for helping him," said Arenadd. "With his speech, too. I've been trying to help him learn, but he won't always listen to me. I think he likes to be monosyllabic just because it's easier."

"He is strong-willed," said Hyrenna.

"Oh yes."

Arenadd fiddled with his beard. "There's something else I wanted to ask you."

"Ask."

"This might sound a bit odd, but I've always wondered about it," said Arenadd, hoping he sounded casual enough.

"Yes?" said Hyrenna.

"Can people come back from the dead?"

Hyrenna gave him a silent yellow-eyed stare that lasted so long he began to wonder if he'd offended her in some way, or worse, given too much away.

Finally, the griffin stood up. "No. There is no magic that can do that."

"But if a griffin had the power—"

"It cannot be done," Hyrenna repeated. "The instant the heartbeat stops, the soul flees, never to return. There is no coming back, for man or griffin." She walked away, leaving Arenadd alone, full of a terrible, dark fear.

Almost without thinking, he put his hand to his neck and kept it there, breathing deeply. His skin was cold, his heart still and silent. Dead.

All of a sudden, he wanted to cry. He sat down on a rock, his head in his hands, and tried to fight off the tears aching in his throat. If Skandar could not help him, and the spirits had refused, what was left for him?

There must be a way. There has to be. There has to be.

The spirits had done more than torment him. Skade had told him they offered advice—what had they told him to do? *Go back to the North, blackrobe.* But they'd said more than that.

"My own pagan ways," he mumbled aloud. "Seek out the Night Eye. The moon."

He felt a little calmer then. The spirits had said to go to the North, and he had. And they had hinted that the Night God could help him. And why not? She was the god of his people, his own guardian, in a way. Her eye had been shining on him on the night of his death. Perhaps she had done something as well.

That was when he saw that he had to stay with Arddryn. *The ceremony,* he thought. *I have to be there. I have to see the Blood Moon; I have to be at the circle if that's when the moon is powerful. There's magic in the land. Magical places. If the stones are magical, then maybe they have the power. Maybe.*

33

The Blood Moon

After that night he stopped thinking of trying to leave. He stayed in the gorge and worked even harder to try to fit in and learn all Arddryn and her friends had to teach. Many of those living in the gorge were fighters: veterans from Arddryn's rebellion, or their offspring, who had been taught their parents' skills. They were happy to help him develop his skills in combat, armed and unarmed, and that was one area where he excelled.

As time passed, he knew that he was changing. He felt stronger, calmer, more confident, free now of the anxiety he had lived with for months on end. Now that he had enough to eat every day, he put some weight and muscle back on and began to take on the lean, wiry physique of the others in the gorge. He even began praying to the moon when it rose in the evening, muttering to it in the Northern tongue just as the others did, though he didn't know if he truly believed in it.

But if he was changing, it was nothing compared to what was happening to Skandar. The dark griffin returned to the gorge most nights, choosing to roost on the cliff top overlooking it, as Hyrenna did. He visited occasionally, but quickly became uninterested in Arenadd's daily life and took to spending most of his time rambling through the mountains doing whatever he chose. He often flew away with Hyrenna and didn't return for days on end, and Arenadd knew she was teaching him in much the same way as Arddryn was teaching his human.

Whatever Skandar was learning, it showed in him more and more as the weeks went by. He became calmer, more settled and peaceful in himself, free of the nervous tension he had once carried everywhere. His conversation became more complex, and he became, if not friendly, then at least no longer openly hostile toward humans.

With his company, and with the presence of the other Northerners who had begun treating him as one of their own, Arenadd began to feel more at home in the gorge. He stopped having nightmares. The lingering sense of guilt and shame over Eluna's death—and Rannagon's as well—began to leave him little by little.

Only one thing stopped him from completely accepting his new life, and that was Skade. Once the initial shock had worn off and he settled down in the gorge, he began to miss her. He found himself thinking about her constantly, wondering if she was safe and worrying that she wasn't, and agonising over what she might be going through while he was gone. Had Saeddryn explained what he was doing? Had she told Skade that he would be back, or that he would be gone forever?

If Skade thought he had abandoned her after all, what would she do? Would she come to try to find him, or leave Eitheinn? Or would she actually act on the wild threat she had made and tell Saeddryn about what he was? He didn't think she would. Even if she did, nobody would believe her—how could they? But he still wanted to see her again, more than anything else.

Saeddryn didn't come back to the gorge. He kept watching out for her, counting the days and hoping to see her, and even asked Arddryn if she was coming. Arddryn said it was unlikely she would visit before the Blood Moon, and looked oddly pleased about it.

Two months—two moons, as the Northerners put it—passed without any sign of her. The second full moon waned into the next month, and then began to wax once more. The Blood Moon was approaching. Arenadd watched the moon every night, noting the gradual increase in size. A crescent became a half-moon, and then began to swell outward into a perfect white globe.

Arenadd already knew the time had come when Arddryn woke him up one morning. "It's time. Come."

Arenadd crawled out of his shelter and found her waiting, clad in a heavy bearskin robe, with a strip of leather tied around her head to cover her ruined eye. She said nothing but beckoned him to follow her. Arenadd rubbed a handful of snow into his face to wake himself up, and obeyed. The others in the gorge must have been either absent or still asleep, because the entire settlement was deserted and silent. They walked through it and to Arddryn's cave via the track.

Inside, Arddryn gave him something to eat and sat down to light a small clay lamp.

"I'm sorry t'wake ye so early," she said. "But ye have to prepare. The Blood Moon is tonight, an' we have things t'do before."

"I understand," said Arenadd.

"Good. Come here." Arddryn stood up and motioned for him to come closer. "Look," she said, holding the lamp close to the wall so that shadows moved over the images carved there.

"What do they mean?"

Arddryn ran her fingers over them. "They're stories. Written in pictures. Look here. See? Here." She was indicating the figure of a human cut into the stone. It was clearly male, tall and clad in a long robe like Arenadd's own. "This is Taranis," said Arddryn. "King Taranis, our ancestor. Ye see here—the crown on his head? It was given to him by the moon itself, in the form of a woman. Aye, the one-eyed woman, the one Southerners call Scathach. She was our god, an' the moon is her eye. See her, here? There, that's her, givin' him the crown an' her blessin'."

Arenadd examined the carving. "I see."

"Ye've heard the tale of Taranis," said Arddryn. "We all have. But there's not many know the whole story, who Taranis really was an' why he could do what he did."

"He's a legend," said Arenadd. "People in legends can do anything. Some people even say he could fly."

"Oh, but he could," said Arddryn. "He could fly."

"Why, did he have wings?" said Arenadd, unable to stop himself.

She gave him a sharp look. "Ye can stop that now, or I'll turf ye out of here before ye can blink. *Think*, Arenadd. What do the stories say? What did Taranis have?"

Arenadd shrugged. "I don't know, magic? Some sort of blessing?"

Arddryn prodded him. "He had *help*," she said. "He had Taliesin, didn't he? His great friend, the sorcerer, the one who made him chief of chiefs and went into battle beside him."

"Oh, yes. Of course. Where is he?"

"There," said Arddryn. "There they are. Taranis an' Taliesin together."

Arenadd looked at it, and faltered. "But that's—Taliesin was a—?"

"Of course he was," said Arddryn. "Don't ye know anythin'?" She touched the carving and smiled her warped smile. "Humans have no magic. Griffins do. An' Taliesin was one of the most powerful ever lived."

Arenadd scratched his beard. "Taranis was a griffiner, then. So that's how he could fly."

"Aye, an' that's how he united the tribes," said Arddryn. "With Taliesin beside him, no-one could fight him. No-one except other griffiners. But that ain't why Taranis died. Ye know the story?"

"Taliesin betrayed him."

"So he did," said Arddryn. "Taranis, see, he was a great man, an' great men lean toward foolery. Taranis became arrogant, self-centred, thought he was invincible. He started takin' his partner f'granted, an' that's why Taliesin left him." She prodded him again, hard. "There's nothin' a griffin gets from ye he couldn't get from someone else. Havin' a griffin choose ye is an honour, boy, the greatest anyone could ever have. If ye treat yer griffin wrong, if ye think ye can do as ye please, if ye think ye can take an' give nothin' back, ye'll find yerself alone when ye need him most, an' that'll be the end of ye."

"I know," said Arenadd.

"Now, I've seen the way ye are with Skandar," said Arddryn. "Ye're patient with him, an' that's good. He's no genius, but he's cleverer than he looks. Now he's used t'ye, he won't leave ye easy. If ye're going t'fight, ye need him beside ye."

"Yes, of course, but—"

"I want ye t'understand that," Arddryn interrupted. "I mean it, Arenadd. If ye fight, ye fight together. Never try t'fight alone. That's for ordinary men an' women. Ye're a griffiner, an' ye fight with Skandar or not at all. Understand?"

Arenadd nodded with as much sincerity as he could muster. "Of course I do. I won't forget it."

"Good. Good." Arddryn was breathing heavily as she snuffed out the lamp and put it aside. "Now let's go."

They left the cave, and she led him through the pass and deeper into the mountains, until they reached a tiny valley. Tall pine trees grew there, and they walked in among them. Snow covered the ground, and as Arenadd walked through it he saw he wasn't the first to do so. There were tracks everywhere. He had never been to this place before, but it looked as if others had many times. Bone ornaments were hanging from the trees, spiralling gently in the early morning breeze, and as they pressed on, Arenadd saw they were following a defined path, which ran alongside a small stream. Trees lined it, spaced at regular intervals, and shapes had been cut into them at eye height: the phases of the moon, each one represented by a few lines. Further on he heard the sound of voices, and they emerged into a clearing and found the others all waiting in a ring around a silver pool.

Arenadd stopped at the edge of the clearing and looked uncertainly at them. They were standing at perfect intervals around the pool, each one in front of a tree, and he found it difficult to tell who was who. All of them, men and women, were bare-chested, clad in nothing but simple fur kilts. Their faces were covered by masks carved from dark wood and inlaid with copper and silver, each one a different animal. Bear, fox, stag, wolf, snake, crow, boar, their eyes big and blank and staring.

Arddryn didn't hesitate. She walked forward, and a woman wearing a fox mask came to her and silently handed her a mask of her own, this one of a great beaked griffin with silver eyes. She put it on and took her place by the pool, where a space had been left.

She turned to Arenadd. "Come forward."

Arenadd did.

"Tell me yer name and yer tribe," she intoned.

Arenadd straightened up. "Arenadd Taranisäii of the Wolf Tribe."

"And why have ye come here among us this day, Arenadd Taranisäii?"

"To be initiated," said Arenadd.

"Do ye swear this in the name of the moon and the night and the stars, and the great god of the night that watches over us all?" said Arddryn.

"I do swear it."

"Then come forward to the pool and name me as yer chief an' swear to honour me an' do my will," said Arddryn.

Arenadd hesitated, but he knew he had no choice. He went to the spot indicated and knelt in front of her. "I recognise you as my chief and swear to do your will. I swear it by the moon and the night and the stars, and the great god of the night that watches over us all."

Arddryn touched him on the shoulder. "Rise, Arenadd of the Wolf Tribe."

He did.

"Take off yer clothes," Arddryn commanded. "Cast yerself into the pool an' wash away yer boyhood. Ye shall emerge from it a man."

Arenadd looked at the pool. There was ice around its edges. Even with his robe on, he felt cold. But he shrugged it off and put it aside, along with his boots and trousers. Naked and shivering, he stepped toward the pool. He nearly slipped on the ice at the edge, but managed to recover, and stood there, staring at the freezing water. The prospect of going into it made him feel sick, but he took a step forward until he was ankle deep.

The cold hit him like a hundred tiny daggers. He gasped and began to shiver. For an instant he was gripped by the urge to run out, grab his robe and simply make a run for it. He looked back and saw Arddryn's mask staring at him.

I can't do this. I can't bloody well do it! This water's half-frozen. If I go in there it'll kill me!

He stopped. For a moment he stood there, frowning, and then he started to laugh. He laughed harder and harder, a dark, cracked laugh with an edge of madness. Then he threw himself forward, into the pool.

The water folded in over him and took him into itself, and he sank to the bottom. The shock of it nearly knocked him unconscious, and moments later the pain hit him and he jerked violently, struggling to get away from it. The pain bit into him, affecting every inch of him. His skin burned, his eyes ached, his head pounded, his limbs went numb and then seized up and refused to move, and he was floating head-downward, helpless and close to blacking out.

But it only lasted for a moment. As he hung there in the water, panicking, something awoke inside him. Without any warning, a massive, powerful jolt went through him, making him convulse. His heart gave a single beat, and the strength came rushing back into his limbs. His fear vanished, and he began to move, thrusting upward from the bottom as hard as he could.

His head broke the surface, and he sucked in a great gulp of air and began swimming back to the edge. Solid ground rose up beneath him, and he found his feet and staggered onto dry land, coughing and shivering. The others were still there, but none of them made a move to help him, and he returned to Arddryn and made a clumsy bow to her. She inclined her head in acknowledgment and gave him a fur kilt of his own.

"Now ye have proven yer worthiness," she said while he put it on. "And shown yer strength. Ye are ready to be marked as one of us."

The man in the wolf mask came forward carrying a long bone needle and a stone jar. Arddryn took it and opened it, revealing that it was full of blue pigment.

"Now be still," she commanded. "Do not flinch."

When Arenadd saw the needle he quickly guessed what they were about to do. But he said nothing and stood as still as he could, bracing himself. The wolf took the needle and dipped it into the ink before stabbing it into Arenadd's chest. Arenadd gasped and gritted his teeth but didn't move.

The tattooing took a long time. Arenadd continued to keep as still as he could, though he ached all over with cold. The needle punctured his skin again and again, slowly moving over one side of his chest and then up onto his left shoulder and down his arm to his elbow. A large patch of skin was covered in bleeding puncture marks and ink, and he could see the intricate spiral patterns underneath.

Then, at last, it was done, and the wolf silently withdrew.

"Now," said Arddryn. "Leave here. Ye must go back to the gorge. Take a bow an' a knife, nothin' more, an' go out into the forest. Ye must hunt a deer or a wolf or a bear or a boar—whatever beast ye can find. Hunt it alone, kill it, an' bring it back whole for us to see. Then, when that is done, ye must go back to the place where ye killed it. Stay there, pray, contemplate, bathe yerself in the spirit of our land. When night comes, go to the circle, an' go alone. Ye must be there by moonrise, before the moon has cleared the trees. When the Blood Moon begins, it will be time. Now go."

Arenadd nodded wordlessly and left, pausing to pick up his clothes. He waited until he was well away from the pool before he put his trousers and boots back on, though he left his chest bare. He had to keep the tattoos clean.

Back at the gorge, he bundled his robe away in his shelter and slung his bow and arrows over his good shoulder. He found his knife and hung it from his belt. There was no sign of Skandar or Hyrenna anywhere as he left the gorge, and he wondered where they both were. Off flying together again, perhaps. There was no reason for either of them to take part in the ceremonies; this was a human thing, after all.

Arenadd spent most of that day hunting. It wasn't easy; he was still inexperienced, and most of the game seemed to have moved away from the gorge. He knew a few good hunting spots that Nerth had shown him, and he visited those one after the other. Most of them were a good distance away, though, and he spent a fair portion of the day simply walking to them. His shoulder and chest continued to throb horribly though the cold helped to numb them a little.

Some time after noon, he happened across a large white deer. He stalked it as Nerth had taught him to do, and finally managed to kill it with a lucky shot. After that he had to drag the carcass back to the gorge, which was far easier said than done. Several times he began to think he'd have to cut it up in order to get it there, but he persevered, tying the deer's forelegs together and hauling it through rocks and fallen trees and snow-drifts, up several hills and back to the gorge. It was further than he had thought, and with the burden of the deer to slow him down it was evening by the time he arrived. The settlement was still deserted, and he laid the deer down beside the remains of the communal fire and collapsed next to it, utterly exhausted. Sweat had soaked into the tattoos, making them sting, and his hair clung to his head.

He ate several handfuls of snow to cool himself down, and did his best to clean the dirt and deer hair off himself with a few more. Once he had his breath back, he got up and reluctantly left the gorge again.

He knew he could never get back to the place where he'd killed the deer and return in time, so he simply walked a decent distance from the gorge and chose a flat rock in a clearing to sit down on and began his contemplation. He had no idea what he was supposed to be contemplating and spent quite a long time just sitting there, his mind a blank. Eventually, feeling tired and a little irritated, he took a comb from his pocket and began to drag it through his hair. It had become quite tangled during the hunt.

The rhythmic dragging of the comb helped to soothe his jangled nerves, and he began to relax. So this was it. He was becoming a true Northerner, just as his father had always wanted him to.

Dad! He started, suddenly remembering the little urn of ashes sitting in his shelter. He had completely forgotten about his plan to take it to the circle with him. *Don't forget to take it,* he told himself as he ordered his fringe and tucked a few stray bits behind his ears.

The sun was beginning to go down, and he continued to absently comb and re-comb his hair and think about his father. Their relationship had always been a little strained after he had become a griffiner, of course, and Arenadd had flatly refused his father's plans for them all to go to the North.

"I should've listened to you, Dad," Arenadd muttered. "But no-one ever does, do they? We never listen to our parents until it's too late. And I paid the price for it. We both did. And so did Eluna. But I hope you're proud of me now."

He sighed and lost himself in memories of his childhood and the times when he and his parents had been happy together. He thought of his friends, too. Gern, who had died, and Bran, his best friend, who had done so much for him ever since they were children together. And Flell, too. Sweet Flell.

Arenadd shut that memory away. He didn't want to think about Flell ever again or see her face, those blue eyes, so like her father's, and the horror he had seen in them that night. *Arren, what have you done? What's happened to you? You're not my Arren any more. You've changed, you've changed, Arren, what have you done?*

He stood up abruptly and stuffed the comb back in his pocket. Night had fallen. Very soon, the moon would rise. It was time.

When Arenadd returned to Taranis Gorge he found the deer carcass gone, but there was no other sign that anyone had been there during his absence. He took the urn and left immediately, following the track up out of the gorge.

He hadn't been back to the circle since that first day, but he found the way easily enough, climbing the slope until he was up on the plateau and then walking on through the snowbound forest until the trees began to thin and he saw a light ahead.

He reached Taranis' Throne and found them all there. Long wooden staves had been stuck into the ground to form a ring inside the stones, and their tips had been wrapped in cloth soaked in animal fat and set alight so that the entire circle was illuminated. The light played over the masks, lighting copper-covered eyes and inlaid spirals, fangs and horns. The Northerners had stationed themselves between the stones. At the centre, four more burning staves had been placed around the altar, and something was lying draped over it. Arenadd wondered what it was, but he had no time to look closer. Arddryn was there, frail but imposing in her griffin mask.

"Welcome," she said. "Welcome."

Arenadd bowed to her. "I have come," he said, hoping this was the right thing to say.

"Ye have come to the sacred circle, on the night of the Blood Moon," said Arddryn. "Are ye willin' to do what must be done, to appease the spirits of the night an' the stars an' the moon, so that they will bless ye an' accept ye?"

"I am," said Arenadd.

"Good. The moon rises now. Drink this."

He took the carved wooden cup she offered him. It looked to be full of wine, and he took a sip. The liquid was thick and warm and tasted nothing like wine. He gagged on it. "Ye gods, what is this?" he said, forgetting himself for a moment. "It tastes like blood."

"Drink," Arddryn repeated.

Arenadd forced himself to obey, but the cup seemed to take forever to empty. He gulped it down, his mouth filling with the horrible metallic tang of what he knew was blood, fresh blood. When he was done, he gave the cup back.

"Good," said Arddryn. "Now turn an' face the moon."

Arenadd did. It had risen high over the treetops, a bright silver orb. But something strange was happening. The moon should be full, he knew, but it wasn't. There was a patch of darkness at its edge, as if a shadow was moving over its surface.

"The Blood Moon," Arddryn intoned, from behind him. "It's coming. See, darkness begins to swallow the moon. The darkness of shadows, the darkness of death. The moon's power waxes an' wanes; when it is full, it is strongest. But when darkness comes, when our people are in danger an' our land defiled, the moon begins t'be swallowed, just as the South swallows the North an' takes what is ours for itself. When the dark time comes, we must honour the moon an' give up our own blood to bring its power back an' bring the Blood Moon that protects an' blesses us. Ye, Arenadd of the Wolf Tribe, must do this."

While she spoke, Arenadd could see the shadow moving slowly but inexorably over the moon's surface, smothering its light. "My gods," he breathed. "It's really happening. It's disappearing!"

"It's dying, Arenadd," said Arddryn. "Wanin' for the last time. If ye don't do somethin', we'll all die."

Arenadd turned to her. "What do I do? Tell me."

"Take this," said Arddryn.

It was a copper dagger, its blade etched with the phases of the moon, and very sharp. Arenadd gripped the hilt. "Tell me what to do."

"Go into the circle, Arenadd," said Arddryn. "Ye will know what to do there."

Arenadd nodded. He took the urn from his pocket and put it down at the edge of the stones, and then walked toward the altar. Arddryn went to stand between the stones where he had entered the circle, and looked on silently with the others.

When Arenadd reached the altar he saw at once what was happening. The thing lying on the altar was a man, naked and tied hand and foot. Arenadd had never seen him before. He was middle-aged, a Northerner with a scarred, tough frame decorated with blue spirals. He looked up at Arenadd with dull, mute terror.

Arenadd came on until he was standing over him, and looked down at his face, taking in his lined features and pointed beard. The man's chest was heaving; he was paralysed with fear, his skin slick with sweat.

Arenadd looked up at the sky. The moon had darkened even further; now the shadow covered more than half of it and was encroaching over the piece that remained. Only a crescent was left.

Then he looked at the man again. He could feel the dagger in his hands, its hilt cold and slippery. He was sweating, too, he realised. But he felt calm.

"What's your name?" he asked.

The man stirred. "Ouen. Ouen. Please—"

"I'm Arenadd." He closed his eyes for a moment. "I am Arenadd Taranisäii of the Wolf Tribe. I am the destroyer of Eagleholm. I am the man without a heart."

The crescent was growing thinner and thinner. Even without looking up he could feel the light dimming.

"Please," Ouen repeated. "Please, don't."

Arenadd looked at him, taking in his wide eyes, the mouth drawn back into a terrible grimace, the trembling in his hands. He was looking at a man who knew he was about to die and whose very being screamed out for life, for freedom, for a chance to run from the circle and be safe and alive once more. He gripped the dagger and brought it forward, so the tip was pointing straight at Ouen's heart. One thrust and it would be done.

And then, as he hesitated, it happened. The shadow slid silently over the moon, extinguishing its white light completely.

From the edge of the circle, the masked men and women let out a low collective groan. On the altar, Ouen stilled, his eyes fixed on the emptiness where the moon had been. "No."

Arenadd felt nothing. "Join me, Ouen," he rasped, and brought the blade down with all his strength.

His aim was true. The dagger went in up to the hilt, and blood spurted from around it. Ouen gasped and jerked, and then was still, the dagger buried in his chest.

As Arenadd let go of the hilt, he heard a great shout from the Northerners. In that same moment, light came from above, dim red light. He looked up and saw the moon had returned. But it was no longer white or silver. It had turned a dull, ghastly red.

The Northerners started up, shouting as one. "Blood Moon! Blood Moon!"

Arenadd turned to them, wanting to go toward them and out of the circle, but something compelled him to look up once again. He did, staring fixedly at the red moon. *It's beautiful,* he thought, and then he was falling, toppling forward and downward, into an endless dark dream.

* * *

A renadd.
         Arenadd opened his eyes. "What? Who's that? Who's
there?"

Arenadd, look at me. See me. See me. See.

Arenadd looked around. He was still in the circle, but something had changed. The Northerners were standing in the same
places as before, but they looked different. Then he realised
that the masks were not masks at all but their real faces. Women
with the heads of animals were staring at him. The altar was
still there, but Ouen's body had vanished, leaving only a pool
of blood. The sky was black from edge to edge, swallowing up
everything outside the circle, as if it were floating. Stars glit-
tered, but the moon had gone.

"Where is it?" he said. "Where did it go?"

Arenadd. I am here.

He realised that there was light behind him. He turned, and
there she was. A woman, tall and elegant, bare-breasted, with
a silver mantle thrown over her shoulders. Her hair was pure
black, like the night, and her skin was white as snow. In one
hand she held a sickle. In the other she had a silver orb; it was
the moon, somehow able to fit into her hand, even though it
looked the same size as before.

The woman regarded him, unsmiling, and he saw that one
of her eyes was gone. She had no scar, but where her eye should
have been there was nothing but a blank hole.

Arenadd knelt. "My lady," he breathed.

She came closer. *Rise.*

He did. "You're the Night God."

*Yes. I am the moon; I am the stars; I am death and darkness.
I am the mistress of the North, the mistress of all tribes.*

Arenadd looked around. "Is this a dream?"

This is truth, she said. *Arenadd, tell me what it is you seek.
Why have you summoned me?*

"I didn't mean to summon you," said Arenadd. "I didn't
know—"

*You do not know many things, but I will tell you. Thank
you for coming here, Arenadd. Thank you for coming to
the North. Here, my power is strongest, and here is where*

you belong. Here is where you have always belonged, in my land.

"I don't understand. What do you want from me?"

What I want is what you gave me, said the lady. *And you— you are looking for something. I feel it in you.*

"My heart," said Arenadd. "I came here because I wanted to find some way to lift the curse on me."

You have already asked another, said the lady. *I can taste it on you.*

"Spirits," said Arenadd. "I found a place where they are and I asked them to help me."

And they refused.

"Yes."

They are Gryphus' creatures, said the lady. *The Southern god has no love for you or for me or for any of our people.*

"But can you help me?" said Arenadd.

The lady didn't seem to hear him. She lifted the silver orb and put it into the empty socket in her face so that she had two eyes, one black, one silver. *My power is weakening,* she said. *My chosen people have been subjugated and humiliated. Gryphus' followers have taken all they have, and if my people do not remember soon, I shall die. The sun and day and light shall triumph, and all will be lost.*

"Arddryn's people remember you," said Arenadd.

They cannot last forever. Arenadd . . . Her voice faded, and for a moment the glow that surrounded her faded, too. *Arenadd, you must know . . . what you have come here to learn . . . it was I who brought you back.*

For an instant, a memory flashed in front of his eyes: the bright glow of the moon that shone on him and Skandar, reflecting in the griffin's eyes as he looked up at it and died.

"You?"

You are a Taranisäii, said the lady. *You are a true Northerner, and by that you are linked to me. It was I who guided Skandar to you and I who blessed him with the power to bring you back and give you the gifts you have now. I command you, Arenadd, to use them.*

"Gifts?" said Arenadd. "What gifts?"

Her shape wavered. *You are the man without a heart,* she breathed. *The lord of the shadows, the master of death. You feel no remorse; you cannot be stopped. It is in you to kill. You have killed many men so far—how did you feel, Arenadd? What was in you when you killed them, when you saw their blood and heard their screams?*

Arenadd trembled all over. "I—nightmares, I felt—"

No. How did you feel? Tell me.

"I enjoyed it," Arenadd whispered. "It made me feel like—it was easy. I enjoyed it."

Yes. Death is yours, Arenadd. Its power, its glory, its mystery, I have given you that power.

"But why? And what powers do I have? I'm only a—"

You walk, she said. *You are dead, but you walk and breathe and speak and know. And there are other things, other powers, other gifts. If you accept me and agree to do my will, you shall uncover them, and then no man or griffin shall be able to stop you.*

"So I came back for a reason?" said Arenadd.

Yes. I have brought you back for a purpose. It is a purpose you have already begun to fulfil, and I am pleased.

"What purpose?"

You killed Lord Rannagon, she said. *When you returned, it was the first thing you did. Now you have come to the North, and I can tell you—*

"Rannagon? Why was killing him so important?"

Rannagon was a descendant; his family was one blessed by Gryphus. He was born to be an enemy to my people and an enemy to me. You have killed him now, but there is more you must do. She held out a hand, and images began to waver in the air between her and Arenadd, vague shapes of people. *Rannagon's blood is all but gone. Only three people are left living who carry it. You must find them . . . and kill them.*

Arenadd looked at the images and saw faces forming inside them. Faces he knew. "Erian. The Bastard. And—and Flell."

They must die, said the lady. *All of them. You must do it.*

Arenadd didn't recognise the third face. "Why?"

Because I command it. Gryphus protects the Southerners, and he wants them to dominate this land forever. He will act to stop us, and when he does it will be through one of these three humans. You must kill them before it is too late.

"I'll kill the Bastard," Arenadd promised. "I swear it. I want to kill him."

And the others, said the lady. *They must* all *die. Do this and I will give you the North. I will give you back your heart. You shall have power, riches, all you could ever ask for.*

"And if I fail?"

Fail and I shall punish you, the lady hissed. *As I punished you at Herbstitt.*

"That was—?"

You saw the Bastard, and you ran from him. If you had not succumbed to weakness and fear, you could have killed him that day. You disappointed me and were punished. Arenadd's legs buckled suddenly. *If I wish,* said the lady, *I could do it to you again. Disappoint me, betray me, fail me, and I shall take away your strength. You will be blind, voiceless, helpless, but aware, and you will be buried and will lie beneath the earth and feel your body slowly rot away until nothing is left.*

Arenadd began to gasp for breath. "I won't! I won't, I swear!"

Then rise, said the lady, and his strength returned at once. *Rise, and swear to do as I have commanded. You are my creature now, Arenadd Taranisäii. You shall do my will, and every Northerner shall bow to you and call you Lord and Master.*

Arenadd looked into that great glowing eye and bowed low. "I'll do it. I swear. I'll do what you want me to, no matter what it takes."

She smiled. *Then go and be blessed, Arenadd.*

34

Master of the Night

Arenadd blinked. When he opened his eyes again he saw Ouen's body lying in front of him. He turned sharply, looking for the lady, but there was no sign of her. He was in the circle and surrounded by the Northerners in their masks, his hands stained with blood. The moon glowed softly overhead, now an ordinary silver-white orb with no trace of red anywhere. It was over.

Arenadd stared blankly for a little while, before he suddenly became aware of the cold. He walked away from the altar, toward Arddryn, his mouth a thin line. She saw him coming and pulled off her mask. "Arenadd, are ye all right?"

Arenadd ignored her. He picked up the urn from by her feet and removed the lid. When he turned it over the ashes poured out and were caught up by the wind and carried away, like a flock of tiny griffins taking flight. "Goodbye, Dad," he murmured.

Arddryn patted him on the shoulder. "Ye did well, Arenadd. Ye did very well. Welcome to our tribe, an' welcome to manhood. Ye're one of us now, through an' through."

Arenadd looked blankly at her. "Thank you."

She showed a hint of fear when she looked back. "Yes, now come, come. We'll go back t'the gorge now, t'eat an' celebrate."

Arenadd said nothing. He walked with the Northerners as they left the circle, only just hearing their loud and cheerful voices. They crowded around him to congratulate him, and he acknowledged them with nods and a few brief words. They noticed his solemn air and quickly lost their enthusiasm, and they walked back to the gorge in near silence.

There, Arenadd sat down on a rock and waited while the others lit the fire and began to cook the deer, which they had butchered in his absence. He ate what was offered to him but said nothing. Around him the others sang and told stories and talked about the past and the present and the future, but Arenadd only sat and stared at the fire, cold-eyed and brooding. When wine was brought out he drank several cups in quick succession but didn't break his silence.

Later on in the evening, when things began to quieten down, Arddryn came and sat down beside him. "How are ye?"

Arenadd said nothing.

"I know ye're feelin' a little shocked," said Arddryn. "It's normal. Nothin' t'be worried about."

Silence.

"If ye're feelin' bad about Ouen, don't," said Arddryn. "He forfeited his life when he killed that griffiner. Only reason we didn't kill him straight off is because we needed him for the Blood Moon. He understood that. Ye did what ye were supposed to, an' brought the Blood Moon, an' that was the final test."

Finally, Arenadd looked up. "I'm going back," he said.

Arddryn stared at him. "Back? Back to where?"

"Back to the village," said Arenadd. "You can't stop me. I have to see her."

To his surprise, Arddryn grinned. "I thought ye were thinkin' that, when ye started askin' after her. Well, don't worry; I won't stop ye. She'll be expectin' ye."

"What?" said Arenadd. "You mean Saeddryn?"

"Of course I do," said Arddryn. "She likes ye, ye know. She told me so."

"That's . . . nice," said Arenadd.

"An' so it should be," said Arddryn. "I know ye're good together, an' that makes things better."

"I suppose so."

She prodded him. "Of course, now ye're a man, ye can take a wife."

Arenadd thought of Skade. Would she make a good wife? He honestly didn't know. "I think there'll be time enough for that," he said, not really paying attention.

"Aye, an' that time is now," said Arddryn. "I meant for ye t'go back to Eitheinn already, ye know. I don't mean for ye t'stay here an' do nothin'. Now ye're initiated, there's things I want ye t'do."

"What things?" said Arenadd.

"Things such as—" Arddryn fixed him with her good eye. "Things such as take my Saeddryn as yer wife."

Arenadd started. "What?"

"Ye heard me," said Arddryn, unmoved. "Saeddryn will make a good wife for ye, an' I trust ye to treat her kindly."

"But I don't want—"

"What ye want ain't what matters," said Arddryn. "I am yer chief, an' ye swore to obey me. I command ye to honour that an' marry Saeddryn."

Arenadd thought quickly of Saeddryn. She was older than him but pretty enough, and brave, too. Fierce, though less fierce than Skade, and less unpredictable and aloof as well. And human. But he knew he couldn't marry her. "I can't do that," he said. "I'm sorry, but I can't."

Arddryn put her cup down. "Now ye listen t'me, Arenadd." She rubbed her hand over her face, over the terrible scar. "I'm old," she said, her voice suddenly cracking. "Too old. I'm eighty-seven, I'm nearly blind and I can't lift a sword any more or draw a bow. Some mornin's I can barely get out of bed. I ain't gonna be around much longer; I've lived beyond my years already. When I die, these men an' women are goin' t'need a leader. Ye, Arenadd, are the only one can be that. Ye're a Taranisäii, a griffiner; ye're young an' strong, a fighter an' already a leader. Yer name has already spread through Cymria, an' every darkman in Tara knows ye're an enemy to the griffiners. If ye were t'raise a banner they'd flock to it. But ye can't do it alone." She sighed. "Saeddryn an' me don't always see eye to eye, an' not just because I've only got the one now. She blamed me 'cause—well, I forbade her t'marry, see. An' she had men wanted to make her theirs, an' some she liked enough t'say yes to. But I told her she could marry no-one but another Taranisäii. I believed a man from our line would come here one day, an' I was right. Now ye've come, an' Saeddryn is very happy. She told me so."

"She did?"

"Aye. She said, 'Mother, for a long time I hated ye for what ye forced me t'do, but I swear I'll never be bitter again. Ye were right. I know he's the one for me.'"

Arenadd grimaced. "I see."

"So go to her," said Arddryn. "Tomorrow. Go to Eitheinn an' ask her t'be yer wife. She'll be expectin' ye. Come back here, an' ye'll be married at the circle. After that, it'll be time t'begin. With Saeddryn beside ye, ye can rally the North an' take the fight back t'the griffiners."

Arenadd stood up abruptly. "My head hurts. I'm going to bed."

Arddryn sat back, regarding him coolly. "Sleep well."

Arenadd turned his back on her and the other Northerners and walked slowly to his shelter, where he quickly slid into a shallow, painful sleep in which the voice of the Night God whispered endlessly.

He woke up at dawn the next day to a griffin's screeching and vile pain in his chest and shoulder that flared up as soon as he moved. The tattoos had bled during the night and glued his skin to the furs beneath him, and once he had pulled himself free and crawled out into the open air they began to bleed again. His head ached, too, and his stomach, and he groaned to himself as he set about trying to clean the tattoos with snow. He managed to get most of the dirt and hair off, and found a roll of bandages in his shelter to cover them with.

He found his robe bundled around his sword where he had left it, and pulled it on. He put the sword aside and began to gather his belongings and stuff them into his pockets. Once the shelter was empty except for his bow and arrows, which he left where they were, he strapped his sword to his back and walked away from the settlement as quietly as he could. No-one else was up yet, and the gorge was still and silent.

Arenadd didn't stop walking until he was well away from it, up on the plateau at the edge of the trees. From there he could see most of the sky, and the dark shape of a griffin circling over the gorge.

He cupped his hands around his mouth and sent out a call. *"Arenadd! Arenadd!"*

He continued to call until the griffin screeched back and turned to fly toward him. Skandar landed and ran to him. "Arenadd!"

Arenadd scratched him under the beak, feeling strangely relieved to see him. "Skandar. How are you? I haven't seen you since the day before yesterday."

"I am good," Skandar said proudly. He cocked his head. "You hurt?"

"I'm fine," said Arenadd. "Where did you go yesterday?"

"To valley," said Skandar. "Hyrenna building nest. Eggs."

"Has she laid them yet?"

"No," said Skandar. "Not lay yet. I help build nest, she teach me. When lay eggs, I go."

"I see. Well, that's good." Arenadd took a deep breath. "Skandar, I'm leaving. Now. Today."

Skandar's head jerked upward. "What? Go? Go where?"

"I'm going to Eitheinn to find Skade, and then I'm leaving," said Arenadd. "I am not going to live here for one more day."

"But why go?" said Skandar. "This home. We come here, live, you say."

"Yes, I know. But I can't stay here. I'm sorry, but I can't."

"Why?" said Skandar. "Why you not want to stay?"

I took part in a human sacrifice and then a god told me to kill Flell, and Arddryn wants me to marry my cousin and start a war. Other than that, I love it here. "Skandar, we're getting mixed up in things we shouldn't. If we don't get out of here now we'll never be able to leave."

"What things?" said Skandar. "Where we go?"

"I don't know. Listen, Skandar—it's Arddryn. She'll only let me stay here if I do what she tells me, and I don't want that. I didn't come here just so that I could be made use of. I'm nobody's tool."

"But I do not want to go," said Skandar, almost forlornly. "This home. My home. I am happy."

"I'm glad you are," said Arenadd. "I really am, Skandar. I wanted to repay you for all you've done, by giving you back the home I took away from you. I'm not going to do that to you again. So if you want to stay here, you should."

"But if I stay, you go, I will not see you," said Skandar.

"Yes, Skandar. I'm sorry."

Skandar shoved at him. "Not want. You stay. Stay with me, Arenadd."

"Skandar—"

"Not want," the griffin repeated. "You my human. You . . . my friend."

Arenadd softened. "You're my friend, too, Skandar. We've come a long way together, haven't we?"

"Stay," said Skandar.

"Skandar, Arddryn wants me to fight a war," said Arenadd. "Do you know what that means? She wants me to fight griffiners—hundreds of them."

"I know," said Skandar. "Hyrenna say. Other human, wrong human—our land, our territory, we drive them out." He hissed. "We fight. You, me, fight together."

The sun was beginning to come up. "Well," said Arenadd, "I have to go to Eitheinn anyway—you know, the village. Arddryn wants me to go and talk to Saeddryn. Do you want to come?"

"I come," Skandar said immediately. He bent his forelegs and lowered his head. "Come."

Arenadd got on his back. "Let's g—"

The rest of his sentence broke off into a yelp of surprise as Skandar leapt into the air. It had been a long time since Arenadd had ridden on his back, and the take-off nearly unseated him. But he managed to steady himself, and Skandar flew upward, levelled out and made for the village at a leisurely pace. Arenadd knew the griffin had insisted on coming partly out of fear that if he went there alone he would not return.

In a way, though, he was glad. The thought of leaving the gorge without Skandar had been a painful one, almost as much as the thought of leaving Skade behind. Deep down, he knew he couldn't allow himself to abandon either of them.

His spirits rose higher as Skandar did and he could see more and more of the lands below them. They began to move southward, and the gorge fell away behind them like a bad dream. He saw Taranis' Throne become a circle of pinpricks against the snow, and the more it diminished the greater his sense of relief. Even the memory of the previous night's vision felt less real and frightening now. It couldn't have been real. *Gods don't talk to people,* he told himself sternly. *They don't care about what we do, and they don't come down and command us to do things. And I'm nobody's creature. If she wants something done, she can do it herself. I don't care.*

He reassured himself with thoughts like these for much of the rest of the flight, until Eitheinn came into view; he straightened up, trying to look past Skandar's head. They passed over the village and then circled around, and Arenadd was soon able to see Saeddryn's home and the barn attached. Skandar must have seen it, too, because he landed in the street close to it.

Arenadd scrambled off his back and dusted himself down. "Well, here we are again! Shall we—?"

He stopped abruptly, as he saw something that bothered him. Frowning, he turned to look around at the houses, trying to discern the thing that looked different.

Nothing much had changed on the outside. The houses were as tiny and simple as he remembered; the dirt street was slick with snow. And yet something was different.

There was no-one around. No-one tending the fields. No sheep in the pens.

"Where *is* everyone?" said Arenadd.

Skandar stirred. "Smell. Something smell."

Arenadd scuffed at the ground by his boot and saw something else odd. "There's charcoal under the snow here. Someone's been burning something." A deep foreboding began to stir inside him. "Come on," he said. "We have to go and see Saeddryn."

He hurried toward her house, with Skandar following. The door was hanging partly open; one hinge had been broken, and snow had blown in through the gap and piled up on the floor inside.

Arenadd shoved it out of the way. "Saeddryn! Saeddryn, are you—?" He stopped dead just inside the door, staring in horror.

The place was in ruins. Some of the furniture was missing; the rest was broken into pieces. Snow had fallen down the chimney and clogged up the hearth, and the cupboards were open and empty. The bed in the corner had been torn apart, the flagstones on the floor levered out.

"Oh no," Arenadd moaned. He turned abruptly and ran back through the door, shoving past Skandar. Ignoring the griffin's offended hiss, he scrambled toward the barn and through the door.

The barn, too, was deserted, its contents gone or destroyed. It looked as if it had been deserted for weeks.

Skandar pushed his way in. "Gone!"

Arenadd suddenly felt dizzy. He sagged against the wall. "Oh gods. Oh dear gods. No. Skade."

"Smell in here," said Skandar. "Griffin smell. Human smell. Old."

Arenadd straightened up. "Come on," he said. "We have to see if there's anyone left in the village. They can tell us what happened."

When they emerged from the barn, they found that there were people still there. A handful of them had congregated outside the barn and were waiting. All of them were old, and fear and anxiety made them look still older. They regarded Arenadd and Skandar dully, keeping well back.

Arenadd went toward them. "Please, I'm not here to hurt you. I'm a friend."

One man ventured a little closer. "Who are ye?" he said, speaking Cymrian. The sound of it took Arenadd by surprise. He himself had been speaking Northern, so used to it by now that he hadn't even thought about it. It was strange to hear Cymrian again.

"What happened here?" he said, in Cymrian, the language feeling clumsy in his mouth.

The man rubbed a hand over his face. "Griffiners," he mumbled. "Dozens of 'em. Guards, too, lots of those. They came here one night, before dawn. No warning, no sign, nothing. No-one had any chance t'run or hide. They went into everyone's houses, woke 'em up, started askin' questions. All sorts of questions. Do ye know griffish, have ye ever been up to the circle, have ye ever seen a griffin up here—if they didn't like the answers they got, they hit people."

Arenadd swore. "What did you tell them? What did they find out?"

"I dunno," said the man. "It was all such a mess."

"And Saeddryn? And Skade? What happened to them?"

"Saeddryn didn't—she was the only one knew where t'find the people what lives up in the mountains. Ye an' the others what lives up in the mountains. Her an' Rhodri an' Talfryn. They was there when the griffiners went to her house. Rhodri got free an' ran in t'help her get away, an' Talfryn attacked the bastards. Some of his friends helped. They all died. Talfryn attacked a griffin, got his head half tore off—after that everyone went mad." The old man's face twisted in anguish. "They just started killin' people. Everyone started tryin' t'run or fight, an' the griffiners an' the guards tried t'stop 'em, but the griffins started killin', an' no-one could stop them." He looked up at Arenadd and added, quite matter-of-factly, "Most of the village is dead."

Arenadd's stomach twisted. "But Skade. And Saeddryn. What happened to them?"

"Saeddryn an' Rhodri tried t'fight back," said the man. "They was cornered, an' Saeddryn got her sword—once they saw she had it, they went for her. She was captured. Rhodri, too, an' some others the griffiners could protect."

"And Skade? What about her?"

"They took her, too," said the man. "Went in an' dragged her out of the barn. She started bitin' an' screaming at them, an' they put manacles on her an' took her away with the others."

"Where did they take her?" said Arenadd.

The man's voice broke. "I don't know. I don't know. It was a whole moon ago. They'll be all the way t'Malvern by now. Eitheinn's finished. They took all the sheep an' horses, burned the crops, took whatever we had. We're the only ones left, us an' two babies. They stayed away from us because we're old, but what's the point? What's the point in livin' this long just t'see our sons an' daughters die? What's the point in seein' this an' knowin' everything we spent our lives toward came t'this? If they can just come an' take it all away."

Several of his friends came to try to comfort him, and Arenadd felt sick. "Oh gods. Skade. And Saeddryn. Those bastards. Those *bastards*. If they've taken them to Malvern, they could— what Saeddryn knows—what *Skade* knows—oh my gods."

Skandar nudged him in the back. "What happen?"

Arenadd turned sharply. "Come on," he snapped. "We have to go back, fast."

"Where Skade?"

"She's not here. Come on, let me get on your back, we have to go back to the gorge."

Skandar squatted to let him on, and took off without arguing, apparently pleased to be going back to his new home.

"What happen?" he asked as they flew, the wind carrying his voice back to Arenadd.

Arenadd leant forward to speak into his ear. "Something awful has happened. Skandar, the griffiners have been to Eitheinn. They've taken Skade and Saeddryn. Very soon they'll know where we are. We have to warn Arddryn."

Skandar snarled. "My land! They come, I kill." He put his head down and sped forward.

Arenadd's mind raced. It was full of horrible visions. Skade captured, dragged away to Malvern in chains, locked away in a dungeon, tortured. Skade, his love. Skade, who knew his secrets. Fierce Skade.

And Saeddryn, too. He remembered the look on the old

man's face, and thought of Arddryn. What would she do when she found out what had happened? What could either of them do?

The journey back passed in what felt like no time at all. Skandar, if anything even more agitated than his friend, made a rough landing in the gorge, which nearly threw Arenadd off his back. He recovered himself and slid off as the others came running.

"Arenadd! Where have you been?"

"Where's Arddryn?" said Arenadd.

"Home, I think. What's happenin'?"

Arenadd turned sharply to point at the man who had spoken. "Listen. I want everyone gathered here in the gorge. And I mean everyone. If anyone's away, go and bring them back as fast as you can. Understand?"

"But we need to catch something for—"

"Just do it!" Arenadd roared. "Now!"

The man gave him a startled look and ran away.

"As for the rest of you, I want you to start gathering your things," said Arenadd. "Bundle everything together. And I want someone to keep watch. Some of you climb up into the trees, as high as you can, and keep your eyes on the sky. If you see anyone coming, raise the alarm. I'm going to go and get Arddryn now, and I'll be back soon."

He had slipped back into the commanding voice he had used at Eagleholm when he ordered the guards, and it worked now. The Northerners ran to obey. Arenadd turned to Skandar. "Skandar, can you find Hyrenna? Someone has to tell her what's happened."

Skandar nodded. "I go," he said, and flew off.

Arenadd ran out of the gorge at top speed, his hair flying. He scrambled through the track to Arddryn's space and, finding it deserted, went straight to the cave, shouting. "Arddryn! *Arddryn!*"

She was inside, on the bed, sitting up sharply and groping for her dagger. "What? Who's there? Arenadd?"

Arenadd grabbed her by the shoulder. "Arddryn, get up, quickly. Something's happened."

She caught his tone and got up as fast as she could, tousled but fully alert. "What is it? What's happened? Have ye been t'Eitheinn yet?"

"Yes. Arddryn." Arenadd took a deep breath. "Eitheinn's been raided."

Her grip on his arm tightened. "What? What d'ye mean, raided?"

"Griffiners," said Arenadd. "A lot of them, and some guards as well. They came in before dawn, without any warning. They've—Eitheinn's in ruins. They killed a lot of people, destroyed all the farms. There's only a handful of old people left, and a couple of babies."

Arddryn faltered. "But—when? Why din't anyone tell us?"

"Because they couldn't," said Arenadd. "Anyone who could have come up here was killed or arrested."

"An' Saeddryn? Where is she?"

"They took her," said Arenadd. "Skade, too."

Arddryn gaped at him. "But—but—Saeddryn—where'd they take her?"

"They must have taken her to Malvern," said Arenadd. "The raid happened at least a month ago. They'll have her there by now, in a cell. Arddryn, we have to leave. If Saeddryn hasn't already told them where we are, she soon will. I know what the griffiners do to people they want information from."

She hit him. "Don't ye tell me, boy. Ye think I don't know? Think I need t'be told, do ye? Think that?" Her furious tone faltered and fell away without any warning, and she sagged. "Saeddryn—oh, by the Night God, not my little Saeddryn."

Arenadd supported her. "Arddryn, please. We need you. The others have got to move out of the gorge, and fast. I've already told them to start packing their things and sent someone to fetch back anyone who's away."

She straightened up. "Someone has t'watch the sky."

"They already are. I told them to climb into the trees."

"Hyrenna—"

"Skandar's gone to find her. Come on, Arddryn. There's no time."

She took his hand. "Leavin' this cave—not easy. It's been home so long."

"You'll find another one. Come on, I'll help you pack your things together."

Arddryn nodded, and the two of them gathered up her meagre possessions. They rolled them up in her sleeping furs, and

Arddryn put on most of her spare clothes for warmth and to save space. Then she helped Arenadd to conceal all signs that she had lived in the cave, even rubbing dirt over the carvings on the walls.

When they were done, they left the cave together and piled stones over the entrance, hiding it from view.

"Now," said Arenadd, "we'll get the others together and then—"

She waved him into silence. "I'll go an' talk to 'em, Arenadd."

"Oh, of course, I didn't mean—"

"There's somethin' else I want ye t'do in the meantime," said Arddryn. "We can hide the settlement well enough—break up the shelters an' suchlike—but we can't hide that griffin."

Arenadd had nearly forgotten him. "Oh."

"Kill it," Arddryn said briefly. "An' make sure ye finish the job properly. After that, burn the body. We don't want anyone findin' it."

"I will. See you later." Arenadd dashed off.

He went further along the pass and entered the little alcove where the griffin was housed. They had built a cage out of logs, and the griffin lay huddled in the middle of it, wings, beak and legs still tied together. Arenadd had been bringing him food; the others seemed almost completely indifferent as to whether he survived or not. The griffin never said anything when his beak was untied, only ate what he was given and then subsided again, dead-eyed and still.

Arenadd found him dozing and cut away some of the bars so he could get into the cage. As he stood over the griffin, looking at him, the creature stirred and opened his eyes. They were yellow and had probably once been bright. Now, though, they were empty and resigned.

Arenadd made up his mind. He struck. The griffin jerked as the blade hit him, and the ropes fell away from his beak. He opened it wide, stretching his jaw, and looked at Arenadd, expecting food.

Arenadd kept well back. "I want to talk to you," he said.

The griffin just stared at him.

"I want to know your name," said Arenadd.

The griffin sighed. "Eekrae."

"Your name's Eekrae?"

"Yes."

"It's a good name," said Arenadd. "Now listen, Eekrae. Have you ever heard the name Erian Rannagonson before?"

Eekrae looked up at that, which was all the answer Arenadd needed. "Yes."

"He's at Malvern?"

"Yes. And Senneck."

"Who's Senneck?" said Arenadd. The name was vaguely familiar.

"Erian is Senneck's human," Eekrae mumbled. "Senneck is beautiful."

Arenadd rubbed his ear. "Senneck bit a piece off my ear. So, they're in Malvern—do they live there?"

"Yes."

"Elkin took them in?"

"Yes."

"Did she give Erian a post?" said Arenadd.

"Yes," said Eekrae. "He is the assistant to the Master of Farms." He shivered. "No, the Master of Farms now. The old Master is dead. He died in—in the circle."

Arenadd snickered. *Master of Farms. I'll bet he's proud of himself.*

He moved closer. "Listen to me, Eekrae. I've been sent here to kill you."

Eekrae made a little rasping noise in his throat. "Kill me, then."

"But wouldn't you rather be free?" said Arenadd. "Because I can let you go instead, if I want to. Wouldn't you like that? To fly back to Malvern? To be back in your own nest?"

Eekrae said nothing.

Arenadd finally made his decision. "Now listen," he said. "I can set you free. But you have to do something in return."

Eekrae looked up. "What must I do?"

"Take me with you," said Arenadd. "And after that, I want you to carry a message for me. That's all. Can you do that, Eekrae?"

And Eekrae said, "Yes."

35

Heartless

Skade had lost track of the time she had spent in the cell. They had put her in it as soon as they arrived at Malvern. Several times she had been taken to a different room and questioned, but the questions were perfunctory: they asked for her name, where she was from, why she was at Eitheinn and how much she knew about Saeddryn. Skade had eventually told them her name, but refused to say anything else. They asked; she sneered and hissed and said nothing. When they began to use intimidation—threatening her with rape and torture—she turned violent, lashing out at anyone who got too close. Her claws, at least, were one weapon she still had. They hit her, she hit back, and once she broke free and instantly hurled herself at a guard who tried to stop her escape, biting a piece out of his ear before they managed to subdue her. Eventually it reached the point where she ceased to speak entirely and took to attacking everyone who came within reach.

After that they apparently decided she was more trouble than she was worth and left her alone.

She sat huddled in the corner, shivering slightly and scratching at the floor. The claw on her forefinger was slowly being worn down by the amount of time she had spent doing this, but she didn't care. The cell was dimly lit by a single torch, protected by a metal bracket, and she watched its light flicker over the dust and cracks on the floor and lost herself in thought.

Arenadd had abandoned her. She knew that by now. She had believed him when he looked her in the eye and promised to return, and she had waited for weeks, believing he would come. But he never did, and nor did Skandar, and she didn't know where they were or if they would ever return. When Saeddryn had returned alone from the mountains, Skade asked after them. Saeddryn said that Arenadd had decided to stay up there and wouldn't be returning for a long time, if he returned at all. Beyond that she wouldn't say anything, such as what he and Skandar were doing there and whether there was anyone else there with them.

Skade didn't believe her, and her silence only made her more inclined to think she was lying. She stayed in the barn and spent most of her time eating or sleeping, slowly recovering from the journey. Using the sword taken from the dead griffiner at Guard's Post, she practised the moves Arenadd had taught her. Saeddryn, seeing this, offered to teach her more, and she accepted.

That was how she spent most of her time, day in and day out, as two long months passed. By the end of the first month, she had already begun to realise that Arenadd was not going to return, and by the end of the second she knew it for certain. After that, everything had gone downhill. She went off her food and became lethargic and aggressive by turns. In the end Saeddryn became wary and began to leave her alone. Skade stayed locked away in the barn, forbidden to leave it during the day lest someone see her. Sometimes she was gripped by appalling urges for violence that led her to attack one of the beams that held up the ceiling, hacking pieces off it with her sword. Saeddryn finally lost patience and took the weapon away from her.

It was only days later that the griffiners came. Skade was woken up by the commotion outside, and for a few moments, hearing voices speaking griffish, she thought that Arenadd had come back. But as she ran to the door she heard the screams, and after that she caught the scent and heard the sounds of griffins she didn't know, reeking of aggression and malice.

In that moment, it was as if all her pent-up frustration and misery rose up inside her in a single burst, and she launched herself in a frenzied attack at the first person who entered the barn.

That was how her time at Eitheinn had ended, and here was where her journey had ended. She didn't believe that she would escape from the cell or that they would release her. Perhaps they would sell her into slavery. Or maybe they would simply kill her. She knew very little about human justice and could only guess. But she wouldn't tell them anything, no matter what they said or did. She had sworn that to herself.

So she had sat alone in her cell, waiting for her time to come, but it never did. She had slid back into the same lethargy and despair that had affected her at Eitheinn. Now she sat and stared listlessly at the plate of food that had been placed next to her. She had eaten the salted beef, but couldn't summon the energy to touch the bread or beans that came with it.

The chains clinked whenever she moved. They had manacled her to a ring in the wall by her wrists, to stop her attacking the guards when they brought her food, and she picked at a spot where the metal had left a sore. It was becoming infected.

A sound at the door made her look up sharply. This couldn't be more food arriving.

The door opened, and Skade squinted as light fell over her face. She could see someone standing in the doorway and hauled herself to her feet, dragging at the chains. "Come near me and I will kill you," she rasped.

The intruder didn't move, and she heard a quick muttering of voices. "Should I just—?"

"Go in," a second, rougher voice commanded. "Don't waste any more of our time."

"Yes, sir."

The first speaker entered the cell, and Skade blinked in puzzlement. This wasn't one of the guards. It was a woman— Northern, wearing a slave collar. She was middle-aged, and her face was etched with lines of grief and worry. She came closer, holding out a hand. "Please, don't worry," she said. "I won't hurt you."

The voice was soft and nervous and had an accent Skade recognised. "Who are you?" she said.

The woman fiddled with her hair, a gesture that made Skade's heart leap. "My name is Annir," she said. "Please, you have to come with me. You won't be hurt."

Skade stared at her. "Annir?" The name was familiar. Distantly, achingly familiar.

"Yes." The woman held out her hands. "See? I don't have any weapons. I'm just a—just a slave. Will you come with me?"

"Where do you want to take me?" said Skade, suspiciously.

"Out of the dungeons," said Annir. "They're not going to kill you."

"Well then, what are they going to do?" said Skade.

Annir looked furtively over her shoulder and came even closer, just out of reach of Skade's claws. "I think they're going to set you free," she said in a low voice.

Skade regarded her. She had had a little more practice at reading human faces and eyes, and she couldn't see any trace of a lie in this one. The eyes, though. There was something about them, something that made her heart beat faster. All humans looked more or less the same to her, of course, but still . . .

"I cannot go with you," she said at last. "I am chained."

Annir held up a key. "Here. If you promise to stand still, I'll take them off."

The gentle tone finally managed to soothe Skade, and she relaxed and held out her hands. "I will come, then," she said. "Take them off."

Annir inserted the key and quickly removed both manacles. She withdrew as soon as the second one had been unlocked, holding up her hands to defend herself, but Skade only stood and rubbed her wrists. "Curse them. If they do not set me free, I shall kill them."

"Don't worry, I'm sure it won't come to that," said Annir. "Come, follow me."

She turned and walked out of the cell, and Skade followed warily at a distance. The instant she stepped through the doorway, however, hands grabbed her by the shoulders. More grabbed her elbows and wrenched her arms behind her back, where her wrists were shackled together yet again. It all happened so quickly and efficiently that she had no time at all to react.

Held firmly between two guards, she found herself looking straight at Annir. She bared her teeth. "Liar!"

Annir looked helplessly at her. "Please, just do what they tell you; they're not going to—"

The guard standing beside Annir smacked her in the face. "Shut up an' get movin'. Go up an' tell 'em they're a-comin' now."

Annir clutched at her cheek. "Yes, sir."

"Now, you," said the guard, turning to Skade while Annir left. "I don't want anythin' from you except 'Yes, sir' an' 'No, sir,' understand? Try anythin'—anythin' at all—an' I'll tear your tits off."

Skade hissed at him and said nothing.

The guard nodded to the two holding her. "Move it."

They moved off, marching her between them up the corridor. She tried to break away from them at first, but one of them hit her in the head so hard that stars filled her vision. Stunned and bleeding from a cut above her ear, she stumbled between them without any further resistance. Their short journey ended in a small room at the end of the corridor, the same one where she had been interrogated. But this time there were other people waiting for them.

Skade blinked, cringing as her head exploded with pain. Eight people, four of them guards. The other four were in manacles: Saeddryn, Rhodri and two Eitheinnians who had been arrested on the same day as she had.

One of her guards saluted. "Got the last one, sir. Sorry for the wait; she's madder'n ever."

"Bring her here."

Skade allowed herself to be taken over to the other prisoners, and was made to stand just behind Saeddryn. The Northerner shifted backward slightly and managed to brush Skade's hand with her own. "Skade! Are ye all right?"

"I am not hurt," said Skade. "What is—?"

"Shut up," a guard commanded. "Now." He moved to stand in front of the prisoners so they could all see him. "We're takin' you out've here. There'll be guards flankin' you the whole time, so don't even think about tryin' anything on. Behave an' you'll get fed. Do anythin' to piss me off, you get a beating. The choice is yours."

"Where are we goin'?" Saeddryn piped up.

He hit her. "Did I say talk? No? Right. Now move. Go on, move!"

The prisoners were taken out of the room and marched in single file up and out of the dungeons, with guards in front and behind them, swords drawn. Once they had ascended to the upper levels of the prison complex, they were led out through a gate and into the open air. More guards were waiting, standing around a large cage on wheels that had a pair of oxen yoked to it.

The captain signalled to two of them to open the door at the back of the cage and gestured at it with his sword. "In."

They climbed up one at a time and sat down on the pair of benches provided. The door was closed behind them, and the guards took up new stations: two climbed up onto the driver's seat, and others perched on special ledges that ran around the outside of the cage. Those that remained behind guarded the door, and they waited there like that for some time until the gate opened again and Annir came through.

She took a few steps back, and bowed low. "Master."

Inside the cage, Skade tensed when she saw the griffin emerge. It was female, thin and long-legged, with pale brown feathers and blue eyes. She approached the cage and sat on her haunches, looking haughtily at the prisoners. Skade snarled at her.

Annir's master came close on the griffin's tail. He was a boy, younger than Arenadd, stockily built and clad in a fine blue velvet tunic. His face was round and snub-nosed, decorated by a sprinkling of freckles and a pair of bright blue eyes. Those, coupled with his tousled sandy-brown hair, made him look almost comically similar to his griffin.

One arm was bound in a sling. He waved the other at the guards. "Put her in the cage."

"Yes, my lord."

One guard opened the door and gestured at Annir, and she climbed up into the cage without argument and sat down next to Skade.

"Now—" The boy shifted uncertainly and cast a quick glance at the griffin. She looked back stonily, and he stood up a little straighter. "Now, if everything's in order, we should go."

"Yes, my lord," said the captain. He nodded to the two men holding the reins, and they lashed the oxen into motion. The cage lurched and began to roll forward, toward another gate that would lead them out into the city. That was opened, and they were out of the Eyrie and away. The boy and the griffin followed behind until they were in the open, and then the boy climbed onto his partner's back and she flew away. Skade watched them fly ahead of the cage as it wove through the city, passed out of it and began to follow the main trade road that headed northward.

"Maybe we are being set free," she muttered aloud.

Saeddryn leant forward. "Skade, d'ye know what's goin' on?"

Skade looked up. "No." She nodded at Annir. "But she does."

Saeddryn gave her a distasteful look. "And what d'ye know, blackrobe?"

Annir glared back. "Don't you dare talk to me like that, girl.

I've spent more of my life living free than you've been breathing, and I will not be called a blackrobe by you or anyone."

"Put on airs if'n ye want," said Saeddryn, unimpressed, "but that ain't gonna change much of anythin'. Now what's goin' on? Where're we goin'?"

Annir shook her head. "All I know is that we're being taken somewhere out in the countryside. Lord Erian—"

"Erian?" Skade said sharply.

"Yes, Lord Erian, my—" Annir's face twisted. "My master. He's agreed to meet someone there. I don't know who, but he needs us with him."

Saeddryn looked troubled. "But who? It couldn't be—" She checked to see if the guards were listening, and then leant forward. "What've ye told them? What do they know?"

"I told them nothing but my name," said Skade.

Rhodri shook his head. "They asked some questions an' roughed me up some, but I din't tell 'em anythin' much. Just my name. I kept sayin' I didn't know nothin' about anythin' else."

The other two gave similar replies.

"Good," said Saeddryn. She leant forward even further, her voice a mere whisper. "So it seems they don't know anythin'. They mustn't think we know anythin' much, or they would've tortured us properly. Or maybe they was just waitin' for approval from up top. They don't just torture everyone; they got to get permission first. They can't hang us; all they know we've done is resist arrest, an' who wouldn't? Everyone in Tara hates the Eyrie. They could've sold us for that, but seems they ain't interested. Maybe they're gonna set us free. They can't keep us locked up forever."

Annir didn't look happy. "I don't think so. There's something big going on behind this, I'm sure of it."

Saeddryn gave her another unpleasant look. "An' what would ye know about it?"

"Everything," Annir snapped. "I happen to be Lord Erian's personal slave, and I saw him while he was planning this. I've never seen him so anxious. And why would he be coming with us if this was just a routine prisoner release? Well? Why would *I* be coming?"

Saeddryn stared at her. "Just who are ye, anyway? Have I seen ye before?"

"I'm Annir."

Saeddryn squinted. "Annir, from where?"

"Idun village. What's your name?"

"Saeddryn."

"Oi!" a guard's voice interrupted. "No talkin'!"

They kept quiet after that, and the cage rumbled on for most of the rest of that day. That night they stopped at a roadside inn, and the prisoners stayed out the back in their cage and were provided with food that was at least fresher than what they had had in the dungeon. Skade slept that night leaning against the side of the cage, and dreamt of flying.

The journey resumed early the next day and continued until noon. The guards had become less attentive now, no doubt tired from all the time spent on the road, and the prisoners could talk again.

"Where d'ye think we're going?" said Rhodri.

"Who knows?" said Saeddryn. She looked up at the griffin still flying above them. She was low enough for them to be able to see the colour of her feathers. "Who's this Lord Erian, anyway?"

"The Master of Farms at Malvern," said Annir. "His griffin is called Senneck."

Saeddryn glanced at Skade. "And how do ye know him, Skade?"

Skade shook her head. "It does not matter."

"But if it could give us some clues, then it does matter," said Saeddryn. "Who is he? Ye've heard his name before, so don't lie about it."

They were speaking in the lowest whispers possible—so quietly they could only just hear each other—but Skade checked the guards anyway and leant very close to Saeddryn to reply. "He is the son of Lord Rannagon."

Saeddryn didn't move a muscle. "An' what is he doin' here?"

"He is Arenadd's enemy," said Skade. "He wants to kill Arenadd for killing his father. He came to the North to find him and sold both Arenadd's parents into slavery. Cardock told me before he died."

Saeddryn pulled away from her. "Damn him!"

Skade, however, was looking at Annir. Those eyes—and not just the eyes, she thought suddenly. There were the brows, too, and the line of the jaw. All familiar. Her pulse quickened, and she leant forward. "Annir, why are you the Bastard's slave?"

"I was a prisoner," Annir said briefly. "At Norton. My husband and I were locked up there. Lord Erian found us there and had us sold."

Skade's eyes widened. "Your husband. What was his name?"

Annir sighed. "His name was Cardock, and I don't know—" She stopped dead, and every guard there jerked awake, at the cries of astonishment from both Skade and Saeddryn.

"Here!" one shouted. "Stop that right now, damn you!"

They had to wait quite a long time before calm returned and the guards' attention lapsed again.

"Cardock!" Saeddryn exclaimed in an undertone. "Ye mean Cardock Skandarson? Cardock Taranisäii?"

"Yes," said Annir. "I don't know what happened to him. I haven't seen him since the day we were sold."

Skade leant very close to her. "He is dead."

Annir just stared. "What?"

"I was there when he died," said Skade.

"Where? How?" Her voice was sharp now, urgent and no longer concerned with whether the guards might hear.

"He was killed by a—" Skade was silenced by a blow to the back of the head, delivered by the guard perched just behind her. She turned and tried to bite his hand, and then lurched backward and nearly fell off the bench as the cage came to an abrupt stop. They had driven off the main road and over a field, toward a patch of large pine trees, and Senneck had come down to land just in front of the cage, hissing disdainfully as the oxen shied.

Erian got down off her back. "We're there," he said to the guards. "Come on, you know what to do."

The guards nodded and went into action. The cage door was opened and the prisoners were made to climb out. The guards surrounded them in a ring and herded them toward the trees, with Senneck and Erian following. When they were at the very edge of the patch, they halted and the captain addressed them.

"Now," he said, "I want you to walk. Go into the trees, an' don't stop walkin' until you find a clearin' with a big yew tree in it. Stop there, an' don't move. We'll be followin' at a distance." He unshipped a crossbow from his back and loaded a bolt into it. "If you turn back or try to run, you're dead. Now march."

Saeddryn was the first to step toward the trees. "Follow me," she told the others. "Keep together."

They formed up and followed her. Skade cast a baleful glance at the guards and especially at Erian, and went, too. They walked on until they saw the clearing ahead, then the captain stopped them and gave Annir the key to the manacles.

"Unchain 'em."

Annir did, and the guards gathered up the chains. After that the captain nodded silently at them, and they walked into the clearing. Skade pushed ahead, every sense alert for signs of trickery. She heard a noise behind her and looked back to see the guards spreading out, ringing the clearing, with their bows at the ready. There was no escape from here.

She walked toward the yew tree. It was indeed big, its trunk dark and gnarled. Low twisted branches were laden with poisonous red berries. She could smell their aroma, all sharp and acidic, mingled with the scent of pine needles—and with something else. Some other scent, a dark, cold dangerous scent, a wonderful scent.

Skade's mouth opened to say the name, but she was too slow. In that moment, a tall robed figure dropped out of the tree in front of her, and she was enveloped by a pair of arms.

"Skade!"

Skade jerked in shock but returned the embrace. "Arenadd!"

Arenadd held her close. "Skade. My sweet Skade."

They parted reluctantly, and he looked her up and down. His face looked different: thinner, older, more worn and troubled. But his smile was genuine and his eyes warm with concern. "Have they hurt you?"

"I am fine," said Skade. "Arenadd—"

Annir was already rushing toward them. "Arren! *Arren!*"

"Mum!" Arenadd grabbed her and kissed her on both cheeks. "Thank gods, thank gods, thank gods. I thought I'd never see you again! And this—" He touched the collar. "Damn them. You'll get it off, though, don't worry. Skade knows how to take them off, don't you, Skade?"

"Yes—"

Annir grabbed her son's arm. "Arren, you have to get out of here," she said. "For gods' sakes, run! They're here—guards, a griffiner—"

He pulled away gently. "I know. I was expecting them. Don't worry; it's fine. It's all been arranged."

"But—"

Arenadd looked past her and raised a hand in greeting. "Good afternoon!"

It was Erian he was waving to. The boy had entered the clearing and was coming toward them, Senneck close beside him.

"Arenadd, what's going on?" Saeddryn demanded. "Why are ye here?"

He looked back at her. "Exchange of prisoners."

"Exchange of—?"

Arenadd walked toward Erian. "Hello, Bastard. I take it you got my message."

Erian stopped to look at him. "Arren." His face was twitching with hatred.

Arenadd grinned widely. "What's the matter? Is your arm hurting?" Without any warning, he started to laugh. "I think it must be! Arrows hurt!"

"I've kept my part of the bargain," said Erian. "Now give me what you promised, murderer."

"Oh, you'll get it!" said Arenadd. His voice was high and manic. "You've got it! All of it! Everything you need!" He giggled. "See?" He reached over his shoulder. "See here? See? I've got a present for you!"

The sword gleamed as he pulled it out of its sheath on his back. Erian and Senneck both tensed, but Arenadd didn't try to use it. He held it out, blade pointing at the ground.

"Ever seen this before?" he said. "I have! It's—" He giggled again. "It's your father's sword. I took it from him after—" He stopped again, laughing so hard he was bent double and nearly staggered over. "After I killed him! Hahahah! Because I killed him! Yes, that's right! And you saw me! Did you see the blood, Bastard? Wasn't it pretty?"

Skade stepped toward him. "Arenadd!"

Arenadd turned sharply. "Back off!" he yelled. "Keep away from me, slut, or I'll kill you, too!"

Saeddryn grabbed Skade by the shoulder and dragged her away. "Keep away from him."

Skade didn't hear her. She had seen Arenadd's eyes. They were wide and staring, full of a light she had never seen before, not even during his worst moments.

Arenadd paid no further attention to her. He turned back to

Erian and threw down the sword. "There! Take it! I don't need
it any more; I can kill people with just my hands. D'you want to
see? I'll show you!"

Senneck started forward. "Enough! Where is your partner?
Where is Darkheart?"

Arenadd stared at her for a moment, and then started to
laugh again. He laughed so hard he couldn't speak, and everyone there stared at him, either angry or bewildered.

"Answer me!" Senneck screeched.

"He's—" Arenadd breathed deeply and managed to control himself. "He's dead!" he yelled at last, and broke into a
fresh wave of mad giggling. "You wanna know why? Because
I killed him! One griffin, two griffins, what's the difference?
I wanted to see him die; so I waited until he was asleep, and
then I cut his throat." Another giggle. "You should've seen the
blood, Bastard, it was beautiful, like rubies. I drank some of
it—oh, it tasted so good!" He gestured at Senneck. "You should
kill her, see what it's like! You'll never want to stop. It's better
than wine."

Senneck looked skyward. "I saw no griffin in the sky," she
said to Erian. "I think he is telling the truth. And I cannot smell
anyone else in the trees. He is alone."

"*Are* you alone?" said Erian.

"Oh yes!" said Arenadd.

Skade finally shook herself free of Saeddryn and ran forward. She grabbed Arenadd by the arm and dragged him sideways. "Arenadd! Stop it! *Stop it!*"

Arenadd snarled and grabbed her by the throat. "I said
keep away from me!" He dragged her toward him, squeezing
tightly with both hands. But he didn't squeeze so tightly that
she couldn't breathe. He turned slightly, so that his back was
to Erian, and looked her in the face. "Run, Skade," he said, his
voice low and suddenly normal. "You can't help me. Get them
out of here." He let go abruptly and shoved her aside, so that
she staggered and fell.

In the trees to his left, one guard raised his crossbow. Arenadd saw him and waved wildly at him. "You shouldn't do
that!" he said, his voice mad once again. "If I die, you don't
get the rest of what I promised!" He stepped closer to Erian.
"Which is everything! I can tell you everything. I know where

the rebels are, I can tell you where to find them and I can tell you who their leader is. Everything."

"No!" Saeddryn screamed. "Arenadd, don't!"

But Arenadd only laughed. "The leader's a griffiner! A rogue griffiner, that's right!" he cackled.

"That's enough," Erian snapped. "Come here or the guards will shoot."

Arenadd nodded and began to walk toward him, holding out his hands. "See? See? I'm not going to fight. Just like I promised. You let them go, you get me and everything I know. See?"

Erian approached him cautiously, holding a pair of manacles in his good hand. Arenadd came to him and stood there placidly, holding out his arms. He put up no resistance at all when Erian snapped one manacle shut around his wrist, and stood there as he opened the second and brought it down to close around the other.

And then, in the instant before the manacle snapped home, he made his move. His hand jerked sideways so the manacle closed around nothing. His knee came up, catching Erian hard in the groin, and as he fell, Arenadd rammed into him, knocking him over. His free hand came up, holding a long dagger, and he brought it down, point first, straight at Erian's throat.

He wasn't fast enough. Senneck leapt. Her beak lashed out, catching him hard on the wrist and sending the dagger flying. But Arenadd wasn't done yet. Heedless of the guards running out of the trees, he lurched forward and wrapped his fingers around Erian's throat, squeezing as hard as he could.

Moments later the guards were on him. They grabbed him by the arms and shoulders, trying to pry his hands away, but he held on grimly, teeth bared, snarling and berserk. Erian's face began to turn blue, and his mouth gaped wide as he gasped for breath.

Finally, a guard hit Arenadd hard in the face and he reeled backward. His hands relaxed their grip, and Erian struggled free. The guards dragged him away and threw him down, shackling his wrists together behind his back.

Arenadd, lying on his front, looked straight at Skade. "Skade!" he yelled. "I have to tell you something! *Skade!*"

The guards grabbed his legs, intending to chain his ankles as well. He rolled onto his back and began to kick out at them, knocking several over before they closed in and began to hit him, aiming for his gut and groin.

Skade screamed and tried to run to him, but Saeddryn grabbed her. "No! There's nothin' ye can do!"

Skade struggled. "No! Arenadd! Let him go! Let him go! *Arenadd!*"

Arenadd was still struggling. "Skade!" he yelled back, his voice broken up by cries of pain. "Listen! *Skade!*" They finally managed to subdue him and chained his legs together. "Skade!" he shouted, as they hauled him to his feet. "I have a heart! I have a heart! Take care of it! Please, Skade!"

Skade broke free of Saeddryn and ran, but Rhodri and another Northerner stopped her, and the three of them pulled her away; she fought at every step, screaming Arenadd's name. But Saeddryn had been right. There was nothing she could do. They had him now, and they would not let him go. This was the way it had to be.

Saeddryn took charge now. The other Northerners followed her command and ran away through the trees as fast as they could, and Skade went with them, tears streaming down her face. No-one tried to go after them. The Southerners had kept their word.

Arenadd, hanging from the grip of the guards, saw them go and felt some relief shine through the haze of pain that had taken hold of his mind and body. They were free, all of them. He had kept his promise.

His moment of triumph didn't last long. He kept his gaze on the fleeing prisoners for as long as he could, but his view of them was blocked by two pairs of eyes. Blue eyes, one pair griffish, one pair human, both staring at him with utter hatred and contempt.

This time, Erian didn't glance at Senneck for approval. He stepped forward and grabbed his enemy by the hair, lifting his head and forcing him to look him in the eye. "Arren Cardockson, I have you now."

36

The Seed

"*Kraeiai kra, ae ee oa ae ka ee,*" said Kraeya, forming every syllable slowly and carefully.

Bran cleared his throat. "Uh, *kraeiai kra ae ee oh . . . ka ei?*"

Kraeya chirped at him. *"Ee ae!"*

Bran sighed and kicked a chunk of wood out of his path. "I know, I know. I'm tryin'. I'm a slow learner."

"Try again," said Kraeya.

Bran nodded. "Sure."

She repeated the sentence for him. This time he was closer to the mark, but they had to do it several more times before the red griffin was satisfied.

The two of them walked along Tongue Street side by side, enjoying a few moments' relative peace, and time alone together. It had been a long while since they had had much of either.

After the destruction of the Eyrie, matters in the once-proud griffiner city had rapidly gone downhill. More than half the griffiners had left, never to return, and the hatchery had been all but emptied. Its occupants had flown the coop, some choosing humans to take with them and others going alone. Only a handful—the sick, the crippled and the very old or young—were left, still looked after by Roland and Keth.

The remaining griffiners had been joined by young, ambitious fighting men and women who had come from Canran, Wylam and Withypool, all after their share of the pickings. As far as Bran knew, almost half of Eagleholm's lands were gone now, taken over by its neighbours on both sides. As for the rest, it was still running, though without an Eyrie Master or Mistress the structure was quickly falling apart. Not that there weren't plenty of candidates trying to take that particular honour for themselves.

Since Lady Riona's death there had been six different Eyrie Masters or Mistresses. Few had lasted more than several weeks and at least two of them had claimed the position at the same time. Both newcomers and Eagleholmian griffiners had fought each other for the post, but with loyalties constantly shifting and nobody holding enough support to last long before being assassinated, it was little better than a farce. More than once, the fighting had spread into the city and the population at large had joined in. Entire blocks of houses and public buildings had burned down, and on the last occasion the fire had taken a large chunk of the platform with it. With the old Master of Building dead and no-one there to appoint a replacement, almost nothing had been done to repair the damage, and these areas were now home to dozens of scavengers. Little by little, piece by piece, the city was tearing itself to bits.

Bran had kept well out of it. Having not sworn loyalty to Lady Riona—or to anyone else for that matter—he was free to choose whatever side he liked, and had chosen none of them. He had continued to fulfil his duties as captain of the city guard as well as he could; with the Master of Law dead he had to sentence most of the criminals he arrested himself. Several of the temporary Eyrie Masters had tried to win his support, but he had avoided them or made excuses, secure in the knowledge that they wouldn't last long enough to make much trouble for him. Few did.

In the meantime, he continued to try to learn griffish as well as he could, and to get used to Kraeya's constant companionship and how it had changed his life. The language was harder than he had expected, though.

"Good," said Kraeya after his fourth attempt.

Bran tried it again, and grinned. "I got it."

The street became rougher underfoot, and the two of them slowed. Bran put his hand on the hilt of his sword, and Kraeya raised her wings slightly. They had entered one of the burned patches near the centre of the city. Up ahead, the wreck of the Eyrie was silhouetted against the late afternoon sun. As they walked toward it, shapes lurched at them out of the ruins, holding their hands out and muttering.

"Sir, spare an oblong? Sir, please . . ."

"Just one, sir, please . . ."

"Spare an oblong, sir?"

Bran put his head down and ignored them, knowing that if he gave money to one of them the others would be encouraged and harass him until he threw them the entire contents of his money pouch. Kraeya walked with dignity, pretending not to see them, but hissed when they came too close. They backed off, but not as far as they might have done once. They were getting more desperate, and that made them bolder.

He couldn't help but be relieved when they passed out of the burned area and stopped at a house that was still intact. It had fallen into disrepair lately, and there was a heap of garbage beside the door, but so far it had escaped the fires and the fighting.

Bran knocked on the door. He had to wait for some time before it finally opened.

Flell peered through, looking apprehensive and exhausted. "Oh, Bran." She appeared to relax.

Bran smiled and held up a bag. "Hello. I've brung you some oranges."

Flell sighed and opened the door all the way. "Come on, come in."

Bran entered, and Kraeya came close on his heels, ducking her head to fit, though the door and the house had both been made large enough for a griffin to enter. Thrain scuttled between her paws, cheeping, and Flell scooped the chick up in her arms and walked ahead into the study.

Bran sat down in a chair in front of the cold hearth, and Kraeya took up station behind him.

"D'you want something to drink?" said Flell.

Bran nodded. "Yeah, thanks."

She gave him a cup of wine and sat down in the other chair, leaving Thrain to perch on the back. Nowadays she moved slowly and awkwardly, her once-slim frame hampered by her swollen breasts and abdomen. Her belly looked a little bigger to Bran every time he saw her. He tried not to stare. "So, how are yeh? Ye're lookin' well."

Flell smiled wanly. "Lord Arn came to see me."

"What, again? I thought you said you din't want t'see him again."

"Of course. I said it again, but he talked me into letting him in again. He's becoming very . . . persistent."

"Yeh ain't gonna say yes to him, though, are yeh?" said Bran, a little anxiously.

The way Flell looked at him then made his heart ache. "I really don't have much choice."

"Yes, yeh do," Bran said sharply. "What's wrong with yeh, Flell? Yeh ain't some little girl needs lookin' after. Yer a lady. A griffiner."

Flell looked surprised, but only for a moment. "Thank you for saying that, Bran. It's kind of you. But you don't understand. I really don't have any choice. I have to marry, and soon. My father's fortune is all but gone now, and I can't look after this child on my own for long. Everyone already knows I'm carrying a bastard, but if someone marries me before it comes they can claim it as theirs. It's my only hope." She closed her eyes for a moment. "I've asked Lord Arn to come again tomorrow."

"He'll be dead the day after that," said Bran. "You know that, don't yeh? If he goes an' does what he's thinkin' of doin'—"

"I know that," Flell snapped back. "Do I look like an idiot to you?" She stood up abruptly, apparently embarrassed by her outburst. "I'm happy that you came to see me, and thank you for the oranges. I appreciate it, but—"

Bran clutched at his cup. "Flell, siddown, will yeh? I've got somethin' t'say."

She reluctantly obeyed. "What is it?"

Bran hesitated and took a gulp of wine. "Listen, over at the barracks today, Dan asked me—well, everyone's noticed I've been comin' here a lot, see, an' they've bin askin' questions."

"What sort of questions?" Flell said sharply.

"I think yeh know," said Bran. "The sorts of questions people always ask. An' today, Dan said—asked me—he's my mate, right, an' I trust him. He said, 'Bran, what're yeh doin' goin' over there all the time? Me an' the lads've bin wonderin' about it.' I said it was none of his business, but he said, 'Look, there's no point lyin' about it, we know what's goin' on. Why don't yeh just tell me, mate?'" Bran took a deep breath and drank more wine. "So I gave up an' told him the truth."

Flell jerked upright. "What? Bran!"

Bran soldiered on, ignoring her. "I said I din't mean for it to happen, an' neither did you, an' it was just one of them things a man can't stop. After Arren left, an' that stuff happened, you was miserable an' lonely, so I comforted yeh, an', well—" He shrugged and drained the rest of the wine. "An' that's the way it is."

Flell was giving him a frosty look. "I see."

Bran put the cup aside. "It doesn't matter, right? Kraeya an' me, we're leavin'."

"Where are you going?" said Flell.

"Well, we ain't left yet because we din't know where t'go," said Bran. "Thought of Canran, but they're a load of nether-eye-kissin' bastards over there. Withypool's too far. Anyway, what'd we do there? No." He laced his fingers together and sighed. "No, we can't go there. It ain't right. There's somethin' else I gotta do, and Kraeya said it's all right with her."

"What is? You're not going to leave the country, are you?"

"Nah. I wouldn't know what t'do with meself in a place like Amoran or what-have-you. See, my business here is done, like. They won't have much use for a guard captain here. Time'll come soon enough when someone decides it'd be better if I weren't around any more."

"I understand," said Flell. "So, where are you going?"

"There's somethin' I gotta do," said Bran. "Flell, we're goin' north. T'Malvern, an' probably even further."

"Why?"

"Why? What d'yeh mean, why?" said Bran. "There's someone yeh an' I both knew an' lost. North's where he's gone, an' I'm goin' after him."

Flell tensed. "Why do you want to find him? Bran, you know he must be dead by now. Even if he was going there, they must have caught him. Erian would have—"

"Erian!" Bran sneered. "That brat came out of the belly of Carrick's village doorknob, an' he couldn't find a thorn bush if yeh stuffed it down his pants. No, Arren's still out there somewhere. I can feel it in my gut. He's in the North now."

"But why do you want to find him?" said Flell. "What good could it possibly do? Do you want to kill him?"

"Again? No. Flell, listen to me." Bran looked her in the eye. "I failed him. So did you. Don't close yer eyes to it; yeh know it's true. We all failed him. He was our friend, an' we abandoned him when he needed us. If we'd stood by him, odds are this wouldn't've happened at all."

Flell looked away. "I don't want to talk about it."

"But we did fail him!" said Bran. "An' there's somethin' else I—"

"Listen," said Flell. "There's no—"

Bran reached out and clumsily took her hand. "No, listen. I've got t'tell yeh, Flell. Listen. Look, Arren talked t'me, see. After Gern died an' yeh disappeared. I kept visitin' him, tryin' t'keep an eye on him an' help him when I could. He din't always answer the door, an' he stopped comin' to the tavern much any more—I hardly ever saw him. An' then one night he came t'find me there—somethin' had happened to him."

"What something?" said Flell.

Bran shook his head. "Someone'd attacked him. Broke into his house, wrecked all his furniture, stole everything he had. Then they beat him up so bad he couldn't leave for days, an' they put that slave collar on him."

Flell started. "What?"

"It's true. I saw what was left of his house, an' I saw the state he was in. His face was swollen, he had broken ribs—it was amazin' he hadn't died. An' he was terrified. He said it'd happened because he told us someone was tryin' t'hurt him; he wouldn't say who, but—"

"My father," Flell whispered. "He told me after he attacked those men in the tavern."

"I thought that's what he must've said," replied Bran. "But he got worse. It got worse. Gern died, an' Arren believed they'd killed him. He thought they was gonna kill me, too, an' yeh. It was horrible how he was then. I've seen people look at me the way he did—when they was on the way t'the scaffold. He was frightened for his life. An' someone was out t'get him. It couldn't be just chance."

"But my father—"

"There's more," said Bran. "I went t'see him afterward. I told him about what was happenin', said Arren needed to be protected an' I thought someone in the Eyrie might be workin' against him."

"What did he say?" said Flell.

Bran shook his head. "He wouldn't listen. He said it was only to be expected that people'd be like that to him now he din't have Eluna any more an' that if he couldn't live in the city without gettin' into trouble he could leave it an' go back t'Idun. Then when I kept at him he got nasty. Said it wasn't proper for

me t'be usin' my position t'do favours for my mates an' that if I
kept pokin' my nose where it wasn't wanted there'd be trouble
for me. He hinted I'd lose my job an' maybe worse. So I left
it alone. I had to." Bran scuffed at the floor with his boot. "I
was a coward. After that I should've seen somethin' really bad
was goin' on, but I ignored it. Shut my eyes, told myself it was
nothin'. I started keepin' away from Arren, makin' excuses—
an' then it was too late."

Flell let go of his hand. "Yes. He told me the same thing he
told you."

"What? You mean yer father?"

She nodded. "After what Arren told me, I went to see my
father and told him the story, and asked him to do something to
help him. He said he would try and do something, but he also
said—he said Arren had been disgraced and that every griffiner
in the city disapproved of our relationship and believed it was
unhealthy and dangerous. He said he trusted me enough to let
me make my own choices, but he wanted to advise me to stop
seeing Arren completely. He said Arren had become violent
and that there were rumours all over the city that he was losing
his mind. He said, 'I don't want to force you to do anything, but
I'm afraid for you. If you were hurt . . .'" Flell shuddered. "And
after that every time I thought of Arren I remembered that. I
was frightened. I realised I was pregnant, and I didn't know
what to do. So I stayed away."

"Neither of us knew what t'do," said Bran. He glanced at
Kraeya. "An' that's why we're goin' north. I have to find him,
Flell. There's got t'be somethin' I can do."

"Bran, he's a murderer," said Flell. "There's nothing anyone
can do for him. When they catch him they'll execute him."

"No. Listen. Arren was my best mate. What happened to
him was my fault, an' I have t'do somethin'. If I can reach out,
find the man he was before all this, then maybe—I dunno. I
gotta try. That's all I know."

"Well, go then," said Flell. "And good luck."

"I'm goin'," Bran said, and nodded. "In a few days. But
what're *you* gonna do? Stay here an' marry that idiot Arn? Sell
the house an' run off to Eire? What?"

"I don't know," Flell said honestly. "I'll find something."

Bran stood up. "But that's why I came t'see yeh, Flell. I want
you t'come with me."

She stood, too. "Bran, I really can't—"

"Why not?" he demanded. "I'm a griffiner, ain't I? I'm young an' strong, I got a sword, I know how to lead an' organise. If I was part of a great ol' family line, I could get a good post— maybe even Master of War at Malvern. If I married right."

"Now listen—" Flell began.

"Listen t'what?" said Bran. He clutched at her hands. "I ain't no fancy thinker, I don't know much about books an' suchlike, but I know some stuff. Like, I know a man's gotta take responsibility for his blood, an' if a woman needs help he oughta give it."

"Bran, this child isn't—"

"It's mine," said Bran. "Yeh an' me made a mistake, right? That's what half the city thinks."

"Well . . ." She faltered.

"Don't yeh see?" Bran said wildly. "C'mon, think about it! If yeh marry me, you an' I can go to the North together, away from all these madmen an' women. I'd be a father t'the child; we'd be a proper family. All three of us together."

"But Bran—"

He clutched her hands, his big ones nearly engulfing hers. "I *love* yeh, Flell," he said at last. "I've loved yeh for years. Ever since Arren introduced us. But I never said nothin', 'cause— well, I was some dumb guardsman who couldn't read, an' you was a great lady, beautiful an' clever an' gentle an' all the things I'm not. But you ain't weak. 'Pretty like a flower, tough like a thistle, that's our Flell.' That's what Arren used t'say, remember? Look at yerself. You deserve better'n this. Better'n Arn an' this ruin. I can offer yeh better, I swear. If yeh wanted me to, I'd build an Eyrie for yeh. Anythin'."

Flell smiled. "Bran, you're babbling."

There was a moment's slightly shocked silence between them, and then Bran burst out laughing. "See?" he said. "That's what I was talkin' about! Flell the thistle!" He became serious. "But I meant it. You an' I have both got unfinished business. We gotta find Arren, an' we gotta save him."

"From Erian?"

"From Erian, and himself."

About the Author

"A lot of fantasy authors take their
inspiration from Tolkien. I take mine from
G. R. R. Martin and Finnish metal."

Born in Canberra, Australia, in 1986, Katie J. Taylor attended
Radford College, where she wrote her first novel, *The Land
of Bad Fantasy*, which was published in 2006. She studied
for a bachelor's degree in communications at the University
of Canberra and graduated in 2007 before going on to do a
graduate certificate in editing in 2008. K. J. Taylor writes at
midnight and likes to wear black.

For news and author contact, visit
www.kjtaylor.com.

**Don't miss
the third book in the Fallen Moon series**

K. J. TAYLOR

The Griffin's War

THE FALLEN MOON, BOOK THREE

With the dark griffin Skandar, Arren—now known by his true name, Arenadd Taranisäii—wants to free his people.

Gathering an army, wielding Skandar's power to move through the shadows, Arenadd seems unstoppable. But his nemesis is journeying to the Island of the Sun, seeking the one weapon that can kill Arenadd, the man without a heart . . .

Coming March 2011 from Ace Books

penguin.com

Don't miss
the first book in the Fallen Moon series

K. J. TAYLOR

The Dark Griffin

THE FALLEN MOON, BOOK ONE

Despite his Northerner slave origins, Arren Cardockson
has managed to become a griffiner. With his griffin,
Eluna, he oversees trade in the city of Eagleholm, but
he knows his Northern appearance means he will never
be fully respected. When Arren and Eluna are sent to
capture a rogue griffin, Arren sees a chance to earn
some money and some respect, but his meeting with
the mysterious black griffin begins a dangerous chain
of events . . .

Available now from Ace Books

M774T0910

Explore the outer reaches
of imagination—don't miss these authors
of dark fantasy and urban noir who take you
to the edge and beyond . . .

Patricia Briggs	Anne Bishop
Simon R. Green	Marjorie M. Liu
Jim Butcher	Jeanne C. Stein
Kat Richardson	Christopher Golden
Karen Chance	Ilona Andrews
Rachel Caine	Anton Strout

31901050354069

M15G0610